C12

MOTHERS AND DAUGHTERS

The four books that make up this novel—*Amanda, Gillian, Julia* and *Kate*—span three generations and nearly thirty years of time. Except that Kate is Amanda's niece, none of these women is related, but their lives cross and recross, linked by Julia's son David.

Julia Regan belongs to the "older" generation in the sense that her son David was old enough to fight in the war. That he ended the war in the stockade was due more to his mother than to himself, and the book devoted to Julia shows what sort of woman she was—why, having gone to Italy before the war with an ailing sister, she constantly put off her return to her family—and why, therefore, David is the man he is.

Unsure of himself and bitter (for good reason) David finds solace in Gillian, who had been Amanda's room-mate in college during the war. He loses her because he does not know what he wants from life. Gillian is an enchanting character who knows very well what she wants: she is determined to become an actress. In spite of the extreme tenderness and beauty of her love affair with David (and Evan Hunter has caught exactly the gaieties and misunderstandings of two young people very much in love, when a heightened awareness lifts the ordinary into the extraordinary and the beautiful into the sublime) she is not prepared to continue indefinitely an unmarried liaison, and she leaves him. When, eleven years later and still unmarried, she finally tastes success, the taste is of ashes, and she wonders whether the price has not been too high.

Amanda is considerably less sure of herself than Gillian, though for a time it looks as if her music will bring her achievement. But she has in her too much of her sexually cold mother to be passionate in love or in her music. She marries Matthew who is a lawyer, and, without children of their own, they bring up her sister's child, Kate, who, in the last book, is growing up out of childhood into womanhood—with a crop of difficulties of her own.

Unlike all his earlier novels (except in extreme readability) *Mothers and Daughters* is not an exposure of social evils, but a searching and sympathetic study of people.

Mothers

and Daughters

EVAN HUNTER

*I don't care who you are, woman:
I know sons and daughters looking for you
And they are next year's wheat or the year after hidden
   in the dark and loam.*
                                    Carl Sandburg

CONSTABLE
London

First published in Great Britain 1961
by Constable and Company Ltd
10 Orange Street London WC2H 7EG
Copyright © 1961 by Evan Hunter
ISBN 0 09 452980 9
Reprinted 1961, 1976, 1981
Printed and bound in Great Britain
by Mansell Ltd, Witham, Essex

CONTENTS

BOOK ONE: AMANDA . . . 7

BOOK TWO: GILLIAN . . . 147

BOOK THREE: JULIA . . . 278

BOOK FOUR: KATE . . . 422

BOOK ONE

AMANDA

SNOW. She heard the shovels scraping on the campus walks when it was still dark, and she sat bolt upright in bed and thought *Snow!* and then almost called out in excitement to the bed across the dormitory room until she remembered Diane had changed rooms and the bed was empty. The word *snow* rushed into her mind again, and she threw back the covers and rushed to the window. The floor was cold. She hopped from foot to slipperless foot as she wiped the window clear of condensation and peered out over the campus. Snow, and it was still falling, whispering, hushed. Snow, and the university lights were almost obscured in a dizzy swirl of white. A sudden gladness clutched at her heart, squeezing an unconscious grin on to her face.

"Oh, good, it's snowing!" she said aloud, and she ran back to her bed and pulled the quilt to her chin and crossed her arms over her breasts and lay in the darkness smiling, thinking of Minnesota and the woods, and walking behind her father and her sister when they went out to cut down the tree for Christmas, the air so cold you could break it off and hear it tinkle in your fist, the snow thick and silent underfoot except for the steady crunching of her father's boots. She lay in bed with the smile on her face and she could not sleep. She thought of the way the snow would bank high against the kitchen door behind the rectory, and the tight snug snowed-in feeling of the house at evening prayers, the fire blazing high in the stone fireplace, the smell of pitch, the crackling spit of new wood, she could not sleep. Dawn broke against her window in silent greyness, sunlessly.

She got out of bed wide awake, and quickly took off her pyjamas. "Whoo!" she said. "Whoo!" She put on her underclothing quickly, the cold bringing out goose bumps all over her body. She put on a skirt and her thickest sweater, and then she went down the hall to wash and brush her teeth. The dormitory was still. She was the only person alive in the entire world.

The campus was a line-drawing that November day, black and

white, everything so sharp and so clear. She felt she could see for miles, beyond the low brick wall hemming in the university grounds, and into the town of Talmadge itself, and beyond that into all Connecticut and New England, and to exotic places over the sea, her visibility was limitless that day. The snow lay untouched on the open campus fields, and banked high on the sides of each walk. It seemed totally flat and one-dimensional, artificial. The bare trees behind it were black in silhouette against the grey sky. There was no colour that day. It was odd. Even the red brick of some of the buildings seemed colourless.

She stopped on the low flat steps of the dorm and scanned the grounds, her eyes travelling in a slow circle, and then she pulled off one of her red mittens and scooped up a handful of snow. She held it in her palm until her hand stung, and then she bit into it, smiled, and tossed the remainder of the snow into the air. She wiped her hand on her coat and started out across the campus, walking rapidly, her hand tingling from the snow.

She passed the three chapels guiltily, well she would say her morning prayers while she practised, and then went on past the Old Campus on Fieldston Street, and then turned abruptly right on to Townsend and past the Townsend Memorial Library and the Townsend Law Buildings, each building topped with a wig of snow so that it resembled a British barrister begging a point of order. She was anxious to get at one of the pianos in the rehearsal room. She was hungry, but she could get a cup of coffee from the machine in the basement of Ardaecker. She could not bear the bustle of the student cafeteria this morning, not this glorious morning when she was feeling so wonderfully alive.

I love it here, she thought, but I do miss home, but I love it here, and again she marvelled at the miracle of being here at all. She could remember first receiving the Talmadge catalogue, and the frightening entrance requirements for the School of Music and the major in composition. Did she know modal counterpoint? Could she harmonize chorale melodies in the style of Bach? Apprehensively, she had read through the list of topics to be covered in the examinations: the rudiments of music, the perception of rhythm and pitch, modulation, non-chordal notes, altered chords, two- and three-part fugue writing, three-part motets.

She had looked up at her father suddenly and said, "This is impossible! They're out of their minds!" and then immediately buried her nose in the catalogue again.

There would be keyboard tests in reading scores of two to four staves in different clefts (including alto and tenor clefts), tests in transposition, in harmonizing figured and unfigured parts, an oral test on the theory of music. And, to cap it all, she was required to submit at least four original compositions, one of which had to be polyphonic in character, "such compositions to be delivered to the Talmadge School of Music not later than 1 March 1941."

"They're out of their minds!" she had said again.

And yet she had done it, and here she was starting her third semester, and it seemed she had been here for ever. Had she really known anything at all about music before she entered Talmadge? How in the world had she ever passed the entrance exams? miracle, that was all, The power of prayer. She drew in a dee breath and felt the cold air hammering her body to life again. She smiled suddenly. There was a tinge of expectation to the day, somehow, as if something were going to happen, oh, she just wished it would, just around the turn of the walk, still she knew nothing would happen, but wouldn't it be great if something did? But she knew nothing would.

And then she heard footsteps on the walk ahead of her, and for an instant her heart stopped and she caught her breath. She felt as if she had made a pact with the devil. Now I've done it, she thought, and stopped stock still, waiting for God-knew-what blinding explosion of evil.

She almost laughed aloud when Morton Yardley came into view around the bend.

"Morton!" she said, relieved. Her voice rang on the campus stillness, startling him. He stopped on the path and peered out from under the hood of his Mackinaw, billows of vapour steaming from within the cowl.

"Oh, hello, Amanda," he said.

She smiled. "Hello, Morton."

"It's too cold," Morton said.

She liked Morton. He was one of the few boys on campus she could talk to. She had first met him in her class on Bach's Organ Compositions. He was a divinity student taking the course as an elective, and really a pretty fair organist, not as good as her father of course, but with a good keyboard sense none the less. He had been puzzled by the tonality of one of the preludes, and she'd stayed after class explaining it to him, liking him instantly even though there was an air of displacement about him, as if he had already taken a personal vow of poverty and chastity. She had hardly ever seen him without his hooded Mackinaw. He wore it well into the spring, always with the hood up, as though he had secretly joined a monastic order ages ago and was only going through the motions of an uncloistered life. He always made her smile. He had a round cherub's face, and a well-padded paunch, and guileless blue eyes,

and a very high voice, the physical equipment of a jolly Friar Tuck.
And yet he was an oddly solemn and detached boy, a thin boy
wearing a fat boy's body, a boy who walked with the curiously
sedate and pensive motion of an old man talking to pigeons in the
park. Still, he made her smile.

"Winter intimidates the soul," he said, somewhat balefully. "It's
too cold. If the sun is God's eye, why doesn't He open it today?"

"But it's a wonderful day," Amanda said, smiling.

"Well, for you, I guess," Morton said. He saw the puzzlement
on her face and added, "Or don't you know yet?"

"Know what?"

"Well, never mind."

"Know what, Morton?"

"No, never mind. I've got to hurry. I'm late for chapel."

She caught his arm and stepped into his path. "Don't I know
what yet?"

A rare and secret smile crossed Morton's face. "Where are you
going now?"

"Ardaecker. What should I know that I don't know?"

"You'll see."

"Don't be mean, Morton!"

"I'll talk to you later. When are you eating lunch?"

"Fifth hour. Morton, what . . ."

"I'll meet you in the cafeteria. I'll buy you a cup of coffee,
okay?"

"All right, but . . ."

Morton retreated into his cowl and started off down the path in
stately dignity. Amanda stared after him, her hands on her hips.
An expression of disappointment crossed her face, a translation of
emotion into exaggerated grimace, the honest and direct translation
of a seven-year-old, curious on the face of Amanda Soames only
because she was nineteen. The expression faded. She stood watching Morton a moment longer, and then she turned and continued
walking towards Ardaecker Hall.

She unslung her shoulder-bag, took off her jacket, and threw it
on to one of the benches along the basement wall. She dug into
her purse, found a nickel, and quickly put it into the coffee machine.
Sipping from the cardboard container, the steam rising about her
face, she walked idly towards the bulletin boards on the wall
opposite the benches.

She was alone in the building. She could hear the huge oil
burner throbbing somewhere beyond the solemn green lockers with
their hanging combination locks. The basement walls were painted

a sterile pale green. Three overhead light globes cast a harsh glow on to the concrete floor. The heating ducts and vents overhead were painted in the same cold green, and the water pipes were covered with astringent white asbestos. She walked idly and slowly, unconsciously female, totally unaware that she added a badly needed tonal softness to the otherwise drab basement. She never thought of herself as beautiful, or even as attractive. "Vanity is a sin," her mother had taught, and she'd accepted this unquestioningly, startled sometimes by the sight of her own naked body in the mirror, surprised by the lushness of it, as shocked as if she'd seen a naked stranger, and embarrassed.

The boys at Talmadge did not find Amanda beautiful, but they did think she was attractive. If there was nothing unusual about her shoulder-length blonde hair, or her brown eyes, or her mouth, or the gentle curves of her body, she was still pleasant to watch because she looked so incredibly soft. One of the freshman boys had probably described her effect most accurately during a cafeteria discussion which caused Morton Yardley to leave the table quite suddenly. They were speculating on Amanda's potential when one of the boys asked, "Did you ever try to kiss her? It's like invading France."

"I never even think of kissing her," another boy said. "In fact, I never even think of sleeping with her."

Morton, eating a sandwich at the other end of the table, retreated further into his hood.

"Yeah, yeah, you never think of sleeping with her," the first boy said.

"I mean it. I swear to God. Never *with* her."

"Then what?"

"She's the softest girl I've ever seen in my life. I think of sleeping *on* her," and it was then that Morton put down his sandwich and left the table.

Unconsciously female, Amanda tossed the empty coffee container into the big trash barrel and studied the first of three bulletin boards. There were the usual notices assumed to be of interest to Music majors; a meeting of the Gilbert and Sullivan Society, a new award for the best violin-cello duet composed by an undergraduate, a dance recital to be given at the University Theatre in co-operation with the Drama School, a revised schedule of fees for practice rooms, *Fifteen dollars an hour, that's outrageous!* she thought, a special rehearsal of the marching band before the Yale game on Saturday, had she promised Diane she would go? She wished Diane hadn't joined a sorority, it made it so difficult to keep up with her, still the Sig Bete house was closer to most of her classes.

She made a mental note to call Diane, and began scanning the second board. Blah-blah, the usual garbage, there was still a notice there about the Hallowe'en Ball, didn't they ever take anything down? Her eye was caught by a frantic, hand-lettered note.

> * IMPORTANT * IMPORTANT *
> I have lost three pages of an English theme due in Eng 61.12 on Friday, November 13th! Please, please, if you have any information, please contact me, Ardis Fletcher, locker number 160 in Baker Dorm.
> * IMPORTANT * IMPORTANT *

Amanda smiled and moved effortlessly towards the third and final board. It was just like Ardis to have lost those pages. If the rumours about her were true, she'd lost just about everything else she'd owned by the time she was fifteen. There didn't seem to be much on the last board. She was turning away when she stopped, alarmed because her name had leaped out at her suddenly from one of the typewritten pages. Even as she moved back towards the bulletin board, she knew that this was what Morton had meant, and she felt an anticipatory excitement. She read the notice with slow deliberation, allowing the excitement to build inside her.

TALMADGE UNIVERSITY
School of Music

November 9, 1942

NOTICE TO ALL MUSIC MAJORS IN COMPOSITION

In re all musical compositions submitted for consideration for annual Christmas Pageant. Drs. Finch and MacCauley have now judged all submitted songs, ballets, and incidental music and wish to announce the selection of the following compositions for inclusion in the show:

INCIDENTAL MUSIC

Introduction and Prelude .... Ralph Curtis...
Vamp 'Til Ready .... George Nelson...

SONGS

Still and Bright .... Francine Bourget
U.S.O. Blues .... Louis Levine
An einem gewissen Morgen .... Margit Glück

BALLETS
Winterset .... Amanda Soames
Surprise Package .... Amanda Soames

She stood before the bulletin board, and she read the notice a second time, and then once again, and she thought, Both ballets are mine, and she thought, This is one of the happiest days of my life, and there in the silent basement she began weeping.

"You should have told me, Morton," she said to him later.
"What?" he asked. "I can't hear you."
She raised her voice above the student roar in the cafeteria.
"You should have told me!" she shouted. "About the Christmas Pageant."
"And spoil the surprise? Not a chance." He sat opposite her at the long table, spooning vegetable soup into the cave formed by the hood. "I wish I could have been there when you read the notice."
"Morton, do you know what I did?"
"What?"
"I began crying."
"Why?"
"Because I was so happy."
"You're crazy."
"It's what I did," Amanda said. "I can't help it. I cry easily."
"Did I congratulate you?"
"No, you didn't. And don't think I didn't notice, either."
"Congratulations. I'm very proud of you. You want some coffee?"
"No. Aren't you warm? Why don't you put down that hood?"
"I feel fine. Listen, are you going to the game Saturday?"
"I don't know. I don't remember whether I made plans with Diane or not. Why?"
"I thought we might go together," Morton said, shrugging. "It's in New Haven, you know, and I *have* got the car."
"Oh, all right," Amanda said. "Morton, can you imagine it? Both ballets are mine. Do you know how many were submitted?"
"How many?"
"I don't know, but plenty I'll bet. Morton, do you think I really have talent?"
"I guess so. Yes. Yes, you do."
"I mean, really. I mean, do you think it's really *professional* talent. I don't mean by college standards."
"Now, how would I know, Amanda?"

"I'm only asking your opinion."

"I don't know the difference between just ordinary talent and professional talent. What's the difference, Amanda?"

"Well, professional talent . . ."

"Is what people pay for, right? Well, people are going to pay to see the Christmas Pageant."

"That's different. They only go because it's tradition."

"I would say, off-hand, that if you have to ask whether or not your talent is professional, chances are it isn't."

"That's a nasty thing to say, Morton."

"I wasn't trying to be nasty."

"I *will* have a cup of coffee. Wait a minute, Morton. Just a minute. Do you know how I feel?" She leaned across the table, her eyes bright. "I feel as if the day is just starting. I feel as if that notice was only the beginning."

"How do you mean?"

"Morton, you won't tell this to anyone?"

"I promise."

"Your word of honour?"

"My word of honour."

"I feel as if this is going to be the most important day of my life."

"How can you possibly tell that?"

"I just feel it. Inside."

"Well, okay," Morton said, and he shrugged.

"Don't you believe me?"

"Sure, I do." He stood up. "Cream and sugar?"

"Yes. One sugar. Morton?"

"Mmmmm?"

"Do I sound silly?"

"You never sound silly, Amanda," he said seriously, and he walked away from the table to join the line at the counter.

Amanda sat at the table, listening to the voices all around her, a part of the babble of conversation, the rush of sound, the clatter of trays and utensils, surrounded by people she knew, all talking about familiar things. She felt suddenly proud. It was good to be here, in this chair, at this table, in this cafeteria. She even felt a sudden sympathy for Ardis Fletcher who came bouncing into the cafeteria from the far end, her red head bobbing, wearing a tight, pale blue sweater, a string of pearls knotted about her neck, swinging wildly as she walked. She raised her hand the moment she saw Amanda, and came over to the table swinging pearls and hips, leaving a host of turning male heads in her wake.

"Hi," she said wearily, and she collapsed at the table and rolled her blue eyes. "Oh, what a day, what a day."

"Did you find your missing pages?" Amanda asked.

"No, damn it, I ..." She stopped. "I'm sorry. I forgot you don't like swearing. Do you suppose someone stole them?"

"Why would anyone want to do that?"

"I don't know," Ardis said. "It's a pretty good theme, you know."

"I'm sure it is."

"Somebody probably stole those pages," Ardis paused. "They were always stealing from Shakespeare, did you know that?"

"No, I didn't."

"Sure. They still are. Half the movie plots today are stolen from him. The artist doesn't stand a chance in today's cut-throat world." She rolled her blue eyes expressively. "I just came from home," she said. "I went through my entire room, I turned it upside down, everything. I found things I didn't even know I owned, letters from when I was at camp two years ago, can you imagine? But no pages. And I walked to school and turned over every scrap of paper in the gutter. Now where could they have gone, would you please tell me? I'm convinced that inanimate objects can get up and walk around, did you get your call?"

"What?"

"Your call. There was a long-distance call for you."

"When?"

"About a half-hour ago. One of the girls told me. I thought you'd ..."

"Long distance? From where?"

"You're supposed to call Operator 23 in Minneapolis. Didn't you ...?"

"Oh, my gosh!" Amanda said. "I'll bet it's happened!"

She rose from the table suddenly.

"Drink my coffee!" she said.

"What?"

"Morton," she answered, and rushed out of the cafeteria.

"Mother?" she said into the phone. There was a terrible electric crackling on the line, and she had to shout. "Mother, is that you?"

"Amanda?" she heard her mother say weakly. "This is Mother. I've been trying to ..." and then the voice faded completely.

"Oh, for the love of ... Mother? Mother!" Angrily she jiggled the hook on the wall phone. "Operator? Operator!"

"Operator, yes?" the voice said.

"Operator, we've been cut off."

"Your party is still on the line, Miss."

"Well, I can't hear her, so what good is it if she's still on the line?"

"One moment, please."

There was more crackling and then the background noises of a telephone exchange came on to the line, an operator haggling with a soldier in Fort Bliss who was trying to reach New York, and then the background noises were cut off, and there was a clicking, and a hum, and then the operator came back and said, "Here's your party, go ahead, please."

"Mother?"

"Amanda? What *is* going on with this telephone?"

"Did she have it?" Amanda asked.

"Yes, dear."

"Is she all right, Mother?"

Two girls in the dormitory reception-room began shouting at each other and Amanda yelled, "Keep quiet in there! I'm on long distance!"

"Well, pish-posh!" one of the girls yelled back, but they quieted down.

"Mother, is Penny all right?"

"Yes, she's fine, darling."

"What was it? What did she have?"

"A girl."

"Oh, that's nice," Amanda said grinning. "A girl. But she's all right? Penny?"

"Yes, she's fine. I've been trying to reach you since ten o'clock, Amanda. Don't they let you know when you have phone calls?"

"I've been in class, Mother. Mother, what's her name? The baby's?"

"Katherine."

"That's a good name."

"Yes."

"I like it."

"Yes."

"How's Dad?"

"He's fine. I left him at the hospital. I had to get back for the church social tonight. How's school, Amanda?"

"Oh, wonderful. Mother, two of my ballets were chosen for the Christmas Pageant!"

"That's good. Don't they call you to the phone when you have a call, Amanda?"

"Yes, sure they do. I was in class. Mother, would you tell Dad?"

"Tell him what, darling?"

"About the ballets. About mine being chosen."

"Yes, of course I will."

"Mother, does Frank know yet? Did someone contact him?"

"Well, darling, he's in the Pacific Ocean. We sent a cable, but Lord knows when that'll reach him."

"Doesn't the Navy have some sort of a system?"

"I'm sure they do, Amanda, but they *are* fighting a war, you know. We're going to get a letter off to Frank tonight, in case the cable goes astray."

"That's good. How does she look? The baby?"

"Like a baby."

"And Penny's all right?"

"Yes. She's tired, but otherwise . . ."

"Tired? Was it very hard, Mother?"

"Don't trouble your head about that, Amanda. You're too young to be worrying about such things."

"Well, I . . ." She fell silent.

"Amanda?"

"Yes, Mother?"

"I thought we'd been cut off again."

"No, I'm here."

"It's time we said good-bye, anyway. This is long distance, you know."

"Yes, Mother, tell Penny I love her, and tell Dad about the ballets, don't forget."

"I won't forget."

"I'll see you on Thanksgiving. Do you think Penny'll be out of the hospital by then?"

"Yes, I'm sure she will."

"Good. Okay, Mother, I'll say good-bye now."

"God love you, darling."

There was a click on the line, and then a hum. Amanda put the phone back on to the hook, stood with her hand on the receiver for a moment, silent, and then turned towards the reception-room. "Hey!" she yelled. "My sister just had a baby!"

"Well, pish-posh!" the same girl yelled back, and Amanda burst out laughing and ran up the three flights to her room. She threw open the door and went directly to the calendar on the wall over the desk. She picked up a black crayon and circled the date instantly, 10 November 1942.

"There," she said. "Kate, that's a nice name," and she laughed again and threw herself on to the bed. She kicked off her loafers, rolled on to her back and lay there grinning, looking up at the ceiling.

My sister had a baby, she thought. Well, what do you know?

Good old Penny. "A baby is God's divine gift," her mother had said once. Well, you did it, Penny. You sure did it, old Penny. I wonder what it was like. It probably hurt like hell.

She sat up suddenly, almost as if she had said the word aloud and wanted to be certain no one had overheard her. But she expected to be alone, and the girl standing in the doorway startled her.

"Oh!" Amanda said.

"Hi," the girl answered. "Did I scare you?"

"Yes."

"I'm sorry, I didn't mean to. Is this thirty-five?"

"What?"

"Thirty-five. Is this room thirty-five?"

"Yes. Yes, it is."

Amanda sat in the centre of the bed, shoeless, watching the girl in the door-frame. The girl was wearing a Navy pea jacket over a grey flannel skirt. The collar of the jacket was pulled high against the back of her neck, a dark backdrop for her reddish-brown hair. The hair hung in wild bangs on her forehead, was brushed sleekly back from the bangs to fall in a smooth cascade to the nape of her neck. The girl smiled. Her smile was radiant. It lighted her green eyes and her entire face. She put down her suitcase and her handbag and studied the room, still smiling.

"This is *marr*-vellous," she said. "I didn't expect it to be so grand." She began unbuttoning the pea jacket. Amanda watched her silently. The girl took off the jacket and tossed it over the suitcase. She was wearing a dark blue cashmere sweater with tiny pearl buttons. She was slender, with good breasts and wide hips. She could not have been older than seventeen.

"You must be Amanda something-or-other," she said.

"Soames."

"Soames, that's right. The woman in charge of Female Berthing sent me over. Female Berthing, isn't that a scream? They make it sound like a maternity ward." The girl laughed. Her laugh was deep and throaty. Her green eyes never lost their sparkle. They darted about the room, absorbing everything, continuously searching, continuously amused, always aglow. Amanda, startled and somewhat annoyed at first by the intrusion, felt her annoyance dissipating. Oddly, she wanted to laugh. There was something contagious about the liveliness of this girl's face, the impish grin, the glowing green eyes.

"Well, what . . . what's this all about?" Amanda asked.

"Didn't Female Berthing call you? And I thought she was so efficient. I guess I'm your room-mate. If you don't mind, that is. I'm sorry about getting here so late, but my mother and I had a slight difference of opinion." She pulled a grimace. "Is it okay?"

"Well, I . . . I guess so. I mean . . ."

"Good. I think it's going to be *marr*-vellous. Is there a john anywhere? I've had to go for hours. The one on the train was a pigsty."

"Yes," Amanda said. "Yes, down the hall."

"Thanks." The girl paused in the door-frame. "Amanda Soames," she said, testing the name. "Which way? Right or left?"

"Left. The second door," Amanda said, her eyes wide.

"I'll be back."

The girl vanished into the corridor. A second later, her head appeared around the door-frame, disembodied, cocked to one side, the long red-brown hair dangling limply over one eye, the impish grin on her mouth, the green eyes sparkling.

"My name's Gillian," she said, "my *first* name, isn't that a scream? Laugh now so you can get it out of your system before I come back."

The head vanished again. Amanda stared goggle-eyed at the empty door-frame. And suddenly the head reappeared, like Alice's Cheshire cat, floating again in the door-frame, disembodied, grinning.

"Gillian *Burke*," the girl said.

And the doorway was empty again.

The incident involving Gillian Burke took place in the University Theatre shortly after the Thanksgiving vacation.

Amanda was rather surprised by what happened because she'd known Gillian only as a room-mate up to that time, and she hadn't suspected this deeper side of Gillian's character. And even when it was all over, she never really knew whether the incident was a revelation of character depth, or whether the entire thing had been an exhibition of Gillian's intuitive showmanship. She could not ignore the persistent knowledge that the incident catapulted Gillian into the role of a campus celebrity within a single week, and she often wondered if Gillian hadn't promoted the entire thing with just such an end in mind. But hadn't there also been a measure of humiliation for Gillian, and would she wilfully have caused herself such embarrassment? The entire affair was contradictory and puzzling. But then, so was Gillian Burke.

Amanda learned almost instantly that living with Gillian was going to be an experience unlike any she had ever had before: refreshing, exasperating and, in a way, annihilating.

The first thing was the swearing. Amanda thought she'd better settle that at once. She had been raised in a home where "Hell" was always spelled with a capital letter and was never used except in sermons by her father and then to illustrate the torments of brimstone and fire. "Bitch" was a female dog. "Can" was a container usually made of tin. "Ass" was what you didn't covet your neighbour's wife or. "To lay" meant to place upon—not necessarily upon a bed. There were other words which Gillian used, and which Amanda had truthfully never heard in her home but which she suspected were scrawled upon the back fences and sidewalks of Minneapolis. In any case, they offended her ear, and she decided to put a stop to the flow of profanity immediately.

Gillian had just returned to the room after dinner. She promptly reached under her sweater and unclasped her bra.

"There!" she said. "Loosen the damn harness!"

"Why do you do that?" Amanda asked. She was sitting up in bed, reading an English assignment.

"Why do I do what?" Gillian answered. She went to her own bed, pulled back the quilt, brushed crumbs from the sheet, and sat abruptly.

"Curse so much."

"What?" Gillian looked up. She had taken off her right loafer and sock and was examining her big toe. She peered at Amanda through a hanging curtain of red-brown hair.

"You curse a lot."

"Who?" Gillian said. She flicked her head, tossing her hair back over her shoulder. "Me?"

"Yes. Every other word out of your mouth is a swear word."

"I hadn't noticed," Gillian said, and she went back to examining her toe.

"Well, you do," Amanda said. "Curse a lot, I mean."

The room was suddenly hung with silence. Amanda bit her lip. She felt there was going to be an argument, and she did not want one. And yet, she had to settle this swearing thing. Across the room, Gillian was studying her big toe and nodding, as if she had finally got the message and was pondering it before answering. She uncrossed her legs, leaned back on the bed, propped by her arms, and still nodding said, "What is this? A formal complaint?"

"Yes, I suppose it is," Amanda answered.

Gillian said nothing. She rose suddenly, went to the desk for one of her books and then walked stiffly back to her bed with it.

"I think we should settle this," Amanda said. "If we're going to be room-mates, I think we should settle this."

"It's settled," Gillian answered.

"I don't see how."

"What the hell do you want me to do? Shave my head and take the vows?"

"No, but I think——"

"This is the way I talk," Gillian said. "This is *me*." She nodded emphatically. "It shouldn't surprise you to realize I'd sooner change my room than my personality."

"I don't see that cursing adds anything to your personality."

"Well, I don't see that muttering all those prayers adds anything to yours."

"I was raised on prayer," Amanda said.

"And I was raised swearing."

"Well, that's no answer."

"No, I guess it isn't." She put down her book. "I'll contact Female Berthing. I'm sure she can find another room for me."

"Maybe you'd better do that."

"I will. In the morning."

There was silence again. In the silence, Gillian took off her clothes and got into her pyjamas.

"I'm sorry," Amanda said. "I just . . . I'm just not used to such language." She paused. "Nobody in my house talks that way."

"This isn't your house," Gillian said, and she got into bed.

"No, but——" Amanda cut herself short and frowned. "Wh . . . what do you mean?"

"I mean this isn't Crackerbarrel Falls, Minnesota. This is Talmadge University, part of the great big wide world. And there's an even bigger world outside Talmadge. And this may come as a great shock to you, but there are millions of decent God-fearing people in this world who aren't considered lost souls because they say 'hell' or 'damn' or——"

"That's enough, Gillian!"

"Okay, the thing is settled. I'll change my room tomorrow. But you're here for an education, Amanda. And it just might include something more than Beethoven's Fifth."

"I don't see how——"

"I'm a person," Gillian said flatly. "You're going to meet a lot of people between now and the time they bury you. It's entirely up to you whether you're going to ask *all* of them to please change rooms."

"I don't know what you mean."

"I mean that's a fine way to live, if it's what you want. But if they keep changing rooms, you can bet on one thing, Amanda."

"What's that?"

"*Your* room'll never change."

"Maybe I don't want it to change."

"Great. You're nineteen years old, and everything's set already. Don't move any of the furniture, Amanda might trip and fall."

"I don't see how listening to a lot of swear words is going to round out my education. I don't expect to be hanging out in . . . in bar rooms or . . . or pool halls . . . or . . . or . . ."

"Neither do I," Gillian said. She sighed deeply. "Let's forget it. I'll call Female Berthing in the morning."

She did not call Female Berthing in the morning. In the morning, Amanda said to her, "Well, I . . . I think we were both a little hasty. But since you know how I feel about it, couldn't you make some kind of an effort? I mean, couldn't you at least *try*, Gillian?"

Gillian grinned. Her green eyes suddenly sparkled. "I'll try," she promised.

There was a joke current that year, a joke about two nuns who went to see one of the most foul-mouthed plays on Broadway. They sat shocked through the first act, appalled through the second. During the third act, one of the nuns reached under her seat and began groping around on the theatre floor.

"What is it?" the other nun whispered.

"I dropped my goddamn beads," the first nun whispered back.

The influence of Gillian Burke was not quite that strong. And yet, Amanda found her ears growing accustomed to the sound of profanity. And whereas she never once used any of Gillian's words herself, she came to accept them as a part of Gillian, an essential part without which Gillian would have seemed somewhat pallid. There was, Amanda discovered, a great deal about Gillian which at first caused annoyance, and then gradual acceptance, and finally seemed to be part of the natural order of things.

The mess, for example.

Amanda was a neat girl who took off a sweater and immediately hung it in the closet, who made her bed each morning before classes, who put her books in the same spot on the desk each evening when classes were done, whose life was governed by an orderly, efficient routine. Gillian, on the other hand, seemed to have no respect for her own possessions, no concern for time, no patience with the ordered cadence of the world around her. Her habits infuriated Amanda at first. Amanda was a music student whose early study of the piano had been strictly regulated by the unwavering beat of a metronome. When she looked at the signature of a composition, she knew instantly the key and tempo, and she knew these would remain constant until the composer indicated a change. The world of music was rigid and unbending. In 4/4 time, there could never be *five* quarter notes—until Gillian came along.

At first, Amanda was at a total loss. She would come back to the room to find Gillian's sweater hung over a chair, her blouse on the desk, her slip and bra scattered on the floor, her stockings trailing over door-knobs, her books opened or closed wherever Gillian happened to drop them, the radio blaring, cookies crushed into the hook rug before Gillian's bed, the bed still unmade, Gillian herself lying naked in the centre of it, or, on at least one occasion, covered only by a copy of the *New York Times*.

She spoke to Gillian about the condition of the room, and Gillian promised to be more careful. But instilling order into the chaotic frenzy of Gillian Burke's life was an impossible task. Amanda found herself picking up after her room-mate, folding her sweaters, placing her loafers neatly on the floor of the closet, even making her bed—and then rebelling against all this when she noticed something telling about Gillian's seeming disorder.

She noticed that no matter how disrespectful of her own possessions she seemed, Gillian would never touch anything belonging to Amanda. When she tossed her bra casually across the room, it never landed on Amanda's bed. When she left unwashed glasses around, or open boxes of crackers, they were always on *her* side of the room. She never imposed her disorder upon Amanda, and Amanda realized it was unfair to impose her order upon Gillian. So she stopped trying. She learned that Gillian's very lack of order was an order in itself, and her own possessions went undisturbed. In the midst of the maelstrom, she was certain that Gillian would never flop down on her neatly made bed, would never move so much as a bobby pin from where Amanda had placed it. The two separately revolving worlds managed to wheel about the sky without colliding.

She learned besides that Gillian's seeming slovenliness had very little to do with the girl's honest concern for cleanliness and good grooming. She had never known anyone who bathed as often as Gillian Burke. "Cleopatra bathed in milk, did you know that?" Gillian said. "I wish I could play her. I'd *adore* playing her." The tiniest blemish, the smallest unexpected bulge was studied by Gillian absorbedly before the full-length mirror on the closet door. For Amanda, who took her flesh for granted, the interest seemed abnormal, almost narcissistic. Gillian would suddenly move close to the mirror and sweep her hair on to the top of her head, holding it there with one hand. "Do you think I should wear my hair up? Does it make me look older?" Or she would put her hands on her hips and scowl at her mirror image and say, "I need to gain a few pounds. Actresses shouldn't be too thin." And once she stood before the mirror nude and suddenly said, "Look, Amanda, a Javanese dancing girl," and struck the angular pose of arm and leg, and moved her head in the short quick movements of the dance, and in that moment even her eyes seemed to slant Orientally. And all at once, Amanda realized that Gillian considered her body only another of her tools. Gillian wanted to be an actress, and learning her own body, its potential and its limitations, was part of her training. Still, Amanda wished she would spend less time before the mirror, and less time in the bathtub.

Her body and her clothes were the two standing edifices in the wake of her personal hurricane, and the clothes completely mystified Amanda. She would never understand how Gillian did it. No matter where she dropped her skirt—on the floor, at the foot of her bed, over a chair—when she put it on the next morning, it never seemed rumpled or wrinkled. It looked, in fact, as if it had just come back from the campus cleaners. Gillian took a long time dressing each morning, in complete contradiction to the speed with which she disrobed each night. It was almost like watching the slow and painful construction of a skyscraper which was destined to be blown to smithereens at sunset. The result was impressive. Gillian's figure carried clothes well. Her waist was narrow, her skirts hung on wide hips, dropped in a sleek smooth line over good legs. She wore her sweaters modestly loose, as if denying her own rich femininity. She spent a great deal of time applying lipstick to her generous mouth, brushing out her long straight hair, trimming her bangs. And at sunset, *boom*! The dynamite was exploded, the entire structure collapsed, the meticulously designed skyscraper was utterly demolished.

It was a building, Amanda soon learned, which had no foundation.

"I don't like pants," Gillian said, and the oracle had spoken, but Amanda missed the meaning of the Delphic sibyl, thinking her room-mate was referring to slacks. She should have known that Gillian chose her words as carefully as she chose her clothes; she would not have said 'pants" if she'd intended to say "slacks". Gillian Burke did not like pants, and she did not wear pants.

"But don't you get *cold*?" Amanda asked.

Gillian winked and flashed her impish grin. "I'm warm-blooded," she said, implying more than her words actually stated, implying—Amanda knew—more than was true. For despite her cyclonic habits, despite her sailor's vocabulary, despite her concern with things physical, Amanda knew that Gillian's actual experience was almost as limited as her own. And this, perhaps, was the one real bond which allowed them to live together in harmony.

The explosion in the little theatre was quite unlike anything

Amanda had come to expect from her room-mate. Or maybe Amanda was simply unprepared for such an outburst. She had been in Minnesota for Thanksgiving and had returned to Talmadge carrying the news that her brother-in-law Frank had been killed in a night action off Guadalcanal. The War Department telegram had been brief and to the point, barely sympathetic in a journalistic way. But by piecing together the news stories of the naval engagement, Penny had come to the dull realization that her husband had been killed before he'd learned of the birth of his daughter. And this magnified the tragedy; this made death an even bigger thief. On the train back to Connecticut, Amanda had wept openly, surprised when she realized she was weeping not for her dead brother-in-law but for her sister, who had to bear the burden of remaining alive. She returned to school with an aching emptiness inside her.

Gillian, on the other hand, was bursting with energy after the holiday. She immediately tried out for a part in the Christmas Pageant and was given a small role, nothing more than a walk-on actually. "That's only because I'm a freshman," she told Amanda. "All the fat parts went to juniors and seniors. I can outact them all."

But whatever she told Amanda, she worked diligently at the part, and seemed moderately content with it until someone heard her singing during a rehearsal one day and decided she'd be just right for one of the songs in the show. She was an excellent mimic, and her command of dialect was impeccable. So whereas her voice was small and rather undistinguished, Dr. Finch, who was directing the show, felt her true ear was perfect for the particular song he had in mind. He told Gillian only that he was fattening her part with a song. He did not tell her *which* song until the day of the explosion. Amanda was sitting out front in the darkened theatre that day. Morton Yardley was slouched in the seat beside her, his hood up over his skull. From the back of the theatre, Dr. Finch called, "Gillian! Gillian Burke!"

"Yes?" Gillian answered from somewhere backstage.

"Where are you, Miss Burke?" Dr. Finch shouted.

"Here I am," she said, and she came onstage carrying a container of hot coffee, sipping at it and peering out over the footlights. She was wearing black slacks and a black sweater. The overhead row of Lekos cast a burnished glow on her hair. "What is it?" she called to the darkness.

"I'd like you to try that song, Miss Burke," Dr. Finch said.

"Oh, okay," Gillian answered.

"Pete," Dr. Finch called to the piano player, "would you give Miss Burke the music, please? Can you read music Miss Burke?"

"No, I can't."

"Well then, would you listen to it once, please? Pete?"

The piano player nodded and began playing. Gillian, sipping at her coffee, straddling one of the chairs onstage, cocked her head to one side and listened. The song was a pleasant ballad with a pastoral quality. She found herself humming to it as the music filled the theatre. When the piano player stopped, Dr. Finch said, "How do you like it, Miss Burke?"

"I *love* it," Gillian answered. "What's it called?"

"'On A Certain Morning'," Dr. Finch replied.

"May I see the lyrics, please?"

"Pete?" Dr. Finch said, and the piano player leaned up over the footlights and handed Gillian the sheet music. Watching from the third row in the orchestra, Amanda whispered, "She's so professional."

"What?" Morton said.

"Gillian. She's so very professional. She looks as if she's been on a stage all her life."

"Oh. Yeah," Morton said, and shrank back into his hood.

Gillian was studying the sheet in her hands. She was silent for a long time. Then she looked up, directing her voice towards the back of the theatre, unable to see Dr. Finch, but shouting in his direction.

"I thought this was 'On A Certain Morning'."

"It is," Dr. Finch said. "The 'certain morning', of course, is Christmas."

"Um-huh," Gillian said.

"What's the trouble, Miss Burke?"

Gillian was thoughtful for a moment. Amanda, watching her, saw a curious expression cross her face. She seemed troubled . . . or was it calculating? Amanda couldn't tell which.

"That's not what this says," Gillian called to the back of the theatre. "This says," and her pronunciation was flawless, considering she had never studied German in her life, "'*An einem gewissen Morgen*'."

"Yes," Dr. Finch said patiently. "That means 'On A Certain Morning' in German."

Gillian nodded briefly and emphatically. "Count me out," she said. She walked to the footlights and handed the music back to the piano player.

"What?" Dr. Finch said. "I beg your pardon, what did you . . . ?"

"I said count me out!" Gillian said, louder this time. She put up one hand to shield her eyes from the lights, squinted towards the back of the theatre and said, "Can you hear me all right? *Count me out.*"

"I don't understand," Dr. Finch said, puzzled, coming down the aisle on the right-hand side of the theatre.

"I won't sing it," Gillian said.

"Why not?" Dr. Finch stood just alongside the piano now, looking up at Gillian. A bunch of kids had come from backstage and were watching her nervously, not knowing whether to giggle or panic.

"It's German," Gillian said.

"It's *what?*"

"It's German, it's German. *Isn't* it German?"

"Well, yes, but . . ."

"I won't sing it. That's all. I won't sing a German Christmas song while the Nazis are cooking Jews in ovens! That's that!"

"Miss Burke, this song——"

"I don't want to sing it," Gillian said, and she walked off the stage.

"Oh my gosh!" Amanda said to Morton. "She doesn't know what she's doing." And she left her seat abruptly and ran backstage to find Gillian, but she had already left the theatre. She caught up with her outside. Gillian was walking with her head bent, her hands thrust deep into the pockets of her pea jacket.

"Gillian!"

She stopped and waited for Amanda to draw alongside. Then she began walking quickly again.

"Why on earth did you do that?" Amanda said.

"I don't like Nazis."

"German is not synonymous with Nazi."

"Oh, isn't it now?"

"No, it isn't! That song was written by Margit Glück. She——"

"I don't care who wrote . . ."

"She's a student here, a refugee! She escaped Vienna, and German is her native tongue, and she writes brilliantly, and you had no right to do what you did, Gillian!"

"Oh," Gillian said in a very small voice.

"Yes, damn you!" Amanda answered. "Oh!"

The college newspaper ran the story the next day. It told exactly what had happened in the little theatre, and then printed an interview with Margit Glück, composer of '*An einem gewissen Morgen*', in which Miss Glück said she was "surprised and saddened" by the incident. Dr. Finch, commenting on the *cause célèbre* to one of the college reporters, said, "Tempers are traditionally short in rehearsal periods. I'm sure this is simply a matter of misunderstanding. Miss Glück and Miss Burke are essentially opposed to the same ideology.

Miss Burke simply reacted emotionally, the way an actress would be expected to, I might add."

Gillian Burke refused to talk to any of the campus reporters. Instead, she went to Margit Glück's dorm the day after the interviews were printed, found her room, and apologized to her. They were both in tears by the end of the session, and some enterprising student recorded the tearful scene on film and sent the snapshot to the newspaper. A fresh recounting of the story appeared the next week, together with the heart-rending photo. Both Gillian and Miss Glück came out of the whole thing rather well, but it was Gillian who really carried the field. She had shown artistic temperament and true patriotism. She had been called "an actress" by Dr. Finch, a respected campus authority. She had refused the vulgarity of publicity by avoiding any of the campus reporters. She had gone privately and in all humility to Miss Glück, and apologized. That someone had taken a picture of the soul-shattering meeting was not Gillian's doing, but the picture and the new story *did* get wider circulation than the original story had, and the picture proved beyond a doubt that this was "simply a matter of misunderstanding" that Gillian had been big enough and humble enough to set straight immediately. The Christmas Pageant, which was a big student draw each year anyway, sold out immediately the day after the new story appeared. Gillian Burke became a well-known campus figure in her first month at school.

Amanda never knew whether that moment of silence on stage had been a moment of calculation. And she never asked Gillian.

The girls were plentiful in Honolulu, but David Regan fastidiously stayed away from them. There was something too impersonal about the whores, something mechanical and precise, something that made the act of love completely loveless. Besides, though he would never admit this to himself, he had been frightened by the training films he'd seen in boot camp, images of which flashed across his mind whenever he was tempted by a passing skirt.

The ship had come back to Pearl at the beginning of the month, ostensibly for repairs in dry dock. But everyone in the crew knew that the *Hanley* was there for reassignment to a picket destroyer squadron. The men of the *Hanley* weren't too ticked by the prospect. The average life of a picket ship on station, they had been told—and they repeated the story with the relish of true heroes—was three minutes. Hardly time to say a final prayer. So they made the best of their time in Hawaii. David would go to Waikiki in the afternoons and swim alone. Sometimes there were nurses on the beach, and the wives of officers stationed at Pearl, and he would watch them in their trim swimsuits and think of the girls he knew back home in Talmadge, think especially of Ardis Fletcher and the things they had done together. Once a young Wave came over to him where he lay on his blanket and asked for a match. He had taken out his Zippo lighter and thumbed it into flame. The girl looked at him archly as she drew in on the cigarette. She blew out a stream of smoke and said, "Thanks."

"Don't mention it."

"You off one of the ships?" She stood with one arm crossed over her waist, the other resting on it as she puffed on her cigarette. She was not really a pretty girl, really too thin in the blue bathing suit, her teeth slightly bucked.

"Yes," David said. "The *Hanley*."

"Just get back, or are you heading out?"

"Just got back."

"From where?"

"Tassafaronga."

"Guess you saw some action," the girl said.

"I guess so," David answered.

The girl was silent, puffing on her cigarette. Behind her, three boys on surfboards rode in towards the beach. The girl's hair and eyes were brown, he noticed. Her teeth were too large but she had a good mouth. She didn't seem nervous at all, and yet something in her eyes told him this was very difficult for her.

"I saw you here the other day," she said suddenly.

"Mmmm?"

"Why do you come alone?"

"Just like that."

"Are you a lone wolf?" she asked coyly. She paused. ' Is that what you are?"

"I guess so."

"Well," she said, and she paused again. The pause lengthened. "How old are you, anyway?" she asked.

"Eighteen," he said.

She studied him speculatively. "Well," she said, and again fell silent. "Well, I don't want to intrude on your privacy." She looked at him steadily for a moment, flicked the cigarette away, and began walking back towards her own blanket. He almost called out to her, and then decided not to.

He ate alone at the Royal Hawaiian that night. He ordered pork chops and lots of milk, and then he bought a scarf in the gift shop, a silk scarf with a picture of the islands on it, and he had it sent to his mother, Julia Regan, in Talmadge, Connecticut. Then he went back to the ship. He didn't know how early it was. They were demagnetizing the hull and everyone had been asked to turn in his watch for safekeeping ashore because the process could do something to the movement, he didn't understand quite what it was about. They were showing a movie on the boat deck, something with Joan Crawford. He changed into his dungarees and then went to watch the last two reels, thinking of Ardis Fletcher back home.

On December sixth, they left Oahu for Nawiliwili on the near-by island of Kauai. There was supposed to be some sort of celebration in honour of Pearl Harbour Day the next day. The scuttlebutt said that the people of Nawiliwili were going to give a *luau* on the beach for the officers and men of the *Hanley*. The scuttlebutt, usually accurate because it filtered down from the radio gang who saw all communications even before the captain did, could not have been more wrong. There was no *luau* on the beach. Instead, on the seventh, a group of seventeen-year-old high-school girls came aboard at about 1100 for a tour of the ship. The men were asked to put on shirts for the visitors. As they worked painting the ship (the civilian workmen at Pearl had left this task to the technicians, the sailors who had learned early in their naval careers that scraping and painting were recurring diseases), the girls went through the ship wide-eyed, ogling the guns and the torpedo tubes and the masts and the blinker lights and the signal flags and the depth charges. The men of the *Hanley* greeted their visitors with remarkable restraint. Like perfect gentlemen, they went about their painting, brushes dipping and swishing. There were no catcalls and no whistles. But three hundred pairs of eyes hungrily devoured the fresh young bodies under the thin tight skirts and full blouses, and three hundred tongues licked lips in anticipation of the evening. There would be a dance that night, the scuttlebutt said, at the local high school. These sweet young maidens would be in attendance, the scuttlebutt said. Greedily, the paint brushes dipped and swished.

This time, the scuttlebutt was right.

The men of the *Hanley* put on their whites and shined their shoes and combed their hair and visited the pharmacist's Mate. They found the local high school, and they heard the music inside, and they marched in like conquering American heroes, ready to celebrate Pearl Harbour Day, but there wasn't a girl to be seen for miles.

Instead, there were the local boys.

Apparently, the good mothers of Nawiliwili had heard of the destroyer tied up at the dock, had heard their good daughters telling about the school trip to the destroyer that morning, had rightly surmised the sailors aboard that ship would invade the high-school dance that night, and had wisely decided to keep their daughters home and in their own safe, snug beds. The men of the *Hanley* blamed the local boys for this act of perfidy. The local boys blamed the presence of the sailors for their own lack of female companionship. Unfortunately, a lot of the sailors had bought out the local liquor store before heading for the high school. When they saw there were no women, they began drinking. Within a half-hour, the fight started. David left the moment it began. He caught a cab to town and went to the local movie. The picture he saw, and he could not suppress a wry grin, was ' The Virgins of Bali ".

He got back to the ship at about 2340, just as the watch was being relieved. Mr. Devereaux, one of the new communications officers, was unstrapping the forty-five from his waist and handing it to Mr. Dinocchio, the ship's navigator. When he saw David, Devereaux turned and said, ' Hey, you're in one piece!"

David came up the gangway and saluted Mr. Dinocchio who was strapping on the forty-five. Dinocchio returned the salute lazily.

"Didn't you go to the dance, Regan?" Devereaux asked. He was a short man with coal black hair, brown eyes, and a wide chipmunk grin. He had thick black eyebrows which always seemed slightly askew, and he spoke with something of a sneer in his voice, as if thirty-six years of living owed him more than a miserable existence as a lieutenant j.g. aboard a Navy destroyer, an attitude strengthened by the fact that life aboard the *Juneau* had been more formal but at the same time more civilized than this.

"I went, sir," David said.

"How'd you escape the melée?" Devereaux asked, his eyebrows askew, a twinkle in his brown eyes.

"I left when it started, sir."

"Good boy," Devereaux said in admiration. His eyes flicked to the dock. "Take a look at this. Here's an example."

Two sailors were stumbling towards the gangway, arm in arm, weaving drunkenly. Their whites were stained with blood, the jumpers torn, the trousers streaked with grass marks. Cautiously, they helped each other up the gangway, releasing their supporting embrace on each other to salute the ensign on the fantail—which ensign had been taken down at sunset—and then to salute Mr. Dinocchio who regarded them with sour Boston distaste

"Reques' permission to come aboar', sir," the first sailor said.

"Yeah, come ahead, Nelson, come ahead," Dinocchio said.

"Ditto, sir," the second sailor said.

"All right, all right," Dinocchio said, annoyed. "Come on, go get out of those clothes. You're all full of blood, both of you."

"Sir," the second sailor said, "do you know who is the bes' buddy inna whole worl', sir?"

"Who?" Dinocchio said.

"This fella here. Nelson. This fella. Yeoman Firs' Class Rishard Nelson. The bes' buddy onna ship, inna Navy, inna whole wi' worl'!" The sailor waved his arm grandiosely and almost fell over the side. Nelson caught him and held him up.

"No, sir," Nelson said to his friend. "No, sir buddy-boy, nossir. *You* are the bes' buddy inna worl'."

"No, *you* are."

"No, mate, *you* are the bes', abso-lutely!"

The second sailor turned to Dinocchio. "Okay, sir, so tell me summin, willya, sir? Would you?"

"What is it, Antonelli?"

Antonelli grinned. "Sir, why should my bes' buddy inna worl' hit me onna head with a whisky bottle?"

"I thought you was a gook," Nelson said.

"I ain' no gook."

"I *thought* you was one."

"Buddy, you nearly bust my head. You know that, buddy?"

"All right, let's hit the sack," Dinocchio said, "before I put you both on report."

"Two buddies?" Antonelli asked, astonished. "Sir, you would put two *buddies* on report?"

"Come on, come on, shove off."

The sailors embraced again and wobbled off towards the aft compartment, arm in arm.

"You should see some of the others," Devereaux said. "Arbuster came back with a broken arm. Do you know him? A gunner's mate?"

"I think so, sir," David said. He hesitated a moment, and then said, "Well, good night, sir. I guess I'll turn in."

"Just a second, Regan," Devereaux said.

"Sir?"

"Have you got a minute?"

"Yes, sir."

"Let's take a walk aft, have a cigarette."

"Yes, sir," David said, puzzled.

"What a vessel," Dinocchio said in his broad Boston accent. "This ship is the last stronghold of baaa-barism in the Pacific fleet."

"Things are rough all over, Lou," Devereaux said. He grinned his chipmunk grin, added, "Don't forget now, the skipper wants to be wakened as soon as everyone's aboard," and then began walking with David towards the fantail. The garbage cans had not been dumped. They were stacked just forward of the fantail depth-charge rack, and they stank to high heaven.

"We picked a spot, didn't we?" Devereaux said, grinning. "Let's just walk, shall we?"

He handed David a cigarette and then lighted it for him. The two began strolling up the starboard side of the ship. It was a beautiful night. The mountains of Kauai nuzzled against a soft wheeling black sky.

"Is something wrong, sir?' David asked. The gun, he thought. He knows about the gun.

"No, Regan, nothing at all. I just wanted to talk to you."

"What about, sir?" David asked apprehensively. This had to be about the gun. Somehow Devereaux had learned about the forty-five. I should have turned it in, David thought; I should have turned it in long before this. He had acquired the automatic shortly after the engagement in the Santa Cruz Islands, quite by accident, a simple matter of having the side arm strapped to his waist during small-arms instruction, and hearing chow-down being piped, and absent-mindedly wearing the gun into the mess hall. And afterwards he had looked for the gunner's mate who'd served as instructor and had not been able to find him, and had been called to stand his own watch, and had put the gun into his locker for safekeeping. And then, somehow, it had been too late to turn the gun in. It was Government property, and he was afraid they'd think he'd stolen it. That would mean a captain's mast, at least. Besides, there was something reassuring about the presence of the gun in his locker, resting in lethal power under his handkerchiefs.

"As you must realize," Devereaux said, grinning. "I am the newest officer aboard in the communications division. Technically, I outrank the four ensigns in the division, but tenure and longevity seem to be on their side—so I've been assigned the somewhat distasteful task of censoring the men's mail."

"Yes, sir?" David said, and felt instantly relieved. This wasn't about the gun, then; the gun was safe. But what . . . and he thought of some of the letters he'd sent to Ardis Fletcher. Was *that* what this was all about? Were the letters——?

Devereaux laughed suddenly. "I'm an English instructor by trade, Regan. I teach at U.C.L.A. when I'm not nursing radar. You should see some of the letters that come through. Unbelievable. Positively unbelievable."

"Yes, sir," David said. "Sir, if my letters——"

"Especially some of the Southern boys. Not that I'm in any way prejudiced against our Dixie brethren, but they use the language as if it's a foreign tongue. It rankles. I respect English. It's my trade."

"Yes, sir," David said. He wet his lips. That's what Devereaux was getting at, the letters to Ardis. He'd used some pretty strong language in those letters. Well, what the hell, he was writing them to Ardis and not the whole damn Pacific fleet! He was beginning to resent the idea that letters written to a girl, *personal* letters written to a girl with whom a fellow had been, well, *intimate*, could be read by some jerk from U.C.L.A. just because he had a silver bar on his shoulder. He knew his mail was censored, of course, but the censor had been someone faceless up to now. How could he ever write another personal letter knowing that Mr. Devereaux with his crooked chipmunk smile was going to read it before it got mailed?"

"Your letters are refreshing, Regan," Devereaux said suddenly.

"Sir?"

"Your letters."

"Yes, sir."

"I enjoy them."

"Yes, sir," David said, and he thought, You son of a bitch, you've got a lot of gall reading my personal mail and then telling me you enjoy it. "Yes, sir, thank you," he said coldly.

"Oh, say," Devereaux said, "I didn't mean . . ."

"What *did* you mean, sir?"

"I wasn't interested in content, Regan. I was only interested in style."

"I thought the two were inseparable, sir," David said, and Devereaux studied him appreciatively for a moment. The night was still. They could hear the water lapping against the steel sides of the ship.

"Ever tried any real writing, Regan?"

"What do you mean, sir?"

"Stories! A book?"

"No, sir."

"Ever felt like it?"

"No, sir."

"You should."

"Why?" David asked flatly.

Devereaux shrugged. "I think you'd be pretty good."

"Thank you, sir, but——"

"Regan, I *teach* creative writing, and I read a great deal of student material, and I think you have potential. I'm sorry if you felt I was intruding on your privacy by reading your mail. I have to read it, anyway. It's my job. I didn't ask for it, but I've got it. I only wanted to say that if you ever *did* decide to try your hand at a short story or anything else, I'd be happy to look at it and offer my suggestions and criticisms, for whatever they're worth."

"Thank you, sir."

Devereaux threw his cigarette over the side. It arced towards the water, its tip glowing, and then suddenly hissed and went out.

"Sir, I'm sorry, but some of those letters were pretty personal."

"Of course, Regan."

"And I guess I felt a little funny, knowing you'd read them."

"Of course."

"And thank you, sir, for your interest, but I don't think I'd like to be a writer."

"Why not?"

"I just don't think I would, sir, that's all."

"What does your father do, Regan?"

"He's dead, sir."

"Oh, I'm sorry. What *did* he do?"

"He was an art director, sir. With an advertising agency."

"Well, Devereaux said. "That's very creative work."

"Yes, sir."

"I should think——"

"No, sir, thank you. Is that all, sir? I'm pretty tired. I'd like to hit the sack."

"Sure, Regan, go ahead."

"Thank you, sir. Good night." He nodded and began walking aft in the darkness.

"Regan?"

David stopped.

"Think it over," Devereaux said.

When Gillian Burke got home for the Christmas vacation, the first thing her mother said to her was, "Well, how's the big actress?"

"Just fine, thanks," Gillian said quickly. "I've been offered a part in a Broadway show. I'm replacing Helen Hayes."

"I asked a serious question," her mother said.

"It sounded just about as serious as hell. I'm tired, Mom. I've been on trains for the past two and a half hours." She paused. "I want to go to bed."

"It's only five o'clock."

"Are there laws about when a person can go to bed?"

"Of course there aren't laws!"

"Then, would you mind? I'm exhausted, and I'm about to get the curse, and I feel . . ."

"I see your language hasn't improved now that you're a serious student of the drah-mah," her mother said.

"I *am* a serious student," Gillian answered heatedly. "And, Mother, I think you should know that *ridicule* isn't going to help one damn bit. I'm enrolled at Talmadge, and I'm going to keep studying at Talmadge, so why don't you just get used to the fact that——"

"Your father spoiled you," Virginia Burke said.

"I thought he spoiled Monica."

"He spoiled both of you. She isn't even coming home for the holidays, your charming sister."

"She's in California, Mom," Gillian said wearily. "Do you want her to spend her entire vacation on a train?"

"There are planes," Virginia said flatly.

"Servicemen are travelling home."

"What do I care about servicemen? Monica's my daughter."

"Servicemen are very sweet-oh," Gillian said. "I'm going to bed. Wake me when Dad gets home, will you?"

"Very *what*?" Virginia said.

"Sweet-oh," Gillian replied, and she went into her room.

She didn't bother to undress. She took off her loafers—she had refused to get all dolled up for a train ride—and then crawled in under the blankets and was asleep almost immediately.

When she awoke, the room was dark. She lay in the darkness for a moment, disorientated, and then realized where she was. She yawned sleepily and raised her arms towards the ceiling. Well, here we are, she thought. Back at the old manse. Everything cheerful and gay, the darkies singing in the south forty, the smell of magnolias oozing through the windows, the candles being lighted on the long dining-room table downstairs, *Scarlett O'Hara stretched her arms to the ceiling and wondered whether she would wear the new organdie or the taffeta, after all the Tarleton twins were coming, and that was an occasion. Besides, there was talk of war in the air, war between the States, and she wanted to be dressed properly for the outbreak of hostilities.*

The old manse, Gillian thought, and she climbed out of bed and walked to the window, raising the shade and looking out over the Bronx rooftops, and the lights of the Woodlawn Road–Jerome Avenue elevated structure in the distance. She turned away from the window, snapped on the dresser lamp and looked at the clock.

At first she thought it had stopped. Then she heard its ticking, and she looked at the time again. Eleven o'clock. Hadn't she asked to be awakened when Dad got home? Didn't they *ever* do anything she asked them to do?

She went to the door and opened it. She could hear the sound of the radio in the living-room.

"Mom?" she called.

"Yes?"

"Dad still up?"

"He's not home yet, dear," Virginia said.
"Didn't he come home for supper?"
"No, Gillian."
"Well, didn't he call?"
"No, he didn't."
"Well, where is he?"
"I don't know, Gillian."

She closed the door, leaned against it for a moment, shrugged, and decided she needed a shower. She began getting out of her clothes. She paused at the full-length mirror behind the door, studying her body. I was bigger when I was fifteen, she thought. I'm losing weight in all the wrong places. She shrugged again, examined a blemish near her jaw, and then went into the bathroom. Her father had not yet come home by the time she'd showered and brushed out her hair. In the living-room, her mother was knitting and listening to the radio.

"Not back yet, huh?"
"No, not yet," Virginia said.
"He probably got stuck downtown."
"Probably."
"This is his busy season," Gillian said. "Christmas."
"Yes, I know."

She stood silently watching her mother. "I think I'll go down for a walk," she said.

"You just took a shower, Gillian."
"What's that got to do with it?"
"Did you dry yourself?"
"No, I left myself all wet. I like to walk in the cold all wet."
"Don't be sarcastic, Gillian."
"Well, Mom, of *course* I dried myself. Do I look like a cretin?"
"It's too late for a young girl to be walking around the streets alone," Virginia said.
"Hey, why don't you come with me, Mom?" she said, suddenly inspired. "It's pretty nice out. Kind of bracing."

Virginia looked up at her daughter. In the amber glow of the single lamp burning in the living-room, the two—mother and daughter—looked very much alike, the same red-brown hair, the same green eyes, the same angular face, the same bone structure, they looked very much alike.

"No," Virginia said. "Thank you, Gillian. I want to finish this sleeve."

"Finish it tomorrow. What's so important about it?"
"I promised Monica she'd have it for her birthday."
"That's not until February."

"Still," Virginia said, and fell silent.

"Okay," Gillian said. She shrugged awkwardly. "Okay." She started out of the room, thinking, My birthday is in January. Oddly, she could not remember what her mother had given her the year before. "Well, I'll go down then, okay?" she said. She looked back into the room. "Okay?"

Her mother did not look up from the knitting. "All right, Gillian," she said.

She met some of the kids in the cafeteria, and they sat drinking hot chocolates. Gillian told them all about Talmadge. One of the girls said Ohio State was a very nice place because the Navy had a V-5 programme there and a lot of handsome fellows were training to become officers. The girl was studying to be a teacher, and Gillian said, quite suddenly, "Are you preparing to be a teacher or a mother?"

"A teacher, of course."

"You sound as if you went all the way to Ohio to date sailors."

"Gillian, that's not fair!"

"All right, I'm mistaken."

"I can get all the dates I want right here in the Bronx!"

"Good. Why don't you go to Hunter College? It's right on Kingsbridge Road."

"It's an all-girls' school, Gillian!"

"Oh, I see," Gillian said, and at that instant her father walked into the cafeteria. He was a tall man with brilliant red hair and wide shoulders, his face as uneven as if it had been hewn from obstinate stone. He never wore a hat, and his face always looked flushed, and his blue eyes had a way of nailing you to the wall when he spoke to you. He ran a shoe store downtown on Second Avenue, but he was always being mistaken for a detective. When Gillian was a little girl, she used to tell the other kids her father was an F.B.I. agent.

"That's your father, isn't——?"

"Shhh," she said. She watched him secretly as he went to the counter, got himself a cup of coffee, and then walked to a table at the rear of the cafeteria. She smiled.

"Excuse me," she said to the girls and she rose, the smile still on her face, and began walking towards the rear table, suddenly wishing she were wearing heels. She walked directly to the table, and she stood there and said nothing until her father looked up at her. He didn't recognize her for an instant.

"His," she said.

"Gillian," he answered, "how arr yuh, darrlin'?" with the exaggerated brogue he used whenever he was feeling particularly good. He stood and embraced his daughter and then kissed the top of her head. "Sit down, Gilly. When did you get in? What *arr* you doin' down in the streets at this hour, shame on yuh, do yuh want someone to be draggin' you into the bushes?"

"Oh, Dad," she said, smiling, ducking her head, embarrassed somehow because he always made her feel like a little girl no matter what he said, and wishing again she were wearing heels. She squeezed his big fist on the table. "Why are you so late, Dad? Didn't you know I was coming home?"

"I did, darrlin', I did, but we were doing a lot of business downtown, and I just couldn't turn them away, would you like a cup of coffee? Gilly, you're looking *marrr*-vellous, school agrees with you, I see. I told your mother it would. How arr yuh, darlin' ?"

"I'm fine, Dad," she said, grinning.

"And are you learning your trade?"

"I am."

"Good, good, let me get you a cup of coffee."

"No, Dad, that's all right. Let's just sit and talk."

"Did you come down by train?"

"Yes."

"None of the kids coming home by car?"

"There's only one girl from the Bronx who has a car, Dad, and she's a stiff-oh. I'd rather have walked."

"A stiff-oh, eh?" Meredith Burke said, and he burst out laughing, a laugh that erupted from his barrel chest and filled the near-empty cafetaria. Gillian laughed with him.

"Really, Dad."

"I know, I know," Meredith said. "My, you're looking fine, Gilly. You've got a sparkle in your eyes, and a good high colour. Have you seen your mother?"

"Sure."

"Is she still angry?"

"I don't know," Gillian said, shrugging.

"She'll get over it. You see, Gillian, she doesn't know what we know, now does she?"

"What's that, Dad?"

"She doesn't know you're going to be a *grrrreat* actress, now does she? She thinks you're going to take all those lessons and then go knocking on producers' doors or wherever it is starving young actresses go knocking, and then taking parts in summer stock, and bits in the chorus, that's what your mother thinks. But we know, don't we, Gilly?"

"Yes, Dad."

"Sure we do." He nodded. "*I* know, Gilly. I *know*," He nodded silently and then he said, "Gilly, do you know what I'd like to do right now?"

"What, Dad?"

"I'd like to go into the bar on the corner and show off my grown-up daughter to my friends. What do you say, Gilly? Have you taken to drinking beer yet?"

"Oh, Daddy, I'm under age," she said, smiling. "They wouldn't serve me."

"Do they serve you in Talmadge, Connecticut?"

"No, but we sneak beer into the dorm from the grocery store," Gillian said, giggling.

"They'll serve you here," he said. "They'd damn well *better* serve my daughter. Come on."

He rose and extended his arm to her, and she looped her hand through it, smiling, and thinking again, I *should* have worn heels.

David showed Mr. Devereaux his first story a few days before Christmas.

It was a story about a man drowning.

He was a little embarrassed about showing it to the j.g., especially after he'd so vehemently objected to the idea of writing one. But one day while he was leaning on one of the depth-charge racks and looking out over the water, he began thinking of that day at the lake. And all at once, he wanted to write about it. He'd typed up the story on one of the ship's machines, and gave it to Devereaux the next day.

"It's all in capital letters," he said. "There're only caps on the radio shack's typewriters."

"That's all right," Devereaux said. He glanced at the first page. "*Man Drowning*, huh? That's a good title."

"Yes, sir." David looked at the manuscript uneasily. "Sir, maybe you'd better let me have it back."

"Why?"

"Well . . . it's pretty bad."

"Let me be the judge of that, all right?"

"Well, sir, if you want to waste your time with——"

"It's my time, Regan. Don't worry about it."

"Still, sir, it's pretty bad," David insisted.

David was right, Devereaux discovered. Not only was the story pretty bad, it was very bad. It was, in fact, totally lacking in quality, totally devoid of any talent. The worthlessness of the manuscript presented Devereaux with a peculiar dilemma. He was aware that, had he not prodded David into trying his hand at fiction, David would have gone along writing uninhibited and emotional letters to Miss Hot Pants in Talmadge, Connecticut, and never given a thought to more ambitious stuff. But Devereaux *had* planted the thought in David's head, and this was the result of that seed, and the result was pretty awful. So what to do about it now?

Devereaux was disappointed. But more than that, for a reason he could not understand, he took David's inability as a personal affront, as if a horse he had bet upon heavily had somehow let him down in the stretch. He admitted to himself that David Regan did not possess the tiniest shred of talent, and then he was irrationally annoyed by the lack of talent. How could he have been so fooled?

I made a mistake, that's all, he reasoned. The kindest thing would be to tell young Regan I made a mistake. He has no talent. I was wrong. That's the kindest thing to do, and that's what I will do.

But that was not what he did. Perversely, he continued to believe that David had wilfully tricked him into a false belief. Perversely, and completely unconsciously, he pursued a course over which he had very little real control.

He asked to see David three days after Christmas, long after he had read the story, long after his initial disappointment had had an opportunity to harden into an angry resentment. The black gang had discovered babbitt in the engines and reported it to the captain, who had asked that the *Hanley* be sent back into dry dock. The two met in Combat Information Centre, the radar shack. A small palm tree which the boys had brought aboard and decorated with homemade Christmas ornaments sat in the centre of the plotting board, lighted from below.

"Come on over here," Devereaux said, and they went to the table just inside the doorway, on the bulkhead behind the Sugar George. The radarmen usually stood voice radio watch when they were in port, a duty which had been curtailed while the ship was in dry dock. A radio receiver was on the shelf above the table, the earphones dangling. Devereaux unplugged the phones and threw them to a corner of the table. He snapped on a light. "This is a pretty good story, Regan," he said. "Why'd you choose to write about a man drowning?"

"I don't know, sir."

"My name is George," Devereaux said, and then wondered why he had said it.

"Sir?"

"George. Call me George. Let's cut out this officer–enlisted man bunk. We're here to get some *real* work done, aren't we? This is a little more important than twiddling radar dials."

"Yes, sir."

"*George*," Devereaux said.

"George," David repeated hesitantly. He wet his lips.

"Good. Why'd you start your story this way, David?"

"Because that's the way it . . ." David stopped. "I don't know, sir. It came to me that way?."

"Is this a true story? Is that it?"

"No, sir."

"George."

"George. It isn't, George. I made it up."

"Who's the man in this story, David?"

"Nobody I know, si . . . George."

"Your father?"

David was silent.

"Your father, David?"

"Yes, sir," he said softly.

Devereaux nodded. "That's all right. That's a good way to begin. A lot of writers use personal experiences as a springboard. Is this the way he died, David? By drowning?"

"Y . . . yes, sir. That . . . that was the way it happened."

"I see. Well, I'll tell you what I'd like you to do, David. That is, if you really want to, if you think you've got the stamina it takes."

"Wh . . . what's that, sir?"

"I'd like you to rewrite this story."

"Why, sir?"

"Because I think we can sell it."

"Sell it?"

"To one of the magazines. Oh, you won't get much for it, but it'll be a start. What do you say, David?"

"Well, George, I . . ." It was easier to say the name now, somewhat easier, but still a little strange. "I don't know, George. Do you really think it has a chance?"

"Absolutely," Devereaux said. "Now here's what I think is wrong with it."

He did not tell David everything he thought was wrong with it. In his honest opinion, everything was wrong with it, and nothing was right, and his criticism would have filled three volumes of tiny print. But he did point out a few of the errors to David, and all the while he wondered why he didn't simply tell David the truth.

He was pleased, he was almost delighted when David let him down once more with the revisions. If anything, the rewrite made the story worse than it was originally. Devereaux suspected this would happen, but the horror of the writing soared beyond his wildest dreams. This was terrible, absolute garbage! How could he have been so fooled by those letters?

"This is beautiful," he said to David. "But I'll tell you something, David, do you mind?"

"No, what is it, George?"

"I think it still needs a little work. Now, take this middle section . . ."

David took the middle section and, as it turned out, also the end section and, for good measure, a paragraph in the beginning section and sat down in the gear-locker opposite the radio shack to begin his new revisions. George Devereaux had no idea how much pain was involved in the rewrite, but he probably would not have discouraged David even if he had known. The pain for David was excruciating. Somehow, all the fluidity of his letter-writing left him the moment he sat down at the typewriter. The radiomen's machine had keys which were blank, and David stared down at their empty faces and despaired he would ever get a word on paper. He was a bad typist to begin with, and the unlettered keys made composition enormously more difficult for him. Silently, he struggled in the tiny compartment, telling himself he could do it, he would do it, and knowing somehow he would never finish this story, knowing he could never polish it enough to satisfy Mr. Devereaux.

The greatest pain was the pain of memory.

The more he struggled with the story, the sharper the memory became. And, paradoxically, the sharper the memory became, the more difficult it was to put on paper. For whereas the day of his father's drowning, 9 September, 1939 would always be clear in his mind, the memory seemed to extend beyond that into a murky distance, extend in fact to the summer of 1938, more than a year before the drowning, so that the edges of the memory were hazy and vague, but painful none the less. Nor did he understand why he should consider his mother's trip to Europe an essential part of the drowning, a prelude to it, and yet the twin memories were irrevocably linked, the trip to Europe seeming to flow inexorably into the summer of 1939 and that fateful day in September at Lake Abundance, Connecticut.

The fringes of the memory were blurred, like double-exposures of the mind. Picture overlapped picture until there was no sense of time, no proper sequence of events, until the mind reeled with the task of sorting and cataloguing, each picture leading inevitably to that final image in September, the thing he saw through the binoculars as he looked out over the lake, each picture a seemingly separate and unconnected event, and yet overlapping towards an overwhelming conclusion. He did not know where it began, he only knew where it ended.

There was something about Aunt Millie being sick, he remembered hearing talk about this as early as, yes, it must have been the spring of 1938, yes, his mother standing slender and tall in a green bathing suit at the kitchen phone, yes, they were at the lake, they had just opened the house, he could remember the scent of pines, yes, her brown hair pushed back over one ear as she held the receiver and nodded, "Yes, Millie, yes, I understand," the sun limning the profile David had inherited, the scent of pines, the sounds of the lake outside, and then another image, the end of June, the lake house waiting for them, the Talmadge house about to be closed for the summer, the sheets covering all the furniture, the big mahogany dining-room table, the gentle clink of silverware, his father's lean face bent over his soup bowl, "Arthur, it's her lungs," the *clink-clink* of silverware, the shine of the overhead chandelier on sparkling glasses, *clink* against white china, "She wants to go away for a while, Arthur, somewhere dry," his father looking up from his soup suddenly, attentively, "She's asked me to go with her."

July, and the full onslaught of real summer, the trees hung with lush foliage, David hitting croquet balls on the lawn in front of the lake house, the sound of mallet against ball, and beneath that the sound of a whispered conversation, the red and blue awning, the lawn chairs painted red and blue, the lawn a thick summer green, and the trees dressed in a shining gaudiness, "There's going to be a war," Arthur Regan whispered. "Why does she want to go to *Italy*, of all places?"

His mother's voice quietly persistent, her fingers moving in her lap, rolling a tall wet glass between the palms of her hands, the glass flashing in the sun, never raising her eyes or her voice, "The climate, Arthur."

"She can go to Arizona."

"That's true. But she wants to go to Italy."

"She can go alone, then."

"No, she can't, Arthur."

"Why in the name of God must *you* go with her?"

"She's sick, Arthur."

"She's not *that* sick!"

"She has a chronic bronchial condition, Arthur."

"Then let her hire a nurse. Or a travelling companion."

"She's my sister. I won't have her going off to Europe alone."

"Goddamnit, Julia——"

"The boy."

"Never mind the boy. You listen to me. If a war breaks out, you'll be right in the middle of it!"

"War is not going to break out."

"No?"

"No. Hitler and Mussolini may be mad, but they're not going to mount a winter offensive."

"Now just what do you know about——?"

"I know that smart generals are afraid of winter offensives, that much I know. And Millie and I will be back before the spring."

"You won't be back before the spring, Julia, because you're not *going* anywhere. You're staying right here in Talmadge."

"We're leaving on August first, Arthur. And we'll be back in January. Now stop behaving like a child."

The airport in New York, the immense imposing bulk of the aeroplane, its giant wings casting deep shadows on the concrete strip, his mother and his aunt climbing the ramp and then turning back to wave, the door of the plane closing, the engines suddenly roaring into life, the propellers spinning, a flutter of newspaper scraps across the concrete, image upon image, frightening, crowding into the small compartment across the passageway from the *Hanley's* radio room, images, sounds, the telephone call from London. "David? David, darling? Is that you?"

"Yes, Mom."

"How *are* you, darling?"

"Fine, Mom."

"Are you all right? I can barely hear you."

"I'm fine, Mom."

"David, I saw the changing of the guard today. David, I do wish you were with me."

"How's Aunt Millie, Mom? Will you be coming home soon?"

"She's all right, darling. Let me talk to your father again."

The cards from Paris, *This is the Eiffel Tower. Millie and I had lunch here yesterday. You can see the whole city of Paris. Guess what, David? Even the children here speak French, ha-ha. Your loving mother, Julia,* and the cards on the long road to Rome. *This is Dijon. They say it is a little Paris. I am sending you some wonderfully tasty mustards,* across into Switzerland, *Berne is like a toy town. There are marvellous medieval statues and a clock that does everything but explode,* over the Alps into Italy, *Stresa reminds me of Lake Abundance, you step out of your hotel and go right into the water,* across the Italian peninsula, *Everything is sere and sunny, the fields are straight out of Van Gogh, the sun is brilliant, tomorrow we will be in Milan,* and then *Rome! I can't believe it! A fabulous city all gold and white, a city within cities a city beneath cities. Yesterday I walked along the very road Caesar took on his way to the Forum. I could feel the ghosts of dead assassins, and everywhere these wonderful Italians whose faces speak volumes. I shall go back to Rome often. We are only two hours away here in Aquila, and the drive is a beautiful one, and I feel time in that city, I feel time beneath the streets and in the air, I feel history. I shall go there often.*

The first snow came to Talmadge at the end of November. He

could remember crying in his room alone because his mother was not there to see the model aeroplane he had started, watching the snowflakes falling outside his window, and then a new rush of overlapping images, a flurry of speed. "David, we're going to Aquila for Christmas!" He could not believe his father's words, weeping and laughing at the same time, hugging his father, feeling his father's coarse moustache against his cheek, and then feeling his father's own tears. "We're going to Italy, David. We'll take her home with us!"

She was waiting for them in the garden in the villa. She was wearing a yellow dress and a wide-brimmed straw hat, and only a sweater was thrown over her shoulders although it was quite cold, she looked a little chubbier, "as round as a partridge," David's father said, and he hugged her, and she said, "David, you're getting to be a man," and he blushed and said, "I tried out for the handball team in school, Mom," and she hugged him, and he felt suddenly happy in the garden in the villa outside Rome. They went everywhere in those two weeks, *everywhere*, the Spanish Steps, he counted them, St. Peter's where he rubbed the foot of the bronze statue where the toes were worn away, the Coliseum, "Look, David! See the lions!" his mother shouted, and he turned abruptly to see three scraggly alley cats roaming through the ruins, and Hadrian's Tomb, the Castel Sant' Angelo sitting across the golden Tiber with the midday winter sun bright overhead, everywhere, they did everything, he ate *tortoni* at an outdoor café while his mother and father sipped their *aperitifs* and he watched two German officers sitting at a near-by table, the swastika bold and black on the white field of their armbands, it did not seem as if a war were coming, the black taxicabs beeping along the streets, the long shutters in the windows of the hotels and apartment buildings, Aquila, 2,360 feet high and bitter cold, the skiers in their heavy sweaters, and the garden bright with winter sunshine where they sat bundled against the cold and his mother poured hot tea, Father watching with his blue eyes aglow, Aunt Millie coughing discreetly into her handkerchief. Rome, and a cold, clear blue sky, a city of white and gold, a city within cities, a city beneath cities, and the promise that Julia Regan would come back with them to Talmadge when they left. He could not understand why they left Aquila without her. He could not understand why she had to stay in Italy longer.

Talmadge in the winter. January and February, the doldrum months. Lake Abundance caught in the grip of ice, the skating parties, he fell and bruised his hip once, there was a new girl in town, he became aware of her at once, her name was Ardis Fletcher, the boys said you could do things to her, her father was an engineer,

March and a sudden burst of warmth, the forsythias blooming unexpectedly and then withering under a new attack of undiminished winter, she had told them she'd be home on April tenth, he had circled the date on the calendar in his room, 10 April, 10 April, hurry home, please.

In April, there was a cable. MILLIE ILL AND UNABLE TO TRAVEL. DEPARTURE DELAYED. LETTER FOLLOWS. LOVE JULIA.

Love Julia. Cablegrams had a blue border. He hadn't known that.

The promised letter did not arrive until the next week. Millie was unexpectedly worse, it said, she had begun coughing badly, and each night her temperature soared. A specialist had been consulted, every hope this was simply a temporary thing and not something more serious like pneumonia, in any case impossible to consider travelling home at this time, darlings, how terribly I miss you, understand and forgive me, it is imperative that I stay here with Millie, know that you have all my love, Julia.

June of 1939, the war talk stronger now, the world certain that Hitler would march, the letters continuing from Julia in the villa at Aquila, two a week, one to Arthur, one to David, at the end of June he kissed Ardis, her mouth was soft, she kept it open, "*Everyone here seems convinced that Hitler is bluffing. In any case, there does not seem to be a climate of preparation for war, no matter what you felt at Christmastime. I know this is foremost in your mind, Arthur, but believe me, darling, Millie and I are in no immediate danger. She is improving rapidly, and I expect we shall be leaving for home in July. I shall contact the steamship lines today on my way to the post office. I'm sure we can book passage for the last week in July or, at the very latest, the first week in August.* Carissimi, vi voglio molto bene. *I will be home soon.*"

Julia Regan came back to Talmadge on August twenty-eighth, three days before Hitler marched into Poland. Millie was with her, looking remarkably well for her ordeal, but drawn somehow, her eyes curiously averted, as if her long illness were something shameful.

David held his mother's hands and looked into her face and said, "You look different," and she smiled at him, a rare and peaceful smile, and said, "But so do you, my love." A hundred things to tell her, a thousand things, "Did you see my finger? It's all swelled up from where a baseball hit it," a million things to show her, the strange wild flowers blooming on the edge of the lawn. "Mom, I got an eighty-five in my geometry end-term," so much to show, so much to say, "Tad Parker is shaving already, did I tell you? He wants to be an actor, Mom," and his father's eyes smiling, Julia Regan was home. Julia Regan was home again.

The image blurred, the focus changed, the molecules of memory swirled like fragments of dark metal in a magnetic field, black against white, and from the vortex there emerged a penetrating single memory, the sharp relentless memory of that single day, September, yes, that single fall day at Lake Abundance, yes, crystal-clear, knife-edged, horrifying.

It was Saturday, September ninth.

There was clear bright sunshine that day, and suffocating heat.

"Why don't we go to the lake?" he said.

"Yes, that's a good idea."

The lake was still and calm. There was not a ripple on its surface. It mirrored the pines. His mother was in green.

"Let me take your picture, Mom," he said.

"Arthur, get in the picture."

"No. I want to take the boat out."

"Arthur . . ."

"I said no."

Sorrow? Pain? What was it that flashed suddenly in his mother's eyes? Fleeting, and then gone, she smiled for the camera. Click, the shutter went.

He saw the boat edging out from the dock. The lake was still and silent. All was still. The world was still. Behind the boat, the lake broke in a pie-shaped wake. There was stillness. A bird screamed into the shimmering heat from somewhere in the tops of the pines.

The boat was white on pine-stained water. His father was wearing a silly red straw hat which she had brought back from Italy. David saw the boat get smaller and smaller as his father rowed to the centre of the lake. The red hat became a tiny dot in the distance. From somewhere in the pines, hidden, the bird screamed again and across the lake another bird answered.

"Where are the binoculars, Mom?" he asked.

He adjusted the focus. He could see the boat clearly now. The boat, and the lake beyond, and his father's face shaded by the wide brim of the silly red hat.

"What's he doing, David?"

"Getting ready to throw out the anchor, I think."

"Why? He didn't take a fishing rod, did he?"

"No, he didn't."

The sun was intense. He could feel it on his head and shoulders. The lake shimmered. The bird was silent now. David could see his father clearly as he stooped to pick up the heavy anchor, an anchor too big for so small a boat. He hesitated a moment, his hands holding the anchor over the side. Then his hands opened.

Watching through the binoculars, David saw his hands opening. The anchor was gone. In the boat, the rope was swiftly paying itself out, coil after coil, following the anchor Suddenly.

Suddenly.

"Mom!"

His father was going over the side.

"Mom, he's caught in the——"

"What? What is it?"

"The rope! The rope! The rope!"

The scream hung on the silent shimmering air, the single word echoing and re-echoing across the lake, the rope, the rope, the rope, the rope, assaulting his ears in waves of echoed sound. He held the binoculars tightly because all reality was suddenly imprisoned in the circle of their focus, there was nothing real except in the twin tubes he held in his hands, reflected in the lens, the shouted word died out, and through the binoculars he watched the lake, waiting for his father to surface, waiting, waiting, he could hear the ticking of the watch on his wrist, loud in the sudden terrifying silence.

"*Dad!*" he shrieked.

He was running towards the lake front. He had thrown away the binoculars, and he was running now, his heart hammering in his chest. He felt the water touch his trousers, I'm wearing sneakers, he thought, and he made a shallow dive, his arms thrashing immediately, his legs wildly kicking as he swam towards the boat and the widening circle of ripples on the water.

The boat was so far away.

He was crying when he reached it. The tears ran down his face, and his arms and legs were weak, and he trembled with exhaustion, and he repeated over and over again to the awful red hat floating on the water, "Dad, Dad, Dad . . ."

It was not very long before George Devereaux discovered he hated David Regan. The idea did not surprise him. He accepted it calmly and even recognized that the hatred had possibly been there from the very beginning, a thing which had been growing steadily over the months. He knew, too, that he was acting somewhat childishly in expecting David to meet impossible standards, but the childishness did not disturb him. He did wonder about it, though. He was, after all, thirty-six years old, and he had been disappointed by students before. But if the boy had no talent, why had he put him through the ordeal of a rewrite? Why, indeed, even though his original premise had been strengthened, did he still persist in asking for more revisions on the same terrible story?

He has to be punished, Devereaux thought.

But he would not leave it at that. He was an intelligent, educated man and he wanted to know why David had to be punished. So he turned the question inward and the answer he found was *He has to be punished because he has to be punished*. He has to be punished because he fooled me. But I've been fooled before, I have singled out a student and come up with a dud. Why does this boy have to be punished. Why am I behaving so childishly? He has to be punished, all right, admit it, he has to be punished because *I* made a mistake, yes, that is why. I've been away from teaching for too long a time. Maybe I'm losing my touch, my grasp. Maybe all this naval communications bull is beginning to suffocate me. Maybe I don't know a good story from a bad one any more. He has to be punished because he has taught me I'm getting rusty, that's absurd.

He recognized the absurdity at once.

He was certainly not putting the boy through the ordeal of constantly rewriting a story about his own father's drowning simply because he was beginning to doubt his own professionalism. That was specious reasoning, and George Devereaux was too honest to allow it to pass unchallenged. And so, as the revisons progressed, he continued to probe his own motives more deeply, and he finally concluded that he missed his students, that was it. And, because he missed them, he was elevating David Regan to the position where he represented *all* students, he was trying to make him the embodiment of every good student he'd ever had, a role David could never possibly fill. But that was all, that was the only reason. He missed his students.

And then he began wondering which of the students he missed particularly, and he began to call up names and faces, and he began to remember excellent stories which had been submitted in his classes, and he began to remember the wonderful quadrangles of the U.C.L.A. campus, and the young co-eds in sweaters and skirts, fresh-looking, carrying their books to class, stopping to chat with fellow students, always in the casual postures of the very young, Ardis Fletcher, the entrance gates to the univer . . .

He caught himself and quickly said to himself, I'm thirty-six years old with a pregnant wife and an eight-year-old son, cut it out.

But the name came into his mind again, Ardis Fletcher, and with the name a flood of co-ed memories, those sweet fresh faces in his classroom hanging on his every word, Ardis Fletcher, so innocent those faces, he would quirk his eyebrows purposely and twist his mouth into an enigmatic little grin, he would deliver his lecture to each and every one of them personally. "He makes you feel as if he's talking to you alone, doesn't he?" he had overheard one of his students say, Ardis Fletcher, I'm thirty-six years old, my wife's name is Abby, she is pregnant, I have an eight-year-old son.

He realized, without shock—it was amazing how none of these revelations seemed to shock him, he accepted them quite calmly, as if he had known them all along—he realized that perhaps he did miss his female students more than he missed any of the male students, well, perhaps he did play up a little to the girls in class, but that was only natural. He was only human, and there was something terribly gratifying to one's ego, all those sweet clean-scrubbed faces and those innocent eyes searching, so what if he did become a somewhat vain male at times, what if he did assume the role of a freshman matinée idol, even Abby said he had bedroom eyes, what was wrong with that, so long as he never touched any of them. Except that once. And even that was not my fault and not as if I *actually* touched her, she only rested herself, it was quite casual, on my arm, a gentle soft touch, she wasn't even aware, cushioned by the wool of her sweater, on my arm, how soft, how young, "Yes, Mr. Devereaux, I understand, but I thought I covered that in the second paragraph, here, do you see, here," how soft, but he had not touched her, not really.

Her name . . . he had fogotten her name, it was not at all like Fletcher, not anywhere near Fletcher, nor was she a redhead. Black hair, he could remember that well, falling in a hanging curtain over one eye as she leaned over the desk, soft against his arm, he could remember, not a redhead, Alice, yes, that was it, Alice.

And he sighed and admitted that possibly, just possibly, the letters from Regan to the girl in Talmadge had only possibly reminded him of a life he had loved, yes, of course, the campus and the pretty young girls and the balmy California air, Alice, yes, all right, even Alice, all those things, the letters from Regan had recaptured for him a youthful recklessness he once had known, that was all, and so he'd naturally been impressed, the letters were quite vivid, quite a good style the boy had, *I wasn't interested in content, Regan. I was only interested in style.* Face to face with it, now, he asked himself whether this was true, and he knew it was not. I *should* have, he thought, but she was such a child, and yet she was not unaware, I should have, that was no accident, the pressure against my arm. I should have, I *should* have!

So.

He sat in his cabin and stared at the grey bulkhead and thought, So. So let the boy go. Let him alone. What did he do? Knock over a round-heeled kid in Connecticut? Let him go. Let him go.

But he was still angry.

He was angry because he had recognized something about himself, and the knowledge was somewhat painful. And he was further angered because he believed that David, no matter how much anguish the revisions brought on, could not possibly be in as much pain as he was in at this moment. It seemed terribly unfair to him. Unfair that this kid with peach fuzz on his face could have this sweet ripe Ardis Fletcher in Connecticut, and unfair that this encounter which he had provoked with his letters should leave him relatively unscathed while it was causing his instructor such pain. Oh, what the hell, I've been in the Pacific too long, he thought, eight months is too long a time, I'm not thinking clearly, I'll tell Regan tomorrow that his story stinks to high heaven and will he please stop bothering me with it.

And perhaps he would have done just that, perhaps he would have spoken to David earnestly and sympathetically, told him that sometimes these things didn't work out and David shouldn't take it too badly, perhaps he'd have recognized that the pain involved for *himself* was becoming greater than whatever perverse satisfaction he derived out of punishing David, perhaps he'd have dropped the whole ridiculous thing if the skipper of the *Hanley* had not summoned him to the wardroom the next day.

"Sit down, Mr. Devereaux," he said. "Smoke?"

"Thank you, sir, no," Devereaux answered.

"Mind if I light up?"

"Not at all, sir."

Devereaux was familiar enough with the ways of the Navy to realize that all this parlour chit-chat was the prelude to some fancy chewing out. He wasn't particularly disturbed nor particularly nervous because he'd been chewed out before, and by experts. One senior officer aboard the *Juneau*, in fact, had been a first-class demagogue and the captain of the *Hanley* could never hope to achieve the same subtle heights of derisive oratory. So he waited patiently while the captain lighted a cigar and shook out the match and waved his hand before his face to clear the room of smoke.

"Now then," the captain said, and he smiled pleasantly at Devereaux, and Devereaux waited, watching with casual interest, not at all frightened or apprehensive, watching the captain as he would watch a movie being shown on the boat deck, uninvolved, impersonally, almost bored.

"I understand you were a teacher in civilian life, Mr. Devereaux, is that correct?"

"Yes, sir."

"Very interesting occupation," the captain said.

"Yes, sir," Devereaux answered, knowing full well that the captain did not think teaching was interesting, the captain thought only sailing the high seas was interesting, only being the hero commander of a naval warship was interesting. "Yes, sir, it is."

"Taught writing, didn't you?"

"Yes, sir."

"Regular discoverer of budding Hemingways, huh?"

"Some of my students were rath——"

"Good writer, Hemingway," the captain said. "Don't you think?"

"Yes, sir."

"How about Regan?"

"Regan, sir?" Devereaux said, puzzled for a moment.

"Yes. David Regan. Radarman, isn't he?"

"Oh. Oh, yes, sir. Regan." Devereaux nodded.

"What about him?"

"Well . . ." Devereaux shrugged. "What about him, sir? I don't understand."

"I understand you've been giving him writing lessons."

"Who told——" Devereaux cut himself short. "Not lessons exactly, sir. I've been helping him with a short story he wrote."

"That's very nice of you, Mr. Devereaux."

"Thank you, sir."

"Very nice."

"Thank you sir. The boy——"

"But of course, Mr. Devereaux, there are certain naval regulations which forbid fraternization between officer and enlisted man, as I'm sure you are well aware. These regulations are based on the sound facts of naval warfare, Mr. Devereaux, the premise being that the power of command is weakened when the person giving the command has become too friendly with the person receiving the command."

"Sir, I assure you——"

"I understand perfectly well, Mr. Devereaux, that *you* are aware of the responsibilities of being an officer in the United States Navy. However, I have never trusted the limited intelligence of the enlisted man, and I never shall. I should hate to have a friendship encouraged which would limit the fighting performance of any man aboard my vessel."

"Sir, Regan is quite intelligent, and he recognizes the limitations of any relationship between an officer and an——"

"Yes, that's all well and good, Mr. Devereaux, but someone overheard him calling you 'George', now that stuff has got to go, Mr. Devereaux, it has got to go."

"Sir——"

"Regan happens to be a pretty important person in the fighting structure of this ship, Mr. Devereaux. His battle station is on the bridge, and he is our communications link with Combat Information Centre, a man who can understand all this newfangled radar gobbledegook and who can give it to Mr. Peterson, our executive officer, without any hesitation or doubt. He is also capable of sifting information and reporting it in the order of its importance without a moment's hesitation, and I don't think I have to tell you how vital that is to us on the bridge who are trying to command a ship under combat conditions."

"I realize that, sir, but I can't see the harm of working with him on a——'

"I would not like Regan to become confused, Mr. Devereaux. I would not like him to start calling me 'Donald', for example, which happens to be my name, nor would I like him turning to my executive officer and saying, 'Fred, many bogeys', or whatever it is those radar boys say, I wouldn't want that to happen, Mr. Devereaux."

"Sir, if I may say so, that's reducing it to the absurd. I can assure you Regan would never——"

"You can assure me, Mr. Devereaux, that these classes in English composition will be terminated immediately. That is what you can assure me, Mr. Devereaux."

The wardroom was silent.

"Are there any questions, Mr. Devereaux?" the captain asked.

"None, sir."

"Very well, then."

"May I be excused, sir?"

"You may be excused, Mr. Devereaux."

Devereaux went back to his cabin and almost punched a hole in the bulkhead with his closed fist. This was the first time in his naval career that he had received an order which positively infuriated him, an order which seemed ridiculously unfair, most arbitrary, and downright undemocratic. We are supposed to be fighting the fascists, Devereaux thought, and the biggest fascist of them all is right aboard this ship! It never occurred to him that the captain was doing him a favour, was offering him an easy way out of a situation which had become inexplicably complex. All at once, Devereaux became a champion of democracy. All at once Devereaux became a person terribly interested in the rights of the common enlisted man.

And this provided another dilemma for Devereaux and, naturally, he blamed his predicament on David and allowed his anger to feed the fires of his hatred. The truth was that Devereaux didn't care at all about the welfare of the enlisted man. Devereaux thoroughly enjoyed all the privileges of his rank and accepted them as the indisputable rights of a man who held a Master's degree and who taught at a university in civilian life. He would no more equate himself with a member of the deck gang than he would with an ape. And whereas he admitted that radarmen were perhaps high on the Navy's scale of intelligence, he none the less knew that no radarman on the *Hanley*, and perhaps no radarman in the entire fleet, was as intelligent or as educated or as cultured as he, George Devereaux. He knew nothing at all about David Regan except that he had been intimate with a girl named Ardis Fletcher and that his father had been drowned in a Connecticut lake, and more about him he didn't particularly care to know. Knowing as little as he did, he was certain that David's background and education were not equal to his own, that David's I.Q. was undoubtedly lower than his, and that David was about as important to him as the man who swept the streets back in Westwood.

And yet the captain's order annoyed him, and he convinced himself that he *was* concerned about the rights of the enlisted man while all the time he knew the order was in keeping with a naval regulation that met with his approval. That was the damn thing about David Regan, he told himself. He forced you into these stupid situations where you believed one thing and professed another, where you were compelled to examine with scrutiny your own motivations, and where you always came out the loser.

The next morning, after quarters for muster, he told David what the captain had said, and David instantly suggested that they forget all about finishing the story.

"No," Devereaux told him. "You go on with the rewrite. Leave the story in my mail-box, and I'll type up any suggestions I have and leave them for you in the radar shack. We're going to finish that story, David!"

Two days after the *Hanley* came out of dry dock, she was ordered to take part in a battle problem involving an American cruiser and five other American destroyers. Considering the fact that the *Hanley* had been in a great many real battles, it was no surprise that the men looked upon the exercise as something of a lark. There was, in fact, something of a holiday air aboard the ship that day as she manœuvred off Pearl in simulated combat.

David, at his battle station on the bridge, was not immune to the general feeling of gaiety. It was nice to be involved in combat where no one could get hurt. He snapped his radar bearings to the exec, sifted the look-out reports, translated messages from fire control, and generally enjoyed the balmy weather and the mild breeze blowing off the open water. As always, he wore sound-powered phones on his head, the mouthpiece of the set strapped around his neck. And, as always, the left earpiece was in place over his left ear so that he could hear any messages which came over the phones, but his right ear was uncovered so that he could hear any commands given on the bridge. The radar shack was in TBS contact with a squadron of Wildcats flying in support of the group, and George Devereaux was the communications officer directing the squadron and reporting its position to the bridge. Three borrowed Army B-24s were approaching the ships, simulating Japanese bombers, and Devereaux had given the Wildcats their interception vectors and was reporting their progress at regularly spaced intervals. In the meantime, the ships were engaged in some fairly complicated defensive manœuvres against a mythical surface attack force, and the radarmen were constantly calling up ranges and bearings to the bridge, the manœuvre constructed so that each ship in the group took accurate position from a previously designated guide ship. The skipper kept pacing the bridge and listening to the signalmen as they reported the flags which appeared on the cruiser, the flags telling the rest of the force which turns they were supposed to execute. As soon as the turn was executed, the radar beamed in on the guide destroyer and called up the range and bearing and the skipper gave orders to correct or maintain direction or speed as the radar indicated. And all the while, Devereaux kept calling up the progress of the fighter planes waiting for that moment of contact with the approaching B-24s, that moment when he would hear the fighter pilots shout "Tallyho! Tallyho!"

The moment came unexpectedly and somewhat confusedly.

The skipper turned to David, wanting the position of the guide destroyer, and started to say, "Regan, get me a range and bearing on Sugarfoot."

All he got out was, "Regan, get me a ra . . ." because at that moment the phone on David's left ear burst into sound.

"Bridge, Combat," Devereaux said. "Tallyho, tallyho, three bogeys, zero-four-two, range one-oh-five, angels two."

David, assaulted by the sound from the radar shack in his left ear, catching the captain's words in his uncovered right ear, did a very normal and natural thing which was immediately misinterpreted by the captain. He held out his hand like a traffic cop and waved it at the captain, shushing him as he listened carefully to the urgent message coming over the phone. The captain clamped his mouth shut and stared at David. David turned to him, caught in the excitement of the imaginary battle.

"Wildcats report enemy contact, sir," he said. "Three bogeys at zero-four-two, range one——"

"Get off the bridge, Regan," the captain said.

David blinked. "Sir?"

"I said get off the bridge! Now!"

"Sir?" David repeated.

"Did you hear me talking to you a moment ago?"

"Yes, sir, but——"

"But what?"

"Sir, Mr. Devereaux——"

"Mr. Devereaux *what*?"

"Sir," David said, "the Wildcats, sir. They spotted . . ." and he fell silent, recognizing at once that it was futile to argue with an officer, especially when he was a full commander who happened to be captain of the ship. He took off the earphones, unstrapped the mouthpiece, and looked at the captain. "Re . . . re . . . request permission to leave the bridge, sir," he said.

"Permission granted," the captain snapped.

"Who . . . who do you want to . . . to take the phones, sir?"

"You may give them to the executive officer, Regan."

"Yes, sir," David said. He handed the phones to Mr. Peterson. Peterson took them without a word. David turned to the captain again. "Sir? Sir, where should I go?"

"Cruiser flying Turn-One-Answer, sir," one of the signalmen shouted.

The captain shoved David aside and turned towards the helmsman. "Right fifteen degrees rudder," he said.

"Right fifteen degrees rudder, sir."

The captain turned to the engine order telegraph operator. "All engines ahead standard," he said.

"All engines ahead standard, sir."

"Coming around to zero-three-five, sir."

"Meet her."

"All engines answer ahead standard, sir."

"Very well."

"Steady on zero-three-five, sir."

"Very well," the captain said. "Mr. Peterson, range and bearing on Sugarfoot. Tell Combat to send up another talker."

"Sir," David said, "should I——?"

"Get the hell off the bridge!" the captain bellowed, and David nodded and went down the ladder quietly.

As soon as they got back to Pearl, the captain called Devereaux into his wardroom. He told Devereaux all about David's misbehaviour and explained that the *Hanley* had been anticipating a command from the cruiser and that a range and bearing on the guide ship had been essential at that moment, and that had the *Hanley* failed to execute the turn command promptly and properly and be in position on schedule, he, the captain of the *Hanley* would have appeared singularly foolish and incompetent in the eyes of the admiral who was aboard the cruiser. In view of this, he was making mention of Devereaux's behaviour on his next fitness report, and would Devereaux please tell Regan the captain wanted to see him in the wardroom immediately.

David came into the wardroom and stood before the long mess table. The captain sat at the far end, scowling. The captain informed David that *his* commands and *his* requests took precedence over any other commands, requests or reports aboard this vessel and David had better understand this at once. In order to help his understanding, the captain was restricting David to the ship for a month and he was asking the senior communications officer to make certain that David stood only mid watches when the ship was under way. In port, in addition to standing his usual voice radio watch, David would relieve whatever seaman was standing the gangway mid watch. He would resume the duties of his usual battle station under surveillance and would promptly be relieved of such responsible duties the next time any such laxity was evident. And, the captain told David, he was lucky his behaviour hadn't resulted in a captain's mast which, as David knew, would have gone into his service record. David thanked the captain for his kindness and left the wardroom.

And the very next day, a gunnery officer discovered the missing forty-five.

The gun-locker was directly across the passageway from the pharmacy amidships. No one would have thought of taking an inventory of small-arms if the ship had been out there fighting real battles. But fresh from dry dock as she was, time on everybody's hands, the senior gunnery officer decided it was time to do a little premature spring-cleaning. So he assigned an ensign and two gunner's mates to put the gun-locker in order, and that was when the ensign discovered the number of actual guns did not tally with the number of guns listed on his clipboard. Actually, Arbuster, a gunner's mate second class discovered the discrepancy long before the ensign did, but he casually and patriotically decided not to mention it. The ensign, on the other hand, was somewhat eagerly bucking for his lieutenant's bar, and he reported the missing gun to the senior gunnery officer who in turn reported it to the executive officer who in turn reported it to the captain.

The squawk box erupted at 1400, directly after the midday mess.

"Now hear this!" it said. "All hands muster on the port side amidships! All hands muster on the port side amidships!"

The men of the *Hanley*, accustomed to peculiar requests and commands, none the less considered this one to be peculiar indeed. They dropped their paint buckets and their scraping tools and their steel wool and reported amidships where they waited in an uneasy knot for whatever was coming. Most of them suspected they'd be pulling out for the islands again. None of them, with the possible exception of Arbuster the gunner's mate, ever once suspected what actually came.

The captain appeared at 1405. Dramatically, he stood on the boat deck before the torpedo tubes and looked down at the men who clustered on the main deck. As was usual with the captain of the *Hanley*, he delivered a little preamble before he got down to what was really troubling him.

"As you know," he said, and the men still didn't know anything, "the effectiveness of a fighting ship depends on a great deal more than the skill of the men aboard her. It depends, too, on spirit and trust and respect. Each man aboard this ship is a vital member of a team, and we've got to respect each other and the job each of us does, or this ship will cease being an effective fighting machine. Respect is the key word. Respect for a seaman second class as well as respect for the captain of this vessel. Respect."

The captain paused and leaned over the boat-deck rail in a confidential way. He was wearing suntans, the scrambled eggs of his rank gleaming on the peak of his hat, the silver maple leaf glistening on the collar of his shirt.

"A forty-five is missing from the gun-locker," he said abruptly. He paused.

"I know why that forty-five was stolen," he said in a whisper, and he paused again.

The men of the *Hanley* looked up at him and began to wonder what he meant. The captain kept nodding his head sagely on the boat deck and the men, none of whom would have interpreted the theft in such a manner had the captain not planted the idea, suddenly got the gist of his whispered words. Someone had stolen the gun so he could put a bullet in the old bastard's head. The idea, now that they thought of it, seemed like a good one, perfectly reasonable and sound. They began wishing that whoever had the gun would carry out his plan. They began visualizing the captain being carried ashore in a basket. The captain kept nodding, and now the men were nodding, too, fantasizing the entire crew in dress uniforms, the big guns going off in salute as they carried the captain into the waiting motor launch, dead. Captain and crew kept nodding at each other, fantasy in total empathy with delusion. The captain broke the stalemate.

"I have asked the officers in each division to conduct a search of every foot-locker aboard this vessel. You will report to your sleeping compartments at once, and open your lockers, and stand by for inspection. That is all."

The men dispersed silently. There wasn't much to say. Many members of the crew began thinking of the various weapons stashed in their lockers, the Japanese pistols they had bought in Honolulu or from the Marines in the Santa Cruz Islands, the Lugers they had picked up, the Italian Barrettas. They began thinking of these and wondering how they could dump them over the side before that locker inspection, but the prospects looked pretty dim. The prospects looked especially dim for David Regan.

He had recognized instantly that the gun the captain was talking about was the gun that he had inadvertently taken with him to the mess hall after small-arms instruction that day so long ago. And that gun was now buried underneath his handkerchiefs in his foot-locker in the forward sleeping compartment. He tried to get there before any of the officers arrived, but by the time he reached his locker, two officers from the communications division were already there. One of them was George Devereaux.

"Okay, men, let's get this over with," Devereaux said.

The men fell in grumblingly before their lockers, and stooped down, and pulled out their dog-tag chains from beneath their undershirts, the keys to their lockers dangling with their identification plates. They opened the locks, and flipped up the tops of their lockers, and then waited while Devereaux and an ensign named Phelps conducted the search. David opened his locker and shoved the automatic clear to the rear, heaping a pile of tee shirts on to it. The officers seemed somewhat embarrassed by their task. David, standing by his locker, began wishing that Devereaux rather than Phelps would search through his gear.

"All right, Savarino, you want to move these cigarettes?" Phelps said.

"What's under that mattress cover?" Devereaux asked.

The officers were moving down the line methodically, ill at ease, conducting the search in a studiously casual but none the less thorough manner, Phelps on one side, Devereaux on the other, alternating. David was suddenly sweating. He wiped his lip.

"Where'd you get this bayonet, Stein?" Phelps asked.

"On the Canal, sir."

"Get rid of it right after inspection, you hear me?"

"Yes, sir."

"All right, Regan, step aside," Phelps said.
"I've got it, Phelps," Devereaux put in.
"I thought . . ."
"I've got it," Devereaux repeated.

He knelt before David's locker and began moving the clothing around carefully, committing his invasion of privacy like a gentleman. His hands stopped on a cigar box. He opened it, saw a pile of photographs and—even though he'd never seen her in his life—instantly recognized the top photo as the girl in Talmadge, Ardis Fletcher. He suddenly bit his lower lip, shoved the box to one side, and thrust his hands to the back of the locker. His hands met resistance and stopped. He glanced up at David. David wiped sweat from his lip again.

"All right, how's it going down here?" a voice asked from the ladder.

The sailor closest to the ladder shouted, "Atten-*shun*!"

Devereaux got to his feet, his hands empty, and turned to face the captain as he came down the ladder.

"At ease, at ease," the captain said. "Have you turned up that piece?"

"No, sir," Phelps said.

"Mr. Devereaux? You giving these lockers a thorough check?"

"Yes, sir, we are."

The captain walked to where Devereaux and David were standing side by side. He glanced into David's open locker. "Where'd you learn to square your gear, Regan?" he asked.

"Great Lakes, sir."

"That's a pretty sloppy job, isn't it? Irish pennants all over the place."

"Sir, I'm afraid *I* made a mess of that locker," Devereaux said.

"Nobody asked you, Mr. Devereaux." The captain squinted his eyes, studying first Devereaux, and then David. "Step aside," he said.

"Yes, sir."

The captain knelt before the locker. He picked up a pair of socks, threw them back into the locker, and then saw David's cigar box. "What's in there, Regan?"

"Some . . . some pictures, sir."

"Open it."

"Yes, sir."

David knelt and opened the box. His hand was trembling.

"You nervous, Regan?" the captain asked.

"A little, sir."

"Why?"

"I . . . I don't know, sir."

The captain glanced at the contents of the box, nodded, and said, "Very well, move those jumpers for me." David picked up the jumpers and put them on to the pile of tee shirts which were covering the forty-five.

"What's behind those shoes, Regan?"

"Nothing, sir."

"I saw something back there, Regan."

"No, sir, I . . ."

"I *saw* something, Regan."

"Oh. Oh, yes, sir. A pair of binoculars."

"Give them to me."

David moved his black shoes on to the pile of jumpers and reached to the back of the locker for the binoculars. He handed them to the captain.

"Are these government property, Regan?"

"No, sir. I bought them in Honolulu."

The captain glanced at them and handed them back. "All right, move those jumpers."

"Yes, sir."

"*And* the tee shirts."

"Yes, sir."

With his back to the captain, David squeezed his eyes shut for a moment, and then picked up the jumpers.

"Come on, Regan, on the double."

"Sir . . ." Devereaux started, and then hesitated.

"Yes, Mr. Devereaux?"

"Sir, I've searched this locker and . . ."

Again, Devereaux hesitated. David, his hands on the pile of tee shirts which were shielding the forty-five, looked up at Devereaux. *He's going to tell*, he thought. *He's going to say he found the gun.*

"Yes, what is it, Mr. Devereaux?" the captain said.

"Sir, I think I should tell you——"

"Captain down here?" A voice from the top of the ladder asked.

"He's here, sir," one of the seamen answered. The captain turned as Levy, the senior gunnery officer came down the steps.

"Oh, there you are, sir."

"What is it, Mr. Levy?"

"I think we've found the piece, sir," Levy said.

"Where?"

"Seaman first-class has it, sir. Claims he bought it from a dog-face. A soldier, sir."

"Where is he?"

"Aft sleeping compartment, sir."

"Let's talk to him," the captain said. "Carry on," he called over his shoulder, and went up the ladder.

"Does he want us to continue the search?" Phelps asked.

"I guess not," Devereaux answered. "They found the gun."

"I'd better find out," Phelps said, as he went up the ladder after the captain.

Devereaux turned to David. In a tight whisper, he said, "Take that gun topside and throw it overboard."

"Now, sir?"

"Now. Move!"

"Yes, sir!" David grabbed the gun and tucked it under his shirt. In thirty seconds he had thrown it over the side, but he still wondered what Devereaux was about to say when he'd used the opening words, "Sir, I think I should tell you——"

Devereaux, on the other hand, knew exactly what he'd been about to say. He'd been about to say, "Sir, I think I should tell you I've found the gun. I was going to report to you privately, sir. I didn't want to embarrass young Regan before his shipmates."

That was what he was about to say. He had been spared the statement by the intrusion of Sol Levy, the gunnery officer, and the news that a seaman first-class had the missing forty-five. As it turned out, the forty-five really had been purchased from a soldier, but it was considered stolen government property none the less, and immediately confiscated. By the time the search was resumed, David had already disposed of the weapon. Devereaux, unfortunately, had not disposed of the nagging knowledge that he'd been about to inform on David to save his own skin.

The thought was a new one to him, and he examined it carefully, examined too the inborn American aversion to the informer. He did not enjoy casting himself in the role of the rat. And yet, undeniably, he had been about to tell on David, would have told on David in the next instant. Anyone would have done the same thing, he thought. It was a matter of Regan or me. What do I owe him anyway? Nothing. I only owe number one, George Devereaux. Still the idea of informing was not a palatable one.

I didn't tell on him, he thought. But I was about to. Well, maybe I would have changed my mind in the last minute, maybe I would have said, "Sir, I think I should tell you I've searched this locker thoroughly, and you're only duplicating my effort," maybe I would have said that if Levy hadn't come down the steps at that moment, maybe I would have protected Regan after all.

But he knew he'd been about to inform, and he knew he *would* have informed if he hadn't been interrupted. And he knew, too, that contact with David Regan somehow brought out all the worst elements of his personality, somehow reduced the private image of himself to a person he didn't even know and, worse, a person he despised.

I have to destroy him, he thought.

At first, he thought he was referring to this image of himself, he image he hated, this person who did things George Devereaux would not have done, this childish man who thought longingly of young girls, this vindictive man who insisted on punishing, this timid man who would not face up to the captain, this intolerant man who mouthed democratic principles, this disgusting man who was an informer.

And then he realized he did not want to destroy this image at all. He only wanted to destroy the source of this image, the one person who caused him to see himself so unflatteringly, David Regan. Unconsciously, he began to plot against David, continuing with the revisions all the while, plotting, plotting, there seemed to be no way of eliminating him, of reducing him to nothingness, no way of ripping David out of his life.

Until that April night in Pearl.

David, carrying out the details of the captain's punishment for his transgression on the bridge, was standing the gangway mid watch. He wore his dress whites and a guard belt carrying live cartridges, and he held a twenty-two rifle at parade rest, more or less. The officer of the deck was a man called Sammener, and he ran a loose watch, and he realized that no Japanese spies were going to blow up the *Hanley* while it lay in port, and so he didn't much care whether David leaned on the rifle or held it on his shoulder or slouched in the most casual parade rest he had ever witnessed. Sammener simply didn't care. Sammener was sleepy, and he detested mid watches, and the gunner's mate standing watch with him was a deadly mid-Western bore who had nothing to say, so Sammener wrote a few letters to his wife, and watched David at the foot of the gangway stifling yawns and standing a very sloppy parade rest watch. The captain was aboard and asleep, and so there was no fear he'd come back to the ship from liberty and raise a fuss.

"What time is it?" Sammener asked the gunner's mate.

"Oh-two-hundred, sir," the gunner's mate replied.

"In English."

"Two a.m., sir."

"Thank you," Sammener paused. "Listen, go get us some coffee, will you? I'll be asleep here in a few minutes."

"Yes, sir. Where should I get it, sir?"

"The radiomen should have a pot brewing."

"Yes, sir."

"Get some for the gangway watch, too." He cupped his hands to his mouth and shouted, "You there! At the gangway! You want some coffee?"

"Yes, sir, I'd like some," David answered.

"Fine. What's your name again?"

"Regan, sir."

"What are you, Regan? A radarman?"

"Yes, sir."

"What are you doing on gangway watch?"

David grinned. "The captain's idea, sir."

"He's full of them," Sammener mumbled. "Go get the coffee, Mercer. Make it fast. I'm about to drop."

The coffee came at 0215. Sammener sent the gunner's mate down with a cup for David, and David shifted the rifle to his left hand and sipped at the hot cup of coffee. The coffee was good. He'd been very sleepy before the coffee came. It seemed as if he'd been standing mid watches for ever, and yet it had only been a few weeks, and still he never seemed to be wide awake any more Night after night, he came to dread that hand on his shoulder waking him at a quarter to midnight, and then standing on the dock watching everyone returning from liberty, not getting back into the sack until four a.m., and then being awakened again at six to start the Navy day, he never seemed to get enough sleep lately. He almost wished they were back in combat. The captain would never enforce such ridiculous punishment if the ship were in . . .

"Well, well, David, having a little cup of coffee?" the voice said.

David turned. "Oh, hello, George," he whispered.

George Devereaux put his hands on his hips and studied David with his chipmunk grin, his eyebrows askew, his brown eyes glinting. David smiled back.

"Sir," Devereaux said.

"Huh?"

"*Sir*," Devereaux repeated, still grinning. "I believe I am an officer in the United States Navy, and as such I am entitled to the respect of an enlisted man, as exemplified by the use of the respectful title 'sir'." Devereaux paused, still grinning. "Respect, that's what the captain said. Respect is the key word."

"You're absolutely right," David answered, sipping at his coffee, and then smiling as he took the cup away from his mouth.

"I am absolutely right, *sir*," Devereaux said.

"You are absolutely right, *sir*," David affirmed, hitting the word hard, grinning.

"That's better," Devereaux said. He lost his balance for an instant and wobbled on the deck, catching at the handrail of the gangway for support and then straightening up to face David again. David suddenly smelled the whisky fumes on his breath.

"Now get rid of that coffee-cup," Devereaux said.

"Sir?"

"Put down the coffee-cup."

"Yes, sir," David said, grinning, wondering what kind of a game Devereaux was playing, but grateful for anything which broke the monotony of the long watch. He put the cup down on the deck.

"Atten-*shun*!" Devereaux shouted.

David snapped to attention, smiling.

"What's so funny, Regan?"

"Nothing, sir," David said, still smiling.

"Take that smile off your face!"

"Yes, *sir*!" David answered, and immediately pulled a serious face, his mouth grim, his brows pulled down.

"That's better," Devereaux said, nodding. His hands reached out for David's kerchief. "That's a pretty sloppy knot, Regan."

"Yes, *sir*!"

"And your shoes need shining."

"Yes, *sir*!"

"And you need a haircut."

"I haven't been ashore, sir."

"There's a barber aboard, Regan."

"I know, sir. But there didn't seem any sense in getting a haircut when I'm restricted to the——"

"Are you questioning my judgement, Regan?"

David smiled again. "No, *sir*!"

"What's so funny?" Devereaux said, and David suddenly realized he was smiling alone; Devereaux's face was dead serious.

"Nothing, sir," he said. The smile dropped from his mouth.

"I tell you your shoes are messy and you need a haircut, and you think that's funny, do you?"

"No, sir, I don't," David said.

"Very well," Devereaux answered. "Get a haircut. Shine those shoes."

"I will, sir."

"Very well," Devereaux said, and he started up the gangway. He saluted Sammener and said, "Well, well, look who's standing the deck watch. Ole Jonah Sammener. What's doing, Jonah? Got any girls aboard? Is there a wild party going on in the bosun's locker?"

"You look as if you just came from one," Sammener said dryly.

"What are you drinking, Jonah? Coffee? The whole watch is drinking coffee. A fine alert bunch of men we've got guarding our lives while we sleep the sleep of innocents." He nodded, and seemed to remember David standing on the deck. He wheeled towards the gangway, went down it rapidly, and walked to where David was standing at its foot. David did not move.

"I believe it is customary to salute an officer when he approaches, Regan," Devereaux said.

David snapped to attention, his left hand moving over to cross the muzzle of the rifle in salute. Devereaux touched the peak of his cap and snapped a salute in return. David remained at attention. Devereaux kept studying him. The chipmunk grin had vanished completely. There were only the hard brown eyes now, staring from beneath the crooked eyebrows.

"I thought I told you to get a haircut," Devereaux said.

David, puzzled, did not answer.

"I'm talking to you, Regan! You *still* need a haircut."

"Sir, I . . . I'm on watch, sir."

"And a pretty *sloppy* watch, I might add."

"Hey, George, come on aboard," Sammener yelled from the quarterdeck. "You're waking up the whole ship."

"You just keep out of this, Jonah," Devereaux said over his shoulder.

"Sir," David whispered, "I think maybe——"

"Never mind what you think, Regan!" Devereaux snapped. "I'm not interested in what you think."

"Sir, I only meant——"

"Yes, what *did* you mean, Regan? I wish you would say what you mean. We've been rewriting *Man Drowning* until it's coming out of my ears, and I still don't know what you mean. Can't you say what you mean? Just for once? Can't you, for God's sake, spit it out in clear intelligent English?"

"I'm sorry, sir," David said. "I've been trying to, but——"

"Don't be so sorry. I'm sorry enough for both of us. I'm sorry I ever read your letters and ever made the mistake of thinking you could possibly in a thousand years write even a single paragraph of nteresting prose. Don't go telling me you're sorry, Regan."

"I'm sorry, sir, but——"

"I said don't tell me you're sorry!"

David stared at Devereaux, wondering how this had suddenly got so serious. He's drunk, yes, he thought, but still this had got so serious all at once. He glanced towards Sammener who had washed his hands of the entire affair and was leisurely sipping his coffee on the quarterdeck.

"What made you think you were a writer, Regan?" Devereaux asked.

"I never thought that, sir. It was you who——"

"Don't contradict me! What was it, Regan? A burning desire to get that magnificent event on paper?"

"No, sir, I . . ."

"Man Drowning, Man Drowning, Man Drowning, how many times has he drowned since we first started the story?"

"I don't know, sir. There have been a lot of revis——"

"What makes you think anyone would be interested in reading about some fool who's too stupid to avoid getting caught in an anchor line?"

David felt his right fist tightening on the barrel of the rifle.

"I . . . I don't know, sir."

"No one. That's who would be interested. No one. A colourless little man goes out in a rowboat and——"

"Sir!"

"What is it?"

"Sir, I . . . I'd rather not discuss the story now, sir."

"Ahh, he's sensitive," Devereaux said solicitously. "The sensitive artist. How literary. If you're so literary and so sensitive, Regan, why did you choose to write about such an insensitive clod? Why did you——?"

"Sir, that's my father," David said quietly. He could feel an uncontrollable anger boiling inside him. His fist was tight on the barrel of the rifle. He hoped he would not cry. His eyes blinked as he tried to stifle the anger.

"Oh, your father. Oh, forgive me, Regan."

"That's all right, sir."

"Yes, your father. I didn't realize your father was the idiot who——"

"Stop it, Mr. Devereaux!"

"——stepped into a rowboat and allowed his foot to——"

"*Stop it!*"

"——get caught in an anchor line, that takes brains, a damn fool is what that man was, a goddam stupid——"

His first impulse was to raise the rifle and fire it.

He controlled the impulse somehow, bringing the rifle up, his right hand almost going to the trigger, and then he decided to swing the rifle, and he started to do that and simply threw the rifle away and smashed his right fist into Mr. Devereaux's face. Devereaux reeled back against the gangway, and David went after him, his eyes brimming with tears, his heart pounding.

"That's my father," he said, and he struck Devereaux again as Sammener put down his coffee-cup and came running down the gangway, his hand going for the forty-five at his side.

"Regan!" he yelled. "Are you out of your mind? Regan, cut it out!" He seized David's arms and pulled him away from Devereaux. "What's the matter with you?"

"I'm sorry, sir," David said, trembling now with the realization of what he had done.

"That's a fool stunt, Regan," Sammener said. "You . . . you better get below. Mercer, wake . . . wake the next man on the watch list. Come on, Regan, we'd just better . . ."

Devereaux straightened up from the gangway and wiped his hand across his nose. He looked at the blood on his fingers and then smiled his chipmunk grin and said, "Just a second, Jonah."

"He lost his head, George," Sammener said. "I'll have him relieved and——"

"He lost his head indeed," Devereaux answered. "I think we'd better wake the captain."

On April seventh, David Regan stood a Captain's Mast, and it was recommended at that primary court that David's case be presented before a Naval court martial. On April sixteenth, he stood before a board of officers on the *Juneau* and was found guilty of violation of Article 90 of the Uniform Code of Military Justice which stated *Any person subject to this code who strikes his superior officer or lifts up any weapon or offers any violence against him while he is in the execution of his office shall be punished, if the offence is committed in time of war, by death or such other punishment as a court martial might direct.*

The lawyer charged with David's defence pointed out that George Devereaux had been returning to the ship from a liberty and was not actively engaged in "the execution of his office", but the defence was reminded that an officer is in the execution of his office when engaged in any act or service required or authorized to be done by him by statute, regulation, the order of a superior, or military usage. In general, the court advised, any striking or use of violence against any superior officer by a person subject to military law, over whom it is the duty of that superior officer to maintain discipline at the time, would be striking or using violence against him in the execution of his office.

It was pointed out to the court that George Devereaux had provoked the attack upon himself, and that he was drunk at the time of the attack, but the prosecution maintained that Article 112 of the Code, the article relating to drunkenness on duty, did not relate to those periods when, no duty being required of them by orders or regulations, officers and men occupy the status of leisure known as "off duty" or "on liberty", which status George Devereaux was occupying at the time of the attack.

They could have given David a dishonourable discharge in addition to whatever punishment they decided upon within the specified limits of the Code. Instead, and because of the mitigating circumstances—the attorney for the defence constantly harped on a duality that permitted Devereaux to be engaged in "the execution of his office" where it suited the prosecution's case, but to be "off duty" or "on liberty" where it did not—David was sentenced to five years at hard labour without pay or allowances, but his punishment did not include a dishonourable discharge.

On May third he was put aboard a transport in irons, and shipped to the Naval Retraining Command at Camp Elliott in San Diego, where he began serving his term.

Aboard the *Hanley*, the captain called Devereaux into the wardroom and delivered a flowery speech, the true substance of which was contained in the four words "I told you so".

The girls from Phi Sig had somewhere acquired an Army Air Corps parachute, painstakingly dyed it a shocking red, and hung it from the ceiling of the gymnasium in a billowing canopy of brilliance. The Omega Epsilon girls had hand-fashioned dozens and dozens of long-stemmed roses, threaded them on strings, and trailed them from the gym ceiling so that the room was bathed in a literal shower of flowers, the huge silk parachute serving as an umbrella to protect the dancers from the crêpe-paper downpour as they circled the floor to the beat of the band at the front of the gym. The dance had been labelled, appropriately though perhaps unimaginatively, The Shower of Roses Ball. The beat of the band throbbed through the hall, pounded the dancers, fired the feet of Amanda Soames, who swirled about the gym in yellow taffeta, amazed that she was here, going round and round in the arms of a stranger beneath the Army Air Corps parachute somewhere acquired by the girls from Phi Sig.

Her intentions, up to six o'clock, had certainly been honourable. She had worked in the rehearsal room on the second floor of Ardaecker Hall until almost five-thirty, immune to the bright May sunshine that lazily sifted through the open windows, sitting at the piano and striking chord after chord, translating each note to the manuscript paper that rested on the piano rack, clamping the pencil between her teeth as she struck yet another chord, fascinated by the task she'd set herself. She was working with a blue-moon tune, a typical I-VI-II-V front phrase arranged in the key of C, strings carrying the first four bars, with flutes picking up the countermelody on the second four. She struck a C-major seventh, and then an A-minor ninth, and a D-minor ninth, and a G-dominant with a flatted ninth thrown into the chord, a bit too dramatic, perhaps, but that was the influence of Gillian Burke. She worked hard, and her intentions, up to six o'clock, had certainly been honourable.

"Make it big!' Gillian had said. "Arrange it as if you were Scriabin!" waving her arms, aware of the mirror behind her. Her knowledge of classical music never failed to surprise Amanda. Gillian seemed to be a hopeless "Nutcracker Suite" addict, and yet she was able to identify obscure symphonies after hearing only the first few bars, a terrifying feat of memory, which even Amanda could not duplicate. Her musical sense, too, was uncanny. It had seemed outrageous to Amanda even to attempt so pretentious an arrangement for a popular ballad like "'Til Then", and yet she began to recognize the showmanship inherent in such an approach, and eventually admitted that it would be effective, and never once forgot that it was Gillian who had said, "Make it big!"

At five-thirty she had gone back to the dorm, and immediately into the shower down the hall. She had just turned on the water when Gillian burst into the room, threw off her robe, and took the stall alongside hers. In a matter of three minutes, as the steam rose from each booth to provide a background for their conversation, they were both shouting at each other heatedly over the drumming noise of the water, and Amanda had begun to regret leaving Ardaecker, begun to wonder why on earth she had gone back to the dorm at five-thirty.

"I told Morton I was staying home to study tonight!" she shouted.

"Are you married to Morton?" Gillian shouted back.

"Of course not!"

"Are you engaged? Are you pinned?"

"No, but——"

"Do you even have an understanding?"

"No, Gillian, but——"

"Hurry up. It's getting late."

"I just wouldn't want him to think I lied to him."

"You didn't lie. Call him up and tell him you're going out, if that's what's bothering you."

"Well, that isn't what's bothering me, exactly."

"Then, what is, exactly?" Gillian turned off the water and came out of the stall. Her hair was soaking wet, plastered to her skull, her lashes hung with glistening drops of water. She picked up her towel from the wash-basin and began rubbing herself briskly.

"I don't even know this fellow," Amanda said from the stall.

"So what difference does that make? Will you please get out of that shower?"

Amanda turned off the water, pulled off her shower-cap, and said loftily, "It makes a difference to me."

"Here's your robe."

"I haven't dried myself yet."

"Dry yourself in the room. They'll be *here* at eight."

"I don't care what time they'll be here because I'm not . . . Gilly, I'm wet! I can't put a robe on when I'm . . ." but Gillian had thrown the robe over her shoulders and was pulling her towards the door. "Gilly!" she protested, but somehow they were in the corridor, Amanda clutching the robe around her, Gillian sweeping her along towards their room. Amanda walked directly to her own bed, sat heavily in the centre of it, crossed her arms over the front of the robe, and said, "Now stop it, Gillian. I know what I want to do."

"And what's that? You're getting your bed all wet."

"I don't care about the bed. I want to stay home tonight."

"Why?"

"I have work to do."

"What work?"

"On the arrangement. It's already a week over——"

"It'll wait another week. Besides, you can knock it off in ten minutes, and you know it."

"I can't! I haven't even begun any of the intricate scoring, and I couldn't hope to——"

"You can do it tomorrow. This is Saturday night, Amanda. Date night. All across America, in cities, in towns, in hamlets, in *shanties*, for God's sake, it's date night! Since time immemorial——"

"Don't get dramatic, Gillian. I can't stand it when you start emoting."

Gillian threw a towel at her and said, "Dry yourself. We haven't got much time."

"I'm not going."

"You have to go. I promised Brian you would."

"Brian is an ape."

"He's very sweet-oh. Besides, you're going with his friend, not him."

"His friend is probably an ape, too."

"His friend is a lawyer."

"Good for him."

"And besides, he isn't even Brian's friend. He's his brother's friend."

"Whose brother?"

"Brian's."

"Then how does Brian know him?"

"He doesn't. They're in the Army together, this fellow and Brian's brother, and Brian's brother asked this fellow to stop off in Talmadge to say hello on his way to New Haven, and this fellow was good enough to do that, and Brian thought he should try to get him a date for tonight. So the least you can do——"

"I don't owe Brian anything. He's *your* boy-friend."

"He's not my boy-friend. He's just someone I see every now and then."

"All the more reason why I shouldn't——"

"My God, Amanda, you'd think we were leading you to the electric chair!"

"I just don't like the idea of you and Brian making dates for me. Or . . . of fixing me up with . . . with soldiers. What does Brian think he is? A . . . a . . . a marriage broker?"

"Who's asking you to marry this fellow, huh? Is anybody asking you to marry him?"

"No, but . . ."

"All I'm asking you to do is to help out your room-mate when a soldier—a *soldier*, Amanda, a member of the armed forces——"

"Here we go again."

"——fighting a war to preserve *our* freedom, took the trouble to come all the way from——"

"He was on his way to New Haven, anyway."

"——from Arizona to deliver a message from Brian's brother. The *least* we can do, Amanda——"

"What was the message?"

"How do I know what the message was? He's very handsome, Brian said."

"Who is?"

"This fellow. Matthew Anson Bridges. Isn't that a *marrr*-vellous name?"

"No. I detest people with three names."

"Get dressed, Amanda."

"No. I'm staying here."

"Here's your underwear, Amanda."

"I don't even *know* him."

"Amanda, there *is* such a thing as a blind date, which is a common American custom and not at all degrading or shameful. Will you please put on your bloomers and stop wasting time?"

"I *loathe* the word bloomers."

"Amanda, it's almost six-thirty."

"I'm in no hurry, Gillian." She paused. "What's he like?"

"I haven't met him. Would you like Brian's description of him?"

"For whatever it's worth, yes."

Gillian immediately hunched over into the hulking pose of a gorilla, her arms trailing, her jaw protruding. She began shuffling around the room, alternately scratching her head and her chest. When she turned to face Amanda, her eyes carried the blank stare of a sub-species animal.

"Uh . . ." she said. "Uh . . . he's about . . . uh . . . six feet two inches in his socks, Gillian . . . uh . . . and he has this black hair, yeah, and these brown eyes and . . . uh . . .oh yeah . . . a black moustache and——"

"A black moustache!" Amanda shrieked.

"I'm only quoting Brian," Gillian said, straightening up and walking directly to Amanda's closet. "He's also a captain in the Judge Advocate's office and doing work someplace in Arizona. He has a great suntan, Brian said."

"How old is he?"

"Twenty-six," Gillian said, opening the closet door.

"Twenty-*six*!"

"Well now, just what's wrong with twenty-six?" Gillian asked, turning, her hands on her hips.

"Twenty-*six*!"

"Yes, twenty-six, twenty-six. What shall we do, bury him?"

"Twenty-six with a black moustache," Amanda said, and she pulled a face, her eyes flaring with new determination. "No. Absolutely not." She took her robe from the bed and pulled it on over her bra and panties. "No, Gillian. I'm sorry. No."

"Which dress do you want to wear?" Gillian said from the closet.

"I'm not going."

"Wear the yellow. It's a good colour for you."

"I'm not going. You can call Brian and tell him . . ."

Gillian threw the yellow taffeta on to Amanda's bed and went to her dresser. She opened the top drawer, rummaged about in it for a moment, and then said, "Haven't you got a pair without a run?"

"Gillian, I have no intention of——"

"Amanda, put on your stockings and your dress and your shoes and stop behaving like a little——"

"Gilly, he is twenty-six years old, and——"

"Yes, and he has a black moustache, and he forecloses mortgages on widows' homes, and you are going to that stupid Falling Roses Ball with him if I have to carry you there unconscious. Yes!"

The green eyes flashed for an instant, and then the impish grin claimed Gillian's face.

"Come on, Amanda," she said gently. "Have a heart. I promised Brian."

Now, sweeping about the floor in the arms of Matthew Anson Bridges, Amanda was forced to admit that he didn't seem terribly old after all. And he did have a marvellous suntan, and a very soft way of speaking, she supposed that was because he came from Virginia. She had never known a Southerner before, and somehow Matthew Anson Bridges—it was strange, she couldn't think of him as just a first name, she had to link all three names together, the way she had first heard them—Matthew Anson Bridges reminded her of all the stories she'd read about the Old South. She could almost visualize him astride a horse, assuring a plantation widow that his troops were only in pursuit of the Yankees, Ma'am, and would not loot or pillage. And yet he didn't have a *real* Southern accent, it was simply a soft way of speaking. Well, she supposed all educated Southerners spoke that way. He danced very well, with a firm guiding hand in the small of her back, and a very light grip on her free hand. It didn't seem at all like dancing. Their feet seemed to be slightly above the floor of the gym, not touching anything really. There was almost a feeling of flying, weightless, in the arms of Matthew Anson Bridges, sweeping about the floor now.

"*When I hear that serenade in blue,*
"*I'm somewhere in another——*"
"Do you like Glenn Miller?" Amanda asked.
"*—world alone with you*
"*Sharing all the joys . . .*"
"Yes," Matthew said.
"He's in the Army, too, isn't he?"
"Yes. The Air Corps."
"Do you like our parachute?"
"It's beautiful."
"He's a captain, too, isn't he? Glenn Miller?"
"Yes."
"*And as we dance the night away*
"*I hear you say . . .*"
"Is something wrong?"
"No."
"You seem angry."
"I don't like to talk when I'm dancing," Matthew said.
"Oh. Well, excuse me."
"You're excused."

Around and around, barely touching the gym floor, he doesn't like to talk when he dances, well, well, well, the strong silent type, Mr. Matthew Anson Bridges, but he does dance well. He's probably counting the steps. Talking probably confuses him, throws him off count. And she burst out laughing.

"Something?" he said.
"No. No."
"I don't like secret laughter," he told her.

"What *do* you like, Mr. Bridges?"

"Call me Matthew. Everyone else does."

"What do you like, Matthew?"

"I like honey blondes who look as if they just fell off a peach tree."

She stared up at him suddenly.

"The song's over," he said. "I do like Glenn Miller, and I think your freshman band and your teen-age vocalist just slaughtered one of the prettiest songs he ever recorded."

"Me?" Amanda said.

"Huh?"

"The . . . the peach tree?"

"Oh. Yes. Would you like a drink?"

"I don't know if I'm flattered."

"Why not?"

Amanda laughed. "Peaches are yellow and red and fuzzy."

"They are also ripe and soft," Matthew said. "Come on."

"Where are you going? The punch bowl's——"

"I think Brian has a pint in the car."

"Well . . ."

"What's the matter?"

"I'd like to dance some more," Amanda said.

"The band's taking an intermission."

"Yes, I know. When they come back, I mean. Oh, there's Gillian! Gilly! Over here!"

Gillian, wearing a vibrantly electric-blue silk, took Brian's hand and walked to where Matthew and Amanda were standing.

"Hi," she said. "How are you two getting along?"

"We're discussing fruit," Matthew said, and he smiled at Amanda.

"I think we ought to get out of here," Brian said.

"Why?" Gillian asked.

"I don't like gymnasiums. They always smell sweaty."

"I want to dance some more," Amanda said.

"Isn't there someplace else we can go to dance?" Matthew asked Brian.

"Sure. There're a hundred places in Talmadge alone. If we——"

"I want to stay here," Amanda said. "I think it's lovely."

"I thought we might find a place where we could sit at a table."

"No, I like it here."

"Defence rests," Matthew said, shrugging.

"You're a lawyer, Brian tells me," Gillian said. She smiled slightly, her green eyes catching Matthew's, holding them in an intense gaze.

"Yes, that's right."

"It must be fascinating. The law."

"It is. I only wish I were practising it."

"Aren't you?"

"I'm something slightly higher than a clerk," Matthew said smiling.

"Isn't that Virginia?"

"Isn't what Virginia?"

"The accent."

"I didn't think it was that obvious."

"I'm an expert," Gillian said. "I'll bet I can pin-point the town."

"Go ahead."

"Say something else. Say 'I think we should take the ferry to Newport News'."

"I think we should take the ferry to Newport News."

"I think we should take the car to New Haven," Brian said.

"Richmond," Gillian said.

"Not quite," Matthew answered, "but pretty close. That's remarkable. Brian told you, didn't he?"

"I didn't say a word," Brian swore. "She's uncanny, that's all. Gilly, do the Russian story, will you?"

"No, not now, Brian. If you live in Virginia, why were you heading for New Haven?"

"Army business," Matthew said.

"Will you go to the theatre there?"

"I hadn't thought so. Should I?"

"Yes, you should. They're trying out a wonderful show at the Biltmore. At least, I think it's still there. It may have already moved to New York. It's called *Sons and Soldiers*."

"A musical?"

"No, no, a straight drama."

"Who's in it?"

"Geraldine Fitzgerald plays the woman," Gillian said. "And there's a new actor called . . ." She paused. "Gregory something. I can't remember. He's very tall, with dark hair and brooding eyes, and a strong profile."

"I'll try to see it," Matthew said.

"The band's starting," Brian said. "Are we getting out of here?"

"Shhh," Gillian said, "they're playing our song." She winked at Amanda and led Brian on to the floor.

"How old is your friend?" Matthew asked.

"Eighteen." Amanda paused. "Does that make her old enough?"

"Legally, do you mean?"

"However you prefer."

"I prefer honey blondes who fall out of peach trees. I thought I told you that. I'm going for a drink. Will you come with me?"

"I'm not thirsty," Amanda said. She hesitated. "But I'll go with you."

"Shall we tell them we're leaving?"

"Why? We'll be back."

"Yes, of course," Matthew said.

He took her arm and led her out of the gym. It was a dark night, almost moonless. They walked slowly towards the car.

"Why'd you ask how old Gillian was?"

"I was curious. She seems older somehow. And yet I knew she was just a kid."

"How old do you think *I* am?"

"I don't know."

"Guess."

"Two things I'll never guess at are a woman's age or her weight."

"I'll give you a hint. I'm finishing my sophomore year."

"That isn't a hint at all. You can be a very bright sophomore, and therefore quite young, or else——"

"I *am* very bright," Amanda said.

"Yes, and quite young."

"And how young is quite young?"

"Younger than Gillian," he said.

"Really? You don't believe that."

"No. I know it isn't true. But you seem much younger than she does."

"Why is that?"

"Search me. Here's the car."

He opened the door on her side. She hesitated.

"Go on," he said. "Get in."

"I told you. I don't want a drink."

"Get in, anyway. I hate to drink alone."

"All right," she said. She got into the car, and he slammed the door behind her. She immediately tucked her skirts around her, but they wouldn't stay put because of the crinoline petticoats. The door on his side of the car opened, and he slid on to the seat, leaned over and thumbed open the glove compartment.

"There we are," he said, reaching for the pint. He unscrewed the cap and held the bottle out to her. "Sure you won't change your mind?"

"I don't drink," she said.

"See what I mean?"

"No. See what you mean about what?"

"Your youth. How old are you anyway, Miranda?"

"Amanda," she said. "I was twenty just this month."

"Amanda, of course." He tilted the bottle to his mouth. "Happy birthday, Amanda." He took a quick swallow, screwed the cap back on, and put the bottle into the glove compartment, slamming it shut. "There."

"Is that all you're going to have?" she asked.

"Isn't that enough? Did you think I was an alcoholic?"

"Well no, but . . ."

"Somehow all this undergraduate nonsense gives me the willies. I needed that drink. But I feel perfectly fine now."

"I'm terribly glad to hear that. I'm sorry our dance seems childish to you," she said, slightly miffed.

"It does," Matthew admitted.

"But of course we aren't experienced citizens of the world who——"

He kissed her suddenly. One arm moved swiftly across the back of the seat, his right hand capturing her right shoulder. His left arm swung over simultaneously, his head was suddenly moving towards hers, his lips found hers, held them, pressed tightly against them. She pushed him away and caught her breath.

"Hey!"

"Hey," he mimicked.

"I . . . cut it out."

"Why?"

"I . . ." She shrugged. "Just cut it out. Let's go back."

"Don't you like the way I kiss?"

"No."

"Why not?"

"I just don't. I'm going back. Are you coming?"

She was in his arms again suddenly, swiftly his mouth descended, she could feel the bristles of his moustache, again she pulled away, and again she had to catch her breath.

"Now . . . now stop it," she said.

"Why?"

"I don't like it, I don't know you, your moustache, I don't like it, stop it."

"No," he said, and he pulled her to him, and she found herself succumbing to the warmth of his mouth, gentle now, not at all harsh, the warm enclosing embrace of his arms, she felt a sigh murmur through her body, and she turned her face from his and buried it in his shoulder. Weakly, she said, "I don't think . . ."

"Neither do I," he answered, and he kissed her again.

She did not mind the moustache at all, she hardly noticed it any more. He touched her face with his hands, and she murmured gently, his hands were on her throat, his fingers touched the hollow of her throat, his mouth was on her ear, and suddenly his hand dropped, touched the neck of her gown briefly, and then pressed into her flesh beneath the gown, under her bra, she felt her breast caught in his hand, and she tried to sit erect, she felt suddenly violated, felt suddenly as if her body were not her own, felt his mouth on her cheek, felt his lips again, his tongue exploring, his hand tightening on her breast, shocked, she sat shocked, trembling with outrage, his hands on her body, and finally she pushed him away violently and moved to the other side of the car, and said nothing, and opened the door, and got out and then turned, her breast suddenly cold now that his hand was no longer there, she was sure she looked naked, she was certain her breast was exposed so that everyone could see it. She turned, and very coldly said, "Good night, Captain Bridges," and as she stalked away from the car she heard him say behind her, "Good night, Miranda," and she was sure there was a smile on his face.

Gillian did not get back to the dormitory room until two o'clock that morning. Amanda was waiting up for her, sitting with the pillows propped behind her, wearing blue cotton pyjamas, her blonde hair caught with a blue ribbon at the back of her head.

"Hi," Gillian said.

"Hi."

Gillian went to her bed and flopped on to it. "I'm pooped."

She lay silently for close to five minutes until Amanda thought she was asleep. Then she stirred and sat up and took off her high-heeled pumps without touching them with her hands, and then she walked to Amanda's bed and said, "Unzip me, will you?" She hung limply in the dress while Amanda pulled down the zipper. She threw the blue silk on to the foot of her bed, took off the rest of her clothes, turned out the light, got into bed naked, and pulled the covers to her throat.

"Gillian?" Amanda said.

"Mmmm?"

"Aren't you going to ask me anything?"

"About Matthew's pass, do you mean?"

"Matthew's . . ." Amanda's brow knotted. "How . . . ?" She leaned forward slightly. "Did he . . . did he *tell* you?"

"No, I figured it out for myself. Why else would you leave the dance so suddenly?"

"Well, he didn't really do anything," Amanda said.

"All right. I'm sleepy, Amanda. We'll talk about it tomorrow, all right?"

"All right."

The room was uncommonly dark. The night was almost moonless and the shade was drawn and Amanda sat up in bed and stared into the darkness and saw nothing and felt only a need to discuss this with Gillian, and yet she waited, waited until she was sure Gillian was asleep, and then tentatively she whispered, "Gillian?"

"Mmmm?"

"He said you seemed older."

"Mmmm."

"It was really a mistake to go to the dance with him."

"Mmmm."

"A soldier, I mean. And twenty-six."

"Mmmm."

"Gillian, he kissed me."

"That's nice. Amanda, go to sleep."

"Do you kiss a lot of boys?"

"Yes. Mmmm-huh."

"Do you let them . . . ?" Amanda paused. The room was silent "Gillian?"

"Mmmm?"

"Nothing. Never mind."

Across the room, lying naked in her bed, with the covers pulled to her throat, Gillian suddenly felt all sleepiness leaving her. She listened to her room-mate breathing in the darkness, and the room was suddenly very small, and she felt a tenderness wash over her, and at the same time she thought, Oh God, why me, why must I be the one? and she lay in the darkness for several moments longer, breathing evenly and half tempted to pretend she was already asleep, and yet feeling this tense uncertain need coming from across the room and threading its way cautiously through the darkness, and feeling very very old all at once.

"Amanda?" she said.

"Yes?"

"What did he do, honey?"

"He touched me, Gilly. My breast."

"Were you frightened?"

"Yes."

"Did you like it?"

"No. I got out of the car." The room was silent. "Gilly?"

She knew what was coming. She lay in bed staring up at the darkness and she thought, I must be careful, she is so young, I must be very gentle, oh, she is so goddam young.

"Gilly, do you . . . Gilly, do you let them? Boys? Touch you?"

Gillian took a deep breath. "Yes, Amanda."

"All of them?"

"No," she said. "Not all."

"But . . . but you don't *like* it, do you?"

Now here we are, she thought, here we are, and how can I tell Amanda that yes, I do like it, how can I tell that to Amanda and hope she will understand it, and not, not, oh God, why did it have to be me, why isn't her mother here, why aren't mothers around when you need them most?

"Gilly? *Do* you like it?"

"Yes, I do."

"But Gilly, it's so . . . so private. I mean, it's so personal. Gilly, you don't really like it, do you?"

"Yes. I do."

"Gilly, Gilly, I feel like crying."

"No."

Amanda was suddenly silent. The room was pitch-black.

"I never have, Amanda," Gillian said.

"I didn't ask."

"But I never have."

"All right."

"But I will," Gillian said. "When I want to."

Again the room was silent. There was something in the silence. Something of youth and of innocence, gone and about to go, something of girls and of women, and a touch of familiar friendship, and a touch of strangeness, and an intimacy bred of this familiar strangeness, so that the two girls in the Connecticut night felt a kinship they would not have known were they truly blood relatives, a kinship bred of the lonely dark hours of the night and the silence of the room and the tiny sound of evenly spaced breathing. For those moments in the silent room, they were closer than sisters, closer than mother and daughter, and they heard each other without speaking.

After a long while, Gillian sighed and said, "I think I'm going to leave Talmadge, Amanda."

"What? What did you say?"

"Talmadge. I don't think I'll be back in the fall. I'm not getting enough here. I'm too far ahead of them."

"It's a wonderful school. You can't mean——"

"It's only a school, Amanda. It's only make-believe. There's too much to do in the real world."

"I don't know what you mean."

"I'm not sure I know what I mean myself. I just have a feeling that I've learned everything I can learn here, that this is no closer to the theatre, the *real* theatre, than . . . than . . . Siberia is, I guess.

And I haven't got much time. I really haven't. I can't afford to waste any of it here with a bunch of silly kids who are only doing make-believe stuff. Don't you feel that way, Amanda?"

"No, I . . . I never thought of it that way."

"Because there's so much out there, Amanda, do you know what I mean? Don't you ever get the feeling that there's so much out there to do and to see and to know? Amanda, don't you ever pass an apartment building and look at all the lighted windows and wonder who lives up there, and sometimes feel so sad that you don't know them, that you'll never know them? Amanda, I could cry when I think of all the people there are in this world that I'll never know. In Talmadge alone, for God's sake, in New York millions of people rushing along the streets, busy, busy, with their own worlds, and I'll never even know them well enough to say hello, or even to smile as I pass them. And then I think of China, and I wonder how it is to be Chinese, and I wish I could speak Chinese and Italian and Russian, and I wish I could read all the books there are, and listen to all the music, and know all the people, walk down the street and say hello to everybody, just hug everybody as if they were part of my family and I'm very glad to see them, we haven't seen each other in a very long time, and we have all sorts of things to tell to each other, and we're not strangers the way everybody is—don't you feel that, Amanda? Don't you want to *know* people?"

"No. No, I've never——"

"Never, Amanda? Never?"

"But, Gillian, you can't know *everyone*. You can't expect to."

"No, I know, I know. I can't do that. But that's why . . . don't you see, Amanda? I just . . . I think of somebody out there who is like me and who I will never meet. And it makes me sad. He's out there, and I don't know who he is, and I'll never get to know him, and I just feel that if we knew each other, if we got to know each other, we could be so rich, don't you ever feel that way? I know it's silly, but I know he's there, maybe he's a Frenchman or something, and maybe I'll pass him on the street and we won't even say hello or smile, we just won't know each other, and he'll be the person, he'll be the one, Amanda, the one person I really *should* know. I get scared when I think of it. I get absolutely terrified. Suppose I should live out my life, and I die, and I never get to know this other person who is also living out his life, and he'll die, too, and we'll never have known each other, never."

"But why do you have to leave school, Gillian?" Amanda said. "I don't understand that. I don't see how leaving——"

"I've just got to get out of this fake place and stop *pretending* to be an actress. Don't you see how that can fool you, Amanda? Don't you see how all those dopes on the college newspaper think they're bigshot reporters or columnists when all they're doing is writing drivel that's fake and not anything that has any worth by the standards of the *real* world? Amanda, nobody cares what's happening in college. It isn't real. It just isn't real."

"What makes you think the world is?" Amanda asked.

"I know it is."

"How do you know?"

"I know. Nobody's kidding out there. Out there you work, and you eat, and you live. I want to live. Amanda, I think I . . . Amanda, don't you feel very important?"

"What do you mean?"

"Important. Just important being alive and being a girl . . . a woman? I . . . Amanda, I think that's very important, being a woman. I mean, I know you got offended when Matthew touched you tonight. Well, I don't feel that way, I feel quite flattered, I feel so good when I'm desired. I like being the way I am, and I like to think that someone wants to touch me, that it's exciting for a man to touch me because I'm a woman. I enjoy everything about being a woman, Amanda. And I think it's important. That's why I have to get away from this trivial little-girl stuff, to get out there and see what's happening and know what's happening and to . . . to live because that's what being a woman is. Because . . . Amanda, I want to have babies. I want to have dozens of babies. I want to meet that person I don't know yet, oh I *wish* I meet him, I wish he doesn't pass me by and not know me, I want to have dozens of his babies. And when I meet him, I really want to be a woman, I want to have reached the point when I come to him where I really am a woman, where everything he ever thought of as womanly is me, and, Amanda, I'll bring all this to him and we'll be so rich because he'll be bringing to me everything that's a man."

Gillian paused.

"I have to leave Talmadge," she said very softly.

"I see."

"There's so much to do."

"Yes."

"This is May," she said. "And then there'll be June, and the semester will be over." She paused. "I won't be coming back."

"Yes."

"Amanda, don't . . . don't be so afraid. Don't be so afraid of life."

"Yes, Gillian."

The room was silent.

"Good night, dear," Gillian said. "I'm very sleepy."

"Good night, Gillian." Amanda paused. Almost inaudibly, she said, "I'll miss you."

The town of Talmadge, Connecticut, became a different sort of town during the summer months, and Julia Regan—who hated the town anyway—hated it more during that loathsome hiatus. The change never really occurred until after final examinations were over at the university and the students began leaving for their homes. It was then that the town settled into its colonial stupor and became a lazy sort of fly-buzzing town, with giant maples spreading dappled sunshine on the wide walks of the main street, the twin steeples of the First Congregational Church dominating the hill and the town, white against blue, and far in the distance the walled and dormant university. The townspeople were really quite proud of the university, and yet they sighed a deep sigh of relief whenever June rolled around and they could reclaim the town for themselves and watch the slow lethargic change that came over it. Actually, the change began with Memorial Day, or at least the beginnings of the change began then. For it was then that the town began reminding itself of its history and its rural character, then that it began tentatively shrugging off the label of "university town", a label that, unfortunately, put the emphasis on the first word. And since Memorial Day each year became the unofficial day of the beginning of the metamorphosis, it was Memorial Day that Julia Regan came to loathe as a symbol of all that was decadent and stultifying in Talmadge.

On that Memorial Day in 1943, she stood in the school courtyard with her friends and neighbours and watched the preparations for the annual parade to the town hall. There were three fire-engines lined up in the schoolyard, side by side. The hood of each complicated-looking machine carried the gold lettering TALMADGE, CONN., FIRE DEPARTMENT, and the brilliant engines only made the sun seem more intense. They had been polished especially for the parade, and all that gleaming brass and red-hot enamel glowed in the noonday sun, reflecting dizzying bursts of brilliance, which were giving Julia a headache.

The Talmadge Volunteer Fire Department, a group composed of 90 per cent hick townie and 10 per cent Madison Avenue commuter, a fraternal group who never attended the same Talmadge parties together but who were expected none the less to extinguish fires with great communal camaraderie, stood about in the schoolyard in their blue dress uniforms looking ill-fitted and ill at ease, and possibly hoping that a sudden fire-alarm would put an end to their discomfort. Julia Regan, leaning against the wall with her secrets churning inside her head, watched a totally inept pack of cub scouts marching back and forth before the red-and-gold engines in blue-and-yellow slovenliness. The scout leader had greying temples, and his uniform was too tight, and he shouted orders like a martinet, and Julia wished he would hush, and she wondered for perhaps the fiftieth time why she bothered to attend these false town functions in this false-front town. She leaned against the shaded brick of the school building, a woman of thirty-nine, her long brown hair braided into a bun at the back of her neck, her eyes closed as she listened to the "Hup-tup-tripp-fuh" of the troop leader and heard the chaotic cadence of the eager cub scouts and thought, He is dead.

"Hello, Mrs. Regan," the voice beside her said, and she opened her eyes, smiling automatically even before she knew who was speaking.

"Looks like it's going to be a good parade," Ardis Fletcher said.

"Yes," Julia answered. "It does indeed." She smiled limply. It was a smile reserved for women, a smile that tried to convey a fragility in direct contradiction to her physical structure. She was a tall, slender woman with a strong and beautiful profile, and the smile she turned on her female friends was one that better suited her sister, Millie. And yet the attempt was not unsuccessful. Despite the big-boned evidence of her body, Julia was thought of by the women of Talmadge as delicate and gentle, if a bit spirited. The men of Talmadge looked at Julia somewhat differently. She had learned very early in life that it was not necessary for a woman to be readily accessible to all men so long as she gave an impression of accessibility. The smile she flashed to men held the possibility of intimacy, promised an arduous and passionate woman if only one could reach her, a mysterious lingering smile with more than a touch of sensuality in it, and yet the smile of a lady. And so, to her credit, the men of Talmadge looked upon her as a good-looking widow—spirited, to be sure—who could possibly, just possibly, and only with the most infinite delicacy and patience, be had. The smile she turned on Ardis Fletcher was her woman-smile, but it was wasted on Ardis, who at nineteen was concerned with nothing more subtle than the shape of her own body, which was about as subtle as a tornado. If anything, Ardis with her bright-red hair and sparkling blue eyes, her short skirt and contour-hugging sweater, supplemented the dazzling splendour of the fire-engines and the cub scouts and the school band, which had lined up beside the fire-engines in a glittering display of tuba and cornet and trombone.

"Have you heard from Davey?" Ardis asked, and Julia flinched at her use of the diminutive in referring to her son, and noticed too that Ardis did not look at any woman she spoke to; her eyes instead wandered over the eligible male members of the holiday crowd, and one of Julia's secrets caught in her throat, the fact that her only son David was not in the Pacific any longer but was instead in the naval prison at San Diego, California. A convict. Her David was a convict.

"Yes," she answered in her low, steady voice. "I got a letter only yesterday. He's doing fine."

"I haven't heard from him lately," Ardis said. She pulled down on her sweater, apparently feeling it wasn't quite revealing enough the way it was. "Don't you think that's kind of funny?"

"Does he usually write to you often?" Julia asked.

"Mrs. Regan, *all* the boys write to me often," Ardis answered, and she smiled suddenly, taking Julia into her confidence with that single gleaming burst of enamel, allowing her to join the sorority of worldly women, an honour Julia didn't particularly desire on that hot day at the end of May.

"Well, David's been busy," Julia lied. "His ship is on a secret mission." A secret mission, she thought. My entire life has been a secret mission.

"Oh, how exciting!" Ardis said. "Doing what? Is it the invasion? Are they going to invade Japan?"

"Dear, he wouldn't even tell *me*," Julia said gently. "His own mother."

"But you have been getting mail from him?"

"Oh, yes. I told you. I got a letter only yesterday." And another letter the day before that, but not from David, another letter, he is dead, *egli é morto*. Memorial Day. A day for memories, a golden day, and my son's harlot stands here in the hot sun and wiggles like a chorus queen, what secrets does she hold in that empty head of hers? How many men and boys have known the loveless white thighs of Ardis Fletcher, were you the first for him, Ardis?

"Tell him to write to me, will you? He's kind of cute."

"I will. And thank you, Ardis."

"Sure," Ardis said, and she swivelled off in an elaborate synchronization of hip and thigh and leg, and Julia could not resist shaking her head in slight displeasure. Still, she supposed they had to learn somewhere. She supposed there was an Ardis Fletcher in every town in America, on every city street, a vast auxiliary army of willing young ladies who performed initiation rites on the back seats of automobiles, in vestibules, on living-room couches, on grass as green as green as her skirt she stained her skirt that day the white skirt with the pleats, the sun was so hot and her skirt became wrinkled and stained with grass his hand under her skirt one thick brown hand rubbing at the stain and the other hand beneath her skirt the knuckles pressing hard against her thigh she had stained her skirt and she twitched with new desire he could smell in the golden hot sunshine, he kissed her again.

The festivities were about to start, she saw. The fire-engines had revved their motors impressively, and the fraternal smoke-eaters had lined up behind the engines, ready to eat carbon monoxide if nothing else. The cub scouts stood at the ready, waiting for the signal to "Fuh-hut *motch*!" The brownies stood by, two by two, little girls, she thought, daughters, she thought, ready to walk down the town's back road to the town hall where a retired Navy commander would give a speech, after which the local American Legion troop would fire a twelve-gun salute, and Taps would be played by the town's best bugler, the town's second-best bugler played the echo from behind the school building.

"Come on," someone shouted, and she turned her head and looked across the road to where an old Ford was parked, a boy in a hooded Mackinaw sitting behind the wheel, a girl leaning out the window, her blonde hair hanging over one eye, waving her hand. "Gillian, come on! They're about to start! We'll miss it, Gillian!"

She turned as the girl called Gillian moved away from the fire-engines and broke into a girlish run across the schoolyard, a slender girl in sweater and skirt, her russet hair bobbing at the back of her neck, a curiously satisfied grin on her mouth. "I'm coming, Amanda," she shouted to the parked Ford, running past the ranked town band, and then on to the macadam road where summer sat suddenly still and golden.

A butterfly touched Julia's wrist.

She glanced at it, and then she heard the girl named Gillian say to the other college youngsters in the Ford. "I'd never seen a fire-engine up close before," and she turned again to look at the girl as she got into the car, and she thought, She moves with such grace, she is so lovely, and then the band began playing "Be Kind to Your Web-footed Friends". Julia hastily found a seat on the grassy bank lining the road, and the parade started with the fire-engines creeping at a snail's pace up the sticky road, followed by the stiff-backed and proud volunteers, and then the martinet leaning into an imaginary head wind and the cubs marching behind him with the vigour of ignorant stragglers. The brownies, buttressed by three firm-busted matrons, nodded at Julia as they filed past proudly, and then the town band wearing blue and white, trousers and shirts, blouses and skirts, blowing their horns and pounding their drums, and the townspeople crowding and shouting and cheering, and the girl Gillian leaning out of the back window of the Ford across the road, her eyes bright, her face aglow with a secret delight, secrets, Julia thought, secrets, I shall have to do something, of course, now I shall have to do something, I will see someone tomorrow, of course I will have to do something. The parade had passed, the parade was over. The Ford coughed itself into life and began driving towards the town hall, and the people of Talmadge, Connecticut, got off the banks and brushed their trousers and their skirts and began trudging up the hill behind the distant music of the school band, like a band of guerrillas carting a cannon across Spain.

The retired Navy commander was in the middle of his speech by the time Julia reached the town hall. She wondered briefly if her son had struck a commander, *I think we should wait a while, Mother, before telling anyone I'm back in the States*, his letter had read, *and then simply say I've been assigned to the shore patrol here at Camp Elliott. I think that would be best, don't you?* Why did trouble always come in batches, she wondered, and of course she would have to do something now, she couldn't simply, no she had to do something, tomorrow, she would take care of it tomorrow. She joined the Talmadge townsfolk and the Talmadge commuters who stood around in slacks and sun-glasses and made faces indicating they were above all this patriotic and sentimental corn, and at the same time made complimentary and contradictory faces that indicated they relished all this corn and sentimentality, the nation being in the grip of a war for democracy, or whatever they were calling it this time, *egli è morto*. Julia bent her head and sat on the rock near the giant oak, the rock carrying a plaque that explained that Hessian forces had been driven from Talmadge, Connecticut, in 1779 by the Continental Army, and that the parish house had been burned by the retreating British. She heard the buzz of something in the new green grass and saw her first bee of summer and was then aware of the girl Gillian leaning against the tree and listening intently to the words of the retired Navy commander, her arms folded across her white sweater.

The American Legion rifles went off, and then the town's best bugler played Taps while the smoke from the rifles drifted across the town hall lawn, and then the echoing chorus came from behind the school building and someone jokingly whispered that next year they were going to have an echo of the echo with the third bugler stashed away in the hills of the next town, and Julia saw the girl Gillian frown momentarily and turn to shush the jokester. She kept her eyes on the girl. The distant notes of the second bugle hung like the rifle smoke on the sticky noonday air, faltering, unclear, magnified somehow by the heat, and magnifying it in turn, reminding everyone that summer was truly about to start. She looked at the girl Gillian and saw a thin sheen of perspiration on her upper lip. The girl was listening to the notes coming from the second bugle hidden behind the old school-house, listening with her head bent in silent thought, and then she lifted her right hand quite casually and brushed it gently across her lip, and suddenly Julia Regan wanted to weep.

And she knew this moment would be captured for her for ever, encased in a permanent indestructible bubble of time, the sound of the bugle echoing on the still and silent air, the thin sheen of perspiration on the young girl's lip, her head bent in rapt silence as she listened, and her slender hand coming up casually, unconsciously, in a gesture that seemed so very familiar to Julia, a gesture that somehow recalled for her in a sweet rush of painful memory her youth, and she watched the girl Gillian until the moment was gone and there remained on the rock with its historic plaque only the thirty-nine-year-old woman named Julia Regan whose life had been secret after secret after secret in the golden sunshine, and then the echo died.

Oh, the summer went by somehow. Somehow the summer went by as all summers do, in fat and lazy reticence. Although they were dying on the beaches in the Pacific and there was sugar and gasoline rationing and it was difficult to get new tyres for old cars, the summer of 1943 went by. Summer storms came and went with sudden fury, and people read the newspapers anxiously to see how our boys were doing, and there was a change in the physical face of America, uniforms everywhere. In Norfolk, Virginia, it was difficult to see anything but white hats bobbing down the main street on any afternoon after three-thirty, and the Army Air Corps took over a great many Miami Beach hotels, and 4-F became an expression that could cause fist-fights in bars. But somehow the summer went by, and somehow there were still relics of peace, and somehow the war seemed very distant.

On the beaches of America, the record players spun all the popular songs, "Do Nothin' Till You Hear From Me." and "They're Either Too Young or Too Old," and "Mairzy Doats," and kids lay on the sand in sun tanned splendour, clean young bodies and clean white teeth and straight legs, and hummed to the whirl of the records and twisted straws in empty Coca-Cola bottles and listened to the distant rush of water against sand, and the war was very far away. Somehow the amusement parks managed to keep their Ferris wheels spinning, and here was black-market gas to be had, and butchers got richer and fatter selling black-market meat to favoured customers. Every now and then, someone was startled to see a gold star in the window of a neighbour, or shocked to learn that an American transport had gone down with all hands and the son of a neighbour or relative was aboard. But the church socials went on, and the dancing continued, and girls and boys alike wore their hair in pompadours, and the Windsor knot came into popularity, and skirts were shorter, and perhaps morals were too, some of the war wives were whooping it up in a fling at second childhood with the teen-agers whose attitude was Kiss Me My Sweet, and a burlesque revue assembled by Mike Todd and called *Star and Garter* was still knocking them dead on Broadway. Somehow the summer went. War wasn't all that much hell after all. War to Americans, in fact, war to the Americans at home—who waited for letters scrawled from muddy Sicilian ditches by men who crawled with lice, by men who huddled together while Stuka bombers screeched out of the sky and tanks loomed on the horizon—was kind of exciting.

There were motion pictures like *The Watch on the Rhine*, which made everybody hate those dirty Nazi bastards, and *This Is the Army*, which made everybody love our patriotic boys, and *Casablanca*, which made everbody love a song called "As Time Goes by", and people were watching time go by, laughing it up and drinking it up and loving it up, strange girls in strange towns met strange soldiers, and generally everything was a little looser and a little more frantic. War in fact, well war, to get right down to rock bottom, to get right down to the core of human reaction, to get right down under all that patriotic folderol and all that war-is-indecent and inglorious and disgusting, and nobody wants all this senseless maiming and killing, war when all was said and done was downright fun.

And somehow the summer went by.

"She's screaming again," Penny said. "I can't stand her when she screams."

The baby's cries came from the open second-story window of the frame house in Otter Falls. Penny, sitting with her mother and her sister, put her hands over her ears and said, "Mother, make her stop."

"It won't hurt her to cry a bit," Priscilla Soames said. "She has to learn sooner or later that she won't be picked up every time she——"

"Mother, make her stop!" Penny said sharply, and Amanda, sitting on the porch steps, turned to look up at her sister.

"I'll go," she said.

"No!" Priscilla said. "Stay where you are, Amanda."

"Why does she have to cry?" Penny asked, and Amanda continued to stare at her, and she suddenly wondered when Penny had stopped being her sister, when she had become only a somewhat thin and gaunt stranger who complained about her baby constantly, who never confided in Amanda at all any more, who seemed to roam the old wooden house in a silent angry world of her own. "What right does she have to cry? I'm the one who should be crying. *I'm* the one!"

"Penny..."

"Make her stop, Mother."

"Penny, if you'd just——"

"I'm leaving. I'm going to town. I can't sit here and listen to her scream all day long."

"Penny, I'll pick her up," Amanda said gently, and she rose from where she was sitting, and again Priscilla said sharply, "Stay where you are, Amanda!"

Amanda sat and looked up towards the second-story window. Penny rose swiftly and slapped her own thigh, a curious gesture that seemed to start as a simple flattening of her skirt, but which became exaggerated in the execution, ending as a vicious slap that sounded flat and hard on the summer air. In the church, Amanda's father began playing the organ, and Amanda became aware of the clicking of her mother's knitting-needles, like a meticulous metronome beating out a steady rhythm for the organ notes that floated fat and round across the lawn and the high shrill cries of the baby upstairs.

"I've got to get out of here," Penny said, and she bounded down the steps, and Amanda watched her walk purposefully across the lawn and into the garage. She heard the old Chevy starting and then saw Penny back the car out of the garage and down the driveway, her long blonde hair streaming over her shoulders. The car pulled away from the house. The sound of its engine faded, leaving only the sounds of Kate, and the organ, and the knitting-needles clicking. And then the baby fell silent, shimpering herself into stillness. The organ notes rolled from the church. The knitting-needles continued their steady subdued clatter. Priscilla Soames rocked herself back and forth in the rocker, and Amanda sat on the porch steps, her hands clasped around one knee.

Priscilla did not look at the needles or the brown sweater she was knitting for the Red Cross. She looked out over the lawn instead, and at the blue jays that darted in the branches of the old maple. When Amanda recalled the scene later, she would remember that her mother's face had remained expressionless throughout the entire discussion, and then she tried to remember when she had *ever* seen any expression on her mother's face, and she could not remember a single time. The face was always placid, always in strong repose. She wondered once—many years later when she was already married —whether her mother's face remained calm and expressionless even in orgasm, and then, of course, she wondered whether her mother had ever experienced orgasm, and then she realized this was all part of the unconscious resentment she had nurtured that day on the porch in Otter Falls, the knitting-needles clicking, the organ notes trembling over the grass.

Her mother's hair was blonde, touched with strands of white. Her face was long and thin, her eyes blue. They followed the darting motion of the jays unflickeringly, emotionlessly.

"You'll be going back to school soon, Amanda," she said. Her voice was flat, as flat as the Midwest plains that had bred her.

"Yes," Amanda answered. She heard her father's fingers falter on a difficult passage, and she smiled and thought. No, Dad, that's B-flat, and she tilted her face to the sun, happy that Kate had stopped crying, wondering where Penny had gone and how soon she would return.

"This is your junior year, isn't it, Amanda?"

"Yes," Amanda said.

"What do you expect to do, daughter?"

"What?"

"What do you expect to do?"

"I don't understand."

"With your life."

"Oh, I . . ." Amanda paused. She had never once thought of what she expected to do with her life. She had always considered it a foregone conclusion that she would write music. Somewhat inspired by Gillian's enthusiasm, she rather imagined she would eventually end up writing musical comedy for Broadway. But she had never given it any definite thought, had never sat down to ask herself what she would do when she was graduated from Talmadge. In her mind's eyes, she imagined things would simply happen to her without any conscious direction or will. She would leave Talmadge eventually, and things would simply happen. She turned to look at her mother, but Priscilla's eyes were still on the frolicking jays.

"I guess I'll write music," she said.

"I see," Priscilla answered.

"I thought you knew that."

"No, I didn't."

"Well . . ." Again Amanda paused. "That's what I'm studying, you know. Composition."

"Oh, yes, I know that," Priscilla said.

"Well . . ." Amanda frowned. "Well, that's why I'm studying it. So I can write music." She hesitated because she didn't wish to seem solicitous, and yet she suddenly felt that perhaps she'd overestimated her mother's intelligence. Perhaps her mother truly did not understand what she meant; perhaps it needed translation. "Composition is writing music, you know," she said hesitantly.

"Yes, I know," Priscilla said. She dropped a stitch, and her eyes moved momentarily from the jays as her hands recovered the stitch, and then shifted back to the maple again.

"Well," Amanda said, and she shrugged, but the frown remained on her forehead. She listened to the annoying click of the knitting-needles, and she suddenly wished that Gillian were there with her to explain to her mother, to tell her about seeing things and doing things, the way she had done that night several months ago. And yet she knew Gillian could not help her now, Gillian was out of her life, they had said their good-byes at the end of June, she probably would never see Gillian again as long as she lived. She sat in silence and she thought, Well, what did you think I was going to do with my life? I'm going to write music, what did you think? Why do you suppose I'm going to school?

"What kind of music did you plan to write?" Priscilla asked, as if she had read her mind.

"You know." Amanda shrugged.

"Serious music? Like Bach? Or Beethoven? Like that?"

"Well, nothing that ambitious, I guess," Amanda said and she shrugged again.

"Then what sort, Amanda?"

"I thought . . . maybe musical comedy."

"I see. For the stage, do you mean?"

"Yes. That's right. For the stage."

"I see."

Again the knitting-needles clicked, filling the silence of summer.

"Amanda," her mother said simply, "what makes you think you have any talent?"

She wasn't quite sure she had heard her mother correctly; it sounded as if her mother had said . . .

"What?" she asked.

"What makes you think you have any talent?" her mother repeated.

"I . . . I don't know." She paused. "I got into Talmadge, didn't I? And I . . ."

"Yes, of course you did, darling. You play piano beautifully."

"Well, then . . ."

"Do you have the talent, Amanda?"

"Mother, I don't think I understand you," Amanda said, hearing the infuriating words reverberating inside her head, and wondering why they infuriated her so, but sitting tightly controlled on the front porch as her mother's chair rocked back and forth and the jays chattered in the maple and the knitting-needles clacked like subdued machine-gun fire.

"You play piano beautifully," Priscilla said, "and it's wonderful for a young girl to get an education at a fine school like Talmadge, but if you don't mind my saying so, Amanda, I'm being perfectly frank with you, dear, the way only a mother can be frank with her daughter, I really don't think you're a genius or anything, do you?"

"Well, no, I . . . I guess I don't. But . . ."

"And it does seem a little presumptuous to me . . . not impossible, mind you, but a little presumptuous for a young girl to consider . . . I just wonder, Amanda, if you have the talent *necessary* for something like that, that's all, dear. I simply wonder about it. And naturally, I'm concerned, because I wouldn't want to see you wasting your life in pursuit of something elusive. Or, more than elusive, impossible. Though I'm not saying it *is* impossible. I'm just concerned, that's all, Amanda. I was hoping you'd meet a nice boy and——"

"Yes, but I'm studying composition," Amanda said, somewhat dazed.

"Yes, I know, dear."

"Don't you see? That's so I can——"

"Yes, I know, dear, and you'll find your education wasn't wasted. I can assure you of that. Any husband would be delighted to have a wife who can——"

"But, Mother, I'm studying so I can——"

"I think you should ask yourself, Amanda, if you have the talent."

"I . . ."

"You're old enough now to be frank with yourself, daughter."

Amanda nodded and said nothing.

"Do you understand what I'm saying?" Priscilla asked.

"Yes," Amanda answered. There was an edge of sharpness to her voice. Priscilla's eyes suddenly moved from the jays and rested on her daughter.

"Good," she said. "I'm glad you understand."

"Yes," Amanda said. "I understand."

They stared at each other and Amanda thought, I'm going to hit her, and then instantly thought, God forgive me, and lowered her eyes. Inside the house, the baby began crying again.

"It's Katherine," Priscilla said. "She's awake again."

"I'll pick her up," Amanda said, and she rose from the steps and smoothed her skirt and started for the front door.

"No," Priscilla said. "Leave her be."

"I'll pick her up," Amanda said without looking back at her mother. The screen door clattered shut behind her. She went through the cool dim house and upstairs to Penny's bedroom. Kate was sitting in the middle of her crib, bawling loudly, her face red, her cheeks stained with tears.

"Oh, what's the matter, snookums?" Amanda said, and she held out her arms and picked up the child and put her over her shoulder. "Do you have a little gas, honey? Is that what's the matter? Here, baby. That's a good baby. That's a sweet honey-child. See? All gone now. No more crying, all right? That's a good honey." She rubbed the palm of her hand gently on the baby's back, holding her blonde head cradled against her own and thinking, *Do* I have the talent? and hating her mother for making her wonder about it, and then shrugging the hatred aside and thinking, Mother only means well. "There, that's a good baby. Come on now, smile for your Aunt Mandy, give your Aunt Mandy a great big smile, *there* you are, that's my baby, oh that's my sweet baby." And she suddenly hugged Kate to her fiercely, wondering again, *Do* I have the talent?

She wondered about it for the remainder of the summer. And at last she decided her mother was right. She played piano beautifully, yes, and she had done a few compositions of which she was very proud, but that didn't necessarily indicate she had any of the real requisites for a career in music. Wasn't that what Gillian had meant that night? About the falseness of college and the standards of the real world? Wasn't her mother simply repeating what Gillian had said? And yet, if Gillian had been there, if she could have discussed this with Gillian, she was sure . . . but of course they both meant the same thing. And of course, she did not have the talent, she simply did not have the *real* talent.

She faced the knowledge, and somehow the summer went by. She supposed she was relieved. It was good not to have to wonder about something like that. And yet, oh and yet if her mother had only said something other than what she'd said, that was the part that hurt, oh if only her mother had said, Amanda, darling, go write your music, go write your beautiful music, oh if only her mother had said that, and yet it was good to know, good to have the uncertainty gone if only the other thing wasn't gone, too. She did not know what the other thing was. It had something to do with her mother's not wanting anyone to pick up Kate when she was crying, and it had something to do with that deadly awful clicking of the knitting-needles, and the way her mother had said, "What do you expect to do daughter?"—not using her name, not saying "Amanda", but saying "daughter" instead, and by using that word somehow denying the relationship.

She faced her life. She looked ahead and she faced her life, knowing that something was gone now, something was missing, but facing it none the less with a weary sort of sad hurt inside her, looking forward to her return to Talmadge, but not the way she usually anticipated the beginning of school, not with that same rush of excitement she had known even when she was a little girl buying a pencil-box and a stiff-backed composition book in the local store, not with that same excitement that seemed to vibrate in the very air of autumn. Something was gone, and she could not escape the knowledge that her own mother had taken it from her, had stolen it from her.

Somehow, the summer went by.

When her mother came into the apartment, Gillian was curled up in one of the living-room chairs, reading Gassner. Her mother's arms were full of bundles, and there was a curious expression on her face, as if she'd been hit by a bus.

"Hello," Virginia said cheerily, "hello." She put down her bag and her packages on the hall table, removed her hat, fluffed her hair, and said, "Were there any calls, Gillian?"

"Nope."

"Would you like a cup of coffee? I think I'll make some."

"I just had some milk."

"Oh. Well, I think I'll have some anyway. My, what a beautiful day it is. All the trees are beginning to turn, Gillian. It's like a painting. My, what a day." She walked out of the living-room, and Gillian could hear her humming to herself as she began filling the coffee-pot in the kitchen. Gillian stared at the empty door-frame, shrugged, and picked up her book again. After a while her mother came back into the living-room, sat down with her coffee-cup, and began sipping at it, smiling somewhat idiotically. Gillian glanced at her over the top of her book, shrugged again, and went back to reading.

"Gillian, guess what happened to me?" Virginia said.

"What?"

"Aren't you curious?"

"Sure I am."

"I was just coming out of Alexander's. You know, right on the corner of Fordham Road and the Grand——"

"Mom, I know where Alexander's is. I was only *born* in this——"

"I'm sorry, dear," Virginia said cheerfully. "I'm sorry, I'm sorry," almost singing the words.

"Well, you always say things like that. Yesterday you asked me if I remembered Aunt Mary. Well, now how could I possibly forget Aunt Mary, since I only know her from when I was two inches high? I know I've been away at college, but——" and she cut herself short, thinking, I'd better get away from *that* little subject right this minute, and feeling again the fear and guilt within her, the knowledge that everyone in the house still thought she was going back to Talmadge on the fifteenth. She had lied about registering by mail, had lied about her plans, had withheld the fact that she had already placed a deposit on an apartment in Greenwich Village, well not really the Village, more or less the outskirts of the Village, actually if one wished to get fussy, the very tail end of the Village or, to be positively accurate, the waterfront almost, but still an apartment of her own, and lucky to get anything at all these days. Still, she had lied, and she could not find the courage to tell her mother and her father that she was not going back to Talmadge, that she was going to register at a real dramatics school downtown, and that she was moving out so she could be closer to the theatre district. That was the part she knew would bring down the roof, the part about moving out.

"You must forgive my little idiosyncrasies," her mother said, still cheerfully, so cheerfully that Gillian was certain now she'd been struck by a bus and had her brains addled.

"Sure," she answered.

"Anyway, I was coming out of Alexander's when I bumped into this man, literally *bumped* into him, Gillian. One of my packages fell to the sidewalk. There wasn't very much in it, just some socks I picked up for Monica. She *should* have come home for the summer, don't you think? Why was it necessary for her to go to summer school?"

"I guess she wants to finish quicker," Gillian said patiently.

"For what? What's her hurry?" Virginia shrugged, as if unwilling to discuss unpleasant subjects, the cheerful smile coming on to her mouth again. "Guess who it was, Gillian?"

"Guess who *who* was?"

"The man who knocked my package down."

"Who?"

"Barry Murdock."

"Who's he?"

"Barry *Murdock*," Virginia repeated, and she opened her eyes wide as if expecting Gillian to recognize the name immediately.

"Well, who's Barry Murdock?"

"Why, he wanted me, Gillian," Virginia said, and she lowered her eyes. For a moment Gillian thought her mother actually meant "wanted". Then she realized that what this Barry Murdock had wanted was to marry Virginia. She remembered hearing her mother mention him once before, and she nodded briefly and raised her book again.

"He's still very handsome," Virginia said wistfully. "He picked up my package for me."

"Did you thank him?"

"Of course I thanked him. We had a drink together."

"I didn't know you drank, Mom," Gillian said, suddenly interested.

"Oh, all I had was a little whisky sour."

"I see." Gillian paused, studying her mother. "Where was this?"

"At Thwaites'. You know, on the parkway."

"Yes. You drove there?"

"Mmmm."

"With this Barry Murdock?"

"Yes." Virginia paused. "He never married."

"That's too bad."

"He told me he'd never found another girl like me."

Gillian nodded, studying her mother.

"I was rather pretty, you know."

"Yes," Gillian said.

"And slender. Of course, after two children . . . well, I can't blame you girls for that. But I used to be very pretty, Gillian. Your father thought so. *And* Barry, of course."

"Why didn't you marry him, Mom?" Gillian asked sharply, suddenly annoyed, feeling that this talk was disrespectful to her father.

"Oh, I don't know. Your father had a great deal of charm, and he loved me very much in those days." Her mother nodded. Gillian thought she detected a sadness in the nod, and then Virginia shrugged slightly. Her face brightened again. Gillian watched her, feeling something quite curious, something she did not particularly want to feel, and yet something that came none the less. "Did I ever tell you about the boat ride?" Virginia asked.

"No. No, you never did."

"When Barry threw me in the water?"

"No."

"On the way to Bear Mountain?"

"No."

"Oh, that was awful, just awful!" Virginia said. "I had made the box-lunch. We all belonged to this club, you see, Barry, your father, and me. It was an Irish sort of club—that is, everyone in it was Irish—and we called ourselves The Bunch. We went on all sorts of outings and picnics together, and we held dances, oh we did a lot of things. That was where I met your father, Gillian. *And* Barry, of course."

She wished her mother would stop saying, "*And* Barry, of course," in that strange way, which made Barry Murdock seem more important than Meredith Burke. Suddenly she didn't want to hear her mother's story; she did not want to know.

"Mom——" she started.

"I told Barry I'd made chicken-salad sandwiches, and he said he despised chicken salad and I said well, if you love me you'll love my chicken salad or something like that. You know how foolish girls are when they're young, you know, Gillian."

"Mom, I don't——"

"Well, he said he loved *me* all right, but that didn't change his feelings about chicken salad. He said he was going to throw that box-lunch right over the side of the boat, and we would both starve unless I would feed him with kisses. Everyone laughed, Gillian, except your father, whose date I had refused and who sat on the side of the boat on one of those folding wooden chairs with a dark Irish scowl on his face as if he was ready to take on the whole world, Barry Murdock included. Oh, he was angry that day, I thought he would take a fit. Well, we struggled back and forth, Barry and me, he trying to get the lunch away from me, and me trying to hold it over my head, fat chance I had against those long arms of his. And finally he grabbed at the lunch, and he whirled towards the side of the boat, and me clinging to it, and as he made to throw it over the side, he shoved at me, just playing, you know, and somehow I went over with the lunch. I screamed to high heavens, I remember. All I could think was that I would get caught in the boat's screw, I didn't want that to happen, I was only twenty, and all the world watching when I hit the water. They both jumped in after me, Gillian, your father and Barry Murdock, and they both swam to me, of course I was a very good swimmer, I had learned the crawl at an early age, my clothes were all soaking wet and sticking to me."

Virginia Burke paused, lost in the memory. "I let Barry Murdock save me. I let him put his arms around my waist tight and hold me up in the water. They threw one of those life-savers overboard, and they pulled us back on to the boat while your father, poor dear, floated in the water, angry as could be. You could see through everything I had on, Gillian, clear through my petticoat, oh I was so embarrassed!"

She looked at her mother, not wanting to hear, not wanting to think of her mother as a young girl, not wanting to hear this girl-talk from her mother, this was not right. She wanted to think of Virginia as her mother, the wife of her father, not a young girl who blushed in wet clothing, trembled on the deck of the boat while Barry Murdock looked through her garments. *I don't want to hear it!*

"They found a pair of white ducks for me, one of the boys had an extra pair, and someone gave me a sweater, I think it was your father. The sweater was too large, of course, and all my underclothing had got soaked, so you can imagine the picture I presented that day, everything flying under that big sweater. You know, in those days, Gillian, I was——"

"Mom!" she said sharply.

"He was very handsome," Virginia said. "Barry was." She paused. "He still is." She paused again. "He asked to see me again Gillian."

"Well, I hope you——"

"And, of course, I said no. Of course, I told him I was a married woman with two grown daughters. Of course, I said no. Did he think a little drink could turn my head? 'Ginny,' he said to me, 'Ginny, do you love him?' I said, 'yes, Barry, of course I love him, he's the father of my two lovely girls.' And he said to me, he reached across the table in Thwaites', the cars were rushing by outside on the parkway, Gillian, Lord knows where they were going, all those cars in a rush, he reached across the table, and he covered my hand with his, and he said, 'Does he love you, Ginny? Ginny, does he still love you?' and I smiled. I smiled, Gillian."

"Well, why didn't you . . . well, why . . . why didn't you . . . ?"

"Because what is there to say, Gillian? What is there to say about Meredith Burke, who ended the day of that boat ride so long ago by punching Barry Murdock in the nose and making him bleed? What is there to say about the man who stays away from this house more often than he——"

"Mom, I don't want to——"

"What is there to say about my Meredith Burke and his little blonde book-keeper? What is there to say, Gillian?"

She paused and smiled, but the cheerfulness had gone out of her voice and her face minutes ago, and she smiled in limp confidence, so that her daughter now hated this more intimate view. It was no longer the view of a young trembling girl in wet clothing, but the view of a *woman*, infinitely patient, infinitely suffering.

"'Does he still love you, Ginny? Ginny, does he still love you?' he asked, and his hand on mine was warm, and I smiled, and he said he would like to see me again, and of course I said no." Virginia shuddered suddenly. "It's cold in here, isn't it?" she asked. "You would think they'd be making heat already. Aren't they supposed to be making heat in September?"

Gillian stared at her mother in fixed fascination. She did not know quite how to react. She felt resentment because she had not asked for this sudden intimate glimpse, and she felt anger because she did not want to know about her father and his book-keeper or why he stayed downtown late each night. But she felt at the same time a curious attachment to her mother, felt closer to Virginia than she had ever felt in her eighteen years. And yet, paradoxically, she no longer felt like her daughter. She felt only like another woman, as if both of them had accidentally happened across each other in one of the dressing-rooms in a clothing store and stood partially naked and strange to each other before separate mirrors. The glimpse was startling. She looked at her mother and saw only a strange person whose face and figure were vaguely familiar and yet totally alien. The hair, the colour of the eyes, the wan smile most certainly belonged to someone she had known for a long long time. But the woman had a small birthmark on her cheek. Had that always been there? There were wrinkles at the edges of the woman's eyes. The woman's upper lip was not perfectly symmetrical. She could see a weakness in the woman's chin. She felt like a camera moving in for a terribly personal close-up, coldly impersonal, a camera that moved in cruelly and swiftly to devour the vulnerable face of a pale sad stranger. She kept staring at her mother, not knowing her, and yet knowing her more completely than she ever had.

Virginia rose. She sighed. She picked up her coffee-cup and started heavily out of the room.

"Wait!" Gillian said. Her mother turned. Gillian hesitated, about to say something. She almost reached out with her hand. And then, all she said was "I'm not going back to Talmadge."

Virginia nodded. "All right."

"I'm going to find a school in New York."

"All right."

"I've taken an apartment in the Village."

Virginia Burke paused, but only for an instant. Then she nodded again and said, "All right." She seemed suddenly very old. "Have you told your father?"

"Not yet."

"He'll want to know," Virginia answered, and she walked out of the room.

The letter was on the long table in the dormitory hall when Amanda came back from her five o'clock class. There was a light covering of snow on the campus, and she removed her galoshes before the mirror and glanced cursorily at the stack of mail on the table, and then began leafing through it. She was momentarily annoyed because the letter had not been separated from the pile and put into her box. As a junior, she expected *some* courtesies and privileges. She looked at the pale-blue envelope and the New York postmark and then she studied the impatient hurried scrawl on the face of the envelope and turned it over to look at the flap. There was no name on the flap, only an address, and an unfamiliar one at that. But she knew instantly the letter was from Gillian Burke. She went up to her room, made herself comfortable on the bed, and began reading.

AMANDA DEAR,
I know you think I'm dead by now, but that's not exactly the case, although I am pretty tired and close to exhaustion. It's not easy to furnish an apartment—furnish, she says!—or to get into a new routine of things, and it's taken a lot longer than I expected, and is really much more tiring than it would seem to be on the surface.

But I'm settled at last, or at least as settled as I will be for a while. It has been a long hard pull, believe me. And, as seems to be the case with everything in life, the resistance came from where I least expected it. I thought my mother would be the one to blow her top when I broke the news, but she took it as calmly as Lee surrendering at Appomattox. It was my father instead who hit the ceiling when I told him I was moving out. He wanted to know why, and I told him I was almost nineteen years old and that I owed it to myself as a person and a woman, oh this all sounds so stupid writing it, but I really think I made an excellent case for the emancipation of the American female, a case which unfortunately failed to impress Dad. He wanted to know whom I'd be living with, and I said I would be living alone, and he said "For how long?" He is a terribly sweet man, and I always felt he considered his daughter's business her own business, and yet all at once he was behaving like a real old Irishman worried about virginity and such. He went into a huff for several days, barely speaking to me, and writing an airmail-special letter to my sister Monica in California, asking her (I found out later) to talk some sense into Gillian—me, that is.

Well, he couldn't have picked a wronger person to write to because Monica answered by saying she intended to stay in California after she was graduated, and this totally demolished poor Dad, who began wailing in Irish accents about the ingratitude of daughters and such, and about rats leaving a sinking ship, all very flattering to Monica and me, the rats part, I mean. I must say that Monica behaved like a little bitch. She isn't graduating until June, and she could have withheld her delightful news until then, knowing the trouble I was having. But she didn't. So my father brought over his brother who runs a wholesale paint business on Long Island, thinking I would be impressed by the advice of an older, more experienced man than he, an uncle named Lonnie Burke whom my sister and I detested even when we were little girls and whom we used to call Uncle Long Drawers because he wore them winter and summer and they always showed beneath the cuffs of his trousers. This was the man who was going to convince me to stay on the auld sod! Uncle Long Drawers read me the riot act and warned me of the perils of living alone in a wicked city like New York, especially now when it was filled with servicemen from all over the world. Did I prize my maidenhood lightly? he asked. (Those were his exact words, Amanda.) I assured him that I prized it highly indeed, and that I did not intend opening a bordello on the West Side, which shocked him no end and sent him scampering back to Hempstead, or wherever it is he lives.

My father gave in at last, most ungraciously, it seemed to me. He said he would not give me a penny towards furnishing the apartment or keeping me in food and clothing. And he also said, in a gracious turnabout, that I could return home any time I chose and no more would be said about it. I thanked him for his kindness and then borrowed $200 from my mother and began shopping around for what I needed. I shopped along Third Avenue, and the one thing I'm really proud of is a big brass bed which I picked up for $56, but which I couldn't resist. That is, the *bed* isn't made of brass, only the headboard and the footboard, but it's a big double bed and I have all the room in the world to twist and turn in, which I love to do. The apartment has two bedrooms and a sort of living-room-kitchenette. I stuck a cot in the second bedroom, and I picked up an old sofa on the Bowery for $12 which I was sure was crawling with vermin and lice and which I disinfected and aired for three weeks before I allowed it into the apartment. A boy I know made a coffee-table for me out of an old wooden door—don't you love those people who are so handy and can make all sorts of useful furniture out of old crumby things that no one has any use for? But he was really sweet, and he got some posters for me which I hung all over the place. The posters all say "Loose Lips Sink Ships", but *c'est la guerre*, Amanda, and they do inspire all sorts of clever talk, not that I've much time for socializing, what with my heavy schedule.

I've enrolled in a small acting class which a lovely old Russian is teaching. He's all gnarled, and he talks in a whisper, but what he has to say, Amanda! He teaches what is called the Stanislavsky method, and it's like a new world opening for me. I always thought acting was a very natural and simple thing, but he's taught me how very much there is to know before one can be really good. I think I've learned more in three weeks here than I learned in two full semesters at Talmadge. My class is in the evening. In the morning I make the rounds and then grab a hot dog and rush to Macy's, where I've got a job in the record department. I work from one until closing, and all day Saturdays. It's a particular madhouse right now with the Christmas shopping, but it's usually pleasant, and

I do have to pay off Mom besides managing to eat. On the nights I'm not in class, I go to the Y on 92nd Street where I belong to a little group. We're working on *Hamlet* now, and I'm playing Ophelia—you know, she's the one who goes a little buggo. As you can see, it's a pretty busy schedule, but I love it.

Anyway, here's why I'm writing. I'm having a party on Friday night, Christmas Eve, a sort of combined housewarming and holiday thing. I don't know when Talmadge lets out for the Christmas vacation—last year it was on the 21st—but it occurred to me that you might be in transit from Talmadge to Minnesota and might be passing through New York on Christmas Eve, and I would so much like you to come. You remember Brian, he's coming, and there'll be a lot of New York kids I think you'll enjoy, all of them very sweet-oh and earnest and eager and all that, but it should be a nice party. I can put you up for the night, or the week, or for ever if you like, or you can simply come to the party and then catch your train or your plane, however you want to do it, but please come. I would like to see you again, Amanda. It seems like a very long time, and I do miss you.

I'm enclosing a little card with my fashionable warehouse-section address and directions on how to get there. The I.R.T. stops practically at my front door, give or take a mile or two, but you might prefer trying New York City's taxi system, which I am told is excellent and which I may be able to afford some day. I do hope we win the war because I don't feel like learning Kabuki, not at this late date.

I'm hoping to see you, so I won't even bother wishing you a Merry Christmas right now.

Love and such,
GILLY

There was music in everything, Amanda thought, either real or imagined. She could pick out melody and rhythm wherever she went, whatever she did, the resounding heavy solid sound of the taxicab door, and subdued closing swish of the building's entrance door, and the clatter of the answering buzzer, and the steady clicking cadence of her own high heels as she climbed to the top floor, the hesitant knock on Gillian's door, and then the door opening and the sound of real music inside the apartment, music on a scratchy phonograph, as forlorn as music on a summer beach, and then the subtle radiant music of Gillian's sudden smile.

She was wearing a black dress with a white collar, her russet hair combed sharply to one side of her head, burnished by the light of the candles inside the apartment. Her eyes danced and the smile came suddenly and radiantly, and she held out her hands and said, "Amanda," very softly.

They embraced wordlessly, pulled apart to look at each other, began laughing strangely, in curious embarrassment, and then embraced again and went into the apartment.

"Didn't you bring a suitcase?" Gillian asked. "Aren't you staying over?"

"I took a room at the Waldorf," Amanda said. "I didn't want to impose on you."

"Impose? On me? Oh, Amanda!" And she hugged her again, suddenly and fiercely. "It's so good to see you. You look *marr*-vellous. Sit down, Amanda. You're the first to arrive. We can talk a little."

Amanda looked around the apartment curiously. She had not been overly impressed by the factory neighbourhood or by the garbage cans stacked in the hallway downstairs or by the overpowering stench of food on every floor of the building. She remembered, too, the shambles Gillian had made of their dormitory room, and she half expected to find an apartment cluttered with the litter of careless living.

The apartment, she saw, was painted a blue that was pale enough to be called neutral. Dark-blue drapes covered the openings to the closets, relieving the paler shade of blue and presenting a look of geometric order. The walls were hung with the war posters Gillian had mentioned, together with several bold black-and-white three-sheets announcing newly opened Broadway shows. The couch Gillian had bought on the Bowery, a couch that Amanda had visualized as some rum-stinking horror, had been covered in a bright orange and served as a focal point for the entire room. The coffee-table that stood before it, the one Gillian's friend had made from an old door, had been patiently and lovingly rubbed down to its natural grain and then lightly shellacked and sanded. It reflected the vibrant orange of the couch and the glow of the flickering candles and almost physically drew one towards the main seating area.

The other seats in the room were high stools, like dunce stools, which Gillian had probably bought unpainted and which stood in graceful clusters like tall black and white birds. A real bird hung in a white-painted elaborate old cage in one corner of the room, a parakeet that had undoubtedly been chosen because his plumage matched the colour of the drapes. The bars of the cage danced with the blinking light of a small Christmas tree, which was in the opposite corner of the room. A long table covered with whisky bottles, glowing amber in the reflected light, was against the wall near the tree.

The total effect was one of warmth and order. The warmth was not unexpected; this was, after all, Gillian's home. But the order came as a total surprise. Amanda felt as if she were stepping into a Mondrian that ceased being coldly mathematical and resounded with loudly pulsating life.

"Do you like it?" Gillian asked, and Amanda realized she had been silent during her scrutiny. She turned to Gillian, seized her hands, and squeezed them in delight.

"It's lovely, Gillian," she said.

"Let me take your coat."

"All right."

"Your bag?"

"I'll keep it."

They spoke very softly. They were alone in the apartment, but they spoke as if fearful of awakening a light sleeper. Gillian hung the coat in the hall closet, shoving aside the long blue drape.

"Sit down, Amanda," she said. "How was the train ride?"

"Not too bad. A lot of servicemen, Sailors, mostly. I think they were coming down from the submarine base in New London."

"You look well, Amanda."

"Thank you. You do, too."

"Shall I put on some Christmas music?"

"All right."

"Do you remember the Christmas Pageant last year? '*An einem gewissen Morgen*'?" Gillian said, and she laughed and went to the record player.

"Yes, I remember."

"How's Talmadge?"

"The same."

"Anything exciting happening?"

"Nothing much."

Gillian put a stack of records into place and then went to the long table. "Shall we have a drink before the others get here?"

"All right, a small one," Amanda said.

"Scotch? Canadian?" she asked, studying the bottles on the table.

"Scotch. With a lot of soda."

She mixed the drinks and brought them back to the coffee-table.

"This is the table I was telling you about."

"It's beautiful."

"When did you begin drinking?"

"Oh, I don't really drink," Amanda said, smiling.

Gillian studied her for a moment. "You seem changed."

"Do I? How?"

"I don't know." She shrugged and then smiled. "I guess you're older."

"I'm almost twenty-one, Gilly."

"Do I seem very young to you?" Gillian asked.

"You never did."

"No, that's true," Gillian said, somewhat sadly. "Not even to myself."

"What?"

"Tell me what's new. How's your music coming along?"

"Fine. Just fine."

"Have you written anything new?"

"Well, you know. The usual. Nothing special."

Gillian nodded. The room was very quiet. From the phonograph, a scratchy record intoned "Silent night, holy night . . ."

"I have to get a new needle," Gillian said.

"That *is* bad for the records," Amanda said.

They were quiet again, listening to the music.

"Where did you get the advertisements?" Amanda asked.

"For *The Skin of Our Teeth* and the others? A boy I know. In the Count's class."

"The Count?"

"Yes, my teacher. The Russian. I wrote you about him, didn't I? He used to be a Count before all those Reds marched in. Do you know what he told me, Amanda? He told me the stories about Catherine the Great are all true."

"But how would he know? She was so long ago."

"Court knowledge," Gillian said seriously. "Passed from generation to generation. Can you imagine doing it with a horse?"

Amanda burst out laughing, and suddenly the strain was gone, suddenly there was no longer any tension in the room. "I can barely imagine doing it with a *person*," she said, still laughing.

"You have changed," Gillian said, laughing with her. "You never would have said that six months ago."

"Maybe not," Amanda said. She finished her drink and put down the glass.

"Are you still a virgin?" Gillian asked, lowering her voice.

"Yes." Amanda paused. "Are you?"

"Yes. Isn't it disgusting? I feel like some sort of cripple. Do you want another drink?"

"All right." She followed Gillian to the long table. "Just a little please."

"Okay. Amanda, do you really like the apartment?"

"I think it's lovely."

"Really?"

"Yes."

"Because sometimes I think I'm a little loony, you know, leaving home and coming to live all the way down here. This is a terrible neighbourhood, Amanda, it really is. I'm scared to death when I come home late from rehearsals. There are all sorts of suspicious characters lurking around." Amanda laughed again, suddenly and spontaneously. "I *mean* it, Amanda! I think my landlady is a drug addict or something. She's always got a glazed look in her eyes, even when I've paid her the rent." She handed Amanda the drink. "And there's a sort of vagrants' club that meets on the street corner. I think they were on their way to the Bowery and got lost—don't laugh, Amanda, I'm in terrible danger every minute of the day, now don't laugh, you silly, you'll make me spill my drink."

"I'm so glad to be here," Amanda said suddenly.

"Yes, oh isn't it good?" Gillian answered instantly. "Amanda, why in the world did you check in at an hotel?"

"Oh, I don't know," Amanda said. "I'm about to be unwell, and you know how I get, all moody and fidgety. I didn't want to impose."

"But that isn't the real reason, is it?"

"No," Amanda said. She paused. "I was afraid."

"That we wouldn't like each other any more?"

"Yes." Amanda nodded.

"But we still do," Gillian said simply.

"Yes," and they smiled.

"Amanda, I didn't buy you a Christmas present."

"I didn't buy you one, either."

"I was going to, and then I thought suppose Amanda doesn't buy me one, she'll be very embarrassed. So I didn't."

Amanda laughed and said, "That's exactly why *I* didn't."

"Well, good. Who needs presents? I'm so glad you're here. You know, there's nobody to talk to in this entire city. Would you believe it? I was born here, and I feel like a stranger. It's the weirdest thing ever." Gillian shook her head unbelievingly. "Talk to me, Amanda. Tell me about Talmadge. Is there a lot of snow up there?"

"Not too much."

"I always loved that campus. It's too bad I wasn't learning anything there."

"Morton Yardley . . . do you remember Morton?"

"Yes, what about him?"

"He was drafted, and he objected."

"What do you mean?"

"He's a conscientious objector. They took him away, Gilly."

"Away where? What do you mean, away?"

"I don't know. Any Army prison, I guess. I talked to him before he left, Gilly. He said he simply couldn't kill another human being. 'Can you understand that, Amanda?' he said. 'I just couldn't be responsible for another person's death. I'm not a coward, Amanda, but I couldn't kill.' He made me want to cry, Gilly. I've always liked him so much." She paused, her head tilted to one side. "Do you know what I found out?"

"What?"

"I found out why Morton always wore that hood. Gilly, he was going bald, poor thing. He's only twenty years old. And he was terribly ashamed of it, and so he wore that silly hood all the time. Oh, Gilly, I could cry when I think of him. He's so sad. He makes me so sad."

"Do you love him, Amanda?" Gillian asked.

"Yes," she answered without hesitation. "Oh, not that way. No, I could never love Morton that way. But I do love him, in a very special way, and I guess I always will love him. He's the first person I met at Talmadge, you know."

"I didn't know that."

"Yes. Gilly, I hope they treat him all right. I can't imagine Morton inside an Army jail, can you?"

"No, I can't."

They fell silent for a moment. Then Amanda said, "Do you remember Ardis Fletcher? You know, the sweater girl."

"Yes?"

"She got married. The girls all say she had to, but I don't know."

"Who'd she marry?"

"A boy in the diner. At the cross-roads. Charlie Something-or-other. She quit school, and they're living in town now, over near the gun factory. I saw her once, and she's as pregnant as a goose, so maybe what the girls say is true. Oh, and Mr. Connerly, do you remember him?"

"No."

"In the philosophy department? Did you take any philosophy courses?"

"No, I didn't."

"The short man? With white hair? He always wore those checked vests. Do you remember, Gilly?"

"I don't think I know him."

"Well, he made a pass at one the girls, promised her an A if she . . . well, you know."

"Did she?"

"No, no, she reported him. He's been suspended."

"Wow," Gillian said. She wiggled her eyebrows. "Maybe I shouldn't have left Talmadge!"

"Also, they've banned pledging," Amanda said anticlimatically, and both girls laughed again.

The door-bell rang suddenly.

Gillian looked up and said, "Here's the party." She rose and put her hand over Amanda's. "If I don't get the chance later," she said, "Merry Christmas," and she went to open the door.

There was music in everything, real or imagined.

Music in the steady ring of the door-bell, and the gentle clink of ice in tall glasses, and the pleasant pretty hum of party chatter, and the counterpoint of laughter, the front door opening, feet stamping into the room, shaking away the cold of New York in December, pretty girls in party dresses, and young boys in suits and ties, and older boys in uniform, a music of sound and colour, music too in the gentle swirl of liquor in Amanda's glass. She had never drunk so much in her life, but somehow she didn't care tonight. She felt warm and protected and loved, and so the drinks passed steadily into her hand, and she drank them and laughed with the other guests, all wonderful people, all Gillian's friends, and she danced, and there was always another drink waiting for her, and she sounded very witty and felt ravishingly beautiful, and she was very proud of her good friend Gillian and her lovely apartment and the marvellous people she knew.

In one corner of the room, by the Christmas tree, two sailors and a girl in a red dress were singing "*Adeste Fideles*," their faces angelic in the glow of the candles on the liquor-table near the tree. The record player scratched out its songs, David Rose's "Holiday for Strings", Harry James's trumpet leading "I've Heard That Song Before", Kitty Kallen and Bob Eberle singing "Star Eyes" with the Jimmy Dorsey band, and somehow the carols being sung beside the Christmas tree seemed to blend with the dance music, so that the couples weaving about the floor in time to the music were oblivious to the singing, accepted it as a secondary theme, accepted it as they did the music of the voices and the laughter all around them.

The boy with Amanda was earnestly telling her about the difficulties of getting a part in a Broadway show, and she listened to him with what she supposed was fascinated interest showing on her face, her eyes intently watching his mouth, nodding sympathetically from time to time, not really listening to him, and not really bored, simply enclosed in a warm cocoon throughout which a secret music vibrated. I think I'm a little drunk, she thought, and she listened to the boy in rapt attention, not hearing a word he said.

"... and they immediately ask you for your Equity card. Well, then when you tell them you haven't *got* an Equity card, they say, 'Sorry but we can't use you.' Well, if they can't use you, how are you ever supposed to *get* the Equity card so they *can* use you? Do you see what I mean?" the boy asked.

"Mmmm, yes, I do," Amanda said. "It doesn't seem fair, does it?"

"It's not fair at all," the boy protested. "If you need experience to get the part, but you can't get the part without experience, why it just isn't fair at all."

"It certainly isn't," Amanda said, smiling.

"Say, would you like another drink?"

"Yes, thank you, I would," Amanda said. He took her glass, and she leaned against the wall, smiling, watching Gillian talking to a sailor across the room, and then seeing the sailor's eyes shift to her, and then Gillian turned and looked at Amanda, and Amanda knew the sailor had asked Gillian who she was. Gillian took the sailor's hand and led him across the room, stopping before Amanda, who still leaned against the wall, feeling very much like closing her eyes and listening to the music all around her. Gillian's voice became a part of the music.

"Amanda, this is Rudy. He's been dying to meet you, but he's shy."

"Hello, Rudy," Amanda said, smiling. "Don't be shy."

"You're the most beautiful girl I've ever seen in my life," Rudy said. He was a chunky boy with curling brown hair and dark-blue eyes. He had cut himself shaving, and a piece of adhesive tape clung to his heavy jaw.

"Why, thank you, Rudy," Amanda answered dreamily.

"Would you like to dance?"

"Later," she said. "Someone's getting me a drink."

"Do you live in New York?" Rudy asked.

"No, Minnesota."

"That's a long way off."

"Oh, yes."

Music everywhere, the door-bell sounding again, and the clicking of Gillian's heels as she ran to answer it, "Brian! Hello! My God, what *took* you so long?", a chorus of answering voices from the door, the carolers suddenly bursting into "Deck The Halls", *Somebody flat in there*, Amanda thought, the door closing again, and then a voice joining the harmonious medley of carol and phonograph, a remembered voice with a Southern drawl, "Well, well, if it isn't Miranda!"

She turned her head and recognized Brian first. Hadn't Gillian said something about his coming down from New Haven? And then she saw the older boy in uniform standing alongside Brian, the same features, his brother no doubt, and then the army uniform on the third boy, not a boy, a man, approaching her, and the voice again, repeating, "Well, well, if it isn't Miranda."

"As a matter of fact, it isn't," she said easily. "It's Amanda."

"Yes, yes, Amanda, of course. And how are you, Amanda? Merry Christmas, Amanda."

Gillian walked to them swiftly. "You remember Matthew Bridges, don't you?" she asked apprehensively.

"I remember the captain," Amanda said.

"The *major*," Matthew corrected. "The captain is now a major."

"Matthew Anson Bridges," Amanda said. "Congratulations, Major Bridges."

"Your congratulations are a trifle belated," Mattthew drawled, his moustache askew over his lopsided grin. "I was promoted in June."

"For action in university parking lots?" Amanda asked, and then turned away from him swiftly and walked directly into Rudy's arms. "Let's dance, Rudy," she said.

"Sure," Rudy answered, somewhat bewildered by the exchange. He drew her close the moment they were on the floor, and Amanda pulled away gently.

"Now, now, Rudy," she murmured.

"You're beautiful, Amanda."

"Yes, you are too," she answered. "Everybody is beautiful. But if you hold me so tight, I won't be able to breathe. Now, you wouldn't want me to stop breathing, would you, Rudy?"

"No, I wouldn't want that," he said.

"I didn't think so. So just ... just ... there, that's better. Now, that's much better, Rudy. My, but you're strong," she said, and she made a face to Gillian over his shoulder, and then saw Matthew Anson Bridges mixing a drink for himself and then turning, looking into the room, that same silly smile on his face, his eyes capturing hers, and she felt suddenly embarrassed. She did not turn her eyes away. Not at first. She stared directly across the room, defying him to remind her of her shame, challenging him to behave like the cad he surely was, with that silly mocking grin under his silly black moustache, daring him to force her into remembrance of their shameful secret; he had touched her breast, he knew the feel of her nipple extended and erect. She felt herself blushing, and she thought again, I must be a little drunk, and she lowered her eyes and gave herself to the music, Alvino Rey, was it? her feet following the clumsy graceless steps of her partner, one hand firmly against his chest, forcing him to keep his distance.

He suddenly backed away from her. She didn't know what was happening at first, and then she looked up and saw the grinning mouth and the evil black moustache, and she wanted to run. Rudy grunted and frowned at Matthew and then slouchingly left the floor. Belatedly, Matthew asked, "May I?" and swept Amanda into his arms. His grip around her waist was very tight. She felt herself close against his chest, felt something very hard pressing against her, hurting her—his stupid sharpshooter's medal, she thought—and tried to pull away. But this was not Rudy, this was Matthew Anson Bridges, and she lifted her head and very politely and very softly said, "Please."

"Please what, Amanda?"

'Please let me go."

"Why? Don't you like to dance?"

"I do not like to wrestle!" she said sharply.

His grip relaxed suddenly. She looked into his face and saw that he was still grinning.

"Thank you." She was silent for several moments. "Does it give you pleasure, Major?"

"Does what give me pleasure?"

"Teasing me?" And she knew the words were a mistake the moment they left her mouth.

"Oh, am I teasing you?" Matthew asked innocently. "How do you mean that, Amanda?"

"You know very well how I mean it! You take great pride in your ability to annoy me! Well, if you don't mind, I'd like not to dance with you, Major."

She tried to pull away, but he would not release her.

"Ah, but I like to dance with you, Amanda."

"That's unfortunate."

"Yes, it certainly is." His arm tightened around her waist.

"If you pull me in against that medal again, I'll scream."

"Oh, I'm terribly sorry."

"Yes, I'll just bet you are."

"I am."

"Don't you do any fighting? Isn't it time they sent you to Japan or somewhere?"

"As a matter of fact," Matthew said, "I've applied for transfer from the Judge Advocate's office." He lowered his voice. "I'm leaving for Europe on New Year's Day."

"Good," Amanda said flatly.

"Don't mention it to anyone. It's a military secret."

"I certainly wouldn't want to see your ship get sunk," she said sarcastically.

"No, I know you wouldn't. That's why it's best to be cautious. Besides, I'm going by aeroplane."

"Well, I imagine you're in a hurry to pack and all, so if you'll excuse me," and again she tried to free herself, but his arm was tight around her, unyielding.

"I imagine the war will be over soon," he said.

"That's nice," she answered, seething.

"Yes," he said. "Once I get overseas. No one can hold out against me for very long."

"You might be surprised, Major," she said.

"I'm never surprised by anything," Matthew answered. "Of course, I can't promise immediate results. I'm only going to London, you see."

"Well, cheer up. Maybe they'll send you to Italy, where the fighting is."

"*And* the Italian girls." He grinned. "But I don't speak Italian."

"I didn't know it was necessary."

"It helps, I'm told."

"I don't think we're talking about the same thing, Major."

"Amanda," he answered, "we are talking about *exactly* the same thing." He paused. "I remember, Amanda."

"I don't want to talk about it."

"I remember your mouth and——"

"I said I——"

"——the feel of you. You're the softest——"

"I'll slap your goddam face!" she said, the words surprising her, the strongest words she had ever used in her life. She twisted away from him violently and walking to the long table where the aspiring actor was waiting with her drink she took the glass from his hand and almost drained it at a swallow. Behind her, she could feel the smiling presence of Matthew Anson Bridges.

"I want another one," she said to the actor.

Rudy suddenly appeared at her elbow and said, "I'll get it, Amanda."

She did not remember how many drinks she had after that one, but she knew that everywhere she turned, the silly grinning face of Matthew Anson Bridges was there, his eyes following her, and she wondered why he had to be there to spoil what was one of the nicest Christmas Eves she'd ever known.

"I'm sorry" Gillian explained. "I invited only Brian, but he brought his brother and Matthew. Believe me, Amanda, I didn't know," and of course Gillian hadn't known, but the apology did not eradicate the grinning image of Matthew Anson Bridges, which floated everywhere around the room, no matter how much she drank. She was certain she had never drunk so much or talked so much or danced so much in her life, and she was equally certain that she was getting very very intoxicated, but not in the same way as before, not in that warm dreary way, but in a vengeful spiteful way as if she simply had to show Matthew Anson Bridges that she could erase his face from her field of vision. She knew she shouldn't drink so much. She did not want a hangover on Christmas morning, especially with a long train ride to Minnesota ahead of her. But she continued to drink, and she continued to dance, and she recognized almost at once that Rudy was a dull clod with nothing much to say, but his voice kept droning in her ear, on and on. When even *he* began to sound interesting, she knew she was drunk beyond recall, and yet she didn't feel at all sick, she felt only dizzy. She couldn't remember when the room had begun to spin, but it was spinning now, the parakeet doing somersaults in his cage, the face of Matthew Anson Bridges whirling in a moustache-black pinwheel as he stood talking to a brunette in a green dress and watching Amanda over the girl's shoulder, and Rudy's voice droned on and on in her ear. Oh Lord, am I drunk, she thought.

"What we do is we send out this little *ping*, you see. That's exactly what it sounds like. *Piiiiiinnnnnnnnng*. And it goes through the water, do you understand?"

"Mmm, yes, ver' interesting," Amanda said, her head on his shoulder as they danced. The floor was very crowded. He kept bumping against her and into people, and she wished he would stop doing that, but she was too dizzy to tell him to stop doing that.

"And when it hits an object like a submarine or something," Rudy said, his voice close to her ear, "when it hits an object like that, it sends back an echo, and we can tell from the sound of the echo just what it is we've hit, a fish or a sub, or whatever, do you see? This sound wave goes out until it hits something, do you see? Like this, do you see?" and he bumped his mid-section against hers and she thought, Oh, stop that, but she didn't voice the words. "Like that, do you see? Did you feel that?"

"Mmmm," she said, and she nodded. "Dizzy."

"Did you feel that?" he asked, and he did it again. "Can you feel that?"

"Mmmm, 'm dizzy, Rudy."

"That's all right, honey, just hang on to me," Rudy said. "Now you're not gonna pass out on me, are you? What you need is a little drink, Amanda, that's what you need."

She grunted and shook her head. "Gilly," she murmured. "Wh's Gilly?"

"Oh, she's making a batch of scrambled eggs, Amanda, in the kitchen. Now come on, let's get you a little drink to clear your head, okay?"

"No, dowanna."

"Yes, it'll clear your head."

"Dizzy."

"Sure, I know. Come on, baby, we're gonna fix you up. We're gonna take care of you."

She nodded exaggeratedly and felt his strong arm around her waist as he led her to the table, across the room, pushing his way through the crowd, bumping into her as they walked, his hip against her hip, the music of gurgling liquid. "Music," she said. "Yes, baby," he answered. "Here. Drink it straight this time. It'll clear your head."

She nodded and felt the small shot glass being put into her hand, and then her hand being guided to her mouth, the rim of the glass rapping sharply against her teeth, she winced and tilted her head, "Drink," Rudy said. She felt some of the liquor trickling on to her jaw. "Born the king of a-en-gels," someone was singing, and then she felt the whisky burning its way down her throat, Oooooo strong, she thought, Clear my head, she thought, Rudy's arm around her waist again, tight, the lights of the Christmas tree spinning, "Ooops," she said, losing her balance. "Scuse me," spinning, the couch was a revolving pillar of horizontal orange fire, "Come on, honey, you'd better lie down," Rudy said, the crowd again, pressing in, Stop that, she thought, Your hand, she thought, I'll scream, you know. She banged into the wall, they were in the corridor, "Ooops, scuse me," she said to the wall and then banged into the opposite wall, something firm was cupping her breast, something hard and tight around her back and under her breast. My bra's too tight, she thought. A door was opening, she saw Gillian's big brass bed, covered with coats, not a brass *bed* really, only the headboard and the footboard, the door closed, the room was black, she felt herself stumbling forward, she could smell the coats, the pile of coats, feel the tweed, "There you are, honey, swing your legs up, that's it. Lie down, put your head on the pillow, that's the girl, go to sleep, go on, that's it," she closed her eyes, the room was very black, she took in a deep breath and dropped suddenly unconscious.

"Amanda?" Rudy whispered.

She did not answer. Her eyes were closed, her mouth open.

"Amanda?"

He kissed her suddenly on her open unresponsive mouth and then glanced over his shoulder towards the door. He walked swiftly in the darkness, finding the slip bolt with his hands, locking the door, and then walking back to the bed. He unbuttoned her blouse and pulled her dress up over her thighs, sudden shocking silken touch unmoving, he kissed her again, unmoving, unknowing, exploration crisp and tight, darkness cramped on winter coats unmoving, white and vulnerable. The sound at the door startled him. Someone was trying the knob. He turned in the darkness, eyes wide. Beside him, Amanda breathed heavily and evenly through her open mouth. He crouched over her protectively. The knob rattled again. A knock sounded on the door. He did not answer. He touched her again, reassuringly in the darkness. She lay still, breathing through open mouth, eyes closed. There was silence on the other side of the door, calculating, speculative silence, silence. He crouched.

There was a sudden splintering sound. The door snapped inward, the slip bolt ripping free from the jamb under the force of the kick. A wedge of harsh light opened into the room, almost touching the bed. A man was silhouetted in the doorway. His hand reached for the light switch. The overhead lights went on in awful suddenness, illuminating the brass bed and the unconscious girl and the sailor crouched over her.

Matthew stood in the doorway, looking into the room. He nodded his head once. He closed the door gently behind him and said very softly, "Get away from her."

"Wha . . . who the hell are you?"

"*Get away from her, sailor!*"

"Turn out that light! Can't you see——?"

"I can see," Matthew said. He took four quick steps into the room and seized Rudy by the front of his jumper, bringing back his right fist at the same time and then sending it forward in a straight piston-shaft punch that crashed into the sailor's nose and started it bleeding.

"What the hell's the matter with you?" Rudy said plaintively, feeling his nose.

"Get out of here," Matthew said. "Get out now, before I kill you."

"Who the hell are you?" Rudy asked, paling at the sight of his own blood. "Her boy-friend or something?"

"Yes," Matthew said, and he said it with such conviction that Rudy backed immediately towards the door. He glanced at the bed again, and then looked at Matthew and said, "You son of a bitch," and then ran swiftly into the corridor, slamming the door shut behind him. Matthew stood by the bed and looked quizzically at Amanda where she lay with her blouse unbuttoned, the skirt pulled to her waist. He looked at her for a long time. Then he pulled down her skirt and covered her with his own coat.

He turned out the light and left the room.

. . . . .

Gillian woke her at four in the morning. She was still asleep in the centre of the large double bed. A blanket had been thrown over her. The coats were all gone now.

"Hey, sleepyhead," Gillian said.

"All right," Amanda answered.

"Do you want to go back to the hotel, or will you stay here?"

"Here."

"Shall I undress you?"

"No. Do it myself."

"All right, sit up."

"What time's it?"

"Four."

"My train's at noon. Is everybody gone?"

"Everybody."

"What time's it?"

"I just told you. Four. You missed some good scrambled eggs."

"Mmmm." She sat up and rubbed her eyes.

"You're half undressed already," Gillian said.

Amanda smiled sleepily. "Oh, g'ness, I feel awful." She took off her blouse and said, "Do you have extra pyjamas?"

"I do."

"I'm sorry I passed out."

"That's all right," Gillian said.

"I think I'm . . ." She pulled a face. "Damnit, yes, I am. Will you get my bag for me, Gilly?"

"Sure," Gillian said. She started for the door and then stopped. "Oh, Matthew said to tell you good night. He said he would call you."

"What for?"

Gillian shrugged. "I guess he likes you."

"Well, I don't like him," Amanda said. "Gilly, could you please hurry? I'm really . . ."

"Yes, yes," she said, and she went out of the room.

He tried to reach Amanda the next day.

Gillian, fuzzy with sleep, answered the telephone. "Hello?" she said.

"Gillian?"

"Yes?"

"Matthew Bridges."

"Yes?"

"May I speak to Amanda, please?"

"No."

"What?"

"She's not here, I mean."

"Oh. Well, where's she staying, Gillian?"

"She's not. She went home. Caught a train at noon." "Is it important?"

"I guess not. I just wanted to see how she was."

"Hung over," Gillian said. "What time is it, anyway?"

"Two-thirty."

"I promised my mother I'd be there at two."

"You wouldn't know Amanda's number, would you?"

"No, I wouldn't," Gillian paused. "Is this important, Matthew?"

"No, no, I just . . where does she live?"

"In Minnesota."

"Yes, but where?"

"A town called Otter Falls."

"Otter Falls, right."

' Does that help?"

"Yes. Thank you very much, Gillian. And Merry Christmas."

He hung up and began fishing in his pocket for change. The booth was set at the far end of the Madison Avenue bar. Through the closed glass doors, he could see a WAC lieutenant sipping at a tall drink, her legs crossed. He spread his change on the ledge and was about to dial the operator when he remembered what time it was. Amanda wouldn't even be home yet, not if she'd caught a twelve noon train. He scooped up his change, opened the booth doors, and walked to the bar. He was putting his change back into his pocket when the WAC said, "No luck, Major?"

"No, I'm afraid not," Matthew answered, smiling. He knew instantly that he would pick her up. He studied her casually, with no sense of anticipation, no feeling of excitement, only with the sure knowledge that they would be spending the day, and perhaps the night, together. She was a brunette with clean-chiselled features, her hair curling close to her face. She seemed in her early twenties, with bright brown eyes and a generous mouth. She smiled back at him, and then looked at her watch.

"Well," she said. "I'll give him another five minutes."

"That accent sounds close to home," Matthew said.

"Virginia," she answered "Is that where you're from?"

"Yes."

"Where?"

"Glen City."

"Oh." She did not seem to know the town. "I'm from Charlottesville."

"I've been there," Matthew said, and he smiled lazily. The

WAC looked at her watch again, but with no sense of urgency. "My name's Matthew Bridges", he told her.

"I'm Kitty Newell." She smiled. "Should we salute or something?"

They spent the afternoon in the Central Park Zoo, and then Matthew found an open ticket broker and wangled two seats to *Oklahoma*. They had dinner at Sardi's, saw the show, and then stopped off at Billy Rose's, where they sat at the bar for a nightcap. When they got out into the street again, it was almost two in the morning.

Matthew hailed a cab and said, "Where are you staying?"

"I'm using a girl-friend's apartment," Kitty said. "She's away for the week. Ski-ing."

"I'll drop you off." They settled into the back seat of the cab. Kitty took his arm and snuggled close to him.

"I had a good time," she said.

"So did I. It seems a shame to end the night so soon."

"Yes, it does."

"Would you like to stop somewhere else? For a nightcap to the nightcap?"

"No," she said. "But I think we've got some liquor in the apartment. We can have a drink there."

The apartment was in a brownstone on East Sixty-first Street. She unlocked the door, snapped on the lights, and said, "Do you like it?"

"Very nice," Matthew said. "Your girl friend must be prosperous."

"Her husband is on *Time-Life*," Kitty said, as if that explained everything. "The liquor cabinet is over there. Isn't that luxurious?"

"Very." He walked to the cabinet. "Brandy all right?" he asked.

"Yes, fine."

He brought her the drink, and they clinked glasses.

"You stare, do you know that?" she said.

"I do?"

"Yes. You were staring at me all day long."

"I wasn't aware."

"*I* was." She paused. "I'm glad that ensign didn't show up."

"I am, too." He put down his glass and leaned over to kiss her.

"No, not yet," she said. "Not until I want you so much I can't bear it."

"I want you that much now."

"We've got the whole week," she said. "Let's not rush it."

When she took off her clothes later, he grinned at her and said, "You're out of uniform."

She giggled and said, "Mmmm, don't I know it!" She threw her arms wide. "Am I all right?"

"You're beautiful."

"Oh, liar, lovely liar. But I do have very good legs. Don't you think I have good legs?"

"Extraordinary legs."

"Do you want me very much?"

"Yes."

"I do, too. Now I do. Now, I really do." She laughed suddenly and lustily and then said, "I'm glad you're from Virginia."

He lay in bed for a long while with his hands behind his head, staring up at the ceiling of the strange apartment. Kitty was asleep beside him, her small spiring breasts pressed against his arm. He felt suddenly lonely. It did not have anything to do with the girl, he knew, or with their practised love-making. It simply seemed like a very long road all at once. He was twenty-seven years old and in a strange city at Christmas-time, and he felt like weeping. "I'm glad you're from Virginia," she had said, and those words would remain in his mind long after all memory of her body had departed. He was not a sentimental Southerner. He had severed all ties with Glen City on the day he left for college. But he wondered now how someone whose childhood had been so full of people, so rich with the sounds of life, happened to be alone in a strange town in a strange apartment on Christmas Day, alone with a girl who had touched him deeply when she'd said, "I'm glad you're from Virginia."

He could never think of his home without a feeling of tenderness, even though he knew he would never return there. He could remember the big old house with its pale-blue shutters, and the sudden coolness when you stepped inside, and the voices, there were always voices, the Bridges' home seemed constantly in a state of preparation for some festivity or another. His childhood was a round of family gatherings and celebrations, of holidays shared with laughing relatives, more relatives than he could count, of servants rushing about the house setting the table and preparing food. He could remember the smell of linseed oil, and the sweet smell of magnolias, a Southern cliché, but the house was banked with them and the aroma drifted through the open windows and the blossoms covered the ground like pink-and-white sea shells. He would play with his cousins under the magnolia trees, oh so many cousins, and they would scoop up the fallen petals and let them fall through their fingers while uncles and aunts stood about on the wide front porch in white summer suits and drank from frosted glasses with the pale-blue shutters behind them. Linseed oil, and magnolia blossoms, and the delicate scent of his mother's lavender, or the crisply laundered smell of her starched linen.

There were aunts to kiss, they always hugged him, and afterwards he was embarrassed because they had left lipstick marks on his cheek. Aunt Matilda, who would say, "Matthew, may dove, you have the devil in your eyes. Sally, keep this boy locked up somewheah!" and his mother would smile delicately, and once she winked at him. Uncle Jeff, who came and went to Arizona, who was a gambler they said, miraculously appearing every Thanksgiving and leaving again after New Year's Day, who taught Matthew how to keep an ace kicker. Fidgety cousin Birdie, who played the piano, and who always wore something yellow, her frock, her ribbon, her shoes. "I feel naked without a touch of yellow," she stated. They said she'd married a Yankee in New Orleans, but it hadn't worked out, she used to play all the popular songs. They would crowd about the piano and sing gustily. "Do you know this one, Birdie?" and her thin fingers would ripple over the keys.

They always seemed to be laughing in that house, and telling stories. The family was like an army he was always glad to see. Grandpa Bridges with his head of snow-white hair, who still wore string bow-ties and who still referred to Northerners as "Carpetbagging bastards", and who, Matthew knew from his older cousins, kept a high-yeller girl in Hopewell. "You mustn't smoke, Matthew," Grandpa Bridges always said, a foul-smelling cigar in his hand. "It is bad for the liver and the lungs. Mind you now, son, I am tellin' you this for your own good," his accent so thick you could slice it with a butter-knife. "You're a professional Southerner, Pop," his mother would say, and Grandpa would wiggle his white eyebrows and answer, "Than which there is nothin' better, daughter. When will that roast be done, anyways?"

There was always so much to eat, not only the chickens brown and hot from the oven, or the roasts simmering in blood-red juices, or the yams and turnips and bright-green peas and hot muffins, but all the aunts seemed to have their culinary specialities as well. Aunt Christine with her corn bread that you bit into, crusty and golden on the outside and then crumbling in your mouth so soft, the heat escaping in a sudden puff of steam; Aunt Isabel, who made shortcake afloat with strawberries and giant gobs of white whipped cream; Aunt Lo, who brought jars of orange marmalade whenever she came up from Tallahassee; everyone brought something, everyone gave something as if it came direct from the heart to show their love, not as duty-gifts, not the phony presents of fake families. "I hope the meringue is all right, Sally," Aunt Martha M. would say, and Uncle Rufus would kiss his mother on the cheek and say, "She spent four hours in the kitchen yesterday, Sally, made that house like a blast furnace," and Aunt Martha M. would say, "Hush, Rufe, you know I love to bake."

It was a kissing family and a hugging family, and he loved them all, each and every one of them, even Simmie, who had bad skin and was always lying about his business deals out West. He loved the warmth of the family, and the lore of the family, and its idiosyncrasies, and its shared family intimacies, like having one aunt named Martha M. and another aunt named Martha L. or having two cousins named James and calling one Jimbo and the other Jamey, or calling Grandma Anson "M.D.", which everybody in the family knew stood for "Mother dear," but which outsiders did not know. He loved, too, the intrigue of the family, the vast family network stretching as far west as Sacramento and as far north as Allentown, Pennsylvania, and the stories everyone had to tell when the family met.

He could remember sitting under the dining-room table with his cousin Rita one day, a rainy day, the grown-ups talking and laughing in the living-room, the table cloth covering them like a cave; he could hear the rain lashing at the dining-room window, and the shade rattling. His cousin with her straight black hair and black bangs and blue eyes whispered to him in the darkness, "Well, the reason they took her back from that farm is because the boys were *doing* things to her, Matty." His eyes wide, "What kind of things, Rita?" And Rita suddenly blushing, a year older than Matthew who was twelve, "Well, I don't know if your mother wants you to know about such things yet."

His mother died in August. He could remember the funeral, black umbrellas, rows and rows of black umbrellas, but no rain. It was not like in the movies. He remembered feeling a sense of disappointment. The sun was shining in Glen City that day, so hot, and they carried umbrellas because of the hot sun, with the dust climbing the black trouser legs of the men carrying the coffin, and his father weeping, the tears mingling with the dust on his face, streaking his face, Matthew did not cry. He thought only, They shouldn't be carrying umbrellas when it isn't raining.

The scent of her lavender clung to the silent house. He could hear his father weeping in the library. He went into the room, opening the door slick with linseed oil, the house was so still, he could not remember the house ever being so still. His father turned his head so that Matthew would not see the tears. "I want to be a lawyer," he said to his father, "Like you." His father nodded and said nothing, his face still streaked from the dusty sunny street of the town and the walk to the cemetery. He wondered if his mother had gone to heaven.

There was not as much family any more, it seemed. Somehow, the house did not reverberate with singing and laughter any more. Oh, they came, yes, but it wasn't the same any more, and there didn't seem to be quite as many uncles or aunts or cousins, somehow the old house went still, and even the scent of lavender vanished after a while, leaving only the smell of linseed oil and magnolia and the sweaty smell of the servants. There was not as much family any more. There were girls now. He could remember learning about girls.

He missed the family.

He didn't know why the house had to be so empty all at once. He missed Birdie's songs on the piano, and her touch of yellow. He missed his uncles in their white suits, telling dirty jokes where the ladies could not hear them. He missed the rush of preparation. He missed the scent of lavender.

When he was eighteen and a senior in high school, his father called him into the library one day and they faced each other in that room where, it seemed so long ago, his father had wept and tried to hide the tears and Matthew had not cried at all. His father sat in the overstuffed easy chair, his shoulders stooped, his head bent, an old old man at fifty-four, and Matthew stood before him in his white school sweater with the orange-and-black Glen City letter he had earned on the swimming team, his shoulders broad, his face clean with the vigour of youth. They faced each other.

"Do you still want to be a lawyer, Matthew?" he said.

"I do, sir."

"Then I've got to caution you against the reputation you're building in this town."

"I don't know what you mean, sir."

"You know what I mean, Matthew."

"No, sir, I do not."

"Don't give me the 'sir' baloney, son," Matthew senior said. "I gave my father the same baloney when I was your age, in this very same room, and he probably gave it to my grandfather, too, so we've got a long line of Bridges who are used to it, and unaffected by it."

"Well, sir, I——"

"There is a friend of mine in this town whose name is Orville Kennedy, and he has a young daughter whose name is Helen Kennedy; I believe the name may ring a bell. Orville happens to be my law partner. In fact, we have been practising law together for the past twenty-five years, did you know that, son?"

"Yes, sir."

"Yes, well, Orville tells me that you, my honoured son with all your 'sir' baloney, has been seeing his daughter regularly and leaving the poor girl weak with exhaustion. Is that true, son?"

"I don't know whether she's weak or not, sir."

"I am referring to the allegation of intimacy, son, and not to the state of her health."

"I know Helen pretty well, sir."

"Yes, in the Biblical sense, I'm sure. Orville happens to be a friend of mine. *And* my partner."

"That's too bad."

"What do you mean, that's too bad?"

"That he's a friend of yours. *And* your partner. But I don't see what that has to do with Helen. She likes me."

"That would seem apparent," Matthew senior said dryly.

"Yes, sir, I guess it would."

"But cut it out."

"Why?"

"To begin with, my partner Orville doesn't like it. Helen's serious and you're not."

"I——"

"Don't deny it. If it wasn't Helen, it'd be somebody else's daughter. She's a good girl, son, and she wouldn't behave this way if she didn't care for you. That's the first thing. The second thing is that the reputation you're building isn't going to help you any when you enter the firm. So cut it out."

"No, sir."

"What?"

"I don't plan to enter the firm, sir, and I don't plan to cut it out with Helen or with anybody else."

"What?"

"Yes, sir."

"Maybe you didn't understand me."

"I understood you, sir."

"I'm not *asking* you, son."

Matthew stared at his father and said, "I'm eighteen."

"So what?"

"I just thought you might like to know."

"I know how old you are, and I also know you've been accepted at Harvard and will be leaving for Boston in the fall. That still leaves the summer, and I expect your behaviour to be impeccable from here on, and what the hell do you mean, you don't plan to enter the firm?"

"Yes, sir."

"Yes, sir, yes, sir, *what*? I've got a practice that——"
"Sir, I do not expect to practice law in Glen City."
"Why not?"
"I don't think I like it here, sir."
"Why not?"
"Well, now, I guess it would take me until midnight to give you all my reasons."
"I'm not going any place," Matthew senior said.
"Well, *I* have a date," Matthew answered.
"With Helen?"
"Yes, sir."
"Why don't you like Glen City?"
"It's too small."
"It's a good town."
"And too cold."
"The winters here are as mild as——"
"I meant the people."
"The people are friendly."
"No. The town's changed. It's not the way it used to be."
"How did it used to be, Matthew?"
"Warm and exciting and . . . alive. I guess, alive."
"Do you think you'll find it different elsewhere?"
"I can look, sir."
"I'm an old man," Matthew senior said suddenly and apparently without meaning. His son stared at him for a second and then went to the door.
"I've got to go. I'm late now."
He opened the door.
"I miss her, too," his father said. "You mustn't think I don't miss her, too, Matthew."

His father died in August, the same month that had claimed his mother. He died of cancer, and they buried him alongside Sally Bridges in the small town cemetery on a day heavy with sunshine and dust. He saw his aunts and his uncles for the last time at the funeral. They all seemed different now, like polite strangers—"Sorry, Matthew, awful sorry. Know we share your loss"—polite strangers with polite sympathetic half-smiles. Uncle Jeff looked old and no longer dashing. There were wrinkles around his eyes. Matthew's cousins were all grown up now. Rita was as pretty as could be, but never as pretty as she'd been that day under the dining-room table, her black hair brushed sleekly back, her blue eyes wide as she whispered of family intrigue. Strangers, all strangers, whom he greeted with remarkable calm, no tears in his eyes, no tears on the face of Matthew Anson Bridges. Even when

Birdie, dressed in mourning black, opened her black-silk purse and pulled out a yellow handkerchief, he did not cry, he would not cry. They stood by the open grave together as the coffin was lowered into the dust-dry earth, a family together for the last time. Aunt Christine dropped a flower on to the shining black lid of the coffin. They dispersed later like scattered leaves before a sharp wind. He knew he would never see them again.

He hated Harvard, and yet he loved it. His feelings for the school were much the same as his feelings for Boston. He had chosen Harvard because of its reputation, aware of the snobbery involved, hating himself for succumbing to the appeal of calling himself "a Harvard man", and yet fully aware that Harvard had the best law school in the country. He hated the school because it wore its snobbery like a dicky under a dress suit, clean and starched, and yet seemingly unaware that the stiffly laundered front had no sleeves. He felt the same way about Boston. He loved the Commons and walking across the wide rectangle with the pigeons frightened into sudden flurried flight, but he hated the stupidity of meeting at the Plaza simply because everyone met there, when he would have preferred meeting in the subway. He loved the Boston girls and their insinuating prance, but he hated the tilt of their sophisticated noses or their casual assumption that they were at all cosmopolitan. He loved the cobblestones of the city and the streets where old gas fixtures still stood with electric lamps in them, but he hated the way its inhabitants calmly claimed the glory of a century and a half ago. He loved the River Charles snaking on its way, gold ensnared in the wintry sunlight, loved the banks upon banks of reflecting bay windows. He loved the filth of Scollay Square and the burlesque houses, some of the roughest burlesque he'd seen anywhere, but he hated the contrariness of a city ordinance that forbade a totally naked girl from moving a muscle while she was on stage. "Paaaak the caaa in Haaavaaad Yaaad," the Boston cliché, came to mean something more to him. For in that flat, hard Boston sound, he could hear the echoing lifeblood of the city, a sound that combined the debutante and the slut, the upturned nose and the provocative wiggle. He came to know Boston through its women, the shanty Irish in the bars, and the high-class Jews in West Newton, and the finishing-school girls on Beacon Hill. They were all the same to him, and all inexplicably different—they were all civilized and proper, and they were all savages, and he loved and hated them the way he loved and hated the school.

"Everybody in that damn place talks through his nose," he said once to a girl on Pinckney Street. Rain washed the cobbles outside, winter in Boston, there was a hush to the city, he could visualize

John Adams strolling through these streets, there was that about the town, you could not steal history from it. "I've finally figured it out."

"Whaaat did you figure out, Matthew?"

"Why they all sound the same. There's this old man in the speech department, you see, who has either a nasal drip or a deviated septum, and he's forced to talk through his nose because of this deficiency. But all our hard-working Harvard scholars, anxious to emulate the old bastard, have picked up this monstrous deformity and accepted it as the proper speech pattern for an educated man. I can guarantee, Betty, that twenty years from now, fifty years from now, I will be able to spot a graduate of Harvard instantly because every last one of them will talk through his nose instead of his mouth."

Betty giggled and whispered, "Listen to the rain."

"We're raising a generation of nose-speakers," Matthew said. "The Harvard mouth will eventually become an atrophied organ, like the sixth toe. Harvard men will begin eating through their noses and kissing with their noses, like the Eskimoes."

"Don't you love rain?" Betty said.

"Ultimately, the mouth will disappear entirely on all Harvard men. The area below their noses will consist of blank, shiny skin. They will approach emitting a high shrill whine through their enlarged nostrils, and everything they say will sound like mucus."

Hating the Boston girls and loving them, hating Harvard and loving it, he entered Harvard Law in 1939 with the third-highest average in his class. He had made no real friends on campus, had joined none of the clubs, and he made no real friends in law school, either. He would later think of Boston as a woman, only because most of the people he had known there were females. He wondered once why he wasn't more involved with the people he knew, and then he thought of Birdie taking that yellow handkerchief out of her black-silk purse, and he felt like crying, not knowing why, and he thought, What the hell.

Now, in New York City, on Christmas Day, he lay in bed with his hands behind his head, and he could hear the gentle breathing of Kitty Newell beside him, and he thought again of calling Amanda Soames. She would surely be home by now. He wanted to call her. He wanted to hear her voice. He felt, oddly, that he knew her better than anyone else in the world. But he did not move from the bed, and eventually he fell asleep.

On New Year's Eve, he decided definitely that he would call. He would dial Information and then argue with the operator until she yielded a number for Amanda somewhere in Otter Falls. He was reaching for the phone when Kitty walked into the room. She was wearing only a half-slip, the waistband pulled up over her breasts, wearing it like a short nightgown that ended just below her hips.

"Hey," she said, "let's take a nap."

"What for?"

"It's New Year's Eve. We've got to stay up until the wee tiny hours."

"All right," he said.

"No funny stuff now."

"I promise."

"Because we need the rest."

"I know. What's that thing you're wearing?"

"The latest creation, my dear," Kitty said. "I do hope you like it."

"It's a bit daring," Matthew said.

"Oh, yes. Yes, I know."

"And revealing."

"Do you think so?"

"And pretty damn provocative."

Kitty laughed her deep lusty laugh, turned like a can-can dancer, flipped up the back of the slip, and, still laughing, ran into the bedroom. They went into the Broadway throng at eleven-thirty. They had awakened at ten and consumed half a bottle of Scotch before taking to the streets. They didn't get back to the apartment until four-thirty, and Matthew's plane was scheduled to leave at nine. He put her to bed and then sat by the window in an easy chair, watching the dawn come up over New York, the first time he had seen it in this city. At seven o'clock, he remembered Amanda and decided again to call her, but then realized it would still be the middle of the night in Minnesota. He dressed swiftly without waking Kitty. He nudged her gently before he left.

"Hey," he said.

"Are you going, Matthew?" she asked sleepily.

"Yes," he said.

"Please take care of yourself."

"I will. You too."

"Matthew?"

"Yes?"

"It was nice, wasn't it?"

"Yes, Kitty," he answered. "It was very nice."

He was in London that night.

He thought of Amanda on and off all the while he was in England. He almost put in a transatlantic call to her the day he found out why he was in Europe, the day he learned the Allies were preparing a massive invasion of the French coast, an assault that had been code-named "Operation Overlord". He realized then that even if he did call her, he wouldn't be able to tell her about the invasion plans, and then he wondered why he'd wanted to tell her at all.

Well now, Matthew, he said to himself, it's because you're liable to get killed.

Yes, he admitted, getting killed was a distinct possibility, but he didn't see what that had to do with the honey-blonde girl Amanda, he didn't see what that had to do with her at all. He supposed one of his aunts somewhere might be slightly perturbed if she received a War Department telegram, but he knew little Amanda Soames wouldn't care one way or the other. So why did he feel it necessary to call her and tell her that he was soon going to be in the middle of a shooting war?

Or, for that matter, why was he constantly thinking about little Amanda Soames when she had made it quite clear that she could not stand the sight of him? Well, he didn't *constantly* think of her, that was an exaggeration. But she did pop into his mind every now and then, a full-blown image, and the image of Amanda was always the one in Gillian's bedroom. Why had he watched her so carefully that night, why had he known intuitively what the sailor was up to, why had he followed them down the corridor, why had he stopped the sailor, what had made him feel so protective towards a girl who despised him? *There* was the entire stupidity of the thing, the fact that Matthew Anson Bridges, who had known innumerable lovely and unlovely ladies since that first time on the hill overlooking the town with Sue Ellen—"Don't tear them, Matthew Bridges! They cost me a dollar forty-nine!"—that Matthew Anson Bridges, who had known them all, was now unable to get Amanda Soames, whom he had not known at all, out of his mind. Now, why should such an idiotic thing be?

The promise, he thought.

Yes, the promise.

He knew intuitively what it would be like with Amanda, the innocent honeyed warmth of her, the big golden promise of what Amanda Soames could be, and *would* be when she gave herself willingly and knowingly and unashamedly. That was what plagued him, the promise. But the promise of more than a bed partner, somehow. This was not what he wanted from Amanda Soames, he wanted more from her. The promise extended beyond that into a remembered world of warmth and laughter.

He knew one thing for certain. He knew that if he survived the invasion of France and the march into Germany, if he came alive through all of what lay ahead, he would one day have Amanda

Soames. She would one day give herself to him completely and willingly and fully aware of what she was doing. He wanted the war to be over soon. He wanted the invasion to start. He wanted to get back to her because, in a way he couldn't quite understand, Amanda Soames had become his girl. He did not write to her, and he never discussed her with anyone, but she was his girl none the less, constantly on his mind—yes, damn it, *constantly*—the girl back home, waiting for him.

She was with him when he crossed the English Channel in early June and hit Omaha Beach, and hugged the sand, and heard his buddies scream in terror as they were pinned down by Rommel's booby traps and obstacles, and the cross-fire from the guns in the hills. She was with him in the hedgerows and with him when they took the town of Isigny, and later when they fought their way westwards to the flooded marshlands beyond the town of Carentan, with him on the seemingly endless day-by-day struggle for yards of French earth, southward as town after town fell, La Haye-du-Puits, the muted fire of German Tiger tanks, Coutances, Avranches, August and the encirclement of Falaise, the triumphant liberation of Paris and then the steady drive towards the Rhine, "Kill every Nazi bastard you see," the colonel said, Übach and the heaviest German artillery barrage he had ever been in, his boots were wet, his feet burned and stung and itched, wasn't there any place a man could dry his feet, "Amanda, my feet are always wet, I think of you always, Amanda, love, Matthew," the letters he never sent and never wrote, the ferocity of the sudden German offensive in the Ardennes, Christmas outside Bastogne, trying to relieve the besieged Seventh Airborne, "Silent night, ho-oly night," he remembered last Christmas Eve and her golden body on the big brass bed, January, Amanda, the German towns dropping swiftly behind them now, France and Belgium only memories, the biting winter cold, "I hate the Nazis, Amanda, I hate them all," Amanda, I want you, Amanda, spring and a blush on the air, a daisy growing in the mud, I would like to walk through Rockefeller Centre with you, I would like to see the tulips, VE Day! VE Day! He toasted her in a grubby shattered tavern and thought Amanda, I'm coming home, Amanda, goddam you, I am coming home.

Now they were coming, now they weren't coming, she wished they would make up their minds. Everything seemed in such a state of confusion. Everything seemed to have funnelled down into the month of June and got caught there in the narrow end. Commencement, of course, was the big thing, and most of the problems seemed to stem from that, the year book, the school ring, the cap and gown, the invitations. Now, why couldn't they make up their minds? She realized that Minnesota was a long way from Connecticut, but it wasn't every day of the week your daughter graduated. She had explained a hundred times that she would have to reserve seats for them since commencement was being held outdoors and there were only so many available chairs. Many of the students had big families, she had told them, and it simply wasn't fair to hold seats that wouldn't be used. She could not understand her parents' hesitancy. Nor Penny's either, for that matter. Was it a question of leaving the baby with someone? She simply could not understand, and Penny's last letter hadn't helped to clarify the situation at all. If anything, it only made things more confusing. Penny had written:

My dearest Amanda,

How wonderful to be graduating, how wonderful to be twenty-two years old and stepping into a shining new world with no responsibilities.

I am sitting here on the lawn and Kate is running around on the grass. She has been eating mud, and her face is all covered with it, but at least she isn't crying. I do wish I could come to your graduation exercises, do you realize that Kate will be three years old in November? How the time flies! I can remember you in your high chair. You would stand up, and I would say, "Siddown, Mandy," being all of five years old myself, and you would shout back, "*Stannup*, Mandy!" Do you remember? I don't suppose you do. I seem to be remembering a lot of silly things lately. I suppose Mother has written to you. It's good to have sunshine again. This was such a long, tedious winter.

I was sorry to hear you won't be coming home after graduation, but I'm sure the camp will be very nice. Where did you say it was? Torrington? Is that in Connecticut? And just exactly what does a camp counsellor do? Well, it doesn't matter because the important thing is that you make something of your life, and this is a good start. You always played piano so beautifully. Do you remember the first time Frank came to call on me? You were playing piano in the living-room, and I had discovered a run in my last pair of nylons! Oh, what a mess! I'm surprised he ever came back again. But of course he did.

Oh, my dear Mandy, I wish you every happiness in the world. You are so dear to me, did I ever tell you? I know you don't care for sentimental hogwash, but Frank and I have often talked about how wonderful you are. Will the graduation be outdoors? That should be wonderful, everyone in white. You will wear white, won't you! I wish I could be there. But you know how difficult it would be to leave Kate. She's so young, and I *am* her mother. It's so strange being a mother, Mandy, really I must explain it to you some day. When you get married, perhaps. But then you'll have children of your own, won't you? And you won't need any advice from your old decrepit sister. You know, I miss you a lot. I miss all the talks we used to have. I can remember things so clearly lately. I sometimes sit for hours and things are so clear they seem to be happening all over again. I sometimes tell Kate about all the things we did together, but of course she's just a child, it's not like having someone to really listen to you. Frank was such a good listener. Do you remember him? I sometimes have the feeling that I'm the only one who still remembers him. And Kate, of course, because she was born then. You know what I mean. So close together and all, the birth. So I'm sure she remembers. But no one else. It would make me feel so good.

Well, I must take Kate in for her nap now. She still takes afternoon naps, you know. Mandy dear, please don't worry. I'm sure Mother and Dad will come to the commencement. It's just a question of convincing them that everything will be all right here at home while they're gone. You know how they are. They worry about every little thing. I've had a little cold lately. I don't think I'll be able to come. But we'll see, Amanda, you will be lovely, I know it.

Your sister,
PENNY

She read the letter again now in the June-streaming sunshine of her dormitory room, sitting on the edge of the bed, her blonde hair caught in a glittering trap. She wore a blue robe, and her head was bent as she studied the letter and nibbled at her pencil. She moved her writing pad on to her lap and wrote: "Dear Penny," and then put down the pencil and re-read Penny's letter for the third time. It sounded like Penny, and yet it didn't. It seemed to ask a hundred questions that required no answers, seemed to hint without stating, seemed to ramble indecisively, and yet it was surely Penny writing the letter, but it didn't altogether sound like Penny. "I seem to be remembering a lot of silly things lately. I suppose Mother has written to you." Well, yes, Mother had written, but she hadn't said anything about Penny remembering a lot of silly things, what sort of things did she mean? Or were the two thoughts even connected? Did the reference to her mother have anything at all to do with her statement about remembering silly things? Or, when you considered it, what was so terrible about remembering silly things? Of course, no one had said anything at all was wrong with it, but . . .

that was it . . . that was what she felt about the letter, its . . . its implication, but surely it was an innocuous letter, chatty and loving. Still, it made her feel uncomfortable. And the fact that she could not pin-point her discomfort only increased the feeling. She put down her pencil and walked to the window.

She heard the telephone ringing downstairs, and she thought instantly, I'd better call home. Maybe something is wrong. She was starting for the door when she heard a girl's voice yelling, "Amanda Soames! Telephone!" She tightened the belt on her robe and went into the corridor barefooted, running down the three flights of steps to the reception-room. She lifted the phone, pushed the hair back from her ear, and put the receiver to it.

"Hello?" she said.
"Amanda?"
"Yes?"
"Well, I did it."
"What did you do?" she asked, annoyed. "Who is this?"
"I won the war."
"I'm very glad you did. Would you mind telling me who——"
"Matthew Bridges."
There was a long silence on the line.
"Amanda?"
"Yes?"
"I want to tell you something."
"What is it?"
"I love you."
"What?"
"I love you."
"What? What did you say?"
"I love you."
"Oh, don't be ridiculous."
"I'm in New York. I'm coming up to Talmadge as soon as I can rent a car."
"Why?"
"To see you, of course."
"Don't bother."
"I'll pick you up at eight."
"I can't go out," she lied. "University rules."
"Don't kid me, Amanda. You're a graduating senior."
"All right, I just don't want to see you."
"That's too bad. I have a lot of things to tell you."
"I don't want to hear anything you have to——"
"Eight o'clock," he said. "Wear a pretty dress," and he hung up.
"Now, listen——" she started, but the line was dead. She stared

at the telephone receiver. "He's crazy," she murmured. She shrugged. "Well, he's just crazy, that's all." And all at once she was blushing furiously. She put down the phone and ran up to her room. She slammed the door behind her and then went directly to her bed and sat on its edge with her hands clenched tight in her lap, staring at the closed door, biting her lip.

At eight o'clock on the dot, the knock sounded on her door.

"It's open," she said.

A freshman in sweater and skirt opened the door and leaned against the jamb, smiling. "There's someone to see you, Amanda," she said. "A soldier."

"Thanks," she said. "Would you tell him I'll be down in a minute?"

"He's got ribbons all over his chest," the freshman said.

"None in his hair?" Amanda answered, and shot an angry glare at the girl. "Close the door behind you, would you?"

She went to the mirror and studied herself. Well, she thought, he's here. He really came. So what do we do now? Now we go downstairs and smile a very cold smile and say, "It was very nice of you to come all the way up here, Major Bridges," although it's probably Colonel Bridges by now, or maybe even General Bridges. "It was very nice of you to take such a long journey, General, but I'm afraid it was an impulsive gesture on your part. I really have no desire to spend any time at all with you, and I'm sorry if anything in our past relationship gave you any notions to the contrary. I certainly cannot recall offering you the slightest encouragement, and I don't intend to offer any now. So, if you'll excuse me." Yes, that was well put, that was exactly the way she would say it. She smoothed the pleats on her white skirt, tucked her blouse into it, pinched her cheeks, and then went downstairs.

He did not see her when she entered the room. He was sitting on the couch at the far end, facing the door, as if embarrassed by the indignity of having to wait for a girl in a college dormitory. "All this undergraduate nonsense gives me the willies," he had said once, that first time in Brian's car. Well, that was just too bad, General Bridges, but no one asked you to come here. He looks older, she thought, no he just looks more mature, why there's grey at his temples, but, and she wondered about war for the second time in her life, the first time when her brother-in-law was killed, and now again, wondered what it did to men, and then squashed whatever sympathetic curiosity she was feeling. As she approached, she saw that he was wearing a gold maple leaf on his collar. Still a major, she thought, and felt as if she'd won her first small triumph. He rose suddenly, as if sensing her approach, rose with a clean swift motion from the deep couch. She did not remember him as being so tall. He looked leaner and harder, and she saw the battle ribbons on his blouse and wondered where he had earned them, and then told herself, I don't *care* where. He grinned suddenly, his mouth twisting under that silly black moustache, why in the world doesn't he shave it off? If he tries to kiss me, I will knock him unconscious.

"Hello, Amanda," he said softly.

"Hello," she answered, hoping she sounded cold and distant and sharp, and then seeing the intensity of his eyes and turning away from them.

"You look like a bride."

"Do I?" she said coldly.

"Yes," he said. "Shall we go?"

"Major," she said carefully and distinctly, "I really don't know what——"

"Matthew," he interrupted.

"What?"

"Matthew."

"Matthew," she said, carefully and distinctly, "I really don't know what this is all about, or what strange obsession has taken hold of——"

"Let's discuss it in the car," he said, and he took her elbow and began leading her towards the door. Her instinct was to pull away from him immediately, but there were other girls in the room, watching her, and so she walked stiffly beside him to the front door, and then down the low flat steps and on to the path, and then she pulled her elbow away gently and said, "I am not going anywhere with you, Major Bridges. I think you ought to understand that immed——"

"Matthew," he said. "Then why are you dressed?"

"Did you want me to greet you in a bathrobe?"

"That might have been interesting."

"I'm sure. Good night, Major Bridges." She turned back towards the dorm. He seized her arm, and whirled her to face him. She could feel the pressure of his fingers biting into her flesh. "You're hurting me," she said coldly, and then realized how helplessly feminine that must have sounded. I don't care *how* it sounded, she thought, and said again, "You're hurting me. Now let go."

"No."

"Must I always threaten to slap you?"

"You'll get over that."

"Let go of my arm."

"Will you let go of my heart?"

"Oh, stop that nonsense! You hardly know me!"

"I know you very well, Amanda Soames," he said, and he released her arm suddenly and stood facing her on the path. She looked up at him, believing him for a moment, convinced by the absolute certainty in his voice, and puzzled by his sureness.

"I don't even like you," she said, not taking her eyes from his face.

"You will."

"Not if you keep behaving like a cave man." She paused. "You shouldn't have come up here. Why did you come?"

"To see you."

"Why?"

"I love you."

"Oh, stop it. Really, I'm not a child."

"Then accept it."

"Why should I?"

"Because I never lie."

She believed this, too. Frowning, she walked beside him to the car, a red Ford convertible, the top down. He held the door open for her, and she slid on to the seat. She expected him to kiss her the moment he got into the automobile, but he turned on the ignition instead and said, "How about New Haven for dinner? I feel like an Italian meal."

"All right."

"Think it'll be too breezy with the top down?"

"No. It's a lovely night."

"You're a lovely girl, Amanda."

"Stop that!"

"Why should I? I carried a picture of you all through Europe, and now——"

"A picture?"

He tapped his temple. "Up here. And you're prettier than I remembered. I'm the luckiest man alive."

She felt flustered all at once. She didn't want to encourage this kind of talk, but every time she asked him to stop he simply enlarged upon the theme. On the other hand, if she remained silent, he would accept her silence as approval and she would become an unwilling accomplice in this one-sided game he was playing. She decided to change the subject.

"Where were you?" she said.

"You missed me?"

"No. But where were you?"

"I missed *you*," he said. "Day and night."

"Look, I . . . I didn't even know you were *alive* until you called this afternoon."

"Were you afraid I'd been killed in action?"

"I never even thought about it."

"The thought was too painful?"

"You're deliberately twisting everything I say!"

"I'm a lawyer, my dear," Matthew said, and he smiled.

"I'm trying to tell you that you have never once entered my mind since the last time I saw you that Christmas Eve."

"Ah, you remember when you last saw me?"

"Of course I remember. But you had nothing to do with——"

"I called you the next day, but you'd already left. I spoke to Gillian."

"You didn't."

"Of course I did. Amanda, I told you. I never lie."

"I'll remember that. Why did you call?"

"Obviously to talk to you."

"What about?"

"About how beautiful I thought you were. In fact, I almost called you in Minnesota."

"Why didn't you?"

"Would you have liked that?"

"No," she said.

"Then I'm glad I didn't."

"It's funny Gillian never mentioned your calling."

"Oh, do you still see her?"

"Whenever I'm in New York, yes. Why?"

"I just wondered."

"You found her very attractive, didn't you?" Amanda said.

"She *is* very attractive." He paused. "Are you jealous?"

"Of course not."

"You are," he said. "How's she getting along?"

"Fine." Amanda paused. "You sound interested."

"I'm not interested in anyone but you."

"I suppose I should be flattered."

"Be careful, now. You're giving yourself away."

"What do you mean?"

"Well, you obviously wouldn't be flattered if some gorilla had fallen for you. So, if you're flattered that it's *me*, I can automatically conclude——"

"A good lawyer should never leap to conclusions," she said.

"Where'd you ever hear that nonsense?"

"I read it somewhere."

"A good lawyer should *always* leap to conclusions. The moment a witness drops a piece of revealing testimony, he should be ready to pounce on it."

"Thank God I'm not a witness."

"No, but I find your testimony revealing none the less."

"Are you a good lawyer?"

"I'm an excellent lawyer. Why? Are you concerned about my future?"

"Certainly not."

"You needn't be. I'm very well fixed. My parents took care of that when they died."

"Well, I couldn't be less interested in how well fixed you are," she said airily.

"We won't starve, Amanda."

She ignored his meaning. "We will if we don't get to New Haven soon."

"I'm opening an office in New York as soon as I'm discharged, you know."

"When will that be?"

"In a few months, I imagine. I had trouble with my feet. Trench foot. I'll be getting a medical discharge."

"Then they won't be sending you to the Pacific?"

"No. I'll get out, and I'll open my office, and begin practice right away."

"That should be exciting."

"Yes. I'll be seeing you every night."

Amanda laughed. "I won't be anywhere near New York City."

"Where will you be?"

"Torrington."

"Doing what?"

"I've taken a job as a camp counsellor. For the summer."

"I'll come up every week-end. And when the summer is over——"

"When the summer is over. I'm going back to Minnesota."

"No, you're not, Amanda."

"Of course I am. I *live* in Minnesota."

"You *used* to live in Minnesota."

"I *still* live in Minnesota."

"You're staying in the East, Amanda."

"Sure," she said, exasperated. "Does that make you happy? Shall I just agree with every insane thing you say?"

"Yes."

"All right, then, I'm not going back to Minnesota, and we'll see each other every night, and I'll make curtains for your office, all right?"

"That's very thoughtful of you."

"Matthew, I wish you'd stop this non——"

"Where do you want to live when we're married? Do you like the city?"

"Married!"

"Some people feel the suburbs are better for children but——"

"Children! We're not even . . . we hardly . . ."

"You're my girl, Amanda," he said.

"*Who's* your girl? Are you out of——"

"You're my girl. Remember that. If you so much as look at another man, I'll break both his legs."

She was silent for several moments. Then she said, "Would you mind taking me back to the dorm, please? Really, I've had enough. Would you take me back, please?"

"No."

"Well then, just stop the car, and I'll hitch back."

"No."

"Matthew, please stop this car!"

"All right," he said, and he suddenly swerved to the right, bounced over the concrete shoulder of the road, and came to a stop on the grass.

"Why'd you do that?" she said.

"You asked me to."

"You could have got us killed."

"To live without your love is to be dead anyway."

"Stop talking like that!"

"Why?"

"Because we're . . . we're not . . . not any of the things you seem to think we are. And I . . . I don't want to hurt you, but you're talking as if——"

"Why don't you want to hurt me?"

"Because I don't like to hurt *anyone*! Oh, you're just . . . you're . . . oh, what's the use? Let me out of this car."

"The door is on your right," Matthew said.

Amanda hesitated. "Really, can't you stop?"

"No. I love you."

"But . . ."

"You're my girl."

"I'm not your girl. I'm not *anyone's* girl. Please, you're going to make me cry. Please. Now please."

He took her into his arms gently, and she lay against him, quietly exhausted, her hand on the lapel of his blouse. She did not move when he kissed her forehead.

"Are you hungry?" he asked.

"Yes."

"I am, too."

"Oh, shut up," she said.

"What's the matter?"
"Oh, shut up."
"All right."

She lay in his arms unmoving, the night air warm, the stars unblinking overhead. In a little while she sat up and said, "Let's go to dinner."

"Do you believe I love you?"
"I don't know what to believe."
"Amanda . . ."
"Could we not talk about it, Matthew? Please? I'm really very hungry, and you do make me very angry, and I feel a little mixed up right now, and I'd rather not talk about it. Please, if . . . if . . . if you . . . you . . ." She could not say the word. "If you . . . *feel* the way you say you do, then please respect my wishes and let's go to the restaurant and eat and talk about . . . about . . . b-b-baseball or something, please. Is my hair all mussed?"

"You look beautiful," he said.

She turned to look at him as he started the car, and very gently answered, "Thank you."

She saw the film many years later, thousands upon thousands of stop-action photos spliced together to show the blooming process of a plant from tightly closed bud to extended flower. When she saw the film, she thought, That's the way it was, that's the way you get married, and then she shoved the thought aside because she did not wish to defile a memory that was no longer even that, a blur instead, something that had happened very long ago to a very young and innocent girl.

But that was how it had been, she knew. Photo upon photo flashed in rapid succession upon a screen, no single photo important in itself, the change imperceptible from one still shot to the next, and yet each separate shot essential to the steadily unfolding sequence, each barely discernible change combining to form an overwhelmingly dramatic change, the juxtaposition of a remembered closed bud against a sudden bloom touched by morning sun. That is the way people get married, she thought.

She could remember with certain clarity only the afternoon he first called and the evening that followed. Everything after that seemed as gradual, as inexorable, as inevitable, as that stop-action flower unfolding to meet the kiss of the sun. It was impossible at first. They argued, they fought, she would often crawl into her bed demolished by his insensitivity, shattered to the point of tears, vowing never to see him again. She should have gone back to Minnesota instead of taking the camp job. Why did he insist on coming up each week-end? How had she ever become so involved with such a horrible person? But he would call in the middle of the night, and someone would wake her, and she would walk over the mist-covered grass to the camp office, clutching her robe tightly around her, to answer the phone. She would listen to his apologetic voice, and she would say, "I don't think we should see each other again, Matthew," and he would say, "I love you, Amanda," and she would say, "Yes, but it's impossible," and he would say, "I adore you, Amanda," and the very next week-end he would be back carrying flowers. "I just happened to spot these on the road," a patent lie because he never arrived empty-handed. It was as if he felt his presence was really not enough to give, as if he felt his professed love needed tangible proof. They argued that entire summer long, interminably. "I can't stand you!" she once screamed at him. "I hate you, I *hate* you!" But she continued seeing him.

She should have gone back to Minnesota in the fall. She took a job at a music school instead, and she saw Matthew almost every night. Together, they discovered the city, and in the process discovered each other. And yet there was nothing memorable in what they did, the rides up Fifth Avenue in the double-decker buses, the trip to the Cloisters, the ferryboat to Staten Island, all the tourist things, all the corny motions of strangers trying on a city like a new coat, touching it in exploration, but sharing it—though later she would not be able to remember what they shared. The atheist on Broadway and Fifty-seventh, his stand covered with anti-religious pamphlets? "How are things going?" Matthew had asked him. "So-so," the man replied. "Organized religion still has quite a hold." Matthew grinned and patted him on the shoulder. "You'll win yet," he assured the man. "Have faith." And Amanda had giggled into the upturned collar of her coat as Matthew whisked her away from the bewildered, bewhiskered man.

Incident, she knew, and unimportant. But incident piled upon incident to form a mutual bank of experience and knowledge: "Do you remember the time?" and then compressing memory into a personal shorthand so that a key word, a key phrase, a single punch line or gesture would trigger the memory and bring back vividly the experience itself, cherished because it belonged to them alone, wide-eyed strangers in a city as large as the world. Memory unmemorable. The unvoiced knowledge that a hundred thousand others were doing exactly the same things, exchanging the same glances, touching hands and lips, whispering secrets, telling all in that first sweet rush of romance.

Winter would not leave the city. It took on a personality, villainous, stubborn, wretched. Now that the war was over, now that victory was here, she had almost imagined there would never be winter again, yet here it was, obstinate and vicious, and she longed for spring. And when it came at last, it heightened what she felt for Matthew and left her somewhat giddy. The city itself, always a trifle unreal to her, became a gigantic balmy backdrop for Matthew the man, a Camelot into which he rode bravely and gallantly, wearing her favour. She loved the way he moved, the long graceful strides, the boyish tilt of his head, the purposeful energy of every motion, the way he miraculously translated thought into action without the slightest hesitancy or doubt. She came to know his every gesture and to wait expectantly for it, a small shudder of excitement accompanying the expected move.

She began to wonder what he did when he was alone. Whatever curiosity she had experienced about men in general became a curiosity about Matthew. His new office in the Flatiron Building was suddenly a place of mystery and enchantment, a lair to which her man retreated to concoct and perform manly deeds. She would visualize him reading *The New York Times* behind his desk each morning, and then folding the paper and putting it aside, brushing it away from him with that impatient little gesture of his, gulping a cup of morning coffee (he would be holding the cup in both hands), reading through a brief, dictating to his secretary. She imagined him in court, he had already pleaded three cases successfully, stalking before the jury box and eloquently reducing the opposition's case to something both horrid and stupid, his deep voice rolling impressively (touched with a slight Southern drawl), and she imagined the ladies on the jury watching him with fascination and thinking, My, how handsome he is!

She tried to penetrate to the secret man himself in her fantasies, seeking the Matthew who was not hers but the Matthew who walked alone in a world of men, wishing to embrace this solitary figure as well, transcending the concept of Matthew and Amanda as a couple, and reaching into a private world that belonged to Matthew alone. In this world, she could watch Matthew shaving each morning, could see him leaning close to his mirror, stretching the skin on his face perhaps—did it hurt when he cut himself? She could imagine Matthew in his pyjamas, he would not wear a top, she knew. His chest would be hard, and the pyjama bottoms would curve loosely over his flat abdomen. She wondered what he felt like. When they danced together, when he held her close, she could feel the rigid arc of his masculinity against her, and she longed to touch him now, longed to look at him and learn him. There were so many questions to ask, and she knew she would ask them only of Matthew, knew she could learn from no one but him.

But knowing this, holding in her mind an elaborate past of terrible arguments, tentative explorations, frustrated tears and spontaneous glad laughter, minuscule sharings that piled imperceptibly into a giant conspiracy in which they stood alone; living a present that was heady with spring and the image of Matthew in a city still flushed with victory; imagining a future, constructing an eternity with Matthew by her side; this, all this, like the stop-action photos of the opening flower, was not truly perceived by Amanda. The process seemed quite natural to her. This was the way people fell in love. This was the way people got married. If the memory seemed blurred to her later, it was only because each separate image was almost identical to the one preceding it. If the girl who took Matthew's call in the college dormitory was a tightly closed bud, then the girl who was married more than a year later in her father's church in Otter Falls, Minnesota, was surely the blossom in the final triumphant shot—but she remained unaware of any real change, the memory would be blurred for her for ever.

She stood beside Matthew nervously and listened to her father, and felt a frightened gladness, and wanted to cry, but she had to listen, she was getting married, she was marrying Matthew.

"Do either of you know of any reason why you both should not be legally joined in marriage, or if there be any present who can show any just cause why these parties should not be legally joined together, let him now speak or hereafter hold his peace."

The church was silent. Somewhere behind her, she could hear Penny weeping. She turned her eyes sideward beneath the white veil, her head bent, and stole a glance at Matthew.

"Do you, Matthew Anson Bridges, take this woman as your lawfully wedded wife to live together in the state of holy matrimony? Will you love, honour, and keep her as a faithful man is bound to do, in health, sickness, prosperity and adversity, and forsaking all others keep you alone unto her as long as you both shall live?"

"I do," Matthew said brusquely.

"Do you, Amanda Soames, take this man as your lawfully wedded husband to live together in the state of holy matrimony? Will you love, honour, and cherish him as a faithful woman is bound to do, in health, sickness, prosperity and adversity, and forsaking all others keep you alone unto him as long as you both shall live?"

Amanda swallowed. She looked at her father, and she nodded, and then she said, "Yes, I do."

"For as you both have consented in wedlock," her father said, "and have acknowledged it before this company, I do by virtue of the authority invested in me by the church and the laws of this state now pronounce you husband and wife. And may God bless your union."

He was lifting the veil. His hands moved so gently, so tenderly on the veil. She felt her face uncovered, she tilted her face, there were tears in her eyes, and then his lips met hers, and he kissed her softly and lightly and moved his mouth back and whispered, "I love you, Amanda," and she suddenly grasped him to her, holding him tight, and heard the organ music, and felt happiness, happiness, and took his arm, and smiling at her sister and her mother and her niece, holding tightly to her husband's arm, walked up the aisle to the back of the church where sunlight streamed through the open doors.

BOOK TWO

GILLIAN

DAVID REGAN came back to Talmadge, Connecticut, on a warm spring day in 1947. He was twenty-two years old, but he knew he looked more like thirty. His image in the reflecting windows on the small station platform did not startle him. He could remember once, at Camp Elliott, seeing his face suddenly in the mirror one morning as he was shaving before quarters for muster. He had almost glanced over his shoulder to see who was standing behind him until he realized he was looking at himself. He had leaned closer to the mirror, his eyes wide, his heart suddenly pounding in his chest. And then touched his own face exploringly, like a blind man feeling a statue. And then turned away.

He took a cigarette from the pocket of his jumper now, conscious of the ruptured-duck symbol sewn above the pocket, conscious of the way his hand shook as he lighted the cigarette.

"Help you with your bag, sir?" a voice beside him said.

He shook out the match and turned. One of the Talmadge cab drivers was reaching for his suitcase.

"Leave it alone!" David said sharply. "I don't need any help."

"Thought you might want a taxi."

"I'm walking," he said.

He picked up his suitcase and started down the main street. The town did not seem to have changed very much. There had been a war in Europe and a war in the Pacific, and they had dropped atomic bombs on two Japanese towns and rewritten the history of the world, but Talmadge wrapped itself in springtime and looked exactly the same, the spires of the university in the distance, the sleepy look of the main street, the women in slacks, the shopping carts. Places never change, he thought. Only people do.

He tried to feel something as he walked down the street. He tried to remember a boyhood here, tried to remember buying comic books in Hurley's, *Batman* and *Superman*, tried to remember the town huddled against winter snow, Jack Armstrong on the radio each afternoon, *The Shadow* every Sunday at five-thirty, fishing at the lake, the lake, ah the lake. His thoughts turned off suddenly.

If only he could feel something.

He had thought of this moment for half his lifetime, it seemed. He had spent his youth thinking of this moment, the time when he could return to Talmadge and breathe deeply of free air, walk down the main street of his home town without that P on his back and on his trousers, P for prisoner, the Navy labelled everything. You wore your rating on your sleeve and your rank on your collar, and that P for prisoner branded into the flesh on your back and into the soft grey cushion of your mind, it's over, forget it. Forget it. But he could feel nothing.

He ached to feel something. His eyes, his nose, his ears longed for something that would trigger an emotion, something that would tell him he was home. But there was nothing. He walked silently down the main street of the town, and the bells of the First Congregational Church on the hill sounded the hour, do I remember the bells, please do I remember the bells? But he felt nothing until he passed the naval recruiting office, and then he felt only a terrible urge to spit at the plate-glass window. He walked by rapidly.

He stood before the gate of his house, the lawn rolling new and green to the ancient building, the lawn chairs freshly painted. He could hear birds in the trees. A woman was singing somewhere in the house. Mother, he thought. He felt nothing.

He opened the gate. He stared down at the gate hatch. He walked across the lawn and to the back door. He looked through the screen. She was singing as she stood at the telephone. She was dialling a number and singing, and he remembered a time long ago when she had stood by a telephone talking to Aunt Millie, but the memory meant nothing to him. He stood with his face pressed to the screen, watching her. She looked a little older, but nothing could ever touch the fine bones of her face, age could never destroy that structure. She's still a very pretty woman, he thought, watching her as a secret lover would, but feeling neither love nor hate, feeling nothing, seeing the tall, slender woman who finished dialling her number and then tucked the phone under her brown hair, against her ear. He opened the screen door. It creaked noisily.

She looked up as he stepped into the kitchen. She said, "Hello, this is Julia," into the telephone, and then she turned to look at him, and she said, "Yes?" her eyebrows raised, a slightly quizzical expression on her face, and he realized with grim amusement that she did not recognize him.

"Yes?" she said again. Into the telephone she said impatiently, "Just a minute, Mary, there's someone . . ." and then she looked at him, really looked at him. "David?" she said. "David?" She put the receiver back on to the wall hook instantly, recovering immediately from her initial shock, was there anything from which Mother could not recover instantly? He watched her as she crossed the kitchen towards him, watched as she carefully rearranged her face, the shock fleeing before an opening smile, the eyes studying his face and rejecting what they saw and adjusting the new image to correspond with the memory. He marvelled at what she could accomplish in the space of ten short steps across a kitchen. The smile she flashed at him was gracious and feminine, as if he were a beau who had come to call too early, but who was welcome none the less. He felt a phony theatricality to the scene, and then condemned his own cynicism and tried to think, This is my *mother*, for God's sake, but he still felt nothing. For a moment, her poise faltered on the icy edge of his indifference. Her hands outstretched and ready to embrace him, she stopped in sudden embarrassment, pulled back one hand, and then seemed to feel the motion of the other hand had progressed too far to allow checking. Awkwardly, her hand caught in space, she completed the motion, reaching for his crewcut head running the palm of her hand across the erect bristles, and saying, "David, you look like a Nazi!"

He wondered if she had seen the scar across the top of his skull, a vivid scar in the stiff bristles, wondered if she had noticed that the hair itself had turned grey, almost white, wondered, and suddenly thought of Mike Arretti and Camp Elliott, the leaded billet crashing into his skull, the way the blood was suddenly gushing on to his face, spilling over his forehead and into his eyes, and Mike Arretti watching him and smiling as he fell to his knees.

His mother laughed once, nervously, and then her poise returned again with new strength. This was her son, he could almost hear the words, this was her son and greet him she would, so she embraced him and held him close and said, "You're home," which he felt was terribly stagey, but he answered, "Yes, Mother I'm home," and wondered when they would bring down the first-act curtain, and then wondered if this wasn't all very genuine, if perhaps he was the actor, he was the one fake cog in this big homecoming machinery.

She held him at arm's length. The gesture seemed corny to him. Would she say, "Let me look at you?" God, he hoped she would not say that.

"I'm glad," she said simply.

He was thankful for that. He immediately chided himself for having underestimated her. But he could not understand his attitude, this feeling of being an observer rather than a participant.

"Why didn't you tell me you were coming? I'd have arranged a parade."

He smiled because it was expected of him. "I wanted to surprise you," he said.

"Surprise me! I nearly died when you walked through that door." She tucked a stray wisp of hair under a bobby pin, watching him as she did, apparently pleased with what she saw, or at least presenting a façade of pleasure, which belied that first moment of shocked recognition. You are not fooling me, Mother, he thought. You are looking at a stranger.

"Would you like some tea? How was your trip? Are you discharged now? Are you home for good?"

"Yes, I am. And yes, I'd like some tea."

"You look tired, David."

"I am tired."

"A long trip?"

"Very long, Mother."

"But you're home for good?"

"Yes."

She nodded. She seemed genuinely pleased now. Perhaps she was getting accustomed to him. Perhaps he didn't look quite so strange to her now.

"Did you hurt your head?" she asked.

His fingers went instantly to the scar. He shrugged. "Oh. Yeah."

"But you're all right now?"

"Yes. Fine."

"You look tired," she said again.

"I can use a cup of tea."

"I'll put the kettle on."

He watched her as she moved to the stove. "How's my room?" he asked suddenly.

"Your room?"

"Yes. How . . . how is it?" He shrugged.

"Just as you left it, David."

"I think I'd like to go up there." He watched her warily. "Change my clothes. Get out of this uniform."

"Well . . . well, David . . ." She seemed bewildered all at once.

"What is it?" he asked.

"Well, I . . . I gave your old clothes away," she said. "Last summer. To the Red Cross." She opened her hands plaintively. "I'm sorry, darling, I thought . . . I assumed you'd outgrown them."

"Oh," he said. He paused. "All of them? My clothes?"

"Yes." She bit her lip. "Oh, David, I'm so sorry, really I am."

"That's okay." He shrugged. "I just wanted to get out of this uniform."

"Yes, I should have realized that. You can go to town later and buy some nice things, would that be all right?"

"Sure." He began drumming his fingers on the table top. Julia stood near the stove, watching the tea-kettle. "How's Ardis?" he asked.

"Ardis Fletcher?"

"Mmmm. Yes."

"She's married, you know."

"Oh."

"Yes."

"No, I didn't know. I wondered why she stopped writing."

"Yes, she's married."

"Funny how ..." he started, and then fell silent.

"I think the tea is ready," Julia said. She brought two cups to the table and poured. "Sugar?" she asked.

"No, thanks."

"You used to take sugar."

"Yeah, but in the brig they——" He stopped himself short.

They sat sipping tea in the late afternoon.

"Do you remember the villa in Aquila, David?" she asked.

"Yes, I remember."

"So lovely. So long ago."

"Yes."

She sighed. "Well, you're home."

"Mom ..." he said.

"Yes, dear?"

"Mom, why ..." He put down his teacup. "Mom, I thought you'd come to see me again. I mean, after that first time."

"What, dear?"

"When I was at Camp Elliott. You came once, and then ... well, the other guys ... I just thought you might come again. I mean, I know it was a long trip and all, but ..." He shrugged.

Her eyes opened wide. She looked at him blankly and said, "But David, you know how ill your Aunt Millie had been."

"Yes," he said. He shrugged.

"I think I wrote you about it."

"Yes. Yes, I remember."

"California's a long way off, darling. And Aunt Millie's all alone in the world, except for me. You understand, don't you? I hoped you'd understand, David."

"Oh, sure," he said. "I just wondered, that's all." He wet his lips and nodded. Well, he thought, this is the second time Aunt Millie's picked up the marbles. He lifted his teacup.

"Was it very terrible, David dear? Do you want to talk about it?"

"There's nothing to talk about. It's over."

"Yes. And things will be different now that you're home."

"I suppose so."

Julia smiled maternally. "Tad Parker stopped by the other day. He asked about you."

"Oh? How is he?"

"Fine. He's enrolled at a New York acting school. He still wants to be an actor, can you imagine that?"

"Well, nothing wrong with that," David said, and he shrugged.

"Will you be going to school David?' To college?"

"I guess so."

"To Talmadge?"

"Well, I . . . I was thinking about New York. A school in New York someplace."

"I see," Julia said. She nodded thoughtfully. "What will you study, do you know?"

"I'm not sure yet."

Julia smiled warmly over her teacup. "I always had the feeling you could be . . . well, David, you always wrote such beautiful letters. Perhaps you could——"

"No!" he said, and then realized his vehemence had startled her. "No," he said softly.

The theatre was dark except for the single work light burning in the centre of the stage. Gillian stood in the wings and looked again at the script which had been handed to her not ten minutes ago. A young buxom blonde was onstage, asking the director if she could sit on the floor while reading for the part, would that be all right? She could get the feel of it better that way, she said. The director told her she could sit or stand, whichever put her more at ease, and the blonde promptly collapsed into a buttery heap at the base of the work light, and began reading. Gillian tried not to hear the lines. She concentrated on the script in her hands, thumbing through it, searching out the character's biggest speeches in an attempt to second-guess what they would ask her to read.. She suddenly remembered a time when she was eight years old and had rushed home excitedly to tell her mother she'd been cast in the role of a frog in the school play. "I got a pock in the play!" she shouted. "I got a pock in the play!" She wished it were as simple now. She wished . . .

"Thank you very much," she heard a voice say. "Next, please."

She looked up from the script, and then closed it. Well, she thought, here we go again. Good luck, Gillian. And she walked on to the stage. At twenty-two, she seemed to have acquired that elusively knowledgeable look which all New York career girls were wearing that fall, a look that was rescued from its usual shellacked hardness by the inherent softness of her body, the freshness of her features. Her face had lengthened somewhat, matured perhaps; it was economically beautiful, with startling green eyes, a generous mobile mouth, a finely turned nose. She wore her hair the way she'd always worn it, the russet bangs clinging to her forehead, the mane brushed sleekly to the back of her neck. She moved on stage with an energetic purposefulness that was none the less feminine, almost feline, utilizing a graceful long-legged lope that was hers alone and that she realized was out of character. I am Gillian Burke, she thought, take me or leave me. I want a pock in the play.

"Hello," a voice from the theatre said. "How are you?"

"Fine, thank you," Gillian said. She could not see anyone in the theatre, but she did not shield her eyes, nor did she squint. She looked out at what she imagined to be the sixth row centre, and she spoke in a natural unforced manner, as if her conversational partners were sitting across a table from her.

"What's your name, Miss?" a second voice asked. The voice was tentative, exploratory. She assumed it belonged to the author of the play.

"Gillian Burke," she answered.

The other voice asked authoritatively. "Why did you choose that name?"

That's the director, she thought. "I was born with it," she answered.

"It's an unusual name," the director said.

"Yes, I know." She smiled. "But I guess I'm stuck with it."

She heard something that could have been a slight chuckle. She could not tell whether the sound had come from the playwright or the director. She was suddenly conscious of the work light. She moved a little closer to it, tilting her head upward so that the light caught her cheek-bones and her nose.

"What have you been doing, Miss Burke?" the director asked.

She tried a tentative smile. This was the part she always hated. She knew they weren't truly interested in knowing what she'd been doing. If she'd been doing anything really important, they'd have known about it already. The question was designed to start her talking about qualifications that were insignificant, the carbon-copy professional life of a thousand other acting aspirants in the city. The plot of the story was unimportant, only the lead character was. And the lead character was Gillian Burke, and they would be watching her all the while she spoke. She had experimented with this phase of casting a long time ago. She had decided that the details of her professional past were boring, and she had coupled this with the intuitive knowledge that people would much rather converse than listen. And so, whenever the question was asked—and it was always asked—she had tried to frame her answers in the form of a dialogue rather than a monologue, bringing her inquisitor into the action, creating a fake give-and-take, which was livelier than a simple recitation would have been. She had abandoned this technique when one director said, "We're a little busy here, Miss Burke, and we haven't time to pull teeth. Do you want to tell us about yourself, or shall we forget it?" From then on, she gave the facts straight. They were supposed to be facts, and they were supposed to allow those people in the darkened theatre an opportunity to study her before she began reading, an opportunity to form an opinion about her voice, her face, her experience, the way she moved, an opportunity perhaps to decide whether she was right for the part even before she opened the script. She began her recitation.

"I've been studying with Igor Vodorin for the past four years. I also belong to a group that has been doing repertory at the Ninety-second Street Y, Shakespeare mostly, though we have done some Marlowe and some Jonson. My best roles at the Y were Ophelia in *Hamlet*, and Goneril in *Lear*. I've done summer stock at——"

"Could you speak a little louder, please, Miss Burke?" a voice from the rear of the theatre asked, a new voice, producer?

"Yes, certainly," she said. "I've done summer stock at Westport and Stockbridge, the usual straw-hat plays, but I had supporting roles in two originals that were being tried."

"What were they?" the director asked.

"A comedy called *Martha Walking*, and a melodrama called *Night Flame*."

"Neither of those reached Broadway, did they?"

"No," Gillian answered. She smiled. "But that wasn't my fault," she added quickly.

She thought she heard another chuckle out front.

"I've also done a few radio spots on WOV and WNYC."

"Commercials?"

"No. Dramatic roles."

"Sustaining or sponsored?"

"Sustaining."

"You're Equity?"

"Yes. And AFTER."

"Done any television?"

"No. Not yet. I think . . . well, my agent thinks there's something for me on Kraft." She paused. "I've got an interview this Friday."

"Why do you want this part, Miss Burke?"

"Because I think I'm right for it." She paused for a fraction of a second and quickly said, "No, that isn't true. I haven't the faintest notion if I'm right for it. I want the part because I'm a good actress."

"How do you know that, Miss Burke?"

"I know it."

"Has someone told you?"

"Would that make me a good actress if I weren't one?"

"No, I guess not," the director said. She detected a smile in his voice. "Would you like to read for us now? On 1-23, the speech starting with 'I can tell things without really knowing them.' Do you see that, Miss Burke?"

Gillian opened the script, moved closer to the work light, and found the speech. "Yes, I have it."

"Would you begin, please?"

She read well, she thought, with force and control. When she finished the speech, she closed the script and stood looking out into the blackness. The theatre was silent.

"Ahhh, Miss Burke," the director said, "would you mind turning to 3-17, please?" The speech starting with 'Yes, but Phyllis was always so sweet, so solicitous.'"

"I have it," Gillian said.

"Would you begin, please?"

Her hands had begun to tremble slightly. She hoped there was not a quaver in her voice. She tried to pretend she was not in a theatre, reading to a director and a playwright and God knew how many other concerned people. She read as well as she knew how to read, and then she closed the script again, and again looked out at the blackness.

"Would you walk downstage left, please?" the director said.

Gillian swallowed, pulled her shoulders erect, and walked across the stage.

"Now back to the light, please."

She walked back to the light.

"How old are you, Miss Burke?"

"Twenty-two."

"How tall?"

"Five-five," she answered.

"Would you take off your shoes, please, Miss Burke?"

"What?"

"Your shoes. Would you mind removing them?"

"Oh, yes," she said. She stepped out of her pumps without stooping, using the toe of one foot to remove the shoe from the opposite foot.

"And now would you walk down left again?"

"Without my shoes?"

"Yes, please."

She nodded and walked down to the proscenium.

"Thank you, Miss Burke. Who is your agent, please?" the director asked.

"Marian Lewis," she answered.

"Thank you," the director said. "Next, please."

The words almost leaped into her throat. She could feel them bubbling inside her, almost forming on her lips. Did I get the part? Did I get the part? She felt parched all at once. She stood in the darkness on the side of the stage and stared out at the empty seats, motionless.

"Yes, Miss Burke, thank you," the director said.

She nodded dumbly, picked up her shoes, and went into the wings, wondering the same things she wondered each time. Did they like me? They asked me to read two speeches. They must have liked me. Maybe they'll call Marian as soon as I leave the theatre. Why did he ask me to take off my shoes? I'm too tall, I'll bet. Who's been signed for the male lead? Is he short? Maybe there's a scene where the girl is barefoot, I should have looked more closely. But he asked me how tall I was. Damn it, who *is* playing the male lead? They couldn't have liked me. They'd have said something, they'd have asked me to read more. But they did ask me who my agent was, that's a good sign, oh God, maybe, maybe!

Outside the theatre, she reached into her bag and took out her small appointment book. She thumbed through the month of November, stopped at the page marked with a big 20, and studied her own hurried scrawl:

> Reading, Booth, West 45, 3 p.m.
> F.A.O. 4–6
> Amanda, Michael's Rest. 6.15
> Class 7

She glanced at her watch. It was three-fifty. If she caught a cab, she could be at F.A.O.'s by four, maybe. The cab would cost her at least sixty-five cents, could she get away with a ten-cent tip? No, fifteen cents would be the absolute minimum, although cabbies *did* expect women to be cheap tippers, maybe she could get away with ten. No, she had better figure on at least eighty cents for the ride. Which meant her first hour at the store would net her exactly sixty cents, a penny a minute, a real fat profit that was. Or should she chance taking the bus and being late again? No, they'd fire her, sure as hell. She simply had to begin planning her days more carefully. But what was she to do when a reading came along? I wonder if I got the part, she thought. Will Amanda pay for dinner? There isn't even *time* for dinner with her. I'll have to take a sandwich to class. I wonder if I got the part.

She hailed a taxi.

She didn't seem capable of concentrating on what Amanda was saying. She kept thinking of the telephone and wondering if they'd contacted Marian. She had called as soon as she'd left the store, but Marian was on another line, and Dotty, the receptionist, had asked Gillian to call back at six-thirty. It was now six twenty-five, and she sat opposite Amanda at a circular table, listening to the polite chatter in the bar, and trying to concentrate on Amanda's words, and thinking all the while of the reading that afternoon and the fact that they'd asked her to take off her shoes, asked her how tall she was, asked her to walk for them. Surely that meant something. They hadn't asked the other girls to do that.

". . . but, of course, Matthew's new office is on Wall Street, and that would add at least another half-hour to the commuting time. I don't think he's too keen on the idea, but I'm working on him." Amanda smiled and lifted her drink.

It was amazing how elegant she looked, Gillian thought, amazing how marriage seemed to have changed not only the way she dressed but her face and body as well. She carried herself with a new certainty, as if she had found a secure niche and settled happily into it. She was wearing a stark black dress, sleeved to the wrist, hooded so that only a faint hint of her long blonde hair showed. The dress, fitted through to the waist, flared to a circle of wool-jersey hem. She wore short leopardskin boots. A leopard jacket was draped carelessly over the back of her chair, together with her sling purse. A large circular gold coin showed on a chain at the throat of the dress. Gillian studied her and felt slightly displaced, as if she had stumbled into another time belt in which she remained exactly the same, unchanging, while everything around her progressed towards a vaguely understood middle age. Has Amanda really changed that much? she wondered. Or is it only because she's married? She did not know the answer. But she felt as if she were sitting with a chic and elegant young woman who made her feel like an awkward adolescent.

Quickly, Gillian glanced at the clock behind the bar, and then towards the telephone booth. A grinning, fat man was hugging the mouthpiece. Come on, she thought, hurry up. I have to make a call in two and a half minutes.

"Do you think I'm insane, Gilly?" Amanda asked. "Wanting to live in Talmadge?"

"No, it's a lovely town," Gillian answered. I wonder if I got the part, she thought. They must have liked me. They wouldn't have made such a fuss otherwise. And I heard them laughing at some of the things I said. They liked me from the very start, even before I read for them.

"I always loved it," Amanda said. "And it's really only an hour and a half from the city."

"When the New Haven's on time," Gillian said.

"Yes. Anyway, I'm going up with Matthew this week-end. Just to look around."

"That should be fun."

"Would you like to come along?"

"I'd love to," Gillian said. "But I work on Saturdays, and I have a rehearsal at the Y this Sunday."

"Oh, that's too bad."

Gillian nodded and looked at the phone booth again. Come on, she thought, get out. Get off the phone!

She shoved her chair back suddenly. "Amanda, will you excuse me? I promised I'd call my agent."

"Go right ahead," Amanda said. "Shall I order another drink?"

"Yes, fine. Yes, do that. Excuse me."

She rose and walked away from the table, aware that two men at the bar turned to watch her as she shoved back her chair. She went directly to the phone booth and stared fixedly through the glass doors at the fat man. She turned to look at the clock again. It was six thirty-one. Oh now really, she thought. The fat man continued to grin into the mouthpiece. Oh, you unctuous thing, she thought, you'll be in there all day, and the booth will smell of you after you're gone. She crossed her arms over her breasts and began tapping her foot, scowling at the fat man. Now relax, she told herself. They probably didn't even call. They probably didn't like me at all.

The doors to the booth opened. The fat man grinned at her apologetically, and she gave him a frozen smile in return, and stepped instantly into the booth. She deposited her coin, dialled, closed the doors, and then opened them again immediately.

"Lewis Agency," a voice said.

"Dot, this is Gillian."

"Just a second, Gilly. Did you call your exchange?"

"No. Why?"

"Miss Lewis was trying to reach you there."

"Anything?" Gillian said.

"I don't know. Just a second, she's free now."

Gillian waited impatiently. At the table, the waiter was depositing the fresh round of drinks before Amanda.
"Gilly? Is that you, sweetie?"
"Marian, for God's sake, did they call?"
"Did who call, sweetie?"
"Well, the Theatre Guild people, who do you——?"
"Oh. No, darling, they didn't. How did it go?"
"Oh."
"Did they like you?"
"I thought so. They asked me who my agent was."
"Did you tell them?"
"Of course I told them! Marian, when you ask stupid questions like that, I could . . ."
"Sweetie," Marian said softly.
There was a silence on the line.
"They didn't call," Marian said. "Maybe tomorrow."
"Yes, maybe," Gillian answered.
"About that appointment with Kraft?"
"Yes."
"On Friday?"
"Yes."
"It's with the producer-director, a man named Stanley Quinn. At WNBT. You know where that is."
"Yes."
"Four o'clock," Marian said.
"Marian, I have to be at work at four."
"This is important."
"So is eating, damn it!" Gillian said.
"Sweetie," Marian said softly.
"I can't afford to lose my job. Make the appointment earlier. Or cancel it. I don't care either way."
"That's no way to talk, Gilly."
"I guess it isn't. How many readings do you suppose I've been to since you took me on two years ago, Marian?" She paused. "I'll be at class tonight. If anything happens, call my exchange."
"All right."
"I gave a better reading than anyone else, Marian."
"I'm sure you did, sweetie."
"They asked me how tall I was."
"Did you tell them?"
"Marian, goddam it . . ."
"Yes, sweetie. I'm sorry."
The line went silent.
"You'll be a big star, Gillian," Marian said.

The line went silent again.

"I'll call in tomorrow," Gillian said. "Just . . . just in case."

"All right, sweetie. Good night, now."

"Good night," Gillian said, and she hung up. She felt automatically for her coin in the slot, left the booth, and walked back towards the table.

For the first time in two years, she felt very tired.

The acting class conducted by Igor Ivanovich Vodorin was held in a loft on Sixth Avenue. To the left of the building's entrance was a small bookshop, the window of which exhibited the latest bestsellers together with a discreet display of silk-stocking photos. Gillian looked at the book titles—she had already read *The Moneyman* and *House Divided* and *East Side, West Side*—and then studied the photos, fascinated. She went into the kosher delicatessen to the right of the entrance, bought a hot pastrami sandwich and a celery tonic, and then went into the building. The stairway leading to the loft was steep and dimly lighted, but after climbing those rickety steps for nearly four years, she could have navigated them in total darkness. She did almost that now, reading from an open script as she climbed the steps, reaching the landing by blind instinct, turning right into the small cloakroom where she hung up her coat, and then walking into the large pipe-riddled room that was the studio itself. As she crossed the room to take a seat near the wall, someone said, "Ho, Gilly," and she nodded briefly and mumbled an answer, absorbed in the script. She sat without looking up from the script, unwrapped the pastrami sandwich, stuck the soda-bottle straws into her mouth, and, still not looking up, continued with her memorizing.

Her method of memorization was simple. She would read a sentence and repeat it over and over again in her mind until she knew it. Then she would commit the next sentence to memory, and then repeat both sentences together. She could never understand why anyone had the slightest trouble learning a part. In fact, she couldn't understand why anyone with a bad memory would want to become an actor. But she'd certainly met plenty of actors who couldn't even remember the words to "The Star-Spangled Banner", who were always searching for a new gimmick that would make the task easier. She could not abide sloppy memorization. She held a vast respect for playwrights and the printed word. If someone misread a line, it infuriated her.

She could remember criticizing a student's performance once, and the argument that had followed it. The boy had done a scene from *The Eve of Saint Mark*, and after Gillian had commented on his particularly annoying mannerism of constantly stroking his hair into place, she had said, "And the line is supposed to be 'The host with someone *indistinct* converses at the door, apart'."

"That's what I said."

"No, you said, 'The host with someone *interesting*.'"

"Well..." The boy shrugged. "What difference does it make?"

"I imagine it makes a great deal of difference to Maxwell Anderson. And probably to T. S. Eliot, whom he's quoting."

"I was trying to get the character over," the boy said. "I don't see where one word——"

"Private Marion is not a person who would quote poetry incorrectly," Gillian said.

Igor, who had been listening to the exchange silently, suddenly said, "Of course, he is supposed to be a cultured man, and the mistake is unforgivable. But would you have made the same objection, Miss Burke, if the character had not been quoting from a poem?"

"Yes, I would have," Gillian said. "The words in a play are everything."

"Ahhh?" Igor said, and he opened his eyes wide and moved closer to her. "In a book, perhaps, yes. But not in a play. In a play, the words must be brought to life. It is the actor who brings these words to life, Miss Burke."

"His own words, or the author's?" Gillian asked.

"You would allow no leeway to the actor, is that correct?" Igor asked. He was circling closer to her now, his shaggy head bent, one bony hand looped into the lapel of his brown sweater, his bright-blue eyes fastened to her face. He spoke English that had been learned in Russia and refined in a dozen foreign countries, but which was scrupulously and miraculously accent-free. "You would prescribe specific limits for the actor, is that right?"

"Yes. Where it concerns the language of a play, the meaning of a play."

"Does an actor convey meaning by memorizing *words*?"

"He starts that way."

"But I hope we may supplement words with actions! May we not?"

"Of course we may. I'm talking about the *language* of a play."

"The language and the action are one and the same. They are only tools to express ideas."

"Exactly," Gillian said. "The playwright's ideas. Not the actor's."

"Miss Burke, I hope you are not telling me that an actor is only a harmonica."

"No. I'm simply saying that an actor's job is to play a part the way the playwright heard it in his head when he was writing it."

"I see. Then if we could wire this playwright's head for sound, we would have no need of actors, isn't that correct? An actor *is* a harmonica, after all."

"No, he's not. But if he won't follow the speeches as written, why do we need the play at all? Why don't we all get up and read from the telephone book?"

The class laughed, and Gillian felt she had scored a point. Igor stopped beside her, smiled, touched the top of her head with his hand, and gently said, "We need plays, of course, Miss Burke, and it is important to learn the words correctly. I would be a foolish old man if I tried to convince you that actors are playwrights. We are not. Although I must admit that some of us are better playwrights than those men who lay claim to the title."

The class laughed again, Gillian, delighted, laughed with them.

"But, Miss Burke, will you grant me a single point? Will you grant me, perhaps, that a good actor, a *great* actor, can bring to the words something which the playwright never heard inside his head? A nuance of meaning, a subtlety of expression, an invented gesture which will suddenly present an idea in shimmering clarity? And that by doing this, by bringing this to the very lines the playwright has written, he will *add* to the creation, bring to the idea a *greater* significance? Will you, Miss Burke, grant to an old man this one small and totally prejudiced opinion? May we have the next scene, please?"

She recognized the technique, of course. She had recognized it from the very first. He would question her belligerently, often taking a stand in which he did not believe, simply to draw her out, to force a reasoning process that led to a seemingly self-formed conclusion. She knew this, but she entered each new argument with vigour and spirit, loving the old man for what he gave her: a secure knowledge of her craft, and a soaring pride in the profession she had chosen.

"Gillian?" the voice said.

She looked up from the open script in her lap. Tad Parker, one of the boys in the class, was standing with his arm on the shoulder of another boy. Her eyes touched Tad's face, the tentative smile, the habitual dirty sweat shirt he wore to class, the Army dog-tags rattling under the shirt. And then she looked at the other boy.

"Got it down yet?" Tad asked.

"Oh, yes," she answered. "I was only making sure."

The other boy had not turned his eyes from her. She could feel them on her, ice-blue eyes that seemed emotionless, a face that held something of menace in it, the short-cropped greying hair, he could not be that old, he could not be older than twenty-five or so, the scar nesting in the short bristles, the way he stood stiffly erect beside Tad, his eyes never leaving her, something of menace, and yet something terribly yearning.

"I brought a friend to watch us go through our paces," Tad said. "From my home town."

Gillian nodded, and then smiled.

"David, this is Gillian."

"How do you do?" the boy said.

"Hello," Gillian answered.

"Look, if you've got work to do, we won't bother you," Tad said. He clapped David on the shoulder and led him to the row of chairs behind Gillian. They sat together, and Gillian went back to her script. When Igor entered the loft a few moments later, she did not look up. He walked around the room, nodding at his pupils, exchanging a few words with each of them, and then finally coming to where she sat.

"Miss Burke?" he said.

Gillian smiled. "Good evening, Mr. Vodorin."

Intently, he said, "The reading? How did it go?"

Gillian shrugged.

"No theatrical shorthand, please," Igor said. "Did they like you?"

She was suddenly aware that Tad and his friend, the boy he had called David, were sitting behind her and probably listening to every word of the conversation. "I thought they liked me," she said, somehow embarrassed. "But they didn't call."

"Perhaps tomorrow then."

"Perhaps."

"Patience," Igor said gently, and he put his hand on her shoulder. He took a gold watch from his pocket then, cocked his head to look at it, and said, "Well, we must begin the class now."

She sat at the back of the loft in the folding chair, huddled in her own arms as if suffering a chill, watching the other students as they presented their scenes. Igor had insisted that they work alone for this particular project, and she'd had a truly difficult time finding a monologue in anything but Shakespeare. She had spent three afternoons at the drama library on East Fifty-eighth before coming up with a section from *Dream Girl*, and even that hadn't pleased her entirely, but time was running out, and the project was almost due. She watched her fellow students now, bored by the monologues, and wondering why Igor had assigned anything so elementary. She contributed nothing to the criticisms following each performance. When Igor finally called upon her to do her scene, she rose from her chair, walked swiftly to the platform at the front of the loft, climbed on to it, faced the class, and said, "This is from *Dream Girl* by Elmer

Rice. I'm Georgina. My mother has just called me from off right to tell me to stop day-dreaming. Her last words are, 'It's almost nine!'" Gillian nodded and walked to the centre of the platform. She took a deep breath and began the scene.

GEORGINA
(Leaping up.)

All right, Mother. I'm practically dressed.
(The lights fade on the scene and come up, at left, on GEORGINA's *bathroom, which she enters, talking all the while.)*
Maybe your mother is right, Georgina. Maybe it's time you cut out the day-dreaming—time you stopped mooning around and imagining yourself to be this extraordinary creature with a strange and fascinating psychological life.
(She has removed her negligée and donned a bathing cap; and now she goes around behind the bathroom, invisible but still audible. The sound of a shower is heard.)
Oh, damn it! Cold as ice. There, that's better.
(She sings "Night and Day" lustily. Then the shower is turned off and she reappears wrapped in a large bath towel and stands, her back to the audience, rubbing herself vigorously.)
Still, to be honest, I must admit that, compared to the average girl you meet, I'm really quite complex. Intelligent and well informed too; and a good conversationalist.
(Indignantly, as over her shoulder, she sees someone looking in at her.)
Well, for heaven's sake! Honestly, some people!
(She pulls down an imaginary window shade and the scene is blacked out, her voice coming out of the darkness.)
And my looks are nothing to be ashamed of, either. I have a neat little figure and my legs are really very nice. Of course, my nose is sort of funny, but my face definitely has character—not just one of those magazine-cover deadpans.
(With a yawn.)
Oh, I never seem to get enough sleep.
(The lights come up as she raises the imaginary shade. She is dressed now in her shoes, stockings, and slip. She seats herself at her dressing-table, facing the audience, and brushes her hair.)
If I could only stop lying awake for hours, dreaming up all the exciting things that could happen but never do. Well, maybe this is the day when things really will begin to happen to me. Maybe Wentworth and Jones will accept my novel. They've had it over a month now, and all the other publishers turned it down in less than two weeks. It certainly looks promising.

. . . . .

Igor, standing at the back of the loft, saw Gillian hesitate for a moment, falling instantly out of character. Her recovery seemed complete in the space of ten seconds, but he had seen the sudden puzzled look that crossed her face, and he frowned now as she picked up the scene again, the frown deepening when he realized she had not returned completely, had not fully recovered the intricate characterization she'd been building.

"Wouldn't that be wonderful!" Gillian said. "With a published novel, I'd really be somebody." She paused. The pause was a long one. Igor began walking slowly from the back of the loft. Had she forgotten her lines? No. Gillian Burke never forgot lines. And then he realized she knew the lines only too well, she was listening to each separate line as it left her mouth. She sighed deeply now and said, "Reviews... reviews in all the book sections..." Again she paused. She wiped her hand across her lip. "Royalty checks coming in." And again the long deadly pause, as if she were suddenly understanding the words, suddenly allowing their meaning to penetrate to her secret heart. "Women nudging each other at... at... Schrafft's and... and... whispering... and... whispering: 'Don't l-look now, but that girl over there—the one with the smart hat—that's ... that's... that's Georgina Allerton, the... the...'" She stopped again. She turned to the class. "I'm sorry," she said. "I have a terrible headache," and she walked off the stage.

Igor caught her as she was entering the cloakroom.

"Where are you going?" he said.

"Home."

"Why?"

"I have a headache."

"An actress doesn't go home when she has a show to do."

She looked up into his face. "Igor," she said slowly, using his Christian name for the first time in four years, "Igor, I don't have a show to do."

Igor grasped her shoulders. "You have a stage, you have an audience, you have a part to play. That is a show."

"Igor, I have a creaking platform, and a roomful of kids, and a part played by Betty Field on Broadway last year, that's what I've got. Not a show, Igor. Please, I want to go home."

"To cry?"

"Yes, damn it, maybe to cry. Can't I cry? Is it against the rules to cry?"

"You may cry," Igor said. "I was only concerned that you would be alone. Stay here if you must cry, Gillian."

She nodded. "Thank you. Thank you, Igor. But... I... I'd like to go home. Thank you." She fumbled into her coat, and then looked around the cloakroom dazedly. "My bag. I guess I left it inside."

"Gillian?" he said.

"Yes?"

"You will come back tomorrow evening?"

She hesitated for a long time before answering. Then she simply nodded and went into the loft for her bag. She walked rapidly towards her chair near the wall. Tad had gone to the front of the loft, preparatory to doing his scene. The boy David sat alone in the row behind her vacant seat. His eyes picked her up as she entered the loft and followed her as she moved towards the chair. She met his eyes with her own, and he turned away as if embarrassed. For no reason on earth, she said to him, "My bag."

"What?"

"I left it here."

"Oh."

"Yes."

"Excuse me," she said. She took the bag from the seat of the chair. He was staring at her again. She looked at him, puzzled. "Yes?" she said. He shook his head. "What is it?"

"You . . . you were very good," he answered. His voice was tentative, almost frightened.

"Thank you."

"The scene you just did."

"Yes."

He continued staring at her. He wet his lips. It seemed he would speak, and then something claimed his eyes and he shrank deeper into his chair and said nothing. She looked at him a moment longer, nodded, and then walked rapidly to the door. Tad had already begun his scene. Igor was standing beside the platform, one arm across his waist, his other elbow propped on it, his hand supporting his chin. She tiptoed past the platform and started down the long steps to the street. She was half-way down when she heard the voice behind her.

"Miss?"

She turned. It was David. He stood on the landing above her, looking down at her solemnly, nibbling at his lower lip.

"Shhh," she said. "Tad's doing his scene."

"I . . . I don't know your last name," he said.

"Burke." She paused. "Why do you want to know it?"

"I . . . I thought I . . . I thought I might call you."

"Why?"

He shrugged.

"Are you Jewish?" she asked.

"Why?"

"David always sounds to me like a Jewish name."

"Yes," he said suddenly. He brought his shoulders back. He seemed to have made a decision, seemed in that moment to have decided he would not call her, would not even speak to her any longer. "I'm Jewish. Does it matter?"

"No. Why should I care what you are?"

"Well, then I'm not Jewish," he said.

"All right." She looked at him curiously.

"May . . . may I take you home?" he asked.

"No," she said quickly.

"May I call you?"

"I don't know. I don't think so."

"Why not?"

"I don't know."

"Are you in the book?"

"Yes."

"I'll call you."

"I have to go now."

"I'll call you," he repeated.

She had been home no more than ten minutes when the telephone rang. She picked up the receiver, put it to her ear, and said, "Hello?"

"Miss Burke?"

"Yes?"

"This is David."

"Who?"

"David Regan." He hesitated. "We met just a little while ago. At the loft."

"Oh. Oh yes."

"Well," he said. "I see you got home all right."

"Yes, I did."

"Did I wake you?"

"No."

"I've been trying the number for the past half-hour."

There was a long pause on the line.

"I thought you might like to meet me for a cup of coffee," he said.

"Do you mean right now?"

"Yes. It's only a little past eleven. I thought . . ."

"I was getting ready for bed," Gillian said.

"Oh. Well, okay, I just thought . . ."

"I'm sorry."

"Oh sure. That's all right."

There was another pause.

"Can I see you tomorrow night?" David asked.

"What's tomorrow?"

"Friday."

"I have a class."

"Then Saturday?"

"How did your hair get grey?" Gillian asked.

"What?"

"Your hair. How——"

"Oh. In the Navy. At Camp Elliott." He hesitated. "I was a prisoner there."

"Why? What'd you do?"

"I hit an officer."

"Why'd you do that?"

"He said something I didn't like."

"What'd he say?"

"Something about my father."

"Well, then I guess he deserved it," Gillian said.

"Yeah, I guess so. Can I see you Saturday?"

"All right," Gillian said.

"Would seven-thirty be all right?"

"Fine," Gillian said.

"What's your address?" he said quickly. She gave it to him, and he repeated it four times, and then said, "I haven't got a pencil."

"Will you remember it?"

"Oh sure, I will."

The line went silent.

"I never met anyone named Gillian before," he said.

"It's a silly name."

"No, I like it."

"It always makes me want to laugh."

"I'm glad it's not Lillian," David said. "It could have been Lillian, you know."

"I'd have shot myself."

"Then I'd never have met you."

"Well . . . well, I'll see you Saturday night."

"Yes, at seven-thirty."

"Good night, David."

"Good night, Gillian," he said.

The play was being presented by a City College drama group at the little theatre on the uptown campus of Hunter College, and David bought the tickets on Friday afternoon from a student at

N.Y.U. who had acquired them from a pharmacy major at Fordham. He picked up Gillian at seven-thirty, and they had a drink in her apartment, and then rode uptown on the Woodlawn Road–Lexington Avenue Express. It was Saturday night, but they were almost alone in the subway car; most of the crowd was heading downtown, towards Broadway. The lonely car seemed to stifle conversation. Each opening gambit provided a few lines of talk, which suddenly trailed off into a muttered "un-huh" or a nod of the head. The train rumbled along the track and they sat in the nearly empty car, each separately beginning to develop misgivings about the advisability of dating strangers. David began chastising himself mentally for not owning an automobile. Gillian began looking ahead to a dreadful college production of Ibsen.

"The thing that's *marr*-vellous about him, of course," she said, "is that he still holds up so well today."

"That's Boston, isn't it?" David asked.

"What?"

"The 'marvellous'."

"No. No, it isn't."

"Say it again."

"*Marr*-vellous."

"It's Irish then."

"Yes. Does it sound awful?"

"No, it sounds lovely."

The conversation lapsed again. David wanted a cigarette more than anything in the world. He was sure it would begin snowing the moment they hit the street. He felt in his coat pocket for the tickets, suddenly certain he'd left them home. The tickets were there, but he was still confident it would snow. When the drunk entered the car at 149th Street, he knew there would be trouble. He simply knew it. It was just one of those nights.

The drunk sat opposite them in the nearly empty car. The weather was uncommonly cold for November, but he was wearing only a sports jacket over a thin white shirt. He grinned at them the moment he was seated. Then he waggled his fingers at Gillian and said, "How do you do, miss? Call me Ishmael."

"Hellow, Ishmael," Gillian said, smiling.

"My name is really Charlie," the drunk said.

"Hello, Charlie."

Charlie waggled his fingers at her again, and winked. "Don't mind me," he said. He turned his attention to David. He stared at him for a long time. Then he said, "Mister, your hair is grey."

"Thank you, I know," David answered.

"Thank you," Charlie said. "It'll be all white in a few years."

"I suppose so," David said, smiling. He turned to Gillian. "Does it make me look very old?" he asked.

"Well, I don't know how old you *are*," Gillian said.

"Twenty-three."

"No, you look only slightly older than that."

"You look fifty-six," Charlie said. "How'd it get grey, anyway?"

"In the Navy," David said.

"Yeah?" Charlie got up from where he was sitting opposite them, staggered across the centre aisle, and plunked himself down alongside Gillian. Leaning across her, he said to David, "I was in the Navy, too." He studied David for a moment and then said, "He don't look like a sailor, does he, miss?"

"Not at all, Charlie," Gillian said.

"No? Then what does he look like, if not a sailor?"

"He looks very sweet-oh," Gillian answered.

"That's all right," Charlie said. "Don't mind me."

"Were you in prison for a very long time?" Gillian asked David.

"Four years."

"That must have been awful for you. Let's not even talk about it."

"Listen, don't mind me," Charlie said. "You just talk, you hear? Don't mind me," He nodded emphatically. "You married?"

"No," Gillian said.

"Congratulations," Charlie answered. "You have any children?"

"Three," David said.

"Boys or girls?"

"A little of each," Gillian said.

"Best way," Charlie agreed. "Where you going now?"

"Uptown."

"That's a lucky thing," Charlie said, "because this happens to be a cross-town bus, in case you wanted to know. Listen, don't mind me. Go ahead and talk. I'll just listen, okay? Go right ahead, I don't mind your interrupting."

Gillian laughed and said, "How do you happen to know Tad Parker, David?"

"He's from my home town."

"You're not from New York?"

"Nope. Talmadge, Connecticut."

"Are you serious?" she said.

"Sure, he's serious," Charlie said. "Don't you know your own husband?"

"Do you know Talmadge?" David asked.

"Never heard of it," Charlie said.

'I was asking the lady."

"Oh. Apologies accepted," Charlie said, and he nodded.

"I went to school in Talmadge," Gillian said.

"When? Did you really?"

"Sure. Let me see. 1942? Yes. '42 and '43."

"I was in the Pacific then," David said.

"Guess who discovered the Pacific Ocean," Charlie said. "Who, huh? Can you tell me?"

"Henry Hudson," David said, and Gillian suddenly took his hand.

"Nope."

"Christopher Columbus?" she asked.

"Hah-hah, smart young kids don't even know who discovered the Pacific Ocean. Ferdinand Magellan, that's who. Fer-di-nand Ma-gell-an. An explorer. You bet your life."

"Thank you," David said.

"Don't mind me," Charlie answered.

"Why'd you leave Talmadge?" David asked.

"Excuse me," Charlie said. "I beg your pardon."

"That's all right," David said.

"No, that's all right," Charlie said, "you're excused," and Gillian squeezed David's hand.

"Talmadge was only make-believe," she said. "I much prefer Igor's class. Are you going to school?"

"Yes. N.Y.U."

"Did you say something?" Charlie asked.

"No."

"Excuse me. I thought you said something."

"No, I'm sure I didn't," David said.

"Oh, then excuse me."

"Does that mean you're living in New York?" Gillian asked.

"Yes. On Houston Street."

"Oh, that's a wonderful neighbourhood. I go there to watch Maurice Schwartz. I learn an awful lot from him. Why did you say you were Jewish, David? In the loft."

"I don't know. I read some place that Ernest Hemingway always signs his name as Ernest Ginsberg or Levine or something like that when he registers at an hotel. Because he doesn't want to stay any-place that's restri——"

"That sounds like a Press agent's plant."

"May be it is. I read it in one of the columns. Anyway, I guess I was testing you."

"Why?"

"Because . . . well . . . do you want the truth?"

"Yes. Please.'

"I . . . I was a little afraid of the way I felt when I . . . when I saw you. Then you asked me if I was Jewish, and I figured if I said I was, and it made a difference, then, well, then I'd have had an excuse for ending it right there."

Gillian smiled. "I'm glad it didn't end right there."

"I am, too."

"And I'm glad you said you were Jewish."

"No, I'm Scotch," Charlie said. "Thank you."

"You're welcome, Charlie," Gillian said. "Why didn't you go to school in Talmadge?"

Charlie shrugged. "I went to P.S. 80," he said.

"I was talking to the gentleman," Gillian said, smiling.

"Oh, that's all right, you're excused," Charlie said.

"I wanted to get away from Talmadge," David said. "I wanted to be on my own for a while."

"Did your parents object?"

"Only my mother's living."

"Oh, I'm sorry."

"Well, my father died a long time ago."

"Both my parents are still alive," Gillian said. She turned and peered through the window of the car. "We'll be passing where I used to live soon." She turned back to David. "Do you like N.Y.U.?"

"I did at first. To tell the truth, I'm not sure any more. Everyone else seems to know where he's going, and I guess I don't. Most of the guys are veterans, you know, and . . ."

"Like the lost generation," she said, and nodded.

"Well, not exactly. Didn't you always feel they were a little dramatic about their rehabilitation problems?"

"Oh, I think they were very sweet-oh," Gillian said. "Sitting in their Paris cafés and talking about shooting trips to the Black Forest and the novels they were going to write. That's very sweet and very sad."

"Maybe I ought to leave school and find a Paris café," David said. "Become a sort of a bum."

"No," Gillian said.

"Does that scare you?"

"No, but . . . well, I don't think you should be a bum."

"Why not?"

"There are too many things to do. No one has the right to be a bum."

"That's it," Charlie said. "She hit the nail on the head. Eat, drink, and be merry." He turned to look at the station platform as the train pulled in. "Where are we, anyway?"

"Burnside Avenue," Gillian said.

"That's good," Charlie said, "because I haven't the faintest idea where Burnside Avenue is."

David looked at his watch. "We're going to be late," he said.

"I don't mind," Gillian said. "We don't have to go at all, you know. Wouldn't you rather talk?"

"Well, yes, but . . ."

"Why don't we get off at Fordham Road and walk around a little, and then maybe stop for a drink later? I'd like that."

"You would?"

"Yes, David. I really would."

"Well then . . ." He dug into his coat and pulled out the theatre tickets. He handed them across Gillian's lap to Charlie.

"Thank you, sir," Charlie said with dignity, "but I am not a panhandler."

"These are tickets to a show," David said. "We'd like you to have them."

"Thank you, sir, don't mind me."

"Will you accept them as a gift?"

"Thank you," Charlie said, taking the tickets. "What are they?"

"Tickets to a show."

"Oh. Very well then. Thank you. Where am I?"

"You get off at Kingsbridge Road, and walk to Hunter College."

"Thank you. Are we in Brooklyn?"

"No. We're in the Bronx."

"Thank God for that," Charlie said. "If we were in the Bronx, I'd lose myself completely. Do you know who discovered the Bronx?"

"Who?"

"That's right," Charlie said. "Sir, you are a gentleman. Thank you, don't mind me," he said, and he rolled over on to the seat and fell asleep immediately.

"I like you," Gillian said suddenly, and David did not understand why she chose to say it at that precise moment.

They got off at Fordham Road and walked east towards the Grand Concourse. He bought her a charlotte russe and then later a jellied apple, and they walked to Poe Park, and Gillian pointed out the Poe cottage to him, and then they sat in the darkness on one of the benches and he recited two stanzas of "The Raven", which he had learned by heart in high school. They began talking about poems they both liked, and he told her about a teacher he'd had in elementary school who'd made him memorize "The Charge of the Light Brigade", and how terrified he'd been when it came time for him to recite because she was a monstrous-looking woman who was a little cross-eyed and who was deaf in one ear, so that you had to shout lines you weren't too sure of, anyway. Gillian told him about a teacher she'd had who'd rubbed her nose across the blackboard while trying to explain a problem in algebra. "You multiply *this* by *this*," she'd said, her hand clutched in Gillian's hair, rubbing her nose across the board from one algebraic symbol to the next. They began talking about games they used to play as children, Johnny-on-a-Pony, and Ring-a-Leavio, and I-Declare-War. "And Rattlesnake, did you ever play Rattlesnake?" Gillian asked.

"No, how does it go?"

"Oh, everyone winds in and out, and gets all twisted up, and you chant, don't you know it? R-A-T, T-L-E, S-N-A-K-E spells Rattlesnake! You never played it?"

"No, not in Talmadge. How about Statues? Did you play that?"

"Oh, yes," Gillian said delightedly. "Where you swung the other person out and he had to strike a pose? Yes, I loved that game!"

"And Flinch? No, I suppose that was a boy's game."

"Do you remember 'Oh, I won't go to Macy's any more, more, more, there's a big fat policeman at the door, door, door'?"

"That's strictly New York, I think."

"Did the girls in your town say 'One-two-three a-learie' or did they say 'One-two-three a-nation'?"

"'I received my confirmation,'" David said.

"'On the day of declaration, one-two-three a-nation!' Right! How about choosing sides? How did you do that?"

"'Ink-a-bink, a bottle of ink, the cork fell out, and you *stink*!'"

"Yes!" Gillian said, squeezing his hand. "And what was the one the boys all did? Something about wine? When they were challenging someone to a fight."

"Oh, wait, yes . . . wait a minute." He thought briefly and then rapidly blurted, "'Three-six-nine, a bottle of wine——'"

"'I can lick you any old time!'" Gillian completed triumphantly, and they burst out laughing.

It was midnight before they knew it. They walked across the street to the tavern and asked the bartender if he knew how to make hot rum toddies, and he said, "Lady, this ain't England." They settled for whisky sours. When they reached Gillian's apartment again, it was two o'clock in the morning. She leaned against the door sleepily and said, "David, I had a *marr*-vellous time."

"We didn't do very much," he said apologetically.

"Oh, but we did a lot."

"Can I see you tomorrow, Gillian?"

"Yes."

"It's Sunday. We could spend the whole day together. If you want to, that is."

"Yes, I want to."

"Good. I was afraid . . ."

"Yes?"

"I was afraid you might not want to," he said, and shrugged. The hallway was very silent.

"I'd like to hold you, Gillian."

"Yes. Hold me."

"I'd like to kiss you."

"Kiss me."

He held her in his arms gently for a moment, and then touched her hair. He lowered his mouth and kissed her. She held him tight for a moment, and then moved her head to his shoulder and whispered, "I like the way you kiss."

His hands cradling her face, he pushed her hair away from her ears, capturing it at the back of her head.

"No, please," she said. "Don't do that. I can't stand it."

He released her hair.

"But . . . kiss me again?"

He kissed her, and she tightened her arms around his neck and then released him suddenly and said, "David, I think . . ." She shook her head. She turned away from him, opened her bag, and looked for her key. She unlocked the door and threw it open. She was turning towards him again when his arms encircled her waist. Standing behind her, he kissed her throat, and she turned in his arms and breathlessly found his mouth, and they moved into the dark apartment silently, caught in the dim illumination from the light in the hall. He closed the door with one hand. They clung to each other in the soft dark. She lifted her mouth to his and whispered against his lips, "I've wanted you to kiss me all night long."

"Yes, I wanted to kiss you."

"We're telling too much," she said.

"We're not telling half enough."

"Oh, yes, I *want* to tell you. I've never felt like this before."

"Neither have I."

"I'm frightened. I don't think we should start anything."

"Why not?"

"I don't know. I don't know. Oh, David, kiss me."

His lips found hers in the darkness, parted, he held her close, she whispered, "I don't believe in things like this, do you?"

"I believe in whatever happens."

He could hear a clock ticking somewhere in the apartment. Her voice came into the darkness and the silence, a whispered voice, uncertain.

"David . . . David, do you want to make love to me?"

"Yes."

"I never have," she said. She paused. "Do you believe me?"

"Yes. Of course, I believe you."

"I'm trembling, do you know that? Can you feel me trembling?"

"I can feel you."

"David, don't do this unless . . ."

"Unless what?"

"I'm not a casual person, David. Please . . . unless . . ."

"I loved you the minute I looked at you," he said.

"Oh David, oh David, do I ask for the wrong things? Do I frighten you?"

"No. You ask for the right things. All the right things, Gillian."

"Come with me," she said. "Hurry, come with me." She took his hand and led him down the hallway. Outside the door of her bedroom, she said, "Say it again, David."

"I love you."

"Oh, yes. Oh, you say it. Does it sound strange?"

"No."

"Have you ever loved anyone before?"

"I think so."

"Who? What was her name?"

"Ardis."

"Did you go to bed with her?"

"Yes."

There was moonlight in the room, streaming through the single window. They took off their coats, and he sat beside her on the bed, and they stared at each other very seriously, and suddenly she smiled, and he smiled back at her and said, "I can see your eyes in the dark," and she said, "Touch my breast. Yes. Oh, I want to cry."

"No, darling."

"You're so wonderful. You were so sweet to that drunken man on the train. Charlie. You were so sweet. You excite me tremendously. Should I tell you these things?"

"Yes, everything."

"Hold me. You feel so hard. May I touch you?"

"Yes."

"You make me dizzy."

They leaned back against the pillows, and he kissed her again and then unbuttoned her blouse and said, "Your breasts . . ." and then stopped.

"No, please say everything. Never stop, David."

"You're beautiful, Gillian. You're so beautiful."

"Yes, yes, for you. I'm glad. For you. David, I'm very excited. Are you excited?"

He kissed her again, and she pulled her lips from his and said, "Should I feel embarrassed?"

"No, why should you?"

"I thought I would feel embarrassed. I don't feel that way at all."

"Good."

"Shall I take off my clothes?"

"Yes."

"I mean, is that what . . . I mean, does the girl or . . .?"

"Yes, take them off," he said.

"I act as if there are rules." She took off her blouse, but her hand hesitated on the button of her skirt. She looked at him and said, "David, I don't wear panties." She paused. "I feel embarrassed now. I . . . I suddenly do."

He reached out and she extended her hand, and he pulled her gently to the bed beside him. He unbuttoned the skirt and lowered the zipper and his hand touched her belly beneath the skirt and then moved under the garter belt, flat against her skin and she said, "I know I'm going to die when you touch me. I just . . ." and fell suddenly silent with a soft shocked intake of breath. She closed her eyes and said, "Please," wanting to say more, wanting to ask him to be kind and gentle and not to hurt her and to please make this what it should be for her because this was the first time, but she only said, "Please," and David, understanding all in that single word, answered, "Yes, Gillian."

"I'm afraid I won't be good."

"You'll be lovely."

"I want to be good for you. I want to please you."

"You do please me."

"Take off your clothes. I want to touch you again."

He stood beside the bed and took off his clothes without embarrassment. She watched him, intensely curious, studying his body with wonder.

"It's brass," he said suddenly, and then quickly added, "The bed, I mean."

She thought that was the funniest thing she had ever heard in her life, and she began laughing suddenly, and suddenly he was beside her again, the long length of his body against her, and he kissed the laugh from her mouth, and she felt her brassière loosening, her breasts falling free, his hands suddenly claiming her.

"How do I feel? Tell me how I feel to you."

"Soft. Wonderful."

"When . . . when will you . . .?"

"When you want me to."

"Would you tell me when?" she said. "Because I . . ."
"You're beautiful."
"Am I beautiful?"
"You're lovely."
"My hair is all messed."
"Your hair is lovely."

"David, will . . ." she started, and felt him suddenly inside her, suddenly and without warning inside her, filling her, immense inside her, she wanted to move against him, stretch, enfold, she wrapped her arms around his neck and said "Oh!" in surprise, and then "Oh!" again, and then she bit his ear and pulled back her face and stared directly into his eyes and then thought, How comical we must look, and then forgot entirely how comical they must look because her body was suddenly not her own, her body was suddenly trembling in uncontrollable spasm after spasm after spasm, "Oh!" she said, "it's . . . it's . . . oh!" and she kissed his mouth and pulled her head away again and said, "Do it, do it," her voice rising, "do it, love me, I love it, I love you, do it, *do it!*" and he plunged deeper inside her until she felt nothing but a rolling succession of waves, dizzy on the crest of each wave, falling uncontrollably into troughs of giddy faintness, and then the lurching shock of his release shuddered inside her, and she pulled him closer as a greater spasm echoed through her, pulled him deeper, close to him, close. She stroked his hair as he lay limp against her. She kissed his cheek and his nose and his forehead. She smiled in the darkness, and in a little while, she asked "Was it good?"

"Yes. Was it good for you?"
"It was *marr*-vellous."
"I love you," he said.
"Oh, and *I* love you. Oh, and I *love* what we did. It didn't hurt at all, do you know that? Now you won't believe me. Is there blood? Will there be blood?"
"Gillian, I'll believe whatever you tell me as long as I live."
"I feel I've known you always, since I learned to walk. It's the oddest thing! I feel as if I'm part of you. I feel *wonderful*! Do you love me?"
"I love you, I love you, I love you."
"Will I have a baby?"
"No."
"Did you . . . yes, you did. I didn't even notice. You're very good. And very practised. I hate that other girl." She paused. "I hate that officer who sent you to prison. How could you stand it in prison, David? Didn't you want to explode?" She laughed suddenly. "Oh, my, but you *did* explode, didn't you?"

"I like that."

"What do you like, darling?"

"Your laugh. It's a good dirty laugh."

"Dirty?"

"Yes. Whores laugh that way."

"Oh, what a nice thing to say!"

"I mean, I think they must. You have a beauty spot."

"I have a lot of them."

"I mean, right there." He touched it with his forefinger.

"I tremble every time you touch me. Should I feel this way so soon? I must be terribly wicked. I want to touch you again. Are you going to marry me?"

"Yes."

"When?"

"When would you like to get married?"

"Now. Tonight."

"No, not tonight. I don't want to leave this apartment tonight."

"Neither do I." She laughed suddenly and said, "My father should only see me now!"

"He wouldn't approve?"

"He'd shoot you on the spot."

"Maybe I ought to leave. I wouldn't want to get shot."

"I'd protect you. I'd throw myself across you."

"That would only complicate matters. Look at what you're doing."

"Oh! Oh, look at that!"

"Yes."

"That's amazing! Isn't it amazing?"

"No, I think it's normal."

"Am I very exciting?"

"You are very very exciting."

"I want to excite you. I want you to desire me every minute of the day."

"That could get exhausting."

"I suppose so, but it's what I want anyway. Should I stop? I mean, you're not going to . . . ?"

"No." He smiled.

"Because I can stop, you know. No, I can't, isn't that disgusting I can't keep my hands away from you." She paused. "Do you lik that?"

"Yes."

"May I kiss you?" she asked.

"Yes."

"I meant . . ."

"I know what you meant."

"Do I shock you?"

"No."

"I just want . . . I want to do everything with you. If I shock you, you must stop me."

"How can you shock me? You're Gillian."

"Yes, I am. Isn't that nice?" She paused. "Your belly is good and flat. There." She kissed his stomach and then said, "What should I do?"

"Whatever you want to."

"Tell me," she said seriously. "Tell me how best to please you. Before we part, tell me how I . . ."

"Part?"

"What a silly thing to say," she said, and suddenly threw herself into his arms and hugged him fiercely. "We have a lifetime," she said. "We have a lifetime."

The city was new.

The late-December snow had heaped tons of whiteness upon her streets, turned her into a tundra wonderland devoid of traffic. There was a hush accompanying her rebirth, the silent tread of rubber-shod soles cushioned on snow, the lazy soundless swirl of snowflakes against amber lights, the secret hiss of radiators behind windows rimmed with frost. New and clear with biting cold that tantalized the cheeks and stung the teeth. New and fresh with voices echoing on nearly deserted streets and children sliding down new white mountains. The snow fell still. It melted when it touched your cheeks. It hung incredibly beautiful on the tweed of your sleeve, clung for just a moment, melted, vanished and magically reappeared an inch away, a new star on blue wool fading.

David walked through the snow pulling the child's sled behind him, breathing deeply of the icy air. He had borrowed the sled from his landlady's son, promising him he would return it in excellent condition, telling him it was very important that he have a sled to commemorate this very important day when God had managed to clean the city as no mayor ever had, and finally settling the debate with a well-placed quarter in a small cold fist. The snow whirled about him as he walked, clinging to his eyelashes, tracing wet trails down the back of his neck under his collar. He stopped every now and then to cover his ears with his mittened hands, and then plunged through the knee-deep snow again, anxious to reach Gillian's place before the afternoon was gone entirely. He left the sled in the hallway of her building, and then clomped upstairs in his galoshes. Gillian opened the door at his first knock.

"My God, what happened?" she said. "I've been calling and calling . . ."

"Nothing's moving," he said breathlessly. "No buses, no cabs. I walked."

"From First Avenue?"

David nodded. "Gillian, you've never seen anything like this. The city is——"

"I was ready to call the police. You said you were leaving two hours ago."

"I did. Everything's white, Gillian. The streets, the buildings, the sky, even the telephone wires . . ."

"Come hold me."

He scooped her into his arms and held her tight, her face warm against his frozen cheek.

"Hi," she said.

"Hi."

"Brrr. You make me cold."

"Put on your coat. We're going downstairs."

"Oh, like hell we are," Gillian said.

"I've got a sled."

"Where'd you get a sled?"

"I bribed my landlady's son."

"You brought it all the way from——?"

"Yes, come on. Get your coat."

"Oh no! I'm going to put on my bathrobe and huddle by the radiator."

"Get your coat, Gillian! If I can lug a sled all the——"

"All right, all right, don't get excited," she answered. She pulled him into the apartment and closed the door. "Here, stand by the heat. Take off your mittens. Your coat is all wet. Warm your hands. Shall I make some coffee?"

"No. Get your coat."

"Some hot chocolate? It'll only take——"

"Gillian, it'll be dark soon!"

"Oh, all right!" She nodded her head once, emphatically, and went down the corridor to her bedroom. Smiling, David pulled off his mittens and held his hands out to the hissing radiator. Outside the living-room window, he could see the swirl of snowflakes, large and wet. He heard Gillian coming down the corridor again and turned towards her. She had bundled herself into a fleece-lined ski parka, the hood pulled up over her head. She grinned and leaned against the corridor wall, one hand on her hip.

"You like nice Eskimo girl?" she asked.

"You ready?" he said, laughing.

"Nice Eskimo girl smell of walrus fat, you like?"
"Come on, let's go downstairs before it gets dark."
"You no like Eskimo girl kiss with nose?"
"You'd better put a scarf around your throat."
"Very cheap. You like?"
"Go get a scarf."
Gillian wiggled her eyebrows. "Ten sealskins all night. Very cheap." In a whisper, she added, "Arctic night very long."
David hugged her and said, "Who's your agent?"
"Marian Lewis."
"Thank you very much. But . . ."
"Don't call us, we'll call you," they said together, and laughed.
She took his arm and said, "Where'd you park your sled?"
"Downstairs in the hall."
"I don't know why I let you talk me into these things."
"Where's your scarf?"
"I don't need one."
"It's cold out there."
"Eskimo girl very hardy," Gillian said, and they went out of the apartment. The street was silent with flying snow. The sky was grey. The world was hushed.

"David, we're alone in the universe," she whispered. "Just you and I."

She took his hand.

Like children, they discovered snow.

February, and St. Valentine's Day. He sent her fourteen cards, the first arriving on February first, each card a little bigger than the one preceding it until the last gigantic card arrived on the fourteenth. She tacked them all to the white wall just inside her doorway, and above the fourteen cards, in red paint, she lettered the words DAVID LOVES ME!

When he picked her up that night, he said, "You ruined your wall."
"You ruined my life," she said.
"How did I do that?"
"I can't think straight any more."
"Why did you use red paint?"
"Because red paint shouts. If I had a tall ladder, I would paint it across the front of the building."
"Why don't you rent a billboard in Times Square?"
"Or put up three-sheets on station platforms from New York to Washington. 'David Loves Me.' I think I'll do it."
"He does love you."
"How much?"

"The world."

"Enough to take me to dinner?"

"Well, now, I don't know," David said dubiously.

"Can I bribe you?"

"How?"

"I bought you a present. For St. Valentine's Day." She turned abruptly and went into the bedroom. He could hear her opening the dresser drawer. When she returned, she was carrying a small box in her hand. She held it out to him.

"What is it?"

"Open it."

He took the box. Holding it on the palm of one hand, he began unfastening the ribbon.

"This makes me nervous," he said.

"Why?"

"I don't know why. Yes, I do. I don't need presents from you, Gillian. You're the biggest present I ever got in my life."

"That's very sweet, David," she said softly, suddenly shy.

"I love you," he said.

He lifted the lid. A tiny tie tack rested on the cotton batting. Its rim was gold, encircling a miniature Italian mosaic wrought in delicate slivers of marble, capturing the image of a fly or a beetle or some fantastic insect with wings of red and gold and eyes of bright green, crawling on a background field of blue, skilfully and meticulously put together piece by piece. He looked at the pin and then took Gillian into his arms.

"Do you like it?" she asked.

"I love it."

"It's a tie tack."

"I know."

"It was made in Italy."

"I know."

"You know everything, don't you? Such a smart-oh." She paused. "I picked a bug because I'm crazy about you, and being crazy is being bugs. Did you know that, too?"

"What kind of a bug is it?" he asked, looking at the pin again.

"Why, I think it's the Green Hornet," Gillian said in surprise.

"Seriously."

"Seriously, darling," she said softly, "it's a love bug."

The touch of her, the wonderful touch of her, to be touched by her, to touch her in return. The hard line of her jaw beneath his exploring fingers, the high firm cheek-bones and the sudden surprising gentleness of her mouth in the darkness in a face of planes exquisite to his finger-tips, the taut skin on her neck swiftly curving to the hollow of her throat, he could feel the pulse beneath her skin, beating, her shoulder-bones seemed glistening to the touch, bone-white like polished ivory, slight in his hands. Her breasts and softness there, wide and full, deep to his touch, the satin suddenly erupting in a coarse circle of sex skin, the hard flat buttons of her nipples, and the gentle undercurve where her bosom sloped back towards her body, gliding, the smooth flawless skin of her abdomen, and the yielding flesh of her thighs, the deeper moistness, the ultimate softness, fold upon fold of warmth, the touch of her, the wonderful touch of her.

Gillian was a crowd. She wore a million faces, she was a million people, and he loved them all, and waited for their appearances, like a man familiar with a repertory company. Gillian the lady, impeccably dressed in a tailored suit, with her hair sleekly brushed, her lipstick immaculate, her lashes blackened with mascara, her seams arrow-straight, her high heels chattering in eternal femininity. Gillian the girl child, her green eyes wide in a questioning face, her lips slightly parted as she listened in awe, her body twisted into the ludicrously relaxed postures of the very young, believing in witches and magic and fairy godmothers and princes on white horses. Gillian the flirt, whose eyes flashed at men, who appreciated the wolf whistles that accompanied her provocative sway, who unashamedly used her most seductive voice when setting up an appointment on the telephone, who infuriated him once by starting a conversation with a teen-ager in a black leather jacket in the lobby of Loew's Sheridan. Gillian the madwoman, who kissed him without warning wherever they happened to be, on a bus, in a restaurant, in a pew at St. Patrick's Cathedral where they had gone to escape the bitter cold, who would suddenly seize his hand and run with him down Broadway, who once in a cigar store on Fifty-seventh Street walked up to the counter, put her hand into her purse, and said to the owner, "Don't move a muscle. This is a stick-up!" Gillian the actress, who talked passionately of Stanislavsky and The Method, who left the performance of a play deeply brooding about technique and staging, who tried voice variations and mannerisms on David, who suddenly bent over into the stooped posture of an old woman and hobbled towards him on an imaginary crutch, whose hands moved emotionally when she tried to explain a point of theory. Gillian the uninhibited, who sometimes entered her bed with the rapacious appetite of a nymphomaniac, who experimented with every female wile, who tried on sex the way she would try on spring hats. Gillian the tender mistress, who made love gently and shyly, who brought to the act of love a glowing wonder that was almost religious. Gillian the businesswoman, who totalled her accounts like a book-keeper, who kept her appointment book with stop-watch precision. Gillian the cook, Gillian the waif, Gillian the tyrant, Gillian the vulnerable, Gillian laughing, weeping, sleeping with the sheet curled below the curve of her breast, her red-brown hair spread over the pillow, an innocent smile on her mouth, Gillian the woman.

They could hear the February wind rattling the window on the other side of the room. The brass headboard behind them was cold to the touch. When they spoke, white clouds of vapour trailed from their lips. They had been in a giddy mood all night long, like tipsy partners in a comic vaudeville routine, and now they made love in the same way, feeling silly and passionless, laughing at themselves and each other, totally absorbed in a love that transcended the simplicity of love-making, not caring a jot about their clumsiness, mating haphazardly, an act that was necessary to their mood, silly and inept, but as binding as mortar.

"I'm freeeeeeezing," she said.

"I'll bang on the radiator."

"You'll wake the whole house," she said, and suddenly began singing.

"Talk about waking the whole house."

"I feel melodic." She giggled and began singing again.

"At least sing something appropriate."

There was a silence in the room. A fresh wind lashed the window, and the pane shuddered with its force. Gillian took a deep breath and sang,

"I've got you . . .
       Un-der
             my skin . . ."

David burst out laughing.

"Keep your mind on your work," she said. "Make me warm."

"You sing beautifully."

"I have the feeling you'll be at this all night," she said, and giggled into his shoulder. "I'm not at all excited, are you?"

"No."

"But don't let's stop."

"No."

"Shall I sing again?"

"Yes. What we're lacking is mood music."

"Mood music, that's right. That's what we need," she said, and they both laughed. "Come on, be serious," she said.

"All right, I'm serious," he said, and they began laughing again.

"Now stop laughing," she said. "You'll make me feel unattractive."

"I'm sorry, you're very attractive." He paused. "What did you say your name was again?"

Gillian giggled uncontrollably and bit him on the shoulder. "I'm going to sing," she said.

"All right, sing."

"What shall I sing?"

"Anything you like. You sing, and I'll bang the radiator."

"Never mind banging the radiator," she said, and they burst into explosive laughter.

Giggling, they loved away the night, surprised when dawn timidly touched the frost-rimmed window.

She was wearing a bright-red bulky sweater, and she set his apartment on fire, curled up in the single comfortable chair in the room, talking while he stood at the sink mixing drinks.

"But how are you supposed to get to the heart of a character, David? Don't you see? It's not enough to give a simply surface portrait."

"I don't know how. I'd personally like to see a play sometime where a character walks on stage and says, 'My name is John Doe, I'm twenty-eight years old, I got to S.M.U., and that's all you have to know about me. The rest will happen during the course of the play, so please pay attention.'"

"That's not enough. People don't live only in the present. They've got pasts, David, and everything that's ever happened to them is a part of what's happening to them now. I can't read a line in a script and take it as a self-contained statement. I have to know *why* the character is getting angry at this particular time, what it is that was said or done to him to trigger the anger. And when I know that, I have to look deeper because nothing, David, nothing is born today."

"I think you're making a big hullabaloo about what is essentially a second-rate art."

"Oh, now, just wait a minute," Gillian said, swinging her legs to the floor.

"I read something about a famous actress," David said. "I forget who, Helen Hayes or Katharine Cornell, one of the really big ones, who had this final scene where only her hand was showing on stage, and the motion of that hand alone was enough to put the audience in tears. And when someone asked her what the rest of her body was doing offstage while the hand was provoking such misery, she said she chatted with the stagehands all through the scene."

"That doesn't prove——"

"It proves there was no emotion involved in the *illusion* of emotion. She could have been playing checkers offstage while her hand pulled tears from the audience."

"Well, I can't work that way. I've got to *know*. I've got to understand the character, know everything about her."

"That's impossible. Nobody knows everything about anybody."

"We're not dealing with real people, David. We're dealing with characters."

"That's right! And they're only representations of people. You're creating an illusion. The illusion can never be really complete. If it were, well . . . well, Gillian, why not *really* shoot a person on stage when the script calls for someone to be shot?"

"David, that's silly. If you're——"

"It isn't. Have you ever been shot?"

"Never. What's that——?"

"Then how can you know what it feels like to be shot?"

"I don't. But I know what pain is, and if I know my character well, I can tell you how she would react to pain. I can really *be* in pain when that bullet supposedly hits me."

"And why do you consider that acting? If you really *are* in pain, then you're not portraying pain. And if your play runs for two years, you're going to be a wreck by the time it's over."

"Amen," Gillian said.

"What?"

"That a play I'm in should run for two years."

"Do you want an olive in this, or an onion?" he asked.

"Onions. Lots of them. Six."

"Not five?"

"Oh, all right, five," she said. She grinned. "You sure are hard to get along with."

He dropped the onions into her glass, put an olive into his own, and carried the drinks to where she was sitting.

"What shall we drink to, Gilly?" he asked.

"To you and me," she said. "To us."

"Is that all?"

"And to for ever," she said softly.

He loved the way she walked into a restaurant. She became a curious combination of gourmet and hungry waif the instant she stepped through the door. Her eyes took on a new sparkle, an instant smile appeared on her mouth, she seemed to sniff savoury delights in every breath she took. At the same time, her shoulders pulled back, her head came erect, she walked with the stately dignity of a princess, glancing around the room with imperial disdain while her appetite showed contradictorily all over her face. Even now, wearing slacks and an old trench coat, her face wet with April rain, here in a sleazy Chinese restaurant on Eighth Avenue, she brought an air of excitement into the place, the promise of a fantastic feast in glittering company.

"It smells good," she said to David.

"I'm hungry, are you?"

"I'm only about to perish," she said.

The waiter came over to them and led them to a table. He handed them menus and asked, "You want drink!"

"Gilly?"

"No."

"No, thank you," David said, and the waiter stared at them and then walked off.

"Did you ever notice that all Chinese waiters seem abrupt and surly?" Gillian said. "They really aren't, you know. It's just the way they speak, clipping off the words, delivering them sort of deadpan, so that everything they say sounds like an order for an execution."

"I never noticed," David said.

"Yes. You listen when he comes back. *If* he comes back. He doesn't like the idea of our not drinking. And he thinks we're crazy to be out in this weather."

"He's out in it, too, isn't he?"

"No, he's in the restaurant."

"So are we."

"You know what I mean."

"Besides, the weather is fine compared to what we had in December."

"I loved December," she said.

"I read in the *Times* that it'll be listed in the official records as the blizzard of '47. How about that?"

"How about that?" Gillian said. "We can tell our children. It makes me feel like a pioneer. Now where did he disappear to? If I don't get something to eat soon, I'll begin throwing dishes."

"Didn't you have lunch?"

"No."

"Why not? Damn you, Gilly——"

"Don't damn me, David Regan! I had a reading."

"What's that got to do with having lunch?"

"I got up at ten, and I went down for the mail and found my copy of *Theatre Arts* and before I knew it, it was twelve o'clock. So I had some juice and coffee, dressed, and went uptown. And the reading wasn't over until three, and then I had to rush right over to the store. So that's why I didn't have lunch."

"Did you get the part?"

"No. They were looking for a blonde."

"Can't you bleach your hair?"

"Why should I?" She frowned. "Don't you like my hair?"

"I love it. I thought if it meant getting a part . . ."

"No one suggested it. Besides, I like my hair the way it is. David, I'm getting very irritable. We'd better order quick." She picked up the menu and said, "They have those wonderful butterfly shrimp here. Would you like to try them? The ones wrapped in bacon."

"Good," David said, "and some char-shu-din, all right?"

"No spareribs?"

"Sure, spareribs, too."

"That's two pork dishes."

"Where does it say we can't have two pork dishes?"

"David, we can have *three* if you like."

"All right."

"I'm sorry. I'm starving. Let's just order, all right?" She looked at the menu again. "How about the chicken in parchment?"

"Fine."

"And some soup. They've got fried-won-ton soup. Shall we try it?"

"Fine."

"Okay, fried-won-ton soup, no egg rolls, all right? We don't want to stuff ourselves. And some barbecued ribs, and the butterfly shrimp, and the chicken in parchment. There! That sounds good, doesn't it?"

"You left out the char-shu-din."

"David . . ."

"What?"

"I hate char-shu-din."

"I like it," he said.

She looked at him solemnly for a moment. "Are we having an argument?" she asked.

"No. I don't think so."

"I feel very bitchy." She paused. "Please get the waiter. I'm so hungry, I feel faint. Get the waiter, please."

He called the waiter. Gillian rested her head against the back of the booth.

"You ready to order!" the waiter said sharply.

"Yes," David said. "We want the fried-won-ton soup and——"

"Are the won-tons good and crisp?" Gillian asked weakly.

"Yes, ver' crisp!" the waiter shouted.

"Good."

"And a small order of spareribs," David said. "And the . . . uh . . ."

"Butterfly shrimp," Gillian supplied.

"Yes, and . . ."

"And the chicken in parchment." Gillian leaned forward, smiled, and said, "*And* the damn char-shu-din."

David smiled back at her. "Waiter," he said, "would you please bring some tea and noodles right away? The lady is very hungry."

"You want fried rice!" the waiter shouted.

"Gillian?"

"Yes, all right."

The waiter left the table and returned almost immediately with a pot of hot tea and a bowl of noodles. The tea brought the colour back to Gillian's face instantly. She drank two cups of it, and then sat munching contentedly on the noodles.

"Oh my," she said, "that's much better. Forgive me, David." David was frowning. She caught his expression, and then looked at him quizzically. "What?" she asked.

"Nothing."

"I'll bet I know exactly what you're thinking."

"What am I thinking?"

"You're leaping to the male conclusion."

"And what's that?"

"I was irritable and bitchy and I felt a little faint. I'm sure those must seem like classic signs to you."

"Signs of what, Gilly?"

"Pregnancy."

He shook his head. "I wasn't thinking of that at all."

"You were." She paused. "Would the idea frighten you?"

"No."

"Would it make you angry?"

"No."

"But you wouldn't love me as much if I were fat and bloated, would you?"

"I'd love you no matter how you were."

"Then you wouldn't mind if I were pregnant?"

"No. I wouldn't mind."

"I'm not," Gillian said.

David nodded.

"That's relieving, isn't it?"

"I told you I wasn't thinking that," David answered.

"Then what were you thinking?"

"About char-shu-din. I like char-shu-din."

"Well, we ordered it, didn't we?"

"Yes."

The table went silent.

"David?"

"What?"

"I went to the doctor yesterday."

"Why?"

"To be fitted for a diaphragm." She paused. "I thought . . ." She shrugged. "This tea is very good," she said. "Did you notice about the waiter? The way everything sounds like a command?"

"Yes. Yes, I did."

"What is it, David?"

"I want to leave school," he said. "I want to get a job."

"Well, what's so terrible about that?"

"Why didn't you order a drink?"

"What?" she said, surprised. "I didn't want one, that's why."

"That's not true. You didn't order it because you knew if we both had drinks it would have added a buck and half to the cheque, and you were worried about whether or not I could afford it."

"That's an absolutely paranoid statement, David. And besides, it wouldn't have been anywhere near a dollar and a half."

"A buck twenty, at least."

"You know, we could have stayed home, for that matter. I have food in the house."

"Well, I have to get a job."

"All right, so get one."

"I'm tired of this college-boy allowance. And I'm not learning anything. I'm not interested any more. I have to get a job."

"David, if you want one, go out and get one!" she said sharply, and suddenly realized there was more to this than he was stating, sensed at once that he wasn't truly arguing with her but with something deeper inside himself, and wondered what it was like to be someone without any real goals, her own goals had always seemed so clear to her. Perhaps their relationship changed in that fleeting instant. Perhaps, staring at him across the table while the rain lashed the plate-glass front of the restaurant, she knew that something more was expected of her as a woman, as David's woman. The thought frightened her a little. She felt inexplicably like a stranger to him, felt she was in love with a man she did not know at all. He sat across the table from her in hooded silence, surrounded by a shell she could almost reach out to touch. She was face to face now with the question of whether or not she wished to penetrate that shell, and this was what frightened her. She felt suddenly threatened. If she opened those doors, if she truly explored this man she claimed to love, became for him more than she now was, she had the oddest feeling she would lose her own identity somewhere along the way. She suddenly wanted to run.

The waiter brought their soup and put it down. Gillian picked up her spoon and began chattering nervously.

"You'd be surprised how many places don't serve fried-won-ton soup," she said brightly. "I once had a big argument with a Chinese waiter who told me there was no such thing as fried-won-ton soup, after I'd eaten it at least a dozen times. 'Won-ton soft,' he said. '*Soft*. All light, you fly won-ton, it get hard. You put it in soup, it get soft again. Why bodder fly it in first place? No such thing as fly won-ton!' I almost hit him over the head with the teapot. Oh, this *is* good, isn't it? They *are* crisp."

"Yes," David said.

She watched him and she thought, What do you want from me? What more can I give you than I've already given?

She knew. And when she was tied to the sacrificial stone, and when he drank her life's blood and was nourished by it, and when he found himself somewhere in the maze of her body and her mind and her trust and her faith, what would be left of Gillian Burke? Silently, she weighed her love.

Nervously, she said, "Do you know the Orson Bean routine about the two Chinese who go to an American restaurant?"

"No."

"It's very funny," Gillian said. "You know how he starts his act, don't you?"

"No, I don't."

"He comes out and says, 'How do you do, my name is Orson Bean Harvard, forty-two,' Then he pauses and adds, 'Yale, nothing,'" Gillian laughed and looked at David who remained silently pensive. "It's really very funny," she said, shrugging. "I guess I didn't tell it well." She lifted the spoon to her mouth. Her hand was trembling. He reached across the table suddenly, catching her hand. The spoon clattered to the table top.

"You see," he said, "you're the only person in the world who means anything to me."

The time for decision was past. Perhaps it was past that night they met in the loft.

She covered his hand with her own and smiled. Gently, she said, "We must find a job for you, David."

Matthew was certainly not keen on the idea of moving to the country. As early as last November, when they had made their first exploratory trip to Talmadge, he had stated in his most unsubtle manner, "I do not see, Amanda, why we should join the horde of migratory birds who are flocking out of the city. I happen to like New York. I find it exciting and interesting and convenient. Besides, I was raised in a small town, and I don't think I'd like to live in one again."

"I was raised in a small town, too," Amanda had said.

"I know that. So how can you even consider——"

"Talmadge isn't really a small town."

"A town is either big or small. There are no in-betweens. Talmadge is a small town, Amanda. And it has the added disadvantage of being a university town. How can anyone possibly put up with screaming goldfish-eaters for the major part of each year?"

"Matthew, college students are no longer swallowing goldfish."

"They're sure to be swallowing something."

"That's their business, isn't it?"

"Yes, of course. But my business is the law. And it will take me two hours to get to my business from Talmadge each day. And two hours to return."

"Only an hour and a half."

"Plus the ride from Grand Central to my office."

"You could move your office. You said you were thinking of joining an established firm, anyway."

"Not right now, Amanda."

"You could do it now if you wanted to."

"Yes, but I don't want to."

"Well, let's not decide yet," Amanda had said.

She had said the same thing in February after they'd walked through seven houses accompanied by a real-estate agent who spoke with a German accent and who wore a pencil stuck into a bun at the back of her head. She had shown them four colonials, two contemporaries, and a bastardized version of a Southern manor, which, she claimed, had been copied from a place called Monticello. She had also shown them acres and acres of undeveloped land, which, she proudly stated, were alive with dogwood and cardinals and were a definite steal at two thousand dollars an acre. In the car on the way home, Matthew had said, "I don't trust that woman."

"You don't trust any Germans," Amanda said.

"I don't trust Germans who show me swampland at two thousand bucks an acre, that's for sure. Dogwood and cardinals! Cottonmouths and crocodiles is more like it."

"How did you like Monticello?" Amanda asked.

"Wonderful! But didn't you think the slaves' quarters were a little cramped?"

Laughing, Amanda had said, "Well, let's not decide yet."

It was April now, and the Talmadge countryside was in the midst of a seasonal clash. The sky was leaden, the trees were bare, a harsh wind scraped the rolling landscape. But crocus and jonquil and hyacinth had burst through the stiff upper crust of the soil, and the brilliant green of day-lily shoots lined the old stone walls of Connecticut. The forsythia were opening tentatively, palely yellow because of their sparseness, showing none of the riotous gold that would be theirs when the weather turned really mild. Here and there, a brave magnolia cautiously emerged from its fuzzy bud, the petals closed tight in pink-and-white timidity. The lawns patched the landscape uncertainly, faded brown merging with new brilliant green. The waiting spring cowered before the last chill blasts of winter. There was a look of desolation and expectation to the land.

She fell in love with the house the moment they saw it. The date was carved into a wooden crossbeam over the front door, and she could visualize a colonial gentleman watching a carpenter as he carefully chiselled the numerals into the wood. She followed the real-estate agent into the small cosy entry, saw the winding steps leading to the upper floors, the polished banister. Wide wooden planks, hand-pegged, richly grained, covered the floors, led to the large living-room and the enormous stone fireplace with its baking oven set into one of the walls, its big iron pot hanging on a swinging black hook. The ceilings were low and stoutly beamed. Something primitive and elementary rose in her breast as she climbed the steps to the bedrooms, somehow familiar with the curve of the banister, feeling an immediate intimacy with the house, as if she had lived in it for years and was now returning to it after a long absence. The bedrooms overlooked a small garden and a rolling field, which promised springtime lushness. There was a brook and an apple orchard and an enormous tree that seemed painted against the sky in twisted silhouette.

"I want it," she whispered to Matthew.

"It's probably got termites."

"I don't care if it's got rats."

"We'll see," Matthew said.

They discussed it with the real-estate agent. Amanda was floating on a giant pink cloud, but Matthew was cautious and suspicious. He activated his lawyer voice, to Amanda's secret amusement, and began asking learned questions about taxes, and mortgages, and existing liens on the property. What about Talmadge zoning? he asked. Two acres, three acres, or four? Was there any light industry in town? How far was it from the house to the railroad station? Were the public schools good? How much were the school taxes? And finally he descended into the mundane and asked the agent why there was a large damp spot on the cellar wall, was there a drainage problem? Didn't the north-east corner of the house get a terrible amount of wind during the winter? Who lived next door? Was the town friendly to new-comers? He thanked the agent for his time at last, and they drove back to the city silently, Matthew balancing figures in his head, Amanda planning on where to fit her piano into the living-room.

When they reached the apartment, Amanda went upstairs and Matthew parked the car and picked up the mail. She had taken off her dress and her shoes by the time he joined her. She sat in the living-room with a broad smile on her face, staring at the wall.

"It'll be lovely," she said.

"We haven't taken it yet."

"Oh, but we will. Won't we, Matthew?"

"He said they've already rented the place for the summer."

"Yes, but it'll be ready for occupancy in September."

"Who knows what those summer people will do to it?"

"Matthew, we've already made plans for the summer, anyway. Autumn is a nice time to move. Why did you ask about schools?"

"Well, why not? You're supposed to ask about schools."

"We can start a family," she said, and she smiled again.

"You got a letter from Minnesota," Matthew said.

He put the envelope in her lap and then slid his hand under her slip, grasping the flesh on her thigh.

"Let's start the family now," he said.

"I want to read my letter. Is it from Penny?"

"It looks like her handwriting. You're still the softest——"

"Get your hand out of there," Amanda said, scowling. "You fresh thing," she added, and then opened the envelope. "Do you want to hear this?"

Matthew sighed. "Oh yes, a letter from Penny will positively make my day."

"My dear darling sister," Amanda read. "How nice to be fat, how nice of you to be fat."

"What?" Matthew said.

Amanda shrugged. "How nice of you to be *fat*," she repeated, puzzled. "What do you suppose she means?"

"She's *your* sister," Matthew said, shrugging.

"It must be a joke of some kind. She probably explains it."

"Well, I'm going to take a shower," Matthew said.

"Oh, sit down a minute." She looked back at the letter again. "I am claws," she read.

"I am *what*?"

"I am claws." Amanda stopped reading. She looked up at Matthew.

"Go on," he said, frowning.

"You . . . you better watch out, you better be good. It should not be hot in November when they die."

"Are you making this up?" Matthew asked sharply.

"No. No, I . . . Matthew . . ."

"Read it."

"Matthew, I'm frightened!"

"Read it!" he said.

"It should not be hot in November when they die," Amanda read. The room was silent now. She spoke in a whisper, and she did not look up at Matthew as her eyes followed Penny's wide scrawl. "Amanda, dear, don't you think, dear, you should wear a yellow ribbon for my sailor who is far far away? Now Amanda, why don't you write to me? I am so tired with crying. Don't you help? You used to help me clean the house on November Saturdays, but not hot. Mother will not let me drive the car. Tell her to give me the keys or I will eat her all up. Love the flying rooster bird, the sailor dressed in blue. Love, Penelope."

Her hands were trembling. Everything was suddenly in her head, behind her eyes. She looked up at her husband.

"Matthew, we've got to . . ."

"Yes," he said. "We'll go tomorrow."

Everything seemed the same except Penny. Nothing had changed except Penny. Her mother did not look any older, and her father still smiled with the curious lopsided grin that had the gold filling in the upper right-hand corner of his mouth, and even the child, Kate, five years old now, did not seem to have grown very much, the house was the same, the lawn, the Minnesota air, nothing had changed but Penny.

"Hello, Amanda," she said, "did you have a nice time?" and Amanda looked deep into her sister's eyes and hugged her fiercely. The family reacquainted themselves with Matthew. Amanda's father took him out to the garage to show him his new power tools, Kate had smeared finger-paints on her dress, and Penny took her upstairs to change her, her hand at the back of the child's neck, the long blonde hair trailing over her fingers as she led her up the steps.

They talked in the garden not yet touched by springtime, Amanda and her mother. Priscilla Soames was calm and sensible, quite infuriatingly calm as she walked with Amanda, stooping to examine a new bud every now and then, but walking most of the time with her hands tucked into the folds of her brown sweater.

"What's the matter with her?" Amanda asked.

"Nothing. Your sister is fine."

"I got a letter that——"

"Your sister is a fanciful girl."

"This letter wasn't fanciful."

"No? What was it, daughter?" Priscilla raised her eyebrows and studied Amanda coolly.

"It was a letter from a . . ." Amanda paused. In a rush, she said, "It was a letter from a lunatic."

"Now really, Amanda."

"Did you know she wrote to me?"

"No, I did not. But if you got a letter that sounded despondent, you mustn't——"

"This was more than despondent."

"Your sister has her black days," Priscilla said. "We all do. And she has had more to bear than most. With God's will——"

"Mother, this has nothing whatever to do with God's will. Penny's letter——"

"I wish you would not profane the Lord," Priscilla said. "I can't imagine what you've learned in the East, but this is still my house, daughter, and I won't listen to any——"

"I want to know what's wrong with Penny."

"There is nothing at all wrong with her. Her husband died, that's all. She loved him dearly. When he——"

"That was almost six years ago, Mother!"

"Yes, and does grief set its own time limits?"

"Grief? For God's sake, when I came into the house, she acted as if I were——"

"If you take the name of the Lord——"

"Never mind the name of the Lord!" Amanda shouted, and her mother turned abruptly on her heel and began walking towards the house. Amanda caught her arm. "We're finishing this, Mother," she said tightly.

Priscilla stared at her coldly and said nothing.

"Do you hear me?" Amanda said.

"Don't shout."

"What's wrong with Penny? Have you had a doctor for her?"

"She'll hear you."

"She's upstairs with the baby. She won't hear me."

"In any case, I don't like shouting."

"Have you had a doctor for her?"

"Why should I have had a doctor? There's nothing wrong with her."

"What are you trying to hide, Mother?"

"Nothing. Is this why you came all the way from New York?

You'd have done better to stay there with your husband and your friends, Amanda. There's nothing wrong with your sister."

"I haven't seen her in two years, and the first thing she asks me is 'Did you have a good time?' as if I'm coming home from a date, but there's nothing wrong with her" Amanda paused. "Why won't you let her drive the car, Mother?"

"There's only one car, and your father needs it."

"But you never denied it to her before."

"Your father's parish is larger now. Besides . . ."

"What?"

"Nothing."

"Tell me!"

"Your sister had a slight accident in town a few weeks back. We thought it would be best, until she . . . got over it to . . ." Priscilla shrugged. "Your father thought it would be best."

"What kind of an accident?"

"A small one."

"Then why won't you let her drive?"

"Amanda, I don't like the way you're talking to me."

"That's too bad, Mother, and I'm sorry. What kind of an accident did she have?"

"She hit someone."

"What!"

"Don't start imagining a terrible accident, Amanda. The woman wasn't hurt at all. But we felt it was best——"

"Where was this? The accident."

"On the old Courtney Road."

"What was she doing there?"

"Just driving. Just out for a drive."

"And the woman?"

"Was walking, Amanda. By the side of the road."

"And Penny hit her? That's the widest road in Otter Falls!"

"I suppose it is."

"How'd she happen to——?"

"I don't know, Amanda."

"Did she hit her deliberately?"

"Of course not!"

"Did she?"

"No." Priscilla scowled at her daughter. "Are you this rude in New York? You seem to have forgotten all your manners, Amanda. Of course, I suppose all your friends——"

"Penny needs a doctor," Amanda said.

"She does not need a doctor! She's as sane as——" The word, startled Priscilla. She closed her mouth instantly.

"Yes," Amanda said.

Priscilla did not answer.

"I'm going to call a doctor," Amanda said.

"You're going to do nothing of the sort. This is still my house. *You* live in New York."

"My *sister* lives here."

"It's a little late to be thinking of her."

"What do you mean by that?"

"You know exactly what I mean."

"No, I don't."

"Then I suggest you ignore it."

"No! What do you mean?"

"You chose to live in New York, Amanda. All right, live there. We are quite capable of taking care of ourselves. *And* Penny."

"I don't understand you."

"You understand me very well, daughter. We have never had any trouble communicating."

"Yes," Amanda said, nodding. "Yes, I understand you perfectly."

"Fine. I'll go inside now. It gets a little chilly——"

"What happened, Mother? Did I spoil your plans for me? Was I supposed to come back to Otter Falls and marry the local butcher? And play piano for him beautifully every afternoon?"

"I had no plans for you, Amanda," her mother said.

"Is that what happened?" Amanda said bitterly. "Well, I'm terribly sorry. I'm really so terribly sorry, Mother, that I chose my own life. But Penny is still my sister! And you're not going to pretend she's all right, Mother, the way you pretended I was going to school just to learn how to play piano, you're not going to do that to her, Mother."

"Penny is my daughter," Priscilla said flatly.

"And so am I," Amanda said.

The words hung on the afternoon air. Priscilla did not answer. Amanda stared at her mother long and hard.

At last she said, "You're made of stone."

"Thank you, daughter."

"You're a stone-hearted bitch," Amanda said, and she enjoyed the words, enjoying hurling them in her mother's face.

The laugh shattered the April air. Amanda heard it with more than her ears. It hit her body like a closed fist. She turned towards the house instantly and heard the laugh again, a high, rising, hysterical laugh that came from the upper-story windows. Her eyes widened. She felt suddenly cold, suddenly bloodless. The laugh came a third time, hanging liquidly in the near dusk, trailing off into a hollow echo. The house, she thought. Penny, she thought. And then she said aloud, "The baby! *Kate!*"

She broke into a run across the lawn. She had covered this same ground a thousand times as a child, knew every rock and every blade of grass, but now the earth resisted her, seemed to cling to her as the laugh erupted in the silence again, she clattered up the front steps, fumbled with the door-knob, she could not open the door, she grasped the knob again, it seemed slippery in her hand and suddenly the door opened and she fell into the entrance foyer and saw her own frightening reflection in the hall mirror, wide-eyed, startled, where? she thought, the steps, she ran for the steps and tripped over the hall rug, scrambled to her feet again as a new sound joined the laughter, the sound of Kate screaming, she clutched for the banister, pulled back her skirt and took the steps two at a time, losing one shoe as she ran for the upstairs corridor and Kate's bedroom.

They were sitting in the middle of the floor, mother and daughter. Penny was laughing. She held a lock of the child's long blonde hair in one hand, and scissors in the other, and she snipped the lock quickly, and then held her fingers wide as the blonde tresses fell to the floor to join the scraps of hair on the scatter rug. The child was sobbing, watching her mother, watching the scissors as they moved towards her head again, her face streaked with tears, her eyes puzzled and afraid.

"Penny!" Amanda said.

Her sister turned. There was vacancy in her eyes. She smiled absently and said, "I'm cutting it off."

"Penny, give me the scissors," Amanda said. She held out her hand.

The smile left Penny's mouth. She frowned and rose from the rug. Beside her, Kate began crying again.

"Penny," Amanda said softly, but there was fear to her voice now. The fear leaped the distance between them and seemed to ignite something in Penny's eyes. She gripped the scissors tight in her fist and lunged across the room. Amanda saw the wicked pointed ends of the double blades, saw the utterly incredible vacant horror in Penny's eyes, a look of terrible lost loneliness, and then the scissors flashed towards her breast. She seized Penny's wrist and stopped the thrust, felt the unnatural strength in her sister's arm. Penny punched her suddenly and viciously with her left fist, hitting Amanda over the eye and sending her sprawling to the rug, tumbling over Kate, suddenly spitting out the child's hair, feeling the hair clinging to her face and her lips as Penny whirled on her, smiling now, smiling a deadly cold controlled mechanical smile.

"Penny!"

She drew back the scissors, ready to lunge.

"*Penny!*"

Her sister began laughing, the same high hysterical laugh that had tumbled from the house and invaded the quiet garden. She pushed the scissors at Amanda clumsily, almost blindly, tearing the sleeve of Amanda's blouse, raking her arm, and Amanda thought, This is my sister, this is Penny, this is Penny, this is Penny, fought the idea until it burst from her fingers in a wild open-handed swing that caught Penny on the side of her face and rocked her head backward. She slapped her again, and again, swinging her arm while Penny laughed uncontrollably, and then the laughter turned to sobs and the scissors dropped from her fingers and she fell to the floor beside Amanda and threw herself into her arms. And they sat together in the centre of Kate's bedroom, sister and sister, Penny in her arms weeping, Amanda sobbing and stroking her hair, and the five-year-old child watching them in wide-eyed bewilderment.

They drove Penny to the Minneapolis General Hospital Psychiatric Clinic the next day. She sat on the back seat of the automobile and said nothing, brooding silently, staring through the window. Only once did she say anything, a shouted incoherency, and then she fell into her dark silence again. At the hospital, they told the resident psychiatrist about the events of the day before. He listened patiently, looking at Penny all the while. She sat stiffly in the chair beside his desk, sullenly studying the floor. When he talked to her, she did not answer him. The only notes he made were on superficial things like Penny's age and marital status, the number of people in the family, things a general practitioner might have asked when confronted with a case of the measles. He told Amanda he would like to keep Penny there for observation, and he said that a psychiatric social worker would undoubtedly visit the house in Otter Falls within the next week to talk to her parents. In the meantime, he cautioned them against undue alarm. This could, after all, be just a temporary thing.

They kept Penny at the clinic for thirty days. Amanda stayed in Minnesota all the while Penny was under observation. Matthew had to get back to New York, but he wrote to her every day, and every day she answered, and each night before she went to sleep she prayed for her sister. Once, she went into the church where she'd been married, and played the organ, seemingly alone with the sunlight filtering through the stained-glass windows, and when she finished the Bach prelude, she heard her father's voice. "That was lovely, Amanda," he said, and put his hand on her shoulder and squeezed it gently. During Penny's stay at the clinic, the psychiatric social worker visited their home four times. He was a very pleasant young man who listened patiently and took voluminous notes. When Amanda asked him how Penny was doing, he smiled sympathetically and said he really had no idea, but he was certain she was in good hands. At the end of May, they went to the clinic again and spoke to the psychiatrist who had been assigned to Penny's case. He was a tall, loose-jointed man who sat behind his desk and seemed too large for his chair. When he took off his eyeglasses, he seemed much younger than he was, and oddly ill-equipped to discuss what he was about to discuss. Unemotionally, gently, with a minimum of words, he told them that Penny was a schizophrenic of the paranoid type, and that she needed a period of intense hospitalization and therapy. Amanda listened to his diagnosis and prognosis in stunned silence. Priscilla Soames sat calmly in a straight-backed chair and said, "I won't send my daughter to a hospital."

"She's a very sick girl, Mrs. Soames," the doctor said. Amanda suddenly had the feeling he had been through this very scene a thousand times before. She suddenly saw pain in his eyes, and she wished he would put on his glasses again.

"She's been this way before," Priscilla said.

"No, I don't think so, Mrs. Soames."

"How would you know? She's my daughter."

"Yes, but she's my patient." He leaned closer to her, his big hands awkwardly clasped. "We've had to keep her under restraint for the past two——"

"Restraint?" Priscilla said, and one hand left the bag in her lap, as if she would strike the doctor, and then fluttered aimlessly as she turned to Amanda, seemed to remind herself she would find neither assistance nor consolation there, and then turned helplessly to her husband, who sat white-faced and dazed.

"She's become extremely violent," the doctor said. "We wouldn't have——"

"I don't believe you," Priscilla said.

"Mrs. Soames, believe me. Two weeks ago, she tried to strangle a student nurse on her ward."

"I don't believe you."

"Mother——"

"I don't believe him."

The doctor put on his eyeglasses. He tried to make himself comfortable in the chair that was too small for him. "I wish I could tell you something different," he said. "I wish I could say she's fine, she's well." He shook his head. "But she isn't. She's lost all contact with reality, Mrs. Soames. She soils herself, she's refused to eat . . .

we've been feeding her intravenously for the past few days. She *needs* to be hospitalized, Mrs. Soames. I can't tell you anything but that. She *must* be hospitalized."

"I won't send her to a hospital."

The doctor sighed, not in impatience, not in weariness, the sigh was almost one of sadness. "We can insist on a legal commitment," he said.

The words resounded in the stillness of the room like a hollow slap.

"Then that's what you'll have to do," Priscilla said.

"We'd rather not. If you commit her, Mrs. Soames, you can petition for her release at any time. If we're forced into a legal commitment, she can't return to society until the director of the hospital recommends her release."

"And when I petition for her release," Priscilla said sarcastically, "will they automatically let her go?"

"That's up to the hospital."

"That's just what I thought. I won't commit her." She paused. "How . . . how long would she be put away?"

"I couldn't tell you, Mrs. Soames. Until she's well. We're not trying to imprison her, we're trying to help her. You can send her to a private hospital if you feel a state hospital wouldn't be——"

"What's wrong with the state hospitals?" Priscilla asked quickly, suspiciously.

"Nothing. Some families prefer private care."

"How much does a private hospital cost?"

"That will vary. Two hundred, perhaps three hundred a week."

"We could never afford that."

"The state hospitals——"

"My husband is a minister, not a banker."

"The state hospitals are very good, Mrs. Soames."

"Really? Are they as good as *your* hospital, doctor? Where you look at a girl for a few weeks and then pronounce her hopelessly insane?"

"I never said——"

"I will not send my daughter to a hospital!"

"Would you send her if she had tuberculosis?"

"That's different. You're telling me my daughter is *crazy*!" Priscilla shouted.

"I don't even know that word, Mrs. Soames. I'm telling you your daughter is very ill. I'm telling you we want to help her. If you won't allow us to, we'll seek legal commitment."

"Very well, seek it," Priscilla said, and she rose.

Two psychiatrists signed Penny's commitment papers and attended the hearing before a justice of the superior court in Minneapolis. On 6 June 1948, Penny was committed to the Sandstone

State Hospital in Sandstone, Minnesota. Before Amanda went back to New York, she spoke to one of the hospital psychiatrists. They sat in his office and discussed Penny quietly, like two old friends over tea at Childs.

"Is there really a chance for her?" Amanda asked.

"I don't see why there shouldn't be, do you?" the psychiatrist said. "There's been an awful lot said about the hopelessness of mental illness, Mrs. Bridges, and I'm afraid the layman comes away with an impression of total despair. The fact remains, though, that some sixty to seventy-five per cent of all acute psychoses *are* recoverable."

"I see," Amanda said.

"And even when we can't effect a complete cure, we can hope for considerable modification along favourable channels. We'll take good care of your sister, Mrs. Bridges. Please be assured. We'll do everything in our power to help her."

"But . . . but how? She . . . she won't eat, she . . ."

"We've had very good results with drugs, Mrs. Bridges. Once we can calm your sister sufficiently, once we can begin talking to her, establish a rapport, once we can understand her illness, why, then we can hope that she, too, will understand it, and understand herself as well. It's a matter of leading her back to reality, to environment—as opposed to unreality or mental disease. This can't be accomplished overnight, Mrs. Bridges. But then, neither does a mental disorder develop overnight."

"And this will help her?" Amanda asked. "Once you can talk to her? Once she can talk to you? This will help her?"

"Communication," the psychiatrist said. "There is hope if we can get her to communicate."

I never wrote to any of the people I used to know, Gillian, because the return address on the envelope made it clear I was a prisoner and not just taking a naval rest cure.

They call it a naval retraining command, but that doesn't fool a soul. My mother was the only one who knew I'd been put in jail, and I wrote to her maybe once a week. She told everyone in Talmadge that I was an S.P. at Camp Elliott. I suppose they believed the story. No one's ever mentioned it to me, so I guess they believed it. You're the only person in the world, besides my mother, who knows I was in prison. And I told you five minutes after I'd met you. I guess that proves something.

I'd begun serving my term in May of '43, and at the end of two years I applied for release. I almost got it until someone on the review board remembered that I had struck an officer. The board decided that I should remain in prison for the rest of my term. If I'd killed an old lady in Seattle, that would have been different, perhaps. But I'd struck an officer, you see. So they turned me down. I'd spent two years behind bars, but that wasn't enough.

Gillian, two *days* was enough. But not to the officers on the review board, and so I was turned down. I began thinking of those years ahead of me, another three years of nothing while life went on outside, while people were laughing outside, or playing cards, or drinking beer, or standing near radiators warming their hands, free. I almost cracked. I almost said, What the hell who cares? I'll be here for the rest of my life, who cares? But then they dropped the atomic bomb, and then suddenly the war was over, and I could taste freedom, I figured they had no reason to keep me there any more, the war was over, they would let me go, I could taste it in my mouth. So I stuck with it, the model prisoner, hoping to reapply for release at the end of three years.

I met Mike Arretti during that time.

He'd been at Camp Elliott for quite a while, and he was going to be there for quite a while longer. He was a signalman who'd got stranded in New Orleans with a girl whose husband was in commando training in England. The girl had a six-year-old son and a house in the French Quarter. Mike had hitch-hiked from San Diego, where his ship was docked, on his way to Easton, Pennsylvania, where his wife was. He had a two-week leave, and he planned to spend it with his wife, but he got sidetracked when he met the girl in New Orleans. He moved into the house with her and her six-year-old son, and stayed a week overleave, and then woke up one morning, did a little arithmetic, and figured that his ship would be pulling out for the Pacific the next day.

He didn't have a chance of catching it if he took the train or hitched, so he began calling the various airlines. He learned that one airline would fly him to Dallas and then to Los Angeles for a hundred and one dollars and ninety-seven cents, and that another airline would fly him from Los Angeles to San Diego for ten dollars and twenty-eight cents, including tax, and the whole trip would take about seven hours, and that would get him back in time to catch his ship.

There was only one trouble. By this time, Mike was flat broke, and the girl had been awaiting her allotment cheque, which hadn't come, and between them they couldn't raise the fare. So he tried the U.S.O., which sent him to the Red Cross, which sent him to the Seamen's Institute, but no one seemed able to come up with the cash he needed for that plane ride back to Diego.

In desperation, he called his wife in Easton and said, "Honey, I'm stranded in New Orleans, and I need a hundred and twenty dollars to get me back to Diego, would you wire it to me right away, please?"

His wife asked him what he was doing in New Orleans, and he said he'd been sent there for a signalman refresher course and was calling from the school where he'd got stranded when the rest of the group left, all lies that Mike's wife might have bought if the six-year-old kid hadn't come into the room right then and asked to talk to his mommy. Mike tried to push the kid away from the phone, telling him it *wasn't* his mommy on the other end, but the kid kept yelling, "Let me talk to Mommy! Let me talk to Mommy!" which Mike's wife heard clearly and distinctly. She may have been ignorant of most nautical matters, but she knew damn well they didn't have little kids running around signalman schools asking for their mommies. She didn't know what kind of a refresher course Mike was taking, but she was willing to bet it had nothing to do with blinker lights. So she told him to to go to hell, and hung up on him.

Mike needed that money the way only a man facing a charge of desertion in time of war could need it. He walked into town, found a closed pawnshop, broke in by forcing a window, and stole a hundred and fifty dollars from the cash drawer. He kissed the commando's wife, and then slapped that little six-year-old kid as hard as he'd ever slapped anyone in his life. He might have caught the ship were it not for a delay in the Dallas airport. But there *was* a delay, and he *did* miss the ship, and the S.P.s picked him up the next day. He was charged with desertion and burglary, the burglary charge having followed him cross-country from New Orleans, where the commando's wife had notified the local shore patrol of Mike's little adventure. Apparently, he shouldn't have slapped her son before he left.

So there he was at Camp Elliott, serving something like twenty years, and hoping to be out of prison and the Navy by the time he was eighty-eight or so. We got to be pretty good friends. He was a good talker, and I enjoyed listening to him, and we'd spend a lot of time discussing what we were going to do when we got out. It seemed like a pretty good friendship until the review board examined my plea again in December of '45 and told me my request had been granted, I would be returned to active duty the following May.

I began to get excited then, Gilly. There it was. There was the whole damn world waiting for me. And naturally, the first person I told about it was Mike.

He listened to me silently, nodding his head, and then he said, "You'll be leaving me, huh, buddy?"

I said something like "Don't worry, Mike, you'll be out of here before you know it," or something equally foolish to a man who was facing such a long prison stretch, and Mike simply nodded again.

"You'll be leaving me," he said, as if I were doing him a great injustice.

"Hey, come on," I said. "Aren't you happy? I'm getting out! Man, I'm getting out!"

And Mike nodded and continued staring at me, and said nothing.

I was almost out when it happened. I had ten days to go when it happened.

It was May, Gillian, and very hot. I don't think you've ever lifted a sledge-hammer, and maybe you don't know how heavy one can get after you've been raising it and dropping it for hours. I don't suppose you know the way rock dust can get into your nostrils and under your clothes, either, the fine pumice that drifts on the air after each hammer blow, like powdered glass, crawling into your nose and under your shirt and making you itch, and getting into your eyes until you can't tell the tears from the sweat. I was working side by side with Mike that day. We were wearing the leg-irons, we didn't always. but this was a little way from the prison and there was only one guard for twelve men, and all he carried was a rifle and a billet.

We were working side by side, the hammers going in that sort of mechanical picking-up-and-dropping, which is not really work, only labour. The guard assigned to our work detail had a voice like a parrot. Every five minutes he would yell out, "All right, mates, let's look alive! Let's make little ones out of all those big ones." He delivered the line as if he had just made it up and was testing it for a laugh. Every five minutes his voice would cut through the hanging dust, you could almost set your watch by it, "All right, mates, let's look alive! Let's make little ones out of all those big ones." Twelve men were pounding at the rock pile, and dust was hanging on the air and choking us. You could barely see the man three feet from you, but you could hear that voice drifting through the layers of dust every five minutes, "All right mates, let's look alive! Let's make little ones out of all those big ones."

And suddenly, right next to me, there was another voice.

Mike's.

And it yelled, "Go to hell, you moron!"

I turned to look at him, and suddenly there was a deep silence, Gillian, and into the silence the guard said, "What?" He said it very quietly. He didn't seem at all shocked. He asked the question as if he hadn't quite heard what was said the first time and was politely inquiring about it. "What?" he asked.

And through the hanging dust, Mike answered, "Go to hell, you fat bastard!"

The guard walked over to us. The hammers had stopped. The dust was settling now. We stood staring at him, our legs manacled together, the sweat and the dust and the tears streaking our faces, our throats dry, squinting against the bright hot sunlight as the dust settled. The guard wasn't smiling, but he wasn't frowning, either. He seemed a little hurt, like a night-club comic who'd been heckled by a drunk. He stood very close to us with the rifle hanging loosely at his side, and with the heel of his right hand cupped over the handle of the billet on his belt.

Very quietly he said, "Who said that?"

No one answered. I was shaking. Gillian, I was ten days away from getting out of that place, Gillian. I could see spending another two years on that rock pile. I could see everything I'd worked for vanishing as I stood there in the sun, biting my lip, gripping the handle of the sledge tight, keeping myself from shouting, "He said it! Mike Arretti said it!"

The guard waited patiently. "Well, what do you say, mates?" he asked, and there was more silence. "What do you say now?" Silence.

I had begun crying, Gillian. Not out loud, not so any of the men standing around the silent pile of rocks could tell I was crying, there was so much sweat on my face anyway, and tears from the dust, but I'd begun crying soundlessly, waiting for Mike to say something, waiting for Mike to tell the truth, *waiting*.

"Well now," the guard said. "This don't look too good, does it?" He waited. Then he turned to me slowly. Slowly and deliberately, he turned to me and said, "What do you say, Regan? Who's the wise guy here, Regan?"

I didn't answer.

"Come on, Regan," the guard said. "You know who did the yelling. Now, how about telling me?"

I didn't answer. The guard kept staring at me, and the tears kept streaming down my face, but I didn't answer. The guard nodded briefly, and then turned, apparently starting back for his chair in the shade with the walkie-talkie resting on its seat. It was then that Mike shoved me.

He shoved me with all the strength of his arms, and I went pitching forward, and Mike pulled back on his leg so that the chain pulled up tight. I tripped and went falling towards the guard, grabbing at him for balance as I fell, the leg-iron holding me. I thought I was going to land on my face, Gillian, I thought I'd smash my face on the rocks. I grabbed at the guard's clothes, and he swung around with his eyes wide, his right hand sweeping towards the billet, and then he raised the club, and I tried to say "No!" I tried to shout, "No, I'm falling! I'm only . . ." but he hit me. He hit me once, sharply, on the top of the skull, splitting it wide with his first shot. I was on my knees, clinging to him, when I felt the blood gushing on to my forehead and into my eyes, and I turned and looked at Mike Arretti and I saw him through the blood, standing there and leaning on his hammer with a smile on his face, a smile, Gillian, a *smile*! The guard hit me again, on the shoulder this time, numbing my right side. I fell over into the dust.

It could have been worse. They could have put me in solitary, they could have left me to rot in that goddamed prison. Or they could have refused even to consider any future parole requests. I didn't get out that May, Gillian, but actually they were pretty decent about it. I reapplied for release in December, and it was six months after that when they finally let me go. I didn't leave Camp Elliott until May of 1947. Mike Arretti had cost me a full year.

I saw him in the recreation yard two days before they sent me to Treasure Island for my discharge. He smiled at me, Gillian. The son of a bitch smiled.

The third job David got was in the public library on Forty-second Street and Fifth Avenue. Unlike the other jobs he'd held, he seemed to like this one. He recognized, of course, that it was only a temporary thing, but he felt completely at home in the small room where he worked, the sunlight pouring through the arched window that overlooked Bryant Park, a window surrounded by stone like an ancient cathedral. The books that passed through his hands were sometimes old and yellowed. He received manuscripts faded with time, written in script that was ancient and strange. He handled the books gently and with great respect. Alone in his tower-room, he felt an enormous sense of continuity as history passed through his hands on the pages of dusty volumes and manuscripts. The official title of his job was "Accessioner". One of his duties, among many others, was the marking of all new library accessions with the official library seal. Any book, pamphlet, or manuscript that found its way to his desk was instantly numbered on the page after the title page, and again on page 97 if the material ran that long. Gillian promptly dubbed him "The Lord High Accessioner", and when he'd been at the job for a month and got his first raise, she shopped the stores off Sixth Avenue for a Japanese army medal and a libretto of *The Mikado*. She tore out page 97 and the one after the title page, and on the flyleaf she wrote:

8/10/48

Banzai!
In commemoration raise, from loving, humble, honourable servant,

        Girrian

On Sunday, they went to Central Park to celebrate. They had lunch at the Tavern on the Green, and then wandered leisurely over the paths, directionless, turning each bend by whim alone. They stopped at Cleopatra's Needle, where Gillian read the translation of the hieroglyph for the first time, fascinated by it. "Are those lobster claws?" she asked, looking up at the metal figures at the base of the obelisk.

"Crabs, I think," David said.

"They were probably added later."

"No, I think they're part of the original."

"Do they have crabs in Egypt?"

"They have crabs *everywhere*. Crabs are one of the oldest forms of animal life."

"Oh, such a smart-oh," Gillian said. "What happened? Did you get a book on crustaceans yesterday, huh? Is that what happened, Accessioner?"

They walked west to the Shakespeare garden, where someone had smashed the glass front of the plaque telling why the garden was there. They came upon an old brown house, which seemed to have been transplanted from some Scottish moor. A girl was sitting on the stoop before the locked door, reading a comic book. They stumbled on to the lake suddenly, and Gillian laughed when she saw the hundreds and hundreds of people in rowboats… "I can't understand it," she said in mock puzzlement. "Such a nice day, and nobody on the lake rowing." They took a winding path up from the lake and found an orchid corsage under one of the bushes. Gillian picked it up and held it on the palm of her hand.

"Now thereby lies a tale," she said. "What do you suppose it was doing under that bush?"

"That's where its owner was last night," David said.

"A prom," Gillian said. "They came here after a prom."

"No proms in August, Gillian."

"That's right. A special occasion of some sort then. A birthday. An anniversary. And they were walking through the park, and they had an argument, and she threw his orchid under the bush."

"*Ja*, go on," David said in a thick German accent. "Dot's very goot. Tell me more about your assoziations."

"Your accent is terrible," Gillian said. "Let's hang it on a tree."

"My accent?"

"The flower, David. Come!"

They unwound the wire holding the stem of the flower to its fern and then rewired the orchid to the leafy branch of an elm. The tree stood to the side of the path, the single purple bloom seeming to sprout magically from the end of one of its branches.

"Und now ve obzerve, doktor," Gillian said.

"And that's a *good* accent, huh?"

"No, but I do it with style," Gillian answered.

They sat on a rock several feet away from the elm tree, trying not to seem interested in the orchid or the people who passed by. Three young men in tight jeans and Italian sweaters were the first to spot the flower. One giggled, sniffed it, shoved at his companions, sniffed it again, and then joined them as they went up the path laughing.

"You know what *they* thought it was, don't you?" Gillian asked.

"No. What?"

"The late-blooming faggotry."

"Here are some more customers," David said.

Two little girls had stopped to study the flower. They approached it cautiously, standing several feet back from it.

"Be careful," the first girl said. "It's one of those stingers. Don't touch it. It'll sting you."

The second girl moved closer to the riotous purple bloom. She peered at its petals and then tentatively stuck out her hand.

"Don't touch it!" the other girl shouted.

The second girl touched it gingerly, pulled back her hand at once, and said, "Wow!"

"Did it sting you?" the first girl asked as they walked on. "Huh? Did it sting you, Marie?"

They watched the flower for at least twenty minutes. At the end of that time, an old man wearing striped trousers and a derby hat stopped at the tree, discovered the bloom, raised his eyebrows appreciatively, plucked it from the branch, stuck it in his buttonhole, and went jauntily down the path humming.

"Most of them didn't even notice it," Gillian said sadly.

"Ah, but that's life," David answered.

"Are you observant?" she asked seriously.

"I noticed *you*, didn't I?"

"Do you notice anything different about the way I'm wearing my hair?"

"No," he said, surprised, and turned to look more closely.

"I'm just checking. I've worn it this way always."

"It's beautiful. You're beautiful, Gillian "

"Oh, yes," she said.

"Why do you always think I'm joking when I say you're beautiful?"

"Because I know I'm not," she said, suddenly shy. "But it's nice that you think so. It's terribly nice, David."

When they got back to the apartment, Gillian immediately busied herself with pencil and paper.

"What are you doing?" David asked.

"I'm making up my own Egyptian hieroglyph."

"Why?"

"If Cleopatra could have one, why can't I?"

"All right, go ahead. I want to hear the end of the Yankee game."

"I hate baseball," Gillian said. "Only boors are interested in baseball." She shushed him as he began to protest, and continued working on her drawing, her tongue caught between her teeth, her brow knotted in concentration. She tried to show him the completed sketch in the middle of an eleventh-inning rally. David put her off until the excitement had died down, and then studied her work.

"Where did you find this?" he asked with an air of shocked discovery.

"Why, it just came through, sir," Gillian said, immediately falling into the role of the apprentice. "I was simply sitting there, sir, when this papyrus scroll was put on my desk. I looked for the page after the title page, but there was none, and page ninety-seven was obliterated by Ibis Feathers. I thought I should call it to your attention at once, sir."

"I'm glad you did," David said sternly. "This girl, what was her name? We'll have to fire her at once."

"Which girl is that, sir?"

"The one who obliterated page ninety-seven," David paused, thinking. "Iris, was that it? Iris something-or-other?"

"Oh, yes, sir. Ibis. Ibis Feathers. She used to be a stripper in Union City before she joined the library, sir." Gillian paused. "We put her in the stacks, sir. She stacks very well."

"Very well," David said. "Do you realize the importance of this find?"

"*Is* it important, sir?"

"Miss Rourke, I can't——"

"Burke, sir."

"Yes, of course, Burke. Miss Burns, I can't begin to tell you about its importance."

"Try, sir."

"Sit down on my lap here, Miss Barnes, and I'll——"

"Burke, sir."

"Yes, of course, Burke. Sit down, Miss Byrd, and I'll tell you all about it." Gillian curled up in his lap and threw her arms around his neck. "Mmmm, yes, where was I?" David said.

"The papyrus roll."

"Yes, of course. Thank you, Miss Bikes."

"Burke."

"Burke, Burke, I can't seem to remember that name. Well, Italian names always throw me. Forgive me, Miss Buggs. The papyrus roll. Is it seeded papyrus or onion papyrus?"

"I didn't notice, sir. A little of each, I think."

"In any case, it should go well with ham."

"Is that a dig, David Regan?"

"No, my dear. The last dig I was on was in Australia in 1912. Found a Zulu skull. Remarkably preserved."

"She's very good, too," Gillian said.

"Who's that, my dear?"

"Zulu. Zulu Skull. A *marr*-vellous stripper. Not as inventive as Ibis Feathers, but remarkably preserved."

"Yes, well of course she——"

"Are you happy?" Gillian asked suddenly. "David, are you tremendously happy?"

"I'm happier than I've ever been in my life," he answered.

They tried to reach Penny with drugs first.

They started with the barbituric acid group, shooting her with ten grains of sodium amytal intravenously, varying the administration with oral, intramuscular, and rectal doses, gradually increasing the dosage to fifteen grains. She would scream whenever they hit her with the needle. She would claw and scratch, and they would grab at her arms and her legs and hold her down while the hypodermic was plunged into her arm. The physicians and attendants began to dread that time of the day when Penny Randolph would be taken out of her restraining jacket in preparation for her injection. The narcosis seemed to have nothing but the most minor temporary effect on her. She still refused to eat. She still would spit at anyone who came anywhere near her, hurl obscenities at patients and staff. The moment the jacket was removed, the moment they took it off to get at the veins on her arm, she became assaultive. Once, she seized the hypodermic from the doctor, smashed it on the table top, and attempted to slit her own throat with the broken shard.

By the beginning of September, when Matthew and Amanda moved into the Talmadge house, the hospital staff had already tried veronal, paraldehyde, and hyoscine, and had switched to sodium nucleinate in their treatment of Penny. When they realized this wasn't helping her at all, when they recognized they were no closer to establishing the communication they so desperately desired, they abandoned drug therapy completely, and called Priscilla Soames the next day to ask for permission to use electric convulsive treatment on her daughter.

Priscilla didn't know quite what to do.

The girl she visited each week was certainly not her daughter, not the Penny she had known. But still, could she submit this poor distracted creature to electric shock three times a week, perhaps more? Could she do this to her own daughter? And yet, and yet, she wasn't really her daughter. She no longer recognized anyone, nor did she seem recognizable, her face had changed somehow, changed from the face of someone Priscilla had known and loved to the face of a stranger. She did not know what to do. She turned to God, as she had so often in the past, and she prayed for guidance. The people at the hospital had told her the electric-shock treatments might help her daughter, might bring her to the point where they could at least talk to her. "We cannot help her unless we can communicate," they had said, and now she communicated with her God and asked Him to show her the way.

She prayed formally, in a language she had evolved from the time she was a child, a highly stylized language, which she considered fitting and proper for discourse with the Lord. She prayed formally, but she prayed openly. If Priscilla Soames ever showed what was truly in her heart, she showed it to her God.

My Lord Jesus, she prayed, look upon me with pity. I need Your help, dear God. Please. I am cold. I am alone. I need Your help. Do not let me lose her. I do not mind suffering. I have never complained about the suffering. But I cannot bear the thought of losing her. I have been good. I never wished to be a mother, You know that, You remember my prayers, You remember the terror in my heart. But I have borne him children, I have given him daughters though I know his true desire was for a son. Forgive me, I do not mean to judge. I have been a good mother. I do not plead sacrifice, though I have sacrificed, still I do not plead sacrifice. I beg only for direction, help me, please, help me.

I am cold. I am alone.

I am a cold woman. I know this, dear God, it is the way I am. Oh my God, I have never held a baby's foot in my hand and kissed the toes. I am cold. I know this. He has never said so. He is so simple sometimes, like a child himself, he has never complained, but I know he feels this in me, I know he feels this core within me which does not bend, which never yields. Love is divine, I know this, love is divine. He is so kind to me. He was so gentle, but he is a man of God, and I am cold.

I must, I wish, I must touch another human. Help me, oh please, help me. I cannot lose her, too. I have lost my younger child, how golden her hair was, and her smile, her eyes would light and she would rush to my arms and I would hold her tight against my breast. "Mandy," I would say, but the name was alien to my tongue. "Amanda," I would say, "Daughter," cold, and the arms would sense, the eyes would cloud, but oh, oh, the golden sight of her hair, to kiss the top of her head, to hold her in my arms and kiss the top of her head freely without shame, I am so cold.

I was cold to him at first, tall and proud with his books under his arm. "I am a divinity student, Miss Bailey," delivering the words with an aloofness of purpose, "I am a divinity student," and I studied him with appreciative awe, but I said even then to myself, "Do not love him, do not love this man." Ahh.

Ahhh.

I was a girl once.

She bit me once. Penelope. She bit my breast and the shock of it! I stared at her in my arms, my first child, I could feel her tiny teeth! I laughed. And then I cried. I put her back in her crib. I did not want her to see me crying.

God, help me. Please. Please!

She is my daughter. I know, I know, she is mine, I should not have let them take her from me.

I do not know myself sometimes, dear Lord, I hear myself saying things, and I do not know this person. I look at this grown-up person saying things, I do not recognize her. And no daughters.

I swear, I swear to You, I was not trying to create myself again in my daughters, I swear this to You. I did not interfere, she wanted to play piano, there was no money. You know that, there was none. But we gave her lessons, she played so well, I felt I would burst when I heard her play, but I never said. I watched only, and I listened, but I did not touch her hair. I did not interfere. I did not want Priscilla Soames twice again. They were new, so new, and smelling sweet as rain, both new, my daughters, my babies, I wanted them to be themselves.

Nothing.

Nothing now.

A daughter who has said to my face the things I only dared to say to myself, alone, said them aloud. They ring in my ears, they echo in my ears, said them to me aloud. I have lost her now. I have no daughter Amanda.

Penelope.

Help me, dear God. Should I let them do these things to her? Should I let them? But if she cannot talk, then how will they help her unless they do these things? My daughter, let me touch your hand.

Dear God, I once ran barefoot in the grass. I once picked a daisy.

Gillian saw her father suddenly and only from a distance. There was a brisk October breeze blowing through the city that day, and it attacked the eyes and made them water. Squinting against the wind, she wasn't at all sure that the tall, redheaded man was actually her father. Or told herself he wasn't. And then knew the man was Meredith Burke, knew without question, and watched him without shock, watched him as she would a slightly ridiculous figure in an old-fashioned movie. He had taken the young woman's arm in a manner so courtly Gillian almost laughed aloud. He was leading her through the promenade, past the banks of shrubs, towards the golden statue of Prometheus overlooking the restaurants and the ice-skating rink. He did not see Gillian, and she pretended not to see him, but she remembered with sudden clarity her mother's words— "*What is there to say about my Meredith Burke and his little blonde book-keeper? What is there to say, Gillian?*" There was nothing to say now, either. She watched them dispassionately and thought they made a striking couple, her father with his deep-red hair, and the girl's head bent close to his as they walked, a bright natural blonde, very striking. How young she is, Gillian thought, he looks so old beside her. She felt curiously abandoned. She watched her father, and then quickly looked at the people on the sidewalk, wanting to know suddenly if they had all seen Meredith Burke and his book-keeper, if they were as aware of him as his daughter was, and then silently condemning him for choosing a place as indiscreet as Rockefeller Centre. She left quickly, seeking the shadowed anonymity of Forty-eighth Street.

She called him at the shoe store the next day. He didn't recognize her voice at first.

"This is Gillian," she told him. "Your daughter."

"Well, Gilly!" he said, his voice booming on to the line. "Now, what a surprise!"

"How are you, Dad?"

"Fine, just fine. And yourself?"

"Very well, thank you."

"Well, that's *marr*-vellous, Gilly. It's good to hear your voice."

"Dad, what are you doing for lunch today?"

"Why? What is it, Gilly?" he said. "Is something wrong?" There was a curious concern in his voice. She wondered for a moment whether the concern was for his book-keeper or his daughter.

"Nothing's wrong," she said quickly. "There's someone I want you to meet."

"Oh? Who, Gilly? A young man?"

"Yes."

There was a pause on the line. "Shall I have my shoes shined? Will he be proposing?"

"No, I don't think so. I just wanted you to meet him."

"Just like that?"

"Just like that."

"Where do you want to meet, and what time?" Meredith asked.

She set a time and place, and then hung up. She did not know quite why she was doing this. It's time he met David, she told herself. She dialled David at the library. When he came to the phone, she said, "David, I'm having lunch with my father. I'd like you to join us."

There was only the slightest hesitation on the line. Then David said, "Sure, I'd like to."

They talked a bit longer. She listened patiently and then said, "I have to get dressed. Twelve-thirty, don't be late."

"I'll be there," he said.

She hung up and stood staring at the receiver. When the telephone rang, it startled her. In the few seconds before she picked it up, she thought, It's one or the other of them calling to cancel. She lifted the receiver.

"Hello?" she said.

"Sweetie, this is Marian."

"Hello, Marian."

"I'm glad I caught you. Have you got a minute?"

"Yes, sure."

"What's the matter, sweetie?" Marian asked.

"Nothing."

"You sound . . . distant."

"No. What is it, Marian?"

"Sweetie, do you remember my telling you about this man who's going to shoot a pilot film in the Bahamas? Bimini, or some damn place, I can never remember the names of those islands."

"Yes, I remember."

"The underwater stuff, you remember. He's trying to get Sterling Hayden or someone like him for the male lead, and he needs a girl to play the part of this trouble-shooter sort of broad, but she'll be in every sequence, assuming they sell the pilot, of course."

"Yes, Marian."

"Well, he came into town Saturday, trying to tie up his financing and all that, and looking around for talent. I called ABC and arranged for a showing of that half-hour thing you did, the one with——"

"I remember it, Marian."

"Well, he liked it."

"That's good."

"He'd like to talk to you about the part. He's one of these guys who likes to meet the actress personally and exchange ideas. He has the peculiar notion that actresses should be intelligent as well as talented. He'll probably want to discuss the Berlin airlift—so brush up on your I.Q."

"When is this, Marian?"

"Today. For lunch."

"I can't make it."

"What?"

"I said I can't make it."

"That's what I thought you said. Why not?"

"I'm busy today. Anyway, Marian, I couldn't possibly go charging off to the Bahamas. That's out of the question."

"They'll only be down there for a month or so—to get the underwater stuff and to do the location work. They'll be shooting all the interiors here."

"Here? In New York?"

"No. Probably on the Coast."

"Well, I can't go to California, either."

"Why not?"

"I just can't, Marian."

"Sweetie, there's something I ought to tell you."

"What, Marian?"

"I'm not complaining, but——"

"What *are* you doing?"

"Look, don't be so damn touchy. This is Marian you're talking to."

"I'm sorry. What is it, Marian?"

"Oh, the hell with it," Marian paused. "But look, sweetie, I just about break my neck setting these things up for you, and this is the third one you've turned down. Now what gives, would you mind telling me? Are you still interested in acting?"

"Of course I am!"

"Then why——"

"I don't want to go to the Bahamas. That's that, Marian."

"The Ivory commercial had nothing to do with the Bahamas."

"I don't think I'm going to learn anything by doing soap commercials."

"It's exposure," Marian said.

"Yes, but it's not acting."

"I know a girl who cashes a dozen residual cheques each week. She earns five hundred bucks while she sets her hair in the morning, just opening her mail."

"I'm not starving, Marian."

"You're not working, either."

"Something'll come along."

"Honey, things *have* come along. Would you mind telling me why you turned down the summer-stock job?"

"It was in Ogunquit."

"So?"

"So I asked you to get me either Westport or Easthampton, or the Paper Mill in New Jersey. You——"

"The Paper Mill does operetta and musicals. How could——"

"I sing, Marian."

"Not that good. What was the matter with Ogunquit? It's a great showcase."

"It's too far from New York."

"When did you fall in love with this city, all of a sudden? You can't go to Maine, you can't go to California, you can't go to Bimini, where the hell *can* you go? Can I book a job on West Fifty-eighth, or is that too far uptown for you?"

There was a long silence on the line.

"What do you want me to do?" Gillian asked. "Get another agent?"

"Argh, who'd have you?" Marian said. "Will you do me a favour? Will you please see this guy today? Even if you won't go south, he's a producer, he's got his fingers in a lot of pies. There may be something later on."

"I can't today," Gillian said. "Make it tomorrow."

"He's leaving for Hollywood tonight."

"I can meet him after lunch, maybe. For a drink."

"What time?"

"Two o'clock is the earliest I can get away."

"I'll try. Will you be home for a while?"

"Yes."

"I'll call you back." Marian paused. "We still friends?"

"You know we are."

"I'll call you later, sweetie."

"Okay," Gillian said, and she hung up.

Her father was a half-hour late. She made desultory small talk with David, certain her father would not show up, pleased when she saw him come into the restaurant at last. He looked around with that bright twinkle in his eyes, saw her, and went immediately to the table. He kissed her and then turned to David.

"Dad, this is David Regan. David, my father."

David rose and took Meredith's hand. "How do you do, sir?"

"How do you do?" Meredith said. "Sit down, please. I'm sorry I'm late, but we had a lunch-hour rush." He paused. "I run a shoe store," he said, watching David, as if anxious to get this piece of information out of the way.

"Yes, sir, Gillian's told me," David said. "Would you like a drink? We're one ahead of you already."

"Yes, I would," Meredith said. "You're looking well, Gillian. You should come to see us more often. The Bronx isn't exactly the end of the world." He looked at David. "Bring your young man. Your mother won't throw him out."

Gillian smiled. "I didn't think she would, Dad."

"Come for dinner some Sunday."

"And will you be home?" she asked, and then wondered instantly if the question had not been too pointed.

Meredith raised his eyebrows quizzically. "Why yes, Gilly," he said, "I'll be home."

"Would you like to go sometime, David?"

"Sure," David said uneasily.

"I'm hoping your hair is prematurely grey, Mr. Regan," Meredith said. "Otherwise my daughter's seeing a man who's far too old for her."

"Would that matter very much, Dad?" Gillian said, and again Meredith raised his eyebrows and studied her, but said nothing this time.

"I'm twenty-four, Mr. Burke," David said.

"That's a good age. Are you studying acting, too?"

"No, sir, I'm not."

"I saw Gillian on television a few months back. She didn't tell us she was on, but I happened to catch the show by accident, anyway. You were very good, Gilly."

"Thank you."

"What *do* you do, Mr Regan?" Meredith asked.

"I work for the library."

"Oh? Doing what?"

David shrugged. "I stamp books, I guess."

"That sounds interesting," Meredith said.

"Well, it's all right for now."

"I don't suppose you'd be interested in selling shoes?"

"Well . . ." David said, and look at Gillian.

"There's nothing wrong with selling shoes, you know," Meredith said.

"No, sir, I didn't think there was."

"Do you call everyone 'sir'?"

"No, not everyone."

"Then why are you calling *me* that?"

"You're Gillian's father."

"Oh, I see. Where's our waiter? I'd like some whisky."

It was one forty-five before she realized it. She made her apologies and left the men alone together. As she walked out of the restaurant, she wondered again why she was putting either of them through this ordeal. She shrugged and hailed a cab.

"Are you in love with my daughter?" Meredith asked David.

"Yes, sir. I am."

"She's a pretty girl."

David nodded.

"Where'd you meet her?"

"At the Count's ... Igor's. That's where she's studying."

"Yes, I know."

"Well, that's where we met."

"Where do you live, Mr. Regan?"

"On First Avenue, Near Houston Street."

"Not with my daughter?"

"No, sir. I have my own apartment."

"But you do sleep with Gillian, don't you?"

"That's my business, sir. And Gillian's."

"I wouldn't want to see my daughter hurt, Mr. Regan."

"Nor would I."

"She's a fine girl. With a lot of talent."

"I know that."

Meredith nodded and studied him. "How long have you known her?"

"Since last November."

"Almost a year."

"Almost."

"And you love her, you say?"

"Yes, sir, I do."

"You seem like a very cold person."

David shrugged.

"Do you mind my frankness?" Meredith asked.

"Yes, I do."

"Shall we have more coffee?"

"I'd like some."

The waiter came, and they ordered more coffee. Meredith Burke took his black, without sugar.

"Do you plan on marrying her?"

"Yes."

"When?"

"I don't know yet."

"Why don't you know?"

"I haven't found the job I want yet."

"What job do you want?"

"I don't know yet."

"Or is there any sense to marrying a free-and-easy girl who's already . . .?"

"Mr. Burke," David said, "you're talking about Gillian. I'd hit any other man in the world who talked about her that way."

Meredith Burke nodded. "I wouldn't try hitting me, son," he said. "I would knock you flat on your behind."

"That's happened to me before, too," David said. "But it wouldn't stop me."

"Maybe you're not such a cold fish. Whose idea was this meeting?"

"Gillian's."

"Why?"

"I don't know."

"What are we supposed to discuss? You're not asking for my permission to marry her, that's for sure."

"No, sir. Not yet."

"Would it matter if I said you couldn't marry her?"

"No, sir, it wouldn't."

"Then what's the purpose of this meeting?" He shook his head. "Why'd you agree to it?"

"Because Gillian asked me."

"Oh, I see. You do whatever she asks you to, huh?"

"I love her," David said. "I don't think you know how much."

"Maybe I do," Meredith answered. "Does it embarrass you to talk about love?"

"A little."

"Don't let it. Drink your coffee. How much money do you earn?"

"Sixty-five dollars a week."

"That's not very much."

"No, sir, it isn't."

"I'm very fond of that girl," Meredith said.

"So am I."

"She's my favourite. My other's in California, you know. I doubt if she's ever coming back. Don't hurt that girl, Mr. Regan."

"I won't."

"Women can be hurt. And women can be used. Don't hurt her, and don't use her. She's my daughter, and I'm very fond of her."

"Does it embarrass *you* to talk about love?" David asked.

Meredith smiled. "I do love her," he said gently.

"I thought maybe you did," David answered, returning the smile. "I had the suspicion."

"I've thought of this day. When she'd bring around the man she'd chosen. I thought of it, Mr. Regan. Even when she was a little girl, and damn pretty she was then too. I thought of it." He paused. "I guess I don't like you. But I guess I wouldn't have liked the mayor of Dublin if my daughter brought him to me and told me she loved him."

"I guess I don't like you, either," David said. "But that has nothing to do with how I feel about Gillian."

"You know, you may be a big damn bull artist, for all I know."

"I'm not."

"Well, you'd just better not be. I don't like you now, but I'd like you even less if you were handing my daughter a line."

"I can understand that."

"Yes, and don't go getting her pregnant. I hope you can understand that, too."

"What are you getting angry about?" David asked suddenly.

"Because, to tell you the truth, I can't get used to the idea of your sleeping with her, that's what. I feel like busting you right in the mouth, Mr. Regan. That's what. Goddam it, it annoys the hell out of me."

"Well, calm down. I don't think Gillian would want us to argue."

"What the hell *does* she want? That's what I'd like to know. Why'd she bring us together?"

"Maybe she think's it's time I married her."

"Well then, maybe it is."

"She knows I'm going to marry her. I told her that the day we met."

"That was almost a year ago, sonny. When are you going to get moving?"

David shook his head. "I'm not ready for marriage yet."

"Then you'll never be ready. If you've got to think it over, you'll never be ready. And if you've got to think it over, I'm not even sure you love her."

"*I'm* the one who's got to be sure, Mr. Burke. Not you."

"You seem a lot older than twenty-four."

"I *am* a lot older."

"So's Gillian." He looked at David a moment. "Maybe it's a good match. Who the hell knows?"

"Does anyone ever know?"

"Don't get smart with your platitudes. Are we finished with our lunch?"

"I guess so."

"Don't hurt her, Mr. Regan. If you do, I'll come looking for you."

That night, she asked David how the lunch had gone.

"Terrible," he said. "He didn't like me, and I didn't like him. Why'd you have us meet, Gillian?"

"I don't know," she said, and perhaps she really didn't.

Perhaps she only wanted to remind David that sooner or later the Hamelin townsfolk would have to pay the man with the pipe. Sooner or later, David would have to take her to the altar and swear the sacred vows, sooner or later he would have to do that if he really wanted to keep her. Or perhaps marriage hadn't figured in the meeting at all. Perhaps all she'd wanted was to prove to her father, prove to Meredith Burke with his young blonde book-keeper, that she, Gillian Burke, was also capable of having an affair.

"I don't know," she repeated.

They began the treatment the moment she received the signed permission from Priscilla. They gave Penny three electric shocks a week for a period of five weeks, and then began speeding up the frequency of treatment. For the next three weeks, Penny's brain was invaded by electricity once every day. They would strap her legs and her arms to the long flat table while she kicked and gouged, trying to escape the machine behind her, hating it from the very first, hating it even before the first shock struck her, even before the blinding orange flash suddenly streaked behind her eyeballs, even before the sound shrieked into her head, hating the look of the machine itself, the sentient silence of the machine, the ominous machine, the hateful wired machine! Now she knew when they were taking her to the machine that ate her brain with fire. She could smell them as they came down the hall for her, dirty bastards come to take her to the eating machine, she would shout at them and roll her eyes in her head to frighten them away, but they would carry her down the hall, down the sliding, sloping hall to the wire machine, strap her down, tie her to the slab, she would twist her head and bite and then sense the hum, that awful hum, know it before it came, feel the orange explosion and the crackling spitting sound inside her head, her hands clenching rigidly, her back arching, blackness.

Limp, unconscious, sweating profusely, she would be carried back to the ward and they would wait for her to regain consciousness, wait for a sign that something was happening, something was penetrating the shell. But she did not respond. So they wrote to Priscilla again and asked this time for permission to begin insulin-shock treatment. "It may help her," they said, and Priscilla signed another form.

If Penny had hated the E.C.T., she hated the insulin shocks and the induced comas even more. She knew about the needle. They had done the needle before. They had done the needle to her when she first came here, had stabbed her day and night with the needle, and now there was a needle again, but this time it was an exploding needle, it rocketed into her skull and exploded there in dirty black filth, her eyes would bulge out of her head, she would scream in the blackness, they were trying to make her black, they were trying to explode her brain, they were trying to hit her with a hammer, they were trying to knock her head off with a hammer, five days a week they came with the needle, six days a week, hammer, hammer at her brain, blackness, forty times, forty-five, fifty, and then they stopped. The bastards stopped.

I am claws, I am claws, I am *claws*!

The doctors were already beginning to think of her as a Back Ward Patient.

The period of mourning was almost over.

The libertine days of World War II, the V-girls and the riveters, the tight sweaters and the low-cut blouses, the short skirts and the exposed knees, the what-the-hell attitude of a generation raised for the preparation and the waging of war, the one-night stands, the shoddy false stateside heroics and the unglorified real heroism overseas, the whole frantic pulse of a nation that had followed the war news as it would the results of a baseball game or a horse race, the entire wacky and unpredictable everyday living that was the United States of America during the war years, all this free and easy living, all this dropping of moral standards in the face of something bigger than both of us, baby, a goddam war, all this sudden kissing and spontaneous mating had reached its culmination on VJ Day and then had immediately produced a feeling of guilt in a country as basically Puritan as Cotton Mather.

The first thing they did was lower the hem line. They pretended this was the latest news from the Paris *couturiers*, a hem line that suddenly dropped from a cosy spot an inch above a dimpled knee to some place low on the shinbone. The women all took out their tape measures, and measured up twelve inches from the floor, and then made the startling discovery that even letting out the hems of their favourite frocks would never make them long enough for the new fashion. The longer dresses and skirts appeared sporadically—this was, after all, a nation in mourning, and mourners don't go on spending sprees even though all the magazines were shouting about a war-free Christmas the moment the Japanese surrendered. The girls who first sported the longer lengths were mocked by their sisters, but mourning is contagious and someone had to bear the guilt of that wartime spree. So it started with the women, and the first thing they did was cover up those legs, cover up legs that were famous the world over because they were good strong straight legs, rickets-free, fed on good American sunshine and canned Vitamin C. They covered them up in what they called the New Look, a look that was as old as the Crusades, but a look that ushered in a new sense of morality, a stiffening of the sagging upper lip. The sneer that had first accompanied the new fashion turned into a fixed expression of approval. It was popular to mourn, and if the men of America missed seeing shapely calves and well-turned knees, they told themselves the new style was more provocative, a style that hid more than it showed, a style that encouraged speculation.

The new cars came out, the first since 1942, and colour was the thing. It was odd that a nation in mourning should suddenly burst on to the automotive scene with the rainbow hues that issued forth from Detroit, but Puritanism is a crazy thing at best, and even in 1692 there was a certain exotic quality to the witches they hanged, a certain theatricality to the serious long-panned men who ranted about God and the devil, and who listened to the Salem maidens as they raved in Freudian free-association about the things the black enticer had asked them to do. Black should have been the colour for this guilty people, this nation suddenly blushing, as was every nation in the world, for its wartime extravagances of emotion and rage. But even guilt must have its compensations, and so the automobiles blossomed in radiant splendour, tentatively at first, design still several years behind colour boldness. People began buying the product, telling themselves they were entitled to a new car after all those years of deprivation. The war was over, after all, and if they bought a beautifully coloured symbol of their own masculinity, it could help them to forget those foolish years. Oddly, everyone in America had already forgotten the very real and noble part they'd played in crushing a monster.

The skirts were longer, and the cars were flashier, and people came back to work as if they were returning from a long week-end that just happened to be World War II. The week-end had been a lot of fun, but now there was work to be done. There had been drinking and fooling around, and a little honest killing here and there, but now there was work to be done, now there was a desk to get in order, and the guilt was heavy. The Hollywood machine began grinding out a few sticky-sweet films on readjustment, the best of which was *The Best Years of Our Lives,* and a little Broadway revue named *Call Me Mister* was a smash hit, combining as it did memories of the military with the bewilderment of return to pre-war values. The trouble was, however, nobody could remember what the pre-war values were. The young people who'd gone off to fight the war couldn't remember the thirties except as a time of N.R.A. stickers and poverty, and all this had radically changed the moment the Japanese dropped their cargo of bombs and torpedoes on the sleeping fleet in Pearl Harbour. There was more than a simple diffusion of memory involved in readjustment. There was, in fact, no memory at all. The people who came back, and the people who were there to welcome them, suddenly discovered they were starting with a blank sheet. They had been children before the war, innocent and naïve, thrilling to the high whining voice of Henry Aldrich yelling for his mother, but now they were adults, beset with all the problems of adults, all the fears, all the guilts, all the obsessions. It was no wonder that the club was formed, and that it gained such immediate acceptance.

The club was not the Pyramid Club, although this, too, flourished for a few brief months, a vicarious sort of gambling thrill that replaced the real thrill of weekday dates with servicemen on leave, the real soaring pleasure of reading about the assault on Tarawa, the whole overstaged, overdramatic, overpoetic production that had been a world at war. The club was a better club, the common mortar of which was guilt: the age of the analyst had arrived. It became fashionable quite suddenly to discuss things like ego and id, repressed hostility, Oedipus, Electra, and Orestes. *The Snake Pit* was an instant smash, and audiences all over America cheered Olivia de Havilland as she writhed in the torments of insanity, feeling God knew what relief at her discomfort—better you than me, Olivia —and finally gave her the New York Film Critics' Award. The top motion-picture awards that year, however, were divided among three pictures that were expressive of this new wave of subtler penetration, this psychological exploration of the self: the first, a brilliantly evocative film interpretation of *Hamlet*: the second, a story that probed the emotions of a deaf mute; and the third, a rare study of men searching for gold in the Sierra Madre Mountains. Yes, the clocks had all stopped at fifty minutes before the hour, and a couch was no longer a piece of living-room furniture. The skirts were longer, and the cars were brighter, and all the people were deeper, God, how much deeper they all were! They probed constantly, wanting to know more about themselves and each other, digging, continually asking questions in search of a new identity to fit into this unremembered landscape. In New York City, some restless kids formed a street gang.

And then, because people were able to talk about their guilt instead of really feeling it, the reins began to loosen a little bit. It would be a long time before women began to show those good legs again, but the skirt was already inching imperceptibly higher on the calf. A play by Tennessee Williams involving some fairly macabre types was greeted with enthusiastic acclaim, and a new actor named Marlon Brando electrified New York with his portrait of an animal, Russia began talking about exploding her own nuclear devices, and the pointing finger of the world began to turn in another direction. The readjustment kick was on the way out. The guilt, ingrained as deep as the soul, a guilt that would linger and grow, was temporarily put aside as the war was recalled once again, not with patriotic fervour now, not with the screaming heroics of *Bataan* with Robert Taylor sitting behind his lonely machine-gun as the camouflaged Japanese crept through the mist, fade out, the end, nor with the wild capers of Errol Flynn cavorting behind German lines in the company of downed Allied flyers, not with any of that boiling-point celluloid magic designed to send the young to the recruiting office and the old to the local bank for a war bond, not with any of that, but with a serene contemplation, an attitude of "You know, we weren't *really* so wild in those war days; those war days brought out in us the things that were finest." In a Broadway roster that included such bits of froth as *High Button Shoes* and *Make Mine Manhattan* and *Look, Ma, I'm Dancin'*, there were two solid hits called *Mister Roberts* and *Command Decision*, both of which—in the new tradition of psychological depth and meaningful action—portrayed the inner machinery of men at war, rather than the external trappings like Stuka bombers and night patrols. In Hollywood, a giant movie called *All the King's Men* was being made ready for release. It would explain demagoguery to Americans everywhere. In New York, the Giants followed the lead of the Brooklyn Dodgers and signed a Negro ballplayer named Monte Irvin.

The period of mourning was almost over. A nation that nominated to the presidency for the second time Thomas E. Dewey, a man with a *moustache*, was certainly a nation flirting with the frivolous, a country that could now remember with warm nostalgia a time of sacrifice and common endeavour. The biggest song hit of the day was "Nature Boy", which proclaimed to the world at large that "the greatest thing you'll ever learn is just to love and be loved in return". The big bands were on their way out. Glenn Miller had been killed during the war, and he belonged to the past. The greats of the thirties, Basie and Krupa and Dorsey and Spivak and Goodman, were fading sounds on a new musical scene, which placed the emphasis on vocalists and arranged jazz. The discordant sounds of Stan Kenton and Dizzy Gillespie were as new to the ear as were the slickly bright colours of the automobiles to the eye. A nation without memory needed new sights and new sounds and new heroes. Americans, perhaps unknowingly, were in the midst of a strange renaissance. There were changes in the country, and they seemed evolutionary, but perhaps they were as revolutionary as those that had swept over Russia in 1917.

In the midst of these changes, Amanda Bridges knew a change all her own, physical, spiritual, mental.

There were perhaps two things that occupied most of her waking thoughts before November. These were her sister Penny's illness and the new house in Talmadge. She would arise each morning with Penny in her mind, and each morning she would write a letter to Sandstone, which Penny never answered. And then she would set about doing the thousands of things that any new house, even when it was an old house, needed done. In November, she felt completely changed, almost as if she had been reborn, almost as if a new person had emerged from the office with its clapboard shingles, a new woman. She felt rounder and softer and more female and curiously more sexy, but also a little more shy, and contradictorily a little more noticeable, but productive and real, and closer to God, and closer to Matthew, and closer to the new house and the town of Talmadge, the roots of Talmadge, a little awkward, a little more cautious, a little more recklessly flirtatious. The news did all these things to Amanda so that she was rendered completely unaware of the bigger changes happening around her, she was concerned only with the miracle of change in herself.

In November of 1948, Amanda discovered she was pregnant.

Matthew thought it was incredible.

He was not so much pleased by the news as he was astounded. He knew, of course, that there were certain natural functions that, if not carefully supervised, could very easily lead to this sort of thing, but it was not the simplicity of Amanda's conception that amazed him. It was, rather, the fact that someone like his wife could suddenly become a potential mother. He didn't know if he enjoyed thinking of her as a mother. He didn't know if he enjoyed thinking of her as a wife. Birth and motherhood implied mysteries he could never hope to fathom. He had never enjoyed suspense stories, and he felt that he was mysterious enough for both of them and certainly didn't need anyone shuffling around the house with the great secret of the universe in her belly. There was one secret in the old Talmadge already, and one secret was enough.

The secret gave him immeasurable pleasure. It was a secret he had never divulged to Amanda. No matter what he shared with her, no matter how close he felt to her, the nights they exchanged kisses and dreams, the days when their marriage fell into the expected hiatus of the ordinary and they shared something less than passion but somehow more intimate, he would never tell Amanda what had almost happened to her on Christmas Eve five years ago. He knew he would never tell her this, and he realized their relationship was built on the solid foundation of—not a lie, certainly not a lie—but a truth withheld. Nor was he being facetious. He felt this withheld truth *was* a solid foundation. This was not specious reasoning, so far as Matthew was concerned. He felt that marriage was a totally illogical invention, anyway, and he thought it was far more honest to build a marriage around a withheld truth than it was to build it around anything like faith or trust, which were lies in themselves.

He had learned early in life that there were the weak and the strong, the poverty-stricken and the rich, the outsiders and the insiders, the loved and the unloved, the chaste and the unchaste, all excellent paperback titles, he surmised, but all none the less direct opposites in a world of conflict and contrast. He had carried this a step further and theorized that every human relationship was based upon a principle of greater or lesser possession or involvement. One party had more money, or loved more, or hated more, or was more ambitious or more cruel or more passionate than the party who was his opposite number. And the other person, by simple inversion, did all these things, or was all these things, or owned all these things, to a lesser extent, the More-or-Less Principle of Matthew Anson Bridges. The remarkable thing about his theory was that it could be applied to a personal relationship as well as a business relationship, and it worked exceptionally well when applied to the institution known as marriage.

On his wedding night, Matthew learned that Amanda loved him more than he loved her. He also learned that he was more passionate, more skilled, and infinitely more interested in sex than was his new bride. He felt it was a good thing that she loved him more because he could not visualize the reverse situation, a situation that could make life intolerable for the person on the short end of the stick. Oh, he loved her, all right. He loved her the way any red-blooded boy would love a girl who was beautiful and desirable and witty and talented and provocative. He certainly loved her. He loved her even after he learned that her early-morning beauty was sometimes a bit faded, and her desirability was simply an accident of the flesh, and her wit was sometimes hopelessly rural, and her talent sometimes included the playing of Mozart, Mozart, Mozart all damn day long, and her provocation was all too often unconscious and led absolutely nowhere; he loved her. What the hell, these were two people living together, and she probably didn't like the way he tied his pyjama bottoms or brushed his teeth. There were bound to be little frictions that would arise when two separate and distinct personalities moved into the same house and began sharing the same bathroom. He expected this, and was not surprised by it. There certainly was nothing about Amanda that would send him running into the streets shrieking for a divorce, and he did love her. But he was very happy that she loved him more than he loved her.

He was also happy about his secret. The secret gave him strength somehow. He never alluded to it, never by the slightest hint of word or expression gave any clue to its existence. But it was there inside him, and he often thought of that Christmas Eve, and how he had saved Amanda on the big brass bed, and the secret and his memories of the secret always made him smile a little. He would look at Amanda his wife, a little naïve, a little unknowing, his beautiful Amanda, and smile. Her innocence sometimes amazed him. He often wished he could have at every jury trial four witnesses for the defence who looked like Amanda and talked like Amanda. He would have her sit in the witness chair and answer questions in her unaffected, honest, Midwestern voice, smiling slightly perhaps, her brown eyes wide, her long blonde hair framing an angelic face. He would not coach her beforehand, but he knew she would unconsciously cross her legs to some point during the questioning, and every man on the jury would desire her and then feel an enormous sense of embarrassment and guilt for his lecherous notions. Amanda would continue answering the questions sweetly, totally unaware of the conflict she was causing. But they would believe her if she told them the earth was flat. He was certainly glad she loved him more than he loved her.

And yet, sometimes, he wondered if her innocence wasn't a pose. He never wondered whether he was seeing her accurately, whether Amanda at twenty-five and fast approaching twenty-six, was the same Amanda he had rescued in Gillian's apartment. No, he never wondered that, and never concluded that he was cherishing his secret, nourishing his secret, in an attempt to keep Amanda the constant college girl in tweed skirt and loafers, the inviolate female, pure and virtuous, the symbol of some half-forgotten youth. He never wondered about her as a woman, never thought to ask how *she* felt about herself, never imagined her as anything but a rather beautiful creature who put on lipstick and brassière, who rustled in silk, an amazing young girl who was somehow his wife to watch, to hold, to love—but not as much as she loved him. He only wondered if she affected naïveté because she knew it was appealing. And yet, it seemed genuine enough. She seemed to have an enormous faith in her fellow-man, believing everyone was as honest and as trustworthy as she knew herself to be, believing Talmadge was a real town with real people. Matthew himself had recognized Talmadge for the phony town it was the moment they attended their first cocktail party. He decided then and there that he did not want to become even slightly involved with this bunch of bogus small-towners whose hearts and roots were still in New York. He tried to understand what had attracted them to Talmadge at all. The town was picturesque, true, with some of the most spectacular countryside he had ever seen in his life, especially during the fall when the woods lining the roads became unimaginably beautiful. And the first view of the town as you came around the bend in the road, with the church sitting off to the right on the hill, and the university spires in the distance, and the shaded leafy main street, was undoubtedly worth a great deal to the picture-postcard industry.

But what was there about the town itself, other than its scenic worth, that attracted families from New York and New Haven, depositing them in a no man's land that was half-way between both and close to neither? Was it indeed the university and the shadow of its subtle beauty, its intimations of a scholarly citizenry, a town of knowledgeable, lively, inquiring people? Perhaps so, but its presence seemed only a deterrent to Matthew. Nor had the prices of houses and acreage been designed to encourage impetuous spending. So what was it? He pondered it for a long time, and when he thought he knew, when he thought he'd figured out what brought people to this fake-front town with its fake ideals and fake morality and fake standards, he tried the theory on Amanda, and she sat and looked at him in shocked wonder, as if he were suggesting they walk over to the Talmadge graveyard and disinter a few bodies. Her innocence stared out at him in disbelief. No, this was wrong. No, Matthew, you are doing the town an injustice.

"I'm reading it correctly, Amanda dear," he said, "and if you didn't look at the world through those rose-coloured glasses of yours, you'd realize that this town and the people in this town are as phony as that exhibit they're holding at the library this week."

"And what's so phony about the exhibit?" Amanda asked.

"If you can't see it, Amanda . . ."

"No, I can't, and I wish you'd explain it to me. We're having a showing of old kitchen utensils and things. Now, what's so phony about that?"

"Nothing. Nothing at all. I just thought your postcards were very funny." He grinned, remembering the cards she had mailed just the day before. He had picked them up from the hall table and leafed through them smiling when he read the first one, and then bursting into laughter by the time he reached the fifth.

DEAR LOIS,

If it's at all possible, we would like very much to have you drop off your cinnamon grinder, wooden ladle, apple-sauce cruncher and bread-making bucket at the library on January 14th.

Thank you,
AMANDA BRIDGES

DEAR BETTY,

Please drop off your apple corer, cabbage cutter, long spoon, copper dipper and olive wood bowl at the library on January 14th.

Thank you,
AMANDA BRIDGES.

DEAR MRS. FRASETTI,

Please drop off your mortar and pestle and French onion print at the library on January 14th.

DEAR MRS. NELSON,

Would you please drop off your handsome loaf baker and match striker at the library on January 14th?

DEAR CONNIE,

Would you please drop off your old doughnut cutter, your pewter kettle and your Swedish cooky things at the library on January 14th?

"Did you say phony or *funny*?" Amanda asked.

"Both."

"I think it's a wonderful exhibit and exactly what women would like to see. You're a man. How would you know?"

"I think it's phony as hell in a day and age when everyone's kitchen has mechanical devices that can do everything but change the baby's diaper."

"You're entitled to your opinion," Amanda said, and she shrugged.

"Yes, and my opinion is that Talmadge, Connecticut, is the fakest town in the eastern United States. And that takes in some pretty fancy fake towns like Darien and Scarsdale and New Hope and——"

"Oh, Matthew, what makes a town fake?"

"I know what makes *this* town fake."

"Yes, people like *you*," Amanda said accusingly.

"The first thing that makes Talmadge a fake is that university backdrop hanging in the hills over there. It creates an illusion of higher education when I'll bet half the morons who live here haven't even been through the sixth grade."

"That's not true, Matthew. You know it isn't true."

"All right, maybe it isn't. They got to junior high school, some of them."

"They're some of the brightest people in New York!" Amanda said.

"Then why didn't they *stay* in New York? That's just my point!"

"What's your point, Matthew?" she asked. "Would you please make your point, Matthew?" She had used his first name twice in as many sentences, a sure sign that she was getting angry.

"My point is this. Talmadge is a fake because only the scenery is real, the rest is all imported like those crumby Japanese toys you can buy in the five-and-ten and which break under the slightest pressure. These people are *New Yorkers*, honey. The sidewalk sings in their blood. Every time they talk about how much they hate the filthy city, their eyes gleam with nostalgia. You can't become a small-towner, Amanda. You either are, or you aren't, and they aren't, and the whole damn set-up here is rotten and phony."

"Wow," Amanda said.

"You said it," he answered.

He did not tell her the rest.

He did not tell her what else he had observed about this phony town, because he felt she was a little too naïve to appreciate it, and besides he didn't know quite what her reactions would be now that she was pregnant. He watched her moving about the house and wondered anew about her, wondered if this girl-woman he saw every day of the week was the real Amanda, the true Amanda. Something had happened to her suddenly, and whereas he had been a party to the abrupt prenatal change, he felt excluded now that it was a fact. He watched her from a seemingly great distance, and wondered how he felt about the coming baby. July. Not so very far away. July, and there would be a child in the house. Not simply the two of them any more. A child. To share with. To love.

He wanted Amanda to be the way she was.

He wanted Amanda to be the innocent college girl who had lain unconscious on the big brass bed.

. . . . .

The eyes are looking at her.
The eyes are looking at the girl with the claws.
Penny-ellow, Penny-ellow, Penny-ellow-penno-pee.
Claws.
Tear out the eyes with the rush of the wind on a wintry summer day in summer sky, on fairy feet, oh maiden fly, Penny-ellow-pee, Penelope.
Dead sea and ironbottom sound aloud a crowd of chowder eaters I love you and I will be home soon you are probably as fat as a house now the things I will do to you I love you my penelope your husband Frank Robert Randolph SM 2/c USS Barton DD 599 c/o F.P.O. San Francisco, California, born her of claws.
Sea wash squash the dead sea hero squad the dears the lovely dears of dd squadron number squash the sea.
Lulu had a baby his name was Sonny Jim.
They are looking at the girl with claw eyes the murderers.

It was the beginning of March.
She had been in the hospital for almost a year when they decided to perform the operation. Priscilla went to Sandstone, and they explained very patiently to her, told her all about this thing called a prefrontal lobotomy. The operation would be performed by a neurosurgeon, they told her, a consultant on the hospital's staff. A sharp instrument would be pushed into a portion of her brain, severing certain connections between the brain and the autonomic nervous system. The patient . . .
"No!" Priscilla said immediately.
The patient would experience no pain. There was no great danger in the operation, little more than what one could expect from an appendectomy. But if the operation were successful . . .
"No?" Priscilla said again.
If the operation were successful, they might have their daughter back, Penny might be able to go home again. They understood it was a difficult decision for parents to make, but they had been unable to reach Penny at all, and the operation might help her. They did not mean to imply there would be no changes. Penny might tend to be a little silly at times, passive, vague. She would not be like her previous self, not like the person they once had known. But she would be quieter, and calmer, and perhaps they could take her home. It was a difficult decision to make, yes, but perhaps they could take her home. She would not be the same, no, but perhaps they could take her home.
"And if the operation fails?" Priscilla asked.

"She'll be no worse off than she is now, Mrs. Soames." The doctor paused. "Nothing else has worked. We've tried everything."

"If . . . if it works, will she know us again?"

"Yes. If it's successful, she'll recognize you, talk to you."

"Does it often work?"

"We've had good results. Of course, you must understand . . ."

"Yes?"

"This would not be a cure, Mrs. Soames. Your daughter won't be the same. I can't mislead you into thinking she'd be the way she was before her illness."

"I understand." Priscilla nodded. "How can I let you put a knife into her brain?" she asked, not looking at the doctor, staring at her clenched hands in her lap.

"Mrs. Soames," the doctor said gently, "your daughter is suffering. I can't begin to tell you how much she is suffering. If there's a chance that we can relieve her of her pain, her total sadness, if there's only the slightest chance that we can bring her at least a small measure of peace . . ." The doctor shrugged his shoulders helplessly.

Priscilla was silent for a long time. Then she sighed deeply and looked at her husband and said, "We must, Martin." She turned to the doctor. "Yes," she said. "If there is a chance, yes, do it. God forgive me, do it."

Penny seemed much better after the operation. When Priscilla and Martin went to see her, she smiled blankly and said, "Hello, Mother. Hello, Dad." She seemed so much better. A little slow, perhaps, a little vague sometimes, and occasionally she would laugh or giggle unexplainably, but she seemed at least to have found that small promised measure of peace.

"Kate," she said once.

Priscilla leaned forward.

"She would like Amanda and Connecticut."

"We're taking care of Kate for you, dear," Priscilla said.

Penny seemed puzzled. "Can't you send her to Amanda?"

"I . . . I don't know if Amanda would . . . would want her, Penelope. She's pregnant, you know. Your sister is pregnant."

"Oh, don't tell *me* about being pregnant," Penny said, and laughed. "Kate would like Connecticut."

"My dear, you'll be coming home soon," Priscilla said. "You can care for your daughter yourself."

"My daughter, yes," Penny said, and she nodded. "And the sewing machine."

"What, darling?"

"What?" Penny said, smiling at her mother.

"Did you say . . . ?"
"I said Kate would like Connecticut."
"Perhaps," Priscilla said. "But, dear, when you come home . ."
"I think it's sad," Penny said.
Her mother stared at her wordlessly.
"Don't you think so?"
"What, darling? What is?"
"About Kate."
"Yes. Yes, I do."
"Well, it's a nice day," Penny said. She seemed very thoughtful for a moment. Then she turned to her father and asked, "Do you still have the black hat?"
"Yes, my dear."
"Wear it when you come. It makes me laugh."

Martin Soames wore his black hat the next time they went to visit Penny, and she laughed and told him it would be good to come home again, had they heard from Amanda? She giggled.

"I wish I were a lobster," she said suddenly.

Four weeks after the lobotomy was performed, Penny attacked the nurse who was making her rounds with evening sedations. She hit the woman from behind, striking her at the base of her neck, and then catching her throat between her fingers and attempting to strangle her. A startled patient in the next bed pushed the alarm button, and three attendants subdued Penny and placed her under restraint once more. The next day, she wet the bed repeatedly and had to be removed from it forcibly when they wanted to change the sheets. She kicked over a night table and rushed with her head bent at the stomach of a burly attendant, slamming him against the wall and almost fracturing his arm. They thought it was the end. They sighed and glanced at each other with the utter despair of men who have tried everything they know, men who are fighting a terrible enemy, retreating constantly, weaponless now, utterly routed.

And then suddenly, the next morning, Penny smiled cheerfully and said, "Hello, Dr. Donato, how are you this morning?" and she asked when they would send her home, and she asked how her mother was, and how her daughter Kate was, and she said again, "It would be nice for her in Connecticut."

They took off the jacket.

She tried to hang herself with the bed jacket that night. The next day, she refused to eat. Her eyes had glazed over, and a look of constant and indescribable horror was on her face, a tortured persistent look, the look of a woman trapped in a burning room with no escape. She began to soil herself again. She sang bawdy lyrics at the top of her lungs, she swore, she spat, she reviled God and the universe, she trembled with fear and screamed in rage. In ten days' time, her intellectual and emotional deterioration was almost total; she had become again the patient they had first admitted to the hospital, silent, uncommunicative, lost.

The director called Priscilla and asked her to come. He told her what had happened and then he shook his head sadly and said, "There is nothing more we can do. Nothing." He spread his hands helplessly. "Nothing. Your daughter will probably remain hospitalized for the rest of her life."

They drove home in silence that night, the Reverend Martin Soames and his wife Priscilla.

After a long while, Priscilla said, "It is God's will."

Martin did not answer.

She went into the house and took off her hat. She paid the babysitter and then she went upstairs to look at the child Kate asleep in her bed. She almost reached out to touch her hair, but her hand would not move. She went downstairs again and sat at the drop-leaf desk for a long time. In the church, Martin was playing the organ. Priscilla nodded, picked up a pen, and began writing the most difficult letter she had ever had to write in her life:

13 April 1949

DAUGHTER

Your father and I have just returned from Sandstone State Hospital where we were told that the results of the operation they performed on your sister, though they seemed encouraging at first, have not been at all what was hoped for, there is no hope.

Amanda dear, there is no hope.

We are getting old, your father and I. The child is not yet seven. It was Penny's wish that she come to live with you in Connecticut. She is not a burden, daughter. She is a lovely child and well-mannered, and she needs young people who can give her love. We are getting old.

I would take it very kindly, my daughter, if you would give her a home and the love she needs. I would take it very kindly.

God love you.

Your mother,
PRISCILLA SOAMES

The scene was a particularly difficult one, and David's absence wasn't making it any easier. Gillian kept alternating her attention between the open script in her lap and the clock on the wall. He'll call, she told herself. As soon as he knows anything, he'll call. Now think of the girl in the play.

She looked at the clock, and then turned her attention back to the script, gathering the shreds of her concentration, seeking in herself a key to the girl's character. She loves her husband, Gillian thought, that much we know. All right, so why did Igor ask me to work with an actor I despise? Just because of that, I suppose. The effectiveness of the scene depends entirely on how convincing the girl's love is. Igor's given me something that will be especially difficult for me. All right, I'll be deeply in love with my husband. I'll be charming and warm and sympathetic to him from the moment we step on to that stage. Oh brother, she thought.

She looked again at the clock, and then turned back to the script and began drumming an attitude into her mind. She told herself she liked him, no, better than that, she absolutely adored this simple, untalented jerk, she worshipped the ground he walked on, the last thing she wanted from him was an argument. The girl she was playing had been raised strictly, and on the premise that marriage was a sacrament, that marriage and obedience, and duty to one's husband, the bearing and raising of children, were a woman's only real goals. She was somewhat shy and reticent, a good wife and a good mother. In the scene, she was supposed to discover that her husband had been unfaithful to her, had indeed withdrawn a thousand dollars from their joint bank account and given the money to his paramour. Faced with this moment of truth, the girl was supposed to explode in a complete reversal of character, expressing whatever hostilities had been repressed during the years of her childhood and the eight years of her even-keeled marriage. Gillian made a face. She found the scene and the character difficult to believe, but she supposed this meant only that the character was someone beyond the scope of her own personality. None the less, a good actress was supposed to create believable experience in terms of related, if seemingly obscure, experiences of her own, wasn't she? Gillian sighed heavily, closed her eyes against the clock, and began to probe.

She could understand the girl's upbringing because it was faintly reminiscent of her own, possibly reminiscent of every girl's upbringing, but the similarity ended right there. As any of the embryo actors in Igor's class might have put it, Gillian had "never done the marriage bit". But she had certainly been subjected to the interminable pounding of a marriage-oriented mother, perhaps even a marriage-oriented society. Her own training was not unique. She recognized that possibly every son and daughter in the world were exposed to a childhood of propaganda, the word-of-mouth advertising passed from generation to generation, the key words of which were "when you get married." She thought it interesting that *this* was the transmitted prophecy, an allegation that left no real room for choice. She could not imagine any mother, except in the novels of Colette, saying to her daughter, "When you grow up and become someone's mistress," no, she could not imagine it. Nor would anyone say to her son, "When you grow up and become a bachelor." The word came down with unflinching adult authority, camouflaged in various guises, but always essentially the same:

"Wait until you have children of your own."

"Some day you'll meet a nice girl."

"I've saved my wedding veil for you."

"You want to plan for the future."

The double talk of subliminal direction, which, when translated from the English, always added up to the same four words: when you get married.

Gillian had been subjected to the same subtle dunning approach, perhaps more so because she was a girl and marriage was the dangling carrot of successful womanhood. The training, she supposed, was as much a part of her as her liver or her heart, and although she accepted her relationship with David, accepted her role in the honesty of an unquestioning love that she felt was real and enduring, she admitted to herself that she was sometimes uneasy about it. Somewhere inside this uninhibited girl, there was a girl quite different, a young child who listened to and heeded the words of mother and God, who reeled back in shock at her own impropriety. Perhaps this was why she chose not to meet Julia Regan.

She could remember the first time David had asked her to accompany him to Talmadge on a week-end. She had hesitated a moment before answering, and then had said, "No, I don't think so, David."

"But why not?"

"It isn't that . . . David, I'd love to meet your mother, really I would." She shook her head. "But not now, not yet."

She had turned away from him, avoiding his eyes, suddenly shy and embarrassed. But she knew she could not meet his mother yet, not this way, not the way things were.

She looked at the clock again.

Come on, she thought, think of the character in the play.

She turned her attention back to the script, read two speeches with forced concentration, slapped the page suddenly, and looked back at the clock again.

He should have been here by now. Or, lacking that, he should have called. He should have known she'd be on tenterhooks waiting for word one way or the other. The appointment had been for a five-thirty drink, she had made the appointment herself, she had called Curt personally the moment she heard about the job opening.

"I'm sorry, Gilly," he'd said. "This isn't an acting job. And besides, I'm looking for a man."

"That's why I'm calling, Curt. A friend of mine might be right for it."

"Who? Anybody I know?"

"I don't think so. His name is David Regan."

"Never heard of him."

"Nobody ever heard of you, either, Curt. Until Westport in 1946, and it was *my* agent who got you the job because *I* told her you'd——"

"Hey, what is this?" Curt asked. "Blackmail?"

"Not at all," Gillian answered. "I'm refreshing your memory. Now that you're a big-shot television magnate, maybe your memory——"

"Has he ever worked in television before?"

"No, but who has, Curt?"

"Well, Gillian, to tell you the truth . . ."

"Curt, darling, don't snow old friends. This is primarily an administrative job, and hasn't got a thing to do with television techniques. Will you talk to him, please?"

"Where do you get all your information, Gilly? What do you do, run a spy system in New York?"

"I simply keep track of old friends," she said.

"Yeah, go ahead. Hit the 'old friends' theme one more time."

"If you don't like him, you don't have to hire him."

"I wouldn't hire your *father* if I didn't like him."

"But you will talk to him, Curt?"

"What else are old friends for?" Curt asked sourly.

"You're very sweet-oh," Gillian said. "Can you make it this afternoon? Five-thirty?"

It was almost seven now, and no word from David. She sat on the living-room couch, and looked through the open kitchen door to the clock on the wall, her legs tucked under her, hating the clock, and hating David for not having called, and hating Curt Sonderman, too. She couldn't concentrate on the script, it was impossible. She picked up an emery board and began frantically filing her nails. She felt as excited as if she were applying for the job herself. She knew instinctively that it would be something good for David, and she desperately wanted him to have it. She would not allow herself to consider its ramifications, the possibility that if once he found a good job, a job he liked, a job that offered a challenge and a future, then he might . . . no, she would not allow herself to think in terms of a stupid shopgirl waiting for a man to make her honest, what the hell am I, Bertha the Sewing Machine Girl? She looked at the clock again and frowned. How inconsiderate of that oafish lout, she thought, not to call me when he surely knows I'm waiting. That big fool knows I'm sitting here sandpapering my finger-nails down to the bone and beginning to resemble Venus de Milo, but does he care? He and that other idiot Sonderman are probably drunk in a Third Avenue bar discussing their conquests while I sit here like Elaine the fair, guarding the sacred shield.

When the knock sounded on the door, she leaped to her feet instantly, rushed to it, and threw it open.

"Did you get it?" she asked.

"Hold it, hold it," David said.

"Hold it! It's seven o'clock! Didn't you pass a telephone? Haven't you got a nickel? I've been sitting here——"

"Now hold it, just hold it."

"Did you get it, or not?"

"Good old Gillian, straight to the point."

"Well, what are we supposed to do, you moron? Beat around the bush for an hour? Did you get the job or did you not get the job? If you don't tell me right this minute, David, I'll——"

"I think so."

"You got it," she said.

"Now wait a minute. I only think so. I didn't say——"

"You got it," Gillian said again, and she collapsed on to the couch. "I knew you'd get it."

"I'm not sure I got it. He said he'd call me later tonight. There was someone else he promised to see."

"If he's going to call you later tonight, you got it. Tell me what happened. Tell me all about it."

"Well, I walked in, and this portly guy at the bar——"

"Portly? Curt Sonderman? He was as thin as a rail when I knew him."

"Well, he's portly now."

"That's because he's rich now."

"Yes, the rich are always fat. Stereotype number six-four-five-three-one."

"Don't be such a smart-oh. He came from the bar, yes, go on?"

"And he said 'Mr. Regan?' and I said, 'Yes,' and he said, 'I'm Curt Sonderman. Nice to know you.'"

"Yes, yes?"

"So we sat down at a table and began talking about the job. Do you know what it is, Gilly?"

"I have some idea. But tell me."

"Well, he produces two or three television shows, all of them live variety-type programmes. The commercials on these shows, for the most part, are live too."

"Yes, yes, go on."

"I am. Most of his sponsors have New York advertising agencies, but some of the sponsors are out-of-town firms, the Middle West, California, who——"

"Yes, yes——"

"——who are using Los Angeles agencies with just very small branch offices in New York."

"I see, yes. Go on."

"Will you please stop interrupting me?"

"I'm sorry, go on."

"Well, one of those sponsors had an incident happen on one of the shows where a fresh pineapple was supposed to be sliced, and the pineapple they used looked as if it had been sitting at the bottom of a garbage can for a week. When they showed the . . . what do you call it, Gilly? The film of the programme?"

"The kinescope, the kine, go on."

"Yes, when they showed the kine, the sponsor blew his top and decided to make sure this never happened again. So he called his Los Angeles ad agency and asked them to contact the other out-of-town sponsors on this one particular show, the Sam Martin show, to find out——"

"That's a very big show. He's very big, Martin is."

"Yes, to find out if they'd be interested in getting together to hire a man in New York whose sole job would be to monitor these things, go to the studio when the commercials were being done, make certain the props were the right ones and all in the right places——"

"Yes, I see, yes——"

"——make sure the person doing the commercial had the right copy, generally ride herd on everybody, the premise being that an on-the-spot representative was absolutely essential. Well, the other sponsors thought it was a good idea, and the agency contacted Sonderman, who also thought it was a good idea, and they asked him if he'd take care of the New York hiring for them."

"And he hired you!"

"Well . . ."

"That's your job. It sounds exciting."

"I haven't got it yet."

"How much does it pay?"

"Two hundred."

"What! A week?"

"Yes."

"Two hundred a week! David!" She threw her arms around him and kissed him. "David, you'll get rich and portly!"

"That's only the beginning salary. Gilly. Sonderman's talking about getting the sponsors of the other two shows into the pool. And if that happens, the salary'll go up."

"Let's celebrate!" Gillian said.

"I haven't got the job yet. Will you please calm down?"

"You got it. I know you did. Why didn't you call me?"

"I wanted to get back here as soon as possible. I gave him this number, and I was afraid he'd call while I was frittering my time away in a phone booth."

"Where shall we go?"

"What do you mean?"

"After he calls. After we know you've got the job for sure."

"Gillian, can't we wait and——"

"Oh, I know you got it. What time did you leave him?"

"About forty minutes ago."

"He'll probably call in a few minutes. Curt does things quickly."

"He seemed pretty much on the ball."

"Did he like you?"

"I think so."

"Did you pay for the drinks?"

"Yes."

"Good. Did he ask many questions about television?"

"No. He seemed impressed by the library background. I don't know why. Maybe he figures he needs a human catalogue to keep track of all the products on the show."

The phone rang abruptly, shrilling into the apartment. They both turned to stare at it.

"Curt," Gillian said.

"It's too soon."

"It's Curt. I know it is. He doesn't fool around. I told you that."

The phone kept ringing.

"Answer it," Gillian said.

"I think you ought to answer it."

"It's Curt."

The phone was ringing noisily.

"Suppose it isn't Curt?"

"You've answered the phone here before! For God's sake, David, hurry! He'll hang up!"

"I don't think it's Curt."

"Answer it!"

David walked to the phone and picked up the receiver.

"Hello," he said. "Yes, this is he." He paused. "Yes, Mr. Sonderman." Gillian suddenly clasped her hands together. "Yes. Oh, just a few minutes ago. Um-huh. Yes, I see. Yes. Yes, I see. Yes, I understand. Thank you. Good-bye."

He put the phone back into its cradle.

"Yes?" Gillian said.

David had a dazed expression on his face.

"David! Please!"

"Yes."

"Really? Oh, Da——"

"I start Monday."

Gillian sat on the couch suddenly and began crying.

"I never, never for a minute thought you'd got it," she said.

They were standing on the lawn and waving as the car pulled out. It was May, and the Minnesota sunshine was bright. It illuminated Martin and Priscilla Soames with a harsh flat glare, so that they looked like painted marionettes against a false backdrop, someone pulling the strings attached to their waving hands.

"Wave to Grandpa and Grandma," Matthew said. "Wave goodbye."

Kate lifted her hand and waved. She continued waving until the house and the lawn were out of sight. Then she folded her hands in her lap and looked straight ahead through the windshield. She was wearing a bright-yellow dress and white socks and black patent-leather Mary Janes and a big yellow bow in her blonde hair. She sat quite still beside him and Matthew thought, Great, now I have to make conversation with a child.

"It's always sad to leave some place," he said, and thought, Oh, that's a wonderful beginning. Matthew Bridges, the Uncle Don of the highway. "But I think you'll like Connecticut," he concluded weakly.

The child said nothing.

Matthew shrugged slightly and then pulled a sour face. He glanced at the child to see if she had noticed his displeasure, but she was oblivious to him, staring at the Minnesota countryside as it flashed past. He felt an active dislike for her in that moment, and instantly blamed Amanda for this whole foolhardy venture, but first he blamed Priscilla for her letter, but mostly he blamed Amanda. "You're pregnant!" he'd said. "For the love of God, you're pregnant!"

"A child needs a young couple to care for her," Amanda said quietly.

"You're going to have your own child in July."

"Yes, I know."

"So how are we supposed to . . . ?"

"We can take care of both. We're young."

"I'm not so young any more," Matthew said. "I was thirty-two years old in February."

"You're still young, Matthew."

"I'm getting white hairs in my moustache, do you know that?" he shouted helplessly.

"She's only a child."

"Amanda, don't do it."

"Don't do what?"

"Don't start crying. I can see you're about to cry. Now don't do that, Amanda. It's unfair. Let's discuss this like——"

"Matthew, I want her."

"Why?"

"She's my niece." She paused. "She's my sister's daughter, and I love my sister very much."

"Your mother's been taking care of her. She can continue to——"

"Not the way I can. Not the way we would, Matthew."

Matthew sighed heavily. "And what'll you do in July?" he asked. "When the baby comes."

"We'll manage," Amanda said, and that was that.

Now, sitting beside the silent child on the front seat of the automobile, he was more than ever convinced this was a mistake. You simply did not throw a fully-grown, well, a half-grown, well, she was almost seven, you simply did not throw a young girl like that nto the arms of people who barely knew her.

"You comfortable?" he asked her.

"Yes," Kate said. "Thank you."

"Because it's going to be a long ride."

"I'm comfortable," she said. "Thank you."

"You look very nice," he said grudgingly.

"Thank you."

End of conversation, he thought. How do you talk to a six-year-old kid, well, she's almost seven, hell, she's only six and a half, let's face it. What do six-and-a-half-year-old kids think about, anyway?

"What are you thinking about?" he asked.

"What?"

"I said——"

"Oh, lots of things," Kate said.

"Like what?"

"I don't know."

End of conversation, he thought. Ask a stupid question . . .

"Like my room," Kate said.

"What about your room?"
"My bed had a quilt."
"We've got quilts home," he said.
"May I have one?"
"Sure."
"I liked the quilt," she said, and fell silent again. After a little while, she asked, "Will I have my own room?"
"Yes."
"Where will it be?"
"Upstairs. Down the hall from us."
"Is there a window?"
"Sure." He paused. "It looks out over the orchard. It's a very nice room."
"An apple orchard?"
"Yes."
"That's good." She paused again. "Is my mother crazy?" she asked.
He hesitated. He did not know what her grandparents had told her.
"Well," he said, "she's pretty sick."
"Will she be in the hospital always?"
"Yes." He paused. "Yes, I think so."
"I feel sorry."
"We all do, Kate."
"Will I live with you always?"
"I don't know."
"Do you want me to?" He hesitated only for an instant, but she took her cue at once and said, "You don't, do you?"
"Of course we do."
"She cut off my hair," Kate said. "My mother." She paused. "But it's all grown back now. Will you cut off my hair?"
"Only if you want us to."
"I don't want you to. I like long hair."
"I do, too."
"Do you think I have nice hair?"
"You have very pretty hair."
"You do, too." She looked at him carefully and then said, "When I get big, I'm going to grow a moustache."
Matthew laughed. "Girls don't grow moustaches," he said.
"Why not?"
"Only men do."
"Mrs. Schultz who has the grocery store in town has a moustache," Kate said.
"Well . . ." Matthew pondered this one for a moment. "Maybe

she's a very special person. A woman can't grow a moustache unless she's very gifted."

"Well, I'm very gifted," Kate said. "I can play 'Jingle Bells' on the organ. Grandpa taught me. Do you have an organ?"

"No, but we have a piano."

"I like organs better." She paused. "But I like pianos, too," she said quickly. "Do you play the piano?"

"No. But Amanda does."

"Would she teach me, do you think?"

"If you ask her to. She plays beautifully. She went to music school, you know."

"Maybe she'll teach me," Kate said. "If I ask her."

"I'm sure she would."

"Do you have any doll carriages?"

"No."

"I should have brought my doll carriage. Grandma said there wasn't room in the car, though."

"Well, we'll see about getting you a new carriage," Matthew said.

"Grandma said I wasn't to ask you for anything. She said taking me in was quite enough. That's what she said. Quite enough."

"You can ask for anything you want," Matthew said. He grinned at her and added, "That doesn't mean you'll get it, of course."

The child responded instantly to his joke. For the first time since she'd entered the car, a warm smile broke on her face. She relaxed immediately and said, "That's the dairy up ahead. It's got thousands of cows. Cows are the stupidest beasts in the world, did you know that?"

"I suspected as much."

"It's true. I read it in a comic book."

"Well, then it must be true," Matthew said seriously.

Kate giggled. "See them? All over the fields. All they do is chew grass and sleep."

"And give milk."

"They don't really give it," Kate said. "You have to *take* it from them."

"That's true. I never looked at it that way."

"There's where I went to school," Kate said, pointing. "I'm in the first grade. Is there a school in Talmadge?"

"An elementary school, and a high school, and even a university," Matthew said.

"What's a university?"

"A . . . well, a collection of colleges."

"College comes after the eighth grade," Kate said.

"Yes, but a long way after."

"Can I go to college?"

"Sure."

"Mommy started college, but then she met Daddy. He was killed, you know. During the war. Were you in the war?"

"Yes."

"Were you in the Navy?"

"No. The Army."

"Daddy was in the Navy. Did you ever hear of place called Guardercanal? That's where he was killed. It's in the Pacific someplace. Did you ever hear of it?"

"Yes."

"Were you ever there?"

"No."

"Would you like to go there?"

"Not particularly."

"Neither would I," Kate said. "Are you going to be my stepfather?"

"I don't know," Matthew said honestly.

"You don't seem at all wicked."

Matthew laughed. "Did you think I would be?"

"Stepfathers are supposed to be wicked. I read it in the *Blue Fairy Book*. Did you read that?"

"I think so. When I was a little boy."

"I can read, you know," Kate said.

"Yes, I can see that."

"When did you get your moustache?"

"Oh, I don't remember exactly. When I was nineteen or twenty, I think."

"Are you gifted?"

"No, I'm not."

"But you got a moustache."

"I guess I was just lucky," Matthew said.

Kate nodded. "Maybe I'll be lucky too. Will we pass through Minneapolis?"

"Yes."

"Grandma and Grandpa took me there once. We had lunch. Could we stop for lunch in Minneapolis?"

"Sure."

They came out of the lake country and down along the banks of the Mississippi, past St. Cloud and into Minneapolis and the state university, and they had lunch in Charlie's on Fourth Avenue South, and then drove through to St. Paul, the capitol building shining bright and white in the early afternoon sunshine. May was upon Minnesota and the roads were lined with lady's-slipper and dandelion, stands of white pine, down through Winona, following the banks of the Mississippi, the river frothy green and white as it rushed to the sea, and across into Wisconsin with Lake Superior high above them now, into the real dairy country and the smell of good fresh cheese permeating the countryside, the glimpse of factories, the giant engines waiting to be shipped farther west and east, the Diesel engines, the turbines, the auto frames, pasteurizing machines, tractors, paper, crossing the Kickapoo, the Indian name sounding on the evening air with echoes of massacres and scalp-taking and the ghosts of pioneers, pushing on to Madison, the town still with the ebbing days of a university semester, twilight in the hills behind the school, and then across the state line into Illinois, hitting Rockford and then cutting over to Waukegan, and the sudden magnificent sight of Lake Michigan and the suburbs falling away one by one, Oak Park, Cicero, the national memory of gangsters of the twenties, bootleg whisky and machine-gun chatter lingering in the fast-falling night, and then into Chicago itself and the giant buildings and the blood smell of the slaughterhouse, Kate's eyes wide in her head. They devoured a steak in the Pump Room and went to sleep exhausted at ten.

They cut off the corner of Illinois in the morning, passing into Indiana and the towns of Valparaiso and Plymouth, racing through the rich farmlands of the state, passing through Columbia City and Fort Wayne, another state line falling behind them, the barren stretch of the low flat plains from the border to Akron and suddenly the whir of a city and the smell of rubber hovering in the air pungent and vile, and through to Youngstown and the refineries adding their vibrant glow to the sun's, and then Pennsylvania, across that entire shabby mining state, the houses covered with coal-dust and poverty and dignity, over the Alleghenies and down the bank of the Susquehanna, pushing for Philadelphia before evening fell, passing through Harrisburg and then down through Lancaster and the Pennsylvania Dutch country with the hex signs on the barns and the Amish men in the fields. He was exhausted when they reached Philadelphia and checked into their hotel.

They made New York after ninety minutes of travelling the next morning. She always welcomed you, that city. She sat there on the other side of the river wearing a crown in her hair and smiling with a million banked windows reflecting sunlight, beckoning you to cross the bridges, to drop from the aerial highways and enter her arms, hung with clouds and neon. Busy and frantic, she none the less welcomed you the way no other city in the United States did, with the possible exception of San Francisco. She welcomed you simply by her existence, she made you feel this was the end of the journey and not a whistle stop, this was New York, you'd had them all once you'd had her. They stopped for lunch in Mamaroneck, and then pushed on to Talmadge.

By the time they reached the house, they were old friends.

Amanda watched them, feeling peculiarly excluded.

She had the oddest notion, all at once, that the birth of her own child would be completely anticlimactic for Matthew. Feeling bloated and unbeautiful and awkward and hot, as May squashed Talmadge flat under a blistering unseasonal thumb, she watched her husband and the child and was slightly annoyed by their mutual delight with each other. Now that Kate was here, now that her voice filled the house, now that her hand was in Matthew's, her husband seemed to take on all the stereotyped traits of the new father. Everything the child did seemed to amuse him, and even though Amanda was forced to admit her niece had a delightful sense of humour and a marvellous laugh, which set the timbers of the old house ringing whenever she cut loose with it, she did feel that Matthew's doting attitude was slightly unbecoming—especially when he was about to become a bona fide father in less than two months. Still Kate's laugh *was* contagious, the incongruous raucous bellow of a fat woman watching a stage show. And every time it issued from Kate's lungs and mouth, Matthew would begin laughing with her, and finally even Amanda, who thought these carryings-on were juvenile and nonsensical, was tempted into laughter, which hurt her back and her extended belly. Kate was a mine of misinformation, and Matthew listened to her solemn pronouncements and answered them with a dignity Amanda found foolish and indulgent.

"Do you know what the most dread disease in the world is?" Kate asked once.

"What?" Matthew said.

"Kansas," she answered, without a trace of a smile.

"That's true," Matthew said, "but Biloxi is even worse," and the child giggled uncontrollably.

He read to her each night. He bought books by the dozen, and Amanda could hear his voice drifting down from the upstairs bedroom. "The terrible, terrible, awful old cat, the cat who went down to the sea in a hat, now that was the cat, oh you know the cat, the cat who had never once captured a rat," reading any idiotic story with drama and emotion until finally Kate's inquiring voice would grow fuzzy with sleep, and he would kiss her and turn out the light and tuck the cover under her neck and say, "See you in the morning, Kate," and she would say, "Don't forget. Breakfast," and he would come tiptoeing downstairs with a smile on his face. Amanda, in her last stages of pregnancy, slept late each morning. The two, Matthew and Kate, would cook breakfast and then sit in the kitchen and chatter like jay birds. Kate would tell him all her plans for the day, and he would feel very much like a father, a very real father who listened to the problems of his young daughter and advised her on how to care for a doll's broken neck, or what to tell that snotty kid Iris next door, or how to tighten her skates with a skate key, or even how to blow her nose like a lady. He enjoyed his role immensely. She would walk him down the path to the garage, and he would back the car out, and then lean out the window, and Kate would kiss him good-bye and shout, "Will you be back soon?" and he would answer, "For dinner," and she would yell, "Are you going out tonight?" and he would yell back, "No!" and race to the station.

The question was always the same—"Are you going out tonight?"—as if now that she had found a father, she could not bear letting him out of her sight.

And the answer was invariably the same, too—"No!"—because now that Kate had come to live with them, Matthew had no desire at all to socialize. The child's presence, together with Amanda's ever-expanding universe, provided a ready excuse for ducking Talmadge's week-end get-togethers, which Matthew had never liked, anyway. Talmadge parties, to Matthew, were simply an extension of the fantasy land these well-meaning New Yorkers had created. He hated to attend them, and he hated to give them, and so he was grateful to Kate for her arrival because she introduced them to a Talmadge disease known simply as The Sitter Problem.

"We shouldn't leave her with a sitter," he said to Amanda. "The house is still strange to her."

"You just don't like parties, that's all," Amanda said knowingly.

"What gives you that idea?"

"You never dance with any of the women."

"I dance with you," Matthew said.

"Oh, and a lot of fun that must be for you right now. Look at me. I'm mountainous."

He put his hands on her belly. "You're lovely," he said.

"Some of the women in Talmadge are very attractive, Matthew."

"Are they?"

"Yes, and I'm just a pregnant old sow."

"A pregnant *young* sow."

"Young, excuse me," Amanda said, smiling. "They *are* attractive, admit it. Very chic, and very——"

"Yes, they're attractive. But you're beautiful. And besides, I happen to love you."

But not as much as she loved him.

She watched his growing attachment to the child, and wondered if she were jealous. She found herself hoping the baby would be a boy. She knew that no red-faced wrinkled little girl could possibly hope to compete with her blonde and beautiful niece. Even the word "niece" worried her. She automatically thought of Kate as her sister's child—but she knew that Matthew had already begun to think of her as his own daughter.

On a day early in June, the picture changed somewhat.

She had been sitting out in the sun, her eyes closed, her hands folded over her belly, when she suddenly realized the yard was very still. She sat up and called, "Kate!" and received no answer. Alarmed, she pushed herself laboriously out of the chair, waddled across the lawn, and went into the house. The house was still. She looked in the kitchen and the dining-room and the living-room, but Kate was nowhere on the ground floor. She heard the sound of Kate's voice upstairs then, and she smiled to herself, took hold of the banister, and tiptoed up the steps and down the corridor to where the door of the master bedroom stood ajar.

Kate was standing in front of the full-length mirror. She was wearing a pair of Amanda's high-heeled pumps and one of Amanda's floppy hats. She stood with one hand on her hip and smiled at her reflection in the mirror.

"You're so pretty, Amanda," she said to the glass. "You're so pretty, Mommy."

Amanda backed away from the door silently.

She had suddenly remembered a day in the upstairs bedroom of the house in Otter Falls when a nine-year-old girl named Amanda had put on a dress and shoes belonging to a woman named Priscilla Soames.

The television programme originated from a loft on West Sixty-eighth Street, just off Central Park West. The building was set among several apartment houses, and it had almost no windows in its brick face. Walking up the quiet residential street, one suddenly came upon the featureless brick wall with its six windows in a vertical line illuminating the stair-well, and with two metal fire-doors on the street level set some twenty-five feet apart. The building looked menacing, but all they were doing inside was putting on a television show.

The show was a popular item called *Memos*, which Curt Sonderman as producer had built around a genial raconteur and quasi-comic named Sam Martin. Martin was one of the forerunners of a school of television performers whose stock-in-trade was a lack of talent, a bumbling sort of oafish man who looked like the man next door and dressed like the man next door and even talked like him. In fact, looking at Sam Martin, the man next door had the distinct impression that this was exactly the way *he* would behave if someone suddenly dragged him into a television studio and told him to start talking. Martin said whatever came into his mind, whenever it came into his mind. His opinions were based on a retentive memory for the trivia of life; his mind was an attic cluttered with unimportant knowledge. He was like the man who wore two wrist-watches, one set with New York time, the other set with London time. When asked why he wore the second watch, he replied, "In case anyone wants to know what time it is in London." Sam Martin could not, perhaps, tell you what time it was in London, but he could tell you who pitched for the Red Sox in 1939, which movie won the Academy Award in 1932, how many eggs to use in a pineapple upside-down cake, the best way to repair a hole in a screen, and how to remove ticks from golden retrievers. He could also tell a dirty joke without offending the ladies, and he could describe the latest fashion trends without disgusting the men. He was good-looking enough to provide a low-key sex appeal for the women—and yet not handsome enough to provide any real competition for the man in the house. He could not sing, and he could not dance, and he had a terrible speaking voice, and plebeian sense of humour; he was, in short, untalented. But television in those early days was breeding a new race of untalented supermen who would pyramid their very lack of talent into a talent that appealed to those anxious viewers out there, those dial-happy fickle folk.

In a time when television dramas were trying their best to convince the man in the street that it was perfectly all right, in fact decent and honourable and praiseworthy, to be a slob, Sam Martin came on the air as visual proof of the theory. The television of that day was concerned primarily with the number of cockroaches in the kitchen sink. A new art school was being hammered into existence in the small inadequate studios scattered throughout the city's more undesirable slums, the premise of the school being that no drama was real drama unless it dealt with small people, a premise Aristotle might have challenged had he been alive and involved in the medium. These small people fought to find themselves on the small screen while they simultaneously stepped on small cockroaches every time they snapped on the kitchen light. For a while there, some of the more perceptive viewers began wishing the cockroaches would march through Georgia to the sea, taking all the damn small people with them. It got a little boring, week after week, watching shows that posed such earth-shaking problems as whether or not a Borscht

Belt summer romance would survive the winter, or whether a man who rescued a rich man's son from a sewer would have his life ruined by this act of heroism, or whether a man who found himself unemployed in his fiftieth year could find a new job before the roaches carried him off. But the small people triumphed. Viewers began talking about "ears for dialogue" and "clinical verity" and "the minutiae of life" and "neorealistic objectivity" and "representational integrity", and into this era of the contemplation of the involuting curves of one's own navel came Sam Martin with his midday drivel, his storehouse of worthless observations, his rumpled suit, his featureless face. The viewers could look at him and know with certainty that he, too, was a man plagued by cockroaches.

David Regan worked for the sponsors who employed Sam Martin.
The show was built entirely around Martin, who opened it every afternoon at one-thirty with the line, "Hello, girls," and then he would wink and say, "And you too, fellers." He would tell a few jokes and relate a few items of disinterest, which he had dug from the newspapers and national magazines, and he would tie the stories in with bits of little-known lore from his vast steamer-trunk memory. Then a girl singer would sing a song, and Martin would sell a product, and a boy singer would sing another song, and Martin would sell another product, and tell a few more jokes, and that's the way it went. He was on the air for two solid hours every day. His viewing audience was estimated at close to fourteen million people, and he earned the network millions and millions of dollars in advertising revenue, and all because he had no talent.

The rumours about Sam Martin ran rife through the industry and in the columns of those devoted to scanning the home screen. The rumours maintained that Martin, genial and affable on the air, was really a tyrant in private life, a man who beat his faithful employees with a cat-o'-nine-tails, seduced thirteen-year-old girls, kicked blind men, howled at the moon, and used cocaine. The rumours were dead wrong; Sam Martin off the air was exactly the person he was on the air. Bumbling, smiling, corny, affable, harmless. He had come into television after a dozen years in radio, most of them spent with an early-morning show in Los Angeles where he played records, told jokes, and sold products. In those early radio days, Martin wore glasses and sat behind his microphone, and when it came time to sell the product, he would lean closer to the mike and begin reading from the prepared advertising copy and then suddenly reach up and pull off the glasses and soar into an inspired emotional ad-libbing eulogy which sounded sincere and earnest and utterly honest. One of his Los Angeles colleagues remarked that Sam Martin was the best damn salesman in radio, that every time he pulled off those glasses and began ad-libbing his pitch, it was as if he were making love to a broad. Well, Sam Martin had pulled off his glasses for good the moment he entered television, but he still pitched those products with an emotional fervour that was difficult to match anywhere else in the medium. Perhaps this was his one real talent. Perhaps the salesmen were taking over the world.

If they were, David didn't seem to mind too much.

The fact remained that Martin sold the sponsor's product, and it was the sponsor who hired David as a watchdog over the product's appearance, the man who made certain the commodity put its best foot forward on the video tube. The importance of David's job could not be underestimated. *Memos* originated live from New York each afternoon at one-thirty after approximately an hour and a half of so-called rehearsal. This was not a filmed show, which could be edited and spliced. If a spot remover failed to remove a spot when it was supposed to, the sequence could not be done over again. There it was for everyone to see, and it was David's job to make sure they saw it right the first time around. He usually accomplished this in the midst of a pandemonium starting at noon and relaxing only a moment before the show was beamed. It seemed incredible to David that anyone could possibly know what was going on at those *Memos* rehearsals or that a show with any sense of continuity or form could emerge from that tangled mass of camera cables, monitor tubes, shouting directors, musical cues, patient guests, gag writers, hanging booms, grips, cameramen, frantic assistant directors, electricians, pacing producers, Press agents, audio engineers, stage managers, and make-up men. But a show did somehow assemble itself out of the rubble in the Sixty-eighth Street loft, and the show was remarkably relaxed and professional, a tribute to Sam Martin's intuitive grasp of his audience and a calmness that was genuine and soothing.

There was nothing soothing about the rehearsal on that Wednesday in the first week of June. There never had been a rehearsal, to David's recollection, that went well, but this one seemed to be defying every law of probability in its efforts to become a full-scale riot. It started with Louisa, the girl singer, yelling at Martin about the suitability of her material, she could not sing a sexy song on the air, her stock-in-trade was the homespun stuff. She was the peaches-and-cream girl, so how could she sing a torrid song like this one? She wanted a replacement for it at once. Martin affably and genially told her she was correct, which necessitated a last-minute scramble for a new song, and several hurried calls to Music Clearance, who, it was surmised, put in their own frantic calls to A.S.C.A.P. or B.M.I. and possibly Local 802, and got back to the rehearsal with the word that it was all right for Louisa to sing the song she had chosen, but this brought up the problem of an arrangement for the tune. The band didn't have an arrangement, and it was too late to do one, so it was decided they'd accompany Louisa with piano, drums, and guitar, and Louisa flipped once more at this and went screaming off to Martin, who calmed her and told her their piano player was the best in the business, and didn't Marian Anderson sing "The Star-Spangled Banner" with only a piano accompaniment?

Along about this time, someone from Network Continuity came down and began protesting about an off-colour joke that one of Martin's writers had inserted into the script following a coffee commercial. The man from Continuity was an intense Presbyterian who kept insisting his taste in humour was catholic, but who felt that Martin's viewers might take offence at the story and, following as closely as it did on the heels of the coffee commercial, might associate the joke with the product and not buy the product and cause the sponsor to cancel. The writer protested that he would not be ashamed to tell that joke to his own mother, and the man from Continuity said he didn't know what kind of a mother the writer had but he certainly wouldn't want to hear that joke told to *his* mother, whereupon they almost had a fist fight. Martin smoothed it all over by telling both the writer and the man from Continuity that they both undoubtedly had fine mothers, and fathers too, but that perhaps the joke might cause consternation in certain fringe fanatic groups, and he winked at both of them, and asked the writer to supply a new joke for the spot. The man from Continuity left mollified but righteously indignant, and the writer went back to Martin's dressing-room to prepare a non-offensive joke.

Martin's guest for that afternoon's show arrived just about then. He was a noted theatre personality who was starring in one of Broadway's long-run smashes, a personable enough fellow when he was sober, but he arrived at the loft dead drunk. He began abusing everyone in sight, muttering that he was going to punch that square Martin right on the nose the minute the show went on the air. He resisted all efforts to pour a gallon of coffee down his throat, overturning a scalding-hot pot of the sponsor's brew, and threatening to hit the make-up man, who he claimed was a faggot. Martin took him aside and gave him a fatherly talk about the traditions of the theatre ("You call this crap *theatre*?" the star shouted) and about the responsibilities of performers, and the necessity of rising above petty personality differences, and he cited a forgotten 1925 theatre incident involving John Barrymore, casually comparing his guest to Barrymore, and reminding his guest that fourteen million people would be watching him from coast to coast, and didn't he think he should have a few cups of coffee and a cold shower before they went on the air? The guest star shook hands with Martin and kissed the faggot make-up man, who was married with four children and who thought a faggot was a bundle of sticks, and then went off to shower and to guzzle some very strong black coffee, not the sponsor's.

Some trouble developed in the cable to number-three camera, and the bank of floods illuminating the show's single expensive set suddenly went out, and electricians began scrambling over every available inch of work space, moving ladders and hurling about screwdrivers, and Louisa complained in confidence to the wardrobe mistress that she had just been visited with her menstrual period and didn't feel like singing at *all*, if the truth were known. There was a feeling of mounting tension in the studio as the clock ticked off the minutes to air time. David felt the rising panic, felt, too, an impending sense of doom, the inexorable sweep of that minute hand around the clock, the calamities that kept piling one upon the other in scattered hopelessness, and another feeling, too, the ghosts of George Devereaux and Mike Arretti suddenly crowding into that strident atmosphere and sending a chill of anticipation up his spine. He tried to fight the feeling, tried to disentangle himself from the sticky helplessness of a fate that seemed to weave itself tighter and tighter around him. He knew something would happen. Nervously, he awaited the explosion.

He was holding in his hand a new product supplied by a Los Angeles advertising agency when he approached Sam Martin that day. The product, one among a list of notable and superior commodities touted by the California admen, was a shaving cream called Beards Away! The name made David a little bilious, but there it was, one of those new shaving-cream bombs full of rich creamy lather, which erupted at the touch of a finger-tip. Or, as was the case with Beards Away!, not quite at a touch. Beards Away! had a built-in safety factor that prevented the cream from dripping all over the medicine cabinet when it was not in use. There was a small cap, which screwed on to the nozzle, and it was necessary to remove this cap before pressing the stud that released the billowing lather into the palm of your hand. The product had arrived from Los Angeles together with a directive explaining the use of the can, the part about the nozzle lettered in upper-case type, REMOVE NOZZLE CAP BEFORE PRESSING RELEASE STUD, underlined. David cornered Martin at about ten minutes after one when it was discovered that the set designer had supplied a wrong backdrop for a skit being done on the show, a view of the Brooklyn Bridge when he was supposed to have provided a Paris bistro. That was the way things were going.

"Sam," David said, "have you got a minute?"

Martin turned from his talk with the designer. He was beginning to sweat through his make-up, and the make-up man hovered near by with powder and brush, waiting to touch him up as soon as he could tear him away from all those other people. The armpits of Martin's blue shirt were stained with sweat. A woman from Wardrobe stood behind the make-up man, holding Martin's jacket and waiting to help him put it on.

"What is it, David?" Martin said, turning. He remembered to smile as he turned. Panic was in the air, and the sweep hand of the studio clock marked in one-second intervals seemed to be moving at a faster clip now, panic was something you could touch and breathe, but Sam Martin remembered to smile as he turned.

"Sam, when you're demonstrating this new shaving cream..."

"Yeah, yeah."

"This Beards Away!"

"Yeah, yeah."

"This stuff." David held up the can. "It's important to unscrew this little cap from the nozzle before you press the button. Otherwise, nothing'll come out."

"I know," Martin said.

"Okay," David answered, smiling. "Good luck with the show."

"Thanks," Martin said, and he turned back to the set designer.

At ten minutes before air time, the panic was so thick you couldn't see through it. David remembered the shaving-cream bomb and decided to find Martin again, just to remind him, just to make sure. Martin was looking over the show's time-table when he located him, underlining portions of the script, marking some passages with a red, others with a blue, pencil.

"Sam," David said, "you won't forget to unscrew that cap, will you?"

Martin looked up from the script and very calmly said, "Would *you* like to demonstrate the product, David?"

"No. No, Sam, no," David said, backing away. "I just thought I'd not forget it." And he went to sit in the sponsor's booth while the announcer began warming up the studio audience. He could not shake the feeling of approaching tragedy. Unconsciously, he crossed his fingers as the clock swept towards one-thirty. There was a silence. The monitor in the booth flashed a ten-second station break, and then a telop announcing "*Memos* to follow", and then the theme hit the tube simultaneously with a film clip showing New York City's fabulous skyline and the announcer's voice rode in over the theme, ending with the words "... and now the star of our show, *Sam Martin!*" The studio audience burst into wild prompted applause, and Martin ambled out casually, just as if he hadn't been through the eight inner circles since twelve noon, and said, "Hello, girls," and winked at the camera and then added, "And you too, fellers," and then told a homey joke and introduced Louisa, who sang sweetly and demurely. David relaxed a little, but he kept his fingers crossed.

The shaving-cream commercial came in the second half-hour segment of the show, following the Paris bistro skit, which was finally played against the Brooklyn Bridge backdrop and which, happily, seemed even funnier that way. Martin picked up the attractive-looking can and held it up to the viewing audience and went into a homespun spiel about this new device that provided sudsy lather at his finger-tips, and then said, "Well, this is how it works."

The cap, David thought.

"You just press this little button——"

"*The cap*," David whispered aloud, and a production assistant in the booth turned and looked at him quizzically.

"—and the cream comes out, it's just magic, folks."

He pressed the stud. Nothing happened.

"Oh, Jesus!" David said.

Martin grinned a boyishly sweet grin, studied the can casually, and said, "You're supposed to press this button on top of the can." He shrugged. "Well, let's see." And he pressed the stud again, still not removing the cap from the nozzle, and again nothing happened. David closed his eyes and then opened them and stared at the monitor in helpless fascination.

"All you do is press this button," Martin said again, and again he pressed it, and said, "Now what the h——" and cut himself short and looked at the can of shaving cream as if it were a malevolent Russian weapon. He banged the stud with the palm of his hand. He hit the can on the edge of his desk. He hit it again, and pounded the stud again, and then said, "Well, you go out and buy a can. Maybe you'll have better luck with it than I did," and tossed the can across the stage to the orchestra leader, who, intent on his next music cue, missed the can as it came sailing towards him. The can hit the stage like a falling rock. The cap came loose from the nozzle and suddenly the can erupted in a shower of foamy lather, spraying everyone on the stage with shaving cream.

The call from Los Angeles came not ten minutes later. Curt Sonderman took it in his private office and said, "Yes, I know. It was just one of those unforeseen ... well, how do I know whether the product was explained to him or not? *Regan* is supposed to take care of that, not me. Look, it's *his* job! I've got enough things to do around here without . . . what? Yes, I'm the one who hired him, but . . . Look, don't use that tone of voice with me! What the hell do you do, write crummy advertising copy all day long? Did you ever try to put on a network television show? All right then, *shut up*! All right, I'll get a full explanation. Yes, I'll call you back. After the show! We're on until three-thirty, and I'm busy, and . . . look, *what's* you name, Mac? Get off my back, it'll be taken care of! If Regan has to be fired, he'll be fired. Good-*bye*!"

David knew he was going to be fired. He had known it from the moment Sam Martin first pressed that stud. He ducked out of the sponsor's booth as soon as the can exploded and the audience disintegrated, laughing for a full two minutes at the sponsor's product. He went down the iron-runged steps to the street, and he lighted a cigarette outside the building and he thought, It's happened again, and then he began walking towards Columbus Avenue, wondering what he should do, thinking, I don't want to lose this job, why does it always happen to me?

When he saw the candy store, he entered it immediately and called Gillian. She listened quietly and patiently while he told her what had happened. When he was finished, she said, "Don't lose the job, David."

There was a curious note of command in her voice. He was silent for a moment.

"They'll say it was my fault."

"It was Martin's fault. You did your job."

"But he's the star of the show!"

"Show them he was wrong, David."

"But how? What can I——?"

"I don't care how. Lie, if you have to. Cheat. Steal. I don't care. Don't lose the job." She paused. "Where are you now?"

"In a candy store on Columbus Avenue."

"You shouldn't have run. Go back to the studio, David. Go back and tell them whatever you want to, whatever you have to, but make it good. And call me. I'll be waiting for your call. *Don't lose the job*," she said, and hung up.

He walked back to the building on West Sixty-eighth. He paused outside the street entrance, and then he pulled open the door, and wet his lips, and walked upstairs to the studio. He was trembling. The sponsor had paid thousands of dollars for a one-minute spot, and Sam Martin had blown the thing sky-high before a network audience. It was David's job to make sure things like that didn't happen. That was why they paid him two hundred dollars a week. Damn it, he did not want to lose that income! Damn it, he *liked* this job! Should he go to Martin and plead with him, ask to be taken off the hook? But he *had* done his job, he *had* told Martin about the goddam cap, so how . . .?

I don't care how. Lie, if you have to. Cheat. Steal. I don't care. Tell them whatever you want to, whatever you have to do, but make it good.

Whatever you have to, and an undertone of desperation in Gillian's voice, something he had never heard there before. He suddenly felt he was about to lose more than his job.

He found the typewriter in one of the empty offices. He locked the door to the office, and he sat at the machine, and he thought, Suppose this backfires? Suppose it only gets him sore? No. There had been so much confusion today, he won't remember. He'll back down. He'll take the blame and smooth it over with the sponsor. They can raise hell with a two-hundred-dollar watchdog, but they can't put Sam Martin, star of our show, on the carpet. He took a deep breath and began typing:

MEMO

FROM: David Regan

TO: Sam Martin

In re new product BEARDS AWAY! Specific instructions from the Coast warn against trying to release lather before removing nozzle cap. This is a simple screw-type cap, easily removed with thumb and forefinger. It is essential to show this on camera before pressing the stud on the top of the can. Failure to remove cap will result in malfunction of the can. It's a good new product and deserves the full treatment, Sam. So, at the risk of sounding redundant, please REMOVE NOZZLE CAP BEFORE PRESSING RELEASE STUD.

He looked over the memo. He put the original in an ash-tray and set fire to it with a match. He emptied the ashes into a trash basket, folded the carbon of the memo three times, and stuck it into his inside jacket pocket together with his electric bill and a letter from his mother, and some cards he dug out of his wallet. Then he took another deep breath and left the office.

Curt Sonderman said, "Where the hell have you been, David?"

"Downstairs having a smoke," David said. "Why? What's the matter?" His heart was pounding. He fought to keep his eyes from blinking. His lips felt parched, but he would not wet them.

"What's the *matter*?" Sonderman said. "Didn't you see what happened with the shaving cream? The damn thing went off all over the stage!"

Calmly, smiling, David said, "Come on, don't kid me."

"If you think I'm kidding, you should have taken that call from Los Angeles. Now, what happened?"

"I don't understand," David said. "You mean the can exploded?"

"Yes, the can . . . no, it didn't actually explode. It just . . . look, why didn't you explain the operation to Martin?"

"Pressing the button? Why it's so simple a child can——"

"Don't give me the 'child can do it' routine. Sam Martin had to do it, not a child. Why didn't you tell him to take that cap off the nozzle?"

"Cap off the . . .?" David stopped and looked at Sonderman sceptically. "You *are* kidding," he said. "I told him about that cap at least a half-dozen times. You don't . . . hey, wait a minute! What are you saying? He left the cap *on*? Is that what you're saying?"

"That's exactly what I'm saying!"

"But how could . . . Curt, I told him about that cap personally five times during rehearsal. The last time I told him, there were three people standing there listening to us, a girl from Wardrobe, and the make-up man, and a designer. I got specific orders from the Coast on this. Do you think I'd let him go on without knowing about it? Give me a little more credit than that, Curt!"

"If you told him about it, why'd he leave the cap on?"

"How do I know? You saw the confusion this afternoon. It's a wonder he remembered his own name. Do you think I'm lying? Are you telling me I'm lying?"

"No, but . . ."

"I told him about that cap, Curt!" David said angrily. "I told him at least . . . wait, wait a minute! I even wrote him a *memo* about it. I handed him the memo *personally* when he walked in today."

"What memo?"

"About the . . . just a minute, maybe I kept a copy. Hold on, now." He dug into his jacket pocket and began leafing through the stuff there, finally coming upon the folded carbon copy of the memo he'd just typed. "Sure, here it is," he said. "Here. Take a look at it." He handed the sheet of paper to Sonderman.

Sonderman read it silently. Then he shrugged.

"What the hell," he said. "You can't ask for more than that. You did your job, David. What the hell." He shrugged again. "It was Sam's goof. I'll ask him to square it."

Sam Martin admitted that he'd been in something of a mad rush that afternoon during rehearsal, and anything was possible. Maybe David *had* handed him a memo, maybe he *had* been reminded about that nozzle cap a half-dozen times. The Wardrobe girl and the make-up man and the designer certainly seemed positive they had heard David deliver at least one reminder. "Okay, I goofed," Martin said affably, and he agreed to call the Coast.

The next day, he made a big spiel about the shaving cream, telling his audience a new lather had exploded on the scene (Laughter), a lather so anxious to shave you, it practically bursts out of the can (Laughter). "This is the way you really work this," Martin said, and he carefully unscrewed the nozzle cap. "If you leave the nozzle on, the stuff definitely will not spill or leak out of the can unless you throw it across the studio at a lousy orchestra leader." (Laughter) "If you want to throw things at musicians, I suggest you use rocks. But if you want a good close shave that leaves you feeling refreshed and clean, I suggest you try Beards Away! It works like this." He pressed the stud on the can's top, and a puff of rich creamy lather foamed on to the palm of his hand. The studio audience burst into spontaneous applause. "It looks good enough to eat, don't it?" Martin said. He winked at the camera. "It's good stuff, folks," he said sincerely. "Try it."

Perhaps David grew up the day he typed that memo.

Or perhaps he only lost his innocence.

The Fourth of July fireworks were supposed to start at 9.30 p.m. They had taken the bus to Playland that afternoon and spent the day on the rides and at the various gambling booths. There was only one thing on Gillian's mind. She tried to enjoy what they were doing, but there was only one thing on her mind, and each time she moved away from the thought it returned until she forcibly ejected it, and then stubbornly returned again. Distressed, she tried to talk of other things.

"There's a party Saturday night," she said. "We're invited."

"Oh?" David said. "Who? Where?"

"John Dimitri, you remember him."

"Tall thin guy with blond hair? East Thirty-sixth Street?"

"That's right."

"What kind of a party?"

"The same kind he always gives," Gillian said. "You bring the booze, and I'll supply the records and potato chips."

"Should we go?"

"If you like."

"Whatever you say," David answered.

The thought persisted. She could not shake it from her mind. They leaned against the railing overlooking the Sound, waiting for the fireworks to start. There was the hush of expectation in the crowd around them. David stood behind her, his arms circling her waist. She looked out over the water to the spit of land where she could see men moving about with flares, preparatory to starting the show. She said, "Do you remember Michael Scanlon?"

"No, I don't think so."

"It was a while back. Marian called me about this pilot he was filming in the Bahamas."

"What about him?" David asked.

This is not the right time, Gillian thought. This is not the right place. Showdowns should be played on the main street, in bright sunlight, with dust rising and the town still.

"He called Marian today."

"Yes?"

This is neither the time nor the place, she thought.

"He's finished the pilot and sold it. N.B.C.'s doing it in the fall."

"Good," David said.

She hesitated. There was a deep silence. A rocket suddenly shot into the sky, exploded in an incandescent blue, which tinted the water. The crowd went "Ahhhhhhhhhhh!" She turned in David's arms.

"They get better as they go along," he said.

"He still wants me for the part, David."

"Huh? What part?"

"The girl trouble-shooter."

"Really?" David said. "That's great, Gillian. Why didn't you tell me before?"

Another rocket went into the sky. It burst in a flash of red, exploded, another flash of yellow, another explosion. "Ahhhhh!" and "Ahhhhh!" the crowd went.

"Because he's shooting the series in Bimini."

"Bimini," David repeated blankly.

Silver fishes filled the sky, darting aimlessly against the black wheel of night.

"Yes."

"Well . . ." David paused. A white-hot flare went off over the Sound, illuminating his face. It fell suddenly, and his features were in shadow again. She tried to see his eyes. "Well, are you going to take it?"

"Bimini is a long way off, David."

He nodded.

"Should I take it, David?"

"That's up to you."

"No, not entirely."

"Is it a good part?"

"It's an excellent part."

"Who's filming it?"

"Revue. That's M.C.A., David. It's going to be a big series. Nothing like it has ever been done on television. I couldn't ask for a better showcase."

"Well, it's up to you, Gilly. Wow, look at that one!"

The triple explosion rocked the night, red and yellow and blue trailing to earth in a dissipating stream of sparks.

"David, it's *not* up to me," she said sharply.

"What's the matter?"

"I want to talk about this."

"We are talking about it."

"Not here. Not with all these people."

"What's the matter?"

"I don't feel like discussing something as personal as this in front of a thousand people watching fireworks."

"What's so personal about a television series? It seems to me——"

"David!" she said sharply, and he looked into her face and saw the anger there, and nodded, and took her hand, and led her through the crowd. The amusement park was almost deserted. Everyone was down by the waterfront, watching the fireworks. The music of the merry-go-round filled the night, and behind it, like a syncopated counterpoint, the intermittent sound of the explosions and the deep sighs of the crowd.

"Do you want to go?" he asked.

"Yes. I want to go."

"Then there's nothing to——"

"But I also want to stay."

David smiled. "Did you ever get the feeling that you wanted to go, and still have——"

"I don't think it's funny, David."

"What do you want me to say, Gillian?"

"Are you going to keep this job with Curt?"

"I think so. Yes."

"You're happy with it?"

"Yes, I am. I like television. I like what I'm doing."

"You're earning two hundred dollars a week, David."

"I know I am."

"Do *I* have to ask *you*?"

"Ask me what?"

Gillian sighed.

"David," she said, "I've been waiting for something like this for a long, long time. I've turned down a lot of offers in the past two years because I didn't want to be away from you. I thought . . . I thought you needed me. So I stayed. But this is important, David.

This one could just possibly lead to something. I want to be an actress, David. You know that's what I want. And if there's even a small chance of——"

"Then take it," David said.

"No, let me finish. Please." She hesitated. "I want to be an actress more than almost anything else in the world. I've wanted to be an actress for as long as I can remember. There's only one thing I want more than that, David."

"What?"

"You."

"You've got me."

"No, David. I haven't got you."

"Look, Gilly . . ."

"*You've* got *me*. But I'm not sure the reverse is true."

"You know I love you."

"Yes, I know that."

"So . . ."

"David, will you marry me?"

There was a deep silence. They walked beneath the arching branches of the trees. The calliope music was behind them now. A few lovers exchanged kisses on the benches lining the walk. A skyrocket exploded over the water, its sound muffled and distant.

"Is that what you want?" he asked.

"Yes. It's what I want."

"You're not . . . you know . . . it's not that you're . . ."

"No. You don't *have* to marry me, David."

"I see."

"But, David, I'm not staying in New York unless we do get married."

"Why?"

"Because that's the way I want it."

"Doesn't what I want count at all?"

"David, you've *had* everything you wanted."

"I thought you loved me, Gillian."

"Oh, David, you don't know how much!"

"Then what's this offended-virgin routine? I thought——"

"I'm not offended, and God knows I'm not virginal, but——"

"Are you throwing *that* up to me now?"

"No, David," she said softly.

"All right, now let's take it easy, Gillian, before we both say things we'll be sorry for, okay? Please." He paused. "I know this Bahamas thing is important. I can understand that. And I can see how it puts a certain amount of pressure on . . . on . . . but, well, what's the sense of rushing into anything?"

"Rushing, David?"

"I'm just getting started," he said plaintively. "I could lose this job tomorrow, Gillian."

"I don't think so."

"What do you know about it, Gillian, really? There are a hundred guys waiting to knife me in the back."

"David, the job is yours for as long as you want it. Sam Martin went to bat for you, and the job is yours. You're not going to lose it. If you didn't lose it when that shaving cream——"

"All right, maybe I won't. But maybe I want something better. Did that ever occur to you?"

"Yes, it's occurred to me. I don't expect you to keep this job for the rest of your life."

"Okay, then how can I get married right now?"

"Why can't you?"

"When I'll be changing jobs?"

"Changing jobs? What are you talking about, David? What's one thing got to do with the other?"

"You just said you *expected* me to change jobs, didn't you?"

"There are married men who . . . David, I'm trying not to get angry."

"There's nothing to get angry about."

"Damn it, there's a lot to get angry about! What do you want from me? What do you want me to be, David? Your mother, your girl, your whore? What?"

"I didn't know it was so trying for you, Gillian, I thought——"

"It isn't trying! It's only exasperating! I want to know what's ahead for us."

"Why? Do you think I'm going to lead you into——"

"I'm a good actress, David."

"I know."

"I'm a damn good actress."

"I know. What's——"

"I almost forgot that, David. I almost forgot how good I was."

"If you want to act——"

"I want to be your wife!"

"You sound like my wife already," David answered sharply.

"Is this how it ends?"

"Nothing's ending."

"In fire and smoke?"

"Oh, cut it, Gillian. You're making a big dramatic scene out of——"

"Will you marry me?"

"I thought the man was supposed to ask."

"Yes, the man is supposed to ask," Gillian said.
"What does that mean?"
"*Are* you asking?"
"You know I'm going to marry you."
"When?"
"I don't know when. As soon as——"
"As soon as what?"
"As soon as I know where I'm going."
"And when will that be?"
"I'm not sure."
"And what do I do in the meantime?"
"I thought things were going along fine as they——"
"Well, they're not. Now you know they're not going along fine. Now you know I've had a firm offer to do a television series, which will be filmed in Bimini and which will take me away for at least six months, now you know all that, David. So what are you going to do? I'd like to know exactly what you're going to do."
"I'll be here when you get back," he said. "You're acting as if you're going to become an African missionary. You'll only be——"
"I won't *come* back, David. I'll go to the Coast. There's a lot of work there. Now, how about that, David?"
"I've never heard you talk like this. You sound like a first-rate bitch."
"Yes, I'm a first-rate bitch, and I love you so much I'm willing to forget anything that ever had any meaning for me, and all I ask in return is that you love me enough to make me your wife. That's the kind of nasty rotten bitch I am. I'm going to cry, you *louse*."
"Gillian . . ."
"Oh, go, oh don't, just don't, oh get away, get away."
"What are you crying about?"
"Nothing. Nothing at all. I want to go home."
"I *said* I'm going to marry you."
"When?"
"I don't know when."
"That's not good enough, David."
"It has to be good enough. I love you, Gillian."
"I don't believe you."
"I love you."
"No." She shook her head. "No. I want to go home. I'm going to take the job, David. I'm going to call Marian and tell her I'll take it."
"I don't want you to."
"Then make me a better offer."
"I don't like the whole damn tone of this!" David said.

"Oh, that's too bad, David. Really, that's awfully sad, really. *You* don't like the tone of it! Do you think *I* like it? Do you think I like getting on my knees and begging you to——"

"No one asked you to beg or——"

"No one asked me *anything*! Not a goddam thing! Get away, you make me cry. Why do you make me cry? Get away, please, it's over, go, do what you have to do, find yourself, know where you're going, but without me, David. I can't, I can't. Please, please, I want to go home, people are looking at us, don't make me cry, I don't want to hate you."

"Gillian . . ."

"It's over." She paused and looked up at him. Her mascara had streaked her eyes and was running down her cheeks. "Isn't it, David? Isn't it really and truly over?"

"If you want it to be."

"No, David. Don't do that, please. It's dishonest, David, and unworthy of you. You know it's not what *I* want. I want to get married. I want to spend the rest of my life with you."

"We could still——"

"No. We couldn't. Not any more. Not this way. I want to go to church and be married in a white gown and a veil. That's what I want. I guess I'm a very old-fashioned girl. That's what I want. I don't want it to be ended."

"I can't marry you right now," David said softly. "I can't, Gillian."

"Yes. Then it's over."

"Then I guess it's over."

"Yes, I guess so."

They stared at each other, stunned.

Amanda felt only foolish.

She had not wanted to come to the hospital so soon because she was sure the pains were only minor, afraid they would send her home and tell her to come back in the morning. Standing at the admissions desk, feeling foolish and embarrassed because everyone in the wide world knew exactly why she was there, wearing her big belly like a billboard, she answered the nurse's questions in a very quiet voice.

"Name?"

"Amanda Bridges. Mrs. Matthew Bridges."

Matthew stood beside her. He had knotted his tie so that the bottom end was longer than the top end. One of the buttons on his button-down shirt was unfastened.

"And your address, Mrs. Bridges?"

"1412 Congress. In Talmadge."

"Can't you do this later, nurse?" Matthew asked impatiently. "She's going to have a baby, you know."

"Yes, sir, I know," the nurse answered, smiling. "May I have your date of birth, please, Mrs. Bridges?"

"Oh, for Pete's sake," Matthew muttered.

"May 11, 1923," Amanda said.

"And your obstetrician's name?"

"Dr. Kohnblatt."

"Would you have a seat, please, Mrs. Bridges? I'll telephone upstairs for a chair."

"For a what?"

"A wheel chair," the nurse answered, smiling.

"I don't need a wheel chair. I can walk."

"Well, we'll give you a little ride anyway, okay?"

"I don't want a little ride," Amanda said.

"Come on, Amanda, come on," Matthew said. He took her elbow and led her across the polished lobby to a bench on the wall opposite the admissions desk. "How do you feel?"

"I feel fine. Why do I need a wheel chair?"

"Amanda, I guess they know what they're doing."

"You tied your tie all crooked."

"How do you feel?"

"Fine."

"How are the pains?"

"They're nothing at all. I told you we shouldn't have come yet."

"Dr. Kohnblatt said I should take you directly to the hospital. Those were his exact words, Amanda. Take her directly——"

"Yes, I know. You told me."

"How do you feel?"

"Foolish. I think this is a humilating experience. I think women should have their babies in the fields where no one can see them."

"Listen, Amanda, you do everything they tell you to do, do you hear? You listen to what they say, and you do it."

"Matthew, women have babies every day of the week."

"Well, you don't."

"Don't worry."

"I'm not worried."

"Button your collar."

"The important part is bearing down," Matthew said, buttoning his collar. "I read that some place."

"Yes, I'll bear down," Amanda said, smiling.

"I don't know what you find so amusing about all this, Amanda. I really don't see——"

"Matthew, you sound like a stuffy old——"

"Are you all right? Do you feel all right?"
"I feel fine."
"How are the pains?"
"Tolerable," Amanda said, and again she smiled.
"Here's your wheel chair."
"I won't get in that thing."
"Amanda, do what they tell you to do."
"Mrs. Bridges?" a nurse said.
"Yes, she's Mrs. Bridges," Matthew answered.
"Do you want to get in the chair?"
"No, I don't."
The nurse smiled. "It's a hospital rule," she said.
"Go ahead, Amanda."
Amanda pulled a face and got into the chair. "They'll probably send me right home," she said.
"Can I go with her?" Matthew asked.
"We'll ring down for you as soon as she's changed, sir," the nurse said.
"Where are you taking her?"
"The sixth floor, sir. The maternity floor."
"Oh. All right. You won't forget to call down, will you?"
"No, sir."
"Okay. I'll see you in a few minutes, Amanda."
"Yes, Matthew."
"Are you all right?"
"Yes, Matthew."
"Okay. I'll see you in a little while."
"Yes, Matthew."
"Is that her bag, sir?"
"What?"
"The suitcase. Is that——?"
"Oh, yes. Yes."
"I'll take it, sir."
"Sure. Sure." He handed her the suitcase.
"Now just relax, Mrs. Bridges," the nurse said, and she wheeled her towards the elevators.
In the elevator, Amanda said, "I'm not getting very many pains."
' Well, let's not rush it," the nurse said. The elevator door slid open. "Here we are. We'll just go down the hall here." She wheeled Amanda into a room that was bare save for a bed and a night stand. "Would you take off your clothes, please?" she said. "I'll bring you a hospital gown."
"I brought my own gown."
"Yes, but these are different. They're sort of slit up the side."

She paused and smiled. "It's hospital rules. Did you bring your own slippers?"

"Yes, I did."

"You may wear those. And a robe?"

"Yes."

"Fine. I'll be right back."

Amanda undressed silently. The nurse seemed so young. She wondered suddenly if she had ever had a baby. When the nurse returned, she asked her.

"No," the nurse said. "Never. Dr. Kohnblatt phoned to say he's on the way. Here's your gown. Would you like to see your husband now?"

"Yes, I would."

"I'll call down."

A sudden groan came from the corridor outside. Amanda turned towards the door sharply. "What was that?"

"Nothing. Don't worry about it."

"No, no, what was it?"

"Someone in the labour room."

"My God!" Amanda said.

The nurse smiled. The groan came again. "She's having a particularly bad time," the nurse said.

"Well, can't you close the door or something?"

"Would you like me to close the door?"

"Yes. Yes, I would." The groan came again. "What are they *doing* to her?"

"She's having a particularly bad time," the nurse said again. She went out, closing the door behind her. The groan sounded down the corridor again, muffled somewhat, but the same animal cry, frightening, primitive. I wonder if I'll scream, Amanda thought. I don't feel anything at all yet. Well, a few little tremors down there, but nothing to speak of. The woman says it's like gas pains. I don't think I ever had a gas pain in my life, my God, listen to her scream, you'd think they were pulling out all her teeth!

The door opened suddenly. A middle-aged nurse with a starched look and a toothy grin poked her head into the room. "Hello, mother," she said, and Amanda winced. "I'm Mrs. Ogilvy, the delivery-room nurse. Are you Dr. Kohnblatt's patient?"

"Yes, I am."

He phoned to say he's on his way over. How do you feel?"

"Fine. Listen, can't you do something for that poor woman down the hall?"

"Oh, she's fine," Mrs. Ogilvy said cheerfully. "Is there anything I can get you?"

"Yes, a taxi," Amanda said, and she rolled her eyes.

Mrs. Ogilvy smiled. "It'll be over before you know it," she said. "You're a nice healthy girl."

"Thank you," Amanda said. "Oooh!"

"A little pain?"

"Yes. Yes. A little . . . stronger than the others."

"Have you broken water yet?"

"No."

"Well, don't let it frighten you when it happens."

"I'm not frightened."

"Of course not, that's a good mother," Mrs. Ogilvy said, and she vanished.

Amanda made a sour face as soon as she was gone. Well, where's Matthew? she wondered. She said she was going to phone down for him, and it's only six floors, so what's . . .

The groan came again.

Oh, you poor creature, Amanda thought, why don't they give you something to knock you out?

"Amanda?"

There was a worried look on his face as he came into the room. She felt suddenly protective of him and thought this rather odd. She was the one having the baby, and yet she felt it was Matthew who needed the protection. She almost laughed aloud at the absurdity of the idea.

"Should we begin timing the pains?" he asked.

"No, I think there's time yet."

"Honey, if you're in pain, don't try to hide it."

"I won't, Matthew."

"It'll be over before you know it," Matthew said, and smiled.

"That's what Mrs. Ogilvy said."

"Sure." Matthew paused. "Who's Mrs. Ogilvy?"

"The delivery-room nurse."

Matthew nodded. "There was somebody screaming in the hall."

"Yes, I heard her."

"You'd think they'd have soundproof rooms."

"I don't mind," Amanda lied.

Mrs. Ogilvy came into the room again. She ignored Matthew completely. "Are you ready for your prepping, mother?" she asked Amanda.

"My what?"

"Well, you come along with me, won't you, dear?"

"Where are you taking her?" Matthew wanted to know.

"Mr. Bridges, she'll be all right."

"Shall I wait here?"

"Yes, won't you, please?" Mrs. Ogilvy smiled. "There's a nice view from that window."

Amanda followed Mrs. Ogilvy down the corridor. They went into a small room with a table and a sink.

"Would you get up on the table, mother?" Mrs. Ogilvy said.

Amanda got on to the table silently. She felt suddenly embarrassed.

"We'll just shave you first, and then you can have your enema, all right, mother?"

Amanda did not answer. Mrs. Ogilvy came back to the table with a bowl of lather and a safety razor. "Pull up the gown, won't you, dear?" she said, and Amanda complied silently, certain she was blushing. She could feel the scrape of the razor and every now and then a sharp pain that rippled through her abdomen. It won't be bad, she thought. I won't scream, she thought.

They had taken Matthew downstairs again and given Amanda an injection of something, but the injection did not help to kill the pain. The pain was a constant thing, it seemed, a steady ebb and flow, but the valleys of comparative painlessness were brief and the pain seemed to roll in immediately, mounting to a shrieking crest and then dropping swiftly into a short restful trough and then rising hysterically again to a needle-point sharpness. Her body seemed to be moving of its own accord, the pain was something beyond conscious will or direction, even the screams that came from her throat, which she recognized as her own screams, fuelled by her lungs, propelled by her breath, voiced by her tongue and her lips, even the screams seemed to be connected to the convulsive area below her waist. Her abdomen, her vagina, her lungs, her throat, all seemed to be manipulated by something beyond her and outside her, yet intricately bound with her body, a single sharp pull of razor-honed steel thread and the pain would rumble upward from her crotch to a white-hot spot near her navel, the scream would gather force and burst from her lips, "Shhhh, shhh," the young nurse said, and Amanda shouted, "You never had a baby!" and screamed again. She no longer felt foolish and she no longer felt embarrassed, nor did she feel as if she were in the hands of heartless torturers, she accepted the pain as a part of this thing that was happening to her, this half-glazed, half-drugged thing that was all pain and sweat so far, something stripped of modesty and sex appeal and attraction, something somehow stripped of all the vacuum-packed sterility of the twentieth century, something that was entirely animal, and yet more than that, more than animal because she did not think of herself as bestial, she grunted and she screamed and she twisted in pain and once she swore at her own doctor who had become only a voice beside her, a pair of gentle hands holding her own, she squeezed his hands each time the pain struck her, she could not remember what Dr. Kohnblatt looked like, she could only hear his voice beside her. She did not think of Matthew as they wheeled her into the delivery room, and she did not think of her mother or her sister or her sister's child Kate, nor did she even think of the baby she was trying so hard to produce.

The act of giving birth, the act of pushing that small body out of her own, was somehow disconnected from the concept of giving birth, so that whereas everyone in the delivery room—the doctor, the nurses, the anaesthetist, Amanda herself—was collected there to bring a life into the world, they were all only concerned with the mechanics of producing the child, their only concern was with the work, the labour of giving birth, and the act itself was completely alien to the concept. The lights over the table hurt her eyes. The anaesthetic mask would be placed on her face and then removed, so that she was in a constant state of near-unconsciousness, and into the swimming cloudlike miasma of her brain she could hear Dr. Kohnblatt saying, "Bear down now, Amanda," and she strained and pushed and she was afraid she would soil herself, he seemed to read her mind, he said, "Don't worry about it, push!" and she pushed and the mask came down on her face again, her mind swam, she felt herself reeling, "Push!" Consciousness flowed back to her, she tightened her bowels and her vagina and felt something, felt something move and was suddenly tense, "Scalpel," she pushed again, "No, wait, Amanda," he said, "there, just a little, nurse, she doesn't need more than that, you're doing fine, Amanda, there we are, sponge, now push, Amanda." She could feel the baby coming out. She could feel it wedged inside her and getting the baby out became a challenge, became something they had to accomplish together, she pushed and felt the baby move, "Good, Amanda," she pushed again, "Oh damn!" she said, "oh damn, damn, damn it!" and she heard Kohnblatt laugh and she started to say, What are you laughing at, do *you* want to try this! and Kohnblatt said, "You're doing a marvellous job, Amanda, we've almost got it, push as hard as you can, here we go, Amanda, come on, come on," she took a deep breath and she gritted her teeth and she could feel the sweat standing out on her face and the baby wedged solidly in her crotch, she shoved, she tightened every muscle she owned, she pushed, and suddenly, suddenly, oh suddenly! she felt a sudden shock of exultation, she felt the baby moving out of her, felt herself trembling as it seemed to slide suddenly from within her, oh, felt a wave of excitement surging through her body, free and out, snapping into her brain, "Did I do it?" she asked excitedly, "Yes, you did it, that was it, Amanda!" she felt suddenly proud and joyful, felt a marvellous soaring ecstasy, a jubilance she had never known before in her life.

The mask descended on her face, and she took a deep breath, smiling, grinning. "I did it," she murmured, and heard the baby's cry.

When she opened her eyes, the baby was on her breast, lying with its legs on her belly. She did not move to touch it. She looked down at it peacefully and thankfully and then closed her eyes again.

"It's a fine healthy boy," Dr. Kohnblatt said.

BOOK THREE

JULIA

THE car Julia Regan bought in 1952 was an Alfa Romeo roadster.

Its appearance on the streets and roads of Talmadge, Connecticut, caused no little comment. The town, indeed the nation, had not yet succumbed to the exotic siren call of the foreign car. They had been fascinated by the miniature charm of some of the foreign imports, had indulged their caprice to the extent of purchasing automobiles that seemed both novel and economical, but the indulgence had not yet become a trend, the fascination had not yet become a craze. The car Julia purchased startled the citizens of the town because it was the first such to appear in Talmadge and because it appeared in a burst of low-slung black elegance with red leather upholstery and white-wall tyres and a Pinin Farina front end seemingly composed of peering headlamps and a smirking radiator grille. Julia Regan was forty-eight years old, and something Puritan in the lifeblood of the townsfolk rebelled at the concept of her driving such a flashy automobile.

At the same time, they were forced to admit that Julia's beauty had miraculously withstood the ravages of time, and that she managed to bring an added grace to the clean, wide-canopied, prancing good looks of the automobile. Oh yes, she had thickened a bit about the waist, and her throat and neck were not as taut as they once had been, and the brown hair braided into a bun at the back of her head showed strands of grey here and there. But somehow, Julia was managing to avoid the anonymous abyss of middle age. They would have said she was ageing gracefully if there were any question of her ageing at all; but Julia seemed to have found a constant level somewhere between maturity and old age, and she clung to that unchangingly, effortlessly. There would, they knew, be no in-between years for Julia Regan, no subtle evolution from summer to autumn to winter. They would continue to see her for a long time as youthful, energetic, beautiful. And then one day they would raise their eyes and look at Julia, and she would be old. Suddenly, she would be old. In the meantime, they watched her with a sort of shocked awe, deploring the jazzy sports car but simultaneously respecting and rejoicing in the freedom of spirit that had led to its purchase.

At forty-eight, Julia still moved with graceful femininity. Her voice had deepened a bit, and she spoke rarely and softly, her large brown eyes emphasizing her every word. Her body was neither the ripe ornamental accident of a maiden nor the meticulously structured shell of a matron, but it was a womanly body that resisted every middle-age tendency towards squareness. There was an iron-hard quality to Julia, a stiffness of back, a purposefulness of stride, a thrust of head and chin, which did not invite casual relationships and which provided her with an aura of aloofness. But this was the core of the woman, and not the mould. The mould was soft and rounded. She did not look like a young girl, but neither was she a ridiculously pathetic older woman desperately digging into cosmetics jars for her lost beauty, draping her sagging body with the fripperies of youth. Julia Regan still had good legs and a firm bosom, and she walked with the slightest hint of unconscious suggestiveness, and, as she always had, she still looked desirable and just possibly available and yet totally respectable. The people of the town watched her and wondered about the secret of her youth, and were puzzled by the anachronism. She drove the Italian sports car over the roads of Talmadge with an annoying but fascinating disdain for the opinions of others. And even though her hair was caught securely at the nape of her neck, you could swear it was streaming over her shoulders in the wind.

As far as the people of Talmadge could see, there were only two things that interested Julia Regan. These were her son, David, and the property she had inherited from her late husband, Arthur. Her son was living in New York and, from what they had heard, was doing quite well in television. They always knew when he was coming up to Talmadge for the week-end because Julia seemed more friendly towards everyone just before his arrival. Her son didn't have much to do with the people of the town, even though he'd grown up with most of the boys, but the town accepted that as the way of the Regans. Besides, with so much Talmadge real estate behind them, neither Julia nor David *had* to be friendly if they didn't choose to be.

Julia had inherited two hundred acres of choice Talmadge land when her husband died. In all likelihood, her son David would fall heir to that property one day, and in a town that was as real-estate-orientated as Talmadge, this was a parcel to be reckoned with. There were two constant cries at town board meetings, and these were "Keep the developers out!" and "Stop the sand and gravel operations!" The cries were in perfect accord with the intent of the townspeople. Talmadge had been invented by ivory-tower scholars and discovered by Madison Avenue confectioners. The largest real-estate interest in town, of course, remained the university's, and this seat of higher learning was not particularly interested in finding itself suddenly surrounded by a lot of belching factories. The gun factory on the far side of town was eyesore enough and stuck in the craw of scholar and commuter alike, but was fortunately close enough to the near-by town of Rattigan to be almost physically divorced from Talmadge itself. None the less, it was a constant reminder of what *could* happen to the town, and so the zoning restrictions insisted upon by the university interests largely concerned industry, both heavy and light.

The university's position was strengthened by the commuter attitude. The thing the commuters all loved about Talmadge was its woodsy, rural, dreamlike quality. Any industry introduced into the town would necessitate living facilities for the incoming workers. The moment the town allowed a factory to go up, the commuters were sure the housing developers would come panting in hotly with plans for tract upon tract of identical homes. No, sir, the people of Talmadge did not want to turn this carefully concocted dream into another Long Island housing slum. The zoning regulations prohibited the building of any private dwelling on less than three acres of land, and the going price for Talmadge property in 1952 was three thousand dollars an acre. This meant that a man needed nine thousand dollars before he could even think of breaking ground, and not many men—even in those days of post-war prosperity—had that kind of money to strew around the countryside. With zoning regulations against industry, with zoning regulations that prohibited building except by the rich or the near-rich, Talmadge seemed fairly well protected from invasion.

Julia Regan, the townsfolk estimated, was sitting pretty with her two hundred acres. From what they could figure, the land had probably cost Arthur Regan's father something like fifty dollars an acre when he'd bought it in 1904. The economic spiral was continuing upward, they figured, and they could visualize a day not too far off when Talmadge land would be bringing anywhere from four to six thousand dollars an acre. A little arithmetic told them that Julia could net a cool six hundred thousand dollars if she decided to sell everything she owned right then and there, and six hundred thousand dollars, they further estimated, was just a little more than half a million dollars, and that was not strawberries. They could also imagine a day when the developers would finally invade Talmadge *en masse*, with or without industry. Most of the land closer to New York had already yielded to the bulldozers, and

Talmadge had the added attraction of being midway between New York and New Haven. With a wild stretch of the imagination it could be called a distant suburb of either. If the developers were finally allowed to bring their housing tracts to Talmadge, there was no telling how much real estate would eventually be worth. Julia, the townsfolk estimated, was playing a shrewdly calculating waiting game with her two hundred acres. She might be dead and gone long before Talmadge ever admitted developers, but her son David would reap a huge profit whichever way the wind blew.

Their opinion of Julia's business acumen was strongly bolstered by her choice of an attorney. Elliot Tulley was perhaps the shrewdest lawyer in Talmadge, the man who had defended the gun factory against the university's violation-of-private-schooling-zone case, and won. He was outspoken about zoning regulations and openly stated wherever he could find an audience that "progress could not be legislated against". Most people thought he was a cantankerous windbag, and most people thought Julia's periodic visits to his office were concerned with her Talmadge real-estate holdings. Knowing Tulley's stand on zoning, knowing he had already successfully defended one so-called zoning violation, tying this in with Julia's standoffish attitude towards the town, assuming Julia had no real love for Talmadge or its woodsy, rural aspirations, they automatically concluded that she and Tulley were cooking up a scheme that would allow the great unwashed to descend upon Talmadge in unimaginable hordes. Two hundred acres were two hundred acres, and a widow who lived alone certainly didn't need more than that big old house and maybe four or five acres to roam around in. So why else was she hanging on to the land, except in hope of a bigger profit? Why else did she go up to see Tulley once a month like clockwork?

Once a month, the black roadster would pull up in front of Tulley's office, and the door on the driver's side would open, and Julia would step out gracefully and close the door behind her. She would walk purposefully towards the steps leading to the upstairs office and then climb them, skirt riding a little, good calves and trim ankles showing, damned if that woman ever showed a sign of age! A half-hour later, she would come down, enter her car, and drive off again.

The townspeople knew she discussed zoning on those monthly visits. They could imagine her and Tulley leaning over a Talmadge map and counting and recounting those two hundred acres, dividing them and subdividing them into builders' plots, cackling as they anticipated the huge profit.

The townspeople, of course, did not know that Julia Regan was a woman living almost entirely in the past. They knew she had once been thirty-five years old and had gone abroad with her sister Millicent. They knew she had been to France and Switzerland and Italy. They did not know that day by day Julia lived and relived a time that had begun for her in August of 1938.

She and Millie ate brook trout amandine in Interlaken. They sat outdoors and the evening was delightfully cool. Millie was huddled inside a hand-woven shawl she had purchased at one of the local shops, Julia wore a sweater over her blouse, her long brown hair trailing over her shoulders. The Jungfrau dominated the town. Wherever you walked, you could see the mountain in the distance, pristine and white, jutting into the sky, Looking at it, Julia understood why men went on climbing expeditions. The streams of Interlaken were incredibly blue and green, pellucid, as if they had been concocted on an artist's palette and allowed to run wetly over a pad. The town felt enclosed and tight, and they sat outdoors in front of the sleepy hotel and ate trout caught that day in mountain streams, pan-broiled, crisp and brown on the outside, flaking off white on the fork, crumbling in the mouth. Two German officers were sitting at a table behind them. They talked in guttural whispers, laughing occasionally. Julia was sure they were talking about her and Millie, but she ate her fish and drank her beer in seeming disregard, and afterwards asked the head-waiter if she might have the thick brown bottle to take home to her son.

They talked mostly about their impending drive through the Alps to Italy. It had been Millie's idea to rent a car in Paris, an idea Julia strenuously opposed. Her sister was going abroad on her doctor's orders, and Julia's concept of the trip had been an air flight to Rome and then a train ride east to Aquila, where Millie would find the sunshine and mountain air she needed.

"I'll probably come to Europe only once in my entire life," Millie had said. "I won't let you wrap me up like an invalid and ship me through the continent in a baggage car."

"That's not the point, Millie."

"The point is we're here, and I'm still alive, thank God, and I'd like to see a little of France and Switzerland and Italy before I end up on a porch in the sun. We'll *drive* to Italy, Julia. That's the way we'll do it."

Julia had dropped the argument. Millie was her older sister, and she'd never been able to win an argument with her, even when they were children. Besides, she had learned that spinsters were as stubborn as anything God had ever devised, and her sister was no exception. If Millie keeled over dead on the ride to Italy, even the death would bring pleasure if it was the result of an independently arrived-at conclusion. So Julia had stopped trying to convince her, and they had remained in Paris for four days, and rented a car from a French agency, and the matter had been settled. Or, at least, Julia thought it had been settled.

Now, sitting in midsummer silence at an outdoor restaurant in the cool shadow of the virgin mountains, Millie began to have qualms about the drive. "These are the Alps, you know," she said. "These aren't the Catskills, Julia. I've always been afraid of high places, and there's nothing higher than the Alps, is there? I've heard the roads are bad, and sometimes slippery, and treacherous. Suppose we get killed up there in the Alps? I don't care so much for myself, but what about you? With a husband and a child, a mere growing boy, back in Connecticut? Perhaps we should forget driving. Perhaps there's another way."

The *maître d'*, who could not help overhearing the conversation, assured them that Swiss roads were the best roads in the world. He went into the hotel and emerged seconds later with the concierge, who bolstered the *maître d*'s opinion of Swiss engineering skill. The concierge was a Frenchman, he claimed, and was therefore unbiased by patriotism. By this time, the two German officers—a colonel and a lieutenant—felt compelled to enter the discussion and give their own Teutonic assurances to the visiting ladies. As Julia and Millie listened in stunned fascination, the four men began deciding on the best route to take into Domodossola.

"Who will be doing the driving?" the German colonel asked.

"I will," Julia said.

"Very well, *Fräulein*. It is not a dangerous drive. There are very good passes. From where did you come, please?"

"Lausanne," Julia said.

"Ah, then you have driven through these mountains, and there is nothing between here and Italy which should frighten you."

"How many passes are there?" Julia asked.

"Two. The Grimsel Pass, and later the Simplon. Neither will give you any trouble."

"I think we should put the car on a train," Millie said. "I understand we can do that."

"Yes, *Fräulein*, but the closest place to do that would be at Kandersteg, and this would involve mountain-driving over roads which are not too good. You would do well to take the Grimsel Pass and then drive down the valley to Brig. Then, if you do not feel like attempting the Simplon, you can put your car on the train in Brig."

"Yes, that is good," the concierge said. "That is what you should do. Here, I will mark it for you."

"But the ladies are afraid of driving," the lieutenant said.

"No, I'm not afraid," Julia said.

"They would do better driving to Kandersteg," the lieutenant said.

"Nonsense, there is nothing to be frightened of," the colonel said, and Millie cringed a little at his tone of command. "You will drive directly out of Interlaken, and you will go through the Grimsel Pass. It is a lovely drive. There are goats. You will love it."

"Yes," the concierge said. "And then you will come down into the Rhône Valley. It is beautiful, beautiful."

"Beautiful," the colonel said.

"And into Brig," the *maître d'* said. "And at Brig you will put the car on to a train and go into Italy that way."

"Yes, that is best," the concierge said.

"Be sure to purchase first-class tickets," the lieutenant said. "On the train. Be sure to ask for first-class."

"Write it down. On the edge of the map," the colonel said. "First-class tickets. The ladies should not forget."

"I will write it," the concierge said. "And I will make the route. You will love it. What are you driving?"

"A Simca," Julia applied.

"That is good for the mountains. You will have no trouble."

"You will leave early in the morning," the colonel said. "It will be a lovely trip. It is settled, is it not?"

"Why, yes, I suppose so," Millie said.

"Very well. *Bon voyage!*" He clicked his heels, clapped his comrade on the shoulder, and led him back to their own table.

They awoke early the next day. They had breakfast on the small balcony overlooking the main street of the town with the mist-shrouded mountain in the distance. Occasionally, one of the town's ancient carriages creaked by, but the streets were almost deserted. A man carrying a bundle of wood on his shoulders walked past, glanced up at them, waved briefly and continued down the street, his boots clattering on the empty pavement. They fuelled the car and headed into the mountains towards Brienz, the first big town marked on their map. Millie insisted on filling a gallon bottle with water.

"It's the radiator that causes all the trouble," she said. "The radiator overheats."

To Julia, sitting behind the wheel as town after town fell behind them, the mountains were a challenge. She could not have explained this accurately to Millie, but there was something terribly unwomanly about the act of putting the car on a train and allowing it to be carried into Italy. It was the feminine thing to do, perhaps, but not the womanly thing—and, to Julia, there was a difference.

She was frightened. She would have been lying to herself if she'd pretended the narrow, winding steep road did not frighten her. The road was cut into the side of the mountain, and she could not thoroughly understand the principle because she had always imagined that a road went completely *around* a mountain until it reached the top, instead of climbing it on one face in a succession of zigzagging stages. She learned very rapidly that every time the car completed one of the stages, it ended on the opposite side of the road, so that the trip up was a constant shifting from the side of the road that hugged the mountain itself and the side that hugged nothing but thin air. She felt fairly secure when she navigated the inboard stretches, but the rim of the road terrified her. It seemed to hang out over open space. Nothing separated the road from the surrounding mist except a series of very small, evenly spaced boulders. The boulders, perhaps a foot each in height and length, were painted white and placed on the outer rim of the road at six-foot intervals. She was sure the boulders were there only as guides; they certainly could not have prevented any automobile from hurtling over the edge. The higher they climbed, the steeper the drop became, and the thicker the mist, until finally they were driving in a blinding rain. The road seemed to slope in one direction and the surrounding mountains in another. She had the craziest feeling of being trapped in a Dali world of tilting geometric shapes with rain and mist obscuring vision and presenting a wiper-slashed dream effect. Millie began coughing the moment they hit the rain. She hunched against the door of the car, alternately on the inside of the road, alternately on the side that overhung the drop. She would not look down. She coughed into her handkerchief and she stared straight through the windshield as the wipers hacked at the rain. She did not say a word. Every time one of the buses let out its terrible horn blast, she jumped with a start, and then coughed again, and shrank deeper into the seat.

The buses combined with the road and the rain and the sharply sloping angles to lend a nightmare quality to the ride, adding sound to the landscape, a terrible alarming sound like the bleat of a wounded bull, strident on the mountain air, a sound that materialized from nowhere, a sound impossible to locate, ahead, behind, where? And then the bus itself would appear, either racing past on the opposite side of the road or coming suddenly from behind, swinging out past the driver's side of the car, clearing the fenders by inches, the horn bleating every moment of the way, while Julia clung tightly to the wheel and prayed God she wouldn't be sidewiped and sent hurtling through those puny boulders down the face of the mountain.

They began to see the goat signs. The signs were painted on to the rock walls of the mountain. They were painted in white, and there were no words, simply drawings, unmistakable pictures of goats. The signs frightened Julia because now, besides having to worry about the rain and the road and the buses, she also had to worry about animals suddenly crossing the road. She made up her mind that she would hit any goat that got in her path rather than swerve to avoid him. She was frightened, but she was also excited and exhilarated. Her hair had come loose and clung wetly to her forehead and her cheeks. Her face was flushed. She had unbuttoned the top button of her blouse, and she could feel drops of perspiration as they trickled past her throat and between her breasts. She had long ago down-shifted to second, and she drove in that gear constantly now, listening for the sound of the buses, beginning to know whether they were coming from ahead or behind. There was, too, she realized, at least a two-foot safety margin between her and the edge of the road when she was driving on the outside. She was beginning to get the feel of the auto, to know its width and its length, and the sound of its engine. The first goats they saw were huddled against the side of the road, protected from the rain by an overhanging rock ledge. Julia smiled when they passed them.

"Well, this isn't so bad," she said aloud, almost cheerfully.

Millie did not answer.

The closer they came to the top and the pass, the colder it got. Millie pulled her shawl around her and insisted that Julia put on a coat. Julia wanted nothing less than a coat. The turns were sharp and steep and closer together now, and she fought the wheel like a truck driver.

It was Millie who heard the sound first.

"What's that?" she said. She sat erect on the seat and stared through the windshield.

"I don't know," Julia said.

"A rockslide!" Millie announced.

"No. No, it isn't."

"It sounds like——"

"Shh. Shhh, darling, it's not a rockslide."

They continued driving. She was not at all sure it wasn't a rockslide. She kept listening to the sound over the steady clicking of the wipers.

"It's water," she said.

"Water? What kind of . . . ?"

"I don't know. I'm sure it's all right, though."

"What's that?" Millie said, and again she leaned closer to the windshield. "Up there."

"Oh. Oh, that's it."

"That's *what*?"

"It's a dam, Millie. Don't you think so? Doesn't it look like a dam?"

"How do I know what a damn *dam* looks like?" Millie said.

"Yes, it is," Julia said. "And look, there's a place to park in front of it. We can get out and stretch our legs."

"I'm not getting out of this car," Millie said.

"Well, I'd like to rest a bit. Do you mind?"

"Do what you like," Millie said. "We should have put the car on a train."

"Don't be silly, darling. It's been a wonderful ride so far."

"So far," Millie said ominously.

They parked in the area beside the cement wall fronting the dam. Another car was parked there, carrying French plates. A man and a woman were eating lunch inside the car. They smiled at Julia when she got out of the car and hastily shrugged into her trench-coat.

"*Bonjour*," the woman said.

"*Bonjour, madame*," Julia answered, and then walked to the other side of the road and stood in the rain with her hands on her hips and the trench-coat belted tight about her slender waist, the collar hugging the back of her neck, looking up at the dam and smiling. She heard the frightening sudden bleat of an approaching bus and ran across the road quickly, just as it rumbled past.

She rapped on the window of the car and shouted, "Come on out, Millie. The air is wonderful."

"No, thank you," Millie answered.

Julia shrugged and walked a little way up the road. She felt oddly fulfilled. She was still smiling when she got into the car again. She threw the trench-coat into the back seat with the luggage and said, "There's a sign out there, Millie. We're very close to the top."

"Thank God."

"There's something called Hospiz up there, which I gather is a rest station of some sort. Maybe we can get some tea."

"I'd love some."

"And then through the pass and down into the Rhône. The German officers said it was a beautiful drive."

"The German officers said *this* was a beautiful drive, too."

"Millie, stop being such a fuss-budget."

"I'm cold."

"We'll stop for tea soon, dear," Julia said. "It hasn't been so bad. Really, Millie, it hasn't."

She started the car and backed away from the cement wall. The

French couple waved again and shouted something, which Julia missed. She drove for a few yards in the lowest gear, snapped the gearshift lever into second, and left it there. She concentrated entirely on the curving road now, almost forgetting that anyone was in the car with her. The turns had become hairpin curves, a turn, a steep rising stretch, another turn, another sharp grade, another turn. She watched the road, heard Millie cough beside her, heard another cough, not Millie's, realized it had come from the stuttering engine, reached for the gearshift lever and the brake simultaneously, rammed the lever down into first, but too late. The car stalled.

"Damn," Julia said.

"What is it?"

"We've stalled. Don't worry."

She put the car in neutral and stepped on the starter. The engine whinnied, but did not turn over. She tried it again.

"What is it?" Millie asked.

"It won't start. It's probably flooded."

"What are we going to do?"

"I want to get off this curve first," Julia said.

"How are you going to do that?"

"I'll back up."

"Not with me in the car!" Millie said. She seemed ready to cry. Julia touched her arm gently and smiled.

"It would help me if you went around the curve and made sure I wasn't backing into any buses."

"In the rain?" Millie said.

"Millie, dear . . ."

"All right," Millie answered, and nodded her head curtly. She opened the door on her side and stepped into the rain. Julia, behind the wheel, sighed heavily.

"Anyone coming?" she shouted.

"No, it's clear," Millie said. "Hurry up! And watch the edge of the road, Julia. You'll be on the outside, once you back around the curve."

"All right," Julia shouted. "Here I come!"

She took a deep breath, put her foot on the brake pedal, and released the handbrake. Slowly, she raised her foot. The car began rolling backward.

"Turn!" Millie shouted. "You're heading for the edge! Turn! Oh my God, Julia, turn!"

She yanked at the wheel sharply, her foot poised above the brake pedal, her neck craning out the window, trying to see the white boulders through the driving rain. When she heard the sound of the horn, her heart lurched and she felt suddenly ill.

"A bus!" Millie shouted. "Julia, a bus . . ."

She rammed her foot on to the brake and then realized she was in the centre of the road. In the same instant, she knew that the bus was coming from Millie's direction, around the curve, or Millie would not have seen it. She heard the rising wail of the bus horn as it approached, the warning bleat sounding over the sloping mountain road. Her first instinct was to get out of the car. The hell with it, she thought, we're going to Italy! She took her foot off the brake and prayed the car would gain speed rapidly, prayed she would not roll over the edge, prayed she had not misjudged the turn. She rounded the curve and saw the bus bearing down on the opposite side of the road. She cut the wheel sharply and the bus went past on her right, its horn blasting in righteous outrage. She watched the white boulders, coming as close to them as she possibly dared, until the car was on the straightaway again. She pulled up the emergency brake, put the car in gear, and let out her breath. Millie came back to the car and collapsed heavily on the front seat.

They sat for ten minutes and then Julia tried to start the car again. The engine would not turn over.

"We're so close to the top!" Julia said angrily. "Why did it have to stall?"

"I'm limp," Millie said.

"I'll try it again in a little while. I'm sure it's only flooded."

"What does that mean? When it's flooded?"

Julia began laughing. "I don't know. It's what Arthur always says when the car won't start."

"Someone's coming," Millie said, turning.

"Who is it?"

"I don't know. A man on a motor-cycle. Maybe he's a policeman."

"In the Alps?"

"I'm sure there are policemen in the Alps, Julia."

The motor-cycle approached. The man on it was not a policeman. His bike bore military markings, and he wore a black helmet with an insignia painted into a white circle, and a wide black rubberized poncho. He stopped his motor-cycle near the car, got off, and moved towards Millie's window, seeming to float inside the wide-hanging black cape. The cape was wet and shining. The rain lashed about his face and shoulders. Millie rolled down the window, and he squinted through the rain at her.

"*É successo qualche cosa?*" he asked.

"I don't speak Italian," Millie said. She turned to her sister, "Julia?"

"*Parlo solamente un poco,*" Julia said hesitantly. "*Parla inglese?*"

"*Si, un poco*," the soldier answered. He seemed thoughtful for a moment. His face beneath the black helmet was lean and tanned. His eyes were almost closed against the rain, but Julia could make out their colour even from her side of the car, a startling blue against the burnished face. He could not have been older than twenty-four or twenty-five, but the helmet was deceiving, combining with the rain to cover his face with shifting shadow. "I speak English bad," he said. "*La macchina, che cosa* . . . ?" He paused. "What . . . the car? What is wrong?"

"It won't start," Julia said.

The soldier rested his hands on the door of the car. They were large hands, brown and big-knuckled, a workman's hands, or a farmer's, with short blond hair curling along the fingers like narrow bronze wires.

"*Forse potrei* . . ." Again he paused and mentally translated. "I," he said. He touched his chest. "I maybe help. To start."

"If you'd like to try," Julia said.

"*Si, signorina, vorrei provare, se non le dispaice.*"

Julia did not miss the "*signorina*". She smiled briefly and said, "*Signora*."

"*Prego?*"

"*Signora*," she repeated.

'*Ah, va bene*," the soldier said. "*É sposata*, married. *Per piacere, signorina*," and his eyes twinkled as he repeated the "Miss" again.

"*La macchina, no?*"

He came around to Julia's side of the car.

"Be careful!" she said. "You'll fall down the mountain."

"*No, no, non abbia paura*," he said. He opened the door, precariously close to the edge of the road. "*Permesso*," he said to Julia, and he executed a short courtly bow, smiling at her. She moved over towards the middle of the seat. He climbed in, bringing the smell of the rain with him, and the smell of his rubber cape.

"*Allora*," he said, and he grinned. "*La chiave, ah?*" He touched the ignition key. "*La benzina?*" He frowned, annoyed because he was speaking Italian. "Benzine?" he said. "Gasoline? *Si, si*, gasoline. You have gasoline?"

"The tank is half full," Julia said.

"*Si, vedo*," he shrugged. "*Allora, adesso proviamo*, eh? *Roma no fu fatta in un'ora, vero?*"

"I'm sorry, I don't understand you," Julia said. "My Italian is not very good."

"Well, forget," he said. "We try. *É pronta?*"

"Yes, I'm ready."

"Julia, do you think this is all right?" Millie asked.

"Yes, darling. He's trying to help us."

"*Cosa?*" the soldier asked.

"Nothing," Julia said, and she smiled.

"*Ha paura?*"

"*Si. Un pochino,*" Julia said.

"Do not be fear," he said to Millie, and he smiled. "I am very good racer." He looked at Julia. "That is right? Racer?"

"Driver," Julia said.

"*Si, signorina.* Driver."

"*Signora,*" she corrected again.

He smiled graciously, a slow lazy smile that came on to his face in sudden brilliance beneath the black helmet. "*Ma tutte le donne sono signorine in fondo, non é vero?* In the heart, all girls are maidens, is it not true?"

Julia smiled and did not answer.

"*Dunque,*" he said, and he twisted the ignition key.

The engine turned over immediately.

The soldier began laughing. "*Sono un mago,*" he said. "*Un vero mago. Signorina, la tua automobile.*"

He opened the door and stepped into the rain, and again he executed a small bow.

"Thank you," Julia said. "*Mille grazie.*"

"*Prego,*" he answered. "It was pleasure."

"Well, thank you."

He smiled, came suddenly to attention, saluted the women, and went back to his motor-cycle. He climbed on to the seat, started the bike, waved with one gloved hand, and turned the curve in the road, vanishing in the rain.

"He was nice," Millie said.

"Yes," Julia answered.

"Can we get our tea now? Please?"

"Yes, darling, of course," Julia answered, and she put the car in motion.

They refuelled in the town of Gletsch, a Swiss town set in a deep mountain-ringed pocket, a town gone suddenly German. Julia read hesitantly from the Esso translation booklet, telling the attendant what she wanted done to the car. The day still looked foreboding and grey. Millie did not budge from the front seat of the automobile. She kept peering up at the ring of mountains balefully. When Julia got into the car again, she asked, "More climbing?"

"Nope. All downhill from here."

"Who said?"

"The attendant."

"I didn't know you spoke German."

"I don't. We used our hands. I pointed up and raised my eyebrows, and he pointed down and smiled. Complete understanding."

"What are you so chipper about, Julia?"

"I don't know," Julia said, and she suddenly looked at her sister and seriously said, "I guess I'm very happy to be here. I guess that's it."

"Don't you miss your family?"

"No," Julia said. "Not yet." She paused. "Is that a horrible thing to say?"

"Not if it's the truth." Millie wagged her sister away with her hands. "Don't ask me. Listen, don't ask me. Come on, let's see this remarkable valley."

They came out into the sunshine. They came out into balmy warmth. They came out on to a rolling green vista of hills dotted with cottages, of streams rushing, cutting through the green, of slick-wet rocks, of air you could taste, a blue sky pinned to the edges of the world, bright white clouds hanging lazy overhead, the sound of chattering birds, the hush of unimaginable peace. A grin came on to her mouth. They rolled down the windows of the car, and the breeze touched their faces, a breeze that stirred memory inside her, brought it welling up into her throat. This was summer-time. This was every summer she had ever known, every dreamed-of summer, imagined and real. There was a timelessness to the valley. A timelessness to the slow and lazy descent of the automobile effortlessly navigating the mountain curves, a timelessness to the sparkling fresh bounding water of the streams and the river and the grass beyond, the brightest grass she had ever seen in her life, story-book grass set against a story-book sky. She caught her breath. She held her breath and felt the sun touching her arm where it rested on the sill of the car, and the soft gentle breeze catching at her hair. She could feel her hair fluttering against her cheek. She wanted to stop the car and lie in the thick grass, suck juice from the thick stem of a blade of grass caught between her teeth, spread her hair behind her on luxuriant thickness, open her blouse, feel the kiss of the sun on her naked body. She knew this valley, oh she had been in this valley when the world was new, walked in it alone with the same sun shining overhead, and the same ancient streams, and the same idle smoke drifting from ancient chimneys, her valley. She said aloud, "It was worth it."

She wished she were alone. She felt she was about to cry, and she wanted to be able to cry alone, without her sister there.

She drove slowly. She wanted to savour this time. She wanted to remember every curve, every curious twisting of rock, each rill, each sound, each painfully sweet assault of blue and green and white and sparkling silver. Sensuously, she opened herself to the valley, succumbing to it as to a lover.

They ate lunch in the town of Brig. Everyone spoke German. The ladies' room was filthy. There was one towel on the roller mechanism, and it had been used repeatedly, and fat women in flowered house-dresses rolled the towel and dried their hands on the same smudged material over and over again. There were young men singing and marching in the streets, knapsacks on their backs. They loaded the car on to the train, and made certain they asked for first-class tickets. The ride was fairly comfortable. A man sitting next to them was eating bread and cheese, and for the first time in her life, Julia felt like an American. The man knew what she was, and his knowledge touched something inside her, so that being an American suddenly became something of which to be very proud. She was a tourist, true, and she had heard all about the terrible Tourist and the impression he created abroad, the fat Texas oil millionaire with his Leica camera around his neck and his cigar in his mouth, desecrating the cathedrals of the old world, treating Europeans like foreigners on their own soil, generally playing the stereotyped role of the fat American capitalist boor. She had heard the stories, and she was a tourist, yes, but she felt completely and utterly American, and the feeling was a good one. She did not know whether the man sitting across the aisle eating bread and cheese liked Americans or disliked them or was indifferent to them. Nor did she particularly care. Being American was enough. She had never been farther west than Pennsylvania nor farther north than Massachusetts, nor farther south than Washington, D.C. But sitting in a first-class coach on a train racing through tunnels towards the Italian border, she suddenly felt the overwhelming geographic length and breadth of her country, was suddenly intimate with grain fields and mountains and sea-shores and deserts and canyons and cities and towns. All of America, all of its people and places, suddenly surged into her and became a part of her, giving her an existence separate from her own—and yet indistinguishable from it. She was an American. The title gave her pleasure.

She wondered all at once if she were getting homesick.

Domodossola lay in intense sunshine, a town carved out of the base of a mountain, a town of white walls and tiled roofs, a border town with a temporary border feel. The train had stopped at Berisal on the Swiss side, and the Swiss customs officials had come through and made a cursory check of passports, and then the train had stopped again at a small depot just over the Italian border. The Italian customs men had marched through the compartments with a greater sense of duty and purpose, asking Millie to open one of her bags, which embarrassed her because she had packed all her underclothing on top, never expecting a thorough customs inspection, spoiled by the French and Swiss border men. The Italian who'd been eating his lunch got into a voluble argument concerning his passport, which from what Julia could gather, had not been properly stamped or validated or something, and the Italian customs officials in their green uniforms with their revolvers strapped to their sides seemed in favour of shooting the man on the spot if it would facilitate getting the train into Domodossola. They finally straightened it out. When the customs men left, the lunch-eater muttered "*Fetenti!*" under his breath, and Julia smiled and looked through the window as the train picked up speed again and came into the broiling border town.

DOMODOSSOLA, the signs read.

Domodossola.

She rolled the name on her tongue, savouring it. She knew instantly that she would love Italy. She tried her Italian on one of the trainmen, asking him where the car would be unloaded, and the man pointed across the tracks to where a lone shed stood in the sunshine. He told her to wait there. The flat cars carrying the automobiles would be uncoupled, he said, and attached to another engine, and then brought to the unloading platform near the shed. She understood perhaps one-third of his monologue, but she understood his pointing finger completely, and she and Millie went through the station and walked to the shed. Two men and a woman were already standing there, waiting for their cars. There was no shade anywhere. There was no overhang on the roof of the shed, and the shadow it cast was a meagre one, adequate if one were sitting—but unfortunately, there was nothing to sit on. The sun was intense. A leaking water spout trickled drops on to a flat, shining rock. The sun glistened along the railroad tracks, gleamed from the harsh white walls of the buildings.

"I wonder how long this will take," Millie said.

Julia wiped perspiration from her upper lip and nodded briefly. The Italians had struck up a conversation with each other. She eavesdropped, trying to catch the flow of language, trying to adapt her ear to the sound. She had learned Italian a long time ago, in college, and she'd been only a fairly good student. But she was certain she would learn to speak it fluently now that she was here. Already, she was beginning to pick up the musical cadence.

The wait became interminable. The water-drops ticked off time on the flat rock. No one seemed to know what had happened to the flat cars carrying the automobiles. Every time a new engine appeared in the distance, one of the Italians would say "*Eccola!*" and a feeling of relief would sweep over the small band standing in the sunshine near the shed. But the engine was never the one hauling the flat cars, and the relief was instantly followed by disappointment, and finally by suspicion. From what Julia could gather, one of the Italians was certain the cars had been sent back to Switzerland. "*Queste porche ferrovie!*" he muttered darkly, and she gathered his opinion of Italy's railroads was not very high, despite *il Duce's* ability to get trains in and out of stations on time. The flat cars did not appear until an hour later. When the engine pulled into view, a spontaneous cheer went up from the little group. The Italians began nodding and smiling. One of the men, standing in his shirtsleeves, was perspiring profusely, giant wet blots under his arms and across his chest. He fanned himself with a straw hat and turned his free hand to Julia in a gesture of helplessness and apology, nodding his head. Julia smiled. The train pulled in, and a platform man yanked the chocks out from under the wheels of the automobile and adjusted the unloading platform to meet the deck of the flat car. The three Italians unloaded their automobiles first. Julia drove the Simca off the platform and Millie got into the car and sighed deeply.

"Thank God," she said. "I'm exhausted."

Julia looked through the windshield. A border official in a green uniform was stopping each car. The owners of the automobiles were showing him some sort of identification. Passports, she supposed, and watched as the cars ahead of her were waved on. As she approached the official, he shouted "*Alt!*" and she put on the brake and waited for him to come over to the window on her side.

"*Carnet,*" he said. He extended one gloved hand, palm up.

"What is it you want?" Julia asked, and then quickly translated in halting Italian, "*Che cosa vuole?*"

"*Carnet,*" the man said. His hand remained extended.

"What does he want, Julia?" Millie said.

"I don't know. My driver's licence, I suppose." She opened her bag, found her wallet, took out her Connecticut driver's licence and handed it through the window.

The man shook his head. "*Carnet, carnet,*" he said.

"He must want the registration," Millie said. "All the papers are in the glove compartment, Julia. Give him those."

Julia sighed, opened the glove compartment, took out the papers the Paris auto rental agency had given them, and handed them through the window. The border official leafed through the various papers, shaking his head as he studied each one. Then he handed them back to Julia.

"*Per entrare in Italia,*" he said, "*deve avere il carnet. Nessuno di questi documenti e un carnet.*"

"What in hell is a *carnet?*" Julia asked Millie.

"I'm sure I don't know. Tell him we'll get it in Stresa, whatever it is. Tell him we're in a hurry, Julia."

"*Non tenimo una carnet,*" Julia said. "*Lo prediamo a Stresa. Per piacere, abbiamo fretta.*"

The border official shook his head. "*Lo deve ottenere qui. Non a Stresa. Non potete lasciare. Domodossola senza il carnet.*"

"*Ma dove lo potere avere?*" Julia asked.

"*Seguitemi,*" the man said. He motioned with his hand, directing Julia to pull the car to the side of the road, where she saw one sign hanging over a customs office and another sign for the Italian military police. She drove to a place marked DIVIETO MACCHINE CIVILI and parked the car alongside a motor-cycle.

"Stay here with the luggage, Millie,' she said. "They won't let us leave Domodossola until we get this *carnet*, whatever it is."

She stepped out of the car. The official was waiting for her.

"*Venite,*" he said, and he led her into the customs office. A man sitting behind an old desk looked up when they entered. The office was dim and cool. The shutters on the single window set in the stone wall were closed, blocking the rays of the sun. The men held a conversation in rapid Italian, the only word of which Julia caught was *carnet*. The man behind the desk kept nodding his head. The other went on at interminable length about the *carnet*. It seemed they would never get it settled.

Finally, the man behind the desk said, "*Si, va bene. Portatela alli' Automobile Club.*"

"Do either of you speak English?" Julia asked.

The man behind the desk looked up and smiled. The smile was evil, Julia thought, a horrid evil smile. "*In Italia,*" he said slowly, "*parliamo italiano.*"

She knew he understood English, because he had answered her question. Slowly, precisely, controlling her anger, she said in English, "And in Italy you have apparently forgotten whatever manners you ever had. How do I get this *carnet?*"

The man behind the desk continued smiling. He did not answer Julia. The other man said, "*Seguite,*" and she followed him out into the sunshine again. A tall blond man in an Army uniform was coming out of the military-police barracks next door. He smiled at Julia and said, '*Ah, buon giorno, signorina.*"

She did not recognize him at first. Somehow, she'd thought the soldier on the mountain was an officer, but she saw quite clearly now the corporal's stripes on his sleeves and was a little disappointed, though she couldn't understand why. Too, the man on the mountain had seemed heavier inside his rubberized poncho, and this man who walked towards her now, smiling, was rather thin, and somewhat older than she'd originally estimated, thirty-three or thirty-four, perhaps even her own age. His hair was a muddied blond and this, too, came as a surprise because he'd been wearing the black helmet on the mountain, and yet surely she had noticed that his eyebrows were blond too and that his eyes . . . the eyes. The eyes were the same. Blue, an intense blue, smiling with the rest of his tanned face. It was a face she knew. She turned to him desperately and said in rapid English, "Oh, hello, how *are* you? Can you help me, please? I seem to need a *carnet*, but no one will tell me what it is, and they've been leading me from place to———"

The soldier held out his hand. "*Piano, piano,*" he said. "My English is not good."

She explained again, slowly this time. He listened intently, his head cocked to one side. He pushed a strand of hair off his forehead, revealing a white streak of flesh that the sun had not touched. She kept talking, fascinated by the suddenly exposed skin, as if she had stumbled upon a secret vulnerable corner of the man. The border official seemed weary of the exchange. He leaned against the whitewashed wall with the black FORBIDDEN TO CIVILIAN CARS lettered boldly on it, one hand resting on the butt of the pistol at his waist. The corporal nodded as Julia spoke, making his laborious mental translation. Then he said, "A *carnet* is a paper. it tells, *descrivere*, describes? *si*, your automobile, and that you are not bring to Italy for to sell. *Capisce?*"

"Yes, *si*, but no one told us about it. The Paris agency . . ."

"*Si, ma é necessario.* Is need. It is law." He shrugged.

"*Si,*" she said, and she nodded, distressed.

"*Si,* but is easy. To get this. The Automobile Club . . . ah . . . *come si dice rilasciare?* Issues? Fixes? They fix for you."

"But where is the Automobile Club?"

"In *città.* In town. He will take." He pointed to the border man.

"Could . . .?" Julia hesitated. "Are you very busy now?"

"*Signorina?*"

"Well . . . are you stationed here?"

"*Pardon?*"

"Well . . . could you come with us? To the Automobile Club? I'll never be able to explain all this in Italian."

The corporal nodded. "Ahhh," he said. "Ahhhh."

"Could you?"

"*Cosa?*" the border man asked.

The corporal translated Julia's request.

"*Allora, andiamo,*" the border man said. "*Stiamo sciupando tutto il pomeriggio.*"

"Will you come?" Julia asked.

"*Si, signorina. Al suo servizio!*" He snapped a salute at her, and them smiled, and the three began walking down the street together. From the car, Millie called, "Julia! Where are they *taking* you?"

"To the Automobile Club," Julia called back over her shoulder.

"The *what*? What did you say?"

"It's all right, Millie. I'll be right back."

There was something comical about the procession, and she could not resist smiling. She walked between the two uniformed men, trying to match her strides with their own. The border man walked with a stiff precise cadence, as if he were leading her to a wall to execute her. The notion delighted her. When they raised their rifles, she would say, "To hell with the blindfold!" The corporal, walking with a rather lazy lope, noticed her smile, but said nothing. There was a curious air of inactivity to the town. No one seemed to be employed, the entire town seemed to be out in the main street, idling, gossiping, the men standing in dark trousers and intensely white shirts, or the green army uniforms with their funny tasselled hats, the women barefoot most of them, but wearing brightly coloured dresses as if they had got ready for a ball and forgotten to put on their heels. Here and there, a few of Mussolini's Black Shirts lounged against the walls. The sunshine caught the town in its lazy posture, caught motion suspended, caught bicycles leaning against walls, reflected from silvered spokes, caught water running in the gutter, caught wrought-iron balconies overhanging the main street, caught the brightly coloured cart of the ices pedlar, and the young soldiers standing beside it in green, and the two adolescent girls in bright skirts and white blouses, barefoot, giggling, the town had been frozen by sunshine. The boots of the border man and the corporal thudded on the cobbled street, bracketed the feminine chatter of Julia's heels.

"My name is Renato," the corporal said suddenly, in Italian. "Renato Cristo."

"How do you do?" Julia said in English. "I'm Mrs. Arthur Regan." She paused. "Julia Regan."

Renato smiled his slow smile. In Italian, he said, "You spoke our language very well earlier. It would be a shame, now that you are in Italy, if you returned home exactly as you arrived."

"How do you mean?" Julia asked in English.

"It might be good to practice your Italian," Renato said. He would not speak English now. He spoke Italian, slowly, deliberately, carefully, so that she would understand him. But he would not speak English, and she sensed a challenge in his choice of language, and she responded to the challenge by answering him in English, refusing to give ground.

"I'll have ample opportunity to practice my Italian," she said.

"Why not begin now?" he asked in Italian. "You could learn very easily. You understand me perfectly well, do you not?"

"Yes," Julia said in English. "I understand you very well."

"Then why won't you answer me in Italian?"

"Why won't you ask me in English?"

"I am the man," he said simply.

She looked into his eyes suddenly. His face was very serious. All at once, she was frightened. She put her hand to her mouth, and then looked away. Renato smiled.

In deliberate Italian, he said, "Your Italian is very good. I have lived here in Italy all my life. I am, after all, an expert on the Italian language. I say your Italian is quite good." He paused. "Do you agree?"

"No," she said, still not looking at him.

"But yes."

"All right then, yes," she said in English, an annoyed tone in her voice. She turned to look at him again. "My Italian is very good, all right? Yes."

He stopped suddenly. The border official kept walking, unaware that Renato had stopped, unaware that Julia had stopped beside him.

"Would it pain you to say 'yes' in Italian?" he asked quietly.

"No. I suppose not."

"Then say it."

"Yes," Julia said. In Italian.

Renato smiled. "Good. We will speak only Italian from now on. It will be easier for us."

"Please, please hurry!" the border man said impatiently. He stood in the centre of the street waiting for them, his hands on his hips. "I have other things to do."

They caught up to him and walked the rest of the way in silence. Julia was suddenly aware that the top button of her blouse was unfastened. She moved her hand to it surreptitiously, buttoned it, and then glanced at Renato to see if he had noticed. The street seemed very hot all at once. When they reached the Automobile Club, an old man was out front, rolling down a corrugated-metal door upon which were painted the letters R.A.C.I.

"What are you doing?" Renato asked him.

"I am going home," the man said. "Today is a feast day. I have stayed open later than I should have."

"This lady needs a carnet," Renato said.

"She will have to come back tomorrow."

"She cannot come back tomorrow. She is leaving here this afternoon."

"That is impossible," the Automobile Club man said. "She cannot leave Domodossola without a carnet, therefore she cannot leave this afternoon, therefore she will come back tomorrow."

"No," Renato said. "Open your door, professor. You will give the lady her carnet now."

The Automobile Club man looked at the border official. The border official shrugged.

"I must go to the post office to mail a letter," the old man said. "I will come back in a half-hour. I should go home. This is a feast day. You soldiers are all brigands. You will not let a man enjoy his feast day."

"The lady is in Italy on holiday."

"No one asked her to come to Italy without a carnet," the old man said, "on holiday or otherwise. This is *my* holiday. There are few enough feast days."

"Yes, professor, but you are a kind man who would not turn away a lady so beautiful as this one."

The old man studied Julia with a practised eye. For a moment, she thought she would blush. The border official looked at her, too. Renato stood by with an air of proprietorship, like a cattle breeder exhibiting a choice head of beef. She was somewhat annoyed by his attitude. The men continued to study her solemnly, as though her beauty or lack of it would be the deciding factor in whether or not she got the carnet.

"Well, she *is* pretty," the old man said grudgingly. "I'll go to the post office and return. It will be a half-hour. If you wish to wait, fine. If not, tell me, and I'll go home to my family and enjoy a well-deserved rest on this scarce feast day."

"We'll wait," Renato said.

"Will you take care of the lady?" the border official asked him.

"Yes. I'll take care of the lady," Renato said.

"Very well. When you have the carnet, please return to the office."

"I will," Julia said. "Would you please tell my sister I'll be a little while?"

"Yes, madam," the border official said. He nodded curtly and walked away.

"I'll be back," the old man said. He tested the padlock on the rolled-down metal door, and shuffled off up the street.

"Well," Renato said, and he began laughing. "Welcome to Italy!"

His teeth were very white. When he laughed, his lips pulled back to reveal them, adding visual impetus to the laugh, inviting contagion. She found herself laughing with him.

"Is it always this way?" she asked. "How do you get anything done?"

"Oh, we get things done," Renato said, and he shrugged. "It's hot today. Do you find it hot?"

"Yes, I do."

"Would you like some ices? Do you like ices?"

"I'd love some, thank you."

They walked to the cart. "Two lemons," he said to the ices man. "Do you like lemon? Of course you like lemon. That is the only kind of ices to have on a hot day."

"Yes, I like lemon," she said softly.

"Good. How old are you?"

"What?"

"How old are you?"

"Why do you ask?"

He shrugged. "Why, because I want to know."

"I'm thirty-five," she said unflinchingly.

"That's good," He nodded.

"Why?"

"Is it not good?" he asked. He opened his eyes wide in surprise.

"Well, thirty is better. And seventeen is even better than that."

"Thirty is a bridge," Renato said, "and seventeen is a cradle. You are a good age."

"Thank you."

"Here. Be careful, the cup sometimes drips. You would not want to stain your pretty blouse," he said, and from the way he glanced at her she knew he'd noticed the unfastened button earlier.

"How old are *you*?" she asked.

"Thirty-three." He grinned. "I'm a boy yet."

"Yes, you are."

"But not too young for *il Duce's* magnificent Army, eh?"

"I take it you don't like the Army."

"Oh, I love the Army," he said broadly. "How else would I be able to afford travel? They send me all over Europe with important secret dispatches. I climb on to my motor-bike and deliver messages to generals of all nations. Very important documents. I carried one to Switzerland that said, 'I will meet you for a drink in Geneva on Tuesday.' Highly important, highly official, very secret."

Julia laughed. "Where are you stationed?" she asked.

"Rome. Isn't everyone? Rome is where *il Duce* is. He likes to look out over his balcony and see uniforms, many uniforms. So that's where I'm stationed."

"And where do you live?"

"I live nowhere," he said.

"What do you mean?"

"I was born in Naples, but my father took me from there when I was very young because he wanted to farm, and he had heard of a strip of land just outside Rome. It is rare for Italians to leave the town of their birth, but my father wanted to go, so we went. When my parents died, my sister and I sold the farm. I suppose I live with her now, in Rome."

"I see."

There was a pause in the conversation. They had walked back to the Automobile Club and were leaning against the metal door now.

Renato said, "Will you be going to Rome?"

"Yes. Well, outside of Rome actually. The Abruzzi. I'm taking my sister to Aquila."

"That's not far from Rome," he said. "Only a few hours' drive."

"My sister is ill," Julia said.

"Aquila is pleasant," he said. "Especially if you are ill." His smile widened. "Perhaps *only* if you are ill." He paused. "Will you be staying long?"

"Not too long."

"How long?"

"Why?"

"You always say 'why'. I ask questions, because I want to know the answers. It's not necessary to say 'why'. How long will you be staying?"

"Several months."

"Perhaps you may stay longer."

"No."

"How can you tell?"

"I have a husband and a son at home."

"Yes, and they will miss you."

"Yes."

"Yes, I know."

He was silent again.

"Aquila will be good for your sister," he said at last. "The air is clean."

"Yes, that's what we were told."

"Where will you be staying in Aquila?"

"We've rented a villa."

"How much are you paying?"

Julia laughed suddenly. "You ask *very* funny questions," she said.

"I want to make sure you're not being cheated."

"A travel agent arranged the rental for us."

"There are thieves among travel agents, too."

"Yes, but that applies to everyone, and I would rather trust people, wouldn't you?"

"No, I don't care to trust people," he said. "Nor they me. It doesn't matter. How much are you paying?"

"Two thousand lire a month."

"That's high."

"It's a beautiful villa."

"Will you have a car?"

"Yes."

"Will you come into Rome sometimes?"

"I suppose so."

"Yes or no?"

"Yes, there are things I want to see in Rome."

"I know an excellent guide," Renato said.

"Who?" she asked.

She watched him intently, slightly frightened by what was happening and yet totally free of any feeling of guilt, and the guiltlessness frightened her even more. She knew where this was leading, and yet she felt powerless to stop it. He had said, "I know an excellent guide," and she had said, "Who?" and she knew what his answer would be. She knew he would say, "Me." She was certain he would say, "Me," and she waited somewhat breathlessly for his reply, not sure what her reaction would be when it came, not sure whether she would end whatever was happening then and there, smile pleasantly but aloofly and says, "Thank you, that's very kind, but I don't think so," not sure at all what she would say when he made his offer.

He did not answer at once.

"Who?" she said again, and waited.

"A woman named Maria Scalza," he said.

"What?" She stared at him, surprised.

"Yes. She is a fine guide. If you like, I will give you her number."

"I . . . thank you, but . . ."

"Ahhh," Renato said, "the professor returns." He looked at his wrist-watch. "He said a half-hour, and a half-hour it is. *Il Duce* should send him a medal. He should send us all medals." He raised his arm in greeting. "Ah, professor!" he called. Then he winked at Julia and said, "You're late, professor," and burst into laughter when the old man exploded in rage.

She brought the carnet to the customs office afterwards. Renato waited until they had stamped it and returned it to her, and then he walked her to the car. Millie had fallen asleep on the front seat.

"Where do you go now?" Renato asked.

"Stresa. Just overnight."

"You will like Stresa," he said. "Are you staying at the Grand Borromées?"

"Yes. Have you ever stayed there?"

"Me?" He began laughing. "*Cara mia*, I'm a farmer," he said. "But it's pretty on the outside." He paused. "Like you." He opened the car door for her. "*Arrivederci*. Have a good trip."

"I . . . thank you for your help. You were very kind."

"It was my pleasure, believe me."

"Thank you again."

"*Prego.*"

"Good-bye."

"Good-bye," he said.

She first saw the paintings in one of the palaces where she had gone with her sister Millie in a gondola. It had been a misty day in Venice, the sky spread overhead like a taut translucent skin, grey-white, the sun behind it evenly illuminating the canopy and creating a shimmering glare on the water and the buildings. It seemed as if the sun would break through at any moment. Instead, as the morning lengthened into afternoon, the sky turned ominously grey. When they stepped out of the gondola, it began raining. They ran for the shelter of the building. A bronze urchin stood in the entrance arch, a lovely statue in an angelic pose, his genitals rubbed shining bright by luck-seeking tourists. He stood grinning at them with his small shining penis as if inordinately proud of its glow, and she smiled as she passed it and noticed that Millie turned back for a second puzzled look.

The paintings were on the third floor, a series that showed men and women alike wearing white masks that covered their faces. At first she thought the paintings depicted some sort of masquerade ball, some fourteenth-century Mardi-gras. And then she thought perhaps the plague had visited Venice at one time and the masks were a protection against the disease. Their guide explained the meaning of the masks, an explanation she never quite believed, but which none the less planted an idea in her mind. The guide told Julia and Millie that in those days there was great intrigue in Venice, and it was not uncommon to find noblemen with slit throats floating in the canals on any given morning. In order to protect themselves from homicide and assorted mayhem, the noblemen took to sending their servants out dressed in their clothes and wearing white masks that covered their features. The point of the masquerade, then, was to confuse would-be assassins. No one wanted to run a dagger across the throat of a supposed Count only to discover it was his own brother-in-law who worked in the Count's kitchen. But, as with many another measure originally conceived of necessity, the masks became quite popular and enjoyed a sort of curious vogue. The women began wearing them as part of their everyday dress, and the masks became more ornate, decorated with pearls and jewels, dominoes hid the eyes and the nose, the city was suddenly filled with faceless citizens.

The concept of the masks intrigued Julia.

For the first time in her life, she began wondering exactly who she was, began wondering who was the noblewoman and who was the scullery maid in disguise, began indeed to wonder whether the mask hid the true face or whether the mask was the face itself.

She had never questioned herself along these lines. She had long ago dismissed soul-searching as a particularly obnoxious fictional device, had long ago in fact stopped reading fiction of any sort, because she felt it added nothing to her understanding of herself as a wife and a mother. There were things Julia accepted, and things she refused to accept, and she had always believed that her own freedom of choice was the very fabric of her life. But now she began wondering if her freedom wasn't simply the security of a jungle animal in captivity. She felt undeniably different in Italy. She could not honestly say she had changed in any way, because there was no tangible change she could see, and really no essential inner change she could feel. She seemed to move in exactly the same way, and think in exactly the same way—and yet there was a difference. A mask had been lowered, or perhaps a mask had been raised. She did not know which, and the uncertainty was puzzling. To Julia, there had always been things that were true and things that were false. She had always known exactly which was which, and she had governed her life accordingly, sure of their constancy. Now, she wondered.

She knew she was attractive. There was no doubt whatever in her mind about that. She had known it even when she was a little girl who seriously studied her own face in the big ornately carved mirror in her mother's bedroom. She would look into the glass and touch her button nose and the edges of her eyes, the thick-fringed lashes, the long silken brown hair. Grown-ups enjoyed looking at her, Julia Stark knew that, too. She would play games with her own childish beauty. She would sometimes get all messy on purpose, so that she could come in with smudges on her face and on her clothes, the incongruous grime heightening the visual impact of her delicately boned face and body. When she matured, providence was again on her side. At first, she was terribly frightened by the sudden pucker of her chest. She would stare at her tentative buds in the big mirror and touch them exploringly, frightened to death, fascinated too, fascinated the way she was with the steady, slow growth of the four-o'clocks she'd planted in her mother's garden. The fear and fascination gave way to pleasure and gratitude. She would examine herself critically now, pulling back her shoulders and marvelling at the new ripe slope of her chest. And sometimes at night in the privacy of her bed, she would seize herself in delight and whisper fervent thanks for her bounty. The other girls in the sixth grade were not quite as enthusiastically grateful for the blossoming flower in their midst. She was pretty enough to begin with. She did not need any unnecessary and totally unfair embellishments. The hardest thing Julia had to bear was their hidden envy and their open scorn. She didn't mind the stares of the boys. She clouted one when he tried to touch her, but she connected no thoughts of sexuality to the boy's understandable curiosity. Her breasts were simply a new part of her body, and she didn't like anyone touching her, no matter how scientifically probing the attitude. She asked her mother to take her into Talmadge to Mr. Kannen's clothing store, and her mother helped her in picking out a suitable brassière. She could still remember it. It had been white, and made of cotton, and she found it difficult reaching behind her back to clasp and unclasp it.

She knew she was attractive, yes. This was one of the indisputable and governing facts in Julia's life. She used her beauty unconsciously, the way most beautiful women do, but she used it none the less. She learned in her teens that a pretty girl can get away with a great many more things than her unattractive counterpart. But she never used her good looks flagrantly, never played the outrageous flirt—until she met Arthur Regan. With other boys, she maintained a sort of cool dignity that was sometimes maddening. She was, quite naturally, one of the most popular girls at Talmadge High, and from the time she was sixteen and permitted to date, she never lacked male company on any week-end night. There was about Julia a touch of recklessness, a tinge of heresy, an abandon beneath that pristine exterior, which promised adventure. When she chose to kiss a boy—and she did not choose to very often—she kissed him with an ardour that curled his toes. This, to Julia Stark, was another of the facts of life. If you wanted to kiss someone, you kissed him because you enjoyed it, and you kissed him as if you were enjoying it. Otherwise, you didn't kiss him at all. She never felt guilty about leaving a date on her doorstep with a handshake and a smile. She felt she owed nothing more than her undoubtedly pleasant company to anyone who took her out. Whatever else they reaped in the way of residual benefits was something Julia and Julia alone would decide. If anyone got silly about it, if any boy decided he would try to wrestle his way into her favour, Julia instantly hit him. She found that an open-handed slap had a remarkably quieting effect. Most boys would not risk Julia's wrath. They dated her because she was really very pleasant to be with, and to be seen with. And if she chose not to kiss them, there was always the hope—and hope had surely nurtured less ambitious projects—that one day, oh perhaps one day, Julia would offer her mouth, one day Julia would allow her blouse to be opened, her skirt to be pulled back, one day Julia . . .

The hopes were mostly the stuff of which dreams are made.

Kiss you she would, yes, they knew that. Reports of her kisses were passed around like international secrets among the chosen few. Her lips, they said, did you ever feel softer lips? Her mouth, they said, she kissed you with all of her mouth. Her teeth, they said, she nibbles at your lips, she nibbles at your tongue, she drives you nuts, they said. But more than that they could not discuss, because there never *was* more than that. The boys of Talmadge had run headlong into another of Julia's incontrovertible facts of life. She was not easy, and she was not promiscuous, and she knew without the slightest hesitation or doubt that the man who married her would be the first and only man ever to possess her.

Arthur Regan, she knew from the very beginning, was destined to become a very important fact in her life. There was nothing outstanding about Arthur, it seemed, except his artistic ability. He was, in his sophomore year, the art editor of the school magazine, and a cartoonist for the school paper. He had also had several cartoons accepted for publication by the *Talmadge Courier*, the town's bona fide newspaper, and he was something of a celebrity at school, well aware of his own talents and calmly accepting everyone's prediction that he would one day really amount to something. He was not a good-looking boy at all. Julia had certainly dated handsomer boys. His hair was sandy-coloured and straight. He seemed to wear a perpetual frown over his mud-coloured eyes, and his nose was a little too large for his narrow face. But he fascinated Julia the moment she laid eyes eyes on him, and for the first time in her life she actively began to plan the seduction of a male animal.

The word "seduction", of course, never once entered her mind. Nor would she even admit to herself that she was planning anything at all for the art editor of the school magazine. She preferred to believe that whatever was happening was happening by circumstance and chance alone. And after a while, these carefully schemed accidents became more of Julia's "facts", and she forgot completely that she had lain awake nights thinking up new plots to ensure the ensnarement of young Arthur.

Their preliminary skirmishes served only to make Arthur more aware of her. He was not a good-looking boy, and perhaps he knew it, but his renown had brought with it an attitude of extreme confidence, so that he walked and talked and sounded and felt as if he *were* handsome, as if those who preferred believing instead the evidence of their own eyes were surely candidates for the booby hatch. He knew that Julia Stark was possibly the prettiest girl in that entire high school, and he knew that for some absurdly fantastic reason she was making a big play for him. And whereas he knew for certain that he was one day going places, the only place he wanted to be right now was alone with Julia.

Like two chess players who had finally decided on their opening moves for the game, after studying the board and each other for a long time, Julia and Arthur came to grips. Pawn to King's four, Knight to King's Bishop three, the pieces stared at each other in perfect symmetry across the board—the opening play they had independently and simultaneously chosen was Arthur's ability as an artist.

"I hear you draw pretty well," Julia said.

"I do," Arthur admitted.

"Would you like to draw me something?"

"Why should I?"

"I just thought you might like to."

"Well, maybe," Arthur said cautiously.

"Don't you think I'd make a good model?" Julia asked, and she smiled a bit coyly.

"You might," Arthur said. "It's very difficult to hold a pose for any considerable amount of time."

"I'd like to try sometime," she said shamelessly. "If you'd let me."

"Well, I'll think it over," Arthur said, slightly bored.

"Well, I guess I'll see you around," Julia said.

"I guess so," Arthur said airily, and when he left her his heart was pounding.

She posed for him on the Thursday of the following week. It was spring-time, and the air of Talmadge was afloat in a thousand crosscurrents of aroma. Breezes flirted in the tree-tops, carrying murmurs of far-off Cathay, clouds were billowy with the juices of romance, she was sixteen and he was seventeen, and the world was turning green, the world was opening, it was good to breathe, and good to look, and good to touch. They went to the bird sanctuary at the end of town, and lifted the unlocked catch on the cyclone fence and walked in past the caretaker's shack, and on to one of the hidden paths, crossing freshly unbound streams over rough wooden footbridges, seeing a scarlet tanager suddenly darting through the foliage in a burst of fire, hearing a chatter that went still all at once as they moved deeper into the woods. They found a hidden glade, an oval of grass surrounded by pines. They could hear the wind in the tree-tops, a gentle soughing wind, a sigh, the exhalation of spring. They felt shy in the presence of nature, they were silent, they moved slowly, unwilling to disturb the calm, they averted their eyes as if in the presence of divinity. She sat on a low flat rock. She put down her books, and she tucked her skirts around her and lifted her chin. Her brown hair trailing down her back, she looked at him as he sat opposite her with his pad open in his lap, his pencil poised.

"Well," she said. "Begin."

"I'm trying to find the best place to start."

"Are there different places with different people?"

"Well, I like to find a key to the face and then take it from there."

"And what's the key to my face, Arthur?"

"Your mouth," he said. Quickly, he added, "Or maybe your eyes."

"Or maybe my nose?"

"Well, maybe."

He began sketching rapidly. His sketches were not really too good. He managed to capture each of her features separately, but they did not combine to form the face of Julia Stark.

"They're beautiful," she said. "Arthur, you're really very very good."

"I can do much better. They're not you at all, Julia."

"How *do* you see me, Arthur?"

He was hesitant at first. He did not want to talk about her beauty because this was old stuff to her, but surely he couldn't lie, surely the evidence was hers to see, she *knew* she was beautiful. And suddenly, in the tick of an instant, their relationship reached honesty. And in that instant, Julia Stark fell in love with Arthur Regan. She barely listened to what he was saying, because she knew the words, the words were part of a familiar litany. But he raised his head slowly, and he found her eyes and he debated in that instant with himself, and the debate showed on his face—the lie or the truth? And he decided in favour of the truth and he said very softly. "You're the most beautiful girl I've ever seen in my life, Julia."

She did not prompt him, she did not turn coy or flirtatious, she did not say, "Beautiful? How am I beautiful?" She returned his honest stare and said, "Thank you, Arthur," and he got up slowly from the grass, the world was moving in adolescent slow motion that day, and he walked towards her slowly, and he reached out with one slender hand and cupped her chin, and brought his face down slowly to meet hers, his lips to meet hers. Gently, softly, he kissed her on the mouth.

There was no passion in the kiss. It was a physical act stripped of physicality. It was less a kiss than an exchange of faith, a seal of trust. It shook them both to their roots. They backed away from each other in the same absurd slow motion. They seemed to have achieved a sharpness of focus in the touching of lips, they stood out in vivid clarity against the landscape, the world seemed to shimmer as their mouths parted and they moved from each other and looked at each other and said nothing. Sound would have destroyed the crystal, sound would have shattered spring and trampled youth. They had exchanged an honest kiss, and they were too young to appreciate its rarity, but they knew that something very special had happened to them both, and that it might never happen again as long as they lived.

In time, she forgot that day completely. There were other things to occupy her. There was all this business of loving and being loved, there was this machine of romance, constantly needing lubrication and new parts. There were plans, so many plans. Arthur going off to New York and Cooper Union, she herself going to the University of Connecticut, time-tables to synchronize, where would they meet and when, the announcement of their engagement, and finally their marriage, and Arthur's first job, and a rented house in Talmadge, oh she forgot that day. There was no need for remembering it, really. She loved Arthur and his quiet ways, and the gradual tempering of his ego, and the forceful efficiency and imagination he brought to his work, and the fervent way he discussed art and his role in advertising. She enjoyed the house they moved into, the old Regan heirloom that became theirs when his mother died, a huge sprawling old house with thousands upon thousands of rooms to discover and a wide springy lawn, and wild laurel filling the horizon with subtle pink-and-white each year. You could see the university spires from the old Regan house. Sometimes she would sit out back alone, and her eye would follow the slope of the hill, the town laid out at her feet, the hazy outlines of the college buildings in the distance, and she would feel very much at peace with herself and the life she had made with Arthur.

The birth of David did not change the steady rhythm of her existence at all. The child was another fact to be stored into the catalogue of accepted realities. There were things she believed and things she refused to believe. Arthur, David, her own beauty, the house, Arthur's frenzied work, the child's steady growth, the town, all these were realities. She refused to believe in death. When

Arthur's mother died and the house and two hundred acres of land became the property of the newlyweds, she refused to associate the sudden bonanza with the event that had brought it their way. She simply refused to accept the death. In much the same way, she refused to acknowledge the Spanish Civil War or Adolph Hitler. She knew these things had happened or were happening, she saw the headlines, she understood the meaning of events, but in her mind they refused to become factual; they remained, instead, intrusions from a fantasy world, vague shapes that did not belong in the ordered life of Julia Regan. She did not believe in infidelity and would not listen to town gossip concerning the peccadilloes of this or that citizen. She believed she was Arthur's sole reason for existence—he had told her so often enough—and she accepted this knowledge without a feeling of superiority over him; this was simply the way things were. She herself was the nucleus of a life governed by a selected group of rock-bottom facts, the sole arbiter, the sole censor, the sole judge of what was real and what was not. There was room for only so much in her life, she felt—so much giving, taking, loving, accepting of love, believing. There wasn't time or space for more. She thought herself incapable of more.

And now she was in Italy.

And now, suddenly, she found herself responding in a way she never had—oh yes, perhaps once, perhaps, a silent glade and sunshine, the twitter of a solitary bird, the smell of pine, the memory was indistinct.

Nor was this simply an awareness of her surroundings. This was, instead, a yearning to absorb every sight and smell and sound. Something had happened to her on the drive through the Alps and the magnificent descent through the Rhône Valley to Brig. The same Julia Regan got off that train in Domodossola, but it was a Julia Regan who had been purged somehow. A film had been removed from her eyes, her ears had been unstoppered, her tongue thrilled to new tastes, her fingers explored surfaces, the earth was suddenly thronged with exciting possibilities she had never before considered. She tried to file them away as facts, but there were too many to record, and the strict dividing line between reality and fantasy, the staunch wall of disbelief began to crumble. *Everything* was real, *everything* was believable, *everything* was new for her to discover and hoard. Except, paradoxically, the never-before-questioned foundations of her normal existence. The only unrealities to Julia now seemed to be the things she had earlier accepted as basic facts: her life in Talmadge, her husband, her son.

She felt no guilt.

She had been born again with shining eyes and smooth skin and questioning hands. She heard new sounds and spoke a new melodic tongue, and everything, everything was a delight.

The Venetian doctor was a part of this make-believe world that had suddenly donned the believable garments of reality. In another time, in another place, the doctor would have been summarily rejected, flatly refused as a figment of her imagination. But he swept into the hotel room now as if he had always existed, and despite her nausea and her fever, Julia felt a new thrill of delight, something new was happening, her eyes shone in her pale face. She caught her breath and waited.

Her ailment, she knew, was the usual tourist's complaint. She should not have drunk the water, should not have sampled so generously the new foods that tempted her eye and her tongue. She tried to tell Millie this was nothing to worry about, but Millie—whose life had been lived in the constant presence of medical men—insisted on calling a doctor, and the hotel had promised to send one within a half-hour.

And here he was, and Julia held her breath as he came into the room, the secret delight reaching for her face, setting her eyes aglow. He was a tall thin man with a balding head. He wore a grey silk suit and an outrageous summer tie. He carried a small black bag in his right hand, and he clicked his heels and bowed the moment he was inside the door, first to Millie, and then to Julia, who lay on the bed with the sheet to her throat.

His eyes searched her face. And then his head fell to one side as if it had been suddenly robbed of its supporting bones and muscles; a look of utter tragedy turned down the corners of his eyes, his eyebrows, the ends of his mouth; he hunched his shoulders slightly, he bent one arm at the elbow, the hand opened in mute supplication as he approached the bed. His tragic pose was complete. Julia fully expected him to begin weeping.

"Oh, madama!" he said in English, his voice breaking as he moved swiftly to the bed, lifted Julia's hand to his lips, and quickly kissed it. He clung to her hand, pulling a chair from behind him with his free hand, sitting beside the bed, leaning over her, his face still wearing the tragic mask, every muscle in his body conveying sympathy and grief and continental courtesy. "Oh, madama, I am so sorry, you do not feel good?" he asked.

"Well..."

"Ah, madama," he said understandingly, and stuck a thermometer into her mouth. Julia stifled a giggle. Millie looked at her reprimandingly and the doctor rose suddenly from the side of the bed and walked to where she was standing and asked, "She has been sick long?"

"Since this morning," Millie said.

"Tch, tch, tch," the doctor said, casting a baleful eye at Julia and then turning his sympathetic attention back to Millie. "She has vomit?"

"Yes."

"She has evacuate?"

"Yes."

"Tch, tch, tch," he said and whirled again to the bed. With the skill of a swordsman drawing a rapier, he swept the thermometer from Julia's mouth, studied it, sighed deeply, cocked his head to one side, put the thermometer back into its case, back into his bag, put the bag down beside the chair, sat in the chair, suddenly pulled the sheet off Julia, and picked up her hand by the wrist. For a moment, Millie looked shocked. Then she realized that Julia was wearing a cotton gown that covered her to the shins, and the doctor was only taking her pulse beat. Julia, at the same time, wondered why it had been necessary to pull down the sheet in order to pick up her wrist, but she watched the doctor with a mixture of anticipation and delight, like a child watching a magician, and she would not have halted the proceedings for her life.

"We're supposed to go on to Bologna tomorrow," Millie said.

"Tch, tch, tch," the doctor said, and he shook his head, and dropped Julia's wrist, and then suddenly reached for the hem of her gown and pulled it clear up over her naked breasts. Julia was too startled to speak. Millie made a small stifled animal sound and then stood watching him with her mouth open, motionless. Swiftly, efficiently, the doctor put his head on Julia's chest and began listening. She realized all at once that the man was his own stethoscope, and she almost burst out laughing. He kept his balding head cushioned on her left breast for at least a full minute, and all the while she fought to control her laughter, afraid her strenuous preventive efforts would lead him into thinking she was a convulsive. He pulled back his head quickly, drew her gown down in one short snapping motion of his wrist, barely looking at her, and then he lifted her hand again, holding it like a loving uncle, and a look of utter serenity crossed his face, the sweetest look Julia had ever seen on a man's face, consoling, strengthening, sympathetic, assuring, the look angels surely wore. "Madama," he said, "you will be okay," and he dropped her hand abruptly and began writing a prescription.

"What is it?" Millie asked. "What's wrong with her?"

"*Un disturbo di stomaco*," the doctor said. "She eat, she drink . . ."

He shrugged. "She will be okay. I promise!" He nodded his head in emphasis.

"Can we go to Bologna tomorrow?"

"Tomorrow, no. The day after tomorrow. I promise!"

"But..."

"I promise!" He turned back to the bed again. "Ah, madama, I am so sorry. But you will be okay." He sat by the bed again and picked up her hand. The tragic mask returned. He said, "Oh, poor madama, my poor madama, you feel bad? You feel no good? Tch, tch, tch," and Julia fought desperately to keep the laughter from overflowing, biting her lip, her abdomen aching with the effort. The doctor rose. "I will leave this at the desk for to fill." He waved the prescription in the air to dry the ink. "One pill every three hours!" He clicked his heels and bowed to the bed and to Julia. He clicked his heels and bowed to Millie. Then he came to attention and waited.

"Ah, how much is that?" Millie asked.

"A hundred and seventy lire," he said airily. "That is all."

Millie signed a traveller's cheque for ten dollars, and the doctor bowed again, walked to the door, paused, and said, "If you are trouble some more, call me. But you will be okay. One pill every three hours. It is on the bottle." He clicked his heels again. "Madama!" he said sharply. Then he smiled briefly, semi-tragically, opened the door, and was gone.

Julia fell into a fit of convulsive laughter the moment the door closed.

"What...?" Millie said. "Julia, he was a madman!"

"Oh, Millie, he was marvellous!" Julia said. "Oh, Millie, I have to go to the bathroom! Oh, Millie, I'm so very very happy."

They ate at the Pappagallo in Bologna, a restaurant that had been heavily touted to them before they left the States. The walls of the room were lined with photographs of American celebrities; apparently every movie queen who'd ever crossed the continent had stopped here to sample the food and pose with the chef. Julia had been advised by the doctor—who had visited her once more in Venice and whose name, as it turned out, was Guidobuono—not to take anything but beverages and very light food for the next few days. She ordered clear broth, spaghetti with butter sauce, and a cup of tea. The waiter looked at her quizzically.

"Yes," she said, "that's all."

The waiter did not shrug his shoulders, but his face clearly indicated that he was shrugging mentally. Three Italian women at the next table turned to look at Julia and her sister, and then went back to their meal. The ladies obviously represented three generations of Italian gourmands. The grandmother was a stout woman with a wide bosom and grey hair tightly wound into a bun at the back of her head. She was dressed in black and was at the moment demolishing a huge bowl of *minestrone*. The mother was a plumpish woman in her late thirties, wearing her black hair loose, no make-up, a large diamond ring on her left hand. She was struggling to loosen what appeared to be two dozen clams from their shells. The daughter was a girl of sixteen following in the classic footsteps of her grandmother, either clinging to her baby fat or working up a whole new layer of adult adipose. She wore a cotton frock and a bow in her long black hair. She ate with all the finesse of a truck driver, disembowelling the trout on her plate and then stuffing it into her mouth as if she expected *il Duce* to declare a famine that Sunday. These ladies were eaters, Julia calculated. These ladies had come from a long line of eaters, and their intent was to continue the line indefinitely. They barely spoke to each other. Their eyes were fastened to the diminishing supply of food on their plates, their hands worked busily, their jaws ground, their teeth ripped, their gullets bobbed. Occasionally, they glanced at Julia suspiciously. When the waiter brought Julia's broth and set it down before her, the three stopped chewing simultaneously. Grandmother, mother, and daughter turned their heads at the same time and looked at Julia's plate. Then, as one, they turned to the *pasta* dishes that had been put before them and continued to eat with renewed vigour, as if the sight of Julia's pathetic fare had strengthened some core of mutual resolve in each of them.

The suspicious glances turned almost hostile as the meal progressed. Julia could feel their hot brown eyes burning across the distance that separated the two tables. The sounds of gluttony continued to rise from the table with the three Italian ladies. Julia, at her own table, barely touched the spaghetti, and then sipped only sparingly at her tea. Her sister, who had ordered a complete lunch, was worried about Julia and did not do justice to the food set before her. The Italian ladies were troubled by Millie's wastefulness, but they were thoroughly agitated by Julia's timidity. Didn't she know where she was? Didn't she know this was one of the best restaurants in Europe? How could she so ignore its culinary offerings? What were these American women made of, anyway?

They began grumbling among themselves as they ate their pastry and drank their *espresso*. They grumbled with much raising of eyebrows and pulling of mouths and twirling of expressive fingers. Julia could not hear everything they said, but from what she did hear she understood she herself was the topic of discussion. The hell with them, she thought. There's no Italian law that states that a recuperating woman has to gorge herself, no matter *where* she's eating. When she rose from the table to go to the ladies' room, she threw a frigid glance at the adjoining table. The Italian ladies followed her progression across the restaurant, deciding she was far too thin because she ate like a bird, shaking their heads in concerted agreement on the paucity of her buttocks.

When she came back to the table, the Italian ladies, all three generations, were beaming at her. Surprised, Julia returned their smiles. The ladies nodded their heads, the smiles widened, bright white teeth showed on their faces, grandmother, mother, daughter, all grinned bright approval.

As they walked to the car, Julia said, "What brought on the change, Millie?"

"What change?"

"At the next table."

"Oh. They were concerned about you, Julia. Because you weren't eating."

"Yes, I know that."

"So they asked the waiter to inquire. He spoke a little English, and I told him you'd got sick in Venice. Stomach trouble."

"Did he understand you?"

"Oh yes, very well. I used my hands, of course, but he understood. And he translated into Italian for the ladies. He told them you'd got *incinta* in Venice. Then they began nodding and smiling. The old lady especially. She'd had trouble with her stomach there, too, apparently."

"Well, good," Julia said. "I'm glad we passed local inspec——" She stopped suddenly. "I got *what* in Venice?"

"*Incinta*. Isn't that the correct pronunciation? I'm sure that's what he told them. He patted his belly and said *incinta*. Yes, Julia."

"Oh, Millie," Julia said.

"What is it, darling?"

"Oh, Millie," she said laughing. "He told them I got *pregnant* in Venice!"

"Well," Millie said philosophically, "then so did the old lady."

20 August, 1938

ARTHUR DARLING,

We arrived in the Abruzzi yesterday, stopping in Rome for the morning, and then driving to Aquila and the house we'd rented. The approach to the villa was quite more forbidding than it appeared in the photographs sent by the travel agent. If you remember them, Arthur, it seemed to be a hill-top house situated on a rather level stretch of ground. But actually, it is hung on a mountain on a broad shelf and approached through a steep winding road. But it is lovely!

There is a beautiful garden in full bloom now, and I understand it will flower until the middle of October sometime. The view from the garden is breathtaking and almost unbelievable. You can see for miles. The air is so very sharp and clear that distant objects seem close enough to touch. We were greeted by the full staff the agent promised. We have a cook, a housemaid and a gardener-cum-chauffeur, such luxury! They are named respectively Lucia, Anna, and Giorgio. Lucia is a magnificent cook who won't allow either Millie or me into her kitchen. She does all our shopping—or at least this morning she did all of it for the next week. I suspect she has some sort of arrangement with the local grocer, but the bill didn't run too high, and it's good to know she'll be taking care of this bother. Anna, the housemaid, is a lazy sort of eighteen-year-old with a beautiful mouth and a dreamy look in her eyes. Her fiancé is in the Army and somewhere in Ethiopia, I believe, and she talks about him constantly to whoever will lend an ear. Fortunately for Millie, I'm the only one of us who can understand Italian, and so I've been treated to monologue after monologue about Anna's boy-friend. Giorgio, on the other hand, is an uncommunicative man who must be at least sixty years old. He has white hair and a white moustache, and he smokes those small, twisted, horrid-smelling cigars, but he's really quite efficient at his job. He was in the garden at seven this morning, and didn't leave until seven this evening. He assured me, briefly, that he is an expert driver and would be happy to take me into Rome whenever I desired. I told him that I prefer driving myself, but that Millie might require his unique services sometime.

Rome is a fantastic city, Arthur. Even the sound of its name excites me. Rome! I can't believe it! A fabulous city, all gold and white, a city within cities, a city beneath cities. Yesterday I walked along the very road Caesar took on his way to the Forum. I could feel the ghosts of dead assassins, and everywhere these wonderful Italians whose faces speak volumes. I shall go back to Rome often. We are only two hours away here in Aquila, and the drive is a beautiful one, and I feel time in that city, I feel time beneath the streets and in the air, I feel history. I shall go there often.

Arthur, it is so incredibly still at this moment. It is only ten o'clock, and Millie has already gone to sleep, and I am sitting alone in the garden with a lamp on the table, and the mountain is asleep and hushed. I can see lights somewhere far off in the distance—

Rome? Impossible! But most of the near-by lights went out long ago, and I have the feeling of floating somewhere in the sky, quite free, and a little bit heady. It is difficult to get used to this air. Actually, it is doing wonders for Millie, even in the short while we've been here. I honestly think this is going to help her a great deal. We shall see.

Your letter addressed to me at the Danieli in Venice was forwarded here and was waiting when we arrived yesterday. Darling, of course I miss you, need you ask? And David, dear David! Oh, Arthur, your letter made me so sad. I can visualize the two of you roaming around in that big shell of a house like two lost souls, and I could weep! Please, Arthur, know that I love you and miss you both, and that I shall be home as promised. I think of you both constantly. There is not a minute that goes by when you are not in my mind. Sitting here in the silent garden, my lamp the only light on the mountain, caught in this yellow circle, I feel so terribly all alone, and miss you more than ever. But January . . . ah, that seems so very far away just now. Until then,

I love you,
JULIA

She did not see Renato Cristo again until the third time she drove to Rome. He was sitting at a table in the Piazza Barberini, sipping at a vermouth, his cap pulled through his shoulder epaulet, staring off across the square, the sunlight touching his hair, his big hands on the table in front of him. She came down the Via Sistina, walking with a rather jaunty swing, and at first he thought only that she was a pretty girl, her figure in silhouette against the sun. Then he realized she was an American, the sun-glasses, the clothing, the regal walk, the erect posture, which all American women brought to Europe. He saw her face and recognized her, and watched her as she came down the street, still unaware of his presence. His secret observation pleased him. He sat with his hands on the table, watching her, enjoying the way her legs carried her body, enjoying the quick female motion of her head as she turned to look at the buildings, a sightseer, a tourist, and yet magically more than that. A small smile touched his mouth.

He did not call out to her until she was almost upon his table. She would not have seen him if he had not called. She walked with an intensity of concentration, determined to absorb each and every landmark on the route to an obviously predetermined goal. But there was nothing unique about this sidewalk café, a bar unfrequented by tourists, a gathering place for natives, where the drinks were generous and the food was prepared without regard for the foreign palate, and she was ready to pass it by without so much as a sidelong glance when he said her name.

"Julia," he called, very softly.

She stopped and turned, surprised. She looked at the wrong table first, trying to locate the voice, her mouth turned upward in an expectant, puzzled smile. But she saw no one she knew.

"Julia," he said again, and he shoved back his chair and rose.

She located the table this time. She turned her head slightly and saw him at once, and then took off her sun-glasses in a quick motion of her hand, and shook out her brown hair. He made a small gesture with his hand, inviting her to the table. She hesitated. He saw the hesitation in her eyes. It seemed for a moment as if she would simply wave in greeting, put on the sun-glasses again, and then walk on. A questioning look crossed his face. She nodded swiftly and came to the table. He was pleased when she addressed him in Italian.

"Hello," she said. "What a surprise!"

"Yes. Won't you sit down?"

"Well, I . . . I'm in sort of a hurry."

"You have time for a drink."

"Yes, I suppose so."

He pulled back a chair for her. Again, she seemed hesitant. Then she sat and took off her gloves, and he watched while she performed the operation, not looking at him, pulling off the gloves finger by finger, and then placing them on the table alongside her purse and the sun-glasses. She was wearing a white linen suit, her hair trailing down her back. She wore no make-up. Her nose was shining, her cheeks were flushed, her lips were bare.

"You've forgotten my name," he said.

"No. No, I haven't. Renato." She smiled.

"And Julia."

"Yes. And Julia."

"What would you like, Julia?"

"I'm sorry, what . . . ?"

"To drink."

"Oh. Whatever you're having."

"Some vermouth?"

"Yes, that would be fine."

"Have you had lunch yet?"

"No. I thought I'd——"

"Good, then we shall eat together."

"No, I couldn't," Julia said.

"Why not?"

"I want to get to the Coliseum."

"*Cara*," he said, "the Coliseum has been there for two thousand years. It will still be there after lunch. We will eat together." He snapped his fingers for the waiter and ordered a vermouth. Julia sat with her hands on the table, silent.

"Is something wrong?" he asked.

"No."

"You seem . . ." He shrugged. "Distressed."

"No."

"Would you prefer *not* having lunch with me?"

"Yes," she said honestly.

"But that would be foolish."

"I don't know you," she said. "We met on a mountain."

"And again in Domodossola. You mustn't forget Domodossola." He smiled suddenly.

"No. I won't ever forget Domodossola," she answered. She looked down at her hands again.

"So you see, it's all very proper. Our having lunch together. We're almost old friends."

"Yes, we are. But I don't know you."

"And if we waited to know each other before having lunch together, we'd both be old and incapable of enjoying good food." He laughed. "Americans always insist on *knowing* people. What does it do, this knowledge?"

"I guess Americans are . . ."

"Besides, knowing another person is an impossibility."

"I don't think so."

"An impossibility," he said flatly.

"All you're saying is that you yourself refuse to be known."

Renato looked at her appreciatively. "Perhaps so." He grinned. "See how well you know me already?"

"No, not at all."

"Well, we will know each other better."

She did not answer. The waiter brought her drink. She lifted the glass and sipped at it.

"Mmmm, that feels good."

"You're not wearing lipstick," he said, studying her mouth.

"No. Does it look terrible?"

"It looks very natural."

"Roman women don't use much make-up. I felt a little conspicuous."

"When in Rome," he said, and he smiled again.

"You're always laughing at me, aren't you?"

"Laughing?" His eyebrows quirked upward suddenly. "*Cara*, laughing at you?"

"Yes." She nodded. "I get the feeling you think I'm very stupid and . . . and dazed, I guess, and you find me very amusing. That's the feeling you give me."

"Well, I must explain. It's my face."

"Your face?"

"Yes it's given me trouble ever since I was a boy. Do you see my eyes?"

"Yes."

"They slant upward. In fact, there's some suspicion that my father was a Chinese."

"You're joking."

"Yes, I am. But my eyes slant upward, none the less. And my mouth turns slightly upward too. So you see, in combination they give my face a look of constant amusement, even when I'm most serious. It's a terrible thing, believe me. Men strike me, women avoid me, all because they think I'm smirking at them. I apologize for my stupid face, but there's really nothing I can do about it." He laughed suddenly, the blue eyes slanting, the mouth turning up at the edges.

She watched, and laughed with him, and then said, "No, it's not your face. It's something else, something inside. Be honest with me, Renato."

"All right," he said. "I'll be perfectly honest. I'm not amused by you. Not in the slightest. I'm delighted by you, and delight shows on my face, and I can't help smiling when I'm in your presence. That is the truth."

Julia nodded and lowered her eyes again.

"And as usual," Renato said, "the truth when asked for is instantly embarrassing when delivered. Why should you be?"

"Because . . . because what you said pleased me."

"And so you become embarrassed? Americans, Americans."

"You sound as if you know a great many Americans."

"No, only a few."

"Women?" she asked, and was immediately sorry.

The smile dropped from his face. He looked at her silently for what seemed like a very long time. Then he said, "Julia, I don't want to play the American game. I don't want the disguised question, and the guarded answer. There is enough falseness in Rome. Let's not add to it."

"I'm sorry," she said. She would not raise her eyes. "I . . . I guess I'm frightened."

"Of me?" he asked.

She nodded.

"I'm a simple man," he said quietly.

She kept her eyes fastened to the table top. In a hushed voice, she said, "I looked for you. This is my third time in Rome. Each time, I looked for you."

"You do not have to look any more," he said.

A city is only wood and stone and glass until you are loved there. Julia Regan, in 1938, felt a oneness with Rome that she had never felt for any other place.

Everything about the city was romantic to her, yes, the obvious romance traps like the fountain of Trevi and the Spanish Steps and the church of Santa Maria Maggiore where it reportedly snowed through the open roof in the middle of summer, and the majesty of the Sistine Chapel, and the flamboyant severity of the Victor Emmanuel Monument, all these tried-and-true tourist delights seemed to have been invented and constructed for Julia's pleasure alone, but more than these, there was romance everywhere in the city. And Renato, like a lover to woman and city both, showed off one to the other and unfailingly flattered both.

The cats.

Surely, she told herself, there is nothing at all romantic about the notion of cats or the presence of cats or the habits of cats. But one day Renato mentioned to her that there were more cats in the city of Rome than any other place in the world, and suddenly the discovery of each new cat became a momentous occasion charged with the excitement only a secret can possess. The cats of Rome were their secret. They found cats everywhere, the real cats prowling every cobbled alley, nosing into every uncovered garbage can, squatting contentedly on the hoods of the black taxicabs, stalking the banks of the snaking Tiber, howling to the moon in the triangular square formed by the junction of the Via Sistina and the angling Viale Trinità dei Monti, parading down the steps and through the Via Condotti like shopping dowagers, striped cats, and fat orange cats, and Persian cats, and black cats to be avoided, and a Siamese cat sitting in the window of a jewellery shop beside a clock with an ornately carved jade face, and an emaciated cat on the Via Giovanni who sat up and begged when Renato offered him a thin slice of salami, real cats of every shape and size, appearing as if by magic whenever they turned a corner or crossed a street. Sculptured cats in the friezework of buildings, cats in paintings at the galleries they went to, a lap cat carried by Violetta in the outdoor production of *La Traviata* which they saw at the Baths of Caracalla, the fat Angora suddenly joining the soprano in her aria, wailing to the stars and the crescent moon above, her song more forlorn than the singer's, convulsing the Italian audience, sending them into gales of unrepressed laughter until the diva finally walked to the edge of the stage and stamped her foot and stopped the orchestra and silenced the audience with a glare colder than the September Roman night.

The cats of Rome, and the colour of Rome, colour in the long flat steps gleaming like narrow bars of gold in the musky yellow reflection of the sky's muzzle, the rust red of huddled Roman buildings with crumbling bricks that stained the fingers, the bold reds and blues of the international traffic markers, the bright exploding greens of the trolley cars, the shining wet grey of the fountains and the liquid yellow-green taint upon the stone, colour punctuated by the black shirts in evidence everywhere, the blue-black garments of the traffic policemen and the white of their shoulder-straps and belts, and the deep jewelled black of the taxis, and the white of high-heeled pumps, and the radiance of yellow cotton on young girls, and the olive green of Renato's Army uniform.

The cats, and the colour, and life bursting from the city like seeds spilling from a lush ripe melon, the Via del Babuino and the side street just off it teeming with grocery stores and butchers' shops, the butchers presiding at the rear of each shop behind high counters resembling judges' benches, the meat swarming with the lingering flies of September, the bicycles darting through the narrow street, skirts flapping wildly about strong sun-tanned legs, the smell of garlic suddenly assailing them from the open door of a shop, salamis flaked with white and green on long strings, pepperoni like Christmas lights, provolone like the breasts of a statue carved in yellow marble, mozzarella soaking in white enamel basins, the man who sold strips of coconut at a curbside cart, the chunky brown-encrusted wedges of white sprinkled with water from a miniature fountain on the cart, the hurrying girls in their thin frocks, white and yellow and the subtlest of blue pastels, the serious-looking young men in their soldier suits, the fluttering flags, the flat-footed stamp of leather-thonged sandals, the Tiber like a golden snake in the setting sun's merciless glare, and, far beyond, the dome of St. Peter's dominating the city.

The Borghese Gardens, the paths his father had taught him when he was a boy, secret paths through sun-dappled stretches of woods, memory, memory nudged, slipped, an oval of grass. "See how the sun catches each separate blade?" Renato said.

She sat beside him. She kissed his hands and the hard line of his jaw. "I feel nothing but love for you," she said. "Nothing else. No guilt, nothing. Only love for you."

And yet the memory was there, an innocent kiss somewhere, someplace, some time, the memory held for just an instant, Renato's mouth turned to hers suddenly a fierce devouring mouth, which could be so gentle, his hands on her shoulders, her hair spread brown on grass as green as green as her skirt she stained her skirt that day the white skirt with the pleats the sun was so hot and her skirt became wrinkled and stained with grass his hand under her skirt one thick brown hand rubbing at the stain and the other hand beneath her skirt the knuckles pressing hard against her thigh she had stained her skirt and she twitched with new desire he could smell in the golden hot sunshine he kissed her again.

The room was in a side street off the Via Arenula, overlooking the river and the island of Tiberina. There was a bed in the room, and a dresser, and a naked light bulb over which they hung a coloured paper bag. In September, the room was comfortably cool. Later, in the winter, they bought a kerosene heater, and they put it very close to the bed and huddled together under two heavy quilts. But in September, the room was delightfully cool. They kept the wooden shutters on the single window closed against the sun. The room was usually in shadow. She would remember it as a secret pocket, shadowy, moving with shadows. She would remember it, too, as suddenly bursting with light, Renato opening the shutters and the golden sun limning his naked body, and then splashing over the bed where she lay watching him. She would remember this room as an essential part of her life, and the memory of it would continue to amaze her for ever. There was nothing distinctive about the room except the fact that she shared it with Renato. A bed, a dresser, and a paper-covered light bulb. A shabby room transformed by Renato until there was no room at all surrounding them, no four walls enclosing them. The room itself was essentially meaningless, and yet whatever they did in that room, whatever they whispered to each other, whatever they laughed about or fought about, seemed to be the only meaningful and important things. The room was small, and it enclosed them tightly, but it did not contain them. Instead, it closed out the rest of the world. The walls did not exist for Julia and Renato.

They spoke only Italian in that room. She said things alien to her native tongue, and somehow alien to the person she had always thought of as Julia Regan. She learned vulgar Italian with remarkable facility. She learned in that room that Renato was truly a farmer who could possess a farmer's crude big hands and a farmer's vocabulary when he wanted to. His language excited her. She never knew when his facile charm would turn to brutish obscenity, when his gently stroking hands would turn suddenly fierce. He taught her to say things she never would have said in English, and she found these more descriptive somehow of the love they made. Perhaps she would have blushed in English—in Italian, the words she whispered, the words she sometimes shouted urgently, only stimulated her the more. She felt like a slut sometimes, but there was nothing shameful about the feeling. Oddly, and dispassionately, she began to understand that her love for Renato, and his love for her, was something that prompted and perhaps nourished their love-making, but that really had very little to do with their real physical enjoyment of each other. She accepted the fact that she loved him and would not have been in bed with him otherwise. But she proceeded from that premise to bring a newly discovered harlot's skill and a gutter wastrel's language to their embraces. There was no need for her to say, "Love me," when she meant something quite different, something quite more basic. She knew that he loved her, and the euphemism would have demanded something he supplied with his every glance. Nor did she choose to say, "Make love to me," because this implied to her a fabrication, a construction, the phrase "*farea l'amore*" meant to make love, to build love, there was no need for its use; and it implied besides a selfishness, make love to *me*, rather than a sharing, a mutual giving of love. No, she preferred a word she and Renato coined, a word based on an expression he had learned from the troops. There was nothing poetic about the expression. It was perhaps common and coarse, based on the word "*chiavare*," to key, used in the vulgar sense to express a key entering a lock, "*Si sono fatti una bella chiavata*". But they turned its usage into poetry, they took the verb and used it the way no Italian would ever use it, "*Chiaviamoci*", they said, key me, enter me, let us unlock each other.

Unlocked, locked in each other's arms, they would talk later in whispers. Entered, the key turned and twisted in the lock, opened, unlocked, love found a voice afterwards, not in flowery images of romance but in seemingly inconsequential and meaningless exchanges of thought and feeling and memory, understood immediately, shared instantly, confiscated at once until more than bodies lay entwined, until mind touched mind and in the touching was rewarded and enriched. The accepted premise in that small dark room was that they would make love and enjoy it—but the richest thing they shared was the exchange of what was most important to both of them, the things they would never tell another living soul.

She learned eventually how important the concept of family was to Renato, and perhaps to all Italian men, though she never equated him with the faceless Italians she passed in the street. He was Renato, inimitably himself, impossibly, miraculously her own to touch and see and hear. He would lie back against the pillow with his hands clasped behind his head, and tell her of his boyhood with such unrestrained joy of memory that once she kissed him in the middle of a sentence, and he stopped speaking and stared at her, and said only, "Why?"

"Because I love you."

"No. Tell me why."

"Because I suddenly loved your cousin Mario, too. And your sister Francesca. Will you take me to meet Francesca? She lives in Rome, you said. May I meet her?"

"You are a strange woman."

"Am I strange to you?"

"No, not at all. I meant curious."

"Oh yes, I *am* curious," she said. "I want to learn all about you. I want to learn you everywhere."

"*Tesoro*, stop that," he protested, laughing. "I only meant that you are unusual."

"Yes, tell me more."

"There is no more to tell. You are a very unusual woman."

"Yes, how?" Julia asked. "I won't let you go until you tell me how."

"Then I'll never tell you."

"Tell me, *cocciuto*."

"You are responsive, inventive, passionate, exciting, beautiful, and totally satisfying."

"And American," she said.

"Yes. *And* American."

"That's important to you, isn't it?"

"It's important to me."

"Why should it be? Suppose I were Russian? Or Armenian?"

"I want you to be American. Which is what you are."

"So you can tell your soldier friends you slept with an American?" she asked jokingly.

"Yes, that's why. They'll make me sergeant if I tell them that."

"Only sergeant? I should think an American would be worth more than that."

"Lieutenant then. Or captain. Or perhaps, with an American like you . . ."

"Yes, yes, tell me about an American like me," she said, grinning. He began laughing. "You are a very vain creature, Julia."

"I know. Does that annoy you?" she asked seriously.

"No. You're only vain because you're beautiful. I've never yet met an *ugly* vain——"

"And you're beautiful, too," she said.

"Oh, yes."

"Look at how beautiful you are. *Bello, bellissimo,* look, Renato."

"I was telling you about my cousin Mario."

"Never mind your cousin Mario. He's not this beautiful. No one is this beautiful. Look, you're made of stone, you're a marble statue."

"My cousin Mario——"

"Do you want to talk about your cousin Mario?"

"Yes. I'm very fond of Mario."

"I am, too. Do you want to talk about him?"

"Yes."

"*Do* you?"

"Yes."

"You don't, do you?"

"I do."

"Oh, I know you don't."

"Julia, when I say——"

"Now tell me, *do* you?"

"Julia . . ."

"Renato?"

"Yes, darling?"

"*Chiaviamoci,*" she whispered.

The Piazza Venezia was thronged with thousands of people carrying crude caricatures and hand-lettered banners. Men in Black Shirt uniforms walked in tight groups down the centre of the Corso Umberto towards the square. The students of Rome University had left their classrooms and combined in noisy groups, parading through the city, marching past the United States Consulate on the Via Vittorio Veneto, picking up the frenzy that had begun in the Chamber of Deputies the day before, demanding Italian rights to Corsica, and Nice, and Savoy, and Tunisia. Blackshirted, black-tunicked, their bright silk scarves flapping about their throats, they surrounded the French Embassy and pushed against the restraining lines of the *carabinieri,* and then converged on the square where *il Duce's* balcony was hung with the Italian flag and the Fascist flag, where Renato and Julia tried to find space for themselves against the crush of people.

She glanced up at the balcony, caught in the press of sweating humans, saw the microphone awaiting *il Duce,* felt an electric excitement in the air, something quite apart from the excitement she ordinarily felt with Renato. There were men in shabby suits and caps, women in house-dresses with sweaters thrown over them, students in their brightly coloured Pied Piper hats covered with insignia, "*Il Gruppo Universitario Fascista*," Renato explained, and men selling ices, and over it all the current in the air. It could have been this way when Caesar spoke to the people of ancient Rome, she thought, it could have been this.

"*Duce! Duce! Duce! Duce!*" the crowd began to chant.

They carried banners with *il Duce's* image, the familiar black-and-white drawing that stared down from every vacant wall in the nation, the leader in his black eagled helmet, wearing epaulets on his shoulders, the strong jaw, the eyes in deep shadow beneath the helmet, the mouth firm and sensuous, the words CREDERE, OBBEDIRE, COMBATTERE beneath the drawing. They milled noisily in the square, and those in the black shirts began clapping, and the applause spread to the rest of the crowd as they turned their eyes and their faces towards the balcony, applauding the microphone there. "*Duce, Duce, Duce, Duce,*" they chanted, and suddenly he appeared! A tumultuous welcome went up from the crowd, the applause rose wildly. The cheering deafened Julia. She put both hands over her ears, lowered them only when it seemed he was ready to speak. He was wearing the uniform of a corporal of honour in the Black Shirt Militia. A field hat was tilted at a rakish angle over his forehead. He raised his arms and the crowd fell silent.

"*Duce! Duce!*" a lone Black Shirt voice cried, and then was still.

"Officers," he began, "non-commissioned officers, soldiers, Black Shirts, and people of Rome," and his voice was drowned out by renewed shouting.

"Tunisia!" a group of students yelled.

"Corsica!" from across the square.

"Savoia!"

Il Duce held up his hands, and the square was silent again. He leaned into the microphone. "Tomorrow," he said, "on the plains of Volturara, before His Majesty, Victor Emmanuel, King of Italy and Emperor of Ethiopia, will pass more than sixty thousand men, two hundred tanks, four hundred pieces of heavy artillery, three thousand machine guns, and twenty-eight hundred armoured cars. This aggregation of men and means is imposing, but it represents, at most, a modest and almost insignificant total compared with the total of men and means on which Italy can surely count.

"I invite Italians to take absolutely to heart this declaration of mine. Not despite the African war, but as a consequence of the African war, all the armed forces of Italy today are more efficient than ever. At any time, in the course of a few hours and after a simple order, we can mobilize eight million men. The Italian people should know that their internal peace will be protected and with it the peace of the world."

The students and the Black Shirts were restless. They had come here for amplification of Ciano's statement, had come here to learn whether or not Italy truly attempted to press claims on French lands, or whether the uproar yesterday had all be staged. So far, *il Duce* had told them nothing they did not already know.

"With the most crushing of victories," *il Duce* said, "in one of the most just wars, Italy, with war in Africa, has acquired an immense, rich, imperial territory where for many decades she will be able to carry out the achievements of her labours and of her creative ability. For this reason, but only for this reason, will we *reject the absurdity of eternal peace*, which is foreign to our creed and to our temperament."

"Bravo!" a voice shouted. It was joined by another. "Bravo!" and then another. "Bravo! Bravo! Bravo!" until the square rang again with frenzied cheering and applause. Julia looked around her, suddenly frightened. She took Renato's arm and whispered, "He's just said there will be war." There was a questioning tone in her voice. Renato, smiling thinly, did not answer her. He touched her hand where it clutched his arm.

"We desire to live a long time at peace with all," *il Duce* said. "We are determined to offer our lasting, concrete contribution to the project of collaboration among peoples. But after the catastrophic failure of the disarmament conference, in the face of an armaments race already under way and irresistible from this time on, and in the face of certain political situations which now are in the course of uncertain development, the order of the day for Italians . . ."

His voice rose. He clenched one fist and shook it at the microphone.

". . . the order of the day for Italians, for Fascist Italians, can be only this: We must be strong! We must be always stronger! We must be so strong that we can face any eventualities and look directly in the eye whatever may befall! To this supreme principle must be subordinated, and will be subordinated, all the life of the nation!"

The shout began as a low murmur of approval in the throat of the crowd. It gained in volume and momentum, thundered into the square, rose to the balcony. The flags and banners were waved, the people began to applaud, *il Duce* grinned and put his hands on his hips, thrusting his chin out characteristically.

"Let's go," Renato said.

He took her arm. They pushed their way through the crowd silently. There was a troubled look on his face. She glanced at him nervously, and her hand tightened on his arm again. Behind them, they could still hear *il Duce's* voice, ". . . spirit of the Black Shirt revolution, the spirit of this Italy, the spirit of this populous Italy, warlike and vigilant on sea, on land, and in the heavens!"

"*Porca miseria*," Renato muttered.

". . . how many events, how much history has passed in these twelve months! They have been rich in events the influence of which is felt today, but will be felt still more in the course of time."

"I'm frightened, Renato," she whispered.

"No. Hold my arm."

"I ask you," *il Duce* shouted into the microphone, "were old accounts settled?"

"Yes!" the crowd shouted. "Yes! Yes!"

"And have we marched straight ahead up to now?"

"Yes! Yes! Yes! Yes!"

"I tell you," he bellowed into the microphone, "I *promise* you, we shall do likewise *tomorrow and always*!"

He lay on the bed with his hands clasped behind his head, the trouble still in his eyes. She watched him, wanting to touch him, aware of his trouble and disturbed by it, and still frightened by what she had seen and heard from the balcony of the Palazzo Venezia.

"My grandfather was a tailor in Naples," Renato said, "when I was a little boy, before we moved to Rome." He did not turn to look at her. He kept his hands clasped behind his head, his eyes on the ceiling, troubled. The thin smile was on his mouth, not a smile of remembrance, not the smile he usually wore when talking of his family.

"He was a very tall man with white hair and a white moustache, very respected in the city, a good tailor. He would always wear a suit to work each morning. He lived just outside the Via Roma in a terrible slum, but he was a proud man and when he walked to work each morning, the people in the streets would say, '*Buon giorno, Signor Cristo*,' never Giovanni, but always *Signor*, always Mister Cristo. He was greatly respected, Julia, and I loved him a great deal. I can remember how hurt he was when my father told him he did not want to be a tailor, he wanted to leave Naples to work the earth. I can remember the pain in my grandfather's eyes. Tailoring was an art to him, a very noble profession. He made all my clothes when I was a boy. I was the best-dressed boy in all Naples, though I lived in a slum.

"He would walk to work each morning and be gone until lunch-time when he returned home. My grandmother, Cristina, would have lunch ready for him, and then there would be a little nap, you know, it is still the same today. Then he would go back to the tailor shop and not return home until eight at night, sometimes later, and they would have a small meal, the noontime meal is the big Italian meal, you know that. My grandmother was a very superstitious woman, and she would sometimes do the *malocchio* for the women of the neighbourhood. You don't know what this means? *Favorita*, my grandmother would put water into a dish, and into the water she would put a drop of oil, and she could tell by the way the oil divided whether or not someone in the neighbourhood had put an evil eye on a sick child or caused a man to lose his job. Nonsense, yes. All nonsense. But she practised it like a witch—and always when my grandfather was away at his shop.

"She would also perform feats with *il tavolo a tre gambe*, the three-legged table. This, too, was a fake, Julia. She used the table to call up the dead, you see. A number of women would sit around the table, and my grandmother would mutter her incantations and then call upon a dead person, and he would answer 'yes' or 'no' to her questions by causing the table to knock on the floor either once or twice. It was considered a sin to call upon the dead, but my grandmother was not a very religious woman, and she used the table quite often, even though my grandfather finally heard about it and warned her to stop. You see, the table gave my grandmother a certain notoriety in the slum behind the Via Roma, a popularity—in fact, I suppose, a sense of power. The women would go to her because they hoped to solve their current ills by consulting with the dead, who were beyond feeling or pain, and my grandmother was the one with the answers, my grandmother could work the table.

"Well, one day, my grandfather could not get home for lunch because he was working on a rush order of Army uniforms, very important work, and so he ate a little bread and cheese at the shop and sent a boy home to tell Cristina he expected a big supper that night. He did not get home until nine p.m., starving, and hoping to find supper on the table. There was no supper on the table. Instead, there were three women and Cristina sitting around the table with their hands touching, and at least two dozen other women standing around the room, listening to my grandmother as she recited the words to summon the dead. My grandfather stopped in the doorway of the apartment, unseen by any of the women, and listened. He was really a little curious at first. It wasn't until later that he got angry. Standing in the doorway, he could see his supper boiling in a huge pot on the wood stove. He was very hungry, but he stood in the doorway and listened to my grandmother's incantation and then heard her say, 'Can you hear us, Carlo Stefano? If you can hear us, will you knock once?'

"Well, the table knocked once, and a large 'Ahhhhhh' of

approval went up from the assembled ladies, all except one who said to my grandmother, 'How do we know this is *really* Carlo Stefano knocking the table, and not you or one of the other ladies sitting around it?' This pleased my grandfather immensely because it was exactly what he was thinking as he stood in the doorway. But Cristina had handled scoffers before, and was ready to deal with this one.

"'Carlo Stefano,' she said to the table, 'will you give us some sign that you are truly Carlo Stefano?' The table knocked once, signifying that Carlo, wherever he was, had answered positively. 'Will you let your presence be known?' my grandmother asked, and again the table knocked once. 'Will you give us a sign through something in the room?' Cristina asked and the table answered 'Yes' with a single knock.

"My grandfather was beginning to get a little impatient. He was also beginning to hope the food on the stove would not burn. He folded his arms and leaned against the door-jamb, the smell of cooking food in his nostrils, his stomach beginning to make noises. My grandmother said to the table, 'Will you give us a sign through the broom?' The table knocked twice. *No.* 'Will you give us a sign through the curtains?' Knock-knock, the table said. *No* again. 'Through the pitcher?' *No.* 'Through the ladle?' *No.* My grandmother was beginning to run out of objects when her eye fell upon Fidelio. Fidelio was a mangy alley cat my grandfather had found in Naples outside his tailor shop. He had put a string around her neck and walked her home one evening, and the cat had become a common fixture around the house, usually asleep on the mantel of the fireplace, which is where she was when my grandmother spied her.

"'Will you give us a sign through Fidelio the cat?' she asked, and every eye in the room swung towards that lazy creature asleep on the mantel. There was a long silence. The table would not answer yes or no. My grandfather waited. Every woman in the room waited. Impatiently, Cristina said, more firmly this time, 'Will you give us a sign through Fidelio the cat, who is asleep on the mantel?'

"Again there was a silence. And then the table knocked. Once. *Yes*, the table had answered! *Yes*, Carlo Stefano had answered! The eyes were riveted to the cat. And then suddenly, whether something alarmed her in her sleep, whether she was bitten by an insect, whether she lost her balance, whatever it was, the cat suddenly let out a horrible shrieking sound and leaped into the air, and scrambled to the floor, her back bristling, her tail fat, and Julia, my darling, that was only the beginning. The women had got the sign they were looking for. Carlo Stefano had spoken, dramatically and emphatically, and now the ones at the table leaped up from their chairs, knocking over the table, rushing into the ones who lined the room, screaming at the tops of their lungs and finally, finally in their mad confusion to get out of that room, which was suddenly filled with the presence of death, finally to my grandfather's horror as he stood in the doorway, one of those screaming-rushing, hysterical women banged into the stove and knocked the big pot of supper to the floor!

"'*Stupide!*' my grandfather shouted from the doorway. He stamped into the room and walked directly to the fireplace. He picked up the axe and marched back to the three-legged table and fell upon it with such anger and such fury that my grandmother could only stand by speechless while the wood splinters flew around her. He demolished that table completely. He was a gentle man, and a tailor, but he destroyed that table as if he had been felling trees all his life. And he told my grandmother that if she bought another three-legged table, if those screaming women were ever inside his house again, if he ever came home in the evening and found his supper still on the stove, he would take the axe to *her*, and do to her what he had done to the table."

Renato turned to her. He took one hand from behind his head and cupped her chin, and he looked into her face very seriously and said, "You see, my darling Julia, we have a person in Italy now who plays with a three-legged table, calling upon the dead legions of Caesar, muttering his own incantations to the gullible old women. But there are no longer any tall men with axes, Julia. And even if there were . . . Julia, Julia darling, my grandfather destroyed the table too late, don't you see? His supper had already been knocked to the floor. His supper had already been knocked to the floor."

She knew almost immediately after that day *il Duce* spoke in the Piazza Venezia. All the signs were there, all the symptoms. She knew exactly what they meant. She read them correctly and told herself, *No, this cannot be*, but she recognized the truth none the less, and none the less refused to face it. *Il Duce's* speech had been made on 1 December, she had looked at the calendar before leaving the villa in Aquila to join Renato. And this was 5 December, and all the doubt, all the fear, seemed to crystallize in the letter from Arthur, and the news that he and David were coming to Italy for Christmas. He will know, she thought. He will look, and he will see, and then my world will crumble. He is sure to see. He is sure to know what I know, what I only suspected in November but what I know for certain now. He is not a stupid man. He will know.

She did not want to leave Italy.

But if Arthur read the signs correctly, and he was not a stupid man, what would he demand, what would he ask of her? She could not leave Italy, she could not leave Renato, not now, not yet. And afterwards, when it was over, when it came to an end as it inevitably and always did, what then? And where?

Oh Renato, Renato, she cried out to him alone, but she did not tell him of her doubts or fears. There is time, she thought. There is always time.

They came to the villa in Aquila two days before Christmas. She was waiting in the garden for them. She was wearing a yellow dress and a wide-brimmed straw hat, and a sweater was thrown over her shoulders. Her eyes filled with tears when she first saw them. Not because she felt she knew them, not really, there was another world for her now, and it did not include Arthur Regan, it did not include her fourteen-year-old son who embraced her clumsily, lean and awkward, his face festering with pimples. "David, you're getting to be a man," she said, and he blushed and said, "I tried out for the handball team in school, Mom," and she hugged him to her and wept.

But only because he was a stranger. Only because two strangers had entered her garden in the villa, and she greeted them with the fabricated affection of a wife and mother, but she felt nothing because there was a new life for her now, a new life.

"Hello, Julia," Arthur said. He seemed embarrassed. Arrivals and departures always embarrassed him. He hugged her close, and she felt nothing for him, yes, a sympathy because he was embarrassed by this meeting, but nothing beyond that. Awkwardly, he said, "You're as round as a partridge, Julia. Rome agrees with you," and only then did she see the happiness beneath his embarrassment. She looked more closely at his face. She felt an extreme sense of loss for everything they had ever known together and shared together, somehow nullified by Renato and her love for him, and she thought it sad that love was so exclusive, that love nourished and at the same time killed. She almost said this aloud to Arthur. She almost, through habit, through years of living with a man she had known since girlhood, almost voiced her thoughts and waited for the tilting of his head and the contemplative look in his eyes and the slow, considered answer. She almost confided to him a world that did not belong to him.

"Have you been eating well?" she asked.

"Yes. You look well, Julia."

"Who's been taking care of you, my darling?" she asked. She wanted to know. She touched his face tenderly. She was confused in that moment, confused by an affection different from what she felt for Renato, and yet unmistakably warm.

"We've had Mrs. Donovan."

"She's a good cook."

"Yes."

"Mom, will we go to Rome?" David asked.

"Yes, darling."

"Mom, there was a player from the New York Yankees on the boat coming over!"

"That's wonderful. Was the trip good? Did you have any trouble?"

"It was a long trip, Julia," Arthur said.

"Come inside," she said. "Won't you come inside?"

She had not known whether or not Millie suspected anything about Renato until the day Arthur and David arrived. And then she knew instantly. She had not fooled her sister. The frequent trips to Rome had not gone undetected. Millie knew, but had apparently made a tacit bargain with herself. She would watch Julia and listen to Julia and take her cues from Julia; she would offer nothing of her own volition. They sat in the large terrazzo-tiled living-room that night as the lights on the mountain winked out. David had gone to bed amid much fussing-over by the help, and the three adults sat and watched the lights go out and sipped *espresso*, and Arthur said, "How do you feel, Millie?"

"Much better," she answered. She looked at Julia quickly, as if for approval.

"The air *is* wonderful here, Arthur," Julia said. "Haven't you noticed the difference?"

"Yes," he said, "it's wonderful." He smiled. "When do you suppose . . . it's December already, you know."

"Yes," Julia said, "but . . ."

"We'd planned on staying until——" Millie started.

"Until April," Julia cut in quickly.

"April?" Arthur frowned. "I'd planned to take you back when we left, Julia. You said January. I thought . . ."

"Darling, Millie's doing so well. It would be a shame to take her back to Connecticut in the dead of winter."

"Well, this isn't exactly a tropical climate right here, Julia. In fact, it's damned cold. I mean, I can see——"

"Arthur, can we discuss this later, please?" Julia said.

"I'm going to bed, anyway," Millie said. She took Arthur's hand. "It's good to see you, Arthur. Sleep as late as you like in the morning. I'll ask Lucia to hold breakfast."

"Thank you, Millie."

They waited until she was gone.

"I'd like to kiss you, Julia," Arthur said.

"I'd like you to," she answered.

He went to the sofa and took her in his arms. He kissed her passionately and thrust his hand under her skirt.

"Arthur," she said, "not here, please. The servants . . ."

"Let's go upstairs," he said.

"All right."

"Aren't you glad to see me?"

"Why, of course I'm glad to see you." She took his hand. "Come."

"I . . . I don't know." He shrugged. "Is something wrong, Julia? Is there something you haven't told me?"

"No," she said, "nothing's wrong." She thought, Is there something I haven't told you, Arthur? Is there anything I *have* told you?

"Millie *is* all right, isn't she?" he asked.

She hesitated for a moment. He had provided her with the lie, and she waited before accepting it. Something within her resisted its acceptance, something reacted to his innocence, his trust, something inside her suddenly felt rotten and foul-smelling. She considered the lie, she paused over it, she closed her eyes tightly.

"What is it Julia? I can tell it's something."

She sighed heavily. "Yes, yes," she said.

"What?"

"Millie."

The lie was hard coming. She did not want to lie. She closed her eyes again and shook her head, and he misunderstood the gesture and took her into his arms, the last thing she wanted. Don't comfort me, she thought, don't comfort your whore wife.

"What about Millie?"

"She . . . she's worse, Arthur," Julia said. "I've . . . I've spoken to her doctor. I haven't told her, of course, there's no need to upset her. He . . . he thinks we shouldn't go back yet. He wants her to . . . to stay until . . . until April at least."

The lie was out, the lie was told, she felt herself relaxing in his arms. She was covered with a cold sweat.

"And must you stay with her?" Arthur asked.

"Yes," she said quietly.

"Your son." He made a meaningless gesture with his hands. "He misses you."

"And *I* miss *him*," she said. "*And* you. But what can I do, Arthur?"

"Julia, it's so empty at home without you. I don't feel alive without you, Julia. I don't feel as if I'm really living."

"But what can I do, Arthur? Can I take her home against the doctor's orders? Can I leave her here alone and sick? What can I do? Tell me, and I'll do it."

It was easier now. She marvelled at how much easier it was. The lie had almost assumed a veneer of truth. She was beginning to believe it herself.

"We'll discuss it later," he said. He put his arm around her waist and they began climbing the steps. "There doesn't seem to be much you *can* do. I only wish . . ."

"Arthur," she said, "there's nothing I want more than to be home with David and you."

She choked down the lie.

The biggest lie was waiting for her upstairs, in the bedroom.

He did not seem to know, nor did he seem to suspect, that there was anything different about her. He saw no change, and yet the change was apparent to her, she looked different, she felt like a different person, she knew she even walked in a different way, she was sure he could tell this was not the Julia Regan who had left Talmadge in August. But he did not know, and perhaps the difference did not show to anyone but herself.

Only once did he say something that could have been interpreted as an expression of suspicion, but even then she wasn't sure—he might have been joking. They had entered the church of Santa Maria in Cosmedin and walked through the portico where they found the *Bocca della Verità*—the Mouth of Truth. The carving was a marble disk representing a human face, an old man's face with accusing eyes, and a beard, and a moustache hanging over an open mouth. The mask dated back to the twelfth century, and the legend concerning it was that in medieval times a suspected person was required, in taking an oath, to place his hand in the mask's mouth. If the suspect was swearing falsely, legend held, the mouth would close upon his hand.

Arthur studied the mask and then took Julia's hand and gently placed it inside the marble mouth.

"And have you been faithful to me?" he asked.

She pulled back her hand suddenly, not because she expected the mouth to clamp shut, but only because his question had startled her. Arthur raised his eyebrows.

"Well, now," he said.

Calmly, smiling at him, she put her hand into the marble mouth again. In an exaggerated attitude of piety, she intoned, "I have been faithful to you, dear husband," and they both laughed, but her secret ached inside her.

She showed them around Rome like a paid guide. The tour was painful to her because, perversely, she took them to all the secret places she had shared with Renato. In a side street off the Piazza

Navona and the Bernini fountain facing the church, she led them to a pair of huge doors, which were opened to her when the caretaker recognized her. At the far end of the enclosed courtyard was an arch over a long passageway floored with tile and lined with columns. At the distant end of the long passageway was a large statue.

"Let's walk to the statue," she said.

They started for the arch, and she knew both David and Arthur were expecting a lengthy walk between the columns. She watched their faces for the first signs of recognition, pleased when it came almost at once. The corridor leading to the statue, the columns lining the corridor, the tiles flooring it, the statue itself, were all a magnificent trick, a masterpiece of *trompe l'oeil*. The corridor was perhaps eight feet long, but it seemed more like fifty. The arch was slanted to give an illusion of perspective, the columns grew progressively shorter, the tiles progressively smaller, as one walked through the arch and down the corridor. The statue, which seemed immense when viewed from the opposite end of the arch, was no more than three feet high. She could remember her own reaction to the optical illusion when Renato first showed it to her, and she was pleased now by the reactions of her husband and her son—and yet annoyed somehow.

She took them to the monastery of the Knights of Malta on the Aventine, where the keyhole was set in the massive entrance doors. She asked David to lean down and peek through the keyhole, and when he did he saw a path lined with poplars, and in the distance the dome of St. Peter's, perfectly framed, centred exactly, like a precious miniature. Arthur bent and looked, smiling, holding her hand as he looked through the keyhole. *Chiaviamoci*, she suddenly thought, and her heart lurched; she had not seen him for a week.

Christmas was upon them before they realized it. They had brought her gifts from the States, and she had shopped Rome for days before their arrival. They exchanged their gifts in the villa while the servants beamed and murmured, "*Buon Natale.*" The present she had bought for David was far too young for a boy his age. The days after Christmas seemed to move very slowly for her. She saw happiness on the faces of her husband and her son, but she could not share it. She could only think of their departure. She went through the mechanical motions of showing them the city, but the city was her secret, and she could not really unlock it for them. Time was suspended. She had not seen Renato for eleven days, and she longed for him. But she lived out her lie, and her sister watched the play-acting, expressing neither approval nor censure, moving silently about the villa with her shawl around her shoulders. On

New Year's Eve, she and Arthur went to a night-club in Rome. They stayed until two in the morning, and he toasted her eyes and toasted her mouth and said there were too damn many black shirts in this damn place and he wanted to go home to make love to her. They were both tipsy on the drive back to Aquila. In bed he told her drunkenly, "If anything should happen to us, Julia, I would kill myself." She brought some measure of passion to her love-making that night, but only because she, too, was drunk.

On 4 January, David and Arthur kissed her good-bye and went back to Talmadge, Connecticut.

The townspeople, of course, did not know that Julia Regan was a woman living almost entirely in the past. They knew she had once been thirty-five years old and had gone abroad with her sister Millicent. They knew she had been to France and Switzerland and Italy. They did not know that day by day Julia lived and relived a time that had begun for her in August of 1938.

They did not know.

Matthew was not in the mood for a Talmadge cocktail party, and he told Amanda so the moment he got into the car at the station.

"Neither am I," she said. "I've been shopping all day. But I promised."

"Amanda, I'm exhausted," he said. "And I'm cold. Isn't it cold for November? It wasn't this cold last November."

"I promised we would go, Matthew," she said.

"Who's staying with Bobby and Kate?"

"I got Mrs. Arondo."

"That decrepit sack?"

"She's a very capable sitter."

"I hate Talmadge parties," Matthew said.

"Matthew, please, let's not argue about it."

"I'm not arguing. I'm stating a fact. I dislike Talmadge parties, and I dislike most Talmadge people."

He nodded once, briefly, and fell into a sullen silence, which lasted all the way into the noisy living-room of a sumptuous house set on twelve lovely acres of land. The houses in Talmadge, or at least the ones to which he and Amanda received invitations, were somewhere in the forty- to seventy-five-thousand-dollar bracket. Some had swimming-pools, some had ponds, all had at least six acres of choice Connecticut countryside. There was still a shortage of capable household help in 1952, but the citizens of Talmadge managed very well with thrice-weekly cleaning girls, and gardeners who kept their spacious grounds immaculately landscaped. There was a chicken in every pot and, in addition to that, two cars in every garage, and Matthew had learned very quickly that Talmadge was what might be called a moneyed town. None of the Talmadge men discussed their salaries openly, of course. But then, Matthew had never heard of any men anywhere discussing their salaries openly, except perhaps on the Malay Archipelago where they were paid in amulets and betel nuts. The men of Talmadge were paid in good hard United States currency, and they didn't have to discuss how much they were paid at all. Those cleaning girls and gardeners hadn't come free with the house. Those Cadillacs in the two-car garages hadn't been acquired with soap coupons and a letter of twenty-five words or less. The Talmadge women dressed to the teeth, and they didn't do it on the income of ditch-digger husbands. However much these men earned, Matthew knew it was plenty. He didn't begrudge them a cent of it. He simply wished they had a lot of legal problems and would take them to Bridges, Benson, Summers and Stang.

As befitted men of means, there was plenty of liquor at Talmadge parties. Vodka had not yet assumed consumer proportions bordering on the epidemic, but there were fifths and fifths of Scotch, rye, bourbon, and gin, with a smaller play on rum, wherever Matthew went. The liquor wasn't ostentatiously displayed; you simply knew instinctively that when a bottle ran dry there would be a closetful of new bottles from which to replace it. The replacement was effected quite often. The people of Talmadge drank fast and they drank hard. Matthew was amazed by the number of empty bottles he lined up alongside the trash barrel after a night of even small-scale revelry. He was amazed because Talmadge parties were always full of social chatter and pleasant music and well-groomed men and dazzling women who seemed to be conducting themselves in a perfectly sober and civilized manner, but apparently all these socially civilized sophisticates were belting away at the bottle at a surprisingly rapid clip. Nor did they ever show any of the apparent effects of steady alcohol consumption; not once did Matthew see anyone, man or woman, who he could say with certainty was drunk. There was no falling down at Talmadge parties. Nor was there any stumbling or staggering.

The bottles were set up in a row alongside the ice bucket, and the host served the first drink and refilled the glass when that was gone, and the standing rule was that everyone was on his own after that. Everyone accepted the rule and made the requisite trips back and forth between the conversation groups and the bar whenever his glass was empty. His glass seemed to be empty every five minutes or so. There was the drinking of whisky before dinner—rarely was there a party given in Talmadge that did not include dinner, usually a buffet—and the drinking of wine during dinner, and the taking of brandy or liqueur after dinner, and then the hard drinking began again as soon as the cordials had calmed the stomach, and continued until the early hours of the morning when the party broke up. People got warmer and happier as the evening wore on. New friends became old friends. No one ever got drunk, but the steady consumption of alcohol did much to contribute to a lessening of rigidity, a feeling of warmth and relaxation.

There was always music going at a Talmadge party. The host generally started the hi-fi a half-hour before his guests arrived, warming up the set with *Scheherazade*, a classical introduction that set the tone for an evening of civilized intercourse. He would set up his bottles and his glasses and his soda and his water and his tonic and his ice cubes while Rimsky-Korsakov flowed from twin speakers and his wife yelled from the kitchen, where she was putting the finishing touches to beef Stroganoff for twenty, to turn that thing down, she couldn't hear herself think. The host would shrug a little, wondering what the sense was in having a hi-fi if you couldn't play the records loud. But he'd turn the volume down and then pour himself a little Canadian-and-soda, and sit in an easy chair, and look out at his garden or his fields or his favourite tree, and in a little while his wife would come in from the kitchen wearing a long hostess gown with a sequined party apron over it, and he would pour her a drink, and they would await their guests together, slightly expectant, slightly excited, but enjoying these last few moments of peace and silence accompanied by musical visions of harem maids in filmy baggy pants. By the time the first guests arrived, *Scheherazade* had given way to the LP directly above it, an album of Tommy Dorsey classics, and "Song of India" bastardized the harem girls into musical visions of Lindy-hopping bobby-soxers, and suddenly the Talmadge ritual was set in motion.

"Hi."

"Hi, Joe. How are you?"

"How are you, Frank?"

"Fine, thanks. Good to see you."

"Hi" being a contraction of "How are you", it was perhaps redundant to use both at the same time, but this was none the less the ritualistic form of greeting in Talmadge. The "Good to see you" was mandatory, and used at every social function even if the people shaking hands had seen each other at another cocktail party only an hour before. Only the men shook hands in Talmadge. Women kissed other women on the cheek, and men used this same form of greeting with other men's wives. Talmadge was a very friendly and tolerant town. The invitations usually designated eight o'clock as the time of arrival. But no one ever showed up before nine or nine-thirty or even ten, depending on how many other parties there were that same night, except the people travelling from New York or New Haven, who usually arrived on the dot. These people were promptly made to feel like exactly what they were: outsiders. Within ten minutes, the Talmadge natives had gathered into tight tribal conclaves and begun discussing the latest town affairs while the outsiders breathed deeply of the bracing country air and muttered, "What the hell, let's get drunk."

The dancing did not begin until after dinner some time, when everyone had consumed enough liquor, wine, and cordials to keep the Stork Club open and running for a week. The small talk had run out by this time, the violent arguments about the new novels and plays and motion pictures had been fought, the latest Madison Avenue jokes had all been told, the latest travel experiences had been related, and everyone had been apprised of who was currently pregnant, cheating, or getting a divorce. The party would be settling into a gelatinous stupor threatening solidification, a yawn would be stifled here or there, when suddenly the all-observant host would rise and turn up the record player, the signal for an adventurous couple to break the ice and set the party into its next phase. This phase was labelled by Matthew, who favoured short descriptive titles, the Touch-and-Go Phase. He recognized a variation of his More-or-Less Principle as the driving force behind the Touch-and-Go Phase, the person who was most bored being the first to start dancing, the person who was least bored being the last to join the throng circling the living-room. Matthew, who never liked doing anything on a given signal, least of all dancing, managed to stay on the sidelines at Talmadge parties, watching the behaviour of the natives. They certainly seemed restless, but restless in a totally relaxed way, a paradox that was difficult for him to grasp at first.

It took him a little while to realize that most of the early dancing was being done by husband-and-wife teams, nice ballroom dancing, which they had practised together since they were teen-agers, every nuance of husbandly pressure on the small of the back instantly picked up by the wife, each trick-step speciality executed with precision and aplomb, slightly idiotic grins on the faces of mates, it was Prom Time again in lovely, woodsy Talmadge. Then the record changed, or everyone suddenly needed a fresh drink, and then the couples on the floor were no longer husband-wife teams, or at least no longer this-husband-belongs-to-this-wife teams, everyone seemed to have changed partners, again at a signal, a magician had waved a magic wand and *whooosssh*, the swirling couples were mismatched.

Talmadge was a friendly town, and everyone danced close here, and cheek to cheek here. If a man in the New York subway had stood this close to a Talmadge woman, she'd have clobbered him with her umbrella. But this was Talmadge, and this was the town where it was always good to see you, and where men shook hands with other men but kissed the women on the cheek, so it was all right to dance close here. No one minded it. It was the proper, friendly, social thing to do. It never got unfriendly, or unsocial, or improper. It got damn close to being all of those things, but it never crossed the unchalked line, never broke the unwritten code. A great many male thighs were very very close to a great many female thighs, and a great many male hands reached clear around a female back to that first soft swell of an unfamiliar breast, a soft cheek was flushed and feverish against a bearded one, lips almost touched when their owners pulled back their heads to murmur a word or two, the dipping was sometimes a little personal, a tiny bit intimate, especially during the summer months when clothing was habitually lighter. But all this touching and near touching seemed to reach a per-arranged, quasi-climactic point when the female would say, "I think we'd better rest a little," or the male would say, "Let's have another drink, shall we?" With these words, or a variation of them, the touching of this particular partner had reached its apogee; there was nothing further to do but go. So they went. Touch-and-Go, and *whooosssh*, the magician waved his wand again, everybody changed partners again, the carousel was in motion once more, different horses, new riders, the same old jazz.

Matthew hated it.

He hated it because it was an outrageous lie, and he didn't like lies or liars. He hated it, too, because it was a game of musical wives that had no obvious destination, a game that was a deception, an inspired delusion, a medieval sort of orgy-cum-fantasy in modern dress with self-imposed limits, time-consuming, energy-depleting, and totally frustrating. He hated it. He decided definitely and emphatically to avoid it. If he had to get stone-cold drunk and pass out on the richly carpeted floors of every home in Talmadge, he would manage to avoid this juvenile nonsense.

For however fanciful Matthew's theories, however speculative his ideas, he had never once in the six years of his marriage broken the contract he'd made with Amanda. If he ever did break that contract —and he had considered it, he was a man, and vain, and egotistical, and he had considered it—if ever he did break that contract, he was going to do it in spades and not by rubbing bellies with a Talmadge matron who had already borne three children and was corresponding secretary of the P.T.A.

The Talmadge party that November night was exactly the same as every other Talmadge party he'd ever attended.

Except for Julia Regan.

He didn't meet her until eleven o'clock. He was fairly crocked by that time, so that the inane chatter and the blasting hi-fi unit and the cavorting couples blended into a sort of alcohol-misted din behind him. He was sitting in the dark on the patio, his jacket collar raised on the back of his neck, the lapels pulled closed across his chest in defence against the cold. The door opened suddenly, and a tall woman with an upswept hairdo stepped on to the patio, pulled her stole around her, sighed deeply, and reached into her bag for a cigarette. He saw her face briefly in the flaring match, fine-line, patrician. She sucked in on the cigarette. The match flared again and died. She began walking towards the edge of the patio. Her heels clicked on the slate in the darkness. He had always liked the sound of high-heeled pumps. He listened to the clicking. She has good legs, he thought. He could tell from the sound of her walk.

"You're not alone," he said suddenly.

The woman turned. "I know." She walked towards him. "I thought you were asleep. I didn't want to disturb you."

Her voice was the voice of an older woman. Forty? Forty-five?

"Had enough in there?" he asked. "Ooooops, I should know better. You may be the hostess, for all I know."

"I'm not." She paused. "May I sit with you?"

"Please." He rose and offered her his chair with an elaborate bow. He pulled over another chair, took a cigarette from his pocket, and lighted it. Julia looked at his face in the flare of the match.

"Oh," she said, "it's you."

"That's who it is, all right," Matthew answered. He held the match close to her face. "And it's you, too."

"That's right." Julia smiled. Matthew shook out the match.

"*Who?*" Matthew said.

"Julia Regan." She extended her hand.

He took it. "Matthew Bridges."

"Yes, I know. We were introduced earlier tonight."

"Impossible," Matthew said. "I'd have remembered."

"You weren't paying much attention. You seemed extremely bored."

"I'm never bored at Talmadge parties."

"You seemed to be."

"Never."

There was a silence.

"I thought we could talk," Julia said.

"Aren't we?"

"Not if you're going to be facetious."

"Okay, I *was* bored. I'm also a little drunk, and I was trying to be cute. Okay? What are you, a district attorney?"

"No."

"Then what?"

"Nothing."

"Everybody's something."

"All right, I'm a widow."

"And that's all?"

"What would you like to know? I'm forty-eight years old, I have a son named David who's almost your age, and I live in a big old house right here in Talmadge."

"There's more," Matthew said.

"No, that's all."

"Uh-uh," Matthew said. "There's more."

"You're right," she said quickly. "I don't collect blood for the Red Cross, I don't belong to the National Democratic Committee, and I despise Little Leaguers. I drive an Alfa Romeo, I shower twice daily, and I don't keep pets. Thumb-nail sketch of Julia Regan."

"I'll bet your son is nowhere near my age."

"How old *are* you?"

"I was thirty-five in February."

"David will be twenty-nine in October."

"That's . . . just a second, I was never very good at arithmetic . . . that's a difference of six years."

"Yes. See?"

"I see. You and I are generations apart."

"At least one generation."

"No, no, countless generations," Matthew insisted.

Julia smiled. "We're closer than you think, Mr. Bridges."

The patio was silent for a moment. The sky was clear. Matthew took a deep breath of air.

"Which one is your wife?" Julia asked. "The blonde girl?"

"Yes. Amanda."

"Yes, we met. She's lovely."

"Thank you."

"Do you have any children?"

"I have a daughter almost as old as you are," Matthew said, smiling.

"Really? How old is she?"

"She was just ten." His grin widened. "And I have a son named Bobby who——"

"You didn't tell me your daughter's name."

"Kate."

"That's a nice name."

"Yes," Matthew said, and he nodded. "Bobby was three in July."

"No dogs? Cats? Elephants?"

"A dog. A cocker spaniel. Present to Kate on her last birthday."

"And what's his name?"

"*His* name is Beverly."

"Oh, excuse me."

"Apologize to the dog, not me. Besides, she's been spayed, so your descriptive pronoun is partially accurate."

"And the elephant?"

"No elephants, tigers or rhinoceroses. Rhinoceri." He nodded. "What gives you the most trouble when you're drunk?"

"I don't get drunk."

"*Everybody* gets drunk."

"I'm not everybody. I'm Julia Regan."

"Well, Julia Regan, the thing that gives me trouble when I'm drunk is endings."

"Not beginnings?"

"I mean the endings of words. The plurals. Like mooses and mouses and desks."

"Why desks?"

"That's a very hard word to say even sober. There's a sort of echo on that word. Say it. Desks. Do you hear the echo?"

"Desks," Julia said. "No, I don't hear anything."

"Desks," Matthew said. "Try it again."

"Desks."

"Listen."

"Desks. Why, yes," Julia said. "A sort of sss-kkk echo. How did you ever notice a thing like that?"

"I'm a very observant fellow. Why is it that you don't get drunk, Julia Regan?"

"I don't have to."

"I *have* to. At these parties, I have to."

"Are you very drunk now?"

"No. Not very. Only somewhat. Why did you tell me you were fifty-eight years old?"

"Forty-eight, please!"

"That's right, forty-eight. Same thing."

"Because that's my age."

"Uh-uh," Matthew said, shaking his head.

"Then why did I tell you that, Mr. Bridges?"

"To make things clear from the beginning, right?"

"What sort of things?"

"You know," Matthew said. "You know."

"Yes, I do. I'm sorry. Did I sound discouraging?"

"Well, when you drag out your crutches and your wheel chair and your eighty-year-old son, I can only assume . . ."

"I didn't mean to be discouraging. If you want to make a pass, go ahead and make it."

"Huh?"

"I think you heard me."

"You said . . ."

"I said if you feel like kissing me or touching me, I wish you would and get it over with."

"Well!" Matthew said.

"Well?"

"Well, that's putting it on the line, all right."

"Yes, it is."

"I must be drunker than I thought."

"Why?"

"I don't feel like kissing you right now."

"All right. If you ever *do* feel like it, then kiss me. Quickly, and once and for all."

Matthew shook his head in amazement.

"What's going on inside your head?" she asked.

"That's a line from *Room Service*. 'There's just one thing I want to know, Gribble. What the hell goes on inside that head of yours?' That was a very funny show."

"Don't change the subject, Mr. Bridges."

"Was I changing it?"

"You were."

"Okay. What do you want?"

"I asked you what you were thinking."

"I was thinking I don't understand you."

"What's so puzzling, Mr. Bridges?"

"Are you propositioning me?" Matthew asked.

There was such a tone of bewilderment in his voice that Julia burst out laughing.

"Well now, what's so funny about that?"

"You're *very* funny," she said. "You're like a little boy, Mr. Bridges."

"Call me Matthew," he said angrily. "And don't ever say that again!"

"Which?"

"The little-boy baloney. There's nothing infuriates a man more."

"I'll remember."

"Okay, remember."

"Why are you angry?"

"Because I think you're playing games."

"No, I'm not," she said seriously.

"Then what *are* you doing?"

"Not playing games. Anything but that. I'm trying to be perfectly honest with you because I like you and want to be your friend."

"So you ask me to hop into bed."

"I didn't ask you that, Matthew. I'm sorry. Perhaps I overestimated you."

"Yeah, perhaps you did. It sounded very much to me like——"

"Damn it, keep still a moment!"

"Listen, don't tell me——"

"*Keep still!*"

"I don't like to be told——"

"Neither do I!" Julia snapped.

They were silent.

"Boy, we get along just fine, don't we?" Matthew said.

"We do. And we will."

"What do you want from me?"

"Nothing."

"That's a lie, Julia."

"All right, then. Everything."

"I can't give you that."

"Only a fool would expect it," Julia said.

"I thought we weren't going to play games."

"We're not. We're talking."

"Very small talk."

"You're not very perceptive are you?" Julia asked.

"You're pretty insulting, aren't you?" Matthew asked.

"I only insult people I like."

"Better to be your enemy, then."

"No. Better to be my friend."

"Oh, the hell with it," Matthew said, and again the patio was silent.

"Do you know why we're fighting?" she asked.

"Yes."

"Why?"

"Because now I *want* to kiss you."

"That's right," Julia said.

"Is that your point?"
"That's exactly my point."
"Okay." He nodded. He approached her awkwardly, clumsily cupped her chin in his hand. He lowered his mouth. "I'm going to," he said.
"Please."
Their lips met. Her mouth was very soft. She kissed well.
"All right?" she asked.
"Yes," he said grudgingly.
"Did you enjoy kissing me?"
"Yes."
"Yes, and I enjoyed you." She paused. "Do you want to touch me now?"
"No."
"Why not?"
"Because I like kissing my wife better than I like kissing you," Matthew said, surprised when the words found voice.
"Yes, that's good," Julia said. She smiled. "Would you give me a cigarette now?"
He shook one free from the package and lighted it for her. She smiled at him over the match.
"I feel a little foolish," he said.
"No, please," she said, "you mustn't. Besides, I don't expect this to happen again, do you?"
"No. I honestly don't."
"But I'm glad it happened here and now. I'm glad it's done."
"I am, too."
"And are we friends now?" she asked.
"I guess so. It's been a hell of a long way around the mulberry bush, but I guess so."
They laughed in the darkness.
"Listen," he said.
"Yes?"
"You're an exciting woman."
"Am I?"
"Yes. So don't . . . I don't ever want to start anything, Julia."
"Neither do I."
"So don't ever——"
"I won't."
"Okay."
They were silent.
"Because I'm only human," Matthew said.
"Yes, we all are. But if . . ." She stopped and shook her head. "No, I won't say it."

"Say it."

"No."

"You're starting wrong, Julia."

"Of course, forgive me. I was going to say, if you ever *need* me, come to me. I didn't want to say it because . . . I didn't want you to think . . ."

"That's not what I'm thinking."

"Good, then."

"Well," he said, and he sighed. "I feel pretty good."

"So do I." She paused. "Someone inside said you were a lawyer. Are you a good lawyer?"

"Yes."

"Tell me what it's like."

"What can I tell you?"

"You *seem* like a lawyer," Julia said.

"How do lawyers seem?"

"Oh, I don't know. Legal and . . ." She shrugged.

"Say it. Pompous."

"You're not at all pompous."

"I'm not?" Matthew said.

"Certainly not. Whatever gave you that idea?"

"I don't know. I guess I feel a little stuffy sometimes. No, not that. I guess I feel I *should* be a little stuffy. There's a difference."

"Why should you want to be stuffy?"

"Because I'm a lawyer, and a husband, and a father, and sometimes I don't feel like any of the three."

"How *do* you feel?"

"Sometimes?"

"Yes."

"Like seventeen," Matthew said. "Sometimes my kids will have their friends over to play, and I'll look at them and wonder why any parents in their right minds would entrust the safety of their children to *me*, an imitation father who is only seventeen years old."

"I see. And how old do you feel right now?"

"Are you going to tell me you're forty-eight again?"

"No, never again. We're past that now, aren't we?"

"Yes, we are."

"So tell me how you feel now."

"With you?"

"Yes. With me."

"I feel like your son," Matthew said.

He went to see her for the first time a week later. It was a Saturday, and he was driving into town to do some errands when he passed the

Regan house and suddenly decided to stop. He pulled the car to the kerb, got out, and walked to the front door. At first, there was no answer. He rang again.

"Just a moment," Julia called from somewhere inside.

He waited on the front step feeling somewhat foolish. The events at the party seemed like such a long time ago, seemed almost unreal. He wondered what he would say to her now, wondered if their so-called friendship had not been the result of his alcoholic haze.

She was wearing a robe when she answered the door. Her hair was in curlers. He could see them under the scarf she had hastily thrown over her head.

"Matthew," she said. "How nice! Come in!"

He followed her into the house.

"I was just making some coffee," she said. "Will you join me?"

"Yes, thank you. I'd like some."

They went into the kitchen. She poured the coffee and then turned on the radio to see what the weather would be like. There was something very natural and very familiar about the scene, Julia sitting at the table in her robe and curlers, Matthew in dungarees and a woollen sports shirt, the radio behind them giving the news and weather. He felt totally relaxed and comfortable as he sipped his coffee. They began chatting later, easily, without innuendo, without guile. Before he realized it, he was telling her about Kate and the difficulties they were experiencing with the adoption.

"Ordinarily, it might have been a routine thing, although adoption laws are the most confusing in the world. With Kate, it's become more complicated because two states are involved, Minnesota and Connecticut."

"I see," Julia said.

"We had to make application in Minnesota, you understand. And the law there states that any person who's resided in the state for more than a year may apply for adoption. Naturally, we can't establish residency in Minnesota. But happily, the law says this provision may be waived by the court. Well, we applied for the waiver, and it was refused, so we appealed, and the waiver was finally granted, but that was only the beginning."

"Have some more coffee, Matthew."

"Thank you, I will. There's a matter of consent involved, too, Julia. Usually, the parents' consent is required, except when the child is over fourteen, in which case *her* consent is required, too. Well, Kate's *real* father is dead, and her mother . . . well . . ." He hesitated.

"You can tell me, Matthew," she said gently.

"Her mother is institutionalized, Julia. And since she's been adjudged incompetent, we then needed the consent of the Director of Social Welfare, but this, too, could have been waived by the court. Well, the court wouldn't waive, so we've been waiting for the results of the investigation. There's got to be an investigation and report by the director, you see, after six months of residence in the proposed home. And then, when he finally decides it's all right for us to keep Kate, and to love Kate, the proceedings will be held in a Minnesota juvenile court in the county of residence of Kate's real mother. Ordinarily, the place of venue would have been the adopting parents' county, but here again we run into the Minnesota-Connecticut confusion. Believe me, it's annoying and frustrating."

"But does it look as if it'll go through?"

"Yes, I think so. At last. I'd hazard a guess and say Kate'll be ours within the next six months."

"Well, that's good, Matthew."

"Yes." He smiled. The radio was playing music now. The November wind lashed under the eaves of the old house. The house felt warm and secure and snug. He finished his second cup of coffee, stayed a few moments longer, and then put on his coat and got ready to leave. Before he left, he kissed her on the cheek.

He stopped by to see her regularly after that. He was always welcomed and he never had to call beforehand. Sometimes he dropped in on the way home from work, and Julia would mix a Martini for him, and he would sit in the living-room with her and sip at his drink, and tell her some of the things that had happened at the office, or simply discuss Talmadge affairs, or sometimes discuss nothing at all, sometimes just sit quietly with her and sip at his drink. Once, sitting opposite her, he said, "I want to kiss you, Julia."

"Please," she said.

He went to her, and she tilted her head.

"I need to," he said.

"Please."

But that was the last time, and he felt better afterwards, knowing it would not happen again. He went to her house without guilt, openly, with no attempt to deceive or to hide. He parked his car blatantly in her driveway, with a total disregard for the opinion of the Talmadge townsfolk. He told Amanda that Julia Regan was his friend, and perhaps she was. He did not question his relationship with her too closely. He knew only that he found something in her home, something he had not known for a very long time. He did not ask himself what this something was. He knew it had to do with a relaxed feeling of irresponsibility. He owed this woman nothing. Nothing, really, was demanded of him. He could come to her or not come as he desired. He could talk or remain silent. He could arrive in a sulk and rant in her living-room for a half-hour before leaving. He could tell jokes if he chose to, but no demand for entertainment was ever made. He could think sometimes of taking her to bed, knowing full well he would never take her to bed. She gave, she gave to him out of her merciful bounty, and he took, he took with both hands.

Once, he was moved to the point of tears. He had brought her a gift for Christmas. There was a large decorated tree in the living-room, and Julia was standing on a ladder when he came into the house, putting a star on the top of the tree. He came into the house and stamped snow from his feet, and then blew on his hands, and then looked into the living-room, and saw her standing on the ladder, reaching for the tip of the tree, and stood suddenly transfixed in the doorway, silent, watching her.

"Oh, hello, Matthew," she said. "Is it cold enough out there?"

It seemed to him he had walked into this same room long ago, in Glen City. He nodded dumbly. She came down off the ladder and said, "Come, I'll make you some tea," and embraced him and took him into the kitchen. He was very silent that day. He kept watching her silently, as if discovering her for the first time. They drank their tea in the living-room. The grandfather clock ticked off time in a rigid solid voice. The clock, too, seemed familiar. He finished his tea, and got into his coat again. She was sitting in a large mohair chair, facing the clock. She seemed older that day. He suddenly realized how old she was. His eyes had misted over. He felt he wanted to cry, but he did not, he would not let the tears come.

"Merry Christmas, Julia," he said.

"Merry Christmas, Matthew," she answered.

He went out of the house quietly. Julia sat quite still in the living-room and listened to the voice of the clock.

Time.

Past and present merged in the mind of Julia Regan. October, November, and now December, now January, a new year. They set off the air-raid siren on the roof of the firehouse to welcome 1953. She went to a party at the Bridges' house, and she listened to Matthew tell her about his progress in the adoption proceedings, apparently the investigation had been made and adoption had been recommended, and now it was a question of making the requisite trip to Minnesota. He was slightly drunk. He put his hand on her knee and said, "It takes such a damn long time, Julia. I love that kid. She's my daughter, do you know what I mean? Really, Julia. She's my daughter. But it takes such a goddam long time."

Time.

1939 in Rome. The long wait.

And the threat of war hovering everywhere. Renato gone more and more frequently, Millie on the edge of hysteria, "Julia, we've got to get out of here. I don't care what——"

"You know that's impossible."

"I'm frightened. Julia, if war breaks out . . ."

"There's nothing we can do, Millie."

"Well then, *I'll* go home. Alone."

"You can't do that, Millie."

"Why did you get yourself into this? You're a grown woman! I always thought——"

"There were a lot of things I always thought, too, Millie."

"You make me want to cry. Seeing you like this, helpless, just helpless. You make me want to cry."

"I'm not helpless."

"If war comes . . ."

"Millie, please, please . . ."

April approaching. Spring in Rome. She had promised Arthur she'd be back in April. She sent him a cable stating that Millie was ill and unable to travel. She knew the war was coming, but her following letter said: "*. . . Everyone here seems convinced that Hitler is bluffing. In any case, there does not seem to be a climate of preparation for war, no matter what you felt at Christmas-time. I know this is foremost in your mind, Arthur, but believe me, darling, Millie and I are in no immediate danger.*" Lies. Lies all through May, the promise that she would be home soon, the dangling carrot, I will be home soon, I will be home soon, and knowing it was impossible for her to leave Italy.

Time.

Past and present flowing together, the memory of those months in Rome overshadowing the real spring of 1953 in Talmadge, the opening of buds everywhere around her, how quickly the winter had gone, how quickly it was spring again, how quickly the months went by, and the years, how long ago had it been, how long ago to 26 July, 1939, to that day when Renato held her trembling and sweating in the small room, "*Ti voglio bene*," he said, "*tesorino, non dimenticarlo mai.*" The crying. She would not forget the crying. 26 July. The end was near. It was odd how the beginning was the end. It was odd how time folded in upon itself, how Rome had been the beginning of a life and the end of a life, the pattern was endless, and present merged with past so that sometimes she could not tell which was now and which was then.

Surely she was in the here and now. The Julia Regan who opened the house at the lake again in the summer of 1953 was a flesh-and-blood person who cleaned out bathtubs and straightened cupboards and aired mattresses. I am growing old, she thought, where is 1939? Where is the girl who was born in 1939? Memory is too cruel, she thought. I would abolish years. I would trample time. I want to be in Rome again. I want to be alive again. I want to be loved.

Oh, all I want is to be loved.

The lake held no menace.

David sat on the back porch of the summer-house, his hands folded on his naked chest, and looked out over the still water. August sunshine caught at his yellow swimming-trunks, reflected from the signet ring on the pinkie of his right hand. A man in a rowboat was fishing in the middle of the lake. He watched the man sleepily, half dozing. The pines were almost motionless. A faint breeze stirred the midsummer air. He could hear his mother inside the house, preparing lunch.

Saturday, he thought. Lake Abundance.

All the Saturdays of his early life, all the summer Saturdays at Lake Abundance, and that Saturday in September—he felt no pain. He sat watching the calm surface of the killer lake, and he felt no real pain, only an inestimable sense of loss. Something more than his father had died on that day in 1939. Something more. I seem to lose people, he thought. I seem to have a knack for losing people.

He listened to his mother humming inside the house.

A screen door opened. He turned his head.

The people next door. He had met them last week-end. Cocktails in his mother's living-room. "This is my son, David."

"How do you do, Mr. Bridges? Mrs. Bridges?"

"Matthew and Amanda," the man corrected. Tall, grinning, moustached. David did not trust men with moustaches. The woman—how old? Thirty? Blonde, sun-tanned, restless somehow, she tucked her skirts around her too efficiently, she smoked too much.

"This is their first summer at the lake," his mother said. "I talked them into it."

"You'll like it here," David said.

"We've been going up to the Vineyard," Matthew told him.

"That's a long haul, isn't it?"

"Well, not so bad. There's a plane service, you know."

"I didn't know that."

"Yes. The trip's not bad at all. I didn't enjoy the people very much, though."

"Oh? Why not?"

"Well, it's a strange crowd," Matthew said. "Everyone performs."

"Matthew doesn't like people," Amanda said. "That's his trouble." She smiled at David. She lighted another cigarette.

"I didn't like *those* people, that's for sure," Matthew said. "I hate people who ask 'What do you do?' That annoys me. Everyone there *did* something. Everyone had a label and a profession. I'm a sculptor, I'm a photographer, I write children's books, I composed the music for this-and-this Broadway hit, what do *you* do? I always felt I should recite a brief or something. Everyone performed. It was like an out-of-town tryout for autumn conversation."

"Oh, Matthew, it wasn't that bad," Amanda said.

"It was, honey. You went to a party, and the party was divided into the entertainers and the appreciators. The entertainers played bongo drums badly, or Spanish guitars, or sang songs they wrote in 1920, or recited their newest poem for the *Atlantic Monthly*, or told dialect jokes, or exhibited the latest piece of sculpture with holes in it. And the appreciators were supposed to applaud and make noises of approval. I guess I'm not the appreciative type. I guess I just hate people who ask 'What do you do?'"

"What *do* you do?" David asked, and Matthew burst out laughing.

"I'm a lawyer," he said. "How about you?"

"Television."

"Acting?"

"Producing."

"That must be exciting work," Amanda said.

"I like it," David answered.

Cocktails and small talk in July. The new lake-front neighbours, Matthew and Amanda Bridges. The visiting son from the city. Julia cool in blue cotton. Matthew in dungarees and a tee-shirt, powerful arms and chest. Amanda in slacks and a full white blouse. July and small talk.

The screen door clattered shut.

August.

"Hi!" she called.

"Hello," he answered. He lifted his arm and waved.

"Have you been in yet?"

"No."

"I'll bet it's freezing."

She was wearing a green tank-suit, a soft round girl who walked quickly to the dock before the cottage, as if she would dive instantly into the lake. He watched her appreciatively. She moved in a beautifully fluid, totally female way, and she was pleasant to watch. She shook her head suddenly, walked back the length of the dock and abandoned it, stepping on to the mud bank and walking gingerly to the waterfront, apparently having decided to enter the lake in slow progressive stages. She went into the water delicately and gently, holding her hands up near the full globes of her breasts, shrieking girlishly when the icy water touched the first mound of her body beneath the green tank-suit. The screen door opened and clattered shut again. Matthew.

"Hi, David. Going in?"

"Not just yet."

"It's freeeeeezing!" Amanda called to him. She was standing in water to her waist, slightly bent, delicately dipping her fingers into the lake the way David had seen it done by grandmothers and little girls.

He decided he liked Amanda Bridges.

The sounds on the lake were good sounds, summer sounds. Matthew grinned and ran past Amanda, plunging into the water recklessly. He surfaced instantly and said, "Wow!" and then plunged beneath the surface again. There was a sudden silence during which the distant sound of the spillway seemed very close, all the whispering sounds of summer seemed very close and very loud, the soughing sad song of the mild breeze high in the tops of the lakeside pines and oaks, the languid rustle of heavy leaves against a heat-pale sky, and carried on the stifled breeze, echoing down the rolling bank from the Bridges' cottage, the laughter of ten-year-old Kate playing with her younger brother, and Matthew suddenly surfacing and advancing on his wife, "Matthew, don't! Don't you daaaaare!" the words hanging on the water and the sky, the near buzz of yellow jackets in the close-cropped clover, the lap of the water against the dock pilings, the creak of oarlocks on the rowboats, the boats bobbing near the dock, yellow, red, yellow, and a telephone ringing someplace on the lake, the sounds of summer, sticky-slow and dream-like, far away the hum of automobile tires on a road that rushed against the belly of the lazy countryside.

Amanda darted a frightened happy excited glance at her approaching husband and then dived into the water and broke into a powerful crawl for the raft. She climbed aboard, panting. Matthew followed her, and they both laughed short little laughs of contentment and lay back against the canvas. The lake was still again. David could hear the laughter of the children in the cottage. "No," Kate said in her clear childish voice, "you're supposed to be the milkman, Bobby." He closed his eyes. The sun was hot. He began to doze.

Crackling.

A strange crackling sound.

His eyelids flickered, closed again.

Smell. Thick. Nostrils and throat. The crackle. What . . .

He turned on the chair, hot sunshine covered his right shoulder, his throat felt raw, the smell was thick in his nostrils, heat and the smell of . . .

He sat upright suddenly.

Smoke!

He looked out over the lake first, blinking. They were asleep on the raft, both of them. He turned his head to the right, saw the smoke drifting on the air, heard the crackling sound again, coming from the rear of the Bridges' cottage, the children in the house, fire, he thought, *Fire*, he thought, "**FIRE**!" he shouted.

He leaped to his feet. His shoes. Where were his shoes?

"Fire!" he yelled again, and then ran towards the cottage, across the separating stretch of stone-strewn ground, where the hell are my shoes? he thought, children in the house, oh Jesus, "*Fire!*" he shouted, turned the corner of the cottage, stopped dead in his tracks when he saw the blaze.

He had fought fires in boot camp, fought raging oil fires, held the spray nozzle and suffocated the flames as thick black smoke poured from the open hatchway and heat mushroomed into his face. But in boot camp there had been experienced fire-fighters, teaching the embryo sailors, there was a feeling of absolute control, there was the knowledge that nothing could go terribly wrong.

There was no such assurance here. His mind seemed to be ticking in stop images. The flames. The pump room. The gasoline water-pump. He rushed to the open door, backed away from the flames. I'm in my swimming shorts, he thought, Jesus, what . . . Jesus . . . the flames . . . how? He saw the gasoline can resting against the pump's exhaust, saw gasoline spilling from the open spout of the can, feeding the fire. He reached into the flames. He grasped the charred, hot handle of the gas can and pulled it out of the flames in one sweeping motion, a straight-armed motion that swept the can out of the fire and brought it back past his near-naked body. A sheet of flame followed the open spout as he swung the can in a backward arc. He could feel the heat passing his face, saw the sudden charred sooty streak appear on the wooden door of the pump room. He let go of the handle, the can fell into the bushes, immediately igniting them.

Oh, Jesus, he thought.

A hose. Water.

He turned his head in short jerks. Where was Matthew? What the hell was taking him so long to get off that raft!

"David, what is it? his mother yelled from the porch next door.

"Fire!" he shouted. "Get Matthew!"

He saw the coiled hose at the back of the house. He ran for it. Kate stuck her head out of the upstairs window.

"What's the matter, Mr. Regan?" she asked.

"Get out of the house!" he said. He began unwinding the hose.

"What?"

"Get out of the house!"

"What? What?"

"The house is on fire! Get out of there!"

He ran back to the pump room with the hose. Which? he thought. The bushes? The pump room? Which first? The whole lake front'll go up. The bushes first. First the bushes. He swung the nozzle of the hose. No water. No . . .? I didn't turn it on! He dropped the hose and ran back to the faucet attachment. He turned the wheel and then ran back to the house again. No water was coming from the nozzle. Come on! he thought. He twisted it. Which way? I'm turning it the wrong way! He finally opened the nozzle, sprayed water at the bushes, watched the flames turn to white smoke, and swung back towards the pump room. The flames had reached the ceiling of the room. They'll go through, he thought. They'll get into the house. Was Kate out? Would she have sense enough to take her brother with her? He looked up, saw only the empty window, and then shot the stream of water at the pump.

He saw the cans then. Cans of paint stacked behind the pump. He saw a gallon bottle of kerosene. He saw a can marked "Shellac." This whole damn thing'll explode in my face, he thought. This isn't my house, he thought. I'm crazy, he thought. But he kept the hose on the flames. Go out! Goddammit, go out! He leaned closer into the fire. He heard a crackling crisp sound, smelled the terrifying aroma of singed hair, my chest, he thought, and backed away from the flames. A pair of flaming overalls was hanging over the buckets of paint. He reached into the small room, a coffin set on end, a tiny room with a blazing pump and piles of explosive material. He grabbed the overalls and flung them back over his shoulder on to the ground, turned the hose on them immediately and saw Matthew, wet, panting, what had taken him so long? He did not realize he had been fighting the fire no longer than three minutes.

"The kids," he said. "Upstairs."

"Have you got this?"

"I've got it. Get the kids."

Matthew was gone. He could feel his heart beating against his naked chest. He was beginning to control the flames, but a new fear leaped into his mind. The water. Suppose the water gave out? This was the pump room. The gasoline-pump had to be started whenever the water pressure got too low. It was the pump that provided water, and he was using water by the gallon, and the pump was on fire, what would he do when the water gave out, don't give out, he thought, stay with me, we're getting it, we're controlling it. He turned the hose up against the ceiling, the flames retreated, no, they had taken too secure a hold, the water was beginning to come from the nozzle in a weaker stream now, hold on, he thought, the paint, it's going to explode in my face, get out of here, he thought, leave it, get out, get out, but he stayed.

He stayed leaning into the flames, sweating, covered with soot, stinking of singed hair, his face streaked, his arms black, the smouldering overalls on the path behind him, the staring labels on the cans and bottles, paint, paint thinner, shellac, kerosene, the water giving out, only a trickle now, he threw away the hose. The flames rallied instantly. He pulled a burning shovel from the wooden wall of the narrow room, dropped the hot handle, swore, scraped earth with his bare hands, tossed it on to the shovel handle, and then picked up the shovel again, still hot, but manageable. He was shovelling fresh earth into the room when Matthew came down again. The children were screaming, Amanda was carrying two kitchen-size fire-extinguishers, small cans. She handed them to David wordlessly, he pulled the levers mechanically, the cans were exhausted immediately, Matthew was suddenly at his side with a second shovel.

"I'll take it," he said.

They worked together, taking turns in the narrow doorway, tossing shovel after shovelful of earth into the diminishing flames. Amanda soothed the children, holding them to the wet front of her bathing-suit. Julia was there now, wide-eyed, there were other people now, someone brought a real fire-extinguisher, the danger was almost past. A man in hip-length boots walked into the narrow room and stamped out the glowing embers, smothered charred wood with earth, and then sprayed the fire-extinguisher over everything once again.

The fire was out.

The men stood together in their swimming-trunks. It was over. They stood breathing hard, weary. David was beginning to feel the aftermath of shock now. He listened to the voices around him and felt somewhat dazed, felt as if he would fall to the ground. He did not speak. They asked questions, but he only nodded or shook his head in return.

The child Kate suddenly broke from her mother's arms. She went to David and threw her arms around his neck and then kissed him on his sooty cheek.

Everyone smiled.

. . . . .

"I'm still a little shaken," he said to his mother. "Is there any brandy in the house?"

"Yes, I'll get you some."

"Please. My hands are shaking, would you believe it?"

Julia brought him the brandy in a large snifter. He took a big gulp and then sipped at it slowly, sitting smoke-stained in the big armchair near the window overlooking the lake.

"Do you believe in God?" he asked.

"Yes. Don't you?"

"I do," he answered. "But so many things happen by chance."

"Yes, a great many." Julia said. She sat in the chair opposite him, looking through the window. Her face, in profile, was calm and reposed.

"If there's a God, why does He . . .?" David stopped and shrugged. "They could have been killed," he said. "I was only there by luck. It makes me wish . . ."

He stopped suddenly. He looked at Julia quickly and then took another swallow of brandy, and then turned his attention to the lake outside, silent.

"*What* does it make you wish, David?"

"Nothing."

"Your father," she said softly.

"No."

"Yes," she insisted.

"Yes, it makes me wish I'd been in that boat with him!"

"Why?"

"To help, to . . . to tell him his foot was caught in the line, to . . . to jump in after him . . . to help . . . to *save* him."

"He didn't want anyone in the boat with him."

"How do you know?"

"I asked if I could go along."

"No, you didn't," David said.

"I remember," Julia said.

"No, Mom. I was taking your picture. And you asked him to get in the picture, and he said no, he wanted to take the boat out."

"Yes, but I said I wanted to go with him."

"No, you didn't. He just walked down to the lake and got into the boat, and I watched him through the binoculars, I . . ." He cut himself short and pulled at the brandy snifter. The glass was empty. He rose, walked into the other room, and poured another from the decanter. His mother was still sitting in the chair, unmoving, when he returned to the living-room.

"It wouldn't have mattered," she said suddenly.

"What?"

"If one of us had been with him . . ."

"If we'd gone along . . ."

"It wouldn't have mattered," Julia said.

The room was silent. He could hear the wind in the high trees outside.

"It would only have happened another time," Julia said, almost in a whisper.

"That's silly. He caught his foot in the——"

"He killed himself," Julia said.

David stood in his grimy bathing-trunks with the brandy glass in his hands, staring at his mother's profile, staring at the unflinching set of her face, the strong August sun limning her nose and her jaw, the wrinkles smoothed by the flat even reflected light of the lake, she could have been the same woman whose picture he had taken that day years ago, she could have been that woman, time was being very kind to Julia Regan.

"What?" he said.

"He killed himself."

"What?" he said again, but she did not repeat the words, and he stood staring at her dumbly, and then said, "You don't know that. How could you know that?"

"He told me he was going to kill himself."

He put down the brandy glass and walked to where she was sitting. His mother did not turn from the window.

"He *told* you?"

"Yes."

"When?"

"When I . . ." Julia paused. "A few days before."

"He said those words? He said he was going to *kill* himself?"

"Yes."

"Look at me."

Julia turned slowly.

"When did he tell you this?"

"I told you. A few days before . . . before he drowned."

"And you did nothing to stop him?"

"I tried to stop him."

"Tried? He killed himself, how the hell did you try?"

"I talked to him. I tried to show him I loved him."

"Didn't he already know that?" David shouted.

The question startled Julia. She looked up into her son's face and said, "He knew it."

"Then how was that going to help?"

"Nothing was going to help. He'd made up his mind. He wanted to kill himself."

"Why?" David said.
The question hung on the air.
"Why?" he repeated.
"I don't know why," Julia said.
"He talked to you. You said he talked to you."
"Yes, but he didn't . . ."
"Why did he want to kill himself?"
"I don't know."
David seized his mother's shoulders. "Don't lie to me," he said.
"You know all there is to know."
"There's more. Tell me what it is!"
"Why?"
"I spent four goddam years in prison because——"
"What? What?"
"Tell me why he died!"
"He died because he wanted to die."
"*Why did he want to die?*" David said slowly and evenly.
Julia's eyes held his steadily. Her voice came as slowly and as evenly as his own. "I don't know why," she said. "He never told me why." She paused. "Perhaps he was just tired, David. Perhaps he was suddenly too tired."
David stood by the chair and looked down at her. "I don't believe you," he said.
Julia made no sign that she had heard him.
"But I don't suppose that matters a hell of a lot to you."
"It matters, son."
"Sure, Sure, it does. The way it mattered that I was in California waiting for you to . . ." He shook his head violently. "Forget it!"
"I came to see you," Julia said quietly.
"Once! In four years, you came once!"
"Some get nothing," Julia said, almost in a whisper.
"What?"
"Nothing," she said. "Nothing."
He stared at her for a moment, and then picked up his brandy glass and went into the next room. He took the decanter from the sideboard, and then went upstairs.

He had left the house drunk, and she lay in bed wondering where he was and whether he was all right, and telling herself, He is twenty-eight years old, he can take care of himself, and yet thinking it was her fault that he'd drunk so much brandy, her fault that he was somewhere in the night now probably drinking himself into a stupor, I shouldn't have told him.
She could not sleep.

She threw back the covers and went to the telephone. She dialled, and then waited. He is a grown man, she told herself. She could hear the telephone ringing at the cottage next door. It's almost midnight, she thought. I shouldn't be doing this.

"Hello?" the voice said.

"Amanda?"

"Yes?"

"Oh, hello, Julia." Amanda's voice was edged with sleep. "Is something wrong?"

"Did I wake you?"

"No, no, that's all right. What is it?"

"Could I speak to Matthew, please?"

"Yes, just a moment." She heard Amanda's voice recede: "Matthew, it's Julia," and she heard Matthew answer, "What's the matter?"

"I don't know. Take the phone."

"Hello?"

"Matthew?"

"Yes, what's wrong?"

"I'm sorry to be calling at this hour . . ."

"Don't be foolish. What is it, Julia?"

"David left here drunk. I'm worried about him."

"Where did he go?"

"I don't know."

"You want me to look for him?"

"Would you? He took the Alfa, and I'm just afraid he might . . ."

"I'll get dressed," Matthew said.

"Thank you, Matthew. I appreciate . . ."

"I'll call you later," Matthew said, and he hung up.

"What did she want?" Amanda asked.

Matthew took his trousers from the chair. "David's crocked and on the town. She wants me to find him."

"He's not a child," Amanda said. "Really, I think——"

"I know he's not. But he's Julia's son, and she's worried about him."

"And that's enough to drag you out of bed in the middle of the night?"

"I suppose it is. Julia's our friend, Amanda. For God's sake, David put out a *fire* in this house today, the least I can . . ."

"Yes," Amanda said.

"So?"

Amanda did not answer. As he went out of the house, she said, "Be careful."

. . . . .

He found David in the third bar he tried. The bar was a wood cabin set some fifty feet off the state highway between Lake Abundance and Talmadge. A few dozen automobiles were parked in the gravel parking lot. A neon sign smothered with moths blinked in the summer night, advertising the name of the place, and the single legend DANCING. A cocktail glass fizzing with bubbles decorated one corner of the sign. From within the roadhouse, Matthew could hear a juke-box oozing a Frank Sinatra tune. He opened the door and stepped into the smoky room. There were booths on one side of the table, and a long bar on the other side, stretching from just inside the entrance door to the far wall, which held, in sequence, the door to the kitchen, a telephone booth, the ladies' room, and the men's room. David was sitting on a stool close to the entrance door. Matthew climbed on to the stool next to his.

"You vowed your love," Sinatra sang,
    "From here . . .
        "To eterni-tee . . ."
"Hi," Matthew said.

David turned and studied Matthew with the careful scrutiny of a man who is unwilling to commit himself.

"Ain't *nothing* lasts from here to eternity," he said.

"Maybe not," Matthew answered.

"No maybes about it," David said, and he nodded his head exaggeratedly. "Nothing. The world is ephemeral."

"Listen, how would you like to go home?" Matthew said.

"What for?"

"Your mother's worried about you."

"Oh, yeah?" David began laughing. "She's too late. She should've worried about me a long time ago."

"Yeah, well come on, finish your drink and——"

"Listen, go take a walk, Matthew."

"Let's take a walk together."

"No, listen, you go take a walk all by yourself. I'm pretty happy right where I am. Go on, go take a walk."

"No, I'll stay with you."

"I don't trust guys with moustaches."

"Why not?"

"Because I don't. You need a shave." David paused. "That's just what he said to me. 'You need a haircut, Regan. And shine those shoes.'"

"Who said that?"

"A friend of mine," David answered. "Long time ago. Nineteen . . . forty-three?" He opened his eyes wide in amazement. "You know that's ten years ago? You know that?"

"That's right." Matthew signalled the bartender and said, "A bourbon on the rocks."

"You going to join me?"

"If I can't fight you, I might as well."

"Mister, you can't fight it," David said.

"I guess not."

"Why the hell're you agreeing with me? You don't even know what I'm talking about, and you're agreeing."

"All right, what is it you can't fight?"

"The pattern, the design."

The bartender brought Matthew's drink, and he picked it up.

"Cheers," David said.

"Cheers," Matthew said, and he drank.

"That's right, the pattern," David said. "The same design. There ain't nothing you can do to change it. It's a big cycle."

"That's right," Matthew said.

"You're agreeing again, and you *still* don't know what the hell I mean."

"You mean life is a cycle, don't you? There's a certain pattern to it, an over-all design."

"That's *right*," David said, nodding.

"And it's difficult to break away from the pattern."

"Not difficult, im*pos*sible. Because nothing lasts."

"Some things last."

"Nothing. Listen, did *she* last, huh?"

"Did who last?"

"What's her name? You know."

"No, I don't know."

"Gillian," David said. "That's right. Gillian."

"I knew a Gillian once."

"There's only one Gillian in the world, so it must have been her. Gillian Burke. That the one?"

"That's the one," Matthew said.

"Right! Nothing lasts, and the world is rotten."

"That's a pretty cynical attitude, David."

"Hey, how come you know my name?"

"We've met before," Matthew said, and he smiled.

David leaned closer to him. "Oh, yeah. That's right. Why don't you shave off that moustache? Jesus!"

"My wife likes it," Matthew said.

"You married? Oh, yeah, Amanda, that's right. Beautiful girl. Congratulations."

"Thank you."

"That's who makes the pattern," David said. "Girls. Women."

"I guess so."

"Who else gives birth to babies, huh? That's what does it, right? Putting people on earth, right? So that's where it starts."

"Right," Matthew said.

"So why should it also finish it?"

"I don't think I follow you."

"Why do they kill us?"

"I'm not sure they do."

"No? Oh, no?" David's voice lowered menacingly. "Then *who* killed him, huh? Who was it killed him, huh? If it wasn't her, who was it, then? Would you mind telling me?"

"I don't know," Matthew said.

"Have another drink."

"No, I think I'll——"

"Bartender, bring my friend another whatever-the-hell-it-is."

"Bourbon?" the bartender said. "One bourbon, right."

"Okay," Matthew answered, and he shrugged.

"And another brandy on the rocks," David said. "You know who killed him?"

"Who?"

"She did. You know where she went?"

"Where?"

"Bidili. In the Bahamas."

"Bimini, you mean."

"I said Bidili, diddle I?" David said, and burst out laughing. "That's a joke. I set you up for that one. Where's my drink?" He looked at the bar and said, "Oh, there you are, you little bastard." He picked up the glass. "Left me dead, went off to Bimini. Now that's an example. I was born with her."

"Who?"

"Gillian. Born. Absolutely. No question about it. And then what? She killed me. That's the cycle, buddy. You're born, and you die."

"That's for sure," Matthew said.

"Cheers. Did I say cheers already?"

"No."

"Well, cheers." Both men drank from their fresh drinks. "Now that's what's funny about it, Matthew. It's funny that the same thing that gives life could also kill. I think that's pretty funny."

"I don't think it's funny at all," Matthew said.

"No?" David looked surprised. "Well, *I* think it's pretty mystifying."

Matthew drained his glass and said, "Women are only women, David. There's nothing mystifying about that."

"I think having a baby is very mystifying. Can you have a baby?"

"No."

"Neither can I." David shrugged. "That's the goddam mystery of the century, ain't it? I think it's pretty spooky, to tell the truth."

"Well, yes, but——"

"Now, look, I'm going to tell you something. There's life and death right there, buddy. In one person. It's like she eats her young, I'm telling you. Life and death."

"You sound as if you don't like women," Matthew said.

"I *love* women."

"Then why are you saying they're murderers?"

"Who's saying that? I'm saying that's life, brother, *life*. Look, have another drink, will you?"

"All right," Matthew said. He signalled the bartender and pointed to his empty glass.

"Give and take, Jekyll and Hyde, that's life," David said. "A man is *one* thing. Period. But a woman is a lot of things, and that's why she's so mystifying."

"A woman is a woman," Matthew said emphatically. "That's *one* thing. A woman. And it ain't . . . it isn't mystifying at all. A woman. Period."

"Right. But she's a lot of things."

"No."

"Yes. Look, she's a daughter, right?"

"Well, she's got to be a daughter," Matthew said. "She can't be a son."

"That's right. That's *right*, Matthew! And then she grows up, what does she do?"

"What does she do?"

"She turns around and becomes a mother."

"Well, that's only natural."

"Sure, but it says what I'm trying to say."

"I don't know *what* you're trying to say, David."

"I'm trying to say *there's* the whole secret of life."

"Listen, I don't see the secret," Matthew said.

"Are you a father?"

"Sure, I am."

"Were you a son?"

"Sure, I was."

"Okay."

David nodded and fell silent, as if he had proved his point. He picked up his glass and sipped at it. The silence lengthened.

"Okay what?" Matthew said.

"That's life," David said. "Life is a pattern."

"Life is a fountain," Matthew said, and he burst out laughing.

"Come on, be serious," David said. "You think God is a man?"

"Absolutely," Matthew said.

"Sure, He would have to be," David said, and nodded solemnly.

"But love is a woman," Matthew said, equally as solemn. "And life is love. They're the love givers, don't you ever forget that, David. It's the women who give the love. It's the women who invented it."

"*One* woman," David said.

"Eve."

"No. Gillian."

"More than one woman," Matthew said. "*All* women."

"Look, if you took all the women in the world——"

"Listen," Matthew said, laughing, "if you laid all the Radcliffe girls end to end, I wouldn't be surprised."

"Come on, be serious," David said.

"I'm serious. *All* women," Matthew said. "What does a man need, David, can you tell me that?" He did not wait for David's answer. "Love," he said. "He needs a mother, and a wife, and a daughter. For love. Because they give love. They're the love bringers."

"Mothers," David said, and he pulled a sour face.

"Listen, you need a mother."

"Only until you grow up," David said.

"And *that's* the secret," Matthew said.

"What's the secret?"

"Love."

"The secret is that women are a secret, *that's* the secret."

"The secret is love," Matthew insisted.

"Listen, would you like to pick up some girls?" David asked.

"Can't."

"Why not?"

"I'm an honourable man."

"So?"

"Married."

"So?"

"Couldn't do that to Amanda."

"Matthew," David said sincerely, clapping him on the shoulder "Matthew, drop your scruples."

"Nope. Can't do it."

"Matthew, go home then."

"Got to take you back."

"I'm going to pick up a lady."

"Your mother's worried."

"Tell her to go to . . . go on, Matthew, go home and tell her not to worry. Tell her I can take care of myself *and* her silly automobile, go ahead, Matthew."

"Nope."

"Aw, come on, Matthew, be a good guy."

"You want to crash into a pole, huh?"

"Nossir."

"Okay. Come on. I'll follow you home in my car and see that nothing happens to you."

"That's awfully decent of you, Matthew," David said.

"Don't mention it."

"You're an awfully decent guy, Matthew."

They paid the bartender and staggered away from the bar. Outside, David said, "What's the sense, anyway? Picking up a girl. What's the sense? You know how many girls I've picked up in the last few years?"

"How many?"

"A million."

"That's a lot of girls," Matthew said.

"That sure is a lot of girls, Matthew. And you know something, Matthew? If you put all those girls together, you get one woman, just one single woman."

"That's a very shrewd observation, David."

"Thank you. Will you follow me, or shall I follow you?"

"We'll follow each other," Matthew said, and he giggled.

"No, no," David said. "After you." He executed a low bow.

"No, no," Matthew said.

"I'll *choose* you," David said. "What do you take? Odds or evens?"

"Odds," Matthew said. He clenched his fist.

"Evens," David said.

They faced each other in the darkness of the parking lot, their fists clenched, watching each other shrewdly, staggering a bit.

"Once, twice, three, *shoot!*" Matthew said. He threw out his hand just as David threw out his.

"I can't see the fingers," David said.

"It's mine," Matthew said. "Ready? Once, twice, three, *shoot!*" He looked at the extended fingers. "Yours. Ready? Once, twice, three, *shoot!*" He looked again at the fingers. "What did I have? Odds or evens?"

"Who knows? Listen, Matthew, *I'll* follow *you*, okay?"

"Good. That settles it."

"Good night, Matthew."

"Good night, David. Give my love, okay?"

"Okay."

"That's the secret," Matthew said, and he walked into the night. David watched him a moment, and then waved into the darkness and walked to the Alfa. Love, he thought. That's no secret at all.

"Are you drunk?" Amanda asked.

"Who? Who, me?" Matthew said.

"Oh, Matthew, how did you manage to . . .?"

"Nobody's drunk," he said, "so shhh, shhh, shhh, you'll wake the kiddies."

"Did you find David?"

"I found David."

"Did you take him home?"

"No. I left him to wallow in sin and corruption."

"Matthew, Julia asked you to take him *home*."

"I took him home. I took him home."

"What are you doing there?"

"I'm trying to take off my pants, that's what I'm doing. What does it look like I'm doing?"

"Let me help you," Amanda said. She got out of bed and walked to where he was hopping on one foot.

"Hey, leggo," he said.

"Matthew, stop being so silly. I hate it when you're drunk."

"So who's drunk?"

"You are."

"I can certainly lower my own zipper."

"Move your hand."

"Amanda, do you love me?" he asked seriously.

"Yes. Sit down, Matthew, I'll take off your shoes."

"I want to die with my boots on," he said, and threw himself across the bed.

"Was David as drunk as you are?"

"He was as *sober* as I am," Matthew said with dignity.

"Who drove?"

"We both drove."

"Where did you find him?"

"In a bar."

"Which bar?"

"Who knows? The Bar X."

"Matthew!"

"The Bar Sinister, who knows?" Matthew said, and he laughed. "Iron bars do not a prism make." He laughed again.

Amanda sighed and went to the closet with his trousers. Carefully, she folded them over a hanger. When she turned back to the bed, Matthew was nearly asleep. She went to the bed and took off his socks. Struggling with his long legs, she finally got him under the covers.

"The big brass bed," Matthew mumbled.

"What?"

"Love," he mumbled and rolled over, suddenly opening his eyes. "Hey, he knows Gillian."

"Matthew, will you please . . . ?"

"*David* knows *Gillian*," he said firmly, nodding.

Amanda looked at him in silence for a moment. Then she said, "Where is she?"

"Didn't say."

"Is she in New York?"

"Didn't say."

"Well, Matthew, why didn't you ask him?"

"Because she killed the poor bastard."

"What?"

"Oh, Amanda, would you please shut up?"

"I wonder where she is," Amanda said thoughtfully.

"Asleep, probably, which is . . . where . . . any . . . sensible . . ." and his voice trailed off.

I wonder where she is, Amanda thought, and a sudden pang touched her. She looked at Matthew asleep on the bed, his arm twisted around the pillow. She stood by the bed in her nightgown, and she thought of Gillian, and wondered again where she was, and felt suddenly empty, and thought, You have everything, Amanda, you have a husband and two children and a beautiful house, you have everything. And remembered suddenly a day when her mother had asked her, "Do you have the talent, Amanda?"

She got into bed beside Matthew and lay staring into the darkness for a long time before sleep finally claimed her.

She had heard the Alfa pull into the driveway, had heard her son slamming the door of the car, and then swearing as he stumbled over something in the darkness. She had listened to his noisy progress to the front door, heard him fumbling with his key until he realized the door was unlocked, and then heard more swearing as he made his way to his room. She lay in bed now with the night noises all around her, the sound of the lake, and the sound of a thousand crickets, and she thought, I shouldn't have told him, it does not pay to tell them, I shouldn't have told him.

She had told Arthur in the bedroom of the Talmadge house as they were dressing to go out. She had been sitting before the mirror in her slip when Arthur came in from the bathroom, wearing a robe and drying his head with a towel. She watched him in the mirror as she brushed her hair, counting the strokes, thirty-one, thirty-two, watching Arthur as he hummed and rubbed his head briskly, thirty-three, thirty-four, a smile on his face, throwing the towel on to the bed, turning to look at Julia. She felt a sudden chill in that room. She suddenly knew what was coming. Thirty-six, she put down the brush.

Arthur watched her with his head cocked to one side, humming. She picked up her bottle of nail polish, unscrewed the top, wiped the excess polish on the lip of the bottle, and applied the brush to her left thumb.

"How does it feel to be home?" Arthur asked.

"Wonderful," she answered.

Her hand was trembling. She smeared polish on to her cuticle, wiped it off with a piece of cotton, and then picked up the brush again. She had no reason to believe this would turn into anything more than a normal discussion, and yet she sensed that it would. And sensing it, perhaps willed it. Or perhaps willing it, only then assumed she sensed something out of the ordinary. If only it were over and done with, she thought. If only the duplicity were finished. She should not have come back at all. The boy, the boy, David, ah yes, a mother cannot simply vanish. She sighed and concentrated on her nails, steadily applying the blood-red polish in a smooth even coat.

Arthur walked to the dressing-table. He watched her in the mirror.

"You smell good," he said. "I forgot what you smelled like. I'd know you were back in the house again, Julia, if only by the scent of your perfume and cosmetics. Even if I couldn't see you. Even if I couldn't touch you." He raised his hands and put them on her naked shoulders, lightly, gently.

"Don't."

He did not answer. He met her eyes in the mirror. She lowered them quickly.

"I'm polishing my nails. I don't want to smear them."

He did not remove his hands from her shoulders. She ignored him studiously, but she could feel the weight of his hands on her, even though he exerted no pressure, even though they rested there so lightly, she could feel their weight. She concentrated on her nails, refusing to meet his eyes in the mirror, refusing to acknowledge the weight of his hands on her shoulders. He stood behind her silently, unmoving, as if challenging her to reject him, as if waiting silently and stiffly for her to say "Don't!" once more.

"Aren't you going to dress?" she asked casually.

"It's only seven-thirty," Arthur said. "We're not due for an hour."

"Have you shaved already?"

"Yes."

"Still, don't you think . . ."

"I can be ready in five minutes."

"It'll take me much longer than that."

"I've seen you dress very quickly when you wanted to," Arthur said. His hands were still on her shoulders.

"Yes, but this is the first time I've seen the McGregors in a year. I think I should——"

"We have plenty of time," Arthur said. "In fact, Julia, I don't even know why we're going."

"They're our friends," Julia said.

"Yes, I know that."

"And I haven't seen them since——"

"Yes, and you haven't seen me since last Christmas."

"That's right."

"You've been home for a week, Julia."

The hand holding the brush had begun trembling again. She did not answer him. She held out her painted hand and looked at the finger-tips.

"Aren't you glad to be home, Julia?"

"Why Arthur, of course I am."

"Aren't you glad to see me?"

"I'm delighted to see you, Arthur."

She turned her shoulders slightly, trying to dislodge his hands without seeming to. But his hands remained where they were, following the motion of her shoulders, and she said, "Please, Arthur."

"What the hell is wrong, Julia?"

"I'm trying to do my nails."

"I'm not talking about your nails. I want to know what's wrong. I'm your husband, Julia. We've been apart since——"

"Arthur," she said, and this time she shrugged his hands away with a very definite forceful shrug. "There are certain natural female functions over which I have no——"

"You've been home for a week, Julia. I may be a poor mathematician, but you've been home for a full week."

"That's right," she said calmly.

"That's right, Julia."

"Yes, that's right."

She thought for an instant how stupid they both sounded, and she fought for control of the silence that had descended on the room, and she knew that the next words had to be hers, that the conversation had moved to an impasse, and she wondered suddenly why he was forcing the issue. She turned slowly on the dressing-stool.

Slowly, her words evenly spaced, she said, "What is it you want, Arthur?" as if she were delivering a slap.

He did not answer, and she respected his silence. There was a strength in his silence and the set of his jaw. She respected him, but she would not let it go.

"Do you want me to take off my clothes, Arthur?"

He still would not answer.

"Well, I'm sorry," she said, and she turned back to the mirror and picked up an emery board.

"All right, tell me," Arthur said.

"We're going to be late. I hate walking into a———"

"The hell with the goddam dinner-party, Julia! Tell me."

"Tell you *what*, Arthur? Just what do you want me to tell you?"

"What happened in Aquila?"

"Nothing."

"Then what happened in Rome?"

"Nothing."

"Then where *did* it happen, Julia?"

"Where did *what* happen?" She turned on the stool angrily, her eyes flashing, furious because he had guessed, and wanting him to know, yet enraged because he already knew, and refusing to tell him, and feeling hopelessly embroiled in a stupid situation that he alone had provoked. "Just what do you *imagine* happened?" She looked up into his face defiantly.

"I . . . I don't know," Arthur said hesitantly.

"Then stop accusing me!" She stood up suddenly and walked to the closet. Angrily, she pulled a dress from one of the hangers.

"I . . . I wasn't accusing you, Julia. I simply felt———"

"You simply felt that because I didn't want———"

"Julia, Julia . . ."

"I suppose that whenever you get the damn———"

"No, but, Julia . . ."

"Then let it go, damn it!" She turned on him, the dress in one hand, her eyes blazing, and she saw the sudden embarrassment on his face. He's going to back down, she thought. He only wanted assurance. He only wanted to know I still love him. Tell him, she thought. Tell him you love him. Tell him you want him. Tell him.

Her eyes narrowed.

"Yes," she said. "It happened in Rome."

He didn't answer for a moment. He looked at her, puzzled, and he shook his head slightly, not understanding, or not willing to understand.

"In Rome," she repeated.

"What are you . . .?"

"With an Italian soldier."

"Don't, Julia." He turned away.

"Whom I loved," she said.

"Don't."

"Whom I still love."

"Don't."

"Who's waiting for me to——"

He turned swiftly and sharply, like a prisoner who has withstood the flailing of his torturer for too long, who regardless of consequence would proclaim his manhood, proclaim his humanity, state that there is still dignity here in this destroyed heap of flesh, he turned swiftly and sharply and said, "Don't!" again, like a defiant whimper, and lashed out at her with his right hand, slapping her face.

She did not raise her hand to block the blow. She did not touch her stinging face after the blow was delivered. She stared at him in the silence of the room, and she said, "Yes."

Arthur sighed. His hand dropped slowly.

"Yes, I deserved that," she said.

The room was silent.

"But it doesn't change anything," she said. "It's too late to change anything," and she told it all then, told everything while he sat foolishly on her dressing-table stool with his head bent, and his hands clasped and hanging between his knees, almost touching the floor, told him all of it, while he sat listening and not listening, told him what had happened and what was yet to happen, while he listened soundlessly with his eyes squeezed shut.

"I'm going back to Rome as soon as the war is over," she said.

She paused.

"I'm taking David with me," she said.

"Yes, leave nothing," he answered. "Take everything, and leave nothing. Total up seventeen years of marriage with a zero."

"I'm sorry. A woman needs her children."

"Yes, certainly. And that does it. I'm sorry. That explains everything. I'm sorry. Forgive me for killing you. That is what separates men from animals. The two words 'I'm sorry.' This is what gives men the nobility our novelists are always trying to express, the wonderful nobility of man, I'm sorry. Yes, be very sorry, Julia. You should be."

She said nothing.

"I wish I could curse you. I wish I could say . . ." He shook his head. "You don't seem like a slut," he said almost to himself. He wiped his hand over his eyes, and then passed the hand downward over his face, disguising the action. He was silent for a very long time. Then he lifted his head, and looked directly into her eyes, and very quietly said, "Stay."

She did not answer.

"Stay, Julia. If not for me, then for——"

"No."

"——your son."

"My child," she said.

"David," he answered. "Your son."

"I'm going back to Rome. I have to. You know I have to."

"And me? What about me, Julia?"

"I . . . I can't . . . I can't think about that, Arthur."

"No, don't think about it. Do you know what will happen to me, Julia?" He paused. "I'll die."

"No."

"Yes, Julia. I swear to you, Julia. I'll die, or I'll kill myself, I can't——"

"Please," she said. "Please don't make this any harder than——"

"Please! Please? Who? *Who* is pleading? How can you look at a corpse and say, 'Please, please, don't let me realize I killed you'? What do you want, Julia? A clean conscience besides?"

He did not bother to wipe at his eyes again. The tears ran down his face. He sniffed and said, "No, don't ask me for that, Julia. Not absolution. You're taking my life, and that's enough."

"I won't ask you for anything," she said. "And you won't do anything foolish, either."

"It won't be foolish, Julia. You killed me when you said, 'Yes, it happened in Rome.' That was death. The rest is only ritual." He sniffed and said, "I haven't cried in all the time we've been married, have I?"

"No," she said.

He nodded. "Because I wanted your respect." He sniffed. "I'm sorry." He searched for a handkerchief in the pocket of his robe, found none. "Well," he said. He gave a curious shrug. "Well, you'll have the boy."

"Thank you, Arthur."

"Yes." He nodded. "You'll have the boy."

There was something more in his words, unspoken, yet how could she have really known, there was so much confusion that day. "You'll have the boy" sounded like a promise, not a threat, and yet he had said, "I'll die, or I'll kill myself." Still, how could she have known? And at the lake, the look in his eyes, did she know then, did she know what he was about to do in that rowboat, did she even suspect? She tried to remember, but that day, too, was confused in her memory. Perhaps she *had* known that day at Lake Abundance, when the shutter clicked and the boat edged away from the dock, known she was sending her husband to his death, and let him go because this was the only thing left to him. Perhaps she didn't stop him because she had taken everything else, robbed him of everything else, and now she couldn't steal from him the one thing left, the one thing he could still do with a measure of dignity and pride. Perhaps she didn't stop him because she wasn't that big a bitch yet.

She listened to David snoring in the room next door, listened to the impersonal lake outside lapping at the dock pilings. The night was so still.

She lay alone in the night.

Alone.

The letter had come a few days before Memorial Day in 1943. Her son was in a naval prison, and she was waiting for the war to end, and the letter came in its hesitant Italian hand. She had turned it over to look at the flap, and had seen the name Francesca Cristo, his sister. Hastily, she had ripped open the envelope. The letter spoke of Renato, the letter told what had happened during an Allied bombing attack on the seaplane base at Lido di Roma, fifteen miles south-west of Rome.

"*Mi dispiace che tocca a me di dirtelo, sorella mia, ma egli é morto.*"

I am sorry that it falls on me to have to tell you, my sister, but he is dead.

It was a lovely day, the kind of day David appreciated. Standing by the window in his office, he looked down the twelve floors to the street, saw newspapers sweeping along the gutters on Madison Avenue, the only falling leaves south of Central Park, saw topcoats whipping about the legs of people who rushed into the wind with their heads ducked. There was a pace to the city now that fall was here. Summer died slowly, gins-and-tonics dulled the senses, languid winds lulled the flesh, but in the fall something changed. He smiled and turned away from the window. *The New York Times*, *Herald-Tribune*, *News*, and *Mirror* were stacked on his desk. He glanced at the headlines only cursorily, PRESIDENT INVOKES TAFT ACT IN MOVE TO END PIER STRIKE; SEE PIER STRIKE END BY T-H BAN, and then turned to the television sections and read the reviews of last night's show. Not too bad. Gould and Crosby had liked it, even if . . .

"David?"

He looked up. "Yes, Martha?"

"You've got an appointment at ten with Mr. Harrigan. You haven't forgotten that, have you?"

"No, I haven't . . ."

"Good. On those calls . . ."

"Yes, how'd you make out with M.C.A.?"

"We really did leave that name off the crawl, David."

"How'd that happen?"

"I'm checking it now."

"Well, there isn't much we can do about it, anyway."

"No, but I can send them the cockroach letter."

"Okay, what about that judge?"

"David, he's merely a municipal court judge, you know that, don't you?"

"Yes, I do."

"Do you think he'll be okay?"

"Sure, he's only window-dressing, anyway. It's a strong enough show without him."

"Why not?"

"It might offend him."

"Not if we offer enough."

"Well, whatever you say," Martha said dubiously. "Let me see. Was there anything else?"

"Benton and Bowles."

"Oh, yes. They want to consider the package a little longer, David. They have the feeling a live show would be better for this particular product."

"What's live or filmed got to do with it, would you mind telling me?"

"I'm only repeating what they——"

"Get me MacAllister. No, never mind, it's only ten. Listen, I don't want to spend more than a half-hour with this Harrigan. Come in at ten-thirty and remind me of a meeting, will you?"

"There *is* a meeting at eleven," Martha said. "In Mr. Sonderman's office. And you've got a screening this afternoon at four. You haven't forgotten that, have you?"

"And I hoped to catch an early train!"

"Are you going up to Talmadge this week-end?"

"Yep. It's my birthday."

"No! *When's* your birthday? The fourteenth is your birthday."

"The fourth, Martha. Sunday."

"Oh, for hell's sake . . . Oh, that's awful. Really, David, that's awful. Why didn't you say something?"

"I took a full page in *Variety*. You mean you didn't see it?"

"Now what shall I do?" Martha said. "I haven't anything to give you. I thought it was the fourteenth."

"You can give me a great big kiss," David said.

"All right," Martha answered, smiling. "Your place or mine?"

"Mine, I guess."

"Now or later?"

"Later. I think I heard someone outside."

"Mr. Harrigan, probably. Shall I send him right in?"

"Just give me a few minutes to clear my desk."

"Okay. Happy birthday, stinker. You *could* have said something."

She walked out of the office, and he watched her smiling, thinking how much he liked her and how fortunate he was to have rescued her from the typing pool. Martha Wilkins was a woman in her early thirties, married to an architect, a plain girl who wore her simplicity with such distinction that she created an impression of off-beat glamour. Her dark hair was straight and long in a time when most other women were clipping off their locks with wild boyish abandon. She never wore lipstick to the office, and some of the Sonderman wags claimed she kept her mouth cosmetics-free in order to facilitate the grabbing of a quick kiss by the water-cooler. David had never tested the validity of this theory—and he never would. Their working relationship was too good, a quick give-and-take which he found rare, an understanding, a communication that bordered on linguistic and mental shorthand. *The cockroach letter*, he thought, and then smiled as he remembered the joke that had provoked the Regan-Wilkins label.

The joke involved a man who was flying on a major airline when a cockroach crawled up the side of his seat and on to his hand. The man indignantly sent a letter to the airline the moment he landed in San Francisco. A few days later, he received a letter from the president of the firm, assuring him that the pilot and co-pilot on that particular flight had been suspended pending a full investigation, that the stewardess had been fired without further ado, and that the caterers who provided food for the airline had been notified that their contract would not be renewed when it expired.

"We are distressed about that cockroach, sir," the letter went on. "It is the first one ever reported in the long history of our company. We are doing everything in our power to see that responsible and effective action in the future prevents any such vermin from being carried aboard our aeroplanes or remaining there. I sincerely hope you will overlook whatever embarrassment or discomfort the incident may have caused you, and continue to fly with us in safety whenever your needs so dictate. Sincerely yours, J. Abernathy Michaelson, President."

The passenger, naturally, was very pleased when he finished reading the letter from the president of the airline. Beaming, he figured he had wrongly judged that fine company, and he was determined to fly with no one else in the future. But as he was putting the president's letter back into the envelope, a small slip of paper fluttered to the floor. He picked it up. It was a memorandum from the president, obviously intended for his secretary. It read: SEND THIS SON OF A BITCH THE COCKROACH LETTER.

David and Martha had heard the story together and roared convulsively when the punch line was delivered. And from that day on, any conciliatory letter, any letter of placation or apology, any letter designed to smooth the ruffled feathers of anyone Out There, was immediately referred to by both of them as The Cockroach Letter. M.C.A. who had complained about last night's credit crawl, would receive a cockroach letter in the morning. David smiled again. Your place or mine? he thought. Now or later? Martha Wilkins. He liked her.

A knock sounded on his door.

"Come in," he said.

Martha entered first, swinging the door wide.

"Mr. Harrigan is here, sir," she said.

"Thank you, Martha," David answered, and he rose and walked around his desk, extending his hand to the bulky man who entered the office.

"Mr. Regan?" the man said, taking his hand.

"Yes, sir. How do you do?"

"Fine, thank you."

Martha winked at David as she went out of the office. David indicated a chair alongside his desk and Harrigan sat in it. He was a heavy-set man in his middle fifties with grey hair and dark-blue eyes. He wore a pencil-stripe suit, double-breasted, and he carried a dark-grey topcoat over his arm, a black Homburg in his left hand. He sat as soon as the chair was offered, pulling his trousers up slightly as he bent to sit, preserving the creases. He was from California, and his voice showed it.

"I hope you had a nice trip," David said.

"I did," Harrigan answered.

"Did you fly in?"

"I don't trust aeroplanes," Harrigan said. "I took the train."

"That's a long trip."

"Yes, it is."

"What brings you to New York, Mr. Harrigan?"

Harrigan looked surprised. He put his Homburg down. "You," he said.

"Me?"

"At least I understand you're the man who produces our show," Harrigan said.

"Yes, I am," David answered, puzzled.

He had received a call from the advertising agency the day before, telling him that Mr. Harrigan would be in New York and would like to see David, and would David please extend every courtesy to him since Harrigan did represent the company who sponsored the Thursday-night hour-long dramatic show. David had no idea what sort of courtesies were expected of him. In some cases, "every courtesy" meant dinner, tickets to a show, and a little discreet female companionship. But the agency had been somewhat vague about Harrigan's visit, and now it seemed he had come to New York specifically to see David, and this puzzled him, and also worried him a bit. The show they packaged for Thursday-night viewing was a big one. It had been sponsored by Harrigan's firm ever since it went on the air the season before. David produced the show, and the ratings were high, and he'd thought the sponsor was pleased with what he was doing. But if that was the case, why would Harrigan . . . now, wait a minute, he told himself. Let's not push the panic button. He offered Harrigan a cigarette.

"Thank you," Harrigan said. "I don't smoke."

"Mind if I do?"

"It's your funeral."

David lighted a cigarette, mulling over Harrigan's last words, beginning to get even more worried. "You said you'd come to New York to see *me*, Mr. Harrigan?"

"Yes. About our show."

"We've been getting some very high ratings," David said casually. "Last night, we even outpulled——"

"Yes, the ratings are fine," Harrigan said. "We're very pleased."

David smiled a trifle uneasily. If the ratings pleased Harrigan, then what was it that bothered him? He took a deep breath and said, "I think the *quality* of the show, as a whole——"

"Well, quality is a very nice thing to have," Harrigan said, "but not unless it sells tickets."

"It's selling tickets for you people," David said grinning. "I understand sales are up some 15 per cent since the show went——"

"Yes, that's true. And we want to *keep* selling tickets. I've heard a theory about television shows, Mr. Regan. I've heard that when a show is too good, when the people are too absorbed in what's happening on that screen, they resent the intrusion of the sponsor's message, actually build up a resistance to the product. This theory holds that the duller the show is, the better it is for the product."

"Well, I don't know how valid——"

"Naturally, we're not interested in dull shows," Harrigan said. "It's the business of the advertising agency we hire to make our commercials interesting enough to compete with the liveliest dramatic presentation."

"And they've been doing a fine job," David said, figuring a plug for the ad agency wouldn't hurt at all.

"Yes, and they're happy with the package you're giving them, too."

"Then I guess everyone's happy all around," David said, beginning to relax a little. "We've got a good show, with a Trendex topping——"

"Yes, and we want to stay happy," Harrigan said. "As you know, it's not our policy to interfere in the selection of dramatic material for the show."

"You've certainly given us all the latitude——"

"Yes, we usually see only a synopsis of the script, and aside from certain very minor objections, we've been very tolerant of your choice of material and your manner of presentation. I think you're a bunch of smart creative people up here at Sonderman, Mr. Regan. We are, in fact, thinking of asking you to work up another package for us."

"That's very kind of you, sir."

"Yes, but that's all in the future, and what we've got to talk about now is a script called 'The Brothers'."

"'The Bro——' oh, yes. That's two weeks away, sir. Goes into rehearsal next Friday."

"Yes, I know. I saw a synopsis of the script a little while ago, and I asked our advertising agency to get me a copy of the completed teleplay, and they sent me one last week, and that was when I decided I had better come to New York."

"We're getting a judge to introduce that show, you know. We think it'll add another dimension to it, and point up the allegory."

"Yes, that's very interesting. It's always good to do allegories, especially if they're clear. And this happens to be an unusually fine script, Mr. Regan, make no mistake about it. I'd like you to get more material from this same writer in the future."

"That's easy enough," David said, smiling.

"Yes, the allegory is very plain, and very fine, especially in these trying days of world tension. A wonderful script. I understand you've got two excellent actors for the parts."

"We were very lucky, Mr. Harrigan. A Broadway show folded last week, and the actors——"

"Yes, and I understand you'll be doing a chase scene right on the streets, by remote pick-up, is that right?"

"That's right, sir."

"Yes, it sounds wonderful. A magnificent show."

"Thank you, sir."

"But we can't do it, of course."

"Sir?"

"I said we can't do it."

"You said . . ." David hesitated. He stubbed out his cigarette. "What did you say, sir?"

"Impossible, Mr. Regan. Believe me, I've gone over it thoroughly. I've even considered a rewrite, but the entire framework is based on——"

"I don't understand," David said. "Why *can't* we do it?"

"Tickets," Harrigan said.

"But it's a good show. You just said——"

"Yes, but one man in the show is a lawbreaker, and the other is a policeman who actually condones his lawlessness."

"He doesn't do that at all," David said. "He understands it. The whole point of the show is . . . is . . . it's a plea for understanding. Why, even the title of the show is 'The Brothers'. Don't you see what——?"

"Oh, yes, *I* see, Mr. Regan. And you see. But will our viewers see?"

"Of course they will."

"We think not. We think they will associate our product with an attitude which seems to condone lawlessness."

"That's nonsense," David said.

Harrigan stiffened slightly in his chair. "Yes, of course it's nonsense. But if our product becomes associated with——"

"The possibility is extremely remote," David said, "if not nonexistent. We're not dealing with a bunch of boobs, Mr. Harrigan. The message is as clear as——"

"Mr. Regan, if we allow this show to be done, and if it is misunderstood, we will never sell another ticket as long as we're in business."

"How can anyone misunderstand it?"

"The show seems to condone murder."

"The murder has nothing at all to do with it! If it's the murder that bothers you, we'll change it. We'll——"

"To what? To another crime? How would that be any different? Mr. Regan, I have gone over this quite thoroughly, believe me."

"Look, it's a good show," David said, a surprised tone in his voice. "It's a really good show. Now look, we've . . . look, we've got two big stars, you couldn't ask for bigger names, they'll play beautifully together. Look, Mr. Harrigan, we've got one of the best directors in television. And those remote pick-ups'll knock the viewer right on his——"

"I'm sorry, we'll have to substitute another show for it."

"We've already paid for the script," David said in desperation. "We've signed contracts with the actors. The network——"

"We will honour whatever commitments you have made," Harrigan said, "but we will not do this show."

"What are you afraid of? The network's continuity section has approved it already. A *judge* has read it and is willing to introduce it. I don't see what you're worried——"

"None of those people have to sell tickets, Mr. Regan."

"Your own advertising agency approved it!"

"Yes, and I'll be talking to them as soon as I leave this office."

"Really, Mr. Harrigan, this is silly. With all due respect, sir, I think you're being over sensitive."

"Yes, and with all due respect, I really feel the decision is ours to make, and not yours."

"I'm sorry, but I can't agree with you."

"Then I suppose I shall have to talk to Mr. Sonderman himself."

"If you think that's . . ." David paused. "Why does he have to be brought in? This is my show."

"This is *his* company."

"I have full authority over any show I handle."

"Yes, but apparently you're refusing to exercise it."

"You're asking me to kill a good show! You're telling me our viewers are morons! That they won't understand what we're driving at, that they'll come away thinking we're asking them to go out and shoot people. Well, damn it, I disagree. They will understand it, they will know what we mean, and they'll applaud us for our stand. Look, the hell with it. Go see Curt. Let him handle it."

"Very well. Is Mr. Sonderman in now?"

"I think so. I'll have my secretary buzz him." David reached for the phone.

"I'm sorry this is causing so much trouble," Harrigan said. He glanced at his watch. "I had hoped it would be a simple matter."

"It's a simple matter of knowing what's good for your product," David said. "This would get your product *talked* about. It's a good show, Mr. Harrigan!"

"Would you call Mr. Sonderman's office, please?" Harrigan said.

David picked up the phone.

"I'm sure he will see this my way," Harrigan said.

David hesitated.

"And while I'm in there," Harrigan said, "I might as well discuss that new package with him."

David buzzed Martha. "It's a good show," he said to Harrigan, his voice low.

"Ah, but I know it is, Mr. Regan. You misunderstand me completely."

Martha's voice came on to the line.

"Yes, David?" she asked.

"Martha, would you . . ." He paused. He looked at Harrigan.

"Yes?" Martha said.

"Nothing," he said. "Never mind." He put the phone gently into its cradle. He stared at his hand covering the receiver. "We've got a script being rewritten," he said. "It's about a second honeymoon. We'd planned it for three weeks from now. I suppose I can speed up the writer."

"I suppose you can."

"There may be casting problems. We may not be able to get a star on such short notice."

"I'm sure you will surmount whatever problems may arise, Mr. Regan." Harrigan rose and extended his hand. "I'm not a stupid man, Mr. Regan. I know what's good for our company, and I know what's bad." He paused. "The same way you know what's good or bad for yours." He shook hands briefly and firmly. "Good day. I'm glad we were able to work this out."

David nodded and walked Harrigan to the door.

"Good-bye," he said.

Then he closed the door and walked back to the window and looked down at the street where autumn raced.

His decision annoyed him all that afternoon.

It seemed to him that he had broken faith with a great many people by agreeing to cancel the show. He had certainly broken faith with the writers and the actors, and possibly Curt, too. He tried to visualize the scene in Curt's office, Harrigan indignantly marching down the corridor to the end of the hall, stamping into Curt's panelled sanctuary, and stating, "I have just had a discussion with Mr. Regan about cancelling our Thursday-night show two weeks hence. Mr. Regan disagrees with me. I would like you to handle the matter personally.

What would Curt's reaction have been?

Would he have politely but positively told Mr. Harrigan to go to hell? Would he have reminded him that Mr. Regan was a full-fledged producer with full authority over his own shows and that the final decision would have to be his alone? And would he have also told Mr. Harrigan that he, Curt Sonderman, believed in this particular script and would back Mr. Regan all the way on whatever decision he finally made?

Sure, he would.

The president of Sonderman Enterprises, Inc., would have listened to Harrigan and nodded his fat head and thought about the new package deal being dangled before his eyes, and then he would have gone out to shoot his own grandmother if Harrigan suggested it. And then Martha would have buzzed David and said very quietly, "Mr. Sonderman wants to see you," and David would have gone down that long hall and into the panelled office, and had his ear chewed off about client-producer relationships and the importance of maintaining a cordial liaison with the sponsor. But would that have been the end of it? Possibly, and possibly not.

He had always thought the stories about Madison Avenue head-rolling and back-stabbing were slightly exaggerated until he found himself in a spacious corner office at Sonderman Enterprises, Inc., on Madison Avenue, until he found the word PRODUCER discreetly lettered in gold on his door, and then suddenly knew that if success rarely arrived overnight, it almost always departed that way. Too many familiar faces, too many men and women vanished from the scene, if not the industry, as soon as they committed the single error too many. Antagonizing Harrigan would have been a monumental error. For all David knew, even his initial reluctance to cancel might still bring repercussions. No, defending a single unimportant —well, it was important to *somebody*, it was important to the man who'd written it, and the director who'd pulled it apart line by line, and the actors who were already studying their parts—still, defending a single unimportant show in a successful continuing series would have been taking the silliest sort of risk. Yes, he had done the right thing.

Then why did he feel so lousy?

"What time is that screening?" he asked Martha.

"Four o'clock."

"It's almost that now. Why didn't you give me a warning? I've still got a dozen calls to make."

"I told you this morning, David."

"How am I supposed to remember something you told me this——"

"Hey, take it easy, birthday boy. This is me, Martha Washington. Tony's on the line. Wants to know whether it's true the show has been cancelled."

"Tell him yes, the show has been cancelled."

"It was a good show, David."

"Are you starting on me, too?"

"I only said——"

"I heard what you said. Where's the screening?"

"In 1204."

"I'll be there if you need me."

"All right. Do you want me to make those calls for you?"

"I'll handle them myself when I get back. You've got a run."

"What?" Martha glanced at her nylons. "Oh, damn it," she said, "goddam it," and she seemed on the verge of tears over something as simple as a run in her stocking.

The agent's name was Ed Goff. He was waiting in room 1204 when David got there. He rose and extended his hand.

"Goff," he said. "I think we've spoken on the phone."

"How do you do?" David said. "What have you got for me?"

"A pilot. We thought Sonderman, Inc. might be interested in handling it for us. It's pretty good, if I say so myself."

"Why bring it to us? If you've already laid out thirty to forty grand to shoot a pilot——"

"No, no, nothing like that. This was part of a deal for an anthology. My clients——"

"Who?"

"Ralph Mordkin and Dave Katz. You know them?"

"I've heard of them."

"Sure, well they produced five out of thirty-nine shows for this anthology. Filmed stuff, you understand. They thought this particular one would make a good series. So we added titles and some theme music and we're showing it as a pilot. I think you'll like it. It's pretty good, if I say so myself."

"You already said so yourself."

"What?" Goff blinked. "Oh, yeah."

"What kind of a show is it?"

"Private eye."

"Another 'Man Against Crime'?"

"Yeah, exactly like it, only different. This is pretty good if I——" Goff cut himself short. "Why don't we run it, huh? You can see for yourself."

"What kind of deal did you have in mind, Goff?"

"Well, we can talk about that after we see the show, huh?"

"Let's talk now, and maybe save a half-hour of each other's time."

"You had a rough day, Mr. Regan?"

"Are you my doctor, Mr. Goff?"

"No, but I want a fair showing. If you're not feeling so hot, let's call it off until another time."

"I'm feeling hot enough," David said. "I asked what kind of deal you had in mind."

"Fifty-fifty?" Goff asked tentatively.

"We couldn't consider anything less than sixty-forty. *If* it's good. If it's what it sounds like, our cut would have to be even——"

"What do you mean, what it *sounds* like? I haven't even given you the title of the thing. How do you know what it sounds like?"

"You said it was private eye, didn't you?"

"So what's wrong with that?"

"Television needs another private eye like a hole in the head. This is 1953, Goff. Private eyes are on their way out. Television's growing up."

"Look, take a peek at it, will you? It's a good show. Quality."

"Private eyes are trash."

"Yeah, but this is *quality* trash. Look, can we run it?"

"All right, let's run it," David said.

They turned out the lights and sat in the leather-upholstered chairs facing the mock television set at the front of the screening room. The movie projector inside the set began to whir, and the film flashed on to the fake television tube, just the way it would be seen in a viewer's living-room. David made himself comfortable. The leader flashed, six, five, four, three, two, one on to the screen. The theme music started.

KIN-KAT PRODUCTIONS
presents
JOHNNY THUNDER

THEME UP. SUPERIMP TITLES OVER STOCK SHOT
SUNSET STRIP. SNEAK SIREN INTO THEME.
OPEN CONVERTIBLE SEEN RACING THROUGH
BEVERLY HILLS, PULLING UP BEFORE BIG OLD
HOUSE AS TITLES END. THEME OUT.

FADE IN

1 INT. JOHNNY THUNDER'S OFFICE - DAY - FULL   1
SHOT - JOHNNY THUNDER SEATED IN CHAIR
BEHIND DESK. OLIVER FIELDS SITTING IN
CLIENT'S CHAIR. OFFICE IS ON GROUND FLOOR
OF OLD "WHITE ELEPHANT" TYPE HOUSE IN
BEVERLY HILLS. HUGE WINDING STAIRCASE
SWEEPS UP FROM RIGHT, RISING OFF CAMERA.

THUNDER
I'm not sure I understand this,
Mr. Fields. You claim your
brother is trying to kill you, is
that correct?

FIELDS
My <u>twin</u> brother, that is correct.

                    THUNDER
            And what's his name?

2   CLOSE SHOT - FIELDS - SADNESS AND DES-   2
    PERATION ON HIS FACE
                    FIELDS
            Anthony. We should have had names
            beginning with the same letter,
            don't you think? But my mother
            tried to raise us as if we weren't
            twins, and she started with our
            names. Oliver and Anthony. I
            always liked his name better, to
            tell the truth. Anthony.

3   MEDIUM SHOT - FIELDS AND THUNDER - THUNDER   3
    IS JOTTING NOTES ON HIS DESK PAD.
                    THUNDER
            Yes, go ahead, Mr. Fields. You
            won't mind if I call my secretary
            in, will you? I'd like her to
            take this down accurately.
                    FIELDS
            No, not at all. I want you to get
            it accurately. After all, my life
            is at stake.

4   CLOSE SHOT - THUNDER   4
                    THUNDER
                (Calling to someone o. s.)
            Bess! Bess, would you come down-
            stairs a moment, please?

5   CAMERA PANS BACK SLOWLY TO REVEAL THE   5
    GROUND FLOOR OF THE HUGE HOUSE AND THE
    UNIQUE OFFICE ARRANGEMENT OF THUNDER
    INVESTIGATIONS, HIS DESK IN ONE CORNER OF
    THE LARGE ENTRANCE HALL, THE STAIRCASE
    SWEEPING OFF TO THE UPPER STORIES.
    CAMERA HOLDS ON STAIRCASE, THEN BEGINS
    PANNING UPWARD TO CATCH THE LEGS OF BESS
    CARTER AS SHE STARTS DOWN THE STEPS. THESE
    ARE GOOD LEGS IN NYLONS, HIGH-HEELED
    PUMPS, SHORTISH BLACK SKIRT.

6   CLOSE SHOT – BESS CARTER'S LEGS AS CAMERA   6
CATCHES THEM AT TOP OF STAIRCASE, KEEPS
FOLLOWING HER DOWN, <u>HOLDING ON</u> HER LEGS AS
SHE COMES DOWN THE STEPS.

David recognized the legs. He told himself it was impossible to recognize a person by her legs alone, but he knew those legs in an instant, knew them the moment they flashed on to the screen, the moment the camera panned up that long sweeping Beverly Hills staircase to catch the girl's legs on the first landing, knew instantly from the walk, knew from the way one foot followed the other, the narrowness of ankle, the curve of her calf, even the thighs beneath the black skirt, he knew those legs. He watched the girl come down the steps, watched her legs as if they provided all the suspense, a suspense more exciting than the quality trash Mordkin and Katz, Kin-Kat Productions, had assembled out of a trunkful of 1930 Black Mask novelettes. The girl was walking into a medium shot, legs giving way to hips and waist and bosom. David wiped his hand across his mouth. The camera was pulling in tight on the girl's face, she was walking directly into another close shot, that mouth, the green eyes, colour leaped from the black-and-white screen, he could see russet hair in black-and-white, the same bangs, the same sleek mane brushed to the nape of her neck, the same defiant thrust of lip and nose and . . .

"Gillian Burke," Goff whispered beside him. "Maybe you know her from that underwater series she did."

"I know her," David said. His voice came in a whisper. He was suddenly covered with sweat.

He sat watching her. He listened to her voice. She sounded much the same, that same wonderful voice that was Gillian's alone, he almost began to weep when she said the word "*marr*-vellous," rolling her r's like an Irish washerwoman, she seemed to have lost a little weight, there was a good sparkle in her eyes, he watched her and listened to her. She was the only person on the screen. She pranced through the inanities of the script like a pro in a high-school senior play, she moved through that empty charade like a queen, and his eyes never left her for a moment. And while she worked hell out of a witless script, he watched another drama unfolding in his mind's eye, the drama that had been Gillian and him, and he felt an empty sadness because the real Gillian was as far away from him as was the celluloid Gillian whose image was cast on the blank glass square resembling a television tube. He wanted to speak to her, wanted to say, "How have you been, Gilly? What have you been doing? Are you in love, Gilly? Have you found someone else?" but the girl on the screen was named Bess Carter, his Gillian in a Bess Carter costume, and the girl mouthed absurd clichés, played the private eye's superglossed secretary, the wise-cracking playmate of the hard-drinking, two-fisted, fast-shooting, quick-thinking Johnny Thunder. And yet Gillian showed through, the warmth of Gillian, and the incredible beauty of Gillian, and Bess Carter came alive because of her, Bess Carter romped through the insipid dialogue and the ridiculous action but she was warm and alive and sympathetic and lovable because Bess Carter was only a part pulled over the head of Gillian Burke.

The reel came to an end. The blank glass face in the phony television set was blank again. The lights snapped on.

"How'd you like it?" Goff asked.

"I liked the girl."

"Burke. Great girl. We've already signed her for the series."

"*If* you sell the pilot."

"Naturally. There's no series unless we sell the pilot." Goff paused. "What do you think, Mr. Regan?"

He thought too many things in the few moments before he answered. He thought, It's a crummy pilot, but maybe we can place it. He thought, I would probably get to see Gillian again, I'd *have* to if Sonderman were packaging the thing. I'd have to fly out to the Coast once or twice, wouldn't I? I'd have to meet the people in the show, I'd have to watch some of the shooting. It's a crummy pilot, he thought.

What's the use? he thought.

What the hell is the goddam use? What's the use, because the world always closes in on you. The world is full of people like George Devereaux and Mike Arretti and Mr. Harrigan from California who takes the train in, I don't trust aeroplanes, and who puts his foot on the back of your neck and squeezes you thin like a cockroach, send this son of a bitch the cockroach letter, what's the use? The world was full of spoilers, yes, and some of them were named David Regan, at least one of them was named David Regan, what's the use? You could see Gillian again maybe, you could okay this quality trash, you could commit your firm to a year's option and you could break your back trying to sell the pilot to a network and an agency, you'd be giving Gillian a break, but it's a lousy show.

Yes, let's start worrying about lousy shows and good shows. The Sam Martin spectacle was certainly a terrific show, and you were its chief office boy and bottle washer, that was a magnificent show. As was the science fiction presentation every Wednesday night at 7.30 p.m. on a channel featuring wrestling, assistant to the producer, David Regan, that was a tremendous little show, so let's start worrying about what's lousy and what's good. The afternoon live soap-opera was wonderful, too, associate producer, David Regan, and so was the first real show you produced, the half-hour filmed Monday-night thing, that *really* was a masterpiece, so let's turn up our noses at a private-eye show that has already signed the only girl who ever meant anything to you in your life, let's turn arty and, it *is* good, my Thursday night show *is* good, yes, but what did Harrigan do to you this morning, what did Harrigan force you to do, so let's get arty, right? You stepped on a good story, you knuckled under to the money, so now let's suddenly find scruples when it involves a continuing series for Gillian, David Regan, with the neat gold-lettered PRODUCER on the door.

Yes, who squashed a good script this morning.

Producer.

With scruples. Big-scrupled producer. Go on, take the pilot. Tell Goff you'll handle it on a 65-35 split and he'll kiss both your feet and buy his clients a magnum of champagne. Tell him the girl stays, tell him the girl whose image filled that screen, the girl who came back like a ghost walking down that Beverly Hills staircase in a walk remembered, a walk familiar, her face, her eyes, her mouth, tell him the girl stays, tell him we'll sell the pilot, I'll see her again.

If.

If, of course, nothing had changed. If, of course, this is still the David Regan who entered that Sixth Avenue loft on 20 November 1947, oh yes, that was the date, if this was the same David Regan flinching from the world, unchanged, who found the girl with the big brass bed. Yes, the same David Regan. Exactly the same. Nothing changed. Yes. Certainly. And the same Gillian. The same Gillian, open and innocent and wanting only to be loved, and standing still while I slapped her open-handed across that wonderful face and the skyrockets exploded over Long Island Sound, slapped her with words as effectively as if I'd used my hands. Will you marry me, David? Slapped her with no after no after no, and left her feeling cheap and foolish, assuming she is the same girl, not destroyed, not thrown away and discarded by David Regan, television producer *extraordinaire* who blew it completely on the Fourth of July, 1949.

Four years.

More than four years.

And one day look at yourself, simply look at yourself in the mirror one day, startle yourself with the image staring back at you, and then ask yourself where the kid who stamped books disappeared to. Ask. He disappeared somewhere, yes, we know that, he vanished someplace, the way the buffalo and the bison vanished, and on

Sunday I'll be twenty-nine years old, happy birthday to you, make a birthday wish.

I wish I could run out into a street covered with snow, holding Gillian by the hand.

I wish the world were still and white.

But it isn't.

"It's a piece of cheese," he told Goff. "I'm sorry, but it's not for us."

1 January

Snow. Snow outside. The world is still and white. It is New Year's Day. The new year. Matthew is still asleep. He drank an awful lot last night. Julia Regan never drinks, I hadn't noticed that before. The children are in the living-room, still fascinated with the Christmas gifts. I think we give them far too much. Why doesn't the new year start in September?

I would like to resolve so many things for 1954, but I can't seem to put them in order.

I would like to be a better person.

I don't know exactly what that means. A better woman? A better wife and mother.

A better person, that's all. Better. I think I know what I mean. The house is so very still, the children are so absorbed. I called home last night to wish my parents a happy new year. Mother cried on the telephone.

I *will* be. Better.

It is still snowing.

4 January

Matthew off to station at 7.45. Orange juice and coffee, as usual. He doesn't eat enough breakfast. I don't know how he gets through the day. Kate asked me at table when she could begin wearing lipstick. I told her she was only twelve. She said, "*Agnes* wears lipstick, and she's only twelve." I told her I didn't begin wearing lipstick until I was sixteen, and she answered, "Well, you're from another era." Another era! She barely caught the school bus. Drove Bobby to nursery school, came back to empty house. Limbered up with Czerny for an hour, fingers very stiff, before men came to clean windows. Something wrong with washing machine.

13 January

Wednesday. Meeting of P.T.A. at Talmadge School. Matthew refused to come, is working on Daley brief. Roads very slippery. I am afraid to drive at night on icy roads. Bobby has slight temperature. Called Dr. Anderson. He said to give him a few St. Joseph's and call him in the morning. Meant to try jazz arrangement of "Clair de Lune", but that was before I remembered darn P.T.A. meeting. Must remember to call Phipps tomorrow, accept cocktail invitation. Are we running out of logs for the fireplace? Ask Matthew to call the man.

23 January

Bobby to dentist in afternoon before party. Says he may need braces by the time he's twelve. When he's twelve, Kate will be nineteen, and probably married. She asked me again about lipstick today, and I said firmly NO! Matthew asked why not. I said because she was still a little girl. "A little girl?" Kate screamed. "I'm as old as Agnes!" I told her I was not Agnes's mother, and I didn't care *what* Agnes did. End of argument.

Sunday

I tried to play "Rhapsody in Blue" today, made a total mess of it. Reminded me of Gillian, somehow. Children in a squabble stopped my effort.

I have an idea.

12 February

Received a Valentine card from Matthew and also one marked "From your secret lover". Kate got six cards, all from boys at the school. Bobby complained because he didn't receive any, even though he sent a beautiful hand-made effort to a girl named, of all things, Melody!

February is so depressing.

14 February

My secret lover was Matthew.

He confessed all today. Also bought me an evening bag which must have cost him at least $100 at Lord & Taylor, the idiot. I knew it was Matthew all along. Other men just don't seem to . . . well, I think there must be something wrong with me. At a party Saturday night, a man dancing with me said I was very pretty and I said thank you and changed the subject. He started telling me about the restlessness of modern American women, and again I changed the subject. I don't know how to flirt. That's the truth of it. Matthew is an unconscious flirt, and Julia Regan is an expert flirt, though it looks sort of silly on a woman who must be approaching fifty, if not there and gone already, however well-preserved she may be.

Is it necessary for me to be a flirt? Why do all the men in Talmadge seem to be seeking a love they never had?

I get puzzled sometimes.

25 February 1954

Suppose it were a chorale? Not in the true style of a Lutheran hymn, nor even anything similar to Bach or the baroque composers. But instead something—I don't know. If it could state something definite. If it could have a solidity.

The pump is out again. I called the Brothers Karamazov who always descend on that pump like two vultures ready to pick the bones clean. I asked the fat one why he always smiles so happily when he tells me there's big trouble with the pump. He apologized, smiling.

A church theme? Or more than that, something infused with the sort of thing Copland got in "Appalachian Spring", or Sessions in his early symphonies, an elemental feeling of the frontier, and perhaps the Negro church? It sounds a little sombre, but I'd like to try it, if ever I get the chance. Tomorrow is a meeting of the League of Women Voters. How do I get involved in such stupid projects? We had to fill the bathtub with water while they fiddled around outside, otherwise we'd have nothing to drink until morning. Kate complained because she won't be able to shower. She brought home a record called "Rock, Rock, Rock". Music? Certainly. Elemental, definite, and solid, why bother?

5 March

Bill from the Vultures. $300 to fix a pump! I asked Matthew to call and complain, and he said we were at the mercy of the world's technicians, and I said not if the man of the house were willing to call and complain. This led into one of Matthew's wild theories, this time on castration, of all things! Matthew said the popular theory was that women are castrating the men of America, and then after they have eaten their (I won't use the word he used) go seeking lovers who they feel are *real* men. He doesn't buy this theory. As far as I can understand it, this is what he believes:

Women and men fall in love when they're still girls and boys. They've been raised in a culture which romanticizes everything, and so romance is the keynote. But romance, according to Matthew, is for children. The boys and girls get married, and suddenly the boys are face to face with a world full of killers in which they must somehow survive. They learn. They survive by becoming *men*, by losing the boyishness they once had. So Matthew says the reason for a woman's restlessness is not that the male has been castrated and rendered impotent. Oh, no, Matthew says it's just the opposite, it's simply that the boy has become a *man* at last. But the woman did not fall in love with a man, she fell in love with a boy. She doesn't like this new person around the house. She wants the boy, the romantic boy who wrote her love poetry and spent hours with her on the telephone. So where does she find the boy, the romance? In a lover. I never knew he thought about such things.

I think he's faithful. I would shoot him!

16 March

Bedlam! Absolute! Bobby drank finger-paint.

Don't ask me how finger-paint got thin enough to be drunk, don't ask me where Mrs. Haskell was when he drank the stuff, don't ask me how that nursery school is run when a child can be allowed to drink finger-paint! Dr. Anderson said I had better take him to the hospital in Stamford, which I did, and they pumped out his stomach, some fun, and we discovered Matthew's Blue Cross had run out. Always when you need it. Kate had a fit! We didn't get home until after five, and I was supposed to drive her to Mary Bottecchi's for an after-school party, and she was absolutely frantic. I told her that Bobby could have poisoned himself, and she said, "Fine, it would have saved me the trouble!" and I almost slapped her. I would have, but she seems so adult, and I don't want to destroy this feeling of independence which seems to be a part of this phase. I never would have said anything like that to my mother, but Kate is not me, and I don't want her to *be* me.

In any case, the Amanda Bridges Taxi Service flew into high gear and got Kate to her party slightly late. I seem to be taxiing children all over the countryside. How does Kibby Klein manage with her five kids? Must go shopping again tomorrow. Why do I always look too sexy in a bathing-suit the moment I try it on again at home? Matthew asked me to bend over, and I did, and he said, "I can see your navel," which of course he could do nothing of the sort. But I guess it *was* a little too revealing. It looked all right in the shop. Maybe Matthew is a prude. Maybe *I* am, too.

I tried to get to the piano, but someone from the library came and spent an hour telling me how vitally our donations were needed this year—as if they are not needed vitally every year. I wrote a cheque for $25. I think she expected $50, but that's too bad.

7 April

Well, I finally got something down on paper. It was a lot harder than I thought. I worked for a full three hours this morning while Bobby was gone. The house was absolutely still, my what a relief! I don't know if it's any good, but I managed to fill a page of manuscript, and when I played it back it sounded at least as if I'd got the feel of the thing. I didn't want anything like Schönberg or Hindemith, a cosmopolitan veneer without roots—who was it that said, "I wouldn't be found dead with roots"? But at the same time I wanted to avoid a feeling of unintentional primitivism, or artlessness. It wasn't easy. These are the first several bars where the rather solemn major theme is established. I still have a lot of work to do on the chords, filling them out, making them richer somehow without too much sophistication. But this is the way it goes:

[musical notation: Broadly]

Bach is probably turning over! But I felt pretty good about what I'd accomplished, even though Matthew seemed to shrug it off. I played him everything I had, and he said he liked it, but I don't think he knew quite what—well, I'm not sure I know quite what I accomplished, either, but—well, I don't think someone should expect a pat on the head just because she put a few notes on paper. Still, I guess it was something. May Collins says she is going to open a novelty shop in Talmadge.

8 April

Matthew's car had a flat, drove him to station and Kate to the bus stop at the same time. Took Bobby with us in pyjamas, then back to the house for breakfast, and over to Mrs. Haskell's. She reminded me about the show the kids were doing this afternoon. I promised I'd be there. Met Julia Regan at the post office, had a cup of coffee with her. She was on her way to Tulley's office. Is there something going on there, or am I crazy? She said she was going to have a showing of some slides she took in the Virgin Islands in February, would I let Kate come? I said of course I would, must mark it down on the calendar, it's a Friday evening, 16 April. Connie Regan, no relation, joined us when we were almost finished, said she wished she could do something like taking pictures, and Julia laughed it off. Connie said she gets tired of being referred to as a housewife, which amused me because what is she if not a housewife?

I went to get newspaper and some things at the drug store and was just ready to sit down at the piano when Parsie informed me that Railway Express in Stamford had called to say I'd better pick up the package they have there for me, or it would begin accumulating storage charges. Hopped into the car and off to Stamford, picked up the package, the garden stuff I ordered from Ohio. Had lunch at Tiny's, and then back home in time to catch Bobby's nursery-school show. He was a rabbit. There was some reference in the skit about him preferring finger-paint over almost any other beverage. I think this showed a huge lack of tact on Mrs. Haskell's part, considering the fact that Matthew is a lawyer who was ready to sue her *and* the school at the time of the accident....

Kate marched in after school with three girl-friends and asked me if I had forgotten the pyjama party which I had forgotten completely. At nine o'clock tonight, four boys from the high school came around with a ladder and tried to climb into the upstairs bedroom window while Kate and her girl-friends screamed to high heaven (in delight, naturally). Matthew finally asked them to come in, and we served them cocoa and cookies. I refused to let them dance. The girls were in pyjamas and robes, and enough is enough. The boys left at 10.30, and the girls stayed up another hour discussing them. I told Matthew I thought Kate was a little boy-crazy. He said she was only twelve years old. I don't see what one thing has to do with the other.

I sometimes miss my sister Penny.

18 April

I drank too much last night. Matthew says he remembers a time at Gillian's apartment when I drank so much I passed out. He says he covered me with his coat. I couldn't remember.

Last night Brant Collins said I have the prettiest behind in all Talmadge. I told Matthew that Brant put his hand there while he was dancing with me, and Matthew said that was par for the course. I asked Matthew if he put *his* hand there when he was dancing with other women, and he said, "No, I don't believe in it." I asked him why he wasn't angry now that I'd told him about Brant, and he said we had reached a stage in the development of American culture where it was considered boorish to slug a man for making a refined pass at your wife. I told him Brant's pass hadn't been exactly refined, and Matthew said, "So why didn't *you* slug him, Amanda?" I wonder why I didn't. I think I enjoyed it.

I'm sorry I wrote that. Because I didn't really enjoy it, and I know

Brant is a wolf, but anyway I was fascinated by it. I think it was the first time any man in Talmadge made a real pass at me. There's something forbidding about me, I think. I wish men wouldn't look at me as if I were so pure. Well, I am, I guess. But it's one thing to be pure and another for everybody to know it. Oh, damn it, I sometimes wish—I don't know what I wish.

I'll bet Gillian would have socked Brant right in the nose.

10 May

Tomorrow is my birthday.

I will be thirty-one years old. I thought thirty was a landmark. But tomorrow I'll be thirty-one, and now *that* seems like a landmark. I get the feeling there are so many things to be done. But who wants a novelty shop like May's? I can't see any sense to that. After all, Brant makes a good living. Besides, Matthew would never allow it, I know. Well, anyway, tomorrow is my birthday.

I know every gift I'm getting, except Matthew's. Bobby made me a pot-holder in nursery school, and he spent all day yesterday wrapping it, tempted to show it to me, and yet at the same time making a huge production of hiding it from me. Kate bought me a merry widow, black, the sexiest undergarment imaginable. I wonder what kind of person she thinks her mother is. I have half the notion Matthew helped her pick it out when they went shopping together Saturday. But Matthew's gift is the real question mark. He hasn't given me the slightest clue, but he's been walking around like the cat who swallowed the canary. I can tell he's just bursting with pride over whatever it is he's done. I can hardly wait. I know it's absolutely girlish and foolish to get excited over a birthday gift, but Matthew's spirit is contagious.

Well, I'll know tomorrow.

11 May 1954

Mink!

17 May 1954

I worked in the garden all morning. The soil is still a little stiff in spots, and I got blisters on my right hand. I wonder if Myra Hess digs in the garden between concerts. Nursery school ends next week. I asked Mrs. Haskell why she can't keep them until the end of June, but she said this was the way she's been doing it ever since she organized the school in 1951, and this was the first time anyone complained about it. I told her that down South they'd been doing things a certain way for a long time, too, but that today the Supreme Court voted unanimously to change it. I think she missed the analogy. Thank God Bobby starts at the elementary school this fall!

Spring seems such a long time coming this year.

18 May

I suppose technically, it's a suite. At least, it seems to be naturally dividing itself into four distinct sections, or certainly three sections with a bridge passage. I enjoyed working on this second part immensely, maybe the change of tempo accounts for that. I tried to combine funk with prayer meeting here, using a lively call and response that leads back into the major theme again, something like this:

I think it has a spiritual quality. Matthew raised his hands heavenward and began waggling his fingers when I played it tonight, so I guess he got the message. I wish I knew why his attitude infuriates me. It's as if he thinks I'm simply doing something to occupy time, or to kill time, or to *waste* time. I think that's terribly unfair of him. The suite may be nothing—although I do think it has some good things in it—but it's not a silly novelty shop like May has. So why does Matthew approach it as some sort of game? Like taking a child on his knee and saying, "That's a good girl. Stay out of trouble." I'm not doing this to fill the empty hours. I'm doing it because I want to do it, I want to do *something*. I wish he could understand that. It would make things so much easier.

It's getting too warm to wear the mink.

3 June

Thursday, and Parsie's day off. She rushes out of the house at seven each Thursday, as if she's afraid we'll change our minds about letting her go. I spoke to her last Thursday about making sure breakfast was on the table before she left. So today she must have got up at dawn. The orange juice was sitting there when we came down, having already lost whatever vitamin C it contained when she set it out in the wee small hours. I want to fire her, but Matthew insists she's a good girl, especially with the children. I think Bobby has an ear for music. He sat at the piano yesterday and picked out "Yankee Doodle". Perhaps I should begin giving him lessons.

I am fooling with a variation on the suite in a minor key. It sounds very Russian, which is perhaps not too good a thing to sound in this day and age. I wonder if the Russian people want war. Why would anyone want war? Matthew says everyone does—men and women alike. He says the invention of an ultimate weapon is the most frustrating thing that's ever happened to mankind. It prevents them from doing the one thing they really love to do, and that is waging war. He seems so cynical and bitter sometimes, and yet I know he really isn't. I'm much too dependent on him. I wish I had an original idea of my own. Well, I have the suite.

8 June

I left Bobby with Parsie this morning, and walked over to the university. I don't know why I went, really. I walked through the campus and looked at the young boys and girls worrying about their final exams. They all seem so innocent. The old dorm looked exactly the same. I stood on the front steps for a while, but I didn't go in. I walked from the dorm to Ardaecker, passing the three chapels, and the library, and the law buildings, and then standing outside Ardaecker and listening to someone playing the piano inside. I was going to look up some of my old instructors, but I decided against it.

It's very difficult to go back.

I think we lose ourselves.

I think somehow we lose ourselves, and we go back to old unchanging places, but it's not as if the memory is one of ourselves in that place, no. It's a stranger who stands on familiar ground and tries to visualize another person there, a person so long ago she's unreal. I wish I could really explain what I felt. It is so hard for me to put words on paper. But why did I go back? I think to learn for myself that the person who moved in that university world is not me, Amanda Soames Bridges.

And yet, I destroyed something today. So maybe Matthew is right. Maybe all we want to do is wage war, destroy each other and ourselves. I destroyed a fragile warmth today. I destroyed a memory. I took a stranger to a place I once had loved, and because the stranger did not fit there, because the stranger questioned the validity of a memory, the memory itself was destroyed. I won't go back to the university again.

And yet, it was a part.

19 June

The annual P.T.A. dance.

I still don't know quite what to make of it.

There are two musicians sleeping downstairs, and I'm sure they're both drug addicts. I wonder if Kate is safe. Matthew is out like a light, after all his ranting and raving. The thing that happened was this. Someone on the committee asked me if I knew of a good band they could hire, and I asked Matthew, and he asked one of his partners who used to play saxophone. His partner, Len Summers, said he knew a very good drummer who had a small jazz combo, and he thought they would be happy to come up to Talmadge to play at our yearly dance.

Well, they came up. The first thing that happened was that the trumpet player left his horn outside the Juilliard School of Music in Manhattan. I don't know how anyone could possibly leave his horn on the sidewalk, but he managed to do it, and he made a few frantic telephone calls to friends in New York and they finally located his horn and said they would drive up with it. In the meantime, the band—piano, bass, drums and tenor saxophone—played without the trumpet man. Well, not exactly without him, since he had his mouthpiece in his pocket, and he kept blowing through it like a kazoo, making the most horrible sounds which everyone in the band, I gathered, thought were very cool and progressive. The trumpet finally arrived at about eleven o'clock, and the band went into high gear.

It was along about this time that someone discovered the bass player and the tenor-saxophonist were both smoking a sweetish-smelling cigarette, and Teddy Bernstein, who is a biochemist, said the stuff was marijuana. You can imagine the stir this caused! We're not even allowed to leave whisky bottles on the tables because the dance is being held at the school. Everyone drinks, of course, and everyone gets drunk, but the bottles are all on the floor, under the table—which is where some people wind up by the end of the night. Matthew, who had hired the band, began to hear comments about the marijuana, and about the way the boys were playing really progressive jazz stuff which was nice to listen to, but not very good to dance to. Brant Collins, who was telling me again how beautiful I am, while discreetly exploring everywhere, told me he appreciated this far-out stuff, but not at a "family-type gathering", the hypocrite! Matthew had drunk a lot of bourbon by this time, and was beginning to get a little angry. "These men are *musicians*!" he kept saying over and over again. Not that anyone had denied they were musicians. Everyone had simply stated that they were a little far out, and a little hopped-up to boot. It was Brant Collins who finally went to Matthew and said he thought it was disgusting that a school dance should have hired a bunch of "junkies", an expression he no doubt picked up from Mickey Spillane.

Matthew said he thought it was disgusting that the world was being overrun by people like Senator McCarthy and Brant Collins. Brant wanted to know what, exactly, Matthew meant by that, and Matthew said again, "These men are *musicians*, and entitled to respect!"

"We're *giving* them respect!" Brant said. "More than they deserve."

"Why don't you go dance with some willing housewife?" Matthew said, and again Brant wanted to know what, exactly, Matthew meant by that, and I swear Matthew would have hit him if Elliot Tulley and Julia Regan hadn't stepped in and separated them. The musicians were playing all through this, "How High the Moon"-ish stuff, oblivious to anything that was happening on the dance floor.

Well, the whole thing broke up at one o'clock, without any suggestion of overtime, which is unusual for the P.T.A. dance. The musicians found themselves in another quandary. Apparently the person who'd driven them up had decided to visit some "chick" in

Westport, and they had no transportation home, and no place to sleep.

Brant Collins, who was sticking his nose into this thing all over the place and refusing to let it lie, said, "Go sleep in the street!"

Matthew, at the top of his lungs, bellowed, "In my house, nobody sleeps in the street!"

I don't think he realized how funny that was because he kept repeating it over and over again.

"In my house, nobody sleeps in the street!"

So now there are two musicians sleeping downstairs in the living-room, the bass player and the tenor man, the ones who were smoking the marijuana. Elliot Tulley took the other three home to sleep in his guest-house. The trumpet player forgot his horn at the school, and Elliot had to go all the way back for it. I think that man is trying to lose his trumpet. I read somewhere that nothing gets lost or misplaced by accident.

One of them snores. I can hear him all the way up here.

Maybe I ought to ask Kate to lock her door.

I wish I understood Matthew.

5 July

Lake Abundance. We drove down to Playland last night to see the fireworks. It was jam-packed. I must say I didn't enjoy it. Today we moved into the house here. I refused to take the same house we had last summer. I'm not superstitious, but one fire is more than I want in any lifetime, thanks. David Regan was up for the week-end with Julia.

I asked him about Gillian, and saw immediately that I shouldn't have. He said Yes, he had known Gillian very well. I asked him if he still heard from her, and he said No, he hadn't heard from her since the Fourth of July in 1949, five years ago, and that this was his annual celebration in honour of the occasion. He wasn't drunk, nor had he been drinking, but he sounded very bitter. I told him how talented I thought she was, and I filled him in on some of the things we used to do together at school. He tried to affect indifference, but I could tell he was very interested in everything I had to say. From what I could gather, he must have met Gillian shortly after Matthew and I were married, which would place it sometime after the summer of 1946. My God, we've been married eight years already, time is disgusting. Although he did say something about the blizzard of '47, which I could barely remember, and I did recall seeing Gillian in, it must have been 1947, and her not mentioning David at all, so perhaps they met after that. Whenever it was, apparently it didn't work out too well.

He's a very strange person, I think. I get a feeling of total lovelessness between him and his mother, and yet I know they are mother and son, and I sense a bond between them, but there's more there too, more than meets the eye. Julia seems to lavish more attention and love on my daughter Kate than she does on her own son. Of course, he's a grown man, but still—it's hard to put my finger on it. Kate said tonight that David was "cool". I must agree that he is. He gives less to anyone than any other human being I know. Oh, he's a fine conversationalist and he knows some wonderful jokes—the Russian joke he told, wasn't that one of Gillian's?—and he's remarkably poised and at ease, but he gives absolutely nothing. And the oddest part is that I instinctively feel he *likes* me and Matthew, and yet he gives us nothing.

I don't think these are the Frantic Fifties. I know it's not alliterative, but I think these are the Distrustful Fifties.

I'll bet people will eventually stop shaking hands.

14 July

The lake. Sun. Water. Easy living. Same old stuff. I was tempted to go back home and play the suite today.

17 July

Lake. Swimming. Outdoor barbecue tonight.

21 July

Lake.

25 July

Lake.

14 August

Party at Julia's house. David there with a television actress named Betsy something. In the john, she asked me how well I knew David. She said he had asked her to go with him to Puerto Rico for a week, and she wondered whether she should or not. They would have separate hotel rooms and all, she said, but she wondered if it would look bad. I couldn't begin to advise her. She's only twenty-three years old, and yet I felt she was so much wiser and more experienced and older than I am. Would I go to Puerto Rico with a strange man?

No.

24 August

Lake. I have been reading magazines all week. I refuse to believe that American women are solely concerned with, in the order of importance:

(1) How to convert their kitchens on $500.
(2) 400 ways to prepare potatoes.
(3) *The Royal Box* by Frances Parkinson Keyes.
(4) Toilet training.

I refuse to believe it. I'm not a snob, but I refuse to believe that American women are quite that shallow or quite that self-centred or quite that witless.

In China, the Communists are talking about invading Formosa and President Eisenhower has all but promised the Seventh Fleet will leap to the rescue—but the magazines are worried about the new eye make-ups.

We don't need eye make-up. All we need is a few peepholes in our hoods.

6 September

Labour Day. Barbecue party at the lake. Klein, Regan, Bottecchi, Anderson, Phipps. Broke up early. Drove back to the house in Talmadge. It's good to be home. It's always good to come home again. I sometimes forget how beautiful the house is, or how much it means to me. I tried a few notes on the piano. It needs another tuning after lying idle all summer.

I envy the children in September. Wednesday is Bobby's first day of school, and Kate starts at the junior high. Gave permission for her to wear lipstick. She immediately called Agnes and said, "My mom says okay, so now your mom'll *have* to say okay!" Matthew calls her "the con man".

I am very anxious to begin work on the suite again.

17 September

The minor key section has bogged down. I worked steadily on the passacaglia, needing only a modulation to take me from the restatement of the major theme, but nothing as florid as the Tristan and Isolde prelude—and suddenly it dried up. I mulled around all day before leaving it and going back instead to the revival section which seemed to suggest augmentation. I've given it a dancy counter-rhythm now by using a left-hand arpeggiated figure. Maybe I'm procrastinating. But I *will* get back to the minor key section as soon as I have an idea. And meanwhile, I like this variation on what I had earlier. These are the first several bars:

18 September

Called Fred Carletti about the new garage door. He left chalk marks all over it, claimed that was the way the lumber yard marks its lumber and that the chalk would come off with soap and water. Parsie was out there all morning and the chalk marks are still there. Fred doesn't feel like coming back to sand them, but that's his problem, and I still haven't paid his bill. Saks Fifth agreed the clasp on my handbag must have been defective, and are ready to exchange it. Must give it to Parsie for United Parcel's pick-up truck. Bulbs arrived today, should hire a man to help me get them in.

The woods are alive with colour!

19 September

Invitations out for the party on 2 October. Ask Matthew to check his liquor. Do we need a bartender? Matthew says a bartender inhibits whisky consumption. But it frees Matthew for socializing and being the host. Six of one, half a dozen. Agreed to work on committee for clearing Talmadge roads of empty beer cans dumped by high school kids. Suggested local boy scout troops handle the actual clearance. Zoning meeting at Town Hall Thursday night. Parsie's day off. Must get a sitter. Or can Kate sit?

21 September

First day of Autumn.
I sometimes get so bored.

12 October

Meeting Matthew in town tomorrow for dinner and theatre. He thinks he can get seats for *The Caine Mutiny Court-Martial*.
I would much prefer *Tea and Sympathy*.

The law offices of Bridges, Benson, Summers and Stang were located in an impressive forty-story structure on Wall Street, nor had the location been chosen by caprice. The firm dealt mostly with criminal law, and the Criminal Courts Building was on Centre Street, not five city blocks from Matthew's office.

Amanda Soames Bridges, who enjoyed the unbending logic of music, could appreciate the mathematics that made proximity to the criminal courts desirable. She could appreciate it, but she found it increasingly difficult to enjoy, especially on days like this when she was forced to make the long haul from the midtown shopping area to Matthew's office. She had never liked driving, and she loathed driving in city traffic. The streets seemed more congested than ever, with more taxicabs and more buses, and bigger automobiles, would Detroit never stop making their cars bigger and shinier, were Americans determined to have the absolute biggest of everything in the whole world? The streets, too, were cold and bitter. She could hear the wind whistling over the hood of the car, rattling at the windows, so cold for October.

She pulled into the parking lot on Chambers Street, put the claim ticket into her bag, and began walking swiftly towards Matthew's office building. The sun at four-thirty was almost gone. The wind knifed through the concrete alleyways, cutting through her skirt. I should have worn a coat, she thought. This stole is for a true autumn, but there won't *be* any damn autumn this year. She was grateful for the lobby of the building. She took the elevator to the twelfth floor, stopped in the ladies' room at the end of the hall to comb her hair and repair her lipstick, and then walked down to Matthew's office, pausing just outside the entrance door. She always thought of it as Matthew's office even though there were four names on the door, even though Benson and Stang were the senior partners of the firm. The fact that Matthew's name headed the listing was a tribute to his powers of persuasion, as was the decor of the office itself.

"Look," he had said to his new partners, "it doesn't make a bit of difference to me. You can stick my name on the bottom of the door in letters usually reserved for escape clauses. The door can read Benson, Stang, Summers and Bridges, just the way you want it to. I'm the junior partner, and I really have no business suggesting anything radical."

Stang, fifty-seven years old and sporting a potbelly and a bright checked vest, had tweaked his nose and said, "Matthew, you are the biggest bull thrower in New York City. Say what's on your mind."

"Okay. The sound of Bridges, Benson, Summers and Stang is cleaner. That's what's on my mind. It reads simpler and swifter, and it's easier to remember. It creates a corporate image that is good for our purposes."

"What are our purposes?" Benson asked. Sniffing at a nose inhaler, his long thin legs propped on a hassock, he looked at Matthew sourly and then shook his head as if he were dealing with a maniac.

"To get clients," Matthew said. "To become the biggest law firm in the city."

"We've been doing all right so far," Benson said.

"We're going to do better."

"Sometimes I wonder why we took you in."

"Stop wondering, Harry. I'm just what this creaking combination needs. I've lost only two cases in the past two years. That's right, I'm pretty damn good. And I've got some ideas about how we should decorate the new office, too."

"He's not a lawyer," Benson said dryly. "He's an interior decorator."

"No, I like his ideas," Summers, the fourth partner, said tentatively. He was blond and strapping, a man of forty-two who sweated a great deal. He offered his opinion, and then shrugged.

"Thanks, Len," Matthew said. "I don't think the new place should look like this one."

"What's the matter with this one?" Stang asked.

"It's dusty, its dingy, it looks dirty and creaking and old."

"My *wife* decorated this office," Stang said.

"And it may have been great in nineteen-twenty, but time marches on."

"Now he's a news commentator," Benson said.

"How *do* you think we should decorate?" Stang had asked, leaning forward.

That had been a long time ago.

The name on the door was Bridges, Benson, Summers and Stang. Amanda smiled and twisted the knob.

The reception room started just inside the door with ten feet of grey carpeting flowing back spaciously from the entrance to two low modern couches, which shared a marble coffee-table and a double-bullet wall fixture. A single abstract painting hung on the wall opposite the couches. Beyond the couches, there was more carpeting, which stretched to the reception desk and the girl behind it. Beyond that, and hidden from the reception room, were the filing cabinets, the four separate private offices of the firm's partners, and a conference room. The firm's law library was shelved on glass-enclosed bookcases hanging free on the wall above the filing cabinets. The scheme throughout was clean, almost austere. If it denied a dusty, tradition-filled interpretation of the law, it created instead an atmosphere that was dynamic and businesslike, and not without a subtle beauty of its own. The girl behind the reception desk seemed to echo the aesthetics of the office. She looked up when Amanda entered, smiled, and said, "Hello, Mrs. Bridges."

Her smile was a carefully calculated instrument of greeting, a warm welcome which flashed suddenly on a face that could have belonged to a teen-age model. Annie Ford, at twenty-seven, looked more like seventeen, with tiny bones and compact breasts, her long black hair worn in a page-boy, her brown eyes sparkling with a curious combination of naïveté and worldliness. The top of her desk was covered with legal forms, but it looked scrupulously ordered none the less, as if she had already straightened it for the evening before putting the cover back on her typewriter and heading home.

"Hello, Annie," Amanda said. "Mr. Bridges is expecting me."

"I'll tell him you're here." Annie picked up the receiver, pressed a button in the phone's base, and smiled again at Amanda.

"Is he busy?" Amanda asked.

"He has someone with him," Annie answered, "but I don't think he'll be very . . . hello? Mr. Bridges, your wife is here. Yes, sir, I will." She replaced the phone, smiled again at Amanda, and said, "Would you mind waiting, please, Mrs. Bridges? He'll be about ten minutes."

"Thank you," Amanda said. She walked towards the nearest couch, sat, and picked up a copy of *Life*. She began thumbing through it uneasily. She always felt a little strange in Matthew's office, the unwanted visitor who somehow managed to upset a carefully rehearsed business routine. The telephone rang. Annie Ford lifted the receiver.

"Bridges, Benson, Summers and Stang," she said, "good afternoon." She listened and then said, "Oh, hello, Mr. Cohen. Just a moment, I'll see." She pressed the stud in the base of the telephone, waited. "Mr. Stang, it's Arthur Cohen, on six." She replaced the phone in its cradle, smiled briefly at Amanda, and walked to one of the filing cabinets.

Watching her, Amanda felt a sudden envy.

She knew the envy was foolish. Annie Ford was twenty-seven years old, a bachelor girl who lived in a furnished apartment on Seventy-second Street, who earned eighty dollars a week as a receptionist, who probably dreamed of a husband, and a family, and a home in the country, who probably wished for all the things Amanda already had.

But Annie got up each morning and dressed to go some place.

Annie came into the heart of the most exciting city in the world, and she talked to people on the telephone about matters slightly more important than a United Parcel pick up. She personally greeted people who were concerned with more than a few chalk marks on a new garage door. Annie Ford was part of a successful law office, and she knew what she was supposed to do there, and she did it efficiently and quietly, and she no doubt derived a great deal of pleasure from the knowledge that she was doing it well.

She did not have to wake up each morning and wonder how she would occupy her time for the rest of the day. She did not have to sit through inane luncheons, or serve on meaningless half-witted committees, or shuttle children around the countryside, or doubt the worth of a musical composition that seemed less and less important each day. No! More important! More important to me than anything else in my life!

Now, Amanda.

Now, Amanda dear.

She sat quite still and watched Annie as she filed her legal forms, watched the quick movement of her fingers, the studied concentration on her face.

Oh my God, Amanda thought, I wish I didn't have a mind.

I wish I weren't a woman in this day and age, part of the giant female convalescent ward, we sit around doing water colours or dabbling in oils or baking ceramic ash-trays or weaving baskets or arranging flowers, busy, busy with our hands, doing anything, anything to stop us from realizing we are really useless human beings. Doing anything, and doing nothing.

The only thing I ever created in my life was my son Bobby, she thought.

The telephone on Annie's desk buzzed. She looked up from the filing cabinet, smiled, walked quickly to the desk, and picked up the receiver.

"Yes?" she said. "Oh, yes, just a moment." She turned to

Amanda. "Mrs. Bridges? Would you mind taking the phone, please?"

Amanda put the receiver to her ear. "Hello?"

"Amanda, this is Matthew. Honey, this is going to take a little onger than I expected. Do you think we could meet at the restaurant? Can you keep yourself busy for a little while?"

"I suppose so," Amanda said.

"I'm sorry, but . . ."

"I understand," Amanda said. "What time? Where?"

"Let's see, it's almost five now. Can we make it six-thirty?"

"The stores close at six," Amanda said absent-mindedly.

"What?"

"Nothing. I'll meet you at six-thirty. Tell me where."

The book shop was on Sixth Avenue, in the Forties, a tiny shop set between a locksmith and a hamburger joint. She wandered into it because it seemed to invite browsing, and because she had more than an hour to kill before meeting Matthew at the restaurant. The shop was long and narrow, its walls lined with bookcases and dusty volumes, its centre aisle cluttered with open stalls of remainders. She wished it were not October and cold. A shop like this cried out for a rainy day in April. She could remember cuddling up in the armchair before the fireplace in the Minnesota house, could remember reading *Parnassus on Wheels* and *The Haunted Bookshop*, and later *Where the Blue Begins*, which portrayed dogs as humans and which raised some serious questions about God. She had felt sacrilegious just reading the book. When she'd read one of the passages aloud to her father and then asked him if she should continue with the book, he had nodded in rare wisdom and said, "I really don't think it can hurt you to hear another fellow's viewpoint, Amanda." She'd read only two more chapters, and then closed the book of her own accord.

There was the smell of dust in the shop. The shop was almost empty. An old woman with a flowered hat was picking through the stalls searching for a bargain. A bald-headed man in a tweed overcoat was at the far end of the shop, taking a book down from the shelves, replacing it, taking another book down. The proprietor sat behind a high counter just inside the entrance door, reading Dostoevsky. Amanda browsed idly. She looked at her watch. It was only five thirty-five. Slowly, she worked her way towards the back of the shop. She found a battered old copy of a Nancy Drew mystery. Excited by her find, she decided to buy it for Kate, and then realized Kate had outgrown Nancy Drew. Reluctantly, she put it back on the stall.

"I used to read *Bomba the Jungle Boy*," the bald-headed man said.

"Yes, weren't they fun?" she answered, almost without turning, smiling at the man in an idle reminiscent way, and then moving past him to the other side of the stall.

"And *Tom Swift*," the man said.

Amanda glanced at him, smiled in polite dismissal, and began walking towards the front of the shop.

"Amanda?" the man said.

She stopped. Puzzled, she turned.

"It *is* Amanda?"

"Yes," she said, "but . . .?"

She looked at the man more closely. He had a round face, and a bald head, and the collar of his tweed coat was pulled high on the back of his neck. He looked very sad, a chubby man wearing a very sad face.

"I'm sorry," she said.

"Morton," he answered. "Morton Yardley."

For a moment, the name meant nothing to her. And then the man made a curiously embarrassed gesture, pulling the coat collar higher on his neck, as if he wanted to pull it completely over his bald head, and all at once she remembered Morton Yardley and his hooded Mackinaw. A smile broke on her face. She rushed into his arms spontaneously and hugged him.

"Morton!" she said. "*No!* Morton, is it you?"

"Hullo, Amanda," he said, and he hugged her with great embarrassment, grinning, awkward.

"What are you doing here?" She pulled away from him and looked into his face. "Of *course* it's Morton! Oh, how good to see you!" She laughed, still unable to believe it, and then they fell silent and stood staring at each other somewhat curiously. The hugging was over and done with, the surprise was past, the first rush of honest emotion was gone. Now two strangers looked at each other in the cluttered aisle of a musty book shop, each taking the measure of the other. Amanda touched her hair unconsciously, fluffing it.

"How have you been, Amanda?"

"Fine, thank you."

"Are you married now?"

"Yes. Yes, I have two children."

"How wonderful for you."

Don't let us be this way, she thought. I liked you so much, Morton. Don't let us end as strangers talking about the weather.

"Are *you* married?" she asked.

"No. No, I never married, Amanda."

"Is your parish here in New York?"

"My . . . ? Oh, well, I sort of changed plans." He nodded. "I gave up my ideas about the ministry, you see." He shrugged. "I work in a bank now. I'm an assistant manager. Manufacturer's Trust, do you know it?"

"Yes."

"Yes, well, that's where I work."

There was a long pause. Morton wetted his lips nervously. He really has lost all his hair, she thought, but he still looks so sweet, he is still a very sweet person.

"Do you live in New York?" he asked.

"No, we live in Talmadge."

"Really? Near the school?"

"Well, fairly near. On Congress."

"Oh, yes." Morton nodded. "You didn't marry a professor, did you?"

"No, a lawyer."

"I thought because . . ." He nodded. "Well, a lawyer, that's good. Gee, it must be . . . how many years?" He nodded again, and then was silent.

The silence lengthened. There seemed to be nothing more to say. After all these years, there was nothing to say but How are you? Are you married? Where do you work? Where do you live? She didn't want it to be this way. She wanted to know about Morton, and she wanted to tell him about herself. She had liked Morton too much, had shared too much with him, had touched his life with her own, and been touched in return, had really *known* Morton too well to allow this to happen. You can destroy a place, she thought, you can come to it with all the tricks and veneer of living, come to it with cynical eyes and destroy the memory of innocence, but you cannot do that with people. I won't let it happen with people.

"Could we have a drink together?" she asked. She smiled gently. "I don't have to meet my husband until six-thirty."

"Oh, I'm sorry," Morton said. "I'm sorry, but I can't, Amanda."

"Oh." Her face fell. Maybe you *can* do it with people, she thought. Maybe life is simply a matter of learning that the present has nothing whatever to do with the past or the future.

"I'm going over to the museum," he said. "I have to see this movie." He paused. "Would you like to come with me?"

She almost said no. This was going badly, this was awkward, this was stupid and disenchanting, and she almost said no. She shook her head, not in reply, but as if to clear it.

"I *would* like to come, Morton," she said.

"Good. Gee, that's . . . well, good, Amanda. Good." He grinned.

"Is it far?"

"Fifty-third."

"Let's walk," she said. "Then we can talk to each other."

Morton let out his breath. "I was hoping we could talk," he said.

October dusk had settled on the city. The subway-bound office workers rushed along the streets with their heads bent against the strong wind, their hands thrust into their pockets. The sidewalks echoed with the clatter of high-heeled shoes, the streets with the empty bellow of bus horns. The sky was a mottled deep blue, not yet black, no moon showing as yet, no stars.

"I like this time of day best," Morton said. "Everybody going home. I feel very good at this time of day."

"I do, too."

"Are you warm enough with just that little thing?"

"No, I'm freezing," Amanda admitted.

"It's very pretty. What is that? Mink or something?"

"Yes."

Morton nodded. She had the impression this was the first time he had ever had a close look at mink. There was something very naïve and boyish about him, as if he had learned none of the . . . the tricks of living, as if there were no guile in that entirely open face.

"I'm glad we got out of that shop, Amanda," he said. "You know what I thought? I thought we would shuffle our feet around a little more, and then say good-bye. That would have been sinful, I think. Don't you think so?"

"Yes," Amanda said, smiling. "Absolutely sinful."

"Are you kidding?" He turned to her, his eyebrows raised.

"No. I'm serious."

He smiled. "Good."

"May I take your arm? I'm very cold."

"Sure. Here. Do you want my coat, Amanda? Let me give you my coat."

"No. Thank you, Morton."

"Come on, I don't need it. Look at you. You're shaking."

"I'll be all right." She smiled at him and hugged his arm. "I'm glad we ran into each other, Morton."

"Yes, I am, too. You'll like this picture, Amanda. A friend of mine made it. I don't know what it cost him, thirty cents or something. Anyway, it was very cheap, and it's received all sorts of praise. Do you know you look exactly the same? You haven't changed a bit. Not a bit."

"You haven't either."

"Amanda, I'm all *bald*!" he said, laughing, as if surprised by the knowledge but willing to share it with her.

"But you look the same."

"But you didn't recognize me," he said.

"No, I didn't."

"I wasn't sure it was you, either. Not because you've changed, though. Only because . . . well, who expected to meet you in a little run-down book store on Sixth Avenue?"

"We didn't even buy anything," Amanda said, and she laughed. "Morton, I'm *freezing*."

"We're almost there. We can get some hot chocolate in the cafeteria. The picture doesn't go on until six."

"Why did you leave the ministry, Morton?"

"Oh, that's a long story. I was in the stockade, you know."

"The what?"

"In the Army. Jail. They call it the stockade. Which is sensible since it was designed for cattle and not men. I had a chance to do a lot of thinking there."

"About what, Morton? Ooooo, Morton, do you know where I'm *really* cold?"

"Where?"

"My feet."

"That's why you're cold all over. That's a known fact."

"You're a mine of information," she said, smiling.

"You mean you didn't know that? Anyway, I was locked up there for about six months, here, put your hand in my pocket . . . how's that? Is that better? and then they sent me overseas as a corpsman, you know, non-combatant, the red cross on my arm, the whole business. And then I saw it, Amanda. I saw what people can do to each other." He shook his head. "And I began thinking some more. I'll tell you, Amanda, a funny thing happened. I was out there without any weapon, you know, and . . . and . . . I wished I had a *gun*! But not for self-protection, Amanda, not for that. I wished I had a gun so I could kill the people who were leaving those broken bodies all over the place. That's right, I wanted to *kill*. Now, remember the reason I'd objected in the first place. Now, remember that, Amanda. And here I was *wanting* to kill, and *ready* to kill. Now, that can make you wonder about yourself a little bit, believe me." He shook his head.

"But you were at war, Morton. You had to expect . . ."

"Oh, I know, I know. But I looked into myself, and I asked myself, What's all this God stuff, and did I *really* believe it? Did I really back out of the war because I didn't want to kill anybody, or only because I was afraid of getting killed myself? And if that was my reason, and how could it be otherwise when there I was *ready* to kill, why then I'd only used religion as an excuse. I suppose I could have decided then and there, Amanda. I suppose I could have asked for a gun. I didn't. But I *did* decide the ministry wasn't for me. Are you happy, Amanda?"

He asked the question so unexpectedly that he startled her.

"Why . . ." She squinted her eyes against the wind and looked into his face. There was honesty there and openness, Morton Yardley had not changed at all, Morton Yardley had acquired none of the shellac. And his face demanded an honest answer, no, not demanded because he was not one of those who forced their will. His face simply asked quietly for honesty. And asked for so gently, honesty could not be denied. "I don't know, Morton," she said.

"You look happy."

"Do I?"

"Yes. Here's the museum. You're still very beautiful, Amanda," he said as he pushed open the door, said it into the raised collar of his coat, as if not expecting her to hear it, and yet hoping she would.

"Thank you," she said, because she wanted him to know she had heard.

They drank hot chocolates in the cafeteria off the garden. The garden was deserted. The modern statues defied the cold, bronze and stone standing erect against the wind. The whipped cream dissolved in their cups, and they sat facing each other, discussing old times at the university, and she realized all at once that there was a smile on her face, and that perhaps it had been there from the moment they left the book shop. She felt completely at ease with Morton, completely without façade. There was no need for stupid fencing with him, no need for the clever answer, the provocative question. She felt honest and somehow exuberant. And curiously, she felt more like a woman than she could ever remember.

"Do you get into New York often?" he asked, and she looked into his eyes because she had heard this approach often at Talmadge parties, had heard it whispered in her ear as she danced, had heard it dropped casually as she sat alongside a polished attractive man on a living-room couch sipping a Martini, she had heard it often, and she knew the intent, and she knew the answer, she knew the game. But Morton Yardley did not play games.

"Yes," she said. "I do."

"Good," Morton said. "Because I'd like to see you again."

"Why, Morton?"

"Well . . . I guess because I love you, Amanda."

The words startled her. Not because she hadn't suspected. But only because they were spoken in utter simplicity.

"That's very sweet, Morton," she said, and instantly thought, I don't mean that, it's not what I mean. I'm not parrying, Morton,

I'm not giving the cocktail-party answer to the standard proposition. Believe me, please. I don't mean what that sounds like. "Morton, you're very sweet," she said. "You have a very sweet face."

He looked at her curiously, as if her words had embarrassed him.

"You make me feel very good," she said softly. "You make me feel like a woman."

She thought all at once, How easy it would be. Truly, how very easy. Without guilt, without soul-searching, because this was not the fantasy of the *grand amour*, this was not the excitement of the pale dark stranger, the secret meetings in hotel rooms, the swell of clandestine passion, this was nothing at all like that. Morton was hardly a glamorous figure, hardly the dashing lover, and yet she thought, How easy it would be, and thought, It would be *something*, I would be giving, I would be giving, and looked into Morton's eyes and back to a time when it could have been uncomplicated, and thought, It could be uncomplicated now, and suddenly thought of herself in bed with him. Surprisingly, the thought did not shock her or disgust her. She accepted it calmly, continuing to look at Morton and continuing to feel this strange sort of pulsing warmth that seemed to hover over the table, not a sexuality at all, although she imagined him touching her, but rather a feeling of ease, of emotion without pretence, the thought was exciting. And she knew it could be that, she knew the discovery of another person was always exciting, and she knew she could find in Morton a total adoration, she could see that in his eyes now, not lust and not passion, she knew that somewhere in this strangely naïve man who sat across from her there was still the little boy. There was still trust, there was still hope, there was still, yes, romance. How easy it would be. How easy to turn a door-knob and open a new world, how easy to say, "Yes, let's have lunch sometime," how easy to accept the love of this man, "Well . . . I guess because I love you, Amanda," and to know that a love could be returned, a different love than she had ever given, returned with fierce purpose, the love of a woman trying to find meaning in a world that seemed oddly and stubbornly unreceptive. How easy.

How easy to find something with him, something she had already found with him on the short walk from the book shop, and over hot chocolates already gone, staining the thick white mugs with a residue of brown, something sheltered from the noisy October wind outside and the statues standing defiant in the garden, sheltered. I could love this man, she thought. I could take off my clothing for him unashamed and eager, I could allow him to caress me, I think I would feel rather rich. And savage. And pure. She looked at his thick hands around the thick white mug. How easy it would be.

Yes, and excitement, the excitement of somewhere to go, and someone to meet, a purpose, a life, how easy.

"Hey, the picture's going to start," Morton said. "Come on."

He took her arm and they walked through the museum, and she kept watching him, puzzled because she had not yet made her decision, puzzled because she even considered making a decision, and feeling no guilt at all, she was not betraying Matthew nor her children, she was betraying no one by her consideration of something she had always thought of as betrayal, "keep you alone unto him as long as you both shall live."

They sat together in the darkened theatre. She took his hand and held it. Thousands upon thousands of stop-action photos flashed upon the screen, spliced together to show the blooming process of a plant from tightly closed bud to extended flower. She thought, that's the way it was, that's the way you get married, and then she shoved the thought aside because she did not wish to defile a memory that was no longer even that, a blur instead, something that had happened very long ago to a very young and innocent girl.

But that was how it had been, she knew. Photo upon photo flashed in rapid succession upon a screen, no single photo important in itself, the change imperceptible from one still shot to the next, and yet each separate shot essential to the steadily unfolding sequence, each barely discernible change combining to form an overwhelmingly dramatic change, the juxtaposition of a remembered closed bud against a sudden bloom touched by morning sun. That is the way people get married, she thought.

Six-thirty was not very far away. Six-thirty was a heart tick away when they came out into the cold again, when the sudden cold attacked their faces and their eyes, six-thirty was so very near. They stood on the corner of Fifth Avenue and Fifty-third Street. The street lamps were on, the department-store windows were lighted, they beckoned like potbellied stoves. The taxicabs rushed along the street. Amanda and Morton stood on the street corner with the wind lashing at them. They seemed like lovers. To the passer-by, to the casual passer-by intent on the cracks in the pavement, they looked like secret lovers, and perhaps they were.

"Do you think we can have lunch sometime?" Morton asked hesitantly.

She searched his face, open and sweet, he has such a sweet face, she thought. She reached up and touched his mouth with one ungloved hand.

"I don't think so, Morton," she said.

He smiled. He nodded. He seemed pleased somehow.

"Good-bye, Amanda," he said. He took her hand. He would

have been content with a handshake. She leaned close to him suddenly and kissed him on the cheek, and then awkwardly said, "I've got lipstick on you," and rubbed at the stain with her gloved hand, and then squeezed his hand and said, "Good-bye, Morton," and turned away from him quickly and walked across the avenue against a light, and knew that he watched her until she was out of sight, and told herself the tears in her eyes were caused by the wind.

BOOK FOUR

KATE

SIXTEEN-YEAR-OLD Kate Bridges was curled impossibly into a straw basket chair on the sun-porch, the telephone against her ear, one long leg wound around the leg of the chair, the other draped over its arm, so that arms and legs of girl and chair bathed in sunlight gave an impression of straw-coloured intertwined warmth. Her blonde hair was clipped short, brushed back from an oval face with shining cheeks and shining nose, blue eyes studying the ceiling and then the floor, and then a speck of imaginary lint on the navy-blue cashmere, her free hand picking off a small twisted knot of wool and then dropping to the skin-tight jeans and stroking the faded blue. "Yes," she said, "Agnes, I am not a total idiot, I can understand your problem."

Bobby Bridges burst on to the sun-porch in a spurt of nine-year-old energy, knocking the telephone book from its stand, nearly knocking the phone itself to the floor in his casual awkward growing way.

"I'm on the phone, Bobby," Kate said.

"So?"

"I'm on the phone, would you mind?"

"I can see you're on the phone," Bobby said.

"Do you want me to call Mother?"

"Why? What am I doing?"

"You make me nervous, bumping into everything. Agnes, would you mind holding on a minute? I've got to deal with the vermin." She put the receiver down in her lap and said, "I'll give you three seconds to vanish, Bobby."

"This is *my* house, too. What am I doing?"

"One," Kate said.

"Are you going to town?"

"Two."

"Because if you are, Mommy says you should pick up some model paint for me. Black and red, here's fifty cents."

Kate took the money. "All right, now disappear."

"Who you talking to?"

"None of your business. Bobby, I'm going to call Mother in a minute. I mean it."

"I only asked who you're talking to. What is it, a big senator secret?"

"Now just what is that supposed to mean? I wish you wouldn't use words you don't understand."

"Those pants are too tight. Daddy's gonna take a fit."

"He's already seen them." She picked up the phone. "Just a minute, Agnes." She put down the phone again. "Bobby, this is important. Will you please get out of here?"

"Everything's important," Bobby said. He shrugged his shoulders. "I wish the Russians would drop a bomb on you."

"If it drops on me, it'll drop on you, too."

"I'm impermanent," Bobby said.

"Impervious," Kate corrected.

"Tell Agnes she's bowlegged and has a fat behind," Bobby said, and he rushed out of the room. Kate rolled her eyes to the ceiling and picked up the phone.

"Who was that?" Agnes asked. "Your brother?"

"Yes."

"What did he say about me? I heard my name."

"Nothing. He's beginning to notice girls, that's all."

"At eight years old?"

"He's nine. Don't underestimate him."

"That still seems awfully young," Agnes said. "Frankenstein didn't enter prepuberty until at least eleven."

"Do they get any better at eleven?"

"Worse." Agnes paused. "Well, what should we do, Katie?"

"I think we should forget the whole thing."

"That's only because you don't like Paul."

"I like him very much. But if he wants me to go out with him, why doesn't he call me? I don't see why he has to go through Ralph, and why Ralph has to ask you to ask me."

"He's shy."

"Oh-ho, he's shy."

"He is, Kate. Really, he is. He's a very shy person."

"Well, if he's *that* shy, I'm not interested. What is this, the Miles Standish bit? He's got to send someone to ask you to ask me to go out with him?"

"Well, you see, I *want* to go out with Ralph."

"I understand that, Aggie. I wish you'd quit telling me you want to go out with him. I know you do. That's understood. If you want to date him, then go ahead. I'll sit home and knit."

"But he won't go out with me unless you date Paul."

"That's the most idiotic thing I've ever heard in my entire life!"

"Katie, it's true. I know it."

"You *don't* know it, Ag. You're only surmising. Did Ralph say so?"

"No, but . . ."

"All right, you just call Ralph back and tell him my number is Talmadge 4-0712, and if Paul wants to call me I'll be here for the next five minutes, dressing, and I'll be happy to hear whatever he has to say."

"Ahhh, Kate."

"Well now, really, put yourself in my position. It's degrading, Ag. It really is."

"Why? *Ralph* called, didn't he?"

"Well, what's the matter with Paul? Can't *he* pick up a telephone?"

"I told you he's shy."

"That's not what Mims said. Mims didn't think he was so shy."

"Why? What did he do?"

"Never mind."

"He did, huh?"

"He's not so shy, honey-babe, believe me."

"Well, I'll tell Ralph to tell him to call you. But I'll bet he doesn't. And I'll bet I'll be sitting home alone next Saturday night."

"Aggie, I have to get dressed. Now excuse me, please."

"Are you angry with me?"

"No, but I'm being picked up in ten minutes, and I don't like to keep people waiting."

"Oh?" Agnes said. "Anyone I know?"

"It's only Mrs. Regan. Really, Agnes, stop being such a creep. I'll call you late. If Paul wants to reach me, I'll be here for the next ten minutes. Now good-bye."

"Hey!"

"What?"

"What *did* your brother say about me?"

"Oh, for Pete's sake, he said he'd love to get into a necking session with you, okay?"

"*Bobby* said that?"

"Yeah, yeah," Kate said, and she rolled her eyes towards the ceiling again.

"Wow, he's got problems," Agnes said.

"Honey-babe, the *world* has problems. Even *I've* got problems. I'll call you later."

"Okay."

"G'-bye."

"G'-bye."

Kate put down the phone, extricated herself from the chair and walked out of the sun-porch, a tall, long-legged girl of sixteen with a lithe figure and a coltish walk, not awkward, but not graceful either, a walk that combined womanly polish with girlish directness and succeeded at neither, and yet a walk that was exuberant and alive, a propelling, bursting walk, energy jobbing at each long-legged stride, in each compact tight-filled-jeans explosion of youthfulness.

"Mom!" she called.

There was no answer. She paused with her hand on the banister, impatience on her face, waiting.

"Mom!"

"What is it, Kate?" Amanda called from the back porch.

"What are you doing out there?"

"I wanted to see something," Amanda said. "What is it?"

"Did Parsie iron my skirt?"

"I ironed your skirt," Parsie shouted from the kitchen. "Why'n't you ask *me*, Kate?"

"I didn't know you were in the house."

"Where would I be, if not in the house?"

"How do I know where you'd be!"

"Kate, don't talk that way to Parsie!" Amanda called from outside.

"What way? Where's the skirt, Parsie?"

"Upstairs in your room, hanging in the closet, right where it's supposed to be. If it had teeth, it'd bite you."

"I haven't been up there yet," Kate said. "Why's everyone umping on me? Where's Dad?"

"In the garage, washing *your* dog," Parsie said. She came in from the kitchen, wiping her hands on a dish towel, a big coloured woman wearing a black skirt and a white blouse, and looking at Kate with disapproval.

"Beverly is *everybody's* dog," Kate answered. "Thanks for the skirt, Parsie."

"I ironed your blouse, too," Parsie said.

"Oh, thanks, that's great," Kate said, and she started up the steps.

"Your mother seen those pants?" Parsie observed.

"Nope."

"She ain't gonna like those pants. They're too tight."

"I only wear them around the house," Kate said, and ran up the steps and down the corridor to her room. She closed the door and pulled the sweater over her head, throwing it on to the bed. She unzipped the side of her jeans, took them off, and then stood before the mirror in bra and panties and suddenly shook herself wildly like a burlesque queen. "Zing-zong!" she said to the mirror, laughed, went to the closet humming, took the tweed skirt from its hanger, went to the dresser and turned on the radio, went back to the closet for her blouse, walked to the dresser again to tune in a Stamford station playing popular music, shook herself at the mirror again, studied a small blemish near the flap of her nose, took a half-slip from the dresser drawer, bent over to look at a movie circular on the dresser top as she stepped into the slip and pulled it up over her hips, thwacking the elastic, put on her blouse, stepped into her skirt, zipped it up, and was buttoning the blouse when Amanda came into the room.

She was wearing plaid slacks and an old sweater, her blonde hair caught with a bright-red scarf at the back of her head. The sun had put a fine glow on her cheeks. Her brown eyes were sparkling. "Where are you off to?" she asked Kate, sitting on the edge of the bed.

"Mrs. Regan's coming by for me," Kate said. "She's got to see Dr. Anderson about something, and she called to ask if I'd like a lift. So I said yes. Mom, this blouse has a spot."

"Where?"

"See? Right here near the pocket. Do you think it's all right?"

"You can wear the green cardigan over it. It's a little chilly today, anyway." Amanda paused. "I didn't hear you practising, Kate?"

"No, I didn't."

"Don't you think you should?"

"I will, Mom. You were at the piano all morning, so how could I?"

"What are you going to do in town?"

"I have to pick up some things, and I have to look up the partition of Berlin."

"Are you going out tonight?"

"There's a party at Suzie's. Can Dad drive us?"

"Why don't you ask him?"

"Well, he's out washing Beverly, and I've got to get dressed."

"You buttoned your blouse crooked."

"Did I? Yes, I did. I'm all fingers."

"Thumbs," Amanda corrected.

"Sure. Mom, can I use your white?"

"You've got your own lipstick, Kate."

"I'm out of white. Besides, it looks creepy on you, Mom. I mean it. It makes you look positively eerie."

"Your father likes the way I look."

"Well, he has no *gusto*," Kate said, and she grinned.

"It's on my dresser," Amanda said, shaking her head. "If you pass the drugstore, buy yourself one. Charge it."

"Thanks, Mom. Mom, would you get it for me, please? I still have to comb my hair, and she'll be here any minute. Mom, how old do I look?"

"What? You look sixteen."

"Oh," Kate said dejectedly.

"How old do you want to look?"

"Oh, I don't know. Mom, could you get the lipstick, please? What were you doing outside?"

"I walked down near the brook. I wanted to see what it looked like now that spring is here."

"Same as always, didn't it?"

"Not quite, Kate. It's always a little different."

"Mom, could you get the lipstick, please?" The telephone rang. Kate looked at it for a moment and then said, "Would you answer it, Mom? If it's somebody named Paul, tell him I'm in the living-room talking to a fellow about something, and that you'll get me? Would you, Mom?"

"No, I won't."

"Oh, come on, Mom, don't be a poop. I want to put him on the rack."

"Put him on the rack all by yourself," Amanda said. "I'll get the lipstick for you."

She left the room. Kate looked at the ringing telephone.

"Ain't nobody going to answer that phone?" Parsie yelled from downstairs.

The phone kept ringing.

"Phone's ringing!" Parsie shouted. "Kate? You up there, Kate?"

"I've got it, Parsie," she answered, and lifted the receiver. "Hello," she said. "Kate Bridges speaking."

"Hello . . . uh . . . Kate?"

"This is she," Kate said. She looked at herself in the mirror and nodded. It was Paul. He'd finally found a dime.

"This is Paul Marris."

"Hello, Paul."

"I guess you're wondering why I'm calling."

"Well, yes, that's *just* what I was wondering," she said and made a face at the mirror.

"Did you . . . uh . . . talk to Agnes?"

"Agnes *who*?" Kate said. Her own words nearly convulsed her. She had to cover her mouth to keep from laughing aloud.

"Why . . . why, Agnes Donohue. Your friend. You know. Agnes? Agnes Donohue?"

"Oh yes, Agnes. What about her?"

"Well, did you . . . uh . . . talk to her?"

"When?" Kate asked, and again covered her mouth because she was just being too devastatingly comic for words.

"Today, I guess. This morning, I guess. Didn't you talk to her?"

"I think I did," Kate said.

"Well, Ralph said he talked to her, and she said if I wanted to talk to you I should call you personally. That's what he said, anyway. Ralph, I mean."

"Oh, is that what he said?"

"Yeah. That's what he said. I mean, *wasn't* I supposed to call you?"

"Well, I don't know. It's your dime."

"No, I'm calling from home," Paul said. He paused. "The reason . . . say, is this Katie Bridges?"

"This is Kate."

"Oh, I thought for a minute . . . well . . ." Paul took a deep breath. "You see, *Gigi* is coming to Stamford Wednesday, and Ralph and I thought you and Aggie would like to see it. On Saturday night. Next Saturday night, that is. If you're not busy. I mean, you would go with me, and Aggie would go with Ralph. Together, of course. But, you know, you and me, and Aggie and Ralph. If you're not busy."

"Saturday night, did you say?"

"Yeah, Saturday."

"Next Saturday?"

"Yeah, next Saturday."

"That's . . . let me see . . . that's the sixteenth."

"Yeah, the sixteenth."

"Of May, right?"

"Yeah, May."

"Of 1959, right?" Kate asked, and covered her mouth to stifle a giggle.

"What? Yeah, sure, 1959."

"I think I'm free," Kate said at last.

"Oh, well, good. Then we're set, huh?"

"Yes."

"Well, that's good. I don't know what time the show starts, but I'll check. I'll call you again during the week, okay?"

"Okay," Kate said.

"Listen, will you call Agnes?"

"Why?"

"To tell her it's okay with you, so she can tell Ralph it's okay with her? I mean, I hate to make this so complicated but . . . well, you see, it *is* complicated. You see, this was all my idea, Kate, and I . . ." He stopped short.

"What was your idea?"

"Well, I thought you might like to go to a show. That's what I thought."

"Yes, I would."

"Well, that's swell. So I asked Ralph, and it gets sort of complicated, so would you call Agnes and tell her everything's smooth now, and we're set, okay?"

"Okay."

"Good. Well, I'll see you, Kate. I'll call you during the week, okay? To let you know what time, okay? You got a curfew or anything?"

"One o'clock on Saturday night."

"Well, that's not so bad, is it?"

"No, it's fine."

"Okay, good. Well, okay," Paul said. "I'll say good-bye now."

"Good-bye, Paul," she said sweetly. "I'll be talking to you."

"Good-bye."

"Good-bye."

"So long, Kate."

"So long."

"I'll talk to you."

"All right, Paul. Good-bye." Gently she put the phone back into its cradle.

"What opera was that?" Amanda asked from the doorway. "Here's the lipstick."

"Thanks," Kate said. She took off the cap, smeared the white undercoating to her mouth, and then put a bright red over it. "How do I look?" she asked.

"Lovely. Are you sure you're only going to town?"

"Sure. Where else?"

"I don't know. You . . ." Amanda shook her head. "Leave yourself time to practise before you go out tonight, will you? Who'll be at this party?"

"The usual creeps," Kate said. A horn sounded outside. "There's Mrs. Regan!" She bolted for the door. "Mom, if Aggie calls, tell her it's okay for next Saturday! I'll see you!"

"Kate, your bag!"

"Oh, hell," Kate said.

"Kate!"

"Sorry, Mom. Give it to me, will you? 'Bye, Mom." She kissed

Amanda hastily on the cheek, and rushed down the steps and out of the front door. Amanda stood at the window in her daughter's room and looked at the Alfa Romeo parked at the curb. The door on the side closest to the curb opened as Kate came running down the walk. A tall lean man stepped out of the car and held the door open for Kate. For a moment, Amanda didn't recognize him. And then she realized it was David Regan.

She shook her head, smiled, and went downstairs again as the Alfa pulled away from the curb.

"I almost didn't make it in time," Kate said in the car. "A boy called, and he kept me on the phone for a half-hour."

"You must be pretty popular, Kate," David said.

"Well, it depends on what you consider popular, I guess."

There was a faint smile on his mouth, not a smile of mockery, but a smile that managed to be tolerant and condescending at the same time. She knew the smile was there, but she would not turn to look at him. She sat hunched between him and his mother and smelling the warm close smell of his woollen sweater and a smell like aftershave, but not the kind her father used, and she knew the smile was on his mouth, and she thought, He thinks I'm just a kid, and she crossed her legs suddenly, and then immediately pulled her skirt over her knees.

"Kate's very popular, David," Julia said. "The boys practically camp on her doorstep."

"I'm afraid your mother's giving you the wrong impression, David," she said. She had only begun calling him David in 1957, when she got to be fifteen. Up to that time, she'd called him Mr. Regan, and then she asked her father if it would be all right to call him David, and her father had said, "Why don't you ask *him*?" and she had asked him, and he had said, "Sure, why not? Everybody else does," and so she'd begun. She still called his mother Mrs. Regan though, well, she was about a hundred years old, and that was respect for elders. But David couldn't be much older than thirty-four, and it was really ridiculous for a young woman of sixteen to be calling one of her contemporaries "Mr. Regan", especially when she knew his mother so well, for Pete's sake Julia Regan was practically her best friend in town, next to Aggie Donohue.

"You mean you're *not* a popular girl?" David asked, and there was that same tolerant but condescending tone in his voice.

"Oh, stop it," Kate said. "You're teasing me."

"I am," David admitted.

"Why?"

"Because you're so damn cute," he said, and he covered her hand with his affectionately, and then reached into his pocket for a cigarette. The touch was brief and hardly intimate, but she felt herself tensing as his hand covered hers, felt a desire to turn her hand over and clasp his fingers into hers. And then his hand moved away, he was fishing inside his shirt for cigarettes, she sat silently and stiffly on the seat beside him, scarcely daring to breathe, suddenly flustered. He offered the pack to her. Again, there was the smile on her face.

"Do you smoke, Kate?"

She was tempted to take one, but she knew it would be foolish to smoke here in the car on the way to town where everyone could see her, yet she was tempted because the offered package was a challenge, and yet she knew it was foolish.

"Not right now, thanks," she said, and she knew by the smile on his face that he didn't believe she smoked, although she really did smoke whenever she and Aggie and the other girls got together alone. And even her father had said she could begin smoking when she was eighteen, which was only a year and a half away, she was practically eighteen already, and there was a half-used package of king-sized cigarettes in the back of her dresser drawer where she kept it with the tiny piece of driftwood she had found at the lake the year before, minuscule and whorled, a tree in delicate minature.

David offered a cigarette to Julia who refused with a shake of her head. He lighted up and then threw the match out, lowering the window slightly, turning on the seat. His knee bumped against Kate's, and together they said "Excuse me," and then laughed.

"Now we have to make a wish," Kate said.

"All right," David answered. "What do you want most in the world, Kate?"

She almost said, "You." Instead, she stared straight through the windshield, and said, "I don't know. Besides, if I told you, it wouldn't come true."

"Oh, sure it would," David said. "What do you think she should wish for, Mom?"

"Well, when I was a girl her age . . ." Julia started, and Kate quickly interrupted before she could augment a theme of sweet sixteen, which would remind just everybody in the entire world how old she was.

"Actually, I've got everything I need," she said hastily.

"Have you got a diamond ring?" David asked.

Kate laughed a phony brittle laugh she had heard the married women of Talmadge use at cocktail parties in her house. "No. Shall I wish for one, David?"

"If you want one."

"No."

"Well, what *do* you want? Think hard now, Kate."

"I'd like to go to Europe," Kate said.

The car was still for a moment.

"Mims went to Europe last summer," Kate said into the silence. David said nothing. She could hear the wind whistling over the cloth top of the car, could hear the tires singing against the road.

"*I* may go to Europe," Julia said suddenly.

David turned to look at his mother. Kate saw his eyes in that instant, puzzled, probing. Something odd had come into the automobile with her mention of Europe, and she didn't know quite what it was, a curious tension that caused her to believe she'd said the wrong thing. And yet she couldn't understand what was so terribly wrong about mentioning Europe, everyone was going to Europe these days, she had even heard her parents discussing a trip to Europe.

"I didn't know you'd planned to go abroad, Mother," David said.

Kate noticed that he'd called her "Mother" and not "Mom" as he had earlier, and she knew this meant something because she never called her own mother anything but "Mom", except when she was particularly irritated or annoyed, or when she was threatening Bobby . . . or, wait, when she thought her mother was acting too frivolous and young for her age, like when she danced close to Daddy at a party, that was really degrading for a couple in their forties, well, Daddy *was* in his forties, still, to act like lovebirds on a dance floor. David was annoyed now, and yet all his mother had said was "I may go to Europe", but Kate could definitely feel him tensing on the seat beside her.

"I've planned to go back to Italy for a long time," Julia said, not turning to look at David, her hands firm and steady on the wheel, looking straight ahead at the road.

"To Aquila?" David asked.

"No," she said. "To Rome."

Kate sat between them and had the oddest feeling they were talking in a code only the two of them understood. She said nothing. David sucked in on his cigarette.

"Is this definite?" David asked. "I mean, have you really made plans?"

Julia laughed, and Kate recognized it as the same phony laugh she herself had used a few moments ago. She frowned. The tension in the automobile had somehow become unbearable. She wanted to get out and walk. If only she could say to David, "Let's get out and walk to town."

"Every year since the end of the war," Julia said, "I've made plans to go back to Italy. And every year, something came up to prevent my return. Last year, I thought I'd surely go. And then Millie passed away and . . ." Julia let the sentence trail. "Maybe I'll make it this year. Maybe this year, I'll get back."

"Maybe you don't really *want* to go back, Mother," David said.

"Maybe not. You young people today . . ."

Kate was grateful for that. She almost turned and kissed Julia.

". . . are too psychologically orientated. I'm not of the school that believes nothing happens by accident. Too *many* things happen by accident."

"But nothing's really prevented you from going to Rome, Mother. Yes, Aunt Millie's death. But other than that——"

"David," she said flatly, "I want to go back. I've wanted to go back to Rome for as long as I can remember."

"Then why haven't you gone?" There was something harsh in his voice. "Why don't you go back?"

"Maybe I'm afraid."

"Of what?"

"What you need is a travelling companion, Mrs. Regan." Kate put in quickly. She laughed tinnily. "I'll be happy to apply for the job."

"I might take you up on that," Julia said, and laughed.

The car went silent again. David snuffed out his cigarette. They could see the church now, white against the blue sky, dominating the town as they rounded the curve and headed down the hill.

"Where can I drop you?" Julia asked.

"Where are you going?" David said.

"To Dr. Anderson's office."

"Why?" David said quickly. "Is something wrong?"

"Nothing serious. A little indigestion."

"Daddy thinks he's a good doctor," Kate said.

"He is a good doctor," Julia said.

"Where are *you* going, Kate?"

"To the library."

"I'll buy you a soda," David said.

"Okay," she said casually. Her heart had begun to pound. She clenched her hands over her bag.

"Anywhere along here, Mother," David said.

Julia pulled the car to the kerb, and yanked up the handbrake. "I'll be an hour or so. Will you want a ride back?"

"Not me, Mrs. Regan."

"I'll manage," David said, and stepped out on to the kerb. He held out his hand to Kate. She took it, feeling embarrassed and awkward all at once. They stood on the kerb together, watching the Alfa as it pulled away and turned the corner, heading for Anderson's office.

"Well, where to?" David asked.

"You said you'd buy me a soda."

"I will. Which is the local teen-age hot spot these days?"

Kate squelched her sudden anger. "Well, the teen-agers hang out in the drugstore, but we can get sodas at the tearoom, and it'll be quieter and nicer." She paused. "Unless you have a preference for teen-age hot spots."

"I was deferring to the lady," David said, and he made a courtly bow.

They walked up the main street and turned the corner. Down the block, they could see Julia's car parked near the kerb, outside the doctor's office.

Milt Anderson was a man who didn't believe in mincing words. Everything about his appearance denied nonsense and frivolity. He wore dark-grey suits in his office, severe ties, white shirts. His thinning hair was iron-grey, and he wore unrimmed spectacles on the bridge of his nose, and if he possessed anything even faintly resembling a bedside manner, his wife Nancy was the only person who had ever seen it. He had been practising medicine in Talmadge for forty years. Psychology, so far as Milt was concerned, was a fake and a fraud. Before Kohnblatt, the obstetrician, arrived in town, Milt delivered every baby born there, and he nursed them through their childhood diseases and through every ache and pain they ever had, and he did it all without the faintest knowledge of Sigmund Freud. He was an excellent diagnostician, and he practised medicine as if the human body were an automobile that had to be kept in constant repair. If you needed a clutch job, he didn't try to tell you about it by explaining that the cigarette lighter wasn't working.

He sat behind his desk, and looked at Julia Regan, who sat opposite him, and he said, "I've got the results on that test, Julia. That's why I asked you to come in."

"Shall I make out a will?" Julia said jokingly.

"Maybe you should," he answered seriously. He tweaked his nose, pulled a tissue from the box on his desk, blew his nose heartily, and dropped the tissue into his wastebasket. "I want to explain that test to you, Julia. It's called the Masters Two-Step or the Masters Exercise Tolerance Test, or sometimes simply Cardiogram after Exercise. Whatever you call it, it's designed to supplement the ordinary cardiogram and discover what your tolerance to extreme physical or emotional strain would be. The Army uses it as a routine examination for anyone over the age of forty who's in a responsible position."

He took another tissue from the box and blew his nose again. "Did you ever hear of a doctor who caught a cold?" he asked. He shrugged, threw the tissue away, and leaned closer to Julia. "Whenever I get a patient in here who's complaining to me of easy fatigability or indigestion, I might as well tell you I suspect angina immediately, and I arrange for the Masters test to be taken. Which is what I did with you last week."

"And you've discovered that I have one foot in the grave, and should——"

"I've discovered that there's a definite compromise of circulation to your heart, Julia. You want my opinion, I'd say you were a prime candidate for a coronary."

Julia grew suddenly attentive.

"That's right," Milt said. "And judging from the experience I've had with similar cases, you can expect it within the next two years . . . unless you start taking care of yourself."

"That's a little shocking," Julia said.

"I'm a doctor," Milt answered.

"What do you want me to do?"

"I want you to avoid any strenuous exercise or emotional stress. I'm putting you on a low cholesterol diet, and you'll begin eating unsaturated fatty acids instead of butter and animal fats. We're going to try to stop hardening of the arteries, Julia. You're not such a spring chicken any more, you know."

"I didn't think I was, Milt."

"The way you go racing around in that little car . . ." He shook his head. "Look, Julia, you're in the right age-group for a full-fledged coronary, believe me. You'd just better slow down."

"What does slowing down entail, Milt?"

"I just told you. I don't want you getting overtired or——"

"How about a trip to Europe?"

"Out of the question," Milt said.

"I was planning——"

"Go on," he said. "They'll send you back in a pine box."

Julia nodded. "What about next year?"

"Maybe. It depends on what progress you make."

"This is ridiculous," Julia said.

"Sure, it's always ridiculous when the body starts giving out. It's more ridiculous to drop dead one day, believe me. That's the most ridiculous and humiliating thing that can happen to anyone." He paused. "Would you like to drop dead in the street one day, Julia? Most of the fatal coronaries, you know, happen to people who've never had a clue. No real chest pains, nothing like that. Bam, and there you go. You want that to happen?"

"No."

"Then slow down. I'll prepare the diet for you. I want you to pick it up tomorrow or the next day. I'll give you a call."

Julia suddenly smiled. "How am I supposed to avoid emotional stress, Milt, would you tell me that?"

"That's your problem, not mine. When you're dead, Julia, there's no emotional stress at all. You might just remember that."

"I will." She paused. "It was only a little indigestion," she said. "I thought I had a good heart."

"It's not exactly a rotten heart," Milt said, "but I wouldn't go courting any shock or strain beyond your capacity." Milt shrugged. "Look, it's your life, Julia."

"I know it." She nodded. "I'll be careful."

"You can start by slowing down to thirty miles an hour when you're driving that little bug."

"I will."

"Fine. I'll call you within the next few days."

"Thanks, Milt."

"And be careful," he said to her as she went out of the office.

The tearoom was in the middle of the street. A bell over the door jingled when they entered. Two young boys were sitting at a table near the kitchen, but the room was otherwise empty. David held out a chair for Kate, and she sat and said, "Isn't this better than the drugstore?"

He sat opposite her. "Indeed it is."

"We come here sometimes when we've got plans."

"What do you mean, plans?"

"Oh, things to discuss that we don't want anyone else to hear. At the drugstore, everyone's on the earie."

"I see," David said. He smiled.

"Everyone needs a private place," Kate said, almost in defence, though she really didn't see what there was to defend. "Don't you have a private place?"

"Sure, I do. It's a little saloon on Sixth Avenue."

"Do you drink a lot?"

"No, not terribly much."

"I hate to drink. Even beer. It tastes so awful. Suzie Fox got drunk two weeks ago. On beer. She threw up in the bathroom."

"Poor Susie Fox," David said.

"Do you ever get drunk? And sick?"

"I very often get drunk, but I rarely get sick."

"Well, why do you want to do that?" Kate said maternally, irritated.

"Get drunk? It's very pleasant. It provides an area of blurred focus, a temporary adjustment with the world."

"I wish you wouldn't get drunk," she said, frowning.

"Why?"

"I just . . . well, I don't like the idea of you lying in a New York gutter some place." He began laughing. "Really, David, it's not funny. You're a grown man, and——"

"Kate, Kate, I don't lie around in gutters. And I never get *that* drunk."

"Well, Suzie Fox got that drunk."

"Honey, Suzie Fox is sixteen."

"That doesn't make her exactly an infant, you know."

"I know. But when I was sixteen, I could get roaring blind drunk on three bottles of beer. Unfortunately, I can't do that any more."

"How many bottles of beer does it take now?"

"Beer? Beer is very out."

"Martinis?"

"Martinis are on the way out. On the rocks is coming back in. Very chic." David winked conspiratorially.

"Do you know the Moses and Jesus joke?" Kate asked suddenly.

"On the rocks?" David laughed. "Sure. But how come you know it?"

"Listen, David, cut it out," she said sharply.

"What did I do?"

"You just stop that business. I'm not a baby. Now you just cut it out."

"I beg your pardon, ma'am," he said, and he gave a deferential little nod of his head.

"Yes, and that too."

"What now?"

"What you just did. Just stop the entire whole business or I'll get very angry."

"Yes, ma'am." He was still smiling. "Here's our waitress."

"What would you like, David?"

"Two chocolate sodas, Connie," Kate said. "Do you want anything else, David?"

"No, thank you," he said, smiling.

"Two chocolate sodas," the waitress said, and walked away from the table.

"Hey, I'll let you in on a secret," David said, still smiling.

"Yes, what?" She leaned towards him.

"The man's supposed to order," he whispered.

"What?"

"The man——"

"Oh, hell!" Kate said. "I come here all the time, and I know Connie and you don't, and I was trying to put you at ease, that's all."

"What makes you think I'm ill at ease?"

"You're *always* ill at ease. You're always so tense. It must be television does it to you. Television is a rat race."

"How do you know?"

"I read a book about it."

"Oh, well then, okay. If you read a book, I guess it's so."

"Stop it, David. Look, I'm warning you. Stop treating me that way."

"I'm only——"

"You're only laughing at everything I say, and that isn't fair. I'm not a moron, David. I'm six——" She cut herself off. "I'm almost seventeen years old, and I'm pretty aware of what's going on around me in the world, and I'm perfectly capable of holding an intelligent conversation, so cut it out!"

"Okay, what would you like to talk about?"

"You. What do you do in New York? Besides getting drunk all the time?"

"I don't get drunk *all* the time. I have a drink when I get back to the apartment each evening, and I usually drink something later on in the night. And when I'm in Talmadge, I hardly drink at all."

"The people in Talmadge are very hard drinkers," Kate said.

"Do you think so? The people in New York aren't exactly slouches."

"I think everyone's drinking more nowadays. And everyone's more tense. Don't you feel that? You're very tense."

"I suppose I am."

"It's because of the bomb and those stupid Russians. I don't care what anyone says, I can't see how the constant threat of atomic disintegration can help but affect a person's everyday thinking. Subliminal, they call it. I know it affects me. I wake up each morning, and wonder if I'll still be alive at the end of the day. Of course, I don't imagine they would bother dropping anything on Talmadge, but if they drop it on New York, everyone'll rush out of the city like barbarians, and no one will be safe. Daddy says he wants to buy a rifle. Did you read *On the Beach*?"

"Yes."

"They're making it into a movie, you know. But I don't think it'll be that way at all, when it comes, I mean. I don't think everyone will just go off into a corner to die very nobly and very peacefully. I think the world will just cut loose and become positively animalistic. When the bomb comes . . ."

"When? Not if?"

"Oh, *when* it comes, David. Everyone knows it'll come. *We* all know it."

"Who's we?"

"The kids. The . . . well, the young men and young women of America," she said pompously, hating herself for having said "kids", especially when things finally seemed to be going so well, when he was beginning to treat her like a person at last. "Why do you think there are all these teen-age gangs today, and rumbles in the street? It's because they know the bomb is coming, and they can't see any sense to living up to a moral and ethical code that has become meaningless. When civilization itself may be wiped out at any second, why bother living by its rules? Well, David, look at the quiz-show scandal . . . you don't handle any quiz shows, do you?"

"The firm does, but we're clean."

"Well, anyway, look at that, look at the moral deterioration of all those fine people, David. Do you think it was because of the money? Absolutely not. It's because everyone knows the bomb is coming."

"*I* don't know it," David said.

"You, of all people, should know it."

"Why me?"

"Because you're so hard. Or at least you try to pretend hardness. You're not really hard at all."

"Do I seem hard?"

"Yes, you seem terribly menacing. You're the only man I know who has white hair." She hesitated. "It's very attractive. Agnes thinks you're quite the most attractive man she's ever seen."

"Thank Agnes for me."

"Of course, she has no *gusto*," Kate said, and she smiled.

"Well, what are you going to do when the bomb falls, Kate?"

"Run like hell," she said, and then she giggled. "No, not really. I'll probably find somebody and live in sin with him until the radiation sickness kills us both. I mean, I wouldn't want to die without having . . ." She paused. "Well, who knows what anyone will do in the face of extreme emergency? What will you do?"

"I'll hop on the first plane to Los Angeles," David said immediately.

"Why Los Angeles?"

He shrugged. 'I don't know. I guess it's as good a place as any to die. Also, it's going West. And 'going West' means dying, did you know that?"

"You're lying, aren't you? I can always tell when you're lying."

"No, no, scout's honour." He raised his hand in the three-fingered salute and grinned. "Going West has passed from the vernacular to——"

"I didn't mean about that. I meant about why you want to go to Los Angeles. There's another reason."

"Nope. No other reason."

"Have you ever been there?"

"Nope."

"Then why would you want to go?"

"Just to see it. I understand the climate is nice."

"My plan sounds like a better one," Kate said shrewdly. "Besides, I think we both have the same thing in mind, only I'm considering it a bit closer."

David laughed. "Does your father know you talk like this?"

"Of course. We've resolved the whole thing."

"What thing?"

"The Electra bit. We're buddies now. I've decided to leave him to Mom," Kate said, and smiled again.

"I'm sure Mom is relieved."

"Well, it *can* be a strain, you know," Kate said. "Here're our sodas." She smiled at the waitress. "Thanks, Connie."

Sitting and listening to her, David was enchanted. There was such an impossible combination of reality and fantasy, such a blending of child with young woman, such a mixture of worldly concern with juvenile irresponsibility, that he picked his way through the conversation like a man walking through a mine-field, and yet he was enchanted. He was thirty-four years old and, he supposed, an eligible New York bachelor who circulated in a hip television crowd where the questions were fast and the answers were ready, but he had never come across anything as refreshing as Kate. He knew this was because she was still a child, but he saw no reason to belittle charm simply because it was worn by youth. He found her thoroughly enchanting and delightful, shining and new, looking at the world with untarnished eyes, seeing everything so clearly and so simply.

He wondered suddenly if he had been that way at sixteen. It seemed to him he had always been a little uncertain, a little shy. But then, he supposed everyone looked back upon his youth as a time of awkwardness. There was an awkwardness in Kate, too. She was groping out of adolescence towards an adulthood that seemed so very far away to her, seeking acceptance in a world that, just a short while ago, was the world of the "grown-ups". But it was not the awkwardness that stamped her youth. It was instead a lack of artifice, a lack of sophistication. She had not yet acquired the gloss, the infinite variety, of the adult. She was Kate Bridges, and sixteen, and herself, and certain of the world and of her place in it, and certain too that a hydrogen bomb would fall on her head one day, and yet accepting the certainty with blithe, almost joyful, indifference. She was Kate Bridges.

He felt a sudden pride. He had known her when she was just a little girl, and he sat opposite her now in a tearoom in the month of May, and she chatted with him like a young woman, and he felt an almost paternal pride in being with her, as if he were responsible in some small way for her growth. And he felt privileged to be sitting here with her at this time of her life, before she had acquired the polish, before she had become too fully aware of the world around her, before age stole in and life forced her to toe the mark. And he felt, too, a fondness for her, a protective fondness, an empathy that cried out over the years like a race memory, I was once this young, my eyes were once this clear. He was glad he'd asked her to have a soda with him. He was glad, even with the missiles poised, even with some trigger-happy nut possibly waiting to push the button, he was glad that he could sit in a tearoom in the month of May with a sixteen-year-old girl and feel something that he could only describe as hope.

And sitting with him, she knew only despair. She was certain that he thought her a fool, certain her love for him was flaming out of her eyes, certain he knew and was teasing her, certain everything she said was absurd and juvenile and hopeless. She lifted her glass and some of the soda spilled over on to the table, and she fumbled for a napkin and saw the smile on his face and felt graceless and stupidly infantile and thought, I should never have come, I should have said No. And then she thought of the person she wanted to live in sin with, David Regan in his New York apartment where he came home each night and had whisky on the rocks, probably with some damn television actress or some fashion model. She mopped up the spilled soda and went rattling on about the partition of Berlin and how it was the crux of world affairs today, and about the hopelessness of disarmament, all the while convinced that he wasn't listening to a word she said. She condemned herself for having loved him all these years. She wondered what it would be like to kiss him. His mouth looked so hard, but she knew it would be soft. She had kissed him the day he'd put out the fire, the day he'd saved her life. His cheek had been covered with soot, and she had kissed him and got herself all grimy, and fallen in love at once with the man in the swimming-shorts all covered with soot, a man she had hardly even noticed before that day. And she had kissed him over the years, throwing her arms around his neck and hugging him and kissing him whenever he came up to Talmadge to visit. But she'd stopped kissing him when she became fourteen, and at fifteen she began calling him "David", and now she longed with all her heart to kiss him again, but not in that childish way, he would know how to kiss, he lived in New York.

I can have babies, you know, she thought, talking all the while about the failure of the United States' latest moon probe, bitterly complaining about the stupidity of an administration that made our failures public. I am capable of having babies, you know, David, I'm not quite the child you seem to think I am. Louise Pelzer had a baby when *she* was sixteen, you know, can't you look at me as if I'm something more than an infant? And knowing this was exactly the way he looked at her, and longing to be alone with him, and plotting desperately, wondering if she could suggest a walk over to the bird sanctuary, knowing he would never never never in a million years kiss her or touch her, a boy touched me, you know, she thought, a boy actually touched me, these are not foam rubber, you know. And wondering why he wanted to go to Los Angeles when the bomb fell, and thinking, Oh damn you, David, I *will* be seventeen in November, you know, that's not very far away, you know, David, oh damn you, you are such a cruddy creep.

That November, Gillian Burke came in from the beach driving her sister's convertible, a grey Thunderbird with the top down. She had figured on a forty-minute drive to the studio, but the traffic was unusually heavy, and even before she reached Brentwood, she knew she would be late. Impatiently, she waited out the traffic light near the shopping centre, her fingers moving impatiently on the wheel. The matrons were out in force, wearing their tapered slacks and sweaters, peering into shop-windows, idly crossing the street, their hair done in emulation of the latest Hollywood goddesses, it was amazing how many Kim Novaks and Ava Gardners walked the streets of the suburbs surrounding Hollywood.

There must be something wrong with that light, she thought, and in that instant it turned to green. She stepped on the accelerator. A woman had begun crossing the street, and Gillian almost tooted the horn at her before she remembered the California law, which she always forgot when she was in any kind of hurry. She put on her brakes and waited for the woman to cross. Take all your good sweet time, she thought. Go right ahead. Impatiently, she shifted to first again, stepped on the gas, and caught another red light not three blocks from the last one. At this rate, she thought, I should reach the studio by midnight. The light changed. She stepped on the gas and concentrated on making up for lost time, rushing past U.C.L.A. and the Bel Air gates, catching another red light on Beverly Glen. This was a conspiracy, she was certain of it. Someone was manipulating those lights. Someone had made a little voodoo doll of her, and was determined she would be not only late but hopelessly late. She resigned herself to her fate. There was no sense in getting killed in a traffic accident. No job was that important.

The traffic thickened the moment she entered the Strip. It always seemed to thicken there, but perhaps the reaction was purely psychological, perhaps the clutter of neon tubing, the shrieking signs for the strip joints, the restaurant and night-club awnings, the damn Las Vegas cowgirl towering over everything with her bent knee and her boots and hat made everything seem tight and cramped and suddenly bottlenecked. Psychological, hell, she thought. The traffic *does* get impossible here, and I *hate* this drive. I should have taken Santa Monica Boulevard, well, it's too late to think of that now. Let's go, please. The light is green, madam. Which indicates that it's now legal and proper to set your vehicle in motion. Stop daydreaming, madam. That man on the sidewalk is not Jack Benny.

She smiled, remembering her sister's story. Monica had been plagued by visitors from New York who automatically looked her up the moment they reached the Coast. Fortunately, her house in Malibu was fairly distant from the hotels in Los Angeles proper, or Hollywood, or even Beverly Hills, and most visitors were discouraged by the long drive. But she'd never been able to escape the callers entirely, and one girl in particular was convinced that Monica knew every star in Hollywood intimately and could point out their homes on demand. Monica had been a chemistry major in college and was working for a chemical research laboratory, and hadn't the slighest interest in where or even how the stars lived. But the girl kept asking, "When are you going to show me the stars' homes?" and Monica soon realized that the only way to get rid of her was to show her where the damn stars lived—if only she knew where. She had passed the old ladies selling maps on Sunset Boulevard a thousand times, sitting on their camp-chairs, wearing wide-brimmed straw hats, holding signs that blatantly advertised invasion of privacy for twenty-five cents—but she refused to behave like a tourist in a town she'd come to think of as her home. She would not have bought one of those maps if her life depended on it. Instead, she climbed into the T-bird and drove her visitor through the last Bel Air gate and past the Bel Air Hotel and up through the hills, and every time she saw a house that looked elegant—and they all looked rather elegant—she said "That's Cary Grant's house," or "That's Loretta Young's house," or "That's Jack Benny's house," and her visitor was completely satisfied. Gillian, delighted with the story, asked Monica what she'd have done if Jack Benny had suddenly stepped out of the house she'd claimed was his.

"I wouldn't have skipped a beat," Monica said. "I've had waved and said, 'Hello, there, Jack.'"

The anecdote became an inside joke between Gillian and her sister. If ever they were driving past Bel Air together, one would automatically say, "That's Jack Benny's house," and the other would instantly wave and shout, "Hello, there, Jack."

The joke reached its climax when they were double-dating together one night. Gillian's date was a contract player at Metro who claimed a familiarity with most of the stars. As they drove through Brentwood, he pointed out the land that belonged to Van Heflin.

"Are you sure?" Gillian asked.

"Sure, I'm sure," the actor replied. He pointed to the large, fenced-in field on the corner. "You see that?" Both Monica and Gillian turned to look. "That's Van Heflin's *horse*!" the actor said, and the girls began laughing uncontrollably.

She passed the car-wash joints now, and the supermarkets and the huge signs advertising the Hollywood cemeteries. She'd never known a place where people prepared for death so vigorously. The first billboard she'd noticed upon arriving in Los Angeles in 1950, almost nine years ago, was one that announced FOREVERNESS as the slogan of a local cemetery.

Driving in from the airport, stunned by the flatness of the terrain and the temporary look and feel of the buildings, dismayed by the browning grass everywhere—"Ain't had rain for months," the cab driver told her—she had seen the billboard and suddenly begun laughing hysterically. Today, she no longer found the signs amusing. Perhaps she had simply grown used to them.

She supposed she had grown used to a lot of things in the past nine years. She had even begun to enjoy eating regularly. There was plenty of work out here, especially in television. More and more shows were being filmed here, the medium had forsaken immediacy and succumbed to the technical ease of film, and she had done three of four television shots of which she was really very proud. The rest . . . the rest was nonsense. "Background action!" and Gillian Burke and a hundred others like her would move into camera range. "Is this child supposed to be yours, Miss? Would you please take him by the hand? Thank you." Gillian Burke, good for a television or feature-film restaurant crowd, or a young mother at the bus-stop, or now and then a waitress, another town, another agent, another medium, another union card, S.A.G. this time, tucked into her purse and ready to show at the casting window. She was not lacking for work, no, and she ate regularly. She was just offbeat enough to go unrecognized in a crowd scene, she seemed real and believable on the fringes of the stage-centre glamour, her beauty did not shriek of professionalism.

She would sometimes look at her own face in the mirror, the bangs on her forehead slightly side-swept, the russet hair brushed to the back of her neck, the slanted green eyes. She came over very well in colour. She had played an amusement-park scene for Warners, in colour. There had been a close-up of her on the roller coaster, flash, if you blinked your eye you missed Gillian Burke's big scene. But she had not missed herself, she had seen how well she photographed in colour, and had seen the authentic terror and excitement on her face as the roller-coaster car swept by, actually six feet above the ground filmed in front of a process shot of the sky, she had looked very good. And standing in front of the mirror, she would study her body, study the familiar body, good breasts and hips and legs, she knew they were good, but not this year's model, thank you, not the overblown cowlike commodity they were buying in 1959, and maybe in 1958, and maybe back to the time of Delilah. She would study herself painstakingly, and she knew exactly where she missed, but there wasn't much she could do about it.

One of her friends, a girl of thirty-seven, had told Gillian she didn't care if she spent the rest of her life doing extra work. She didn't even want that meaty character role, the speaking part that brings down the house in the third reel, the hell with that. It meant only two days' shooting, and here's your pay cheque, thanks and good-bye. Gillian's friend wanted the steady extra part, the perpetual girl on the bar stool in a place the star frequented, there all the time, three or four weeks of shooting, that was for her. But Gillian was not an extra, and she knew she was not an extra, and she would not settle for less than what she was.

She was an actress.

They could fill the fan magazines with 38-28-38, they could provide three-dimensional glasses that made the latest siren pop out of the picture and into your lap, they could evolve screens that enveloped you with sight and sound and now even smell, but she was an actress, and this they could not take away from her. She could act hell out of any part they threw her way, and she knew it, and so she waited patiently for the promised trend towards the offbeat, wasn't Shirley MacLaine a star, look at Carolyn Jones, somewhere there was a place for her, Gillian Burke, and she hoped meanwhile that her envy didn't show.

She pulled the car up to one of the booths at the studio gate. A uniformed guard stepped out of the booth and smiled pleasantly at her.

"I have an appointment with Mr. Floren," she said.
"Yes, Miss. What's your name, please?"
"Gillian Burke."
"Just a moment."

He consulted a list of names and telephone numbers encased in Lucite, picked up a phone from the booth counter, and rapidly dialled an extension. He spoke quietly into the phone while Gillian waited. Then he replaced the receiver, came out of the booth, and said, "It's in building number seven, third floor. That's room 306. You can park the car right there, inside the gate."

"Thank you," Gillian said. She smiled, nodded, and swung the car over towards the diagonal spaces. She parked, turned the rear-view mirror so that she could see her mouth, decided her lipstick was fine, and then combed her hair. An electrician strolling by turned to look at her as she got out of the car and bent to take her black portfolio from the seat. She suddenly wondered if her skirt was too tight. She had worn a matching suit over a pale blue sweater. Now she wondered if the skirt was too tight, wondered if she shouldn't have put on some jewellery, a string of pearls perhaps, and instantly checked her legs to see if her seams were straight. Oh, the hell with it, she thought. I'm Gillian Burke. I want a pock in the play.

A white Corvette with zebra upholstery was parked in the space alongside hers. A white poodle sat behind the steering wheel, and Gillian wondered if the car belonged to the dog. She smiled and began walking across the lot. A man in a cowboy suit waved at her. An electric cart buzzed by, a man driving, a blonde woman sitting on the jump seat, her legs crossed, facing the rear. It was a mild pleasant day, without much smog. She sucked deeply of the California air, and suddenly wished it would rain. It doesn't rain enough out here, she thought. Rain gives people a chance to relax. She would not acknowledge what she was really thinking about: the theatre legend which held that rain meant success—if you auditioned when it was raining, the part was yours; if you opened on a rainy night, the show would be a hit.

She found building number seven and walked back towards the elevator banks. Two screen-writers were waiting for the elevator, talking about a scene that was giving them difficulty with the Shurlock office.

"They're a bunch of goddam Catholics there, that's the trouble," the first screen-writer said.

"What's that got to do with it?" the second one answered. "The two people in the scene are Protestants."

"Look, they want us to get them off the bed, we'll take them off the bed."

"Where we gonna play the scene then? The floor?"

"The floor, the ceiling, who cares? You want to fight with a bunch of Catholics?"

"I don't want to fight with anybody."

"So stop fighting with *me*. We'll take them off the bed."

"Where's your integrity, Pete?"

"What's this got to do with integrity? They can do it on a floor as well as on a bed. If it's the bed they object to, so we'll take them off the bed. What difference does it make? We have to be fancy? We have to show them on a bed? You know how many people do it on the floor?"

The elevator doors opened. The screen-writers stepped aside and allowed Gillian to enter first. She stepped into the car and pressed the button for the third floor. The screen-writers came into the car silently. One of them pushed the "2" set into the elevator panel.

Before they got out, one of the writers said, "In *Room at the Top*, they did it on a bed."

"That was British," the other writer explained, and they stepped out of the car.

She got out on the third floor and walked to room 306. She paused outside the door and looked at her seams again, and then wet her lips. Here we go, she thought. Good luck, Gillian. She opened the door. The receptionist looked up as she entered. A small redheaded boy was sitting on the couch reading a comic book.

"Miss Burke?" the receptionist asked.

"Yes."

"You're a *little* late," she said, looking at her watch. "Mr. Floren just about gave up on you."

"I'm awfully sorry. The traffic——"

"Yes, would you go right in, please? Mr. Floren's waiting."

"Thank you," Gillian said. She went to the door of the inner office, took the knob, and twisted it. The door did not budge. She turned back towards the desk, and the receptionist pushed her release button. The door clicked open.

Herbert Floren was sitting behind his desk reading a copy of *The Hollywood Reporter*. He put the paper down when Gillian entered, looked at her in surprise, and said, "That girl never tells me when anyone's here. Lucky thing I'm not a secret drinker. Are you Miss Burke?"

"Yes, I am."

"How do you do?" Floren said pleasantly. He rose and extended his hand. Gillian took it. "Sit down, sit down. What happened? Traffic jam?"

"Yes. I came in from the beach, and I guess I didn't allow myself enough time."

"Crazy traffic in this cockamamie town, well, that's all right, sit down, unwind, take it easy." Floren smiled again. He was a balding man in his early fifties, wearing an impeccably tailored blue suit and a striped grey tie. His nose was too large for his face, and his eyes were shrewd and piercing behind his eyeglasses, but he had a pleasant smile, and he used it extravagantly. "Your agent's been saying very nice things about you, Miss Burke. Very nice."

She didn't know whether an answer was expected or not. She smiled politely and modestly, and kept silent.

Floren nodded. "I saw the thing you did for Warners, the roller coaster. Very nice. I saw some of the television stuff, too. *Wagon Train*, very nice. *General Electric*, very nice."

"Did you see the *Playhouse 90*?" Gillian asked.

"No, I didn't. When was that?"

"Last year."

"Your agent didn't show it. Listen, everybody goofs now and then. You're a good actress, Miss Burke."

"Thank you."

"I'm doing a picture," he said, "*doing* it, I'm up to my ears in it already, a million dollars gone and we haven't even begun shooting. There may be something in it for you, I don't know. How old are you?"

She debated lying. She hesitated for a moment, and then told the truth. "I'm thirty-four," she said, and she watched his face.

"Well, that's good," Floren answered, "because this girl is supposed to be a young mother. Thirty-four's not bad. You look younger, though."

"Thank you."

"Don't thank me. If you test too young, you can forget all about the part."

She sat stunned, scarcely daring to breathe. For a moment, she thought she'd misunderstood him. This was not the way it happened. You did not walk into a producer's office, and he did not begin talking about tests and parts, this was not the way it happened.

"Did you see the kid sitting outside? The little redheaded kid?"

"Yes," Gillian answered. She was afraid to speak. Suppose he doesn't like my voice? You have a good voice, she told herself.

"Listen, what are you so nervous about?" he asked. "Relax. I'm a grandfather already. You've been hearing too many stories about Hollywood producers. You want a cigarette? You want a drink?"

"No. No, thank you."

"You don't smoke? You don't drink?"

"I smoke. I drink."

"Have a cigarette. Here. It'll do you good." Floren came around the desk and offered her the open cigarette box. She took one and he lighted it for her, reaching behind him for the gold lighter on his desk. "They gave me this when I finished my last picture," he said. "Not my *last* picture, God forbid. My most recent one. You interested in this part?"

"*Interested?*" she said. "Am I *interested?*"

"All right, relax, relax." He went around behind his desk again. "I asked you did you see that kid outside?"

"Yes, I saw him."

"We already signed him. He's a good little actor. Done a lot of *Lassie*, and he was in a picture with John Wayne, he's a good kid, we signed him. You're supposed to be his mother. He's got red hair, did you notice that?"

"Yes. Yes, I did."

"Your hair's not as red as his, but we'll see how it shows in the test. I want to test you together. Is that all right with you?"

"Yes. Yes, that's . . . that's fine."

"You'll choke on that cigarette," Floren said. "Put it out. Go ahead, do what I tell you. I never met anybody so nervous in my life. What'll you do during the test? Drop dead? Blow your chance?"

"No, no, I . . ."

"Okay, we're set up downstairs, stage three. I've had a little crew hanging around since two o'clock, waiting for you to arrive. Marilyn Monroe, yet. You know how much they're costing me?"

"I'm sorry. I'm truly sorry. But I had no idea . . ."

"What do you think I called you in for? You know how many girls there are in Hollywood who come around and stick their pictures in my face every day of the week? You think I got time to waste with all of them? Look, if you test okay, the part is yours. You can act, that's what I'm interested in. This is just one scene, and it's played in the foreground while the star is sitting on a bench watching, but it's very important to the picture, it's like a catalyst for the star, you understand? The things you say to your son, they cause a response in the star, you see? So we need an *actress* for it. You'll be on the screen for maybe five minutes all together, unless the director or the cutter decide to snip you out. Five hundred bucks, okay?"

"Okay," Gillian said.

"That's too cheap," Floren said. "What do you want to work so cheap for? You work cheap, everybody'll hear about it. Lucky thing I'm not a big-mouth. I'll contact your agent. He'll probably talk me into a thousand. If you test okay."

"Well . . . well . . . when do I . . . ?"

"I want you to meet the kid first. That schlocky little crew's been waiting since two o'clock, they can wait a little longer, too, it wouldn't kill them. What do they care, it's my money." He lifted his phone and said into the mouthpiece. "Listen, Miss Surprise Package of 1959, would you send Tommy in? Thank you." He hung up. "They sent her over from the mimeographing department. My own girl is on vacation, she's divorcing her husband in Vegas."

The door clicked open. Tommy walked into the office and said, "Hello, Mr. Floren."

"Tommy, this is Gillian Burke."

"How do you do, Miss Burke?" Tommy said, and he shook hands with her. He was perhaps eight years old, but he moved and spoke with all the professional aplomb of a top box-office star. Gillian smiled at him pleasantly.

"How would you like Miss Burke to be your mother?" Floren asked.

"I'd like it fine," Tommy said.

"Sure, he'd like it fine. Eight years old, the little cockeh, and already he's casting my pictures for me. You're going to do a test together. Is that okay with you, Mr. Kazan?"

"That's fine," Tommy said.

"Okay. Sound stage three. They're waiting for you now. Be good, you little vontz, and don't make Miss Burke nervous, you hear me?"

"I'll do my best, Mr. Floren," Tommy said.

"Yeah, you better. And you," he said to Gillian, "stop worrying. Such a nervous girl I never met in my life. You remind me of my daughter, you know that? I got a nervous daughter like you." He smiled and extended his hand. "Don't worry, you hear? You're a good actress. I got starring in this movie a klutz she couldn't act her way out of *Snow White and the Seven Dwarfs*, me, I got stuck with her. Forty thousand dollars a week. Learn your lesson, Miss Burke, never sell yourself cheap." He grinned again. "I like you. Go. Go take your test. Do a good job, or I'll never talk to you again."

"Thank you," Gillian said. "Thank you very much."

"Thank your agent. Thank yourself. Go. Take the test."

She joined Tommy in the reception room outside.

"He's a nice guy," Tommy said.

"Yes," she answered softly. "He's very sweet-oh."

"What's the matter?"

"Nothing."

He held the door open for her. They went into the corridor together and began walking towards the elevators.

"Didn't we work together once?" Tommy asked.

"No, I don't think so."

"On *Beaver*? Did you ever do any *Beavers*?"

"No. Never."

"*Father Knows Best?*"

"No. Not that either."

"Hey, what's the matter with you? You look as if you're about to cry."

"I'm all right," Gillian said.

"It's only a part," he told her, and he shrugged and pushed the button for the elevator.

She could not remember afterwards what she did or said during the test. Floren's little crew, which had been waiting since two o'clock, consisted of a cameraman, an assistant cameraman, an operator, a director, an assistant director, a boom man and a mixer, a recorder, three grips, a make-up man, a hair stylist, a wardrobe mistress, four electricians, three prop men, a handyman, and a script clerk, who handed her a mimeographed script the moment she entered the sound stage. She tried to memorize her lines while a lipstick brush traced her mouth, everything seemed hazy and blurred, a pencil touching the edges of her eyes, a comb being pulled through her hair, someone dusting her jacket, someone else asking her to take her jacket off, lights being moved into place, the assistant cameraman stepping in front of the camera with the synch sticks, raising the diagonally lined clapper, the words TEST, GILLIAN BURKE scrawled on to the slate in chalk, and beneath that TAKE No. 1, SOUND No. 27, and beneath that the date and the name of the cameraman, and the name of the director, and the name of the producer. "You ready, Miss Burke?" the director asked. She nodded. "Okay, quiet and roll!" the assistant director said. One of the sound men, earphones on his ears, waited for word from the recorder and then said, "Speed," and the cameraman said, "Mark it!" The sticks came together, the black-and-white lines met, the assistant cameraman said, "Test, Gillian Burke, Take One," and that was all she remembered. The rest was truly a blur. She had a vague notion that they were stopping too often, that she heard "Cut!" shouted too many times. She thought someone asked her to laugh on the next take, thought someone else asked her to cross her legs, but she could remember none of this clearly, could only remember feeling awkward and clumsy beneath the blazing lights, could remember how professional little Tommy had seemed in comparison.

And when it was over, she was certain she had done badly, was certain there was a sickly smile on the face of the assistant director, was certain the electricians and the cameramen were laughing at her. She put on her jacket, thanked them all, and walked through the stage and pushed open the door, and saw the red light still burning outside and the sign forbidding entrance when the red light was on, and walked slowly towards her sister's car, feeling despondent and foolish and rejected, and knowing she had thrown away the first real opportunity she'd ever had.

She wondered why things never seemed to work out for her, wondered why the underwater television show had lasted only a season and hadn't been picked up for re-runs anywhere, wondered why the Johnny Thunder pilot had never even got off the ground, wondered why the few decent things she'd done never seemed to get the notice she hoped they'd get, wondered why today she had suddenly become all arms and legs, tripping over herself, barely able to speak, allowing herself to be out-acted by an eight-year-old boy, what the hell was the matter with her, anyway?

She could not go back to Malibu that night. She ate dinner in a small Italian restaurant in Hollywood, and then went to a movie. She took a room at the Hollywood Roosevelt afterwards, ordered a double Scotch, and went directly to bed. She slept until two o'clock the next afternoon, dressed listlessly, and then went down to check out and pick up the car. The day was suffocatingly hot. She drove out to the beach in a fog of despair. She never failed to respond to the fresh breeze blowing off the open water as she came down the hill from Santa Monica on to the Pacific Coast Highway, but today she sat lifelessly behind the wheel of the car, hating the sun-bronzed bodies cluttered about the hot-dog stands, the girlish shrieks from the beach, the sun blazing on the water, the breakers rolling in against the high wooden pilings under the shore-front houses. When she reached the Mexican restaurant near Castle Rock, she looked at her speedometer. Seven point four, she thought, and then watched it steadily, knowing her sister's house was six-tenths of a mile past the restaurant, all those damn little Malibu houses crouched behind their highway fences and all looking exactly the same so that you couldn't tell one from the other without clocking the mileage on your speedometer. She made a screeching turn across the highway in the face of an approaching trailer truck and almost knocked over the garbage cans in front of the house.

The gate was locked. She pulled the cord on the hanging bell out front and waited.

"Monica!" she called.

There was no answer.

She went to the house next door and leaned into the open Dutch door of the gate.

"Anybody home?" she yelled.

A man in a brief yellow-nylon bathing-suit was sunning himself on the slatted wooden terrace. He lifted a pair of sun-protectors from his eyes, blinked, barely turned his head towards the gate and said, "She's down on the beach, Gilly. Want to hop over the fence?"

"Thanks, Lou," she said. She reached over the bottom half of the door, unlatched it, walked past him to the fence separating his house from Monica's, climbed on to the bench resting against it, and boosted herself up, legs flashing.

Lou sat up and said, "How'd it go?"

"They tested me."

"Yeah?"

"Mmm," she said, and dropped to the terrace on the other side of the fence. The door of the house was open, thank God for that. She went in, walked clear through the house to the ocean side, walked out on to the deck, and scanned the beach for her sister. She was nowhere in sight. Annoyed, she came back into the house and threw her jacket on to the couch, hating the California modern and the Japanese look of everything in the house, hating the way the house shook each time a new wave crashed in against the pilings, rushing across the beach and striking the wooden logs with force and power, washing up clear under the terrace on the highway side of the house. She went into the bedroom. A fly buzzed against the window-pane. She threw open the window, and the fly escaped. The bedroom was very hot and sticky. She could hear the sound of the surf booming under the house, and far off down the beach, where the expanse was wider and the tide had not yet completely engulfed the sand, the sound of people laughing. She took off her sweater and her bra and cupped her breasts, massaging them for a moment, and then throwing herself full length on the bed, kicking off her shoes, rolling on to her side, and staring at the wall. She could see the small card tacked over the dresser, telling when the grunion were running. She had been on a grunion run only once in all the time she'd been in California. She had been tested for a picture only once in all the time she'd been in California.

I'm thirty-four years old, she thought.

David, I'm thirty-four years old.

She sat up suddenly.

She supposed she should go down for a swim. She swung her legs over the side of the bed, took off her skirt and her slip, and was reaching into the dresser drawer for her bathing-suit when the telephone rang. She lifted it from the cradle.

Naked, sobbing, she listened while her agent told her she had got the part in Floren's movie.

Christmas never came to Hollywood. They could have their parades down Hollywood Boulevard, with Santa Claus sitting on one float and a big movie star sitting on another, Charlton Heston this year, and clowns turning cartwheels in the street, they could do all that but it never felt like Christmas to Gillian who was used to biting cold and the promise or reality of snow. There was something wilted and pathetic about the Christmas trees inside the Hollywood houses, something that made Christmas a fake. Back East it was perfectly all right to cut down a spruce and drag it into the house and trim it with tinsel and balls, that was perfectly all right, and not at all unnatural. But to do the same thing out here, where the sun was shining and the temperature was in the seventies, this somehow seemed anachronistic, and a little sacrilegious as well.

Nor could she adapt to the concept of January first arriving in a burst of sunshine, the year beginning in the middle of a seeming summer rather than in the dead of winter. She had put on the protective coloration of the natives, but Christmas and the New Year were simply unacceptable to her chemistry, and she always went through the charade of buying gifts and presenting them as if she were an impostor from another planet who went through the ritual artificially and without real feeling.

This year it was worse because she worked on the picture all during the week before Christmas and then through to January fourth, with barely time to do any real shopping—she could never accept the Lord & Taylor in Beverly Hills as the *real* Lord & Taylor, everyone knew the *real* Lord & Taylor was on Thirty-seventh Street and Fifth Avenue—rising at six each morning and rushing to the studio and then working until five each afternoon. The director was a meticulous man who insisted on shooting and reshooting each scene until he was certain he had it the way he wanted it. Invariably, when he saw the rushes the next day, he decided that the way he'd wanted it had been wrong. So he shot and reshot the same scenes over and over again. They were using a new fast colour film that enabled them to work later each day, a boon since much of the work was being done outdoors, on location. But by the time Gillian crawled into bed each night after a full day of trying to re-create a freshness she had felt only at the start of production, she was thoroughly exhausted.

When Floren asked that she join him at the studio one afternoon at the end of a day's shooting, her first reaction was to beg off. But she could not forget his kindness to her, and so she accompanied him reluctantly and wearily. He introduced her to the cutter on the picture, a man in his late forties, wearing a white shirt with the sleeves rolled to his elbows, sporting a thick moustache over his lip. In the corridor outside, Floren said, "He's important to you, Gillian. You've got only one scene in this picture, and you want to look good in it. Get to know him, and maybe he'll let you help pick the shots."

She was allowed to watch the rushes all that week. In the peculiar structure of the Hollywood hierarchy, Floren, who was producing the film, had to get permission from the director, whom he had hired, for Gillian to sit in when the rushes were shown. The director didn't like the idea at all. He wasn't even allowing the picture's *stars* to see the daily rushes. But perhaps he remembered that he was fourteen days behind his shooting schedule, and that Herbert Floren was picking up the tab, and so he graciously permitted the intrusion. She sat in the screening room all that week and watched herself play the scene over and over again from more angles than she thought imaginable, juggling the shots in her mind, arranging the scene as she thought it would finally be put together. When they showed the rough cut, though, she finally understood Floren's advice, and was glad she'd shared so many cups of coffee with the cutter in the studio commissary. They had assembled the sequence so that most of it was played on the face of the male star, who sat on a bench behind her. The shots they had chosen illustrated every nuance of emotion that crossed his features as he reacted to her speech and her bitter tears. She hovered on the edge of the scene and the screen; and for almost two of the five minutes, her job amounted to nothing more than voice over. The best shot of her, in fact, was a close-up of the back of her head. She immediately cornered the cutter.

"What did you *do* to me, Hank?" she said.

"I didn't do anything, Gilly," he said. "This is the way he wanted it. Look, it's his picture, not mine."

"Hank, we shot that scene from a hundred angles. You saw the rushes. You know what we——"

"I know," Hank said, "but this is the way he wants it."

"Couldn't we just *try* it some other way?"

"What other way?"

"Well, couldn't we start the scene with that full shot of me, and then as the speech builds come in closer and closer until we're just on my face when I begin crying? We've got the footage, Hank. It's just a question of putting it together."

"How can I do that? This is the way he wants it."

"You could say you just did it to get his reaction."

"With that nut? He'd jump through the ceiling."

"Or you could sneak it in with the rest of the stuff, the next time you——"

"Gilly, that's impossible. This is *his* picture, don't you understand?"

"Yes, but it's *my* scene," she said earnestly. "I don't think you know how much this means to me, Hank."

He studied her silently for a moment. "Maybe I do," he said. "Let me think about it."

He thought about it for several days, and then decided to take the chance. He went through the early rushes again and began the scene with the full shot Gillian had suggested, carefully examining the footage and going from that to a medium shot, and then a close shot, tighter and tighter as the speech gained momentum, cutting back every now and then to the male star reacting on the bench, but for the most part staying with Gillian, closer and closer, full face and profile, finally choosing a tight shot of her eyes as she began crying, and then cutting back to the star on the bench, realization crossing his face as the scene faded. Gillian was on the screen for almost the full five minutes, and for the major part of that time in close-up. Hank spliced the revised scene in ahead of that day's rushes and then sat back to wait for the explosion when the footage was shown. The director was silent as the scene played. He glanced quickly at Hank when it was over, and then turned his attention to the fresh film. When the lights came on, he lighted a cigarette, shook out the match, and with edge geniality said, "When did you take over the direction of this picture, Hank?"

Hank smiled. "You mean the scene on the bench?"

"Have you directed any others lately?"

"I just wanted to try it on you," Hank said. "I can still go back to the other way."

"Okay, you tried it. Now throw it away, okay?"

"Sure," Hank said. "It was just an experiment."

"If you don't mind, I like to handle my own experi——"

"I figure you meant the girl to be in there for a change of pace. We're on Tony's face all through the preceding scene, you know."

"I know, but *this* happens to be his pay-off scene."

"Then why'd you take all that footage of the girl? You must have had *something* in mind."

"Who remembers what I had in mind? All I know is when I saw the rushes, we discussed the way I wanted it cut, remember? Do you recall that?"

"Sure, I do. But did you see that girl's colouring? She's got good colouring, and an interesting face. Look, I may be wrong, but didn't you want that scene to show what the speech was doing to *both* of them? If we stay on Tony, we lose half the power of the scene. You shot some beautiful stuff there, kid. It'd be a shame to waste it. That close-up of her eyes is real artistry, I mean it. Reminds me of some of Bergman's stuff."

"Ingrid's?"

"I was thinking of Ingmar, but what's the difference? Look, it's your picture. Am I supposed to tell you that one thing you shot is better than another? You did them both, didn't you? Either way is great. But I think the essence of what you really want to say is in that girl's face. I know it makes *me* cry, that's all. I've cut a lot of pictures, kid, but the way you shot that girl... well, it makes me cry."

"Well, maybe so. But if we lose——"

"And the beauty of what you did is that we get Tony's reaction at the same time, almost like a double exposure. That take some doing, believe me, getting a multiple viewpoint on the screen, expecially in a crucial scene like this one."

"You think it comes over? His reaction?"

"Absolutely. And do you know why? Because of what you accomplished with that girl. Do you realize the performance you got out of a bit player? It's fantastic, that's all. The camera stays on her most of the time, and it's *still* Tony's pay-off scene. That's the kind of stuff that makes them sit up and take notice, believe me. The oblique approach, nothing head-on, subtle."

"Well, we don't want to get too subtle. If we——"

"Who said it's *too* subtle? With those close-ups of the girl's face? And that shot of her eyes when the tears start rolling? How could that be *too* subtle? Listen, don't underestimate yourself."

"I'm a little worried about that fade at the end, though, aren't you? I don't think we stay on Tony long enough to see——"

"Oh, I've got footage I can tack on to that. Do you want a longer fade there?"

"I think a longer fade might——"

"Plenty of footage. Longer fade's no problem."

"It might round out the scene better, don't you think?"

"It would make the scene *perfect*. Just the way it is, with a longer fade."

"You liked that close-up of the eyes, huh?"

"Beautiful."

"She really cried, you know. We didn't use glycerine."

"It shows. The patience you took with that scene shows."

"Well, let's try it this way for now, okay? We'll see how it fits into the over-all scheme. Maybe we *do* need a change of pace there, get the hell away from Tony for a while."

"I figured that was the way you intended it."

"Probably, but you know how easy it is to forget things. So many damn things going on at once."

Hank laughed. "Boy, you don't have to tell me," he said. "But I think the scene looks just great now, except for that longer fade you want. I'll give you that. It'll round things out just the way you want them."

"I think you're right." He nodded, pleased with himself. "About the rushes, Hank. I liked that third take in the saloon, but the colour looked a little off to me. Can we get another print on that?"

The work on the picture consumed Christmas and the New Year, and late in January she went back to the studio to dub in the sound that had been lost on location. She saw the revised scene for the first time then, and rushed out immediately afterwards to buy a pair of gold cuff-links for Hank, a gift that cost her almost two days' salary. There was nothing more to do now, nothing but sit and wait and hope the picture would eventually lead to something else. Her agent sent her to audition for a part on *Peter Gunn*, and she was terribly surprised when she got it because she was hardly the type of curvacious cutie who paraded across the *Peter Gunn* screen. But that involved only a few days' rehearsal and shooting, and then she sat back to wait again. It was February already, and warmer than any California February she could remember. When Ben Cameron called one day and asked if she'd like to go with him on his boat to Catalina, she accepted eagerly. She would have accepted anything that helped to pass the time.

Ben was an actor she saw regularly, a man who'd made his peace with the world and possibly with himself. He'd come to Hollywood after a long run in a Broadway hit, a supporting role to be sure, but one that had got him a screen test and a studio contract. His story was hardly a fresh one. He'd hung around for seven years collecting his salary and doing almost nothing. When his option finally expired, another studio discovered he was an expert horseman and could fall off horses with great realism. He had since fallen off more horses than he could count. He refused to call himself a stunt man. He was an equestrian expert, and he had fallen off horses as an Indian, a Civil War soldier, a Crusader, a renegade outlaw, a Mongolian chieftain, a Foreign Legionnaire, a regimental brigadier, an Arab, and even a mounted policeman. He earned a good living, and he owned a Chris Craft cruiser and a house in Venice in the midst of the beatniks. Every Friday night, he and his friends would gather at his house and he would cook them a lasagna dinner. Lasagna was his speciality. He was a fairly happy guy. He very rarely thought of his days in the theatre, or of that single long-run play on Broadway.

Once, though, he said to Gillian, "Do you know what I liked best about the theatre? Whenever you came to a new house, a strange dressing-room, there was always something written on the mirror. In one place, I remember, someone had written, 'Don't look up. There's no balcony.' In another place, somebody had written in lipstick, 'Skunk them!'" He had shaken his head wistfully. "Nobody ever writes anything on a horse, Gilly."

They talked all the way to Santa Monica, where his boat was moored. Ben was a good sailor, and she helped him with his lines until they were under way, and then she lay on the deck with her blouse tied in a knot under her breasts, soaking up sunshine. The sky was almost cloudless, the ocean calm. Ben dropped anchor off Catalina, and they ate sandwiches and drank Cokes and then lay back on the deck again. Gillian with her eyes closed, Ben with his hand resting gently on her thigh, the boat almost motionless on a calm sea, the sun intense.

"Want to do some diving?" Ben asked.

"Sure," she said.

"Go on below and change. I'll get the tanks ready."

"I've never dived with a tank, Ben."

"You've snorkeled, haven't you?"

"Yes, but . . ."

"The tanks are easy," he said. "I'll teach you."

"Okay."

She went below and changed into her suit, a one-piece green wool. When she came topside again, Ben had already taken out the masks and flippers and was opening the valves on the tanks. He taught her how to breathe through the mouthpiece, explaining that the regulator would automatically control the flow of oxygen, giving her as much or as little as she needed for normal breathing.

"We'll practice near the boat at first," he said. "Then we can dive a little."

He strapped one of the tanks to her back and laughed when she sagged under its weight. "Crouch down on the edge of the boat," he said, "and fall into the water backwards. Don't worry about the tank. It won't weight a thing once you hit the water. Hold your mask now. Go on, Gillian."

She clung to the boat with one hand, holding her face mask with the other, and then let herself fall back into the water. She bobbed to the surface almost immediately. Her mask had began to cloud. She swam to the side of the boat, pulled off the mask while she clung to the ladder, spat into it, washed it out with salt water, and then put it back on.

"Is the mask tight enough?" Ben asked.

"Yes, it's fine. Aren't you coming in?"

"As soon as I get this tank on."

He came into the water a few moments later. They swam around the boat in idle circles while Gillian got used to the tank and the breathing apparatus. Once or twice, they dived under the boat and surfaced on the opposite side. The ocean was incredibly clear, alive with small fish. Ben had a dagger strapped to his leg. He was a muscular man, and a powerful swimmer, and she felt entirely safe in his company.

"We won't go too far from the boat," he said. "Stay with me all the time, Gillian, and don't panic under water. If you want to go up, just go up. But remember you're in water, and deep water, and try not to react to anything the way you would on land. Don't scream, for example. You'd only lose your mouthpiece, and without it you can't breathe."

"Okay," Gillian said.

"All right, let's go."

They put on their masks again, stuck the mouthpieces between their lips, and dived under.

Blue and pale-gold sifting sunlight down in silence.

Silence.

Weaving underwater plants, fish darting, bubbles from the oxygen tanks.

Down.

Down in silence deep and sunlight shafted.

Even his hair looked beautiful, caught in watery motion, afloat on his head, his long legs pushing effortlessly, the flippers gently paddling, down, sea urchins clustered like heads of medieval maces, spikes erect, silent and brown, a world without a whisper, a striped yellow fish coming up to peer through Gillian's face mask, she almost laughed aloud and then remembered she was under water, remembered the sweet suck of oxygen flowing through the regulator and the tubes and into her mouth, the fish turned tail and darted away. She followed it. Ben was by her side again, ever present, his powerful arms pushing through the water, the dagger strapped to his leg. He pointed, and she looked, a school of tiny silver fish, needlelike, hanging on the water without thread, a cluster of glistening needles, she reached out to touch them and they scattered in hurried silence, re-forming some five feet away, sunlight fanned the water in a spreading golden wedge, down, deeper, wash of sun vanishing in silence, blue so intense, the shocking stillness of underwater colour, the delicate grace of sea life, the lulling rhythm of the water itself, and silence, silence, she saw the shark.

She did not know what kind of shark it was, but she knew it was a shark. She felt panic rocket into her brain, and she knew her eyes had suddenly opened wide behind the mask. She saw Ben back away instinctively, his legs dropping so that he stood erect in the water, like a man standing groundless. He made a placating gesture with his hand, outstretched behind him, a calming gesture, but he did not turn to look at her, he kept facing the shark, which had suddenly come into view and which hung in the water like a white-bellied torpedo circling idly and then suddenly vanishing in a burst of speed. Ben swam closer to her. His eyes kept searching the water, but the shark was nowhere in sight. He gave a slight shrug, and then gestured with his thumb, pointing directly upward, commanding her to surface. She nodded. She noticed for the first time that the dagger was no longer strapped to Ben's leg. It was in his hand.

He gave a scissors kick with his legs and shot upward, and she followed him, pushing down against the water with her arms, thrusting her legs out in kick after kick, and then she saw the shark again.

He materialized from nowhere on a crest of blueness, blue himself, appearing suddenly and dead ahead and swimming towards her in a rush, directly at her, a giant specimen some fifteen feet long, he arced away from her and she saw the white underbelly and the curved mouth, and her first instinct was to scream, and her second instinct was to run. But she could neither scream nor run, she was under water and Ben was somewhere above her, probably on the surface by this time, she tried to remember everything she had ever heard or read about sharks, where was he now? should she splash? should she make noise? should she swim quietly away, where was he? She looked through her mask with wide, frightened eyes, turning her head in short jerks, the wide rubber mould limiting her field of vision, watching, waiting, afraid to move, afraid to attract attention to the bright-green wool of her bathing-suit or the bright yellow of her flippers, where was he? afraid to cause the slightest movement in the water, afraid the motion would attract the shark, he appeared again.

He appeared again, seeing her this time, perhaps he had seen her the first time, but definitely seeing her this time, making a long pass at her, a graceful beautiful swift pass, coming as close as six feet away and then circling off, she remembered something about sharks circling before they attacked, or had he attacked already, was that pass the beginning of his attack? She pushed out with her arms and legs and tried to swim away, but the shark was everywhere. He circled her patiently now, judging his distance, coming closer with each pass, what if he came close enough to tear her flesh with his rough skin, would she bleed, would the blood provoke a frenzied attack? She could see two small fish clinging to the shark, could see them in shocking clarity as he completed another pass. She hung witless in the water as he circled her, wishing Ben would come back, wondering why Ben did not come back with his dagger, paralysed with fear. She felt her mouth going lax, felt the rubber mouthpiece sliding from her lips. She clutched at it greedily, grasped it before it fell completely clear, held it to her mouth, desperately sucked oxygen, certain she was trembling, feeling cold and limp and faint, and knowing she was going to die.

Knowing this.

Knowing it would be terrible and painful, knowing this as the shark cruised silently and patiently, almost as if he were toying with her now, coming closer and closer, his mouth seemingly curved into an evil grin, the water miraculously clear of any other fish, there was nothing in the water but Gillian and the shark, life and death, and she knew she would die.

But don't, she thought. Please.

Please, I haven't begun.

She decided to turn. She decided to swim away from the shark. She decided to find the boat. She hung paralysed in the water.

Turn, she commanded herself.

Swim away.

She looked up. There was no sunlight. She was very deep, she felt heavy all at once, all at once she wondered if her oxygen would run out, and the shark made another pass, terrifyingly close.

Go ahead, she thought. Do it! Get it over with!

No, she thought. No, goddam you! No, I haven't begun.

She felt her arms moving in a breast stroke, felt her feet lashing out in a scissors kick, felt herself moving. She would not look back. She knew the shark was there. She knew he was behind her. She knew he was coming from behind, huge and silent, knew that any moment those terrible ripping teeth would cut into her legs, would sever her legs from the rest of her body. She began to whimper soundlessly behind the mask, thrusting with her arms, kicking with her legs, waiting for the razor slash that would end her life.

Sunlight.

A wedge of light fanned on water, breaking, motion.

Something touched her.

She thought, *The shark!*

She reeled back from the touch, her heart stopping. Something clamped on to her arm, she tried to pull away, her eyes exploding in fear, she saw something through the clouded face plate of the mask, saw, saw, and suddenly relaxed, suddenly went limp, suddenly knew she was about to faint, and felt Ben's arm around her waist.

· · · · ·

"Drink this," he said. He put the brandy to her mouth. She sipped at it, and then turned her face away.

She had told him brokenly and hysterically about her encounter with the shark, and now she leaned against the bulkhead, her eyes wide, staring down at the deck. The boat rocked. She could hear the creaking of the timber. The world was silent, except for the creaking of the timber.

"Ben," she said.

"What is it, Gillian?"

"Thank you."

"I was scared to death, Gilly," he said, and he began sobbing. "I thought you'd drowned. I kept diving down after you, but I couldn't find you."

"The shark," she said, and she shivered.

Ben blew his nose. "Come on, get out of that wet suit," he said. "You'll get a chill." He lowered the straps, took the suit off her, put her on the bunk, and covered her with a blanket. Then he sat on a barrel opposite the bunk and watched her, his face pale. He blew his nose again. Very softly, he said again, "I thought you'd drowned."

The cabin was silent. She kept staring at the overhead.

"Ben," she said.

"What, Gilly?"

"I just thought . . ." She shook her head.

"What is it, Gilly?"

She kept staring at the overhead, her face calm and pale, her eyes wide. She lay still beneath the blanket, and she stared at the overhead and through it and beyond it, and she said, "I just thought . . . he might die, Ben. He might die and . . ." She turned her head into the pillow.

Ben was silent, watching her.

"Ben," she said, "I just hate to think he might die somewhere and never know how much I loved him."

"Try to get some sleep, Gilly," Ben said.

She nodded.

"I'm going to start back," he said.

She nodded again.

"Never know how much I loved him," she said into the stillness.

Elliot Tulley clawed at his bald pate with long thin talons and then studied his finger-nails and then walked to the window and looked down at the wind-swept Talmadge street. The vista never changed. Year after year, the Talmadge main street crawled with life, winter and summer, the faces changed, but the town never did.

He turned to look at Julia, sitting in the leather-upholstered chair alongside his desk, the wall of law books forming a backdrop behind her, her legs crossed, a cigarette burning idly in her right hand as she studied the document. She's still a dish, he thought, but not the Julia Regan who came into this office for the first time almost seventeen years ago, with her head held high, to lay a secret on my desk and to work out a plan. Who the hell are priests? Tulley wondered. Who gets more of the confession business, the lawyers or the sanctified holy men who sit in their little boxes and listen to how many sins you committed last week?

He shrugged birdlike shoulders and walked to where she was sitting, impatiently began reading the document over her shoulder. He was wearing brown sharkskin trousers and a brown vest over a white shirt. The sleeves were rolled up over his scrawny biceps. He should also have been wearing a clip-on bow tie, but it was in the pocket of his shirt, and the shirt collar was open over a prominent Adam's apple and a throat nicked with shaving cuts.

"I thought you knew me well enough to skip over the fine print, Julia," he said.

"I don't know anyone that well."

"You don't trust me, Julia?"

"I trust you, Elliot. But I like to read something before I sign it. And with something like this, I won't get an opportunity to change my mind, now will I?"

"Why not? Do you plan on dying the minute you leave this office?"

"No, not quite that soon."

"Then take the will home with you and read it there. If you want any changes made, I'll make them before you sign. You need two witnesses anyway, Julia. And there are certain formalities I want you to follow."

"What are they, Elliot?"

"First of all, don't pick people who are apt to die before you do. If this will is ever contested, we want people around who can testify to their witnessing signatures. That's the first thing. Pick two witnesses who are younger than you are, preferably *not* a husband-and-wife team."

"That shouldn't be too difficult," Julia said, smiling.

"That's right, someone as old as you are with one foot in the grave already shouldn't have any trouble on that score. Then I want you to get them together, and I want you to say, 'This is my last will and testament. I have read it, and am asking you to sign it as my witnesses.' Have you got that? I'll write it down for you before you go."

"All right."

"Then the testatrix—that's you—signs her name and dates the will. And then you give it to the witnesses to sign it below the attestation clause. That's all there is to it. But they've got to be in each other's presence when they sign it, Julia. You've got that?"

"I've got it."

"Okay. Then now I can tell you this is a lousy will, and I'm sure it'll be contested, and I think you're a damn fool."

"Who'll contest it, Elliot?"

"You want my guess? David."

"Why should he?"

"Why should he, huh? Because he'll think you were out of your bloody mind when you signed it, that's why. Look at it, Julia. You've left half of your estate to be held in trust by a man named Giovanni Fabrizzi quote in the secure knowledge that he will disperse it as agreed upon in prior discussion unquote. Now, what kind of a legal document is that? He can spend the money on a villa somewhere and then claim that was in agreement with your prior discussion. Who'll ever know *what* you told Fabrizzi?"

"I trust him," Julia said. "I've trusted him all these years, and I can trust him now."

"I don't trust anybody," Elliot said. "Not when it comes to a will. Not when it comes to an estate the size of yours."

"There's only one person who could possibly object to the will, and that's David. And I don't think he's that kind of person. Besides, he's taken care of adequately."

"Sure, with half your estate. And the other half goes to a guy in Italy named Giovanni Fabrizzi, and you think David isn't going to raise a fuss? Julia, don't tell me about people and estates. Don't tell me about people and money."

"I still think——"

"And what do you know about Fabrizzi, other than that he's handled a penny-ante transaction over the past sixteen and a half years? This is real money, Julia, this is better than three-quarters of a million dollars. That damn spaghetti-bender may just——"

"Don't talk that way, Elliot."

"I'm sorry. But I don't trust him. You want this money to go where it's supposed to, don't you?"

"Of course I do."

"Then don't trust Fabrizzi."

"How else can I——?"

"I'd like you to change the will. I'd like it to read 'to be held in trust by Giovanni Fabrizzi pursuant to a separate agreement between Mr. Fabrizzi and the testatrix.'" He reached for another document on his desk, handed it to Julia, and said, "This is a rough draft of the separate agreement. It tell exactly where the estate goes, and when. Nothing vague about it, Julia. I'd like you to send it to Fabrizzi for his signature."

"Nothing vague about it," she said, and she nodded. "And when I die, Elliot? What happens to this agreement that is anything but vague?"

"One copy stays locked in my safe, and another stays locked in Fabrizzi's. There *are* such things as secret trusts, Julia. And if a separate document is mentioned in the will, David won't have a leg to stand on."

"And if he contests it, you'll have to show the separate document, won't you?"

"No, I doubt it. A will contest very rarely involves the provisions of a will. Your son can't say such and such a provision is no good simply because it doesn't happen to appeal to him. He would have to base his contest on trying to prove you were mentally incompetent when you made the will, or that undue influence was exerted on you, or something of that nature. But this wouldn't necessitate showing the separate agreement, which is a part of one of the will's provisions. In fact, the separate agreement would be testimony to your mental stability. Only an idiot would leave half her estate to a man three thousand miles away on the basis of a *verbal* agreement."

"I wouldn't want——"

"Julia, I *know* what you wouldn't want. This is Elliot Tulley."

"Yes, I know. I'll think about it, Elliot."

"I suggest you think about it very carefully. And I strongly suggest that you allow me to revise the will and to send the separate agreement off to Fabrizzi for his signature and approval. As your attorney, this is what I suggest."

"I'll think about it."

"Sure, it's only money." Elliot paused. "How's everything else?"

"Fine."

"What were you doing over at the travel agency day before yesterday?"

"Elliot, you should have been an F.B.I. agent."

"How do you know I'm not? Planning a trip, Julia?"

"Maybe." She smiled and picked up her handbag.

"It wouldn't be to Rome, would it?"

"Maybe."

"It's none of my business, Julia, but this is a small town, and a man who's alert can't help hearing things. Milt Anderson says your heart——"

"If I'm going to have a coronary, Elliot, I might just as well have it in Rome, don't you think?"

"It's your coronary," Elliot said, shrugging. "Have it wherever the hell you want." He paused. "I think it's amazing you've managed to stay away all these years, anyway."

"You have to be ready to go back, Elliot. Otherwise, there's no sense going, is there?"

"I guess not. And you're ready now, are you?"

"I'm fifty-six years old, Elliot. I want to see ... I want to go back before I die."

"Everyone wants to go back before he dies, Julia," Elliot said. "Call me as soon as you've decided on the will, please. I want to make those changes as soon as possible."

"Elliot, really," Julia said, smiling. "I do have at *least* a few weeks, don't you think?"

Kate Bridges was seventeen.

She had turned seventeen in November, and now it was March; she had been seventeen for four months and the change was remarkable only in that it was nothing at all like a metamorphosis. The person who emerged from the chrysalis of sixteen still resembled Kate, talked like Kate, moved like Kate, and yet was truly a different Kate, the change was indiscernible and perhaps a little disappointing.

But oh, it was good to be seventeen.

It was marvellous to be alive and at the peak of beauty, to have a strong body and uncomplaining muscles, an appetite for life and living. It was wonderful to know you could laugh robustly and cry in unashamed torment. It was good to be able to magnify all the minuscule problems of living, and shoulder none of its responsibilities, it was good to be young, it was good to be seventeen.

Nor was this Booth Tarkington's seventeen, nor Eugene O'Neill's, this was not that magic age, that long-awaited phase of adolescence when the braces came off and the kisses got longer. Oh yes, it still included idyllic dreams and fresh discoveries, visions of romance and high ideals, it was still all these things, but seventeen had changed. Kate had been born in 1942 while her father was meeting his death on a Navy destroyer. She had been nursed on the waning days of a world war, and weaned on the threat of another, and so war or the promise of war was part of the fabric of her life. And yet the adults had managed to do something to the concept, had robbed it of all its glamour and excitement. If war came, there would no longer be the agony of deprivation, the banners-and-music excitement of seeing a loved one off, the free-and-easy love-making in moments stolen from the battlefront, the weeping alone while the guns echoed far away, the tragedy of death in combat, the excesses a seventeen-year-old could really appreciate. The adults, instead, had invented the ultimate excess, and now war only meant annihilation.

And in annihilation, there was democracy.

There had been a time, back in those swinging days that were the forties, when a sailor in a San Diego bar, a sailor headed for the Pacific where he could very easily have his head blown off, would not be served a glass of beer unless he could prove he was over twenty-one years old. It was still tough to get a drink in San Diego, but it was fairly simple to get one in your own living-room if you were seventeen years old and blessed with modern parents who understood that physically you were capable of doing the same things they did, possibly better, and that mentally you were struggling with the same day-by-day possibility of extinction, with a great deal more to lose since you had experienced a great deal less in the short seventeen years of your life. When the hydrogen bomb fell, if it fell, no one was going to separate the women and children from the men. There would be a blinding flash and ten seconds to say your prayers, and everyone would wonder in those ten seconds who had pushed the button, good-bye Charlie.

So seventeen was a different thing, a new thing, and Kate was a part of this new seventeen, a curious seventeen, which still included a freedom from most adult responsibilities, but which also included an adult attitude of tolerance that permitted participation in many adult activities. You could smoke at seventeen. You could have a drink at seventeen. You could drive a car. You could mix with your parents' friends at cocktail parties, you could even dance with some of the men, you could discuss everything they discussed, no conversation ever stopped suddenly when you walked into the room, no one ever said, "Shhh, here are the kids." It was casually assumed that you were almost an adult at seventeen, not quite, but almost. If you could kill at seventeen, if you could be killed in the indiscriminate indifference of a hydrogen bomb explosion, then surely you could be allowed the courtesy of adult treatment.

Kate was allowed this courtesy, as were most of her friends. She accepted it with a supreme ladylike poise that was sometimes astonishing. She could sit in a group of older men and women and discuss anything they happened to touch upon, perhaps too vigorously and with the extreme conviction of the very young, but none the less intelligently and knowledgeably. She could smile in maidenly restraint at the too-dirty joke told in her living-room—and then later repeat it to Agnes and laugh vulgarly and hilariously when she delivered the punch line. She could listen to a conversation about morality and virginity, knowing she was still pure and relatively untouched, voicing her opinions in a low clear voice, and then pet furiously on the back seat of an automobile with a boy, his hands under her dress, her own hands exploring.

There was in Kate the woman.

They saw this in her, the other women, and the men. They saw in her the woman almost formed, and they were surprised by the glimpse because they could not remember themselves this way at seventeen, and indeed they could not because this was a new seventeen, quite different from what theirs had been. When they told stories of their own youth, they could remember with extreme clarity the single incident that propelled them into the world of the adult, that one memorable instant when their parents at last seemed to accept them as grown-ups, when they crossed the imaginary dividing line. But for Kate, there had been no crossing, there had been instead a gradual disappearance of the line itself. She had helped serve hors d'oeuvres at one of her parents' parties when she was only ten. She had danced with one of her father's friends when she was twelve. She had listened to a conversation about birth control when she was fourteen. There seemed to be no adult aversion to her growing up, no pressure to keep her a child. Instead, the adults surrounding her seemed impatient, even eager, to accept her into their world, to equate seventeen or eighteen with thirty-five or forty. She sometimes felt she was allowing them into her universe rather than being permitted to enter theirs.

The woman was in her—but so was the child.

And they recognized the child, too, especially the women, and saw in Kate something fresh and unspoiled, something that was yet to be determined by, fashioned by, moulded by her contact with ... and here they hesitated. They hesitated because for each there had been a different experience, sometimes sourly admitted, sometimes joyfully, a different experience, but the same knowledge, and they did not hesitate for long. They saw in Kate something fresh and unspoiled, something that was yet to be moulded by ... men. They saw the child in her, and they watched the glow. But they waited for the greater change, waited expectantly, like women at a wrestling match, aware that the match was a phony, knowing the outcome was identical each time, and none the less screaming for blood.

The child in Kate knew fear.

The child was afraid of too many things, afraid of growing up too soon, afraid of never growing up, afraid of being too passionate, or not passionate enough, or frigid, of being popular for the wrong things, or even unpopular for the wrong things, of touching and being touched, afraid. The child Kate could remember sitting in the middle of a room far away, on a scatter rug covered with her hair, while two women struggled grotesquely. The child Kate could remember coming to a strange house and sleeping in a strange room with night noises in the house, timbers creaking, frightening shadows on the wall whenever an automobile passed outside in the night. The child Kate sometimes dreamed of a woman who was insane wandering down long narrow cramped halls, scissors clutched in her hand.

The child Kate wondered if something would happen to her one day, something terrible and horrible, something that would drive her finally mad. Like her mother.

Like her mother.

She confided her fears to David once. She had gone to the Regan house one week-end, ostensibly to see Julia, but knowing it was the week-end and David would be there. They sat in the living-room while she waited for Julia. Outside, the wind whipped under the eaves of the house.

"That's a very scary wind," she said.

"Yes." He paused. "But you get used to it."

Kate shivered. "It makes me think of terrible things."

"Like what?"

"Like losing my mind," she answered quickly and without hesitation. She looked across the room at him. Do you ever think of losing your mind, David?" she asked.

"I've got nothing to lose," he said, and smiled.

"No, seriously."

"No, I don't think I ever do, Kate."

"I do. I keep waiting for it." She paused. "Do you think insanity is hereditary?"

David shrugged. "I have no idea."

"I mean, do you think something terrible could happen to a person, something, well, frightening and traumatic that could cause ... could ..." and Julia had come into the room, and she had let the conversation lapse, but she was still afraid.

She was afraid of her relationship with David, too. And here, too, there was a combination of woman and child, one creating phantoms and the other putting them to rout. The child was quite sensibly disturbed by her love for a man twice her age. The woman could speculate upon the ecstasies of such a love, could envision passionate embraces and whispered promises, but the child reared back in something like revulsion at the prospect of ever being held or fondled by David Regan. The woman could plan supposedly chance meetings, could sit opposite him in a living-room full of other people and plan the quickest and most direct route to his side, concoct the wildest schemes for coming into chance physical contact with him, the resting of her hand upon his arm to emphasize a point, the casual brushing of a breast against his shoulder as she reached for a magazine—and then the child would pick up her skirts and run. The woman wanted him to know she loved him, wanted him to accept this love, use it, abuse it, do with it what he wanted. But the child was fearful that he would laugh, and more fearful that he would act upon a cue from her, act in a masculine and physical way for which she was not yet ready. And so she thrilled in his presence, she quaked in his presence. She schemed in his presence, she defected in his presence. She wanted him, and she was fearful he would take her.

She was seventeen.

It was March.

It was Sunday. Matthew was still in his robe and slippers, reading the newspaper on the sun porch when the telephone rang. In the living-room, Amanda was working at the piano. Beverly, the cocker spaniel, began barking the moment she heard the phone. Matthew scratched the dog's head, shushed her, put down the paper, and went to the telephone.

"Amanda, could you hold it a minute?" he shouted, and then lifted the receiver. "Hello?"

"Hello. Mr. Bridges?"

"Yes."

"This is Agnes. May I speak to Kate, please?"

"Just a minute, Agnes. I think she's still sleeping." He cupped the mouthpiece and shouted, "Kate? You up?"

"Who is it, Dad?" Kate called from upstairs.

"It's Aggie."

"Thanks, Dad."

He waited until he heard Kate pick up the extension. He put the receiver back into its cradle and went back to reading his newspaper. Beverly dozed at his feet, basking in the sunshine. He had finished a cursory reading of the book section when he heard Kate coming down the steps and going into the kitchen. He put down his newspaper, belted his robe, walked past the living-room where Amanda had begun playing again, and then directly into the kitchen. Beverly padded along behind him, sniffing at his bare feet.

"Morning, Kate," he said.

"Morning, Dad."

She was wearing a robe over her pyjamas. Her hair was tousled, and there was still a sleepy look on her face. She opened the refrigerator, poured herself a glass of orange juice, and then said, "Have you had breakfast?"

"Yes. But I'll have another cup of coffee with you."

"Okay," Kate said listlessly. She poured coffee into two cups, and then sat opposite him at the table. "That was Agnes," she said.

"Yes, I know." Matthew put sugar into his coffee, added a drop of cream, and then stirred it.

"I don't know what to do, Dad."

"What's the matter? Trouble?"

He could remember when she was a little girl. He could remember sitting at this very table with her, explaining the use of a skate key. He lifted his cup. With his dangling free hand, he idly stroked Beverly's head where she lay by his chair.

"We're going to the dance at the church tonight," Kate said. "Paul Marris is taking me."

"Mmm?"

"He's going into the Air Force, Dad. He graduated high school last term, you know, and he's enlisted, and he expects to be called by the end of the month." Kate paused. "He'll be gone for four years." She swallowed a hasty gulp of hot coffee. "Do you have a cigarette, Dad?"

Matthew felt in the pockets of his robe, handed her the package, and then lighted one for her.

"Thanks," she said. She blew out a stream of smoke and picked up her coffee-cup again. "He's going to ask me to go steady, Dad," she said.

"Paul is?"

"Yes."

"How do you know?"

"Agnes told me. He's discussed it with Ralph, his friend. He's going to ask me to wait for him." She paused. "He'll be gone for four years, Dad."

"I see."

"I don't know what to do."

The table was silent. A car passed by outside, and Beverly leaped to her feet and began barking.

"Shhh, shhh," Matthew said, and the dog growled once as an afterthought, and then collapsed at his feet again. In the living-room, Amanda kept striking the same chord repeatedly as she transcribed it to the manuscript paper. "Well, do you like him, Kate?"

"Yes, I do, Daddy."

"Well, I think . . ." He hesitated. He suddenly felt inadequate. "I think you should ask yourself whether or not, well . . . if he wants you to wait for him, Kate, this would indicate he's pretty serious, wouldn't it?"

"It wouldn't be like getting engaged or anything, Dad."

"I understand that."

"But I couldn't go out with anyone else, either. I'd be his girl."

"Yes, I know." Matthew paused again. "Well, he's a very nice boy, Kate."

"Yes, he is, Dad. Not at all hoody like some of the other boys around. But . . ." She shrugged. She picked up her coffee-cup and stared into it, and then swallowed another gulp.

"Kate, maybe you're a little young to be tying yourself down to someone. You'll be getting out of school this summer, you'll probably want to make plans for college, you——"

"Yes, I know, Dad. The only thing is, you see, I wouldn't want to hurt Paul. I think he might be very embarrassed if he asked me to wait for him and I said no. You see, I do like him, and he is awfully nice, and I'm very flattered and all, but . . . well, I wouldn't want to hurt him, especially when he's going away to the Air Force. Because I like him, Dad."

"I think it takes a little more than that, Kate. I think you should consider whether there's more than just *liking* him."

"Well, I like him a lot, Dad. But then . . ." She shrugged. "I don't know. Mrs. Regan asked me if I'd like to go with her this summer, you know, when she goes to Italy, and——"

"I didn't know that," Matthew said.

"Yes. So there's that to consider, too. I was going to ask you, Dad," she said hastily. "I wouldn't just accept without . . ."

"I know you wouldn't. But I don't see how the trip would affect——"

"Being away and all, I mean. And suppose I go to college in the fall . . . well, I don't know what to do, Dad. Actually, I may not even *go* to college."

"That's up to you."

"But I still don't want to hurt Paul before he goes away."

"Kate, do you love him?" Matthew asked flatly.

"No." She paused. She looked into her empty coffee-cup. "I love someone else."

"Then that settles it, doesn't it? It has nothing to do with the Air Force or the trip or college or anything but the fact that you love someone else."

"Well, this other person doesn't even know I exist, Dad."

Matthew smiled. "How can *anyone* not know you exist, Kate?"

"Oh, it's possible, all right," she said. She smiled wanly, got up, and walked to the stove. "Would you like more coffee?"

"No, thanks."

She returned to the table, poured herself a fresh cupful, put the pot back on the stove, and said, "Believe me, Dad, it's possible," and the kitchen went silent.

"Kate . . ." he said, and he paused. Go on, he thought, be the father. Make the father speech. He felt very clumsy all at once. "Kate, you're a young girl," he said. That's a wonderful beginning, he thought. Always start with the obvious, especially when your daughter is someone as bright as Kate. "You're a young girl and . . ." He groped for words. Amanda should be doing this, he thought, and then he saw that Kate was watching him, and listening to him intently, and he realized that he'd made the mistake again of thinking she was truly adult, of assuming she already knew what he was about to say. But she didn't. She *was* a young girl, and this was all new to her, and she wouldn't have begun discussing it if she hadn't hoped for assistance. He suddenly thought of the skate key again, holding the skate and showing her how the key worked.

"Kate," he said, "the important thing to think of is . . ." In a split second, he thought, No, don't tell her that, don't tell her to hurt this boy, don't tell her to think only of herself, and he remembered when he was eighteen and he thought of a girl named Helen Kennedy and he wondered suddenly what Paul Marris had done to his daughter Kate. But very carefully, and all in the space of several seconds, he phrased what he was about to say, almost as if he were summing up a case for the jury, but this time he was only summing up a life, so how do you sum up life in a Connecticut kitchen on a sunny Sunday morning to a troubled girl of seventeen, how do you do that? It was so easy with the skate key, he thought, Jesus, it was so easy. How do things get so complicated?

"Kate," he said, "I like Paul, he's a nice boy. I'm glad you've been going out with him. I think Mother likes him, too. I think he's sensible and level-headed and nice-looking, but none of this matters a damn if you don't love him, because there are a lot of nice-looking, sensible, level-headed people in this world, and you're going to meet a great many of them and, Kate, you can like them all, but that isn't love, and if you loved Paul, you wouldn't have to think about it twice, you'd know exactly what you wanted to do." He paused. "I knew exactly what I wanted to do when I met your mother."

I'm doing this all wrong, he thought. I sound like the voice of the ages, the wise old man of the hills, she hasn't experienced this, damn it, she doesn't know that people come and go, she doesn't know what life is all about.

Yes, and do you? he asked himself.

"Kate . . ."

Do *you*? he asked himself.

"Kate, I'd kill anyone who tried to hurt your mother," he said. "I'd strangle him with my bare hands."

Yes, and that explains love, doesn't it? That explains it all to a seventeen-year-old girl who is going to a dance tonight where someone will ask her to wait for him, did *I* ask anyone to wait for me? No, but Amanda was waiting. Amanda was . . .

"Kate," he said, and suddenly realized he could not talk to her, and was filled with a desperate lonely sadness. I cannot talk to my own daughter, he thought. "Kate," he said, "you'll know when you're in love, don't rush into anything," crap, he thought, baloney, bull, crap, nothing, why can't I talk to her, and tell her what, and tell her of the girl on the hill overlooking the town, and tell her of Helen Kennedy, and tell her of the girls in Boston, and tell her of Kitty Newell, all of whom I loved in a way, all of whom took a part of me, Matthew Bridges, and from whom I accepted something, tell her not to hurt, tell her to be kind, "Kate, don't hurt him," he said, tell her of a love beyond the physical exchange, did she know of this already, has she been kissed, has she been touched, what can I tell her, and why can't I speak to her?

So all the platitudes came out, all the father-daughter jazz evolved from a long line of father-daughter conversations starting with Eve and the biggest father of them all, and ending perhaps with Tracy Lord in Philadelphia, and he thought wildly of love as he explained patiently to her, explained that Paul would be more hurt if she accepted his love when she really couldn't return it, thought of his very real and long-ago concern with people until somewhere he had lost the capacity, thought how sad it was to be sitting here with a daughter who was almost grown up, a daughter troubled because she didn't want to hurt someone she liked, and thinking back to all the people he had possibly hurt in the past, and telling her she had a long life ahead of her, and that one day she would find the person she instinctively knew was the right person for her, telling her this while believing there *was* no single right person in the world for any other person, but giving his daughter all the time-honoured crap while recognizing that something very important was happening then and there in the sunny Connecticut kitchen while Amanda played piano in the living-room, recognizing that he was about to lose her because they could no longer talk together.

And sitting there with her, shining and new, recognized perhaps that Matthew Bridges was not a very special unique individual at all. Recognized the falseness of a man who shouted rebellion while slowly settling into a comfortable rut where there was really nothing against which to rebel. Who theorized and observed and complained about the culture, but who had none the less succumbed to it over the years, and was totally at ease within its confines, recognized this, and was shocked by the recognition. Matthew Bridges was a man who got up to catch the 8.04 each morning, and who read the *Times* and who voted without much interest and who went to the parties and the picnics and the dances and who devoted time to his wife in the evening and time to his children on Saturday and Sunday, and yet was losing his daughter this very minute, not to another person, but only because he could not talk to her. Or maybe had lost *himself* a long time ago in the morass of just doing the things that had to be done every single day of the week, like brushing his teeth, or taking Beverly for a walk, losing his own identity in a superficial uniform mass-identity where people spoke in shorthand and where it was important to be liked, but not at all important to be loved.

"It's important," he said flatly and harshly.

He wanted to run. In the stillness of the sunny kitchen with the March cold outside and the echo of his words, he wanted to run because the image of himself was suddenly frightening, an image indistinguishable from the countless others who caught their trains and mowed their lawns and lighted their cigarettes and held their cocktails and made love to their wives and had hopeless conversations with their daughters without being able to speak to them. He wanted to run anywhere out into the countryside because he knew he had once been Matthew Anson Bridges, a person in his own right, a very important individual, and that now he was not that person, but someone else—not even someone else, he was everyone else, he was faceless.

"Oh, Christ, Kate," he said, "keep it!"

She stared at him in puzzlement, there was no communication. She thought he meant something quite different.

"I'd like to get on a train for Boston sometime," he said.

She stared at her father because he no longer was making the slightest sense. She had already decided how she would handle Paul Marris—honestly and simply; no, she would not be his girl—but this was something else. She looked up at him in confusion and said, "What did you say, Daddy?"

"You know what love is?" he said fiercely.

"I think I do."

"Do you know what it is?" he said fiercely. "It's accepting things you don't really want, and giving away the things that mean the most to you."

She did not answer him.

He thought, She doesn't understand.

He thought, For Christ's sake, Kate, your father is a shadow. I loved girls once, do you know that? I killed men once, do you know that? I raced across Connecticut with Amanda once, do you know that? Do you know what I did once, Kate, oh do you know the things I did once?

"Well, he said, "you can take care of it. You're a sensible girl, Kate."

He wanted to run.

"You can handle Paul without hurting him."

He wanted to be Matthew Anson Bridges.

"I've always been able to depend on you."

He wanted suddenly to see Julia. He wanted someone to look at his face, to take his face between her hands and look at it very hard and then say, "Why, yes. It's you." He closed his eyes tight.

Why, yes, of course, it's you.

April came in alive with plans. April always did. You had to do something in April, you had to burst outdoors in a sweater and suck air into your lungs, you had to leave the house and the winter behind, the season demanded it of you. And because life was suddenly sprouting everywhere around you, because there was visible evidence in everything you touched that the world was turning green again, because April had that magic sound in it, April, you could taste the word, you could sniff it, you could hold it in your arms and love it, because April brought with it the promise of sunshine and languid breezes and romance, it was a time for planning, a time for renewed hopefulness.

Julia Regan was going back to Italy.

There were clothes to buy, and she shopped the stores and studied the designers' offerings with all the excitement of a young girl going to her first prom. She bought a Brigance walking skirt in taupe with a geometrically patterned matching top. She bought a Jane Derby afternoon dress in black silk surah. From Grès, for the evening, she bought a brown chiffon, and from Galanos a dark-blue print in Italian silk. At Lord & Taylor's she found a colourful Pucci silk-jersey print, which she purchased, amused because she was going to Italy where the dress originated, but not at all sure she could get it there. At Ohrbach's she found two drip-dry cotton shirtwaists, one in madras and one in khaki. She bought impetuously, but with a practised eye, two Acrilon knits, one in white and the other in black, two pairs of Belgian walking shoes from Henri Bendel, a woollen mohair stole in a burnished mustard, a coral-coloured jersey raincoat that could double as a topper, a dark-green cotton suit from Jax with a matching scoop-necked dressy blouse and a striped tailored blouse, a pair of brown satin shoes and another pair dyed to match the blue Italian silk. She bought a simple black bathing-suit, and a dozen nylons, and a pair of beige walking pumps with a stacked heel, and a travelling clock, and a cardigan sweater, and a large bottle of aspirin, and cleansing tissues, and paperback books for the plane trip. She bought no new jewellery, but she laid out her pearls and her scatter pins and bracelets, and a ruby pendant Arthur had given her when David was born, and a cameo she'd inherited from her mother, and tried to decide which she should take with her, if not all.

There were arrangements to be made, too. She longed to duplicate the trip she'd taken in 1938. She wanted to begin in Paris as she had with Millie—only this time, Kate would be her companion, Kate would accompany her to the Meurice, and then out of Paris by rented car to Fontainebleau and Sens and Dijon where they would stay overnight at the Hôtel de la Cloche, and then on to Lausanne and the Beau-Rivage, and finally to Interlaken. Kate would be with her when they drove through the Grimsel Pass, and down that magnificent valley to Brig. Kate would be with her when the train pulled into Domodossola, white and shining in the sun. There were hotel reservations to be made, and maps to be marked, the entire route from Paris to Rome, and airline tickets to be purchased, and passports to be applied for and acquired, and vaccinations and shots, and travellers' cheques, and a letter of credit from the Talmadge bank, a hundred things to do before they left from Idlewild on the first of July.

She barely had time to think about Milt Anderson's warnings in those hurried days of buying and preparing for the trip. Somewhere in a buried corner of her mind, there was the memory of a car stalled on a mountain curve, a bus rushing past, the frightening lurch of her heart as the horn's sound filled the air, she did not want this to happen again. But she none the less planned her trip to duplicate that earlier one, telling herself nothing could possibly happen, she would avoid the physical and emotional stress Milt had talked about. Kate would make it easier for her.

And then, remembering the true intent of her trip, she wondered whether it was advisable to take Kate with her. But yes, there would be no harm, Kate would make it easier all around, easier to accept whatever physical hardships presented themselves, easier to reconstruct the past—and perhaps easier to adjust to the present. So she stopped questioning her judgement. April was a time for planning, and she planned happily and with joyous expectation.

Julia Regan was going back.

April was a time for meetings.
The panelled private office of Curt Sonderman contained six

executives of the corporation met in high conclave to discuss a television phenomenon known simply as "the trend to the Coast". This, when translated from O'Brian, simply meant that New York City was becoming a dead town where television—live, filmed, or taped—was concerned. The trend was not a surprising one, nor had its development gone undetected over the years. The business of Sonderman Enterprises, Inc., after all, *was* television, and Curt was a shrewd businessman who knew upon which side his onion roll was buttered. But when you've got a going firm in a going city like New York, the natural thing is to believe not what your intelligence tells you is true, but what your emotions want you to believe. So what if they opened a big Television City out there? So what if North Vine was crawling with bright fancy studios, and more and more shows seemed to be originating from beautiful stages constructed for the sole purpose of television broadcasting, instead of the left-over legitimate theatres and converted lofts in New York? So what if every major film studio had subsidiaries that were grinding out more filmed television dramas than the public could consume in a month of Sundays, New York would stand eternal. New York would not succumb to the cry of the cannibals on the Coast, New York would remain the inspiration, the creative centre of that world of video, yeah, the actors and the writers and the producers and the directors would recognize that Hollywood was just so much flesh in the pan, yeah, movies they could make, yeah, but when it came to television, when it came to that newest of mediums, which had its beginnings and its real roots in the East, yeah, nobody was ready to believe that Hollywood could take the ball away from New York.

Yeah.

Well, it had.

And so Curt Sonderman and six producers of Sonderman Enterprises, Inc., one of whom was David Regan, sat in that lush panelled office and pored over figures that explained without a single doubt, no matter what feelings they had about that mecca of creativity named New York, explained precisely and concisely that most of the television work—live, filmed, and taped—most of the really artistic and creative stuff like *Wagon Train* and *Johnny Midnight* and *Peter Gunn* and *Maverick* and *Gunsmoke* and *Lawman* and *Leave It to Beaver* and *The Man and the Challenge* and *The Detectives* and *Air Power* and *The Real McCoys* and *Disneyland*, all these were being done on the Coast. So where did that leave a New York firm like Sonderman Enterprises, Inc., whose business was producing and packaging television programmes for consumption throughout the nation? Where did it leave them especially when New York City was still crawling with investigators who were complaining about perfectly legitimate rigged shows like *The $64,000 Question* and *Twenty-One*, and like that?

"What am I in business for, my health?" Sonderman shouted repeating the words his sainted grandfather had been fond of using. "We're supposed to package shows, we're supposed to produce shows, we're paying enough rent in this Madison Avenue glass slipper each month to support a tribe of Arabs for the rest of their natural lives, am I in business for my health?"

David sat watching him, and said nothing.

"Who's making the money?" Sonderman asked. "Hollywood is making the money. Who's doing the shows? Hollywood is doing the shows. Where have all the actors gone? Hollywood! Where have all the directors gone? Hollywood! Am I out of my mind, staying here in New York! What's in New York, would you please tell me? The Bowery? The Statue of Liberty? Grant's Tomb? What is there in New York that I, Curt Sonderman, should stay here like a baby holding his mother's hand, what is there would you please tell me? Nothing! That's what there is in New York for an honest firm trying to do television business, N-O-T-H-I-N-zero! Nothing!"

"That's not quite true, Curt," one of his executives said.

"Look, buddy-boy, take a look at the books. This was the hottest firm in the business in 1956, and now it's 1960, and we are very quickly falling on our big fat butts. You know what New York has? Legitimate theatre, that's what it has! And a little bit of movies is trickling back, they're shooting up in the Bronx and on the streets. Are we supposed to start producing plays? Sure, try to edge your way into that pretentious crowd. Or movies, maybe? Ridiculous. They can do them better in Hollywood. They've been feeding the public crap for so long, the public is used to the product and respects it like a brand name. *Television* is our business! So where's television? It's in Hollywood, that's where it is."

"Curt, you're getting too nervous," another of his executives said. "You're always getting too nervous."

"Yeah, I got nervous when *Studio One* went to the Coast, and I got nervous when *Kraft* went off the air, and I get nervous right now when I see all these shows and on the credit crawl it says 'Filmed in Hollywood at Desilu' or some other cockamamie mixed-name outfit, yeah, I get nervous. You think I'm in business for my health?"

"What do you want to do, Curt?" David asked.

"I don't know what I want to do. That's why I called this meeting."

"You want to pick up everything, lock, stock and barrel, and go West?" one of the executives asked.

"Maybe."

"Foolish," another of the executives said.

"Look, you said *For Whom the Bells Toll* was foolish when they wanted to do it, so they did it in two parts and it was a big hit."

"It was a lousy job."

"Who's interested in lousy or good? It was a hit."

"The movie was better."

"It is only my pistol, Maria," one of the executives quoted.

"Don't clown around," Sonderman said. "We've got business here."

"It'd be foolish to go West, Curt," one of the men said. "This is just a fad. A few new studios, a few actors and directors with itchy feet——"

"Itchy feet, my nose. That's where the long green is, Hollywood, California. So we're sitting here and watching the industry collapse all around us. That's smart, all right. That's smart if you're in business for your health."

"So what do you want to do?"

This is April. We've still got the season to finish, and with a little luck we won't be selling apples on the street before the fall. But we've got the whole summer to fool around with, while everybody's showing re-runs. I suggest we start fooling around in Hollywood. I suggest we send a man out there to get the lay of the land and to deliver a full report. And if there's room for us out there, then, gentlemen, we are *going* out there!"

The executives fell silent.

"You feel like taking a trip to Hollywood, David?" Sonderman asked.

"If you want me to," David answered.

"When does your show go off the air?"

"The last one's on June sixteenth."

"Can you leave by July first?"

"I think so."

"Yes, or no?"

"Yes."

"I'd like a vote on this," Sonderman said.

The executives voted unanimously to send David Regan to Hollywood on July first, just to scout around. David sat and watched the hands go up all around the table in the panelled room. Oddly, only one word popped into his mind.

Gillian.

It was April, and a time for making plans.

Amanda sat down with her uncompleted suite and read it through carefully, and then decided if she was ever going to finish it, she would finish it this summer. Her own tenacity, her own concentration, sometimes amazed her. The suite would lie dormant for months at a time, untouched, barely thought of in the press of her household duties, and then she would begin working at it steadily again, sometimes devoting as much as eight hours to it in a single day. And then the world would close in again, the petty everyday things that had to be done to keep a home running smoothly, and she would put the work aside, once leaving it for as long as six months before returning to it again. There had seemed no real rush, no real necessity for completing the composition. She wanted it to be perfectly right, and so she had taken her time, knowing it was there, knowing she could always return to it. But now she had an idea, an idea she had never considered before, and the idea presented a new field for speculation, and a definite incentive for completing the suite during the summer.

She was, after all, a graduate of Talmadge University, and some of the music instructors there were rather well known in musical circles, and she had always been a good student and a favourite of many of them. As soon as the composition was finished, she would walk over to the school and renew old acquaintances, casually mention that she had been working on an orchestral suite for a good long time now and had just finished it this summer, well no, really I'm sure you wouldn't want to hear it, no, it's nothing really, well, if you insist, I'll play it for you, though I'm not sure the full effect will be realized with piano alone. And then, yes, she would take advantage of whatever connections they had. Then, yes, she would try to get the work performed, try to get it recorded—but first, of course, she had to finish it.

She was thoroughly satisfied now with the major theme, the section she called Genesis, the opening section with its choralelike overtones. The theme ran throughout the entire work, its solemn ponderous chords appearing in the most curious places, illogically springing up in the Revival section where, and she thought this was an innovation, she had actually used clapping hands as a part of the scoring, two sections of clapping hands in counterpoint to each other and to the timpani and brass. The spiritual section still disturbed her, though, despite the gimmickry of the clapping hands, not really an original concept anyway, Bernstein had used it, though not as flamboyantly, still she wasn't satisfied with the section, it did not have the true ring of an old-fashioned revival meeting.

Nor was she happy with the brief section in the minor key, the section she had titled Episode, somewhat tangential to the concept of the entire work, and with a foreign flavour to it, actually a Russian flavour. She thought Episode described it fairly accurately, a sort of interlude, a filling-in of spaces, a jaunt away from the major theme of the entire work, and yet a section that advanced the first two sections, the introductory section labelled Genesis, and the spiritual, hand-clapping, joyous, happy, loving second section called Revival. Still, it needed work, she knew that.

The last and final section of the composition was called Judgement Day, and it recalled the major theme again, picking up the tempo and enlarging upon it, striking each note sharply and cleanly, with a great deal of brass and a *seque* into strings again. Judgement Day, in fact, borrowed from each of the work's sections, trying to round out a cycle, something begun with Genesis and ending with the final note of the suite, but really a cycle that was never fully completed because after Judgement Day, there would be another Genesis, and another joyous Revival, and perhaps another Episode, and then again into Judgement Day, the cycle was endless and mystifying, somewhat like a medieval round. The problem in the final section— or the problem as she visualized it—was the resolution of the various themes stated throughout the work, themes that certainly needed resolution before the final note was sounded, but which needed resolution in terms of a sudden alteration of tempo towards an overwhelming climax of sound. The last section moved faster, there was the rushing sound of strings in the background, the reeds seemed to flow more swiftly, the brasses tongued their passages in staccato wildness, everything seemed to rush, oh how she hoped it would rush, towards a climax where theme after theme was resolved separately, and where the major theme was stated triumphantly and majestically.

Or at least, that was what she wanted.

And what she did not yet have.

But this was April, and she was brimful of plans. She knew exactly what she hoped to accomplish during the summer. Kate was going off to Europe with Julia Regan, and arrangements had been made to send Bobby off to camp, and this meant that the house would be empty, blissfully, magnificently empty, and that she could spend all day, every day, at the piano until the suite was finished. In the first green rush of April, she made out a tentative schedule, a visual chart that outlined the exact amount of work she hoped to complete by the end of each day. Her chart told her how many new bars she would write, which sections of the work she would revise, where more complete scoring was necessary, when she would tape-record and play back the sections already finished. Her chart was a day-by-day plan of creativity, and she knew that before the summer was through —she had set Labour Day as her deadline—the work would be completed and ready to show to her old instructors at the university. After that, it was anyone's guess. But at least she had a plan.

It was April, and at least she had a plan.

Matthew got the idea for the second honeymoon some time in April.

He got the idea sitting in his office and looking down at the street. The idea came to him full-blown. Sitting there with spring outside his window, he suddenly remembered that Kate would be going to Europe this summer, and Bobby would be going to camp, and he suddenly thought, it would be nice to go away somewhere with Amanda, a sort of second honeymoon.

That was exactly the way he thought of it. As a sort of second honeymoon.

And yet, though he labelled it that, he knew it was something more, knew it meant a great deal more to him. He could remember with painful clarity that day at the breakfast table with Kate last month, and the knowledge that something in him had changed, that he had become a different person than he once had been, a person unexciting and somehow dead. He longed to be alive again. The children would both be away for the entire summer, and he had a vision of the open road with Amanda beside him, both of them free of all responsibility, laughing, haphazardly crossing the face of America, sleeping when they were tired, making love when they chose to, getting drunk if they liked, doing whatever they wanted, whenever and wherever they felt like it, recklessly, foolishly, in complete abandon. It seemed absolutely essential that this spring of all springs, this spring when he had had a sudden and frightening glimpse of himself as some fossilizing organism, this spring he should plan for a summer that would be revitalizing and rejuvenating. He felt it was absolutely essential.

He went next door to see Sol Stang, the senior partner of the firm, and he said, "Sol, I want to take my vacation in July this year."

"Okay," Stang said, "so take it."

"I want a full month."

"You're out of your mind."

"You'd have to prove that allegation with the testimony of either two psychiatrists, or a psychiatrist and a psychologist. I want a full month, Sol."

"We'll have a half-dozen cases coming to trial in July, Matt. We can't spare you for a full month."

"I know you can't. But you can't spare me for two weeks, either, when you get right down to it. But I take two weeks each summer and two weeks each winter, and somehow the firm seems to get along without me. So this summer, I want to take my wife on a second honeymoon. I want a month. That's that."

"Who the hell says that's that?"

"I say it. I'm taking a month, Sol. My daughter leaves for Europe on July first, and my son leaves for camp on July third, and Amanda and I are leaving for parts unknown on July fourth. That's that."

"You know, Matthew," Stang said, "I sometimes wonder why on earth we ever took you into this firm."

"I'm a good lawyer," Matthew said, and he grinned. "I just won a decision for a full month, didn't I?"

"This isn't law," Stang said, "this is economics. And besides, you didn't win any decision. It's been a standing rule of this firm for as long as I can remember that no single partner would take more than two weeks at any one time."

"It's lucky I'm a married partner then."

"You know what I mean, Matthew. It's a rule. It's the way we operate."

"Rules are made to be broken," Matthew said. "The same as laws."

"What?" Stang stared at him, shocked. "What did you say?"

"I said," Matthew repeated slowly, "that laws are made to be broken." As he said the words, he felt again this necessity for rebellion, and wondered instantly whether he really believed what he was saying. And remembered again that day at the table with Kate, and realized anew the terrible need for getting away, and said with firmer conviction—still not knowing if he believed himself—"Laws are made to be broken."

"That's the goddamedest thing I've ever heard any lawyer ever say."

"I'm more honest than most lawyers," Matthew said, smiling.

"What do you mean, laws are made to be broken?"

"Why else do they exist?"

"To protect society. Why do you think?"

"Nonsense," Matthew said.

"Look, Matt, the law——"

"The law is a body of rules and regulations that are supposed to limit the activities of human beings, am I right? It is illegal to stab your mother, or drown your sister, or get drunk in church. All right, Sol, let's assume our laws are perfect, which they're not, and let's assume our judicial system is functioning smoothly and effectively, which it's not, and let's assume that nobody ever breaks any of the laws we've invented. Can you visualize that?"

Why am I doing this? he wondered. I don't even *believe* this. Why am I taking an impossible stand and trying to prove it? Why am I such a goddam phony? A dull conformist who pretends to anarchy? Why?

"I don't know what you're driving at," Stang said.

"I'm simply asking you to visualize a civilization with a rigid code of laws that no one breaks. No one speeds, no one spits on the sidewalk, no one commits assault, or burglary, or homicide. Everyone lives within the law. There are no crimes and no criminals. Can you visualize that?"

"Yeah, go ahead," Stang said, frowning.

"Why do we need the law?"

"What?"

"In a society devoid of lawbreakers, why is there a necessity for law?"

"Well, to . . . to protect the citizen."

"From what? No one is committing any crime."

"Well, to *ensure* that no one does. To guarantee——"

"But you missed my original premise. No one, repeat, no one commits a crime in this ideal society. No one would even *think* of committing a crime. Years and years of respect for the existing law has made crime unthinkable. So why do we need the law?"

"I guess because . . ." Stang fell silent.

"If no one is going to break the law, there is no need for it. Therefore, it seems safe to conclude that laws are only made to be broken. The very existence of law presupposes a person or persons who will one day break it. No mice, no need for mousetraps. No lawbreakers, no need for law. It's simple." He shrugged. "Laws are made to be broken."

He felt no pleasure watching the puzzlement on his partner's face. He felt only an emptiness, a sorrow at whatever had pushed him into this meaningless rebellion.

"There's something fishy . . ." Stang started.

"In summing up, ladies and gentlemen of the jury," Matthew interrupted, "I can only observe that since laws are made to be broken, and since it is a standing rule, or a law, of this firm to limit each partner to an absence from the office of only two weeks, my full month's leave during July of this year will constitute an action necessitated, yea, *dictated*, by the very existence of the nonsensical rule itself. Defence rests, Sol."

"I'm glad you're on *our* side," Stang said dryly.

"A month," Matthew said, "thank you, thank you," and he bowed low from the waist and then went back to his own office, smiling.

And in April, his daughter Kate formulated a plan of her own.

· · · · ·

She did not put the first part of her plan into effect until the beginning of May, when she finally worked up enough courage to translate theory into action. By that time, she had learned that David Regan was leaving for California in July, and this knowledge, rather than her own impending trip to Europe, was what lent urgency to her plan. For whereas she knew that she and Julia would be gone only two months, she had the oddest feeling that if David were allowed to go to California without ever seeing her as a woman, he would never again return East. She was seventeen, and she believed this with firm conviction, never once doubting her intuition.

She was used to making plans, because everything about seventeen involved planning. But the planning she had done up to now was usually a group activity and rarely involved anything conceived and executed alone. This was different. She couldn't even breathe to anyone the slightest hint of what she intended to do or hoped to accomplish. David was her exclusive problem, and so she planned alone all through April and the beginning of May, and when she learned he was going to California, she daringly put her plan into motion.

The plan would only work, it seemed to her, if it were made to appear accidental. If David once suspected she had worked this out in detail, she was certain he would bolt. He still thought of her as a seventeen-year-old, a nice kid who was the daughter of two of his adult friends. She wanted him to know that, yes, she was seventeen, but she was something much more than a nice kid. She was an adult in her own right, and quite capable of loving and being loved. And she wanted him to know this before he left for the Coast.

She began working on Julia weeks before she hoped to launch her main offensive. Like a good general, she studied the terrain and chose her own battleground. She had decided that she and David had to be alone somewhere, away from other people, and she concluded that the Regan house at Lake Abundance would be empty and isolated in May, and would serve her needs excellently. And then, like a good general, she began considering the various approach routes to the house, choosing Julia as the most likely and most reasonable, and beginning her early shore bombardment by casually stating she had begun packing her clothes for the European trip already, and then leading the conversation into the various items of clothing, and finally asking Julia how many bathing-suits she should take.

Two days later, she told Julia she had bought a new bathing-suit, but couldn't find a suit she had worn all through last summer, a suit she was very fond of, a basic essential to her European wardrobe. Julia, unsuspecting, innocent, sympathized with her, and told her it would probably turn up somewhere, had she looked very carefully through the summer stuff that Amanda had undoubtedly packed away at the end of the season? Kate let the matter drop.

But casually, within the next few days, as they discussed passports and hotels, she brought the conversation around to that bathing-suit, "The red one, don't you remember, Mrs. Regan? I wore it all last summer at the lake. I practically lived in it. The red wool."

"Yes, I remember it," Julia said. "I'm sure you'll find it before we leave, Kate."

And again the conversation drifted off into more important matters, or seemingly more important matters; the one thing on Kate's mind was access to the Regan house at the lake.

The next day, she called Julia and said, "I remember now, Mrs. Regan."

"What's that, darling?" Julia said.

"Where I left the bathing-suit. The red wool."

"Oh, good. Did you find it?"

"No, I didn't. But I remember where I left it."

"Where, dear?"

"At the lake." Kate paused. "At your house."

"My house? At Lake Abundance?"

"Yes, Mrs. Regan. Do you remember once at the end of the summer, we came over for a barbecue? And I'd been swimming, and I went into the bedroom at the end of the house, the little one that has the picture of a ship on the wall, and I changed my clothes in there, do you remember?"

"Well, no, I don't exactly, Kate."

"Yes. I put on dungarees and a sweater, don't you remember?"

"If you say so, Kate. But I had the house cleaned thoroughly before I left it, and I don't remember seeing your suit anywhere."

"Oh, I'm sure it's there," Kate said.

"Well, what would you like to do? Shall we drive out some day to have a look?"

"Yes, but there's no real rush," Kate said. "Now that I know where it is."

"All right, darling, let me know when you want to go, will you?"

"I will," Kate said, and she hung up triumphantly.

The first part of the plan, then, had been carried off successfully. She had convinced Julia that the red bathing-suit was at the lake house—or at least led Julia to believe that *she* was convinced it was there. And Julia had offered to drive her out one day. The next part of the plan was to make sure that Julia did *not* drive her out, and this required a little bit of manœuvring and a great deal of luck. For one thing, she had to synchronize David's presence with Julia's absence, and this would not be easy. Julia often went into New York on her shopping sprees, but she went invariably on Mondays or Thursdays when the stores stayed open late, and when she could spend the entire day looking and buying. She had, in fact, once mentioned that she wouldn't dream of going into the city on a Saturday because the stores were unimaginably crowded and the train service was too erratic. But the only time David came to Talmadge was on week-ends, so it was essential that Julia be gone on a Saturday—Sunday would have been equally acceptable, but far too difficult to manage—and it had to be a Saturday when David was there for the week-end. By a series of discreet questions, she learned that David would be coming up on the twenty-first, less than a week away. Desperately, Kate tried to figure a way of getting Julia out of Talmadge.

Her break came unexpectedly. Julia told her that she was going into White Plains that Saturday to pick up a few things she needed, and Kate thought about this all the way home, her heart pounding, and called her the moment she reached the house.

"What time did you plan on going, Mrs. Regan?" she asked.

"Oh, I thought I'd get there before lunch and come back sometime in the afternoon," Julia said.

Quickly, her voice expressing disappointment, Kate said, "Oh, I thought I could join you."

"Why not, Kate? You're entirely welc——"

"I have some library work to do in the morning, Mrs. Regan. Could I possibly meet you there later in the afternoon?"

"How late?"

"Three o'clock?"

"I hadn't planned on staying that late," Julia said.

"Oh well, then never mind. I guess I can get a lift back somehow."

"What do you mean?"

"Well, one of the girls was going to drive me in, but she's going right on to New York, and I don't have a way of getting back home."

Julia sighed and said, "I suppose I can find something to do until three."

"I'd certainly appreciate it, Mrs. Regan."

As soon as she hung up, Kate called Suzie Fox. "Sue," she said, "I need a lift to White Plains on Saturday."

"I'm not going to White Plains on Saturday," Suzie said.

"Yes, you are," Kate said.

"No, I'm not. I have to finish a theme Saturday, and I can't go rushing off to——"

"Suzie, I'd drive myself, but I'm not allowed to in New York State until I'm eighteen. You can——"

"Ever since my birthday, I've become a taxi service to New York," Suzie said.

"When's the last time I asked you for a favour?"

There was a long silence on the line.

"I'll probably fail English," Suzie said. "The theme is due on Monday."

"You won't fail. Two-thirty Saturday. You won't forget, will you?"

"I won't forget," Suzie said wearily.

"Mark it on your calendar."

"I already did."

"Okay, hon, thanks a million."

She was grinning when she hung up. She now knew that David would be in Talmadge on Saturday, that Julia would be leaving for White Plains sometime before lunch and that she would have to remain there until three o'clock. She had arranged for Suzie to pick her up at two-thirty, which gave her at least two hours alone with David. All she needed now was a little co-operation from him.

She was certain she would get it.

The twenty-first of May was a bright cloudless day, somewhat brisk for so late in the month, but a beautiful day with a flawless blue sky and a brilliant sun. She was pleased at first by the splendour of it, and then wondered if the good weather would bring some people to the lake. She did not want anyone at the lake when she and David were there.

She dressed very carefully. Her plan had not taken her beyond the simple premise of adult recognition, but she none the less chose her undergarments with the cold precision of a seductress, the most feminine and female she owned. Over these, she put a straight black skirt, a little tight, and a white silk blouse. She wore no stockings. She knew that high heels would have looked absurd for any Saturday afternoon in Talmadge, and she even debated the advisability of wearing a French heel, but she finally settled for it, and then wondered again whether she looked too elegant. She shrugged, polished her nails, applied her lipstick with a brush, and then at eleven-thirty, she called the Regan house. David answered the phone.

"Hello, David," she said, "this is Kate."

"Hi, Kate."

"May I speak to your mother, please?"

"I'm sorry, she left about a half hour ago." He paused. "Aren't you supposed to meet her in White Plains?"

"Not until later this afternoon. David, did she mention anything about the key?"

"What key is that, Kate?"
"To the lake house."
"No. Why?"
"I think I left a bathing-suit there, and I wanted to look for it. Your mother said it would be all right."
"Well the key is here, if you want it."
"Oh, good. I'll stop by for it in a few minutes. Will you be home?"
"Sure."
"All right, David. Good-bye." She hung up quickly, her heart pounding. Quietly and unobtrusively, she went out of the house. Parsie looked up when she passed the kitchen, but said nothing. Once outside, she began walking swiftly. The Regan house was a good ten blocks away, but she made it in five minutes. She went around back to the kitchen door and knocked on it. David opened the door. He was wearing a sweat shirt and a pair of khaki pants. There was shaving cream on one half of his face.

"Hi," he said. "I didn't expect you so soon."
"I hope I'm not disturbing you, David," she said.
"Not at all. I was just shaving. Come on in."
"I really have to hurry," she said. "I thought I'd have a car, but I don't."
"Just let me get the rest of this off," he said, "and I'll find that key for you."
"All right," she said, and she followed him into the house. He had not taken the bait, had given no sign that he'd even heard her. She sat in the living-room while he finished shaving in the downstairs bathroom. The grandfather clock read ten minutes to twelve. The drive to the lake took at least twenty-five minutes. She wondered suddenly if he'd brought his car up. Suppose he'd taken the train? She tried to remember if she'd seen his car as she passed the garage outside. Nervously, she began tapping her fingers on the arm of the chair.

"When did you arrive, David?" she called to the open bathroom door. "Last night?"
"Yes."
"Did you come by train?"
"No, I drove."
She was glad he could not see the relief on her face. "Traffic heavy?" she asked casually.
"No, not too bad." She heard him turn on the faucet, heard him splashing water on to his face.
"Will you be much longer, David? I may have trouble getting a hitch out to the lake."

"I'm finished," he said. He came out of the bathroom drying his face.

She did not want to ask him directly if he would drive her. She wanted the suggestion to come from him. But the suggestion did not seem to be coming. She glanced again at the big clock, rose, and said, "Well, may I have the key? There isn't a bus running, is there? Would you know?"

"To where, Kate?"

"The lake," she said. "Daddy promised me the car, and then remembered he had to take it in for a . . . a greasing." This was an outright lie, and she wondered if David would notice her father's car was not in the Talmadge garage.

"I don't think the buses begin running until after Memorial Day," David said.

"Well, I'll get a hitch, I suppose. May I have the key, please?"

He went to the kitchen cupboard and took down a jar that was half full of tagged keys. He turned the jar over on to the table and began reading the tags, looking for the key to the lake house.

"How long will you be there, Kate?"

"Oh, just until I find the suit. I can't stay too long. I'm supposed to meet your mother in White Plains."

"How will you get to White Plains without a car?"

"I've already arranged for a lift."

David found the right key. He handed it to her and said, "This is for the front door. It sticks a little, so pull down on it when you open it."

"I will. Thank you."

She turned quickly and started for the door.

"If you like, I can give you a lift there," David said.

"Oh, thank you, but I couldn't trouble you, David." She opened the door.

"No trouble at all, Kate. I haven't anything planned, anyway."

She turned and smiled graciously. "That's very kind of you," she said. "I'd appreciate it."

"Just let me get my wallet and my keys," David answered.

She talked about the trip to Europe all the way out to the lake. She sat on her side of the car with her legs crossed and her skirt demurely pulled below her knees. She didn't want to seem too excited about the trip because she knew this would appear childish to him. Nor did she wish to seem indifferent to it, because she knew he would detect this as a false attitude. She talked about it enthusiastically, and with a sense of anticipation, but all the while she was thinking, I'm alone with him, I'm alone with him.

The lake was deserted when they got there.

It was twelve-forty, and the sun was directly overhead, shining brightly on the water, giving the lake a curious look, as if it were composed of light beams somehow solidified. He parked the car in the driveway and they walked to the front door together. She didn't know exactly what she planned to do now that she was here with him, but at least they were alone. David unlocked the door, and they walked into the darkened house. The living-room smelled of contained dust and moisture and heat. The furniture was covered with white sheets.

"I'll open some windows," he said. "No sense suffocating while you look for that suit."

She went directly to the small bedroom at the rear of the house, knowing full well she hadn't left the suit there, but pretending to search through the empty dresser drawers and the empty shelves in the closet. She could hear David opening the windows facing the lake.

"Find it?" he called.

"No, not yet," she answered. She slammed a drawer shut, and then opened another one.

"I'm going out on the deck, Kate," he called, and she heard the back door of the house open and then close again. She was glad he'd gone outside. For a moment, she'd thought he would join her and watch while she went through the bogus search. But he was out of the house now, and this gave her some time to consider her next move. She went through the small end bedroom methodically, almost as if she were conducting a real search, knowing she would find nothing, trying to work out a feasible plan all the while. When she finished with the bedroom, she walked out into the corridor and opened the door to the linen closet. There were perhaps half a dozen large towels and two blankets in the closet, leftovers from the summer before. She studied them thoughtfully.

And then the idea came to her.

The idea was a simple one, a cliché she had seen represented hundreds of times in cartoons and motion pictures. But as she stood looking into the open linen closet at the blankets and towels, it seemed to her the idea had two distinct advantages. First, it would make David feel extremely masculine and heroic while presenting her as a helpless, dependent female. And secondly, it would give her an excuse for disrobing. She nodded in agreement with the idea.

She had decided she would drown.

Or, at least, she would pretend she was drowning.

He was waiting for her on the deck outside. He was sitting facing the lake solidified by light.

"I couldn't find it," she said. "I was sure I'd left it here." She shrugged. "It was a nice suit, too. The red wool, do you remember seeing me in it?"

"I think so, yes." He kept staring at the lake, seemingly absorbed by it.

"It was my favourite suit," Kate said.

"You looked well in it," David said.

"Did I?"

"Yes."

"Thank you. May I have a cigarette, please?" She sat in the chair opposite him and crossed her legs. David offered her the package and she took one and waited for him to light it. She blew out a stream of smoke. "Thanks." They were silent. The sun blazed on the surface of the lake, reflected dizzily on to the deck. "Mmmm, that sun is good," she said. "Are you in a terrible hurry, David, or can we just sit here for a while?"

"I'm in no hurry," he answered. He was still staring at the lake.

"Mmmm," she said, and she stretched out her legs, bracing her feet on the deck railing, pulling the tight skirt back a little. She closed her eyes and tilted her face to the sun. "Oh, that's really good," she said.

"I hate this lake," David said suddenly.

She did not open her eyes. She was thinking, Wading, I'll say I want to go wading. I'll slip and fall in. The water'll be cold. I have to be careful because he knows I'm a good swimmer. I can do it, though, and I know the water'll be very cold, and that'll be my excuse. I just have to be very careful.

"Every time I come to this damn lake . . ." he started, and then shook his head and fell silent.

She was ticking off the seconds. She did not want to wait too long, what time was it already? But neither did she want him to suspect she was executing a preconceived plan. She waited. She could feel the hot sun on her face and on her legs. She pulled her skirt a little higher.

"It's awfully hot, isn't it?" she said at last. "I wish I *had* found that suit. I'd go in for a swim."

"Water's still probably very cold, Kate."

"I think I'll wade, anyway. Want to join me?"

"I'll watch you from here."

"Oh, come on down."

"Nope. Thanks, Kate."

"Please, David?"

"All right," he said reluctantly.

"Take off your shoes."

"This is against my better judgement," David said, smiling. He took off his loafers and socks, and rolled up the cuffs of his trousers. Together, they went down to the edge of the lake. She chose her spot carefully, knowing exactly where the rocks were most slippery, knowing exactly where the lake bottom dropped off suddenly after a few shallow feet of shelf. She pulled her skirt up over her knees. She was sure he was watching her. She was sure his eyes were on her legs. She was suddenly glad she'd worn the tight black skirt.

The water was very cold. She felt it attacking her feet and her ankles, almost numbing. She gave a girlish little shriek. David stood on the shore, and she turned, surprised to see he wasn't watching her but was looking out over the lake instead.

"Come on, sissy," she said teasingly.

She pulled the skirt high on her thighs, held it there with one hand, and extended the other hand to him. He took it and came gingerly into the water.

"It's like ice," he said.

She squeezed his hand playfully. "You haven't even got your feet wet."

"That's all they're *going* to get wet," he said, and he nodded once, emphatically, and then suddenly dropped her hand.

"Hey!" she said.

"I'll watch you from here," he called, wading back to the shore.

"Oh, come on back here!"

"Well, what's wrong with that? Blue's a lovely colour."

David laughed. "Go on, enjoy yourself. I'll sit here and watch your legs."

She did not miss the reference, and yet there was the usual condescending tone in his voice. He was talking to a child. He was still talking to a child.

She pushed out suddenly against the water.

"Be careful, Kate," he called. "Those rocks are slippery."

The rocks were slippery, yes, and the water was truly very cold, and she had the sudden feeling she might *really* drown if she went through with her plan. She could feel the icy water attacking her legs, rising on her flesh as she waded deeper, over her knees, touching her thighs now. In a moment, she thought. In a moment.

"Be careful, Kate," he warned again.

She would allow herself to slip, the child in Kate thought. She would allow one foot to reach out tentatively and to slip suddenly, and she would throw both hands up over her head, dropping her skirt, and go into the icy water. The child in Kate thought, I'll flounder around a bit trying to swim, laughing perhaps, and then I'll shout, "Help! David, help me!" and I'll go under, and he'll jump into the water and pull me out trembling, my clothes clinging to me, he'll carry me into the house, I'll undress and come into the living-room wrapped in a blanket, the child in Kate plotted as she stood poised on the shelf at the edge of the drop, ready to feign a plunge into freezing deep water.

Go ahead, the child in Kate urged. Take the step. Do it.

But the woman in Kate hesitated. The woman in Kate clung to her skirts, she could feel the slime-covered rocks with the tips of her toes, could feel the numbing water, the woman in Kate weighed the plan silently, the blatancy of the plan, and wondered if it had not been too outrageously conceived. The woman in Kate was suddenly aware of caution and subtlety, and something beyond that, something only unconsciously understood, something that told her instantly and without doubt that the plan was wrong.

She turned and began wading out of the lake.

Clinging to her skirt with one hand, her long legs flashing in the golden sunshine, she extended her free hand to David, and he bent over to reach it, laughing at her sudden reversal. She clung to his hand tightly. He tugged at it, and she came splashing out of the lake and on to the shore. Impulsively, she allowed the momentum to carry her into his arms. "David, I'm *freezing*," she said, "Oh, David, make me warm," hugging herself to him girlishly, and yet aware that her skirt was still pulled up over her thighs, held there where their bodies met in flat contact, sensing he was aware of this, sensing he knew he was holding a woman against him. She broke away from him suddenly and started for the house, holding out her hand to him. He laughed again and took her hand, and they went up the path together, the lake silent, the woods still.

"We're all alone in the world David," she said, and he stopped suddenly and looked at her curiously, his eyes searching hers.

"It was sweet of you to drive me here, David," she said softly, and reached up to kiss him, a fleeting, little girl's kiss, a simple kiss of gratitude, but tinged with slightly more than that, her lips parted slightly for only an instant, the brief increased pressure of her mouth. She pulled away from him swiftly and said, "We'd better go now," as if he had taken a liberty to which he was not entitled.

She thought she detected a difference in his attitude as they drove away from the lake. She thought there was something new in his voice and on his face. When he stopped the car in front of Suzie's house, she thanked him and then reached across the seat to give his hand a gentle squeeze. As she got out of the car, her skirt accidentally rode up over her knees. She went up the walk to the house without once looking back at the car, but she was certain he was watching her.

And she was certain now that he would return to Talmadge after his trip.

The two men sat in the screening room and waited for the third man to arrive. The lights were still on, and they sat chatting idly about production problems, not really too concerned with them, but only killing time while they waited. The third man came in breathlessly and took a seat alongside the others, apologizing for being late, but he'd been in conference with a set designer, what was all the shouting about, anyway?

"Herb Floren wants us to see this," one of the men said.

He was sitting behind the control panel in the miniature theatre, and he pressed a button in the face of the panel now, and there was a moment's wait while the projectionist in the booth upstairs read the signal, and then the lights went out, and the screen was suddenly filled with colour as the film began.

"Are we going to have to sit through the whole picture?" one of the men asked.

"No, just this reel. She's in this reel."

They sat watching the film. The man behind the panel pressed the button asking for more volume at one point, but for the most part the three men sat very still and watched the reel. They didn't know quite what was happening because this was the last reel in the film, and it was impossible to get any true picture of plot development by watching a series of climaxes. One of the men lighted a cigar. One kept coughing into his handkerchief.

"This is the girl," the man behind the panel said.

They watched the new face on the screen. No janitors in the hallway stopped sweeping. The projectionist in the booth did not put down his detective magazine to look at the screen in sudden awe. The three men watched the girl, and the one who'd been coughing into his handkerchief kept right on coughing into his handkerchief. The one who was smoking a cigar kept right on smoking it. The man behind the panel thought he detected a blur on the screen, and he pressed the focus button, and the projectionist put down his magazine and adjusted the focus, and then picked up his magazine again.

The scene was over in about five minutes.

"Is there more of her?" one of the men asked.

"That's it. That's her scene."

"Do we have to watch the rest?"

"No," the man behind the panel said, and he signalled for the projectionist to stop the film. The lights went on.

"I don't know where I got this damn cold," the coughing man said.

"What's her name?" the man with the cigar asked.

"Burke. Gideon Burke."

"That sounds phony as hell."

"So does Rock Hudson."

"What do you think?"

"I think she's too old."

"Look, she isn't Sandra Dee, that's for sure. But nobody says she's supposed to be a teen-ager."

"She comes over maybe thirty-eight, thirty-nine."

"I think she comes over younger than that. Thirty-five maybe."

"So? So that would be perfect, wouldn't it?"

"The girl in the script has black hair."

"So she's got red hair, what difference does that make? We'll change two words in the script, and she's a redhead."

The coughing man put an inhaler to one nostril and sniffed deeply.

"What'd you say her name was?"

"Gideon Burke. Wait a minute. I wrote it down some place." He fished into his jacket and consulted a slip of paper. "No, it's Gillian. With l's."

"That's even worse," the man with the cigar said.

"Well, what do you think?"

"She cries nice," the man with the inhaler said, and he sniffed menthol into the other nostril.

"I was hoping for another name we could stick over the title."

"That costs money."

"What'd Floren give her for this?"

"He wouldn't say. We can find out. She's nobody, she'll work for coupons."

"What do you think, Eddie?"

"I don't know," Eddie said. "What do you think?"

"What colour were her eyes again?" the man with the cigar said.

"Blue, I think."

"No, green."

"Then the colour was a little off. That's the new fast film they're using."

"I thought they were blue."

"She's got buck teeth, did you notice that?"

"No, I didn't."

"Yeah." Eddie paused. "You think she's pretty?"

"She's okay. She's no raving beauty, if that's what you mean."

"Gideon Burke?"

"Gillian, Gillian."

"Where'd she dig up *that* one?"
"Look, what do you think?"
"She married or what?"
"I don't know."
"Well, that could make a difference, you know. We're not shooting this around the corner. She may be married with a houseful of kids, who knows?"
"I can find out."
"Did you hear from New York yet?"
"This morning."
"What'd they say?"
"Sheila won't come out to take a test."
"What?"
"She's too big to test. The hell with her."
"Big television shmearcase, she's too big to test!"
"Look, what do you think of *this* girl?"
"I don't know. What do you think?"
"She's not bad, you know."
"No, she wasn't bad, that's for sure. She cries nice."
"So what do you think?"
"How much does she get?"
"You want me to call her agent and find out?"
"What do you say, Eddie?"
"She's supposed to have black hair."
"Maybe she'll be willing to dye it."
"And she's got buck teeth."
"So she'll see a dentist. Look, we know she's not a beauty."
"You asked my opinion, didn't you? I'm telling you. Her hair's supposed to be black, and her teeth are bucked. If we have to take her all apart and put her together again, we might as well look for somebody else."
"If you're finished with that cigar, would you please put it out?"
"I'm not finished with it."
"So what do you think?"
"Gillian Burke, what a name!"
"This is a big part, Harry. You think we can ool around with an unknown?"
"Who else have we got?"
"What about that one from Fox? What the hell's her name?"
"She's such a big star, you can't even remember her name!"
"If you know a name, and you forget it, that's one thing. But if you forget it without ever having heard of it, that's another. Who can remember a phony name like Gillian Burke?"
"Anyway, Fox is out. They want thirty grand and over-the-title

for her, and I know she got only eighteen-five on her last lendout, so I told them to go screw. They said we were making a big mistake. they said she was a big star. I told them if she was *really* big, she'd be asking a hundred grand and a cut, and not thirty grand which she isn't even worth. So she's out. What do you think?"

"I'll tell you the truth, I had in mind somebody like Liz Taylor." He paused. "*She's* got black hair."

"She's doing *Butterfield 8*."

"She finished that. She's doing *Cleopatra* now."

"Whatever she's doing, we couldn't afford her anyway. We got three stars already. Come on, what do you think?"

"We can get her cheap, huh? This Gillian Burke?"

"I think so."

"What's cheap?"

"Two grand, twenty-five hundred, maybe three tops."

"That's reasonable, Eddie."

"Floren says she's gonna be very big once this picture is released."

"Yeah, they said that about me, too, when I was playing juveniles at Metro."

"What do you think?"

"There's more of her in this picture?"

"No. You want me to run the reel again?"

"No, no that's okay. Why don't you call her agent, sniff around a little?"

"What do you want me to sniff around about? Do I offer the part or not?"

"See how much she wants."

"How high can I go?"

"Offer her a thousand a week."

"The part's too big, Eddie. Her agent would laugh at me."

"Okay, then two grand. Two grand is the highest I'll go for an unknown with buck teeth when she's supposed to have black hair."

"And find out if she's married!"

"And if she agrees to two grand, do I sign her?"

"I don't know. What do you think?"

"What do *you* think?"

"I say sign her."

"Eddie?"

"Sign her, sign her."

Her agent called that night. It was eleven o'clock, and she was asleep when the telephone rang. At first she thought it was Monica. She pulled the phone to her and said, "Hello?"

"Gillian?"

"Yes?"
"Sid."
"Oh, hello, Sid."
"Did I wake you, Gilly?"
"No, that's all right."
"Don't you think it's time you got out of Hollywood?" he asked.
"What?"
"Get away from this place, huh? Change of scenery? Be good for you, don't you think?"
"What's the matter, Sid?"
"I just thought you might like to get away from this town."
"Oh, God," she said, "don't tell me! Please don't tell me."
"What, baby, what?"
"They cut me out of the picture."
"No, no. Matter of fact, Herbert Floren arranged for some people to see that last reel today. Some very important people, Gilly. Some people who are shooting a very big picture with three stars in it and they need another girl for the picture, a big fat supporting part, and they offered fifteen hundred bucks a week which I grabbed instantly."
"What?" she said.
"Yeah, baby, yeah."
"Me?" she said.
"Yeah, who else?"
"Sid, if you're joking . . ."
"Baby, I never joke where it concerns money."
"Me?" she said again.
"Yeah, yeah, yeah. You ready to leave this town?"
"What do you mean? I don't understand."
"Can you leave Hollywood?"
"I'm packed," she said.
"Good, 'cause shooting starts on June fifteenth."
"Where, Sid?"
"Rome," he said.

Maybe it came too late.
And maybe it was not what she expected. Maybe, after years of working, and hoping, and waiting there should have been more. There should have been spectacular fireworks, perhaps, shooting up into the sky in a blaze of trailing sparks and dripping incandescence, there should have been brass bands playing rousing golden marching songs with heartbeat bass drums pounding out the rhythm, there should have been hordes of people screaming approval. She should have arrived overnight, the overnight success, the miracle of

America, she should have arrived in a burst of glittering white teeth smiling in a radiant lovely face, arms outstretched to accept the bushels of offered love, success should have been an overnight shimmering thing, a golden thing, a throbbing, wonderful exciting thing. But it wasn't.

Maybe it simply came too late.

She cried alone that night.

She lay naked on the bed in the house at Malibu with the sound of the surf rushing up under the timbers, the sticky feel of salt on everything, the sheets soggy, she cried. She cried into the pillow because she knew intuitively that *this* was the break, *this* would do it, *this* was the opening door. She had never really felt this way before, all the things she'd done, the good things and the bad, had never made her feel this way before, she knew *this* was the one. And knowing it, felt empty. Knowing it, knowing this was only the beginning for her, the fat supporting role in a picture with three top stars, a picture that would have all the ballyhoo bandwagon behind it, a picture that would probably advertise "And introducing Gillian Burke", she felt empty.

Introducing Gillian Burke, she thought.

And the machinery would whir into motion, and there would be the concocted stories of the overnight success, the dream to feed the kiddies on, this is the story of the overnight success, last night was seventeen years ago when she left home and took the apartment near the river and started classes in a loft with an old man named Igor Vodorin, that was last night, and tonight is this morning, and she was thirty-five years old. And seventeen years of hope and rejection and solid dedication to a premise never doubted and always doubted in a secret corner of the mind, do I have it, do I *really* have it? Seventeen years of extending the deadline, I'll give it another year, seventeen years of watching that girl child march from a glittering wide-eyed youthful hopefulness into a professional attitude of competence and restraint, and then into a barely disguised hopelessness, this was the culminating event of those seventeen years, the door was swinging wide, a big supporting role in a three-star picture, this was it, *this* was the reward.

But too late to be a reward.

Too late to be *anything*. Too 'ate to provoke anything but tears, this was success, hold it in your hand, clutch it tight, it was meaningless. I knew it all along, she could tell herself, I knew this would happen, I know what will happen next, I have dreamed of it often enough, I have gone to sleep with it in my mind, and awakened with the taste of it in my mouth, I knew this would happen one day, and I know what is coming, I can feel it, but it doesn't excite me, and I can only lie here with my head buried in the pillow and cry.

She did not feel like telling anyone.

It was odd that Monica wasn't home. It was odd that on the night it came, Monica was out, and there was no one to tell.

She used to tell people. She used to say, "I'll be on *Dragnet* next week, watch for me," until she learned that all the *Dragnets* in the world did not add up to very much unless *this* happened, so she stopped telling them. Her agent knew when she would be on, and he informed the people who counted, and they watched—maybe—but the others didn't matter, the others followed her progress with only a fleeting interest. She was to them a fringe celebrity, they knew someone who was in a play over in Westport, they knew someone who was going to be on television Thursday night. But they also knew private secretaries and they knew receptionists and editorial assistants, and this girl, this Gillian Burke, was only another person with a job, a slightly more glamorous job, but certainly nothing to go shouting about, a fringe celebrity, yes, someone who could give you the inside story on some of the big stars she'd worked with on the edges of the crowd scene, "Is it true what they say about . . .?" but not someone to consider very seriously because she had not yet been touched by the magic wand of success. She could be as successful as the most successful secretary they knew, but the standards were different here. And so, until *this* came along, until she exploded on the scene as an overnight sensation, and she knew it would happen, there was no doubt in her mind now that it would happen, until success came big and gaudy, why, then she was a failure. Even though she worked as steadily as the receptionist or the editorial assistant, even though she probably earned more money each year than they did, why everyone knew—and so did Gillian—that she was a failure. So she stopped asking them to watch for her here and there. She simply went about her business knowing, believing, trying to maintain belief, that one day she would make it.

And now here it was.

And tears.

Too late. Too much hoping. Too much waiting for that phone to ring, announcing *this*. And staring at the phone silent. Black and silent. Should I call my agent? A pride in the silence of failure. A hopeless, ridiculous pride, I won't call him. I'll wait. And waiting. And waiting. And the phone silent. And the call never coming. I'm Gillian Burke. I want a pock in the play. Well, here it is, she thought. A man on a shining white horse has galloped into your life, a ridiculous man with a big nose and eyeglasses, a man who makes me laugh, a man who is making me cry right now, Herbert

Floren, knight on a charger, here he is, and he has told the others, he has spread the word, a supporting role on the wide screen in full colour with stereophonic sound, russet hair whipping in the wind, green eyes flashing, here it is, Gillian Burke, here's your part in the play, take it, a gift from God, take it, spend it, enjoy it. Now the pattern will change, now there will be success tucked behind your ear like a flower, the overnight success that took only seventeen years. But it *will* be just that to the others, Gillian, never forget that. This is the land of the jackpot, this is the land of the quiz show and the newspaper contest, and in the eyes of others you have struck it rich, your ship has come in, you've pulled the little lever and scored three oranges and now those quarters will come spilling out of the little spout and cover your feet in shining silver, you were lucky, you are an overnight success.

Please, please, she thought, why do I feel bitter?

Success does not come with soaring elation.

Success comes with a sudden taste of blood and a feeling of utter loneliness. Tears alone on a salt-sodden pillow. Alone.

How do you wear success?

You wear it the way you wore failure, I suppose.

You wear it in your throat and on your face. You are a failure because you're daring to go for the biggest prize, and you haven't yet reached it. So you duck people on the street, you see them coming, old acquaintances, and you duck into a doorway and study the items in a shop window, seemingly absorbed in the display, and you lift the collar of your coat because you're ashamed of failure. You do not want them to say, "I hear you're up for such and such a part," you do not want that look of pity and curiosity, she's not as young as she used to be, there are age wrinkles around her eyes. Character, you say to yourself, they give my face character. Did you notice the wrinkles, they whisper, why does she keep trying, isn't she grown-up enough now to quit this nonsense? So you lift the collar of your coat, and you find the empty doorway and duck the old friend, it is shameful to dream. How can you dream in the midst of concrete and steel? How can you dream? I wore failure like a cloak. And I'll wear success the same way, and they'll say, She ducks her old friends now that she's been lucky, now that she's an overnight success.

Yes.

I will avoid the dead.

I will avoid those with the dead dreams, those who stepped on their dreams and squashed them flat, who forgot there were ever such things as dreams or dreamers, who knew dreams only in the eyes of others, and who pitied those, and who told themselves dreams were for idiots, yes, I will avoid the dead men with their dead dreams, yes.

Yes, goddam you, I'm crying tonight, what are you doing? Are you cooking steaks on your patio, are you having friends in for Bloody Marys, are you kissing your neighbour's husband in the kitchen? Well, I'm crying tonight.

Success is not an acceptance of universal love. Success is a roundhouse slap in the teeth of the world.

She lay on the bed and wept into her pillow and thought, in June. I'll leave for Rome, and wondered what it was like to be seventeen.

It began as a day of confusion for Kate, confusion upon confusion, confusion compounded until it built to terror, she would remember it always as the most terrifying day of her life.

It began with hot June sunlight sifting through Venetian blinds, stripes of black and gold, and weird discordant music far away, stripes like a prison, stripes like the bars of a cell covering her bed, and somewhere in the distance a strange music, the same music struck over and over again, the ticking of a clock in the silent gold-and-black-striped prison of her bed.

Ten o'clock.

The house still except for the music drifting up the steps and into her room, the sunshine streaking her bed in parallel bars. Mother, she thought.

She touched her hair reassuringly, and drifted back to sleep.

Thunder.

The echoing roll of thunder in a room gone suddenly black, streaks of lightning in a summer sky, what had happened to the sun? Thunder rolling ominously and downstairs she could hear her mother at the piano, the chords rolling like the thunder itself, but where had the sunshine gone, hadn't there been sunshine? The ticking of the clock again, she looked, she opened one eye and looked as a streak of lightning struck close near by, and she saw the time, eleven-thirty, and she wondered where the sun had gone, wondered what had become of the Saturday sun.

Confusion.

Voices in the house, the piano stopped now, only the voices coming up the stair well, shaking her from sleep, rain lashing the trees and the lawn outside, she rolled over and pulled the blanket to her throat.

"Amanda, look at what I've got. Road maps! Dozens of them! The whole damn country is open to us! We can go anywhere!"

"Excuse me, Matthew, I'm working. Can't you see that?"

"What? Oh, sure, sure. I'm sorry, Amanda."

The music again. Discordant, cacophonous, the same chord struck over and over again, resounding up the stair well, a sudden crash of thunder, Kate sat up suddenly and stared into the room.

"Have you ever been to the Grand Canyon? We could go there, Amanda."

"I've never been to the Grand Canyon, no. Matthew, I'm trying to figure out this passage."

"Honey, can't that wait a few minutes? I want you to look at———"

"No, it can't wait a few minutes!"

Her voice was sharp, a chord punctuated her words. Kate got out of bed in her nightgown and walked into the hallway, and came down the steps quietly. She sat on the third step from the bottom like a little girl, sleep in her eyes. There was a rained-in feeling to the house. She wondered why Parsie wasn't making any noise in the kitchen, and then remembered Parsie's little boy was sick, and her mother had sent her home last night for the week-end. She looked into the living-room. Her father was stretched on the floor. The floor was covered with opened road maps. Lightning streaked outside again. She huddled in her own arms, suddenly frightened.

"Is something wrong, Amanda?" Matthew asked.

"Nothing's wrong."

"Then why the hell can't we———?"

"Matthew, I don't like swearing in the house!"

"Who the hell is———" He cut himself short and stared at her. "All right, Amanda, what is it?" he asked patiently.

"Nothing. I don't want to look at road maps right now. I want to work. If you had any respect at all for what I'm trying to do, you'd take yourself out of here and———"

"Honey, we're *leaving* on the fourth. I don't want to sound———"

"I'm not even sure we're leaving," she said.

He stared at her silently.

"What do you mean?"

"I want to finish this by the end of the summer."

"I know you do, honey' But if you don't finish it by then, you'll finish it in the fall. What's so urgent about———?"

"I want to finish it this summer!" she said sharply.

She was sitting at the piano with her hands in her lap, not looking at him, staring down at the keyboard.

"Amanda, we'll only be gone through July," he said gently. "When you come back in August———"

"I can't spare a whole month."

"Well, why not?"

"Because I can't, because I told you already, I want to finish this now, this summer, and I'll need all summer if I'm ever going to——"

"I just can't understand the rush, that's all. You've been working on that damn thing for as long as I can remember, and now——"

"I told you I don't like swearing in the house!"

"Oh, what the hell!" Matthew said angrily. "Now listen, Amanda. You just listen to me. I managed to take a month away from the office, I thought it would please you, I thought we could be alone together, and now you . . . well now, you just listen. We're going away, and that's all there is to it. You can begin work again when we get back. August is time enough."

"No," she said.

"Well, that's the way I want it."

"Well, that's too bad."

"Yes, you're damned right it's too bad, because that's just the way it's going to be."

"Then you'll go without *me*."

"All right, then I'll go *without* you," he shouted. He stared at her angrily for a moment. Then he let out his breath and walked to the piano and took her hands in his, sitting beside her on the bench, and said, "Honey, I don't want to go without you."

"Then don't."

"Honey, we'd have a whole month together, just the two of us."

"I can't go this summer. I have to finish my work this summer."

"Your work, your work," he said, exploding again, "what's so goddam important, all of a sudden, about——"

She slapped him, suddenly and viciously. As Kate sat on the staircase, she saw her mother slap him, saw his head rock back with the blow and saw his fists tighten automatically and thought in that moment he would kill her. And then his hands loosened, and Kate sat in confusion watching his face, and watching her mother's face gone suddenly cold as if he had said something terrible and unforgivable to her.

"All right," Matthew said very quietly. "All right." He rose from the bench and walked to where the road maps were spread on the floor. He folded them very quietly and very calmly, pushed them into a neat stack and picked them up, and then walked silently out of the living-room. He walked past the hall steps without seeing his daughter. The door slammed when he left the house. A thunderclap ripped open the sky. Lightning flashed, there was more thunder, and then silence. She heard a car starting outside, and then heard the shriek of tires against the driveway gravel. The house was still for a very long time. She expected the music to start in the living-room again. She sat on the steps, confused, and waited for her mother to begin playing again.

But Amanda sat at the piano staring at the keyboard, with her hands in her lap, her face cold and expressionless, the rain streaking the window behind her.

She did not begin playing again.

Kate watched, waiting.

She wondered if she should go into the living-room and say something to her. She had never seen her mother looking that way, and the sight frightened her. Stiff and cold, she sat motionless at the piano and stared at the keys, making no move to touch them. Kate rose slowly and started up the steps. When she reached her room, she lay on the bed and looked out at the rain, and waited for the music to begin again.

It did not begin.

Because Amanda knew.

Because she knew suddenly, or perhaps she had known all along, she knew as the argument with Matthew mounted, she knew as she tried to control her rising rage, knew as she felt her hands tightening, knew when her fury finally exploded against his cheek, knew that she would never, never finish the composition.

And, knowing this, was dead.

And sat dead at the piano and looked at the keyboard in despair. And knew it was false, all the years of false work on it, knew she would never finish it and never wanted to finish it, and sat dead inside because now there was nothing. Now there was nothing to hope for. And knew. Knew it wasn't really very good, never had been any good, knew she would never be satisfied with it, and knew it would always be unfinished. Like her life.

Unfinished and incomplete.

And she didn't know why.

But she sat dead at the piano and wondered what she needed, and hated Matthew for having made her realize suddenly she would not finish the suite. Lifelessly, she stared at the unresponsive keys, and wondered what was to become of her. And wished that her son were here with her, wished she had not sent him visiting today of all days when she needed visual proof that she had at least accomplished *something* in her lifetime. But she was alone.

In a little while, the rain stopped.

Kate was still in her nightgown when she came downstairs later that afternoon. She walked into the living-room cautiously, almost as if she expected what was about to come. Amanda was sitting in an easy chair near the window, her face in calm repose. The sky beyond and outside had been torn apart by the wind. Tatters of clouds streaked the horizon, blue patches showed spasmodically, the day was indecisive, lacking the clean look or smell that usually follows a furious storm. The house was very still. Amanda sat in the chair and stared across the roof at the piano, large and black in the opposite corner, silent.

"Mom?" Kate said.

Amanda looked up.

"Are you all right, Mom?"

"Yes. I'm fine."

"Dad back yet?"

"No."

Kate took a chair alongside her mother's and pulled her legs up under her.

"I can see through that nightgown," Amanda said. "Don't you think you should wear a robe around the house?"

"Well, there's just the two of——"

"Put on a robe," Amanda said.

"I'll be getting dressed in a few minutes," Kate said.

Amanda nodded once, briefly. She didn't seem angry at all, or even irritated. Her face was absolutely calm. Kate looked at her face and tried to remember if it had always looked so calm, so . . . so lifeless. Suddenly she could not remember.

"I wish the weather would make up its mind," she said.

"Why?" Amanda asked. "Are you going somewhere?"

"Well, I have a date tonight, but that isn't——"

"I thought you might be rushing off somewhere," Amanda said.

"No. No."

The room was silent again.

"I've been doing a lot of thinking about you, Kate," Amanda said.

"Oh? Really?"

"Yes." Amanda nodded. "What do you plan to do in the fall, daughter?" she said.

The word sounded strange to Kate's ear, the word "daughter" delivered in such a curiously cold way. She didn't answer for a moment.

Then she said, "Well, we've already talked about this, Mom."

"Yes, I know we have. But it wouldn't hurt to——"

"I'm going to get a job somewhere," Kate said.

"And then what?"

"Then I'll see about going to college."

"You should go to college, Kate."

"Maybe I will. I'm just not sure yet."

"You should go," Amanda repeated.

"Mom, I'm not sure I *want* to go. Maybe all I want to do is get married and have children and——"

"I shouldn't have agreed to this European trip," Amanda said. "You haven't had time to think of anything else. Agnes has been accepted by three colleges, do you know that?"

"Well, Mom, she knows what she wants to do. I just don't."

"You *should* know by now. You're almost eighteen, daughter."

The word "daughter" again, curiously rankling, and a sudden wall between them, so that Kate felt they weren't really talking to each other, they were simply hurling words and sentences that neither understood nor cared to understand. In that instant, she decided she should leave the living-room. She began to rise, but Amanda's words stopped her.

"What *do* you expect to do, daughter?" she asked. "With your life?"

"I'm getting a job in the fall. I already told you . . ."

"I see."

"I thought you knew that."

"Yes, I knew."

"Well . . . that's what my plans are. For now."

She frowned, confused. She didn't wish to seem solicitous, and yet she suddenly felt that perhaps she'd overestimated her mother's intelligence. Perhaps her mother hadn't really understood the first time they'd discussed all this. "When I get back from Europe, I'll begin looking," she said.

"Yes, I understand," Amanda said.

"Well," Kate said, and she shrugged, but the frown remained on her forehead. She sat in silence and thought, Why do I have to know what I'm going to do with my life? I'm going to take a job. Isn't that enough for now?

"What kind of job do you want, Kate?"

"You know," Kate shrugged.

"No, I don't know."

"Receptionist. Something like that."

"I see. In New York?"

"Yes. Mom, we've already——"

"I see."

The room was silent. Amanda kept staring at the piano.

"Kate," she said, "I want you to go to college."

"Well, maybe I will. After I——"

"I want you to go this fall. When you return from abroad."

"I don't think I want to do that, Mom."

"I don't think this is a question of what you want to do," Amanda said. "This is a question of what's best for you."

"Well, I think it's best for me to get a job and——"

"Yes, and what makes you think that'll be enough?" Amanda asked, leaning towards her. "What do you hope to be, Kate? A wife, Kate? A mother, Kate?"

Again, she felt a rage inside her, a rage at the way her mother was using her name, Kate, Kate, like a battering ram, Kate, Kate. "Well . . . well, wh . . . what's wrong with that?" she asked.

"You're a beautiful girl, Kate, and bright, and it's wonderful for a young girl to be going abroad, but if you don't mind my saying so, I'm being perfectly honest with you, I think you're going to need more than a husband and a houseful of children."

"Well, I'm . . . I'm not getting married right this . . . this minute. I mean, I'm only seven——"

"Yes, but it seems wasteful to me, Kate . . . oh, not that working in New York wouldn't have a certain amount of glamour and value, I suppose . . . but I'd hate to see you wasting six months of your life, perhaps a year, when you could be preparing for something important in that time. You could go to school right here in Talmadge, you know. There wouldn't be any real reason for leaving Talmadge. Your grades are good, Kate. I'm sure if you applied even now——"

"Yes, but that's not what I want," Kate said, somewhat dazed. "I *may* go to college later, but right now I want to find a job."

"Yes, I understand, dear," Amanda said.

"Well, that's all there is to it then."

"I think you should ask yourself, Kate, what you want to become."

"I . . ."

"You're old enough now to be thinking of the future, daughter."

Kate nodded and said nothing.

"Do you understand what I'm saying?" Amanda asked.

"Yes," Kate answered. There was an edge of sharpness to her voice. Amanda's eyes suddenly moved from the piano and rested on her daughter.

"Good," she said. "I'm glad you understand."

"Yes," Kate said. "I understand."

They stared at each other, and Kate thought suddenly and for the first time since she could remember, She's not my real mother. My real mother wouldn't be saying these things to me."

"I want to be myself," Kate said. "That's good enough for me."

"Yes, but——"

"I want to be *myself*!" Kate said fiercely.

Her heart had begun to beat against her chest. She rose swiftly and started out of the living-room. Behind her, Amanda said, "Kate?" and she turned.

"I didn't mean——" Amanda started, and then closed her mouth and simply shook her head. Kate waited for her to continue. But she was silent now, and it did not seem she would speak again.

Quickly, Kate went upstairs to dress.

She heard the station wagon starting in the driveway outside just as she was putting on her skirt. The sound of the engine annoyed her because she'd planned to use the wagon herself, and now her mother was obviously tooling off in it some place, and she would have to walk. Where was everyone rushing to all of a sudden, everyone leaving the house as if it were too small to contain the separate lives inside it, everyone getting out and away from each other. She buttoned her skirt angrily. She did not want to be alone in this house. She did not understand her mother. And again she thought, She's not my real mother, and again the image of some isolated soul drifted back to her, a woman with staring eyes and scissors in her hand, back back through long narrow corridors, stop it.

Stop it, she told herself.

But her hand trembled as she put on her lipstick.

The blonde hair falling to the scatter rug, the women fighting for the scissors, their shadows huge and grotesque on the wall, the taste of hair, and the taste of fear, and . . .

Stop!

Please, oh please stop.

She rushed out of the room and down the long flight of stairs. The house was empty, and it creaked with strange sounds she had never heard before. Frightened, she passed the empty living-room with the piano at the far end, silent, and rushed out of the house. It was chilly outside. There was a strong wind, and the sky was falling apart. She suddenly thought of Chicken Little. Someone had read it to her a long time ago, Minnesota, an old house, organ notes coming from a near-by church, Mother, she thought, Mother, the sky was falling apart.

She wished someone were with her.

"Beverly!" she called. "Here, Bev! Come on, Bev!"

The dog came out of the garage and wagged her tail, but she would not go to Kate. She called once more, and then walked swiftly up the driveway and turned left at the sidewalk and continued walking at a fast pace, looking down at her feet, not daring to look up at the sky where the clouds rushed frantically.

It was several moments before she realized where she was going. She was heading for Julia Regan's house.

The Alfa Romeo was parked in the driveway when she got there. As she passed the garage, she stood on tiptoe and looked through the windows to see if David's car was there, but apparently he had not come up for the week-end. She went to the front door and rang the bell.

When Julia opened the door, she said at once, "Mrs. Regan, could we go for a drive, please?"

Julia hesitated only an instant. There was something in the child's eyes she had never seen there before.

"Yes, of course," she answered.

She closed the door behind her instantly, and together they walked quickly to the car.

He had burned out his anger on the parkway, speeding up towards New Haven, stopping at a diner for lunch, and then turning back and heading for Talmadge again.

He sat behind the wheel of the car now with only a weary sadness inside him, the anger all gone, wondering why life never turned out the way you expected it would.

You get old, he thought. The damn trouble is you get old.

Everything seemed the same as he turned off the parkway and pointed the nose of the car towards Talmadge. The noises in the brush alongside the road, the lush June landscape, the pines, everything seemed the same. And as he made the turn into the main street, Talmadge looked placid and peaceful, tree-shaded, the big church on the hill, the shops lining the sidewalks, the women in slacks, everything seemed the same, but you get old.

The anger had dissipated under his foot pressed to the accelerator, his eye watching the rear-view mirror for state troopers, the anger was all gone now. There was only sadness now, and disappointment. He had been deprived of something essential. Whatever her reasons, whatever had provoked her vehemence, she had forced him into relinquishing something he had desperately needed and wanted. And he blamed her now for her insensitivity, her coldness, her inability to recognize this need. He wondered what had provoked her attack. What had he done or said to so infuriate her, couldn't she recognize his need? Damn it, couldn't she see they were getting old? Couldn't she understand that?

Coming up the road that led to the driveway of his house, he still could not understand. He knew only that he had been denied. The denial, he felt, was wilful and impetuous. If she really loved him, if she really understood him, she would have felt his need, and subjected her own wishes to it, especially now when it was so important, especially . . .

He applied his foot to the brake, gently. There was something in the road ahead, just in front of his driveway, a carton of a discarded garment, or . . . no, it was an animal, a mole probably, or a beaver, or perhaps even . . .

He stopped the car on the side of the road.

The animal was a dog.

He opened the door of the car. He knew even before he stepped out that the dog was Beverly. He did not want to walk to her. He saw the blood on the asphalt when he was ten steps away from her. He stopped. Oh, you son of a bitch, he thought. Oh, you bastard, who did this?

"Beverly?" he said, as if by calling her name, by getting no response, he could prove to himself this was not Beverly lying in the road with blood spreading on the asphalt.

As he approached her, he began hoping she was dead.

He looked down at her. There was not a mark on her body, and yet the asphalt was covered with blood, how . . . ? He glanced past the dog, his eyes following the trail of blood she'd left, across the sidewalk, and into the woods beyond. She had come out of the woods then. She couldn't possibly have been hit by a car.

Her eyes, normally brown, had a strange whitish-blue cast, as if they had been drained of all colour, wide and staring in her head. Her body was stiff, as if in shock, and there was a questioning, puzzled look on her face. And as he stood over her, watching, she began to vomit blood, and suddenly she seemed to be haemorrhaging from every opening in her body, and he knew at once she had swallowed something poisonous, knew she had somehow got hold of one or maybe more of those goddamed pellets people were putting around to control field mice and moles, probably softened by the morning rain, a little rancid, Oh you son of a bitch, he thought.

He reached down for her. She whimpered as he picked her up, he had the feeling she would drain away in his hands, had the feeling she would turn to liquid in his hands as he began walking up the driveway to his house, wanting only to take her inside the house some place, wanting only to make her comfortable. "Please, Beverly," he said, "please, Beverly." He walked with her in his arms. He could feel her hot blood on his hands. He was trembling. He wondered, Should I call the vet? What can I do? Oh my God, she's bleeding to death in my hands. "Please Beverly," he said again.

The garage was open.

He took her into the garage and kicked an old pile of rags into place with one foot and then laid her gently on the rags. She whimpered again in pain, and he wondered, What shall I do? Jesus Christ, what shall I do?

"Amanda!" he shouted, and then remembered he had not seen the station wagon in the driveway. "Kate! Kate!" There was no answer. Her blood was spreading into the rags, staining them a bright red, her life was draining out of her as she whimpered in pain, and he thought, I'm alone in the house, I'll call Julia, Julia will know what to do, Julia will help me, Julia.

And the dog whimpered again.

And he knew there was no time to call Julia, no time to pick up a phone and dial her number and explain about Beverly who was bleeding and dying and ask her to come over to help him. Help me, Julia, he thought, and knew Julia could not help him, no one could help him now, he was Matthew Anson Bridges, alone with a bleeding dog in an empty house, alone.

She died before his eyes. She died swiftly. He closed his eyes, and stood over her with his head bent.

He had not cried when his mother died and they walked through the stifling hot sunshine in Glen City, he had not cried when they lowered his father into his grave and cousin Birdie took a yellow handkerchief from her black purse, he had not cried. Now, standing over the dead dog with his eyes shut, the first tear came.

It squeezed from his closed lids, and he felt it slipping down his cheek, swift and hot. And then, as if this single tear released a larger flow inside him, he began trembling, and his shoulders shook, and he opened his eyes, and looked down at the lifeless dog, and began to cry unashamedly and openly, began to cry in great chest-racking sobs because something he had loved very dearly was gone.

He accepted the death.

At long last, he accepted the death, and he cried brokenly in the stillness of the garage.

She saw Matthew's car parked on the side of the road just ahead of their driveway, and she was puzzled for a moment, but not alarmed. She seemed to be driving effortlessly, the wheel in her hands seemed to move of its own accord as she sat with her thoughts and wondered what she had done to her daughter, wondered what it was she really wanted of her life, thinking quite logically and calmly as she had been thinking for the past hour while driving slowly and effortlessly. She turned into the driveway. A lassitude seemed to have come over her, a resignation perhaps, and yet there was no sadness in the resignation, there was instead a sort of peace. She saw the bloodstains on the garage floor as she made the turn. When she got out of the car, she saw the pile of bloodied rags.

"Matthew!" she called.

He did not answer. She listened for a moment and heard an odd sound behind the house, a scraping sound, coming from out back near the brook. A frown came on to her forehead. She quickened her pace and went around the house.

He was standing silhouetted against the slope of the land, beside the brook, a shovel in his hands, digging silently. She walked to where he was working.

"Hello, Amanda," he said. He put the shovel down and looked at her, and then very softly said, "Beverly's dead. I think she got hold of some poison."

Amanda nodded. She could not think of anything to say to him.

"I was just burying her," he said. "I thought this would be a good spot, here by the brook."

"Yes, that's a good spot, Matthew," she said.

He picked up the shovel and began digging again. He had wrapped the dog in a tarpaulin, and she lay beside the half-dug grave as he worked.

"I went for a drive," Amanda said.

"Yes, I did, too."

He had been crying, she could see that. His eyes were puffed and red-rimmed, there were streaks on his face. She wanted suddenly to touch his face.

"Matthew," she said, "do you love me?"

She asked the question as if it had been on her mind for a very long time. The words sounded curiously young in the stillness of the day. The brook was the only other sound as Matthew worked with the shovel, and heard her words, and stopped digging, and looked up at her suddenly and with surprise, surprise at her question, and then another curious sort of surprise as he gave his answer, as if his answer were unexpected and startling even to himself.

"Amanda, I love you more than anything in this world," he said.

She nodded as if she had always known. She lowered her eyes.

"Didn't you know that, Amanda?" he asked.

She did not answer. She kept looking at the ground. When he stooped to pick up the dog, she said quickly, "Let me help you."

She took one end of the tarpaulin, and together they lowered the dog gently into the shallow grave. Matthew gave a curious, uncompleted shrug, and then began shovelling the earth back again.

"Where will we go, Matthew?" she asked.

"Wherever we want to," he said.

"Because . . . I'd like to go, Matthew. I'd like very much to go **with you**," she said.

The trip didn't matter any more, it didn't seem as important any more, but he took her hand and smiled limply and said, "All right, Amanda."

She began shivering in the automobile.

The top was down, and the Talmadge countryside blurred by on either side of the road, and overhead the giant old trees arced, and wind rushed past the car and over it, and she began trembling.

She said, "What am I doing wrong, Mrs. Regan? I don't understand, I don't understand."

And Julia, sitting beside her, driving in the direction of Lake Abundance, took one hand off the wheel and patted her gently on the knee, and tried to console her. The sky overhead had turned a clear, startling blue, cloudless. The countryside was rich and orderly, the old homes, the wide vista of lawns, a peacefulness seemed to pervade the landscape, and in the car a young girl and an old woman tried to understand what was happening.

"She said 'daughter'," Kate said. "'Daughter' and I felt hatred. Why should . . . why is she pushing me this way? I don't *want* to! I want to live my own . . . my own . . . *daughter*! I hate that word! If she's my mother, why doesn't she understand?"

"She was trying to understand," Julia said. "I'm sure she's only thinking of what's best for you."

"It's best to leave me alone!" Kate said. There was anger and desperation in her voice. "If she were my mother, if she . . ."

"She *is* your mother," Julia said.

"Then why can't we . . . she sat there, she sat there like a rock and she said, 'I want, I want, I want!' Well, what about what *I* want? Me! Isn't that important? I'm getting . . . my head is burning, it's . . . everything is rushing inside. I feel as if . . ."

"Kate, now stop it!"

"She hit him," Kate said. "She hit him, and then she sat like a rock and told me what to do, told me cold and . . . I didn't know her, she was . . . her face was different. I looked at her, and I didn't recognize her, she was just another . . . another woman sitting there, cold, cold, nothing . . . my father . . . they ran, everybody ran . . . there's no one there, I feel . . . oh, everything burning! Oh!" She covered her face with her hands. She would not let the tears come, confusion, everything was confusion, she knew she would lose her mind, she knew without doubt.

The car raced along the Talmadge roads, Julia's foot pressed tight to the accelerator as if absorbing Kate's tension and translating it to speed. She sat beside Kate, and she thought, This is what it's like to have a daughter, and she took one hand from the wheel and squeezed Kate's hand, and then recovered the wheel again immediately when she saw the car ahead of her. Kate looked up and through the windshield as Julia prepared to overtake and pass.

"There's a curve ahead," she said.

"I see it," Julia answered, and she signalled and swung the car out, and the nightmare began.

The milk truck filled the road, filled the sky, appeared monstrous and metallic as the small sports car rounded the bend. Kate could see the face of the driver as his eyes opened wide, could hear the terrifying bleat of the truck's horn, an explosion of sight and sound. "Oh my God!" Julia said beside her and wrenched the wheel of the car, skidding into a tight sharp turn as the sleek silvered sides of the truck rumbled past in a horn-blasting rush of air and sound and reflected sunlight, the name of the milk company etched itself into her mind, black letters on the silver truck, the car swerving in a screech of burning rubber, the milk truck gone, the car Julia had passed swinging by on the left, the small Alfa rumbling into a ditch, she thought she heard Julia say, "Renato," and then the countryside was silent again. She sat still and silent, trembling, unable to speak. The other car hadn't even bothered to stop. The truck had not turned back. She sat trembling and hating them. She could hear birds chirping in the woods alongside the road. The Alfa was tilted at an angle, the front wheel in the drainage ditch. She suddenly realized she was covered with a cold sweat.

"Mrs. Regan?" she said. She had spoken too softly; her voice was barely a whisper. She turned her head. Julia was sitting erect behind the wheel, as if in shock, staring through the windshield.

"Are you all right?" Kate asked.

Julia did not answer. Her hands clung to the wheel tightly. She kept staring through the windshield.

"Mrs. Regan?" Kate said.

She turned on the seat.

"Mrs. Regan?"

She reached out to touch her.

"Mrs. Regan?"

And then her hand touched Julia's shoulder, and the scream burst from her mouth in terror as Julia fell over in seeming slow-motion, bending stiffly from the waist as Kate's hand touched her, falling on to the wheel, her forehead hitting the wheel with a dull hollow thud.

"*Mrs. Regan!*" she screamed, and knew she was dead, knew those staring eyes meant death, and was suddenly gripped with a cold knifing fear and a desperately urgent need to get out of that small car. She threw open the door and stumbled into the ditch. Her eyes wide, she ran blindly into the woods.

The experts in death surrounded the small car, two state troopers, a reporter from the *Talmadge Courier*, and Dr. Milton Anderson, who arrived in his automobile and pushed his way through the crowd and pronounced Julia Regan dead after looking at her for only an instant.

"What do you make of it, Doc?" one of the state troopers asked.

"I couldn't tell for certain without an autopsy," Milt said. "I imagine it's a coronary, though, sudden shock, insufficient blood supply to the heart, that's my guess."

"Skid marks all over the road," the second trooper said. "She yanked that wheel over in a hell of a hurry."

Milt nodded. "She did everything in a hell of a hurry," he said.

"Saved the girl's life, though."

"What girl?"

"Found this on the seat of the car." The trooper held out a handbag. "There's a junior driver's licence in it."

"Whose?"

"Katherine Bridges," the trooper answered. "That the woman's daughter, Doc?"

"No," Milt said. "She only has a son. We'll have to notify him."

"You want to take care of that, Doc? There's one thing I hate, it's calling up somebody whose——"

"I'll take care of it."

"We better start looking for this girl," the second trooper said.

"I'll call in for the meat wagon," the first trooper said.

That's the way it ends, Milt thought. Rich or poor, full or empty, they call in for the meat wagon.

Darkness came to Talmadge suddenly and swiftly, because black is the colour of nightmares. A high wind rose, blowing in off the ridges, penetrating the woods where Kate lay huddled to the ground, cold and frightened. She had no idea what time it was. She knew only that the sun seemed to vanish suddenly, the way it had this morning just before the thunderstorm, completely and swiftly abandoning the sky, and that darkness had followed immediately afterwards. She lay in the darkness and whimpered and remembered the lifeless staring eyes of Julia Regan, her face turned sidewards on the wheel, death staring at her inside the tiny automobile, and again she shivered and tried to tell herself she would not go crazy.

But she knew she would. She knew before this day was ended she would lose her mind, and she lay huddled against the ground, feeling the cold wind rushing over her back and her legs, convincing herself she would, knowing she would, until the subtle line between reality and fantasy finally merged, and she wandered through a half-believed insanity, constructing images that were terrifying, almost play-acting a maniac, and then wondering if she had already gone insane, and then telling herself she was completely sane, and then knowing, believing, that crazy people always thought they were perfectly normal, and listening to the wind, and shuddering, and hearing the myriad sounds of night, the insects in the woods, the cars rushing by on the highway, sounds that seemed magnified, a moonless night, and darkness everywhere, the resounding darkness of horror, her flesh was cold, her mind reverberated with the events of the day, sunlight and rain, music and cacophony, the bitter argument, her mother cold and forbidding, her mother, her mother, her mother, she knew she was going crazy.

David, she thought suddenly.

And, thinking of him, all else rushed out of her mind, as if some powerful sucking wind had drawn everything down into a tiny funnel, drawn everything out of her mind to leave it white and blank, with first the single name appearing there on a white, blank screen. David, and then the name fading, and the image of David replacing it. A new rush of thoughts followed the image, lucid and clear, his mother was dead, they would have notified him, he would have come up to Talmadge, he was here somewhere, he needed her.

This was the thought.

He needed her.

She got to her feet. She wiped her face. Her blouse was torn, and she had lost one shoe somewhere in the woods, but she stood up and tucked the ends of her blouse into her skirt, and she took off the remaining shoe, and she thought *David needs me*, and she began walking. She knew instinctively where he would be. She knew because everything suddenly seemed so clear to her, as if the single thought *David needs me* had erased the confusion of the morning and the bitter uncertainty and frustration of the afternoon, and the frightening terror of the monster milk truck and the wide staring eyes of the dead woman on the seat beside her. She knew where he would be, and she went there instinctively.

There was a single light burning in the house on the edge of the lake. She walked directly to the front door, but she did not knock, She opened the door and walked into the house. She passed a mirror in the hall, but she did not look into it.

He was sitting in the living-room with the furniture covered with sheets, facing the window that overlooked the lake. The lamp burned next to his chair. He was sitting quite still, looking out over the lake, when she entered the room barefoot and soundlessly. He did not look up. She did not call his name. She went directly to his chair, and she sat on the arm of it, and he turned to her and looked up into her face, and she reached out gently with one hand and touched the back of his neck. With the other hand, she began unbuttoning her blouse, almost unconsciously, button by button, the hand at the back of his neck softly resting there, the other hand unbuttoning the blouse in a steady inexorable motion, and then she brought his head to her breast. She kept her hand on the back of his neck and gently, tenderly, she brought his head to rest on her breast, cradled there, and she said nothing. She simply held him to her breast with her hand on his head.

She stroked his head. He seemed so very helpless in that moment. Looking down at his face, she could see the lines radiating from his eyes, the set of his mouth, he was really not a good-looking man, but she loved him very much in that moment, more than she had ever loved him before. And wanted nothing from him. The nights she had lain awake thinking of his kiss, thinking of his hands upon her body, these seemed not to have happened, or possibly to have happened to some child she once had known. She held his head to her breast, and she felt a love new to her, but a love none the less, powerful and abiding. He lay against her unmoving. She could hear his gentle breathing. She stroked his hair comfortingly, and she said nothing, holding him to her.

In a little while, she felt his tears on her flesh.

And now there was the will.

Now the shock was done and gone, now that day which had started for him with a telephone call to his New York apartment and the shocking words of Milt Anderson telling him his mother was dead, and the drive to Talmadge, and the body lying cold and lifeless in the mortuary. "Yes, that's my mother," he had said, and left the room and driven to the lake, that day was done and gone.

And the night was done and gone too, the woman who had come to him in the night, not a child he had known, but a woman named Kate Bridges who offered him comfort and solace, who allowed him to cry unashamed, a magnificent woman named Kate Bridges who leaned back into the automobile when he dropped her off at her house and said, "I'll be worrying about you, David. Call me, please," and he had nodded and touched her face gently in thanks, the night was done and gone, too, and now there was the will.

The flowers wilting beside the open casket. The relatives and friends who came to express their sorrow. The funeral procession from the old Regan house through the town to the cemetery on the hill where his father was buried. The open grave with the two gravediggers standing by it silently abused in the presence of a ritual they witnessed over and over again, holding their caps in their hands while the minister read the elegy, and the straps poised over the open earth were pneumatically released and the coffin sank slowly, slowly, into the receptive earth, and he walked homeward silently in the town where he'd been born, in the town where sometimes death came.

And now there was the will.

Now there was the formality of death, now there was only the business of death, the hard transaction of inheritance, and he stood in Elliot Tulley's office with the window facing the street behind him, and life rushing past below, and he talked to him the way he would to an agent trying to sell a dubious property.

"Who's Giovanni Fabrizzi?" he asked.

"He's the person to whom your mother chose to leave half her estate in trust."

"Don't give me any double talk, Elliot," David said. "I understand the will perfectly. Who is he?"

"A man. A person." Elliot shrugged.

"Look, Elliot, I'm not in the mood for this kind of horse manure, believe me. I'm leaving for Los Angeles on Friday, and I want to settle this before I go, if possible. Either you tell me who this man is and what the separate agreement between them is all about, or I'll start suit the minute I get back from the Coast."

"There isn't a court in the land that can force me to produce that document, David. I think you ought to know that."

"Who's Fabrizzi?"

"I'm sorry, but I can't tell you that."

"I've gone over my mother's accounts," David said, "and settled all her unpaid bills. I had the opportunity of looking through her cancelled cheques, Elliot. Why'd she give you a cheque for a hundred and fifty dollars each month?"

"That was something between your mother and me," Elliot said.

"What kind of something?"

Elliot shrugged. "A retainer."

"That's not true. I've seen the cheques she paid you as retainers. They were all clearly marked as such in her records. These other cheques were made out to you in the amount of a hundred and fifty dollars every month since the summer of 1943. Her cheque books do not indicate *why* she made those payments. Suppose you just tell me why, Elliot."

"Suppose I just don't," Elliot said.

"I can get rough, Elliot. There are a lot of lawyers around who'd just love to sink their teeth into a portion of such a large settlement. How about it?"

Elliot shrugged again. "You want some advice?" he asked.

"No, I don't want advice. I want information."

"I'll give you the advice, anyway. Free of charge, which is unusual for me. A, you can't force me to tell you why your mother paid me a hundred and fifty dollars a month or what for. It was a private transaction, and entirely legal, and this is still the United States of America, and you can go straight to hell if you think you'll find out from me. And B, you can contest this will if you want to, but you'd have to show your mother was incompetent when she wrote it, and that'd be difficult to prove since she was an unusually alert and aware woman right up to the time of her death. And in any case, I wouldn't have to show the document mentioned in the will. So my advice is to forget all this nonsense and take your half of the estate and be damned happy you got that much. If your mother left the other half in trust, she had a very good reason for it. That should be enough for you."

"Well, it isn't."

"Well, that's too bad, David."

"The will gives an address in Rome for Fabrizzi," David said.

"Yes, that's true. It does."

"I can always go to Rome."

"I suppose you can. I don't know why you think you'd have more luck with Fabrizzi than you've had with me, but you can always go to Rome. That's true."

"This is important to me," David said.

"I imagine it is. Money is always important."

"It's not the money!" David said angrily.

"Then what is it?"

"I want to know. I want to know why she left her son only *half* the estate." He paused. "I'm her son, Elliot," he said softly.

Elliot spread his hands wide. "What can I tell you, David? Do you want me to break a trust? Well, I can't. Go to Rome if you want to. But don't ask me to be an informer."

"I'm supposed to leave for Los Angeles on the first of July," David said.

Elliot did not answer.

"I can get out of it," David said, almost to himself. "Curt would let me out of it."

"She's dead," Elliot said. "Let her rest in peace."

"What are you afraid of, Elliot?"

"Nothing."

"That I'll find out something terrible in Rome?"

"Only fools go looking for trouble," Elliot said. "Let it lie, David. There's nothing for you in Rome."

The art gallery across the square from the hotel was exhibiting the works of an unknown Sicilian painter, white posters boldly shrieking in huge black letters the single word PANZOLA. A few taxicab stoics nudged the kerb in front of the gallery, indifferent to culture, shining, black, impervious to the clinging Roman haze. David cursed their formidability, squinted his eyes against the glare, and then walked swiftly towards the overhanging green canopy of the hotel.

A bellhop idling in the lobby, enwrapped in his dream of a holiday on Lake Como, leaped erect when he saw David approaching, turned on an instant dazzling smile, and rushed to pull open one of the glass doors.

"Thank you," David said.

"Very hot outside," the bellhop said, grinning, testing his tourist-trade English.

"Yes," David answered. He pulled his handkerchief from his hip pocket and wiped his brow, wondering if the opening of a door warranted a tip. He decided it did not. Nodding briefly to the bellhop, he pocketed the handkerchief and walked into the lobby past Remus and Romulus suckling at the wolverine in bronze, feeling suddenly thirsty and wishing for a Scotch-and-soda.

The concierge behind the desk was busily pasting Italian airmail stamps to the pile of postcards before him. He did not look up when David approached. Wearing the silver-and-blue uniform of the hotel, his eyes distantly bored behind glasses whose rims were a shocking pearl-grey, he voraciously lapped stamps like a jungle cat licking his chops in the entrance doorway to a slaughterhouse.

"May I have my key, please?" David said.

The concierge did not look up from the postcards. The pink tongue darted out, another stamp gathered moistness.

"Your room number, sir?"

"Four-twelve."

"Ah, yes, sir. Mr. Regan, sir?"

"That's right."

"There's a message for you, sir."

He flashed a mercurial and rare smile, and then turned his back to David, his extended forefinger running down the cubby-holes behind the desk. Then he whirled, dropped key and small white envelope on the desk before him and reached for another stamp, his tongue darting out simultaneously.

"Thank you," David said.

He looked at the envelope as he walked away from the desk. A meticuolusly small hand had lettered the name David Regan on the face of the envelope. He turned it over and looked at the flap.

The name Giovanni Fabrizzi sat in the centre of the white triangle and beneath it the man's business address on the Corso. David pressed the button for the elevator, tore open the flap of the envelope, and pulled out a square of white notepaper, which bore the same letterhead and the same studied careful handwriting:

MY DEAR MR. REGAN:

My secretary tells me that you have been calling repeatedly since your arrival in Rome several days ago. I was, as you know, away for a while with my family and have only just returned to my office and my various duties. If it is convenient to you, I would be happy to see you this afternoon at four o'clock.

My very kindest regards,

GIOVANNI FABRIZZI

The elevator doors opened. David stepped into the car. "Four, please," he said.

The elevator boy nodded and set the car in motion. David leaned back against the mirrored wall. A tiny fan tried to stir the hot air in the car. Four o'clock, he thought. Four o'clock and Giovanni Fabrizzi would be happy to see him.

I wish I had a drink, he thought.

The elevator stopped and the doors opened. He walked down the corridor to his room, unlocked the door quickly and walked directly to the small ivory panel resting on the night-table near his bed. The panel was attached to an electric cord, which ran to some mysterious wall connection somewhere under the bed. There were three rectangular buttons on the face of the panel, one beneath another. Each of the buttons was illustrated with a line drawing.

The top button pictured a man in an apron carrying a pair of shoes. He seemed in great haste. The middle button was a frontal presentation of a woman holding a feather duster. She seemed in no hurry whatever, but the intelligent look on her face indicated she was waiting at the ready to rush wherever beckoned. The last button showed a man in tails carrying a tray. He too seemed in a desperate hurry to get somewhere, undoubtedly to the place where he would collect his tip.

Now which of you little people has the keys to the wine cellar? David wondered. The room waiter, of course, and he stabbed at the third button, pulled off his coat and shoes, loosened his tie, and threw himself down on the bed.

In a few moments, a knock sounded on his door.

"*Avanti, avanti,*" David floundered. "Come in, come in." He turned to face the door, thinking how comical it would be if a man the size of the little man on the button walked into the room, a half-inch-high human carrying a minuscule tray. The illusion was shattered instantly by the entrance of a tall gangling man wearing a look of surprise on his sharp features.

"Sir?" he asked.

"A Scotch-and-soda, please," David said.

"Yes, sir," the waiter answered, and departed hastily, the same look of surprise on his face, as if he were a baron who had only accidentally stumbled into this hotel where they'd dressed him as a waiter before he could explain or protest.

The drink arrived not five minutes later. David signed the check and tipped the waiter, and remembered only after he was gone that one didn't tip these buzzards each time they performed a service; one waited until check-out time to drop the brimming sackful of largess. Sighing, he wondered if he would ever grow accustomed to the European way of doing things.

And again he wondered what he was doing here.

Why'd you come to Rome? he asked himself. Why in hell did you come to Rome?

He sat on the edge of the bed and looked through the open shutters to the city beyond. The heat had been insufferable for the past few days, building to an intensity that was felling people in the streets, hanging over the city now in a thick, electrically charged haze, which promised rain. There was blackness in the distant sky. He hoped it would rain soon.

Why did you come to Rome? he asked himself again.

He sipped at his drink.

I came because I don't like the idea of being cheated out of half my mother's estate, that's why I'm here, admit it, face the knowledge, and for God's sake stop inventing fairy-tales!

I'm here because I loved her, he thought.

I'm here because she came back from this place once. She came back and she was no longer the person who had left. And when she returned, there was nothing there any more, nothing but the accidental bondage of birth, the love was gone. And I'm here because I want to know it was *she* who changed and not me, not her son, it was she who came back without love, and not me who was suddenly unworthy of whatever love she had to give.

Fabrizzi knows, he thought.

He had looked up the man's name the moment he arrived in Rome, surprised to discover he was a lawyer, dismayed by the knowledge because he had the sudden feeling he'd be facing the Italian counterpart of Elliot Tulley, close-mouthed, legal, infuriating. His premonitions mounted as he made call after call to Fabrizzi's office, certain he was being ducked, constantly being told by a secretary who barely spoke English that Fabrizzi was away but that she would deliver Mr. Regan's message the moment he returned. And now the note, and the neat careful hand, another lawyer, a Roman Elliot Tulley.

I should go home, he thought, what the hell am I doing here? Who cares? Who cares *where* love goes, who cares *where* it vanishes?

He heard the first rumble of thunder in the sky to the north of the city, saw the lightning flash. It would rain soon, and heavily. He looked at his watch. It was only eleven. There were five hours ahead of him before his meeting with Fabrizzi, there was a whole lifetime ahead of him. He did not relish the idea of sitting alone in his room, waiting out the time. There were gifts he should buy. Something for Curt and Martha. And something for Kate.

Something very special for Kate.

He finished his drink and began dressing. By the time he left the hotel, it was pouring.

He did not recognize the city at all.

Walking in the rain, picking out his gifts and having them sent back to the hotel, he was amazed at how short memory could be, astounded by this timeless Rome surrounding him, a Rome that should have remained sharply etched in his memory, unchanging, and yet a city he barely recognized. He walked through the streets, trying to find the courtyard with the *trompe l'oeil* arch and statue, locating the Bernini fountain, but confused completely by the identical doors in the street beyond. The ancient cobblestones collected puddles of water, which he tried unsuccessfully to avoid. He was wearing a light raincoat, and he ducked from doorway to doorway looking for a time he had known, but the rain had washed the city clean of memory.

It was still raining heavily when he started back for the hotel. It was only noon. There would be time for a drink and lunch, time to change into some dry clothes before his four-o'clock appointment.

He saw her coming down the Spanish Steps.

He had reached the Piazza di Spagna at the foot of the hotel, passed the patient taxicabs clustered like shining black beetles to the left of the fountain, approached the steps that rose in quiet majesty to the Via Sistina above, and began counting the steps idly as he climbed them, very tired somehow, wet and tired, his head ducked against the driving rain, he knew there were a hundred and thirty-seven steps, he remembered counting them when he had been in Rome with his mother so long ago.

The rain swept across the flat steps that seemed to mount for ever to the sky. He kept his hatless head ducked against the relentless spikes of rain, the count of forty-eight, and then perhaps a shadow, it could not have been a shadow because there was no sun that day, a knowledge, a sureness that another person was approaching, and suddenly he knew it was she, he lifted his head, he dared to raise his eyes.

The steps were behind her in a rain-rushing backdrop, her russet hair was the only splash of colour in a monchromatic print. She came down the steps in her peculiarly graceful, peculiarly awkward lope, wearing a grey trench-coat belted tightly at the waist, a grey skirt showing below the hem of the coat, dark-grey pumps, the coat collar lifted high at the back of her neck, her hair consuming the total greyness like a runaway fire lapping newsprint.

She stopped suddenly.

She looked up. The shock covered her face, starting with the sudden rising wings of her brows, startled in flight, piercing the widening green eyes, flaring nostrils in the angular face, spreading to the incredible mouth, distending the lips slightly, ever so slightly, her lope arrested, she stood stock-still.

"David," she said. She whispered the word. There was no relief in the word. There was only incredulity and shock.

"Hello, Gillian," he said.

They stood in the rain. They could have been in Times Square and not on foreign soil thousands of miles from home. It could have been yesterday that he'd seen her last, and not eleven years ago. She was standing two steps above him, a slender girl in a sopping-wet trench-coat, and he held out his hand instinctively, and instinctively she took it, and they both laughed, and then stopped laughing, and she said, "We're in Rome!" again with the same incredulity and shock. They stood in the rain on the Spanish Steps, and he held her hand and listened to her laughter, and he could think of nothing to say to her. Her laughter died. There was nothing to say.

"Shouldn't we get out of the rain?" Gillian asked.

"Yes," he said. He could not take his eyes from her face.

But neither made a move. They stood ridiculously on the steps, her hand in his, and neither moved, and suddenly she laughed again, and clinging to his hand tightly, pulled him down the slippery steps. For a moment, there was no time, no place, only memory full-blown and poignantly painful, the dimly reconstructed image of two innocents running down Eighth Avenue toward a sleazy Chinese restaurant, hand in hand, the sidewalks glistening wet, the thunder booming majestically in the surrounding skyscrapers. The image gurgled away flatly into the sewers of Rome. Eleven years, he thought. A cab door opened and a fat driver in a black cap shouted "Taxi?" and they both shook their heads at the same time and ran down the rain-gutted street.

The yellow-topped tables outside the bar glistened with rain, spanged to the steady tattoo of rain, added a drumming counterpoint to the shouted whisper of rain against the cobbled kerb. A white, rain-brimming Cinzano ash-tray sat in the exact centre of each table on the deserted sidewalk. David threw open the door to the bar. A bell tinkled. She went in first, and he closed the door, shutting out the sound of rain beating on the table-tops. The room was silent. It carried the close tight smell of wet garments in a small and secret closet. She shook out her hair and grinned, and they went to a table together and took off their coats and sat, and then looked at each other for the first time really, looked at each other silently across the table.

She had changed. Looking at her, he saw the change and saw her eyes studying his face and knew she saw the same change in him, and remembered again that it had been eleven years.

The knowledge came to them both at the same time perhaps. Eleven years. The knowledge came to them, and they suddenly wondered who, exactly, had met on the Spanish Steps and extended hands to be touched, who had run through the rain together, who? And with the knowledge, with the mutual understanding that it had been eleven long years, there came the strangeness.

"You look well, David," she said.
"Thank you. So do you."
"Have I changed very much?"
"No," he lied.
"Neither have you," she lied.

They knew they were lying to each other. They studied each other's faces and tried to find what they had known, but eleven years was a long time.

"What are you doing in Rome?" she asked.
"My mother died, and I——"
"Oh, I'm sorry."
"You never met her, did you?"
"No."

Memory touched, a time long ago, a time shared, you never met her, did you?

"She died last month," David said. "I had to come to Rome about the will."

"Will you be here long?"

"No. Just a few days."

A waiter came over to their table. "*Boun giorno, signore, signorina*," he said.

Gillian smiled at him, and said, "*Boun giorno*. Would you like some coffee, David?"

"Yes, please."

"*Per piacere*," she said to the waiter, "*portaci due caff caldi con latte separato*." The waiter nodded and moved away from the table. There was the strong smell of coffee in the room. The place was empty save for an old man who noisily slurped sherbert through a hanging white moustache. "You have to specify that you want the milk separately," Gillian explained, "or they bring you a cross between iced coffee and lukewarm bath water."

"You speak Italian very well," David said.

"Oh, that was fake, David. Really. I learned to say that from our director. He's very sweet-oh, but it's almost the only thing he taught me."

"Your director? Are you doing a show here?"

"A movie."

"That's wonderful, Gilly."

"Yes, it's *marr*-vellous," she said. She saw the sudden look that came over his face, and she stared at him curiously, and then smiled and said, "It's a good picture, and I've got a wonderful part, and everyone is treating me like a star, it's all quite wonderful, David." She smiled again. "Do you like Rome? Is this your first time?"

"I was here a long time ago," he said, and fell silent.

"What are you thinking, David?" she asked.

"I was thinking how long it's been since I last saw you."

"Yes." She nodded. "I feel very strange."

"I do, too."

"We mustn't." She reached across the table to touch his hand, and then drew it back almost at once. "I've thought of you a lot, David. I've thought of this day."

"I have, too."

The waiter came back to the table. He put down two cups of black coffee, and a small silver pitcher of bubbling milk.

"Oh, see?" Gillian said. "They've gone and warmed the milk. Should we send it back? Do you mind hot milk?"

"Not at all."

"All right, then." She turned to the waiter and smiled. "*Grazie*."

"*Prego*," he answered, and left the table.

"Who else but Italians would go around boiling milk?" Gillian said. She pulled the pitcher to her and poured. "You're still in television, aren't you?"

"Yes."

"Producing." She nodded. "I saw your name on some shows."

"I saw some of the work you did, too," he said.

"Really? Which?"

"Oh, some television stuff. And a movie once, I think. It was hard to tell because you weren't on the screen very long. But I was sure it was you."

"The roller coaster?" she asked.

"Yes, that's right."

"The roller coaster," she said, and she nodded. "Well, anyway, here we are."

"Yes."

"Alone at last." She laughed quickly and nervously, caught the laugh before it gained momentum, and sobered immediately. The table was suddenly silent. "I'm glad we ran into each other, David.'

"Are you?"

"Yes." She looked down at her coffee-cup. "Are you different now?" she asked.

"Different how, Gilly?"

"I don't know." She shrugged, her eyes refusing to meet his. "Now that you're successful? I'm different, I know. I feel different, and I look different, I . . ." She paused. "Have *you* changed?"

"I guess we all change, Gilly."

"Yes."

They sipped at their coffee silently.

"It was a very happy time for me, David," she said at last.

"And for me, too."

"There's been so much in between," she said. "Will I see you while you're in Rome?"

"Would you like to see me?"

"Yes. Yes, I would, David." She raised her eyes. "We shared so much, you see, I'd hate to think . . ." She shook her head. "I always cry easily. This is very hard for me, sitting here with you. Maybe I'm not quite as grown up as I thought."

"Shall I get the check?"

"Yes, I think so. I have the feeling . . . I feel so odd all at once, David. I feel . . . I wish I hadn't seen you again. I think . . . I have the feeling something is ending. I feel so very sad. I'm going to start crying in a minute."

He signalled for the waiter. They were both silent while he added up the check. David deciphered it and paid him, and then helped

Gillian into her coat. The old man with the hanging white moustache had ordered another dish of sherbert.

They went out into the rain. The bell over the door tinkled again. The yellow table-tops were still there. Up the street, the cabs were still lined up. Nothing had changed. Everything was still the same.

"Will you walk me to a taxi?" Gillian asked. She thrust her hands into her pockets, and he took her elbow. "Sunny Italy," she said. They walked silently. As they approached the hack stand, she stopped. "I'm staying at the Excelsior," she said. "If you want to, you can call me there."

"Do you want me to call, Gillian?" he asked.

She waited for a long time before answering. Then she said, "I want you to come with me now, David."

"Yes," he said.

"Yes," she answered. "I want you. It's as simple as that." She hesitated and then said, "Hasn't it always been as simple as that, David?"

She was a young girl again, trembling with need and anticipation, as innocent as she had been that first time so long ago, trembling on the brink of discovery. He kissed her gently and with infinite tenderness, and her mouth formed to accept his kiss, curving to fit the mould of his lips, pressing his mouth in tentative exploration, softly, gently, lips that were old friends greeting each other anew and with freshness, partially suspicious of the ardour of an earlier time, filled with wonder at the endurance of memory, the persistence of training. She pulled away from him suddenly and looked directly into his face, her eyes meeting his, touching his nose with curious fingers, and his mouth, and his cheek-bones, and then back to his mouth again.

"I wanted so much to kiss you in the rain," she whispered.

"I love you, Gillian," he whispered.

"Yes, yes, I love you."

"You're so beautiful, darling."

"Yes, call me darling."

"Darling, darling. Gillian, my darling."

"Yes, please. You say it with such love. You do love me, David, don't you? You do love me still?"

"Yes, I do love you still."

"Yes, and I love you. Would you kiss me, darling? Would you please kiss me again?"

He kissed her, and she suddenly hugged him fiercely. "Oh, it's so good to be with you again," she said, holding him tight. "Oh, David, it's so damn good."

His hands were upon her again, remembering again with a memory of their own. Her mouth closed upon his, they moved together with the precision of meshing gears, there was, he could hear his watch ticking in the stillness, a breath-holding, clumsy, time-suspended moment when they joined irrevocably, flesh claiming flesh, and suddenly she began sobbing.

She turned her head into the pillow and began sobbing, and he stumbled on the sudden tears, the world stopped dead with her tears, time stopped, she twisted her head, wrenched it from the pillow, looked into his face and his eyes, her own face tear-streaked, and whispered angrily, whispered in confusion and despair and puzzlement, whispered, "Where did we lose it, David? Oh, David, David, where did we lose it?"

He looked at her, startled for a moment, holding her in his arms and staring at the misery on her face, and then he seized her close in fear, held her trembling body close to his because he did not want to let her go now that he had found her again, didn't she realize they had found each other again? Didn't she know they hadn't *lost* anything? Held her desperately. Clung to her, frightened. Held her, held her, and shook his head, tried to shake the truth from his head, realizing it was the truth, and thinking, Good old Gillian, straight to the point, and then nodding with a weary sort of resignation, nodding, and releasing her, and accepting it as something he had known all along. He had known it on the steps after the first shock of recognition, known it when he took her hand and ran down the street, known it as they sat strangers to each other while the old man spooned sherbet into his mouth. And again when they declared their love feverishly, when they desperately whispered, "I love you, I love you," they could still say the words, the words were always and ever the same, "I love you, I love you," but it was done and finished, drowned by time, and now there were only the words and the empty notions, but nothing more.

And nothing more to say, really.

Nothing.

"I'm sorry." She was sobbing into the pillow. She kept one fist pressed to her mouth and sobbed. "I'm sorry. I'm so sorry."

"Gilly, Gilly."

"I hate endings. Oh God, I hate things to end. I'm sorry, David. I'm so terribly sorry."

He kissed her gently, and he cupped her face with his hands and pushed her hair back behind her ears, and she smiled wanly and said, "You know I don't like that, David."

He released her hair.

He felt a terrible need to leave quickly. He felt he was suddenly in danger. He could accept the fact that it was over, he could accept the knowledge that their love had changed, that it was gone, that there was really nothing for them any more. But he had the feeling that if he stayed longer he would discover their love had never been. The idea frightened him. He did not think he could bear that knowledge. He had to maintain the belief that they *had* loved each other once, had loved each other completely and magnificently, had to believe that time could not obliterate memory—it could change people, yes, but it could not destroy what they once had shared.

"I wish you everything, Gilly," he said. "I wish you everything in the world."

He kissed her once more, gently, and then dressed and quickly left the room and the stranger on the bed.

The office was in an old Roman building, solid with the dignity of time. He located the lawyer's name on a brass plaque set into one of the building's entrance columns and then walked upstairs to the second floor. A blonde Italian girl was sitting behind a desk in the small reception room. He told her who he was, and she went into Fabrizzi's office, returned a moment later, and motioned for David to follow her.

Fabrizzi was standing behind his cluttered desk, a man in his sixties with a full head of shocking black hair, and piercing brown eyes, and a large hooked nose. A thin, angular man, he extended a large hand and pumped David's hand energetically and said in good English, "Sit down, Mr. Regan. I'm sorry, I was away, but the heat..." He shrugged philosophically. "This rain is welcome," he said. "Rome is only for the animals in the summer."

He smiled as David sat. Watching him, David became suddenly nervous and frightened, nervous because he knew immediately he had been wrong about Fabrizzi, frightened because he knew Fabrizzi would tell him what he wanted to know. He sensed this in the man's cordial welcome and easy attitude, and he wondered all at once if he really wanted to know at all.

"Do you know why I'm here, Mr. Fabrizzi!" he asked.

"I think so, yes," Fabrizzi answered, nodding.

"I want to find out about my mother's will," David said. He spoke very softly and very slowly.

"That is understandable," Fabrizzi answered, speaking softly and slowly in return.

He felt suddenly that he knew Fabrizzi very well, felt as if this were an old friend he had come to for advice, a friend with whom he could speak without caution, completely relaxed.

"My mother left half her estate to you in trust, Mr. Fabrizzi,"

David said. He hesitated a moment. "The will mentions a separate agreement, an agreement that specifies how the trust is to be handled. Are you familiar with this agreement, Mr. Fabrizzi?"

"I am."

"And you know, of course, that my mother died last month."

"Yes. Please accept my deepest sympathies, Mr. Regan. She was a fine and noble woman."

"You knew her?" David asked, surprised.

"No, not personally. But I have had dealings with her for a great many years. Through her attorney, of course, Mr. Tulley."

"What sort of dealings?" David asked.

Fabrizzi smiled. "The payments. The cheques she sent every month."

"What payments?"

"Your mother sent a hundred and fifty dollars to me every month," Fabrizzi said.

"Why?"

"I want to know, Mr. Regan, what you intend to do with whatever knowledge you receive from me. I want to know whether or not you plan to contest your mother's will."

"Well, I . . ."

"Because if you do, Mr. Regan, our conversation is ended, and there is nothing more to be said."

"I came to Rome because——"

"Yes, I know why you came to Rome. Mr. Tulley called me before you arrived and said I should be expecting you. We had a long talk, he and I, debating the advisability of letting you know anything more than you already know. The will is legal, and so is the accompanying document. We're not worried about the will surviving the test of legality. But your mother went through a great deal of trouble to——"

"Is that why you went out of town? Because Tulley warned you I was coming?"

"No, no, believe me." Fabrizzi smiled. "My wife can't abide heat. I went to the mountains with her and my son and his family. No, believe me, I was not trying to avoid you. But you haven't answered my question."

"I don't know *what* I'll do," David said. "I just want to know what this is all about. I have a right to know! I'm her *son*!"

"Yes, that's true."

"Will you tell me?"

"If that will be the end of it. If then you will let it drop, why yes, then I will tell you."

"I can't promise you that."

"Then I'm afraid we have nothing to say to each other, Mr. Regan."

"Look, you don't understand. I——"

"I do understand, Mr. Regan. Those are my terms."

David sat still and silent for a long time. Then he nodded and said, "All right."

"This is the end? I have your promise? There will be nothing further said or done?"

"Nothing. You have my word."

"There is a girl, Mr. Regan," Fabrizzi said.

"What?" He stared at Fabrizzi, who stood before the rain-streaked window. "What do you mean?"

"A girl," Fabrizzi repeated, "a girl born in Rome on July 26, 1939."

"Well, what about her? How . . .?"

"The girl's name is Bianca Cristo."

"What's she got to do with——"

"She is your mother's daughter," Fabrizzi said.

He tried to understand what Fabrizzi was saying, but everything seemed confused and impossible all at once. My mother's daughter, he thought. Bianca Cristo, he thought.

"She was born to your mother and a man named Renato Cristo in a room off the Via Arenula. Cristo's sister, a woman named Francesca, served as midwife. Cristo was a soldier. He had been a farmer before he went into the Army, but he died as a soldier in 1943 when the child was four years old. She was living with Francesca at the time. She is still living with her, though of course she is no longer a child."

"Are you saying my mother——"

"Yes, I am saying your mother gave birth to a daughter in Rome in 1939, that is what I am saying. I am saying she began sending monthly cheques to me for Bianca's support in 1943 when Renato was killed. I am saying that half of your mother's estate is being held in trust by me for Bianca Cristo until the time she is twenty-one years old, which will be on the twenty-sixth of this month, that is what I am saying to you, Mr. Regan."

"I don't believe you."

"Ahh, believe me, Mr. Regan."

"No! My mother——"

"Believe me."

"Why would she leave half to . . . to a . . . a girl who . . . who . . .?"

"Her daughter," Fabrizzi said.

"No! What the hell are you telling me? You're telling me my mother and an Italian soldier——"

"Would you like to see a copy of the agreement, Mr. Regan?" Fabrizzi asked.

The office was silent except for the sound of the rain outside.

"Yes," David said, "I'd like to see it."

He left the office with nothing but anger inside him.

Now he knew. Now he knew what he had come to Rome to discover, now he knew what his mother was, now he understood everything, the long delay in 1939 while his father wrote frantic letters to her, now he understood, now he knew that his mother was nothing but a slut who produced a bastard child in Rome, that was his mother, that was Julia Regan, his mother, now he knew. And knew, too, why his father had died that day on the lake, and hated this woman who had returned from Rome, this woman who had dropped a bastard sister in a grubby room off the Via Arenula while her lover, a farmer, a soldier, a cheap . . .

Oh God, he thought.

Oh my God, I wish I didn't know.

Anger and hatred, anger and hatred, repeated in each sloshing stamp of his feet against the wet cobbles. This was where it had gone, oh yes, this was where the love had gone, first to a soldier, and then to a daughter, and nothing was left for the son in Talmadge, nothing but a whore mother who planned on her return, *Every year since the end of the war, I've made plans to go back to Italy*, nothing but a whore who play-acted the part of mother, there was no thunderclap.

He hated her.

He hated the girl Bianca, too, the girl he had never laid eyes upon, the girl who was his half sister, the girl who had stolen love from him. In his hatred, he wanted to see her. In his anger, he wanted to know what the thief looked like. He was filled with an urgent need to get back to the hotel and ask the desk to locate a woman named Francesca Cristo, and he would call her and say, "This is David Regan. I want to talk to my sister. Put my sister on the phone." And then he would arrange a meeting. And he would look at her. It was important that he see what she looked like. He wanted to study the face of the thief who'd stolen love from him, there was no thunderclap.

But the anger and hatred, dampened by the rain, gave way to a sadness, a melancholia bordering on self-pity, as he splashed through the puddles wearing the grey day around him, this is the way it ends, he thought, this is the way love ends. You meet a stranger on a flight of steps, and you take her hand in yours, and your mouth touches hers, and she's a stranger, your life dwindles on the bed of a stranger you once loved more than anything else in the world, your life vanishes completely in the office of a man you've never seen before, this is the way it ends. So chalk it all up, he thought morosely, stand somewhere high above David Regan, and look down on that poor pitiful bastard as if he is not yourself, and ask him what it's all about, and he will tell you it ends in sorrow and in tears, he will tell you all love ends, even a love you carried inside you like a cherished hope. Here, at least, here there was love. At least with Gillian, there was love. But even that had ended in Rome where there's been a beginning so long ago, there was no thunderclap.

But from the anger and the hatred and from the self-pitying moroseness, there came a desperation. He thought if only he could breathe clean air into his lungs, if only the streets could smell clean again after the rain, how he wanted to believe there was something more than duplicity and shallow hopelessness. If only today he had touched Gillian's hand and found Gillian's mouth, truly found her, if only today there had been a beginning, the way years ago his mother had found a beginning with a faceless Italian soldier, spawned a half sister and given to her a beginning, too, a life. I don't know, he thought, I don't know. I want the world to smell so sweet. Oh Jesus, love me, somebody. Somebody please love me.

There was no thunderclap, there was no sudden recognition.

He walked through the rain with his head bent and his shoulders slumped, and he remembered something Matthew had said a long time ago. They are the love bringers, Matthew had said.

He wondered idly what she looked like, his sister. He wondered if she had his mother's eyes or nose or chin.

He wondered if she looked like him.

What love had *she* known, he thought, this girl who'd been born to his mother, what love had been brought to her? A slip of paper every month, was that it? A cheque for a hundred and fifty dollars in hard American currency, was that what *she* knew of her mother? Or did they tell her stories of the American woman who had come to Rome before the war, and found a life, and left a life? Did she asked questions, Bianca? The name seemed more real to him now. Repeating it in his mind gave it reality. Bianca. Bianca. Did she ask questions about the American woman? He found it hard to think of his mother as a woman, solely as a woman, found it difficult to construct an image of her here, in this city, a woman. She suddenly seemed like a person he had never known at all. Not his mother, not whatever *mother* meant, not some distant impossible figure of whom he expected impossible things, but instead a person who'd been in love here, and gone to bed here, and given birth here. A person first, a woman first, and only after this his mother. What had she carried inside her all these years, this woman with the child in Rome? What had kept her away, what could have possibly kept her away, shame, guilt, fear, what? What had gone on in the mind of this woman he'd never known, whom he was closer to knowing in this moment than he'd ever been in his life? He suddenly felt a vast aching sorrow. If there had been a tyranny in silence, there was now a finality in death. If only one or the other of them had held out a hand. It might have been possible. It might have been possible for them to have known each other not as mother and son, but simply as human beings. There was no thunderclap, but he somehow knew for certain that his life was not ending here in Rome. And then he wondered whether there ever were any real endings in life, or whether endings only nurtured new beginnings.

There were people in the streets. He saw them now. They walked with their heads bent against the rain. He could hear them talking to each other. He heard someone laugh. His anger was gone now, his hatred was gone, his self-pity, his desperation, even his sorrow. There was left only a piece of understanding, and not even very much of that, but he could feel the rain hammering him coldly alive again.

He would try to see her. He would call her and say, "Bianca, this is your brother, David. Did you know you had a brother, Bianca?" He would stay in Rome for a little while. And in that time, if it were at all possible to bring love to another person, he would offer love to his sister. If it were at all possible to know another person, he would try to know her.

He walked swiftly across the square.

The rain was cold on his face as he reached the steps and started to climb. He slipped on one of the landings, falling to his knees. But he got up again immediately and climbed the rest of the way without once looking back.

When the telephone rang, she knew it was David.

She left the dinner-table and went to the phone swiftly, and then hesitated before answering it, filled with a sudden sense of dread. Apprehensively, she picked up the receiver.

"Hello?" she said.

"Yes, this is she."

"One moment, please."

She waited. There was a terrible crackling and buzzing on the line. She could hear the operator talking to someone else, and then an Italian voice came on to the line, and the American operator said, "Go ahead, please," and she heard a very faint voice, and then the Italian operator again, and then the American operator frantically saying, "Go ahead, please. Go ahead, your party is on the line."

"Kate?" his voice asked.
"David?"
"Hello, Kate."
There was a long silence.
"I'm in Rome," he said.
"Yes. Yes, I know, David.
"Kate . . ."
"Yes, David?"
"It's two o'clock in the morning here."
"We were just having dinner," she said.
"I hope I didn't interr——"
"No, no," she said quickly.
"How are you, Kate?"
"I'm fine, David."
There was another long silence.
From the dining-room, Matthew asked, "Who is it, Kate?"
"David," she answered.
"*Who?*" Matthew said.
Amanda looked up from her plate. "It's David Regan," she said quietly.
"Kate . . . Kate, listen to me," David said suddenly.
"I'm listening, David."
"Kate, I'm an old man."
"Yes, David?"
"Kate, I was born on 4 October, 1924."
"Yes, David?"
"I shouldn't be calling you. I know I . . . but I just wanted to say . . ."
"Yes, David?"
"It's dark here. My room is very dark. There's only your voice, Kate."
"What is it you want to say, David?"
"I'm coming home tomorrow," he said in a rush. "My plane arrives at Idlewild tomorrow night at nine-fifteen."
She did not say anything. She waited. She waited breathlessly for him to speak again. She thought for a moment the connection had been broken. She heard him sigh. She could visualize him lying in the dark, in a hotel room in Rome.
"Kate, will you meet me at the airport?" he asked.
"Yes," she said instantly.
"Will you?"
"Yes, yes."
"There are things I want to . . . to talk about, Kate."
"Yes, I'll be there. Yes, David."

"If the plane is late or anything . . ."

"I'll wait."

"Please wait."

"David, you don't know how long," she said, and her voice broke curiously.

"Nine-fifteen," he said. "Pan-American. It's flight one-one-five."

"Yes, hurry. Come safely, hurry, *hurry*!"

"Kate?"

"Yes?"

"I won't be able to sleep."

"Sleep," she said. "You must sleep, David."

"Kate?"

"Yes?"

"You'll be there?"

"Oh, David, if I have to walk!"

"I'll see you tomorrow."

"Yes, tomorrow."

"Good night, Kate."

"Good night, my ——"

The connection was broken. She put the receiver back on to the cradle and stood staring at the phone. When she went into the dining-room again, Matthew asked, "Was that David Regan?"

"Yes," Kate said. She sat opposite her mother.

"Isn't he in Rome?" Bobby asked.

"Yes. He's coming home tomorrow." Kate paused. She looked directly at Amanda and said, "I'm meeting him at Idlewild."

Matthew put down his fork. "David? David Regan? You're meeting him at Idlewild?"

"Yes."

"Why?" Matthew asked.

"Because he wants me to," Kate said, and again she looked at Amanda. Matthew saw the glance and felt peculiarly excluded. Bobby seemed about to say something, and then judiciously closed his mouth. Picking up his fork, Matthew looked at his wife and his daughter, and said nothing.

"How do you propose getting to Idlewild?" Amanda asked. "You're not allowed to drive outside Connecticut."

"I hadn't thought of that," Kate said. "I'll take a cab."

There was a moment's silence at the table. Matthew's fork accidentally clinked against his plate.

"I'll drive you, if you like," Amanda said.

"Thank you, Mother," Kate answered. "I can take a cab."

Amanda raised her eyes to Kate's. Very softly, she said, "It's a long trip, Kate, to make alone. You might want someone to talk to." She paused for a moment, as if what she had to say now was very difficult. But when the words finally left her lips, they were really quite simple. "I'd like to go along with you, daughter," she said.

Matthew watched them silently as they faced each other across the table. Amanda smiled tentatively and extended her open hand to Kate. Kate hesitated a moment, and then took the hand wordlessly, her eyes never leaving Amanda's face. He had the feeling something passed between them in that moment, something almost tangible passed between them as Kate took Amanda's hand in her own, a love, an understanding, something he could not quite fathom, something like . . .

He shook his head.

Something like a legacy, he had thought.

"Eat your potatoes, son," he said.

THE END